THE GAMES MASTER

THE GAMES MASTER

Rise of the Black Knights

A Novel by

David Brosbell

THE GAMES MASTER
RISE OF THE BLACK KNIGHTS

iUniverse books may be ordered through booksellers or by contacting:

iUniverse
1663 Liberty Drive
Bloomington, IN 47403
www.iuniverse.com
1-800-Authors (1-800-288-4677)

ISBN: 978-1-4917-5183-1 (sc)
ISBN: 978-1-4917-5184-8 (hc)
ISBN: 978-1-4917-5185-5 (e)

Library of Congress Control Number: 2014921762

Print information available on the last page.

iUniverse rev. date: 01/27/2015

CONTENTS

The Beginning of the End 1
Enter Sand Sorceress 48
Mystery of the Sand 113
Deo's Exit 162
Blood Sport 219
Unexpected Allies 273
Gabriel's Window 321
Here They Come 350
War 391
Absolute darkness 458
Mystical 519

CHAPTER 1

THE BEGINNING OF THE END

The morning sunshine brightened the fearless warrior's hands. He stared at them with intensity, examining the fatigued landscape.

"How did we survive?" Kruno asked himself a question, but he didn't have the answer.

He pulled his sword from its sheath and examined it with absolute respect. The sun's rays reflected off its stunning polished steel gathering in his sky coloured eyes. His mind left him for a moment as he bonded with his weapon. Finally he jammed it into the ground, penetrating the dirt at his feet.

"There is no way we should be here right now."

Kruno turned his thoughts to his pride and joy: his Clorian shield.

He had a deep emotional attachment to his sword. It was of great quality, but wasn't anything unique. His shield on the other hand, was one of a kind, created specifically for him. His rough right hand caressed its smooth silver surface. It was far from ordinary because Clorians built it and because they were its creator it had other characteristics. It could morph, connected to Kruno's will. In its current relaxed state, it looked more like a piece of armour fitted perfectly around his forearm up to his elbow. His beloved shield continued up to his shoulder, but only one side not hindering the mobility of his left arm.

"Brothers, I don't know how we are still here. We were overwhelmed, outmatched, but having our backs against the wall is what we love. The Games Master is dead, and since that moment, it has been a whirlwind. I haven't had a chance to reflect."

Kruno spoke to his weapons as if they could hear him. He hadn't had a chance to really analyze what transpired. He needed the debriefing time, it should have happened a while ago, but he pushed it off to this moment. One he could have in solitude.

"The Games Master taken out by us? He was far too powerful. God was on our side that day."

Kruno dropped to one knee; he could feel that his ripped muscles - which rested on his eye pleasing frame - were still sore, but any feeling was a good one. He drew a cross with two fingers over his heart, kissed the same fingers, placed them on his forehead and then motioned towards the heavens.

"Four of us to start but now only three. Dorious, your name will never be forgotten."

Kruno shed his first and last tear for his friend who hadn't survived. A tear he didn't wipe away, but let it travel through his scruff covered jaw. His dark facial hair submitted to its first hint of grey, after the ferocious life changing battle. Dorious was someone who shaped who Kruno had become and although Kruno saved Dorious's life when they met years prior, it was Dorious that became his mentor.

Kruno repositioned himself and sat on a log, trying to find some sanctuary.

He and his comrades, those who had survived the Games Master, were in Tristan, a town resting between two great kingdoms, a town that seemed to get smaller as the two kingdoms continued to swell. The Dark Realm to the east and the Silver Allegiance to the west. They continued to expand and so did the tension, building towards an inevitable conflict. A war to come, one that Kruno had no interest in being a part of. His focus hadn't changed; he would live independently of any King. He led a group of warriors who looked for adventure and wealth.

The moment the Games Master's heart stopped, fortune was theirs. They had more gold than most could dream of, and although they could live the rest of their lives enjoying it, they would never stop. Kruno had a lifetime goal, a creed even, one that only Dorious had understood. His life was dedicated to the destruction of evil. To hunt down anything that praised the Underworld. Ivan, Christian and now Decan didn't know his credo. It would be nice if they did, but it wasn't imperative.

Decan replaced Dorious because Kruno needed a fourth; he believed it to be the optimum number, comprising a man of magic and three warriors.

Decan was recruited only a few weeks prior. A man with a funny accent and eclectic personality, but an almost perfect warrior skill set. He shared one thing in common with Kruno and that was a weapon made by Clorians. Decan's two swords were special to say the least — they had unique attributes.

Kruno had watched him decimate three men with cockiness, but also with true ease. He was by far the most technically sound fighter of the group and arguably the best Kruno had ever witnessed. He was smooth with perfect form. Decan would take some shaping but Kruno had faith it could be done.

The day had started off as pleasant as it had over the past couple of weeks. They were new to town and people were surprisingly pleasant.

A little too happy, not just to us but to everyone, Kruno thought. *This kind of town displays glee like they live in some kind of utopian society, and this town is far from perfect, that is for sure. Even Dryden, the greatest city, economically dominant with thicker walls than any other and an army arguably the greatest in mankind's history doesn't have such an attitude.*

If he brought this up to Christian or Decan they wouldn't understand and would accuse Kruno of being overly paranoid. Personally he felt this was his unbiased evaluation, but knew releasing his observation would do nothing positive. It would just add ridicule to a meaningless conversation. He would have loved to discuss this with Dorious, but that would be impossible. The dynamics of their group had changed; Dorious was dead and the only person he could bounce these ideas off wasn't himself.

Dorious's glorious departure was significant to Kruno and changed the configuration of the group. His experience and knowledge would be tough to acquire, maybe impossible. As a rule of succession, Decan filled a void but would never truly measure up to the greatness of Dorious. He was skilled, that was evident, but Kruno hoped many more were still untapped.

These boys know me well, but even I have a few tricks I have never pulled out of my sleeve. I am hoping the same for Decan.

The tremendous kindness of everyone in town was a little much to swallow, and Kruno would love to talk to Ivan about it. He had definitely taken the role of senior advisor of the group. Ivan had proved to be a valiant warrior and a decent decision maker. Kruno and Ivan had different styles, but they still complemented each other.

He considered talking to Ivan about it, but Ivan's personality had been changing and he needed to be re-evaluated. Ivan's ability to stay focused had deteriorated over the past few months, and he dipped in and out of this new personality trait, leaving Kruno irritated. Ivan's attention span was never one to brag about, but when Kruno needed him, his mind was always in the right place.

Now, when addressing even the most basic questions, Ivan's mind wandered, eyes glazed over and vision bent into a different world.

I truly hope this is just a small thing to get over and his mind will return.

Leaving everyone out of the decision-making process, Kruno decided to let things slide. It was quite possible that this town was filled with a certain charm and goodwill. High spirits could be a result of a different culture that had been imbedded in this place for generations. He had never been here before, nor had any of his colleagues so he chose to let his feelings of unease slide.

Still something didn't add up. The town had no walls protecting its soft underside. It was too small for any recent victories or to be noticed by the Silver Allegiance.

Why is everyone in such a good mood? The town lacks security but people gallivant around like it has the great walls or army of Dryden, the capital of the venerated Silver Allegiance.

He guessed it could be the surprise that was ringing off everyone's tongue. The Duke of the town had promised something weeks ago. He had mentioned to a few people that he had a surprise for them, a great surprise that would be a gift from him to everyone else. This small token of appreciation ran through the chatty people of Tristan like a wildfire.

Kruno decided to accept that the uncanny, gleeful attitude was a direct result of this anticipated gift.

Tristan had one main road and six intersections. It followed a similar pattern to most towns; commerce concentrated on the main street, the other streets were dwellings and the outskirts of the town was where the farms were located. It had a pub, the Rocking Pony, and a Church at the end of the main street.

The Church had an interesting allure about it. It was probably built many moons ago and had a look of ancient craftsmanship, designed with beauty in mind, no care of cost or timeline to build. A Church and a pub was almost a guarantee to find in any town, no matter how small it was. People needed a place to understand their purpose, and another to forget the burden that it brought.

"Decan!"

Kruno yelled over the voices of the town's people to his new ally, while Decan played with a few children on the street with Christian.

"Kruno, you have to come over here. These kids are great! They believe everything I say. I could tell them I was King and they would buy into it."

Kruno would admit that Decan, even though very strange, was quite amusing. The in-tune warrior seemed to be so different at points, ranging from dead serious to entertaining. While requesting Kruno to join him, he jumped on to his head and did a little spin. The children loved him and while they laughed, they attempted to do the same. He brushed the sand out of his dark hair and it seemed to fall back to the way he liked it; a little unsettled.

Amused but way too serious to ever spin on his head for any reason, Kruno answered with a little laugh and a shake of his head. "Maybe later, good man. Have you seen Ivan?"

Distracted by his own acrobatic abilities, he didn't respond, but Christian stepped up to pass on the information that he had seen Ivan in the Church.

"Thanks boys, and remember those girls are a little young for you."

"I can definitely agree with that, but they all must have moms and maybe a few have sisters. Maybe we can even get you-know-who a little something." Decan pointed to Christian in an obvious attempt to make sure he heard.

"I don't need any help, I am doing just fine." Christian attempted to defend himself with a whiny, insecure response.

"Come on now, Christian, we all know you haven't seen a woman's pleasure area since you jumped into the world."

His reference to Christian's virginity hit a spark and they argued back and forth.

Kruno left them to bicker, and while he walked to the Church to see if he could locate Ivan, he observed the town transforming. The farmers brought forth the best of their harvest and were setting up the last of their food stands. Today wasn't market day, but the event to unfold was anticipated to be such a spectacle that the fruit and meat stands were doubled.

Foolish, Kruno thought, as a lot of it would go to waste unless they were assuming guests from the neighbouring town would join in.

Anyone with artistic skills came to present their artwork on the main street, while music performers and street performers came to entertain. Again this didn't sit right with Kruno, but he would abide by his earlier decision to forgo his uneasiness.

"Excuse me," Kruno asked a farmer already set up.

"Yes sir, how can I help you, anything you like?"

"Sure, pass me some of those."

The farmer grabbed a handful of apples and shoved them in a bag. The whole time he was smiling, like some kind of idiot. His speech was finely articulated, indicating an education, but yet he smiled like a person with a mental deficiency.

"Why are you so happy?" Kruno asked inquisitively.

"I have seen you around here over the past couple of days, you must know that today is the day the Duke will visit and present us with a gift. We have been instructed to treat today like a grand festival. See, everyone is participating, we even have mimes here and other street performers."

"It seems like a grand event, reminds me of Dryden a little, of course on a much smaller scale. You must have slaughtered twenty chickens here and all this fruit, don't you think that is a little overkill? Who the heck are you guys expecting to arrive?"

"Well stranger, I will let you in on a little secret. We really aren't supposed to disclose this but I am sure the Duke won't mind since the announcement is going to be soon. We were told a few weeks ago to prepare food for many. Slaughter what we wished, just make sure it was a plentiful number. We would be rewarded with great bounty."

Kruno had enough of the conversation and decided to close things off. The ridiculous amount of food and all this performance for a town of less than two hundred people. It made no sense. What made even less sense was when Kruno asked how much he owed for the fruit, and the farmer waived the price.

Maybe I am a little too paranoid here. What else do these people have to get excited about? Crappy town, outskirts of the Silver Allegiance, some worthless Duke I haven't even heard of. Let them have their little festival, but I am really looking forward to leaving Tristan. Way too blissful, it's creepy.

Christian and Decan continued to play with the kids on the street. The Wizard dazzled the kids' little minds with small tricks. Dancing fire up his arm and small swirls of sand were his arsenal of entertainment. Christian had to thank the Games Master for the sand trick. Since he witnessed the sand image of the Games Master in the labyrinth, he had been working on his own spell and it had been coming along quite nicely. He was able to create little puppets out of the fine particles.

Decan was somehow able to override Christian's abilities and capture the attention of the kids by the old coin out of the ear trick. A continued quarrel brewed as Christian was envious of Decan.

"Oh, I see Decan, I get a little attention and you have to take away my audience!"

"Christian, I didn't know you were so attached to these little guys. Now you are mad because they like the coin out of the ear trick better than your fancy spells, or maybe they just like me better because I am prettier than you are."

Christian realized his unhappiness was foolish, but didn't care because Decan always had to belittle him. Decan was new to the group. He didn't fight with them in the labyrinth; he didn't face the Games Master. As far as Christian was concerned Decan had to earn his spot in the group, just as he still struggled to do.

"They just like you because you are giving them money, your trick is stupid!" Christian's youth was ever-present.

Decan was on the ground ignoring the young Wizard — as he did regularly — and three kids tackled him, jumping on his chest. Laughing and giggling, Decan pulled them off and made a declaration.

"I love this little town. It puts me in such good spirits."

Christian had to admit he felt quite uplifted himself. While the thoughts crossed his mind, a few ladies in their early twenties approached them. Like normal, the Wizard felt his Adam's apple drop, as if it had doubled in size. On the opposite side of the coin, Decan turned and talked with ease.

"Ladies, well, how are we today? Have we been taking care of your kids?" He looked to Christian winked and said softly, "Don't worry, I will get you a little something."

A beautiful young lady looked to Decan and said, "That is my little sister you have been entertaining."

Under his breath, with a facial reaction that expressed his confidence and pleasure that this situation had presented itself, he said gently, "Hmmm, lovely, isn't she Wizard?" Out loud he bellowed, "Well then, I guess I was the child's guardian for almost an hour and yet I have requested no pay, whatever shall be done to reciprocate my services?"

The woman smiled, already enamoured by Decan. This really irritated Christian. Decan's warrior stature and light eyes combined with his olive skin made him exotic looking in this part of the world, which made him successful with the ladies. On the other hand, Christian's diminutive physique and skin that looked like it had barely seen the sun, worked against him. Height wasn't the issue, he was a little taller than Decan, but his small frame and lack of muscle wasn't desirable. It was as if his body never evolved from adolescence. To him it wasn't fair.

The other women had encircled them and looked up with keenness to hear what Christian had to say, to see if he was as charming as his friend, but nothing would come out of his mouth. It flowed so easily off Decan's tongue, why wouldn't that occur for him?

"Ladies, please meet a great Wizard, a companion of mine, Christian." Decan pointed to Christian, but all the great Wizard could do was raise one hand to greet them.

"Hello Mr. Wizard! And how long is your staff?"

"Good heavens, that is quite the question!" Decan looked over and loudly responded.

Christian attempted to respond, but didn't pick up on the sexual innuendo and started to talk about his wooden staff.

Decan shook his head, giving up on Christian and focusing on one of the women.

"Well then, what shall I call such a stunning lady?"

"You could call me Mrs. Robertson." She pointed back to a large man resting in the doorway of the one of the little houses across the street.

Looking directly at her husband, Decan expected at the very least a shake of the fist and even potentially a charge his way, but he was thoroughly mistaken. The man only smiled and said, "No harm done."

"Weird town, Chris. The men are fine when we hit on their women. Got to love it, I hope there is more of this in our travels."

"Bye boys, nice staff Chrissy." The girls grabbed their kids or sisters and walked away.

"What in the heck was that?" Decan spoke sternly to Christian, "Listen, Christian, you've got to improve your social skills — I need you as my assistant. I can't believe you really described your staff. Anyway, let's go meet some more people!"

On Kruno's way to find Ivan, he passed all kinds of activity and tried not to get too bothered by the whole situation. It was an incredible effort for a small town. The stage was nearly completed where this great announcement was going to be made.

He approached the Church just as Ivan passed through the doors. He had to bend down and turn a little just to fit; doors weren't made with his physique in mind.

"Greetings cousin," Ivan hollered accentuating his chiselled jaw.

"You seem to be in quite the good mood," Kruno commented.

"I must admit, as the day progresses I find this town's energy absorbing into mine. Why the long face, Kruno? Maybe you should have a conversation with the man who rests in all Churches. It has relieved me of some worries I have been dealing with."

"Well, Ivan, that's great! I have noticed you a little off these past few weeks. It's just... never mind." Kruno considered bringing up Ivan's lack of focus and weird characteristics that had been surfacing, but decided against it.

"Come, cousin, let's not worry and enjoy the festivities." As Ivan addressed Kruno, he grasped him by the shoulder. His sheer strength was enough to knock an unsuspecting man to the ground with a basic greeting.

He calls me cousin, but if we are related I certainly got the short end of the stick, Kruno thought with a humorous smile.

"The air is fresh today and the sun shines. To the pub, I hear they will be giving away free beer for this stupid Duke. Free beer and Ivan go well together." Ivan referred to himself in the third person with obvious drinking eyes.

They all ended up at the bar for the Duke's arrival. Ivan and Decan had both pounded back three free pints, and as always, they seemed to be served first. Decan concentrated his efforts on a young barmaid and Ivan's size always got him the attention he wanted from any bartender.

Christian sipped on a beer, but Kruno knew he would rather have wine. In order to attempt to fit in with the others, he would suffer with beer, especially now that Ivan had a drinking partner.

The Duke's arrival was a poor attempt at a royal entry. Three women spread flowers in front of his horse, a few instruments played a song only Ivan knew and for some reason he sang along with it. Everyone's spirits were elevated and it seemed that even Christian was excited, and he actually talked with some lady. Decan approached Christian and talked about something to do with his staff. Things hit a whole new level of strange when Decan kissed Christian on the side of his head.

How many damn beers have they had?

The crowd roared as the Duke, accompanied by nothing more than two lightly armed guards, rode his horse around the podium, attempting to gather all in front. As he trotted past Kruno, his eyes played a strange trick on him. The Duke seemed to move slower than normal. It was a bizarre feeling that usually would only occur when he was absolutely drunk. That didn't add up because he had drunk slower than even Christian and he wasn't even close to inebriated.

He slid his beer on the table with no intention of picking it up again. Looking to his left and right, all patrons of the bar's outer patio were fixated on the Duke.

The Duke smiled at them awkwardly but with confidence. His face was interesting, enthralling on some level. His expression seemed frozen, no muscle movement, similar to a porcelain doll, the kind of doll made for children but that made most adults uncomfortable.

Even stranger was that the only time the Duke's face changed was when he made eye contact with Kruno, and then the frozen smirk seemed to turn a little apprehensive. Kruno shook his head fast with little snaps in order to clear the strange observation from his mind.

Everyone gathered around the front of the stand and awaited his speech.

"Well, I guess we will find out what this great reward or gift is. Three gold pieces says it's not worth more than a horse's ass," Kruno said aloud, but just for his own ears.

"Great people of Tristan, please don't stop drinking on my account. Keep drinking, that is what life is all about." The crowd cheered as they continued to pour beer down their throats. "We sit on the edge of the great Kingdom of the Silver Allegiance. Our little town is key to the security of this monarchy."

In a large apple orchard two towns east of little Tristan, two children were playing. Little Janie, only eight years old, was frolicking with her older brother Jake, who was turning ten in a month. It was a game the boy had the clear advantage in playing, but looking up to and being less intelligent than her brother, she played even though he won every time without fail. Simplistic in nature, the game involved tossing apples at a target.

Becony was a farming community that lay just outside the Silver Allegiance. It had little commerce and trade besides agriculture. It was at least three times the size of Tristan when comparing population and ten times the land size. They relied heavily on trade with the Silver Allegiance for everything outside of foodstuffs and even traded with the Dark Realm a little. It was a pivotal town where the two boundaries came the closest to meeting each other. Becony was a town that really had no King or army's protection, but acted like a buffer state between the two great superpowers.

There were many more buffer states or uninfluenced towns belonging to neither of the two kingdoms, but over the past few years, towns and villages were gobbled up. A lot of political propaganda was aimed by the Silver Allegiance as it grew west and north, and by the Dark Realm that expanded eastward and south. Mergers and questionably amicable acquisitions threw the two kingdoms into a race for power. In time all that would be left would be to turn towards one another.

The two children had been out since morning, as the chores were all completed earlier on. Their mom called to them, but they both conveniently didn't hear her as they were enthralled with their game.

"Janie, what is the next target?" Jake asked, giving her the opportunity to pick the spot he would most certainly hit before her.

She didn't respond but stood still as if God himself looked at her. She was frozen and stared just beyond her brother's head.

"Janie, what the heck is wrong? Stop goofing about," Jake said, at first with irritation, but even over just a few moments he could tell there was something wrong. Fear shot over him and goosebumps instantly took domination of his skin. He turned his head in a blur. He could hear it before he could see it. The air swished with an eerie disposition and the leaves of several trees were tossed aside as they tried to call out... *DUCK!*

The young boy crouched by pure instinct to elude the danger the trees tried to warn him about. His vision finally processed what they had seen — a hairless, red beast, fearsome and large as a horse, soared toward him, not more than ten feet off the ground. The movement of air that he had heard was from the creature's final move in its attack routine. It glided with malicious intent and sheer speed.

Jake dropped as close to the ground as he could to avoid the long reach of this crimson-skinned, vile beast. In a matter of seconds it had closed in on its perceived target, dropped to a diligent attack height and stretched out its long, clawed hand.

Jake's heart stopped and his mind raced to find an evasive solution. With so little time and being so young, all he wanted to do was call out to his mother. He closed his eyes, bracing for the pain he was so certain to feel as his flesh would be pierced in moments.

Jake soon learned he was wrong — his depth perception had anticipated it would have arrived already, but he felt nothing. Instant joy rang throughout his young body, but that abruptly turned into terror as the shadow of the assassin passed right by him.

What followed was a moment he would never forget for the rest of his life.

His sister stood still with a tear in her left eye as the unknown monster gripped her by the hair and ripped her off the ground. Instantly her silence broke as pain and fear combined, forcing a reaction — a scream — one that would haunt her family forever.

She was light compared to the beast's strength, and with ease, the creature shot upward, well above the treeline with Janie in tow.

A sixth sense had struck her mother only moments before her daughter was ripped from the earth in a nefarious act. Knowing something was going to happen, she looked out from the kitchen window to see the red creature rise from the orchard. She saw something dangling from its hands and rushed out to the porch. The scream followed and ripped her soul in two.

Her boy lay helpless on the ground. He didn't move and wouldn't for hours, even after his parents found him. His tears were like an endless stream flowing from his eyes.

Janie's mother fell to her knees and screeched for her husband. Both mother and son, from different parts of the farm, watched the beast elevate, gaining altitude. It rose hundreds of feet and joined a sea of red. The sky looked as if the sun was setting, giving the sky the red shade that often predicted a nice day to come for the farmers. This colour had nothing to do with the sun setting. It was midday and definitely didn't offer any good predictions.

The assailant, just before reaching hundreds of its airborne friends, let the child go.

Many people in Becony had been marvelling at the several platoons of Cryptons as they raced across the sky in battle formation. Most of the villagers didn't know what a Crypton was, but they were just hoping that the beasts were going to pass on by to some other village. Selfish desires, but survival instinct is a human trait. The worst events are better off somewhere else.

Little Janie screamed in pain once her hair was entangled in the unknown creature's fist; it gripped her without concern for gentleness. Its three-inch claws had dug deep into her skin and she instantly started to bleed down her cheeks. It was only a matter of minutes before she was released from a fatal height.

The townspeople, those who had been watching and those who were beckoned to observe, gasped with horror as the young body twisted, turned and with forward motion slammed fatally into the side of a building, before thudding to the ground.

"That creature did that just for enjoyment," a farmer said from the middle of a group of horrified observers.

"Warn the others!" a young man exclaimed urgently.

"Wait!" an elder responded. "If you smash that bell, they may turn on us."

Irritated, the young man watched the beasts fly beyond them. They had no intention of attacking Becony. They had their minds focused on another target. As soon as the last Crypton passed, the young man ran up the tower and frantically clanged the bell in several sets of three, a warning of an invasion to the surrounding towns.

The Duke's speech started to make perfect sense. Kruno felt his words comfort him and relax his mind. He decided to let go of his paranoia.

The air was filled with a beautiful scent, it filled his head with relaxation and it was wonderful. He could feel his lips form a small smile, something like that of an infant seeing a colourful painting for the first time. He wanted to look over to his right and see if Ivan felt the same, but decided he would inquire later because the longer he stared the better he felt.

The words of the Duke started to form a mental picture in the minds of the individuals of his audience. His soft speech was so elegant that it painted utopian images in their subconscious. As time passed it seemed as if all senses were overridden. Decan could feel his skin comforted, as if he was lying on the smoothest silk. Besides the luminous words of the great Duke, music played a mesmerizing ballad in the background.

Kruno's mind started to slip away from him, out of reach of his control, but that was okay. He was always on top of everything, always paranoid and untrusting, but on this occasion he would enjoy this mental vacation.

From the podium the Duke looked on to the crowd. Everyone enjoyed his carefully prepared speech with perfect awe. Each mother, father and child looked on with silence, head tilted to the left or right with a little smirk on their face.

The beast had just released the girl and rejoined the formation. Swooping over hard and with a blow, one of three black-skinned Cryptons smashed into another.

"You idiot, why would you let one of your subordinates create an opportunity for warning?" it said, using demonic tongue.

"Come now, it has motivated the others in the platoon." The first beast looked back to see all the soldiers hungry for more death and blood.

The second beast spoke again, "It's like a feeding frenzy. We have just lifted the spirits of the group. Besides, humans are afraid of power and are selfish. That town will not attempt to warn the others for fear of retribution."

"Look!" a third black Crypton yelled to the others in mid-conversation. It pointed to Tristan. "Our plan is unfolding as we expected. This will be a slaughter."

With a shift of its wing, the first beast flew back to regain the lead of its platoon.

Kruno stared ahead at the Duke, and his mind slipped further away from his normal lucid state. He was ready to fully enjoy the perfect feeling he had when something imperfect interrupted the ballad. Three off beat banging noises unstitched the seamless message being conveyed. He tried to ignore the displaced noise and focus back to ultimate relaxation.

Bong... Bong... Bong...

Each bong got louder and more real. He felt fury build in him as he jumped out of his blissful state. His head filled with anger but settled fast as he tried to make sense of the situation. Like waking up in the middle of a deep sleep, he placed his hands on his face and twisted hard against his eyes.

Bong... Bong... Bong...

"Three bell noises. Three bell noises means danger, a warning, but from where and from what?" Kruno said out loud but nobody was listening.

Against the advice of the elder, the young boy in Becony had run up the tower and rang the warning bell, jarring Kruno.

Kruno looked at the crowd and noticed everyone was in the same trance that he once was.

How long have we been out and what was the reason behind the spell? I need to find Ivan and the others.

Ivan was easy to locate. Being so much taller than everyone else, he found him off to the right. Pushing by a few locals, Kruno found the big man staring off into oblivion. His long northern coloured hair blew across his face, but that didn't disrupt his intense focus forward, as he was also spellbound. Ivan slowly whispered weird things to himself under his breath. Kruno attempted to break his concentration with a verbal assault and shook him to no avail.

The caster, or at least the medium of the spell was simple — the Duke. Kruno didn't even have to look, but knew that he was the vehicle for the distribution of this diversion spell. The warning bells went off again, indicating an impending attack and he needed the crowd back immediately.

Kruno needed Decan and fumbled through the crowd in a mad scramble, and located him near Christian who, to his dismay, was just as affected as the rest of them. Being a Wizard, it was his job to warn them of this kind of threat. He should have been impervious to it. That would be dealt with later, if they lived.

Decan had the same stupid smile as the rest of the horde. Pissed off and needing an efficient solution, Kruno wound up and drilled Decan on the right side of his forehead. He knew how angry Decan would be, but he needed him coherent instantaneously. Besides the pain of a shot to the face, the irritation of leaving the perfect spellbound world would enrage Decan.

He fell straight on his back and was instantly awakened. Kruno stood back for a second and let him deal with this immense anger and orient himself before providing a short briefing.

"Kruno, you will need to explain to me right now why you just hit me before I stand up and make a mess of that pretty little face of yours. I love you man, and many would say you could drop me, but we will find out the proper way!"

"Listen, Decan, we have all been mesmerized and I don't know why — look around and see for yourself."

Decan panned the crowd and drew the same conclusion.

"Okay, how do we rectify the situation?"

Kruno grabbed him by the hand and helped him to his feet. With one arm pointing out towards the Duke, he said, "Our beloved Duke is, at the very least, a vessel for the delivery of this enchantment. Whether he has anything to do with its creation or not doesn't matter, he is expendable."

Just as he finished his words the bell heeded its warning again from Becony.

"Can you make the shot from here Decan?" Kruno asked as Decan drew an arrow from his pack and pulled the pew back. With one eye closed he released the arrow with deadly accuracy. The arrow raced inches above the crowd's heads toward its target and connected. It dug deep into the Duke's face, lifted him off his feet, and before he hit the ground he was dead.

Kruno and Decan knew the reaction to the Duke's death would be doubly magnified; the crowd would be furious over their beloved leader's assassination as well as feeling the loss of a man who made them feel so good while entranced.

The crowd felt their world collapse in an instant and with a sharp pain. They all came to in a matter of seconds and searched to find who killed the Duke.

"I killed him!" Decan yelled out.

Well, that wasn't the brightest thing to say at this particular moment, Kruno thought.

But maybe it wasn't such a bad idea after all. The crowd immediately focused on Decan, and he was able to engage their full attention when the braver members started to advance towards him.

"String him up..." a lone voice bellowed from the crowd.

"I just saved your life and you want to string me up? Each and every one of you has been in a trance, and by guess who? You got it, Duke Jackass." He waited a moment to let it register. "Listen, we are in some kind of danger." The crowd's attention was redirected towards the bell ringing from Becony. Each person drew his or her own conclusion that something was wrong.

"Look to the sky!" Another anonymous individual identified the serious threat looming in the distance.

"We could have just walked away, but no, we decide to assist you and, guess what, nobody cares." Decan mumbled on below his breath slightly offended, "Even more important, pissed off or not, somebody could have recognized the skill of that shot. I bet less than one in a hundred could have made it. Great shot Decan — thank you, oh great Decan — you are handsome Decan — nope nothing."

Kruno knew fear would overtake the crowd and potentially send them into an unorganized frenzy. The crowd was on the cusp of a chaotic response, and he only had seconds to organize the people and give them some kind of chance to defend themselves.

He recognized the sheer number of Cryptons, and their victory would be a simple one.

"Ivan, how long do we have?"

"Eight to ten minutes at most before they are on us. Like a well-armed hunter on a helpless pig," Ivan responded in his normal fashion.

"Listen up, everyone!" Most of the crowd started to break down as they realized they were going to die if they didn't run, but that was exactly the thoughts Kruno didn't want. To flee would be a foolish move.

"LISTEN UP, EVERYONE! I am taking over leadership of this town for this assault. If anyone has a problem with this, stand up to me now. I will kill you with three strikes of my sword or less, and then we can move forward."

The crowd needed someone in this desperate situation, and Kruno was known at least by most as a warrior from the stories told about him. Still, someone in the crowd yelled, "We must run!" and others agreed.

"To run now would be futile. They will pick each and every one of you with ease. Even on horseback you will be hunted down. Together we have a chance to defend against these vile beasts. Anyone strong enough to swing a sword will fight, women and children alike."

"We can't defend against them, there are too many!" a middle-aged man yelled out, and the eyes of the crowd looked back to Kruno with the same expression of fear.

"We *can* defend and we will. If enough of them fall they will leave. Strike their leader and the group will collapse. Now anyone who has skills with a bow, stand to my left."

Nobody moved at first because the leadership role wasn't completely defined.

"NOW!" Kruno yelled intensely.

Instantly they fell into line.

"Where is the armoury?"

"We are a small town, we don't have an armoury," a townsperson responded.

"What about a blacksmith's shop?"

"I don't think so!" the blacksmith said with selfish, foolish greed. "Not without gold are any of my weapons leaving my store."

"Are you the blacksmith? Open your doors and arm your town to defend themselves."

The blacksmith turned and ran. Kruno looked towards Ivan, whistled to get his attention and with a nod gave him the license to kill. Ivan turned in the direction of the fleeing blacksmith and ran after him.

Kruno identified the unarmed and instructed five of them to gather as many weapons from the impending shopping spree at the blacksmith's shop, and told them to bring them back to arm the others. Quickly directing three archers to elevated positions, he grabbed the remaining three, including Decan, to the front line beside him.

"Christian, we will talk later about this," Kruno said, implying Christian's failure in detecting the spell. He ignored how the Wizard seemed to shrink at the realization of what he had done, but Kruno ignored it. "I need you on your game now!"

"I am sorry, Kruno. I don't… I don't…" Christian stammered, knowing he screwed up by succumbing to the spell and was shattered by it.

"That's fine, but just make up for it in this battle. Make sure you drop at least a few of these bastards."

"Consider it done!"

The four front line archers landed on one knee and followed Kruno's lead by lightly digging four or five arrowheads into the ground for easy access.

In a matter of three minutes Kruno had relaxed the crowd, devised a plan and had the group ready for battle.

"Quite the speech you gave there Kruno, oh great leader," Decan said with a smirk. "Not easy bringing this untrained crowd to order. Don't see us having much of a chance here, my new friend. Three platoons of forty or so, that places us at a serious disadvantage. To combat that, including us, we may have thirty battle-ready warriors and another forty who have seen too many summers or too few."

"You sound like you're not too thrilled with our decision to come here."

"Are you kidding me, I can't wait! I live for this."

"I promised you blood and blood you will have," Kruno declared. Decan smiled big and wide.

Kruno made an immediate connection between Ivan and Decan. They both shared similar battle mentality. If they represented core characteristics of their people back home, the battles must be very interesting. Ivan's people, the Northerners, were constantly battling the islanders of Decan's home.

Do both sides laugh as they charge each other? he wondered. *Strange how peoples of such similarity would be at constant battle with one another.*

"Be careful in your words to describe these people. We are guests but they are defending their home. I have seen great things by humans in extraordinary situations. Maybe they will surprise us," Kruno continued.

"Hey brother, you don't have to blow smoke up my ass, this will be a slaughter. Unless someone comes up with some way of protecting this town, every last one of them will be killed. Personally, I will duck out once the battle is on its axis and live on. As for you… well… I don't think things look that favourable. Hey, you gave it a good run."

Decan looked seriously at a shocked Kruno. Kruno was blown away that he would make such a comment. Decan waited a moment and then tilted his head back, barking out raucous laughter. Kruno wasn't sure if he was genuine with the comment or not, but attempted to shake the statement out of his mind.

Christian, strangely excited, broke position and ran up to Kruno.

"Kruno, I have something that could help."

"Kind of busy right now, in four minutes those beasts are going to be in range. Get back in position."

"You don't understand, let me show you something."

Christian stepped in front of the four archers and drew a line in the sand in front of them. He then ran around back behind them.

"Christian, what the heck are you doing? You are starting to irritate me, how many beers did you have?" Decan said.

Christian ignored Decan and grabbed two rocks, giving them to one of the town's men on the front line, who had his long bow on the ground.

"Throw the first rock forward over the line."

Without hesitation he tossed the rock. The rock landed on the other side of the line some ten feet or so, nothing out of the ordinary happened and Decan rolled his eyes, "Amazing! Christian, that was great." His comment reeked of sarcasm.

Still ignoring Decan, Christian spoke the language of Wizards and blew sand from his hand which seemed to land perfectly on the line he drew in the sand.

"What the heck is going on here?" Decan yelped.

"Toss the other rock with the same velocity as the first," Christian commanded.

The townsman did as instructed. He picked up a stone and tossed it over the line. The rock, prior to breaching the line, acted like the other, but once it broke the plane of the line it jetted as if it was shot from a catapult.

Christian attempted to explain how the spell worked and what they would use it for, but Kruno already knew the purpose of the spell, loaded an arrow, aimed at the assailants well out of range and released.

All archers watched as the arrow raced at unprecedented speed towards a group that was becoming more defined with each passing moment.

Even the Crypton generals couldn't wait for blood. The anticipation of mass carnage was too exciting for them. The warning bells had rung a few minutes prior, but nothing was said. The small town really had no way of defending itself even though their stealth invasion was foiled.

One of the beasts envisioned pulling an arm off a warrior as it heard a whistling sound. This noise raced by the beast, and with the noise, brought about the battle's first victim. The arrow shot from Kruno's bow, and aided by Christian's spell, raced past the leg of the first general and dug deep into a Crypton infantry's neck.

None of them really got a good look at what occurred. All they saw was the head of one of their soldiers curl to favour a wound. Its hand reached up to grab something sticking out of its neck and collapsed, letting gravity take control. Helpless to fly or even to talk, its wings folded and it started its rapid descent.

To their joy, blood from their impaled comrade splattered all over them. Each of them licked the blood with ecstasy.

Unable to fully gauge what had occurred, the platoons maintained course and speed until a barrage of arrows started to flood the sky and claimed the next four casualties, one if which was a black Crypton general with an arrow through its jaw and leg.

"Spread apart, double your distance and height," another general bellowed the command, and it was projected to the platoons, who immediately responded. Not exactly evasive action, but splitting up would mitigate the losses that they were sure to endure if they stayed in a close-knit group. This would make them harder to hit from such a distance.

"Seems our adversaries have a few tricks up their sleeves."

"Load... Back... Fire..." Kruno happily released his orders. They watched as another Crypton fell from the sky.

"Excellent… good job little skinny one. Never doubted you for a minute," Decan yelled back to Christian, thanking him for his spell.

"Have I rectified my mistake?"

"Not yet, but that was a good start," Kruno responded. He knew that Christian desperately desired Kruno's acceptance and would forget his fear just to get even.

The Cryptons, in an evasive manoeuvre, spread and Kruno yelled, "FIRE AT WILL!"

Ivan must have eradicated the uncooperative blacksmith, who assumed similar size meant similar skill but was wrong. The men that were to bring back weapons ran with a wheelbarrow full of ordnance, everything from swords to maces, and the crowd was armed.

The enemy approached fast and hard, with many more than they expected receiving the gift of impalement, pierced by arrows ranging from the wing to the shoulder. The first to arrive on the battlefield was one that couldn't control itself after a chest injury. With a crash the beast landed near Decan's feet. He looked down, smiled and then focused on the remaining beasts.

The second to hit Tristan was another victim that slammed into a building, resembling a ball of fire. Seconds prior to the creature reaching striking zone, Christian bellowed words of the mystical language and a fireball raced from his extended hand with the same velocity as the arrows and inflamed the target.

The remainder of the beasts landed with ferocity, most of them positioned themselves on the ground, battle-ready, but the generals positioned themselves on rooftops to command their battalion. Many of the beasts engaged in direct combat, ripping through the inexperienced with relative ease. A few of the brigade took a different direction from the main battle arena and went on to seek and destroy the weak, hunting the women and children.

Decan and his front line backed up, slowly releasing the last of the arrows and tossing the now useless weapon aside. As commanded, the group had positioned itself in a cluster but as expected, it didn't last long. Most of the town broke down in battle and spread out making themselves easy targets.

"We are getting killed out here! We need to engage and destroy the generals. That is our only hope," Decan yelled to Kruno.

Kruno agreed and then released one of his many talents, pointing in Decan's direction, he screamed at the top of his lungs in demonic tongue.

In shock, one of the generals took note, became infuriated, and leapt into flight. Its target was Decan and it hit the ground only a few feet from him. A cloud of dirt burst around the feet of the black Crypton general as it landed.

Decan responded by pulling his two swords from their sheaths at the side of his legs and placing them comfortably together end to end. They magically bonded and grew as they did every time without fail.

Decan began to twist his now double-ended sword over his head slowly as his mind started building his strategic assault.

Kruno called over, "Good luck and God be with you. The enemy you have chosen is ranked class A and in the top tenth percentile."

"Gee thanks, Kruno, and I am not sure what you said, but it seems pissed." He paused for a second and then asked, "What did you say?" He asked with apprehensiveness as if not to disturb an aggravated cobra that possibly wouldn't strike if left alone.

"Something I would never say to a beast of that skill level. They are much more ferocious when they are agitated," Kruno responded as he watched Decan and the Demon encircle each other.

"He does seem quite irritated, what did you say, Kruno?" Decan asked a second time, strangely curious about what enraged it so much.

Kruno's plan was to assist him as he picked up a spear lying next to him. A hand still gripped the shaft of the weapon, but nothing else of the fallen warrior was left.

"Ask it yourself."

As many plans change fast, he realized Decan would have to handle himself. The spear was needed for another beast ready to lay its final blow on the most important of his allies. Normally it would be children, then women, then men but the priority list changed in a situation like this. All able-bodied men would receive his first attention, because they were the only chance at survival. The women were next because a woman whose child had just been slain is an excellent ally. With deadly accuracy he gave the spear flight and it met the back of a beast ready to strike a man. This man was fending off more than one Crypton, a skill level worthy of some assistance.

Kruno poured his focus on the situation unfolding behind him. The majority of the battle was out of his control for too long. He ran a few feet to give the delayed order to the archers that were placed in the buildings to unleash everything they had. The assistance was needed badly.

"I feel it necessary to find out what my good friend told you a few moments ago. I know it sounds crazy because you probably can't even speak common tongue, but I'll ask anyways." Decan spoke to the beast as if he was having a conversation with a new pub mate and couldn't leave his sense of humour out of it.

"Of course I can speak common tongue, but you can't speak demonic, making you less smart, I think."

"Valid point, I can't really argue with your logic," Decan said softy in his normal lighthearted manner.

"Before I death you, I can grant you the request and tell you what other human said." It pointed to the arrow in its quad. "He said you shoot me in leg, so you can use as handle to have way with my ass."

Decan broke into laughter.

"Damn, that is funny, and I guess just as insulting in the Crypton world. Okay, I understand why you are pissed, and I am ready for you to death me now."

He swung his double-ended sword slowly over his head and analyzed how the situation would unfold. Never taking his eyes from his opponent, he stared at its torso. Even though the main assault would arrive from his enemy's offensive weapons — its fists, claws or mouth —he looked to its hips. Decan knew the beast had to get around his weapon in order to inflict a wound. His double sword had a longer reach then its claws. This meant the Crypton needed some kind of distraction. It would have to attempt to confuse Decan in order to move forward, making him think it was going left but then come right. The demon would rely on a deceptive move and then its dexterity to strike, but it would be impossible to confuse its intended direction without moving its hips.

Something wasn't right and Decan could feel it. He remembered what one of his teachers from the Island had told him.

Some creatures don't need to use their mouths to communicate. They can have complete conversations with their minds, but as our ears pick up the sound of verbal communication, our largest organ will let us know when telepathy is being used.

What his old teacher referred to as the largest organ was his skin.

"We can't hear telepathy but we can feel it," Decan murmured to himself.

The small buzz in the back of his neck let him know another one or two creatures were attempting to flank him. With that keen sense of mental communication, they had the advantage, but now that Decan knew he was under siege from behind, and since his sword was in prime attack position for any angle, he quickly spun, driving his sword into the unexpected target. The assailant had slowly moved closer to him and was only a few feet away. Its hands were to its side with claws that needed blood. It was split deep along its abdomen, and with three more quick spins of his weapon, the lacerations inflicted more depth and rose up its chest, across its neck and finally directly to its face.

The general only had a few seconds of Decan's exposed back as he split the flanking Crypton into pieces, but took full advantage. It leapt forward, unleashed its open hand along Decan's back with its claws. Digging four gashes and then followed with a powerful fist as soon as the claws were free from inflicting their wounds.

Decan instantly felt the pain in his back and then the impact from the fist, which pushed him off his feet. Surprised by the reaction time of his adversary he re-evaluated its skill. Wasting little time and ignoring his pain and blood-covered back, he flipped to one knee and swung the sword blade where he assumed the Crypton's feet were. He was right with his assumption, but the beast leapt over his assault.

This gave Decan the opportunity to time his opponent's landing. Just as its feet grazed the ground the beast was tackled hard and driven by Decan's shoulder. The two of them shockingly didn't fall back a few feet, but to their confusion, flew several dozen feet! They crashed hard on the ground. They had crossed the mystical line that Christian created earlier to help the arrows reach such unnatural distances. The line didn't just work for the arrows and rocks, but for anything that breached its plane.

Decan lay on his back with his swords now separated into two weapons because they left his hands. They lay some five feet from him and the general looked up from its stomach. The positions they ended up on left Decan at a serious disadvantage. In the better position and with the human winded from the impact, the Crypton leapt to its feet and charged. It planned to crush him before he could regain his footing. Missing the oxygen to mount a viable evasive solution, he closed his eyes and to the enemy it looked as if he had given up.

Using an ancient trick that only the greatest warriors had the ability to do, he called to his sword with his mind. With only a few seconds before impact, he caught his breath and his weapons slid fast along the ground landing perfectly in his hands, first in the right and then in the left, as he spun to his knee once again. In a fluid motion the general's second last step ended with the complete severing of its foot. The second swing from Decan's other sword carved a good chunk out of its wing. The beast flipped over Decan.

Standing up, Decan knew his enemy was in serious trouble. Rushing to their commanding officer's aid, five Cryptons landed between Decan and the remaining battle, which also left him far from his allies. That little spell that Christian created at the beginning of the battle seemed like a blessing at first, but now seemed like one heck of a curse.

They approached in a careful but uniformed manner. Decan knew he was good but not that good. They would surely cut him down.

Well I guess I was wrong with my little prophecy. It seems like I am the one who won't be surviving very long, Kruno is going to have a good laugh at this.

They moved slowly, and focusing on his evaders, he didn't want them to stall, and continued to think but yelled in his mind.

Well, what are you waiting for? Bring it on! I am cutting at least two of you down!

Two of them leapt into flight and the others charged on foot. His blade, now back to one solid unit, rested at his side, but as they approached he realized that the ones in flight were too high to strike him and the eyes of the others seemed to look beyond him.

They weren't interested in him! The group attacked the severely wounded general instead. What Decan didn't realize was that Cryptons loved blood, even if it was of their own kind and especially that of a general. Whoever claimed the prize of its heart and bit into it would begin a physical transformation, its skin would darken and eventually receive the rank of general.

Floored by what just happened, he turned his head to see the beginning of the general's impressive but futile attempt to defend itself.

Canvassing the battlefield, Kruno recognized immediate assistance was an absolute for any chance of survival. Kruno needed the archers to start their assault. It was important from a strategic point to wait until after the battle had begun to use them. The enemy was now settled and wouldn't be expecting a strike.

"ARCHERS!"

All three of them leapt to a visible position.

"Men first, then women and last children. Defend our warriors, they are our only chance!" Kruno bellowed as he realized that the archers wouldn't last forever. They were as good as dead once a general picked up on their existence. Until then they would be a welcomed part of their defense.

With a quick survey Kruno recognized who was in need of aid. Several warriors were in the process of being ripped apart by the more experienced and numerous enemy.

We are in serious trouble!

He pointed to the archer in the tower first and then identified his first three targets.

One archer directed his volley to two beasts that were circling a warrior who had killed a Crypton which lay at his feet. He looked to be uninjured but definitely tired. A third beast, after snacking on one victim, had risen up to join their little group. Without assistance he would have been a goner. The archer's assault provided a welcome support.

The third archer Kruno would use for himself. He commanded him to shoot individual targets within striking distance of his own sword. Walking up to the first of many he pointed directly at the beast. The beast, not understanding what this meant, looked to Kruno strangely and completely confused until an arrow lodged deeply into its right shoulder. With perfect timing Kruno's sword met the distracted beast, almost splitting it in half. The format was brilliant. He pointed to a second and a third, cutting each one down in a similar manner. Striding with confidence he mimicked his action with each beast with stunning results.

Combing the battleground he noticed a warrior standing out from the rest — several beasts lay victim to his sword. He called to him and the man ran to his side. As he closed in, Kruno realized he was no man but a boy. In great shape and obviously skilled with the sword, the blood-soaked soldier stood beside him.

"What is your name?"

"Zel, commander," he responded with admiration and respect for Kruno. He recognized that his town —where he spent his entire life — was on the brink of destruction and the slight chance at survival, or at least some form of vengeance, was Kruno.

"How old are you, Zel?"

"Eighteen sir, and thanks for the assistance from the tower." Still panting and referring to the archers arrows that aided his success.

Kruno knew Christian could use a guardian and this boy Zel would be happy to fight with such a skilled Wizard.

"God favours you today and I want to exploit that. Find the Wizard, Christian, and help defend him." Scouring the battlefield, he looked past many humans being ripped into pieces but couldn't locate him. "I want to see you survive today. If you possess this much skill today, I want to see the great Zel in the future."

"I will find him and die defending him."

"Today is not your day to die and your comment is the reason why you won't," Kruno responded and pointed in the direction of a beast that was being fried by a lightning bolt. He placed his hand on his blood-soaked shoulder and said, "Go there."

The archers had wreaked havoc on the Cryptons on the ground, and had hidden from the eyes of the generals longer than anticipated, but that ended swiftly. Commanded by a general from one of the rooftops, two beasts leapt to flight from the ground and another two from a roof. The two from the roof easily took over the archer that had assisted Kruno. They pulled him from the window, flew up high and then let him go, but before falling the archer had a chance to pull out his knife from his leg sheath and dig it deep into his aviator.

One archer down.

The archer in the tower saw an aggressor fly towards him. He attempted two shots to take it out but missed both of them; its manoeuvres were too skilled. He fell to his back, lying on the tower floor with an arrow cocked. The diligent beast landed on the side of the tower expecting a timid and curled up victim, but when it looked into the tower floor it witnessed an arrow ready to fire, and from point-blank range it was tossed to the ground with an arrow sticking out of its forehead.

The first archer fell close to Kruno's feet, dead on impact as his bones snapped.

"Archers down to the battle now! Clear the tower and the building."

The tower wouldn't last long. The archer waited on his back with another arrow cocked, and even though he heard the command to get out of the tower, his legs wouldn't move, fear set in. Learning from the error of the other Crypton, two of them took flight and aimed for the legs of the tower. With a hard smash the six-by-six pieces of supporting timber buckled and the tower came crashing down. Two unlucky souls, both women running from their homes, were in the wrong place at the wrong time and were crushed to death, along with the second archer.

On one of the buildings, two Demons talked, a general and a soldier, in demonic tongue, "We have lost General Duka, but overall we have started to take over this battle as planned and this should be a stunning victory. We took some additional casualties from the initial air assault and again from the archers, but both threats have been eliminated."

"The man who killed Duka, does he still breathe?"

"I am not sure but I can find out."

"Yes, find out who he is and who is this?" The general pointed to Kruno, whose undeniable skill was evident as he cut down another two beasts, and just before they noticed him, he had commanded the retreat of the archers.

"He seems to be the commanding officer. This was unexpected to have someone of such expertise on the battlefield." It looked to its superior with fear because the comment expressed an intelligence error and if the comment wasn't accepted, it could be in for a severe reprimand.

"I have seen him somewhere before. That should earn our respect. Our causalities are much higher than expected and men like him may be the reason. Take two of our best and make sure he is out of commission," the general calmly responded.

"Yes sir, I will take Dith and Valus."

Recognizing that they were getting slaughtered, a sanctuary was needed. Kruno returned to his thoughts, *What the heck are we going to do now? Lord, I need your guidance, but of course, if you want my life to end here, then let it be, but if not, help me take these God-fearing people to safety.*

Looking around he got the answer he needed. At first he saw a beast get bounced off an object and then burst into flames and immediately drew the incorrect conclusion that it was another of Christian's spells. Looking more acutely, he could see the impregnable force of their most powerful ally... the Minister!

He had left the Church, and with utmost bravery and faith, walked into the battle while preaching. As long as he didn't attack any of the enemy he couldn't be touched. It only worked with truly evil creatures — they couldn't attack him and if they did they would feel the direct wrath of God. The divinity rules of combat forbid any attack on a person in God's pure graces who was acting purely defensively in nature.

The one beast had attempted to fly into the Minister and, as if slamming into some kind of invisible shield, it burst into flames and bounced in another direction.

Kruno grabbed a random older gentleman — one only barely scarred by the battle — and pulled him to the Minister.

"Submit therefore to God, resist the devil and he will flee from you," the Minister preached while holding a holy book.

Kruno grabbed both their attentions and gave his final order of retreat. "Minister, there is only one place that these people have a chance..."

"Everyone is getting slaughtered, women and children alike… there is no place safe for anyone," the Minister said, interrupting Kruno.

Kruno, needing his attention right away, slapped the Minister to the shock of all three of them, including Kruno himself, but he needed him fully attentive.

"That is the devil himself trying to break your will. You preach of a man that spent forty days in the desert and we haven't even been here for forty minutes. Get a grip. Did you not see the beast flip from you? You are invincible as long as your spirit isn't broken… Now, are you calm?"

"Yes, I am sorry, but there was no need to hit me."

"Fine, I will apologize later, but right now I need you to lead these people to the Church. Get them on holy ground and we will make our stand under God's shield. Under no circumstances will anyone attack from behind the Church's ground or walls… Understood?

The two nodded and the word was hollered by the priest to head to the Church.

Combing the terrain behind him Kruno looked for any of his friends' faces. Ivan, Decan or Christian weren't visible. He knew Ivan was okay; time had passed for them as warriors, as friends, now they were almost family. He could sense his heart was beating fine, but didn't know the whereabouts of Decan or Christian.

The pause to attempt to locate his friends and get the Minister on side was advantageous to the Cryptons who had been commanded to take him down. Circling down from flight, one wasted no time. It landed and led with a heavy right hand. With a quick reaction Kruno used his Clorian arm shield to block its strike, but the power of the beast forced Kruno to punch himself in the face. His nose opened up and began to bleed. The blow was still softened by the shield, but not an ideal injury as it made his eyes water.

"Impressive to sneak up on me like that," Kruno said as he wiped the blood from his face.

"You should feel good, to have me here, to take your life. I am best."

Kruno stepped back and his foot didn't hit solid ground, but he felt a badly gouged body. The body was still armed and he reached down slowly to gain another weapon. Holding his sword in one hand and a mace in the other, he prepared for battle.

The Crypton spoke in demonic tongue to the other two beasts that now stood side by side behind Kruno. They assumed Kruno couldn't understand what they were talking about. They discussed their battle plan. Both Cryptons, or Dith and Valus by name, saw this as an easy victory.

Kruno decided to let them talk about their plans and not release the small vantage he had.

Soldier one will attack as a decoy and the other two will strike from behind. A good plan but too bad I know about it. Well, I have no allies around, no archers, no Minister, none of my posse.

Kruno held his arms extended with the mace pointing to the two beasts and the sword at Dith.

Well, this won't be easy. Have to fight my way through this one, can't really see myself coming out unscathed. Three of them, interesting... could use a little help... Patience, things will work out... They always have! With an easy calm that few would have in a situation like that, Kruno relaxed and waited with patience.

The four of them were just about ready to break into battle. They stood at the corner of a house, only a few feet from the wall. On the wall, just around the corner from Valus and the other Crypton, Ivan walked slowly holding the ultimate king of blunt weapons... a war hammer! Ivan loved many weapons but that was his favorite. The weapon itself was similar to him; large, feared and powerful. Most would never use it because of its weight. To move it with any skill wasn't easy.

Ivan knew Kruno was in a whirlwind of trouble and was coming to his aid. Still the length of the building away, he had to move slowly and quietly in order to surprise the Cryptons.

Come on little brother, recognize that I wouldn't leave you in a situation like this. Hold these guys for thirty seconds and I will make sure they regret encircling you.

Ivan could see the backs of Valus and the other but couldn't communicate with Kruno.

Kruno released his one advantage because a little voice in his head told him to buy time and he spoke in demonic tongue. Directly translated, he told them he thought their plan was a little weak.

"Thanks for your advice, interesting that you would let us know you understood us, ill advised, but we thank you."

Kruno spoke once again but this time in Northern tongue, "I hope my feeling is right, my brother, and you are close by. I would be obliged if you could drop these two while I take the other one… How about on three?"

"What the Hell kind of language is that?" Valus asked Kruno in demonic, not understanding the Northern language. Irritated, it made its decision, "Stupid human must die now."

"One!" Kruno called out in Northern tongue, assuming that his feeling was right.

"Two!" On that count, Ivan realized he was going to be late for the critical timing of the attack and attempted to speed up.

Dammit, Kruno, I am not going to get there in time!

"Three!"

Kruno's plan counted on his sixth sense being accurate and needed Valus and the other hit as he attacked Dith. Ivan, five feet behind heard the final "Three!"

Kruno spun like a windmill, flipped his weapons around, missing intentionally with his sword to distract the beast and leaving it no time to swerve away from the mace that came down hard, cracking Dith's scull.

Seeing their opportunity of an exposed back, the other two leaped into action. Kruno turned his head to see the beasts almost on him.

Damn it, where is Ivan?

Valus and the other knew he couldn't retaliate, and with claws extended, they starved for the flesh of the warrior.

Ivan, dragging his war hammer a few inches above the ground, drove his weapon up. To Kruno he came with such speed that he only caught a glimpse of him. He saw his massive friend's long hair shift to one side, war hammer cocked and a look in his eye he recognized.

The war hammer's powerful impact was second to none and a prize he received from the selfish blacksmith he had to lay out earlier. It met with the side of Valus and satisfied all the prestige the weapon had gained over the years. Valus never saw it coming and only felt a slight pain as its ribs buckled like toothpicks and its spine snapped in half. Lifted off the ground by the power of Ivan, Valus slammed into one of the other Cryptons, but not before it was able to dig into Kruno's shoulder, spinning Kruno and disorienting him briefly.

Kruno turned to watch the third Crypton attempt to get up, but it was smashed with a vicious overhead blow. Like a man trying to hit the bell on a strongman competition — something Ivan never lost at any county fair ever since the age of fourteen — the war hammer went above his head and crashed down, shattering the Crypton's bones. Blood shot up over Ivan's face as he looked up to see Kruno favouring his shoulder.

"What took you so long? Getting slow in your old age?"

"Don't joke at this time, it's not in your nature. I am just glad you heard me, little brother, but I could have used a few more seconds... By the way." Ivan pointed to Kruno's waist where a second wound had opened up. Kruno didn't even realize it was there until Ivan identified it.

"Looks like the first one got me as well."

"I think we got it better, now let's go, we don't need odds like that anymore."

They rejoined the main battle arena to see a very poor scene. As they hopped over mutilated bodies and twisted corpses, things looked hopeless. One of the men in the crowd had some military training or just keen insight, and had all armed men in a circle surrounding the women and children. At a quick estimate it looked as if only fifty or so of Tristan's townspeople remained and a lot less were warriors. Of course the assumption that anyone outside of the main street was dead, or soon to be dead, was probably accurate.

Rushing into the circle, Ivan took position on the circumference and Kruno behind the protected barrier in order to review the situation and come up with something fast.

"We must make our way to the Church!" someone in the crowd yelled.

The Cryptons weren't stupid and realized this would be the only chance for Tristan to not be completely slaughtered. The Crypton general in charge made a smart command, followed by one that wasn't so bright. Intelligently it commanded some fifteen Crypton soldiers to form a battle line between the group and the Church. The only way the humans could possibly break the battle line was to modify their defenses by allocating all armed men towards it. This would expose the soft underbelly for flanking forces to charge and ultimately destroy with a final insurgence. Foolishly its next command was a product of over-confidence as it took half of the battle forces off the ground and set them to torch the village and destroy the remaining human life.

A cry was heard from the first building on the street adjacent to the main battle. A woman's voice shrieked, "You will not touch my baby!"

Funny that Kruno would hear only these words so clearly when all around him women and children screamed as the Cryptons started tossing corpses on the group from above, attempting to damage them emotionally. But he did hear it and looked over to see where it came from. At that moment he saw something he would never forget. With a loud smash a beast was launched through a window and then some twenty feet on to the street.

Kruno had a crazy assumption of what had happened but wouldn't believe it until he saw it. It would turnout he was right and a woman, a mere 110 pounds, threw a 220-pound Crypton warrior farther than Ivan could. For several reasons he had to intercede and one was out of sheer admiration.

"Ivan, take these people to the Church."

"Easier said than done," Ivan responded from somewhere in the crowd.

"Use Christian!"

Kruno ran to the aid of the woman.

Ivan wasn't pleased, and even though Christian was one of the main reasons they destroyed the Games Master, he just didn't like Wizards. Rolling his eyes, he took Kruno's advice.

Kruno started running towards a beast he knew had a bruised ego from being tossed by a female human and couldn't wait to pull itself from disorientation, charge in the house to rip the baby and mother to pieces. Kruno raised his bloody sword above his head and released it. Practicing his sword toss thousands of times, he knew that he had a dead shot and because his presence was hidden from the beast — its life was over.

Without losing stride he instantly changed direction and made for the house, assuming time was not on his side. Most likely there was more than one Crypton in the room. He assumed the woman was dead, but maybe he could save the child or at least satisfy a request, he was sure the dead woman would most certainly want revenge. To his surprise, as he looked through the window while charging the house, he noticed she was alive! A second Crypton held her by the throat and examined her as it was amazed by the sheer power of the woman. Its curiosity would end soon; with a twist of its wrist it could snap her neck.

So it was true. Many folk storytellers had discussed how, in times of extreme circumstances, a woman can use adrenaline to lift boulders or crates to save their children's lives. In most cases it was a friend's friend that did it, but in this case he witnessed it himself.

With the window only a few feet away, Kruno could see the woman hadn't been completely strangled. She still held her baby in her left arm, but was losing strength. He took his side knife, unused in this battle, placed it in his teeth and dove through the window. Thanks to Kruno's speed and fluid agility, the Crypton had no clue he had entered the room, until he had rolled along his back and jammed his blade into its ribs. Quickly he pulled the knife and made three more rapid but deep incisions all along the right side — upper rib, neck, and then deep in the ear.

The Crypton's grip immediately released pressure and the woman fell to her knees. Kruno quickly grabbed the baby in one arm.

"Your baby will live, or I will die. Take one minute to grab your breath and then we are up and out of here. Sorry, we don't have much time. The voices are getting farther away and we must join the others," Kruno said quietly but intensely.

Panting heavily and gripping her throat, her eyes started to swell. She was extremely grateful and tried to thank him, but Kruno pushed his finger against his lips, "Shhh, no time for that."

From a distance a large explosion ripped throughout the town. He wasn't exactly sure what that was, but he knew that was their cue.

"Okay, I need you up. I will hold your baby but you must handle yourself." *Not that I doubt you can. You just tossed a beast twenty feet through a window.* "I need my sword. We will run out, I will pull it from our victim and then head straight for the crowd. Don't let anything distract you. Get into the Church. I will take the little one... Okay?"

She nodded.

"Christian, there are fifteen soldiers standing in our way. If we bring the remaining armed men forward they will rip us from behind, very few if any will survive," Ivan informed Christian.

"Okay."

"What the heck was Kruno thinking? Why would I ask you? *Okay.* What kind of response is that?" Ivan assumed that he didn't understand and reacted quickly which insulted Christian.

"It means I am thinking… relax." Christian's mind wandered as he canvassed the volumes of spells in his mind. Ivan's patience began to wear thin and he started to prepare for an assault without his Mystical aid.

"Okay, let's try this." The magical words left his mouth with beauty, but as relaxing as the words sounded, the results were the opposite. As he spoke he touched the ground and dug his fingers hard into the dirt.

"Well, what happens now?" Zel inquired, still by his side.

"Well, this spell should create…" Christian looked confused and was unsure of the results of his spell until it finally took shape and a crashing *boom!* blasted the air.

The spell created a huge swell of pressure directly below the middle of the battle line. The spell forced energy to a location; it built until it exploded, ripping the ground underneath the Cryptons into pieces. The area where they stood unexpectedly buckled and popped sending all of the beasts on their backs, a few without legs. It also set up one heck of a smoke screen.

The sound was so loud that Ivan and most of the group couldn't hear and were in a daze. Quickly, the Minister was directed forward, even though he was untouchable; they needed him in the Church.

The path was cleared and, as they rushed onto the Church grounds, Kruno, a baby and a woman joined them.

A very bloody, dirty and confused crowd housed the Church. On a good day the capacity was seventy in the main room but most needed to lie down. Warriors had battled for a long period of time and were exhausted, with most of them panting. Warriors and townspeople alike were disturbed, still afraid for their lives and many were wounded. Horizontal occupants filled all of the pews.

Kruno scanned the room to get a damage report and put together a plan. First order of business was to locate all of his crew.

"Boys, gather here — Christian, Decan, Ivan."

As requested they gathered by the entrance in a circle.

"Hold on we have one more — I want... Zel, come here now!"

"Okay boys, if you don't know this is Zel, he is a hell of a warrior. Wait, maybe I shouldn't use purgatory as a positive description in the house of God. Actually, before I say anything else, each of us drop to one knee." The group did as requested. "Thank you, Lord in heaven for blessing our lives. Thank you for bringing us out of the jaws of certain destruction."

Ivan interjected, "And please Lord give us the opportunity to meet each one of these vile beasts in the future so we can exercise revenge."

That wasn't exactly the comment Kruno wanted, but he saw the look in Ivan's eyes and this wouldn't be the time to bring up that God himself was the one who would deliver vengeance.

The group stood up after an Amen and Kruno took command. He discovered that everyone was wounded except Christian, but no one fatally. Kruno had the worst injuries but there were more important things to worry about.

"Okay, we are safe for now. Those creatures can't breach holy soil or they will be breaking divine rules of combat. As long as we don't attack from behind this wall, we are okay. If we fire even one arrow we will have broken the rules of engagement and they will rush this Church. Decan, I want you to talk to the priest... make sure he communicates that rule to the crowd. Some of them are going to change their attitude from being afraid to being very angry soon and will want justice. Also, get him up on that stage and instruct him to put on the sermon of his life."

Decan immediately broke from the group to put the command in action.

"Christian, I need a damage report and hard numbers. Scan the room and tell me numbers of women, children, men and able-bodied warriors. Also let me know what condition they are in."

"How would you like the injured segregated? Slightly wounded, severely wounded and almost dead?" Christian asked and looked at Kruno who had a blank look on his face.

"Go now and don't ask any more stupid questions! Don't heal anyone until I give the order."

Christian let a little spell go and touched Kruno. Instantly the wound on his abdomen closed up, not completely healed but the bleeding had stopped. "Thanks little brother, now go." He appreciated the help but the situation needed to be assessed.

Ivan stood before him and looked for some kind of advice or command, but nothing was said.

"What travels through your mind?" The blank look precipitated Ivan's inquiry.

"That was a tough one, wasn't sure if we were getting out of that alive."

"That's okay, I knew we would. With patience comes answers and solutions. You say that crap all the time. Now what do you want me to do? How do we get them back?"

Kruno was concerned by Ivan's last question. As he said "get them back" he had a strange look in his eye.

"Listen, I need you to evaluate the exterior, and Zel, I need you to find all of our supplies. How much food, water and bandages do we have? Also, I have a task you're not going to like." Zel looked at Kruno with such respect that it didn't matter what he asked, he was going to do as requested.

"I have a feeling we are going to be here awhile. The Cryptons want blood and will try to wait us out. Probably our best chance at survival is to stay here until they have no choice but to leave. I am sure some people in here aren't going to make it. The air will become repugnant and I could see myself eventually starting to think that challenging the enemy might be a better fate than dealing with the putrid odour of decaying bodies. We are going to have to burn the dead immediately in the fireplace. This is our only option."

Zel's response was a nod. He knew most wouldn't be too pleased with cremation but he understood it had to be done.

The leading Crypton general stood outside the Church and decided to fully gauge the situation. Panning the background, it looked like a major war zone for such a short battle. Smoke flew to the sky and with a slight shift of wind blew in its direction. The sweet stench of bodies burning and the thrilling musical sound of the enemy in agony put its mind in a state of morbid comfort. The town was ablaze and anyone left alive was for entertainment purposes only, except for the humans that made it into the Church.

It knew that its blissful moment would come to an end soon. As the thirst for more death would override its mind and take control. This was the curse of being born of malevolence. A constant desire for the destruction of others could only be satisfied for a moment and then a burning sensation for more would take control.

Tilidus was a Crypton general and its intelligence level was greater than that of an average Crypton. Tilidus knew it wanted the rest of the humans and came up with a plan to get them out of the Godly protection. It was Tilidus's idea in the middle of the battle to toss the dead carcasses on the defending townspeople and it had a positive effect. The people had started to crumble as it challenged their mental stability.

How did they get past us? Didn't see that Wizard having the arsenal to blow through our line, tricky bastard. Our plan should have been an absolute success and a human feast should be our main focus right now. I need to draw them out and I know just how to do it.

Tilidus called to some of his soldiers, "Bring the woman here!" Two soldiers were digging into her leg and watching her scream in pain. They weren't pleased to have to hand over one of the last living humans, but wouldn't argue with Tilidus. If they even hesitated for a moment, it would lunge forward and rip their throats from their bodies. One of them dragged her across the ground by her hair and with a powerful toss flung her five feet, where she landed in front of Tilidus.

He grabbed her by the hair. Her leg was bleeding uncontrollably as her artery was severed. Death was imminent for this woman, but her last moments of life would be used as bait.

"People of Tristan, open your eyes and tell me if you are willing to trade for her?" Tilidus yelled to the Church and pulled hard on her hair.

She let out an agonized scream and did something she wouldn't normally do, but the pain was so bad.

The woman screamed for her husband with anger and fear mixed together,

"Jeff... Help... Please... Please... I can't take it anymore!"

Ivan had already commenced his analysis of the exterior to evaluate the potential threat looming outside their divinely protected walls. His eyes were focused in on the young woman being tortured, and the second she yelled for her husband, Ivan cocked his head back to see if their strategy had a taker.

Jeff, her husband, was carefully consoling his little girl about the loss of her mother. He had assumed that his wife was dead and rage had grown to a point of irrational thought. He foolishly leapt to his feet and rushed the door. He gripped a spear and charged. He wanted revenge and once he heard her voice, a voice he never thought he would ever hear again, he snapped and leapt into action.

Ivan understood the Crypton's strategy would precipitate a reaction, but didn't think Jeff would charge without even thinking. He thought that there would be time to intercept, but there wasn't.

Jeff foolishly blew through the doors to witness a horrific scene. Dozens of Cryptons were ripping corpses to pieces, bodies lay strewn everywhere, smoke filled the sky. His town was destroyed and in the centre, in plain view, his wife screamed as her hair was being torn from her head.

Their daughter's tear-filled eyes caught a glimpse of something she would never forget, something that would haunt her memories forever.

Ivan attempted to charge the man but it was too late. He leapt towards his doom. Jeff didn't even come close to his wife and made his daughter an instant orphan. Beasts swooped from the sky and lifted him off his feet.

All excited, one of the less-experienced beasts attempted to breach the perimeter of the holy ground, seeing the door ajar, but was tossed back in flames. Since Jeff didn't toss the spear from behind the walls of the Church, he didn't break the rules of divine combat.

Tilidus laughed, as his plan worked marvellously.

"STUPID, STUPID… STUPID!" Kruno yelled. "The next person who thinks they are going to charge the enemy like that, they will be killed by me before they even get to the door. We have one chance for survival and that is not the way. We are lucky the rules weren't breached or that Crypton could have smashed through our defenses. Nobody does anything without my consent!"

On the flip side, Ivan kind of respected the man for charging into a no-win battle. It was a typical Northern trait to have such a reaction.

Kruno walked beside Ivan to chat. Ivan gave his take on the situation.

"That Crypton general is smart, he speaks common tongue with near perfection and his strategies are militarily correct. This bastard understands human characteristics more than I would like."

Kruno inquired more about the total opposition and Ivan responded, "We are looking at at least sixty enemies, maybe upwards of eighty."

Ivan then looked to Christian who gave hand signals from across the room. After decoding his silent message, Ivan continued, but as he spoke, emotion took over his face. He spoke with anger.

"In here we have twenty warriors left, including us, and four are injured beyond hope. The women and children are slaughtered. Those vile beasts think they can get away with this atrocity? They killed the undefendable while laughing, tossed children's bodies unto mother, to destroy their spirits." He spoke softly, "Don't worry, they will pay."

Ivan began to walk away with a strange look on his face. Kruno was about to investigate a little further, but was called away by other internal issues. Food really didn't matter if they didn't have water, and Zel reported enough water for maybe four days.

Four days of water — two days more, and then we have to attack them head on. It will be a massacre.

Midday gave way to evening, which in turn submitted to night. Seven more died and were tossed into the fireplace for cremation. The townspeople's morale was draining quickly and hope seemed far from reality.

Ivan spent his time in a dark corner, thinking silently, forming some kind of plan. He figured out what had to be done and started to paint his face with a dark dye he had sought and found.

Decan walked over to see what the heck was going on. He discovered Ivan had altered his equipment and made a housing unit for several daggers. He also strapped short spears to his back. Decan questioned Ivan about his intentions, but Ivan didn't respond. He covered his entire body in the dark dye and talked in Northern tongue under his breath.

"Ivan, what's going on?" No response. "Ivan, talk to me?" Ivan got up and started to walk past Kruno. "IVAN!"

Ivan responded with one word and with a look in his eye that meant "don't try to stop me."

"Revenge!"

Kruno knew there was no stopping him. He had seen him in past ventures take down four guys just for striking a woman, never mind maiming large numbers of women and their children.

"I am coming too!" Decan reached for his swords, but Ivan gripped him with all of his might and squeezed his arm.

"NO," the large man insisted. "Me and only me, that's the way it is."

Kruno and Decan stood frozen as he walked up to the little girl who still sat in shock. She hadn't responded to anybody since her father had been killed trying to save her mom. Ivan whispered in her ear.

"They will pay! For your mother, I will take ten."

She nodded with maturity, a maturity that was forced on her by an awful situation. The horrific experience and the pain she felt left her connected with Ivan.

Morning was close to breaking and Ivan had not returned, so they assumed Ivan had met his fate with the best of intentions. Kruno felt a surge of emotion as a good friend might never return. He didn't feel that he was dead, but he had to be. Nothing was said the entire night, a night Kruno would describe as the longest of his existence.

Decan and Christian slept for a few hours, while Zel kept silent company with Kruno. Even though nothing was said, Zel's nods every so often let him know he appreciated Ivan's intentions for his townspeople.

The backdoor opened just before daybreak. Ivan, in a zombie-like state, walked through the door. He was covered in blood and had a few new open wounds, but he was in relatively good shape. Three out of four knives didn't come back and none of the short spears returned. The blood that drenched his skin wasn't his. Strapped to his belt was a bag.

He walked up to the little girl sitting on the edge of a pew and handed her the blood-soaked cloth bag. Her eyes filled with tears. The tears were of admiration for this amazing man, happiness for his return, anger for the bastards that stole everything from her and intrigue to see if ten fell. She was handed the bag, while Ivan turned to the corner and sat down.

Everyone who could observe did so with silence, hoping to see the contents of the bag as she turned the bag upside down, revealing the mystery. Out slid eleven Crypton tongues on to the floor.

"Three for your mom's anguish, three for your dad's bravery and five for your innocence destroyed, but eleven for inspiration," Ivan spoke softly.

The comment was genius and completely understood by this young child. She turned, smiled and a warrior against evil was born in a little girl.

"Tonight I hunt again," he closed his eyes, head resting on his knees.

The rest of the group could only speculate what had transpired that night because Ivan would never reveal. Kruno assumed he waited with patience using their over-confidence to his advantage. The dark worked in his favour as he would have hid and waited. His weapons of choice, the knives and short spears, were quick stealth killers that could be used up close and as a throwing weapons. Decan was fully impressed and couldn't believe that he dropped at least eleven; a new respect dawned for the Hillman.

Tilidus wasn't stupid but was stunned. He wasn't sure how many were dead at first, but discovered the assassin's consistent mark, no tongue. It didn't take long to figure out that many of his warriors were dead and not one human.

It must have been that damn Wizard. Who else could have pulled this off? Tilidus thought to himself. The general was angry but had to admire the abilities of the humans. *The Wizard was able to foil my plan with that unexpected charge spell. A couple of the warriors must have joined him. Some kind of stealth spell or maybe a time freeze enchantment.* Looking around he was able to see fear in the eyes of the soldiers. *Interesting, we are less than fifty now, I don't think we can take another night like this. Our anaconda strategy isn't going to pay off if they can charge us in a day or two evenly matched. I think it's time to use this to my advantage.*

The night was close to pushing the day from its dominion. Ivan, still acting strangely and locked in his own world, sat in a corner sharpening his instruments of death. The remaining townspeople started to feel hope; not because of the Minister or the fact that their shelter was the house of God. It surrounded the Hillman warrior. They appreciated and respected him, but wouldn't dare look in his direction for any longer than a quick glance. His thoughts were written all over his face, and even though he wouldn't draw a weapon on the people in the Church, nobody wanted to test that theory, just in case he was in a killing frenzy-type mentality.

That night Ivan left without a word from Kruno. He let Ivan be because that was what he would have wanted. It killed him to let him go unassisted, but Kruno would respect his strong request from earlier.

It wasn't more than a few hours when Ivan returned. He walked through the front door. He stopped in the middle of the entrance and with all eyes on him he released information even Kruno never would have expected.

"They are gone!"

Such a simple statement but the relief it provided was unprecedented.

Morning broke and the last of the doubt was confirmed, Decan was the first to investigate. Walking on to the street, staring at the sky, he realized they had left.

Tilidus knew they couldn't take another beating like they just had, and it knew the odds were weak for victory, at least in this situation. The decision to leave was uncanny for a Crypton — very humbling, incredibly intelligent.

For the group, emotions were in a paradox; satisfaction from the removed threat yet they grieved for the dead.

"I know you want to bury the remains of your dead. You may want to look through these carcasses for identification of loved ones. Your mind insists that you go back to where your home once stood, to find some of your life to take with you, but I say these are just bodies, anyone who was not in the Church is dead and material possessions are worthless if those beasts come back again. Leave immediately!" Kruno commanded with conviction. "Move on with life and their victory is worth less than it is now. Never mind 'their victory' this was our victory. No way should we have lived. God looked in our direction."

"You can follow us, if you would like, to Innisville," he continued. "We are leaving in ten minutes, not a minute later. Innisville is protected by the Silver Allegiance. You will be safe there."

Looking at the crowd, he scanned for Zel and located him.

"It would be a pleasure if you would join us." Kruno placed his arm around Zel's shoulders and walked beside him. "I have to consult with my group, but I am sure they would be interested in another sword. What say you?"

Zel never anticipated such a request and was overwhelmed, but tried to respond as coolly as possible, "I thought you would never ask." To travel with Kruno and his regiment was the opportunity of a lifetime.

CHAPTER 2

ENTER SAND SORCERESS

The sun on the third day was just about to set when the first glimpse of the Great City of Dryden breached the horizon.

Dryden's magnificent architecture and sheer size captivated the group. One at a time they pulled on the reigns of their horses as it was revealed to them. First Kruno, who was the lead horse, and finally Decan on the rear flank stopped to gather their thoughts as they each were equally impressed.

Kruno had visited Dryden many times and had even lived in its powerfully prestigious borders for a short while, but was just as caught off guard as was Zel or Decan who had never laid eyes on the legendary city.

Ivan seemed the least interested with Dryden, but Kruno wasn't shocked. Ivan hadn't said more than a handful of words since they left Tristan. Even when they dropped off most of the survivors in Innisville and he was glorified for what he had done, his response wasn't much more than a head nod in their direction. Knowing Ivan for so long, Kruno knew that wasn't characteristic of him. A few striking young females from the town gazed at him as the survivors told the story of Ivan as he destroyed the Crypton warriors, but Ivan ignored them. Thinking back, it was quite funny to see Decan's face and hear a few of his comments to the crowd because he wanted his glory projected to the audience. Ivan had all the glory, but as far as Kruno was concerned, he deserved it.

Kruno attempted a few conversations over the past few days with the great Northern warrior, but he was non-responsive.

I am not really sure what happened to you my brother, over those couple of nights, but I feel for you, I really do.

The group consisted of Ivan, Kruno, Decan, Christian, Zel and a handful of Tristan and Innisville people who asked for a guarded escort to Dryden. The people were afraid, which made sense after what they had been through.

If I was a citizen of Tristan, I would be doing the same thing. Seek sanctuary in the arms of the Silver Allegiance, and what better place than the home of their great King? Kruno continued to think, *Even if Tristan wasn't technically a part of the Silver Allegiance, Deo will surely shelter them.*

It's been a while since I have met with King Deo. Time has shifted since our last encounter, but I am sure he is the same welcoming, brilliant man that he has always been. He is a noble character, not just by blood but his demeanor, and it amplifies his right to rule this Kingdom.

Night was approaching, and if they wanted a soft bed and clean dressings for their wounds, they needed to hurry. Getting into Dryden at night was almost impossible. Kruno was sick of sleeping outside and wanted each of his men to avoid infection from the lacerations, compliments of the Cryptons.

"Come, let's ride so we don't spend another night eating from the land and sleeping in ditches," Kruno commanded with words he knew would invoke positive emotion with everyone. "Zel, I believe this is your first visit here, what do you think?"

"It's fascinating!" Zel responded, amazed.

"What about you Decan?"

"This would normally be a time when I would make a sarcastic comment, but even *I* can't do that. We have some impressive castles back home, but nothing like this!"

"Dryden has that effect on a man. It will captivate you."

"Well, I don't know about you Ivan, but I am pretty excited to see what's under Dryden's dress," Decan commented with a smirk and looked in Ivan's direction, but he didn't react.

"Maybe you could use your last battle story to dust off you know what?" Decan continued, attempting to invoke a comment from Ivan. "Actually, probably best you give it to the virgin boy."

"Why do you always have to pick on me? I am just saving myself," Christian responded.

"You know, Christian, you won't wear it out, you can use it over and over again. Something I am personally testing out as soon as we get in there."

Christian crossed his arms in frustration, and Ivan smirked and forced a chuckle.

Zel examined the outer walls as he rode alongside his comrades. It was constructed of a beautiful, off-white material in giant blocks. The walls were higher than anything he had ever seen. The length of the city was tough to guess, and Zel didn't even bother to attempt. Dryden, from its creation, was built to be admired for its beauty and its fortification. The architects spared few expenses when it was designed and even fewer during its construction. Like no other, the city had a series of four walls, one behind the other, with a little more than walking room in between.

There were three ways to attempt to breach a castle wall. The first would be to send catapults to smash its exterior; hence the reason for several walls. It would take days of catapult fire to take down one well-constructed wall, so to take four down would be very difficult and time consuming as they moved towards the city. Each layer had several archer towers to pummel infantry as an enemy would attempt to move forward.

The second way to access a castle would be to smash the gate. The problem with that was that each layer had its own four-inch thick, grated metal gate, which was usually open to promote trade and easy access for residents and welcomed foreigners alike, but could easily be collapsed if an invasion was looming. Another brilliant feature designed purely for military reasons was the last gate. The first three lined up but the fourth gate was thirty feet off centre. The distance between wall three and four was large enough to accommodate larger goods and products moving in and out, but still irritating to merchants. Traders didn't agree with this because it caused a bottleneck in the busy season, but it would cause even more of an issue for an enemy force trying to use a battering ram to smash the last gate. A battering ram usually takes heavy casualties as it attempts to breach one gate, never mind four. To make things even more difficult, its size was restricted as the attacking forces would have to shift and could only uses a ram that would fit in that area.

The third way to breach the perimeter of a castle wall would be to use ladders. The walls were so high that it made it difficult to construct, move and then erect a ladder that size. Plus an added feature of this incredible city was its northern and western walls; they butted up against a great river.

The reasons the city designers positioned the walls in this way was to provide irrigation for the city, a great trading area and the ability to mobilize troops to deploy along the river. It also provided limited options for attacking forces and the resources for a large moat. With walls so high it would be impossible to launch an assault from the north or west. The east and south walls had a moat that was fed by the river, and unlike any other city, Dryden's moat touched the exterior walls, yielding no place for the base of a ladder system.

"City of water or the island city — isn't that what Dryden means?" Christian asked anyone who was listening, but nobody responded.

One of the most amazing features of the city could only really be seen from the exterior. Every city in the Silver Allegiance has its name written in pure silver on the exterior, but a huge statue in the middle of this city supported Dryden's name. The letters were some twenty feet tall and rested in the right hand of a huge arm. The hand looked as if it gripped the letters. The cost attached to such a statue was nothing shy of a small fortune, but it was a testament to Dryden, its people and their beliefs. King Deo started or ended all of his speeches with "and he will raise Dryden up with his victorious right hand!"

They entered the drawbridge, but were halted when a guard held up his hand.

"Hold the gate, please, fine sir," Kruno requested to the guard who was giving the order to seal the gate for the night.

The guard, dressed in light armour with his halberd in one hand and a typical shield with Dryden stamped into it, looked across the bridge and thought for a second before he spoke.

"What is your business here? You should know that the gate is sealed at night. If I give the order to close for the night you are out of luck until the morning."

Kruno responded gently and with patience, "We are looking to seek comfort in one of your inns and seek treatment for the wounded."

Looking over the group, the guard on a power trip decided they weren't going to come in for the night. He waved for the other guards adjacent to the door to come to his side.

"Sorry, maybe if you were a resident I could let this slide, but I don't recognize you and rules are rules. Close the gate!"

"Friendly place this Dryden Mr. Kruno, I hope everyone is as nice as this guy," Decan made sure the remark was heard by all.

Kruno was shocked at Decan's comment. He knew he was cranky, aching and really wanted a stein of beer, but above them twenty archers stood in each tower, itching to fire, and the ten men out front probably could be a hundred with a bellow from the guard. No point in aggravating a man with that much power and someone who was probably looking to pick a fight.

"Watch your mouth pretty boy, or I will make sure there isn't a lady that will look in your direction."

"So it's like that, is it?" Decan responded as his manhood clouded his judgment.

"Just for that you're not coming in until tomorrow, none of you."

One of the ladies from Tristan decided to intervene. She rode up to the guard, covered in dirt, sweat and blood. She stared at the guard.

"What?" He responded.

"You should be ashamed to talk to these men the way you did. Who do you think you are?"

"But..." He attempted to cut her off, but to no avail.

"These men saved our lives, they fought for us against terrible odds when they could have run to save their hides. Do you know when we met them? Do you know how long we knew them for?" She spoke louder.

Attempting to speak again the soldier only murmured a, "But I..."

"I didn't know them, they were complete strangers. They were strangers, but fought for us and they are the reason we are here. Now a stranger asks for you to forgive him for being a moment late, and you tell him and the dozen others that we have to sleep one more night in the cold. If only your mother knew."

Belittled, the soldier didn't even hesitate and motioned to let them in. Decan smiled and dismounted. The soldier laid his shoulder into Decan's as he walked by. Kruno reached out and grabbed Decan to let him know to check his ego at the door, and realized the power of a woman's voice was stronger than a hundred men with a hundred swords.

When entering the city, Decan and Zel expected it to be quiet and lifeless, but that was the exact opposite of what they saw. The group passed the four gates, and as they entered the interior of the city, a great commotion could be heard from the distance. The main street was a broad avenue with merchant shops and eateries lined up on either side. Most of the shops were only two storeys high, but in the distance massive buildings stood.

"I am sure everyone is thirsty, drink." Kruno pointed to what seemed to be a small stream that was running down side of the street.

"The city of Dryden was designed to perfection, some say. The river to the north not only feeds the moat, but it runs through small, man made streams that feed the city. Eight main streets have this system. The west side of the street is for drinking, cooking or irrigation, and the east side is for cleaning and dumping. The streams enter from the north, flow south and leave through the front walls in the moat which follows back into the river," Christian proudly explained.

"Really tough for an army to force you out of your home when you have an endless water supply," Decan said, impressed.

Kruno mentioned he would show them around tomorrow, but first they needed a room, including food and fresh dressings for their wounds. He explained the city was much more impressive in the day.

Canvassing the travellers from Tristan, he figured out they didn't have any currency so he put them up for the week in the first inn they found, paid for their meals and wished them luck.

The city treated them well, just as Kruno had anticipated. Cities of Dryden's size and wealth had a place for everyone, no matter how different. Subcultures for all types were readily available, and even awkward Christian felt right at home. He had travelled with warriors now for many years and still had little in common with them, but here in Dryden there were guilds for Wizards, retreats, even schools. The city boasted one of the most prestigious schools for Mystics.

DSW, or Dryden School of Wizardry, was where Christian spent most of his days. He never formally attended DSW but always dreamed of it. He gladly paid the coins to attend certain one-off classes and was delighted. His name was readily known on campus from the battles he had engaged in with his posse. To many of the students, and some of the professors, he was like a celebrity. Of course he fed off the attention because it was such a welcomed relief from the way the other guys treated him. The professors at the school were some of the greatest Wizards in history. The dean of DSW was head council to King Deo and led the army's magic division.

King Deo embraced magic as a key strategic advantage in battles and boasted a collaboration of the greatest mystical minds anywhere. He was no fool and understood that a healthy configuration of knights, infantry, cavalry, archers and Wizards was a powerful combination.

The city believed in equal rights and that's what Kruno loved the most. Most of the major races had their own community including Hedgemen and Clorians. The Clorians, and their ability to make the finest weapons, was one of the main goals for Kruno's visit to Dryden. He needed Christian to be more independent in battle. Currently someone always needed to protect him because if an attacker breached his defensive parameter, he would be destroyed with relative ease.

Kruno had to meet with King Deo to add credibility to what happened in Tristan, and to find out what his administration's theory was on what transpired, but his affairs kept him away from the palace for longer than he would have liked.

Kruno worried about Ivan as time went on. Each night he became more distant from the group and from him. They all focused on healing, and if it had been anyone else other than, Ivan he might have drawn a conclusion that his mind was psychologically injured.

What happened in Tristan that night would leave a mark on most warriors, but Ivan my friend, you are far from normal. There has to be something else.

The city hosted more entertainment venues than any other — from brothels, to taverns, to gladiator arenas. Dryden had them all. It had the recipe for Ivan to run wild. He loved women, beer and battling, but the Northern warrior became anti-social.

"First order of business is to work on my comrade Ivan. I am going to figure this out," Kruno said himself. "I know you would do the same for me. Second, I need to fix Christian's hand-to-hand combat issues. Lastly, I need to meet up with the King."

Decan entered the dining room of the inn where they had been staying. Kruno, finishing his soup, looked over to an awful-looking Decan. It was easy to figure out what was wrong, but Kruno wanted to pick on him anyway.

"Would you like something to eat? They have a great fish soup, well it doesn't smell that great but it is tasty."

Decan's hand raced for his mouth to stop him from vomiting everywhere and he responded in a quiet but irritated tone, "I guess you weren't with me last night?"

"How could you not remember if I was there?" Kruno probed with a smirk.

"Lots to drink, way too much to drink. I can't remember a damn thing after we left Lue's tavern. I woke up this morning with one serious headache," Decan said as he placed his head in his hands.

As he spoke, two women walked up from behind Decan, reached over and simultaneously kissed him on both cheeks. The larger of the two slid her hand down and grabbed between his legs and whispered, "Good day, lover."

"Not exactly the best Dryden has to offer?" Kruno commented as they left earshot.

"What can I say? I am a lover of all shapes and sizes," Decan said with a little smile and changed subjects, "What are you doing today?"

"Well, that is what I need your help with. Sometime over the next few days, once your hangover is gone, I need you to go to Xavier's Weaponry Cluster. I don't care what it costs but we need something for Christian."

"What is Xavier's and why for Christian?"

"It is an area of Dryden run by Clorians. We need you to find him a weapon that will help with his close combat skills, they are pretty weak."

"You mean he is continuing on with us? I thought we had enough of his abracadabra, hokey pokey, look at me with my wooden staff."

"Always a joker Decan. Even with the serious hangover you've got, you can still muster something up — impressive."

"Yep, always a joker."

"Besides helping him out, I am sure you could find something worth your while to buy. They are the best weapon makers in the known world. This is where I got my arm shield. Their weapons can almost think — actually, I've always assumed your swords were Clorian."

Decan stood up slowly, grabbed a pitcher of water off another table and said, "Okay, back to bed I go."

"Why did you get up in the first place?"

"First and foremost I needed this," he said, lifting his jug of water, "and second, very few ladies are welcomed during a hangover stage, and as you astutely pointed out, they weren't even close to meeting the requirements."

Kruno thought for a while about how to assist Ivan, and after the day of visiting old friends in the town — bouncing in and out of a few taverns — he realized he needed advice from home, Ivan's home. The journey north was too far and arduous, so Kruno would send a letter.

"How can I help you?" a small greasy haired man asked.

"My name is Kruno and I need to send an urgent package. Where do you travel to?"

"Kruno, a well-known name, pleasure to meet you. I am Larry and we travel anywhere. If you are looking for speed, nothing beats our slingly travel teams. One of our messengers will travel with a slingly and personally deliver it." Larry motioned for his prospect to follow him to the back of the barn.

"As you can see we have four different teams, this is the one I would use for your package." He pointed to a version of a horse stall, but it had a twenty foot poll in it and a nest near the top. The area was covered in straw. At the bottom of the stall was a little green creature, not more than a foot and a half tall. It was gathering hay when hot, wet fecal matter struck it on the side of the head.

Kruno immediately broke into laughter. The little green creature flipped its lid and kicked the pole. The slingly, a winged animal about five feet in length, was coming in for a landing on the top level and looked as if the assault was malicious in nature. "I see they get along well. Can they speak common tongue?"

"Yes... well enough," Larry quickly responded to the buying question. "How long to Vard?"

Vard was the capital city of the North, home of the great King that ruled Ivan's people of the peninsula. The Northern Kingdom was split into three states, each with their own Kings. They all worked well together and often had joint efforts for expansion, trade or defense. The Lower Peninsula was where Ivan was born and Vard was the city where his relatives resided. It hadn't been long since Kruno had joined Ivan to visit the amazing Northern Kingdom — a trip he would never forget and would love to repeat. He would send his letter to Sven, Ivan's cousin, someone Ivan was close to and Kruno had spent a lot of time with.

"Vard! The North!" Larry exclaimed with an uneasiness Kruno didn't like, and the creature that just got shat on looked over strangely as well. Larry continued, "That will probably be a few days and be expensive."

"Have you ever been to Vard?" a stranger from inside the barn yelled over.

"Of course, who asks?"

"Then what would be your route?" He didn't reveal himself.

"Well, stranger, this gentleman is in a hurry and the shortest distance between two places is a straight line," Larry answered with what he thought was a brilliant answer.

A human dressed in coveralls with a thick red beard finally came around the corner and said, "That is a death trap! You would have to fly over the Algerin forest, quite possibly the most dangerous area to fly over. You would be shot out of the sky within minutes of travelling over the forest perimeter. If you were able to avoid attack from the ground then you would be surrounded in air by a dozen different creatures which would rip your little slingly to pieces and this poor man's message would not make its destination." With confidence that rises in a man on the fringe of winning a debate he continued, "I don't think you know what you're talking about, I don't think you have even been to the North."

Kruno looked over to the man and asked if he had intimate knowledge of the North. The man's name was Cardis and he brought Kruno to come see his method of travel, which was an Adas. After seeing his Adas he knew he was the right man for the job. This legendary creature was only really found in the North, bred in captivity like horses. Their name means horses of the sky in Northern tongue. Northern warriors used these beasts in battle, to attack from the sky and as intelligence gatherers. They were exclusively controlled by the North because of Northerners' ability to control certain beasts, like Adas. Others couldn't control them. The Adas would have to be willing to work with this man.

"How did you get one of these?" Adas were large, winged beasts able to carry the weight of a Northerner with relative ease. They were agile, with sharp claws as their primary offensive weapon. They had four wings that could move independently. The rider sat in between the front set and the back.

"I lived in the North for many years, close to Vard, near Ahus. After a while I was given one of these beasts as a token from a Northerner of royal blood."

The decision was easy. Cardis, on his Adas, would take the urgent letter north. A message that would be more critical than Kruno realized at the time.

Christian was engaged in a conversation with a group on DSW's lush grounds when Decan rode up. He overheard Christian talking about some great spell he cast in battle. Enthralled, the audience listened on the edge of his words.

"Christian, what you talking about now?" Decan called.

Christian turned and looked nervous, fearing Decan would steal his thunder and his moment of fame would come crashing down.

One of Christian's groupies retorted, defending their new hero, "Back off warrior! He is a great Wizard and will blow you off your horse."

Decan mentally prepared a comment that would surely destroy his partner, but at the last second took the high road and said, "Surely I know, Christian is my brother in warfare and I wouldn't want to make him cross."

Christian was shocked at this small, uncanny gesture and was relieved that his status would remain high among this group. His reputation was a critical factor to advancement at DSW and the upper hierarchy of wizardry, something he desired most of all.

"This is Decan, one of the warriors that rides with me. Our combined effort in battle is essential to our dominance in the theatre of war."

Christian said his goodbyes and the response of the crowd was of anticipation for his next visit. They really didn't want anything to do with Decan, but really cared about Christian. For a show, Christian didn't jump on the horse, but used a levitation spell to awe his audience. A young, awkwardly cute female walked up and sensually slid her hand down the storyteller's leg and told him to come back soon.

As they road for Xavier's Weaponry Cluster, Christian thanked Decan for his restraint.

"Well, don't get overjoyed as if this is a turning point for me and you."

"You mean you and I?" Christian corrected him with a smile.

"You see — this is why you are still a loser. I meant to say me and you because I am more important. To continue, the only reason I didn't say anything back there is because I saw the young lady in the crowd, even though she wasn't the prettiest of things, she could have helped with your little no-action problem. I am sympathetic to the lonely penis."

Christian continued to smile and even though Decan couldn't see him, he responded, "Stop smiling!"

The two rode through a part of town Christian wasn't familiar with. He knew where it was but had never been. Decan, of course, being his first time in Dryden had never seen anything like it. Clorians ran this part of town, right next to the area Dwarves primarily occupied. Dryden was a multi-ethnic city and subcultures had populations into the thousands. It was more than just acceptance by assimilation; areas like Xavier's could exist in a similar fashion to their homeland. Clorians came from Cloria, arguably the most beautiful part of the known world.

They were firm believers in living with nature and it could be seen in their everyday life. The streets in Xavier included a little bit of their homeland. They were lined with gorgeous trees, plants and strange but beautiful little animals. Colour was the first thing one noticed. Natural bright blues, greens and lavender overwhelmed the senses.

Clorians weren't great warriors and ranked well below humans, but they made the best weapons. How they were made was kept a secret. There was an element of magic used when creating them, even though they didn't have traditional wizards. Their weapons were special, made over long periods of time, almost alive and ridiculously expensive.

Leaping from his horse Decan's feet hit an unexpected softness and a Clorian greeted him, "Welcome, Decan!"

Decan had met a few Clorians before and wasn't shocked by their physical appearance. They had a light blue skin, completely hairless and with natural tattoos. Their skin would change shades a little based on their state of mind and almost looked like the surface of water.

"You must be the man I am supposed to meet?"

"I am Disha and the female you are supposed to meet."

"Sorry, I didn't know. I have trouble telling the difference," Decan said, feeling slightly embarrassed.

"Not to worry, I have the same problem with humans."

Decan went to tie up his horse and Disha interrupted explaining it wasn't necessary because the horse would be fine. The Clorian then placed her hand on the horse's head, rubbed it a few times and the horse slowly lowered itself into a relaxed state.

I didn't know anyone had this kind of control over animals other than the Northerners.

They followed her toward a tiny building. Its exterior was built with stunning white granite and there was an entranceway but no door; instead, water poured perfectly downwards from the top of the entrance to the bottom. All three walked through the water doorway.

"Great, now I am soaked, seems a little silly to have..."

Disha stopped immediately and turned sharply. She shot out her hand in his direction and opened her fingers. Every single drop of water jumped from his skin. Decan stood in amazement as he felt the water flee from him, float through the air in slow motion toward the door, and it was gone.

"Now that was excellent!" Decan looked down to evaluate his body. "Feel free to do that anytime." With a whisper he commented to Christian, "That kind of turned me on a little."

"Are you kidding me? You didn't even know she was a female until a few moments ago."

"Well, a lot has happened since then, don't you think?" Decan spoke with conviction and then winked at Christian.

"What is with water for a doorway? It's not exactly great fortification."

"Water frozen solid is ice, heated it is skin-melting steam — within seconds I can choose either. Actually, wooden doors are quite inferior."

Decan nodded his head and tried to come up with a response, but couldn't drum up anything and decided to just move on.

Oddly enough, the room inside was quite large. The walls were covered with weapon after weapon. Projectile weapons occupied half of the room, from bows, to spears, to darts. The second part consisted of armour and the last was heavy weapons. He was mesmerized as he looked and touched many of them.

"So when did you talk to Kruno?" Decan inquired.

"Hmmm, let's see, four years, two months and nine days ago."

"That is just ridiculous. We have only been here five days, is that some kind of Clorian joke I don't get?"

"We fitted him for his shield a long time ago."

"Great memory, four years, two months and nine days, I can't remember what I did a few nights ago. Who would know that off the top of their head and how did you know we were coming?"

"We have been building Myst... oops, sorry, you don't have that name yet." She looked at Christian in a way as if she had revealed a secret and then continued, "I mean, we have been building *Christian* a weapon for a long time, and it was just finished."

Decan was more confused than ever because Kruno didn't even know Christian then, but decided not to ask any more questions. Some things were best just left alone.

Disha led the two gentlemen into a big room behind the cashier's desk. One silver staff, about six feet in height, leaned against a wall.

With a big smile, Disha introduced Christian to his new weapon.

"This has taken us years to build and we specifically designed it for you." Christian really didn't understand how it was possible, but just decided not to ask how a person could create something for someone without ever meeting them.

Disha then asked for an absurd forty-seven gold pieces.

"Are you insane? I could buy two dozen swords with that! You want forty-seven gold pieces for a staff."

"Inside your bag you will find exactly the amount needed to purchase this weapon." Disha provided insight.

Decan opened the bag to find exactly forty-seven pieces of gold and normally would be impressed, but he had just walked through a water doorway and had water blown off him with the flick of a wrist. It wasn't as impressive as it would have been at the start of the day.

"First, that is an insane amount for a staff, secondly and most importantly, Kruno mentioned that I could use the remainder to buy something for myself. I could only imagine that an impressive community like yours that has soft, almost-living streets, the ability to create fantastic weapons and have water doorways, which is really cool by the way, must have some kick ass version of beer."

"We don't normally negotiate, but since your master has a Clorian shield, Christian is buying a staff we designed and you have swords that are Clorian, then I will give it to you for forty-five pieces. Now the rule is that you must spend that money here. Not in my store but in Xavier's and today."

Decan agreed to the terms. Disha told him about their version of beer and explained that with two gold pieces he could experience the best they had to offer.

Christian grabbed his new staff and was blown away that Kruno was willing to make such an investment. Holding it confidently, he started to handle it with relative ease, testing its balance and giving it a quick spin, but still couldn't figure out why it was so special.

"It will take you time to learn the complexity of your weapon. You will need to bond with it, teach it, as it will teach you. It knows you are the master, but you don't speak a common language yet. It is the finest of its kind and an unusual request for so many reasons. Magicians are too proud to buy weapons from us because they feel they can do it better. Also they aren't usually too excited about close combat and shy away from it. If you can master both arts and humbly continue to accept assistance as you have today, you Christian, will be a deadly adversary to anyone who crosses your path."

"What is all the love for Christina today?" Decan used the female version of his name on purpose to irritate. "First the losers at DSW love you off, second we buy the most expensive weapon I've ever heard of, and then you are prophesized to be great."

Disha found Decan amusing, kind of like a human would with a pet dog. She smiled and decided to explain in more detail what they had just purchased.

"Give me your weapon!"

She pulled the weapon from his hand and then tossed it aside quickly as would be done if something was burning hot. Before the staff even hit the ground it changed, as razor sharp spikes, long enough to penetrate a hand in a dozen places, jettisoned from the smooth shaft.

"We have enchanted it with several features and this is the first. If anyone touches your staff without your permission they won't hold onto it for very long. As you can see, the defense spikes will split through anyone's hands."

The two humans were impressed. Christian then was told to pick it up, and just before contact, the staff morphed back to its original state.

"Christian, may I see your weapon?"

"Sure."

This time he handed the weapon over and nothing happened.

"See, since you gave me permission, the staff's defenses weren't triggered." She continued, "Let me show you a few things to get you started. This staff's ability to learn is amazing. Don't look at it as an inanimate object. We have taught it a few things, triggered by common tongue. Let me show you an example."

The Clorian manoeuvred the staff, and turned toward a thick wooden pole in the room about eight feet away. With a quick jolt she snapped the head of staff and shouted, "RELEASE!" To the amazement of the two men, the end of the staff split into a dozen pieces of wire, which fired outward with little blades on the ends and dug into the wooden pole. With a twist of the wrist, the cords tightened and she yanked them backward pulling pieces of the pole with them.

"Okay, not only am I impressed but I am going to borrow that."

Christian was amazed with his new weapon. They spent another thirty minutes learning the basics, but it would take time and patience to utilize the weapon to its fullest capabilities.

Several hours earlier, Kruno had arrived at the main political building where King Deo resided and conducted most of his business. He knew it would take a long time before he could pass all security checks. The King and his guards weren't foolish and provided little opportunity for assassins. He knew the King fairly well and was at one point offered to be a Silver Allegiance Elite or SAE. As Black Knights were to the Dark Realm, SAEs were to Dryden and the Silver Allegiance. They were the best Knights in the Kingdom and greatly respected. Even though some of the SAE knew him, he would have to go through a series of interviews over a long period of time before being accepted.

Kruno hated being unarmed. Like most warriors, even when he was bathing or sleeping or with a woman, he had a weapon within reach, but an absolute requirement to see the King was to disarm.

Finally he entered Deo's chamber. The room was glorious and Kruno was sure even Deo himself, after walking through the doors hundreds of times, would still be impressed. The ceilings seemed to touch the sky, the walls were made of the finest marble and a series of stunning oak tables, enough to seat hundreds, filled the room. Before this King, the room hadn't held a table and it was just one big open space, built to impress but more so just because it could be built. Deo was a smart man and not as flashy as most leaders of such power. He found it was a big waste of space and made this a room for many political and social gatherings.

Along the walls were portraits of great Kings of the past, dating back dozens of generations. Other portraits and inscriptions were mounted as well — great Wizards, warriors and other residents who lived astounding lives.

At the very end of it all was the throne. A few servants were scattered throughout the room and guards at every door, but besides that, it was empty.

"Who is this man who demands to see me?" a voice bellowed from the corner behind a pillar. "Does the King have time for every last beggar on the street?"

Four armed SAEs moved in front of the man who yelled. Their body armour was a mixture of plate mail and chain mail. They moved with a steady, focused walk, one that would normally set off alarms with Kruno, but he was sure that nothing was astray.

"This man claims to be someone I know, but I don't know him." The King was visible now. His long beard was more grey than brown, giving insight to his age. It pointed towards a well fed short frame. It was Deo surely, but his body language was one of aggression, which was confirmed by his command to surround Kruno.

Time has passed but not that much. My appearance isn't that different... Not armed, somehow pissed off the most powerful King in his castle, with four armed SAEs. Hmmm, this isn't exactly ideal.

"King Deo..." Kruno attempted to speak, but he was cut off by one of the Knights.

"You dare speak to the King without being asked to speak? And you are not kneeling."

"He is right, on your knees, traitor," Deo commanded.

Now, completely surrounded and on his knees, he waited for what was next. Kruno's mind raced to consider his options; his first thought was of how to disarm one of the men if it got any worse. What would be his next course of action after that? The second thought pondered the serious label he had been given.

Traitor, why would I be a traitor? Maybe the King has lost his mind or been fed poor information. I better figure this out in a hurry.

"You better answer this question as fast as you can. After it's asked, I will count to ten, and if you haven't answered it to my satisfaction, then you will be done," Deo informed him, his intensity evident in his unwavering glare.

Looks like the King has become a real prick. This is a power trip if I've ever witnessed one. I guess he forgets what I have done for him.

Deo asked if he was ready, and Kruno nodded, giving his full concentration to how to answer as he waited for the question.

"Name every woman you have bedded, in alphabetical order, since the last time we saw each other."

Kruno took a second to digest the question and then looked up at a King with a smirk on his face. The guards themselves were confused as the situation seemed to change.

"Well, that is going to take a lot longer than a count to ten," Kruno replied, awash in relief.

Tension broke as the King laughed and said, "I was pretty sure you had swung the other way, making the answer very easy."

The guards backed off and Kruno himself started to laugh.

"I didn't want you grabbing my ass. If I embraced you and the rumors were true, then you would have a problem. Grabbing the ass of a King is a very serious offence and mine is irresistible."

"So this is what you do for entertainment these days?"

"I don't have as much free time as I would like these days, so I have to make do. I had you there, didn't I? I bet you had figured a way to disarm one of my men though, hadn't you?"

"He wouldn't have had a chance," one of the guards spoke out, defending himself.

"Don't underestimate this man. He is the best I have seen with a sword, next to Bruno of course."

"Any time, old man!"

Kruno kept silent to the challenging words, knowing the King would put his man in his place if the Knight crossed the line.

After a few moments of chatting with the King, he was led into the war room with Deo's arm around his shoulders. The war room held no more than thirty people at capacity. It was made more for comfort and lighting. There were maps all over the place and one very detailed one on the main table.

Deo pointed to the detailed map and to what looked like a speck just outside the Silver Allegiance's borders.

"Tristan, you were there, so I hear. Some of the transcripts that reached me were disturbing but vague. Reports say that the town would have been completely slaughtered if it wasn't for you, a Northerner and a few others."

Kruno described the battle to Deo and two SAEs that were waved in as if they were supposed to be a part of the discussion. He went into detail about the town's susceptibility to the magic, the invasion itself and whatever he deemed key knowledge for his audience.

Bruno, the King's best SAE and military advisor, jumped in immediately, "This attack sounds to be premeditated to me. Any clue who would have commanded a battalion of Cryptons and used it to annihilate a town so close to our borders?"

Deo knew that Kruno and Bruno knew each other, but introduced the second SAE as Clinton. Bruno and Clinton were both typical SAEs. They were tall, superb physical specimens, well-armed and bald. Being bald had more pros than cons; the primary reason was to eliminate an area of the body that could be grasped in battle. This was something that had started a long time ago, but now was a requirement for any SAE.

Deo looked blankly around the room and called out, "Rizzian, Master Wizard, are you here?"

From a bright window, an old bearded man materialized to Kruno's amazement. He was dressed in a magnificent red robe with a unique silver and gold design. Rizzian was the most respected Wizard in the known world. He was a brilliant designer, executer and teacher of spells. He was the Dean of DSW and head military council alongside Bruno.

Kruno was in the war room with the King and two of the greatest military architects of the Silver Allegiance. This was no coincidence. It would be impossible to organize this attendance. He knew this was more serious than he expected.

"Okay, gentlemen, how come I am a part of this meeting?" Kruno inquired. "I have only heard of this room, yet today I am invited in as if we are going to have tea and biscuits, then Bruno and Rizzian show up." He needed to understand why he had been given the honour of being a part of such a meeting. "Question is, how can you even trust me?"

"The fact that you asked the question is the reason we can trust you." Rizzian, with his smooth words that slid from his mouth, said, "Prepare yourself for military intelligence that would impress even the North."

With a wave of his hand the map on the main table jumped to life. Its geographical area covered Dryden up to the massive island of the northwest, the entire Northern Kingdom and Far East beyond the condemned area and far south to the land beyond the great sea. It showed every city name and was colour coded, showing a Silver tinge that represented the Silver

Allegiance and another area that was shaded black to represent the Dark Realm. It showed the battles of the past and how the borders had moved for both nations over the past two decades. The conclusion was simple: the Dark Realm had grown as far east and south as it could and the Silver Allegiance owned most to the land up to the Northern Kingdom, as far west to the sea and down to the mountains. There wasn't much more independent land the two superpowers didn't own.

"You are receiving sensitive information but your input is needed," Bruno commented sternly. "As you can see, there is only a small strip of land that is a buffer zone between the Dark Realm and us. They have aggressive plans for growth, have always envied us and have nowhere else to go, unless they want to attack the North, which we know they wouldn't consider."

"You think that the Dark Realm is behind the assault?" Kruno asked, shocked.

"If they are, that is a declaration of war. Breaching the buffer zone would be a sign of future intent to proceed into our territory," Clinton said and seemed to salivate at the opportunity of war.

"We have an agreement with the Dark Realm that neither of us would attempt to annex buffer towns. If they were to use Cryptons we couldn't blame them. It would be an interesting strategy," Bruno added.

"If they were to use Cryptons then they would be dabbling with dark magic! I don't think that makes any sense," Kruno said, fully understanding that Cryptons were demons born from purgatory and could only be manipulated by a group that practiced dark magic or that had made an agreement with controllers of the Netherworld. It would be a fool's way to power, something the Dark Realm wouldn't consider, he was sure of that.

"Dark Realm, dark magic," Clinton said.

"Come on guys, I know you aren't the biggest fans of them and propaganda is a great tool, but this is a little farfetched, isn't it? The Dark Realm was created as a name to intimidate — there is no correlation."

"I won't use a propaganda strategy based on lies, it could only backfire. This attack on Tristan is just one of many actions that have made us assume this could be true. When we expand our Kingdom, resistance is met, but we fight with rules and for the betterment of not only our lives but theirs as well," Deo informed Kruno. "We give new communities schooling and a sense of law. Lately the Dark Realm has changed. They have done horrible things to their enemies. Stories from reliable sources speak of women being raped, and then used as slaves, baby girls tossed over walls because they are of no immediate use. If children are old enough, they work to service the original members until they die due to exposure to the elements or of malnutrition."

"We can't communicate with the Dark Realm any more," Bruno added, helping give Kruno full understanding of what they faced. "They have closed their borders to us. Three of my men were hung for stealing just two weeks ago. These men would never have conducted such an act. They accused them of the crime because the Dark Realm needed a reason to keep our eyes out of there, and as a bonus they got to murder our soldiers."

Kruno was shocked but knew why he was brought into the room and understood why this meeting was required. He was childhood friends with Zoran, a high-ranking official with the Dark Realm, out of their capital, Pra.

"So you want me to visit Zoran and see what is going on?"

"You have no true affiliation to the SA and have a relationship with General Zoran. He would know what is happening. I am not asking you to put yourself in danger, just look into his eyes and tell me what you feel. He will be different if he is under the influence of the Netherworld," Deo requested, fully understanding it was a difficult thing to ask.

"And here I thought I was just going to pass on some information and then head to the pub."

Rizzian didn't pay attention to Kruno's comments, but continued to explain further, "If the area is affected by such evil, you will be able to tell because you are a man of God. An eerie feeling will loom in the air. People will be eccentric and have trouble socializing. Your friend Zoran will be strangely invigorated about stories of hardship and evil. Evil entities will watch you but attempt to stay incognito. The longer you stay, the more comfortable they will become, the more likely they are to err and reveal themselves."

"Gentlemen, I am off," Kruno announced to his group, mounting his horse for the long ride to Pra. "I am doing a favour for King Deo and will be gone for several weeks."

"Where are you headed?" the young Wizard inquisitively responded.

"Going to see an old friend, Zoran of Pra."

The reaction was the same for everyone but Ivan. Decan and Christian were both shocked and requested to come with him. They both knew the journey shouldn't be too arduous, but nonetheless, anything could happen on the road, and a party was always better off than one individual.

"Christian, you take your time here and use it to your advantage. DSW is a great school, meet with Rizzian to help advance your skills, and also learn how to use that staff. I am sure Decan can assist with some manoeuvres," Kruno elusively commanded looking down from his steed.

"What do you mean, meet with Rizzian? How am I supposed to do that?" Christian felt a wave of fear run over him. Although meeting Rizzian had been a lifelong dream, he was nervous.

"Why not ask for a favour when you are doing one for someone else?" Kruno said and Christian looked back with confusion. "I have arranged it."

Christian, with joy and intimidation, was blown away to meet someone as great as Rizzian.

"You're welcome."

"Sorry — thanks, Kruno! I am blown away, first my staff and now this. I don't think a simple thank you is strong enough."

"You deserve it. Walking with us has privileges, lots of perils as well, but a few privileges."

"Well that's great lovebirds, but what about me, when do I get some of these privileges?" Decan jumped in.

Kruno shook his head in jest and smiled.

Ivan stood there as if in another land. He didn't offer to come with Kruno, which made little sense. Normally he would have insisted and even if Kruno said he would have to go into Pra alone, Ivan would have camped out in the field adjacent to the city just in case.

"Ivan, when I get back, beer's on me." Kruno looked for a positive response but didn't get one. Instead Ivan slowly looked in his direction and nodded his head.

"Decan, can I borrow you over here for a second?" They moved out of range of the others. "Listen, something is really wrong with Ivan. I need you to keep an eye on him — actually, don't let him out of your sight."

"Something wrong with Ivan — are you kidding me? There are many things wrong with him. He is way too big, clumsy, ugly, full of gas..."

"Seriously, Decan, we need your help here," Kruno interjected. "I know him and I've never seen him like this before. Shortly, some assistance should arrive that will solve our problem. Check out The Messenger. It's a business that sends letters or parcels via land, sea or air. Cardis was the deliverer and should be back any day now. Please get an update on what transpired."

"What am I looking for?"

Kruno explained what he thought Decan needed to know and headed for the gates.

Something is seriously wrong, but I am sure my message will bring the assistance we need. A little bit of home should help Ivan, that and time will be the key to bringing him back, at least I hope so...

In a dark room, lit only by candlelight, two people moved in perfect motion. A man's barely visible figure mounted a young brunette from behind and engaged in erotic activities. Hours seemed to have passed as they continued with their rhythmic engagement. She screamed as if sex had never been that good before, turned her face to look back at him and exposed her beauty; something she knew drove all men wild. Her hands stretched forward touching the lifeless cold stone wall as she was rocked forward, but to her it felt amazing, everything she touched felt incredible. The man threw his fingers through his soaking wet hair so he could truly see his accomplishments slowing down for a moment.

"Is that all you've got!"

He reached forward, put his hand into her hair, grabbed as much as he could hold and pulled back hard. The pain was very real but it was mixed with pleasure. With her back arched, her head touched his cheek. Both glistened from sex-induced sweat, and she smiled.

Waiting a few moments, she retaliated from his aggressive tug by digging her nails into his shoulder and ripping his skin. Blood immediately started to pour out of the wound.

Angered, he tossed her sideways flipping her around. Lying on her back she looked up at an impressively toned body. He was angry at first from the lacerations, but anger quickly turned into excitement. Her naked body turned him on. She was possibly the best he had ever seen — large round breasts rested on a flat stomach. She put her foot up to attempt to stop his advance, but he pushed open her legs with relative ease, pulled her hips towards him and thrust forward. His blood dripped from his wound and landed on her breast. The sight was exhilarating and prompted a more aggressive stage. He reached over and grabbed a leather strap. She let him wrap it around her neck and he tightened it.

She couldn't breathe but it was exhilarating. His hand fiercely gripped one of her breasts and continued to pleasure her. He stared intensely at her face and saw her colour change. Her mind wondered if life was over. She knew he had the legal right to kill her and it would be a great honour if he elected to end her life right now. It crossed his mind but this one was way too beautiful.

Just before she blacked out he released the tension. She struggled for breath as he thrust harder — her plight drove him wild. She grabbed a small bowl with smoke coming from it, and lifted it for each of them to inhale. The smoke ran quickly to their brains, and the world became enhanced. It infected their eyes as things became dazed yet colourful, and pleasure mounted. They were both enchanted by the combination of wild lust and the smoke-induced high.

The door to the room was flung open and slammed into the wall. A loud voice bellowed from the threshold.

"Zoran, you disgust me. Stop this demoralizing behavior and meet with me."

Zoran, the lead general for the Dark Realm, answered to few people and he was pretty sure he was going to kill the bastard who ruined the moment.

"Who dares interrupt me?" Extremely high on sex and drugs, he sobered up fast when he saw the Wizard Gabriel in the doorway.

"I do, and let me tell you, Kings don't spend time doing this all day. You want to be King, but you spend time with all of these whores."

"I am no whore."

"It certainly looks that way, sassy wench."

Zoran was not a big fan of Gabriel. They didn't like each other much, but Gabriel was one of few people Zoran couldn't touch.

Zoran, stark naked and in front of Gabriel, turned and looked to the woman on the bed, "I could have killed you."

"It would have been an honour," she replied sensually while caressing herself.

"I like screwing you too much, you may have to hang around for a while. Take a bath, prepare another and maybe she will die and we will watch."

Zoran met with Gabriel in his chambers. The room was filled with books, flasks, powders and liquids. Small creatures were caged up or dead. The room smelt terrible and Zoran wasn't pleased he was summoned to this area of the castle.

"You are supposed to be a great Wizard, yet you can't invent a spell that makes it smell better than this?" There was no response so he continued, "Don't enter the room like that again, especially when I am with a woman. Try knocking first."

"How I am supposed to know that you are with a woman, conducting such disgusting activities? I don't know how you get such pleasure violating your body."

"That's easy, always assume I am with a woman, I usually am," Zoran smirked.

One jealous of popularity and the other of unique abilities, it was a classic Wizard-Warrior standoff, but they both knew battles were won with a combined attack of magic and swords. They didn't like each other but needed one another.

The Wizard's fingers drew an invisible square on an empty part of the room. With a few words, the dark, cold stone wall changed into what appeared to be a window. Through the window he could see a bird's-eye view of a man on a horse riding with haste.

"I have ears all over the land. Creatures in my command listen to the conversation of thousands and report to me when any one of a hundred words is said. I was told of a conversation hosted a few days ago in Dryden. Four men said Pra, Dark Realm and Zoran. Then this man left right away and speedily headed in this direction. Do you know this man?"

"I need a little more than that."

"This man has far too few scars for the number of lives he has slain. He is respected among most that he meets, he is confident about many things. He is tied to your past, but it has been many moons since your last encounter." The Wizard nebulously explained what he knew, not that he could see him any better, but he could feel certain things. "I can read a lot more about most people, but with him that is all I get. He has a magical ability about him. It hinders my capacity to read any further. This is extremely uncanny for a warrior."

"This man could very well be Kruno."

"I have heard of him before, and if I have heard of him he might be a problem."

Zoran's mind drifted back to his old friend and he responded with relative confidence, "He should be fine, he is an old friend and could be a great ally if we could convince him."

"But he rides from Dryden. Does he have a covenant with the Silver Allegiance or any other?"

"Not to my knowledge. He is a man who is ruled my no man, a true barbarian. I heard he was offered a seat as an SAE beside Deo and he turned that bastard down. That must have pissed Deo off." Zoran laughed. "Let me know when he arrives. Let's be on the safe side and keep things from his eyes until the time is right."

Kruno woke up and realized that for mid-spring there wasn't a bird in sight; it was very strange. Normally he would wait for nature to let him know it was time to rise, but nothing stirred. Although he pushed this small observation aside, he didn't realize it was an omen.

He looked down from a hill at Pra, the greatest city in the Dark Realm. He laughed a little when thinking back to the meeting with Deo.

I can't remember who made the comment Dark Realm, dark magic but that was funny. The Dark Realm is just a better name than the Silver

Allegiance, just a little more intimidating. I think it pisses them off a little because they came up with a name that makes people tremble. It's important for me to come here to make sure these two great powers don't come to arms, especially over speculation. He continued to think. *On the off chance that Deo is right and there is some connection with the Underworld here, Deo has himself another sword. If either of the two were to commit to the Netherworld and have any part in black magic, I would be the first man to join the other side. Once someone is under the influence they must be destroyed, that applies to individuals and nations alike.*

He rode up to the city and had to appreciate its fortification and beauty. It wasn't Dryden but still impressive. The walls of Pra were said to have been built of a mountain that once stood adjacent to its location. A combination of their greatest architects, builders and magicians supposedly constructed the walls and some of the buildings. What was strange in the equation were the magicians. They never usually got involved with building, but in this case they were a major part of it.

The city was fortified with high walls, fused mountain rock for strength, and each wall bowed out many feet from the top. The reason for this design was to make a ladder attack impossible. One more critical and unique feature that separated Pra from any other city was its moat. The moat was full of boulders, which didn't make any sense.

Esthetically the city had beauty as the outer walls were crystallized with a mystical, unidentified substance. The crystal exterior had a black tinge to it and always looked different each minute during the day. The sun would bounce the rays back like a prism. It really looked like a massive jewel, which was fitting as Pra meant just that.

As he got closer, he entered a line of merchants, peasants, farmers and many others attempting to gain access to the city for many reasons. There seemed to be a tremendous amount of activity. He noticed a lot of them had canvas covering their goods and when he tried to peak in he was met with resistance. What he could see was a lot of iron and metals that had been recently mined. Also many of the carts carried weapons, which were probably spoils of war or they were for a new blacksmith shop.

"What's your name?" a guard asked as he motioned him to dismount.

"I am Kruno."

The guard looked at him for a second and then pointed to the ground.

"Get off your horse now!" He seemed angry.

"Whoa, whoa, relax friend, it's no big deal. I will get off my horse."

"Where are you coming from and what is your business?"

"I just left Dryden and..."

"Dryden? Are you part of the SA?" the guard interjected immediately, with his voice raised. "We have no need for SA here, maybe you should just turn around before someone that isn't so forgiving hears this conversation."

Three other guards started toward Kruno and the guard.

Kruno was irritated to say the least. *Another guard on a power trip, just like trying to get into Dryden.* He knew he could cut him down with one blow, but it wasn't worth it. He could see that a few of the guards had blood on their weapons and the dirt on the ground had wet spots. These guys were trigger happy and ready to unsheathe anytime.

If this guy draws his sword, I am going to smash him in the side of the face before he even knows what hit him, but I think it's time to take the high road.

"Listen, sir, I am not part of the SA, I am just here to see an old friend," Kruno commented, sucking up his pride.

"Who are you here to see, jackass?"

Another time, another place, I will remember your face. My old teacher's stupid sayings come in handy because I would love to teach this guy a lesson, but not today.

"I am here to see Zoran."

The words surprised the guard and he immediately dropped to one knee. The guard started to question if he had been giving the wrong person attitude.

"You're a friend of Zoran?" the guard asked.

Kruno nodded.

The guard looked him in the eye and examined his posture. It was evident that Kruno was confident. He put his hand up to halt the advancing guards and said, "Please proceed."

It was strange for him to drop to one knee just because Kruno had said Zoran's name. Devotion to a ruler is one thing but that was extreme.

Kruno decided to stand back and watch the guards from a distance. He was here to observe and he took that task seriously. He watched them being rough on more than one occasion. One such guard went too far as he slapped the mother of a small boy and then kicked him in the head. The others that witnessed this action laughed. Kruno didn't react right away. That would satisfy his urge to put him in his place, but he waited for the guard to separate himself from the group. He followed him as he went to urinate against the castle wall.

Wrong corner, nobody can see us, time to teach you some manners.

The urinating guard felt something cold in an area he didn't want to feel it. Kruno had snuck up behind him, and with his dagger drawn, put his hand around his mouth and blade between his legs.

Kruno made a stern and quick comment, "Between your legs is a blade that I will use to remove your testicles if you make one little peep. Do you understand?" The guard nodded slowly. Kruno continued softer and slower. "If I ever hear of or see you kick a child or smack a woman again, I will remove your balls because you aren't a man. If this is the way you treat women and children, I don't care if you have daddy issues or your comrades think it is fun to abuse your power. I hope you understand, but to confirm this really needs to sink in…"

To hammer his point home, Kruno smashed the guard's face against the wall. His forehead immediately opened up and he was knocked out cold.

The interior of the city was like most major cities and offered a commerce centre catering to all man's needs. From prostitution, to pubs, to merchants who carried produce or clothing, to blacksmiths weapon shops — Pra had it all, but it was no Dryden. Kruno attempted to keep the words of King Deo out of his mind because he wanted to form his own opinion of this place. Kruno assumed it was all speculation or the means to create a propaganda case for war for Deo's supporters.

The people of the town were no doubt strange. He spent a few hours riding through town and going from shop to shop. The attitude of everyone was grim, they acted as if their lives were in a state of dearth. Shop owners tended to have one of two characteristics — extremely aggressive or morose. It was different but not too weird to conclude anything.

With some relatively easy directions, he was able to locate the main political building. Its exterior was as brilliant as the exterior walls. It had a beautiful, crystallized finish but it was abnormally designed. First, the building was unusually tall and each floor had a balcony on all sides. Kruno assumed it would be the ultimate last stand for archers to fire down on potential invaders, but the main reason he concluded was for entertainment. The main square was in front of it and all trials were probably conducted here. Hangings were obviously a regular thing as he noticed three bodies that still dangled.

Kruno found himself curious about the endless lineup of caravans heading into one building. He wanted to know what was in them and more importantly what was already in the building.

"Well, look who it is." From behind, Zoran called out to his old friend. "I had a feeling you were in town."

"Great to see you, it's been way too long, but how did you assume I was in town?" Kruno said with confusion as he reached out to embrace Zoran.

"I heard one of our guards was missing for a few hours and when he rejoined his post, he looked like he had been trampled by a horse, but he wouldn't talk about what happened. How many people would consider attacking a guard without killing him? Also, who would be so confident in their words that they wouldn't sound the alarm?"

"Well, he deserved it," Kruno said with a smile. "I watched him hit a woman and then kick a small child. I was blown away, but blade to balls and a head to smash, he learned his lesson."

"Bring this guard to me!" Zoran yelled his order.

"Don't worry about it Zoran, I am sure he will think twice about making that mistake again."

"Kruno, I just want to talk to him, no big deal. They should also know who you are. I am hoping this isn't a onetime visit and I want to make sure access isn't a problem. So what do I owe the pleasure?"

The two of them chatted and Zoran lead them to a gaudy room on the fifth floor of the main political building. Jewels decorated the gold plated walls, a long wooden table and chairs, which were obviously carefully designed with rare wood, solely occupied the room. In Kruno's opinion it was way too much, but it definitely portrayed an image of wealth. The room had a large opening that led to the balcony and provided an impressive view. The city was bustling, that was easy to see.

It had been many years since he had seen Zoran. They grew up together and were close once. Even though Zoran had a few years on him, one thing hadn't changed and that was his obsession with his physical appearance. For such a successful and respected warrior it was a weird personality trait. He kept extremely well groomed, thin goatee trimmed every day, relatively short hair that somehow seemed to stay in one perfect position even in battle, dressed nice and bathed often.

"You have done really well for yourself, Zoran. Your name is attached to great success. The Dark Realm has spread its Kingdom all the way to the eastern dead lands, very impressive."

"I am now the highest ranking general, pretty impressive from where we started, eh Kruno?" he continued after plucking some fruit that was delivered to the room by one of the servants. She had bowed to the floor and waited for him to call her. After she was done, she fell to the floor and kissed his feet.

"Did she just kiss your feet?"

"These feet will one day be running this Kingdom. King's feet are worthy of such praise, I believe."

"Desires to be King… well, they may have a few steps to go before that is awarded, and future King or not, I don't kiss anyone's feet."

"A few more steps indeed, but something Zoran will achieve one day, with my help of course." The comment came from the doorway as two Black Knights entered the room. Their armour was dazzling, black plate mail with carvings and designs all throughout. Each Knight's armour was different from the other. The Dark Realm did a remarkable job of making their Knights feel special.

Kruno's ability to analyze a potential threat never turned off. Without even thinking he sized up the two Knights. One in particular stood out because the plate mail armour on his legs had a special feature — housing for several knives on each leg. He also had a sword mounted on his back, but the knives were of interest and had to be taken into consideration. Only a man with incredible talent with throwing knives would make such a request to custom design his armour.

"We've gone as far east as anyone in their right mind would want to go. Things are great here — wealth, opportunity and fun. Would you not agree, gentlemen?" Zoran asked his two prized Knights and they nodded in his direction.

"This is Kruno, an old friend of mine. I am sure you know his name, and these two are my top Knights, Baccarat and Valin, I am sure you know their names."

"The great Kruno, we have all heard your name, a man who travels the country side killing anything that challenges him. I am sure even dragons would cower from your path," Baccarat commented with little expression on his face, but with a deeply sarcastic tone. He was the second Knight that Kruno noticed, and unlike his comrade, he had no knives and only an immense sword as his primary weapon.

"Actually, I've never heard of you Baccarat," Kruno responded perfectly. The comment angered the other man.

Zoran smiled as he found the little verbal battle amusing, "Now, now, boys, we are all friends here. Kruno, your name has echoed throughout the land, a Predator, the Games Master, plus many more I am sure."

"I am really not concerned about my name," Kruno said, his tone serious.

"Don't be foolish! We all want our name to boom throughout history. You're no different."

Kruno didn't respond but instead looked to Valin, "Do you speak or just stand there?"

Valin didn't respond but just smiled in his direction.

Kruno could have continued but realized three Black Knights were in the room with him. One was a friend, so he didn't want to test the boundaries. They were to be respected. The intense training they had gone through since they were children had virtually eliminated pain, taught them how to defend and attack with stunning ability. If they had been granted the right to wear the Black Knight armour, they were well skilled.

The mood changed over time as Zoran and Kruno continued to talk about the past and the two of them laughed and reminisced about old friends. Kruno made sure that he engaged the two Knights in some of the conversation to lighten things up a little.

Kruno noticed that many servants entered and exited the room with the respect that would make a Minister jealous. Each bowed to the ground and Zoran called them over when he was ready. One messenger waited nearly twenty minutes with his face on the ground, as if lifeless until the general commanded him to come.

"Zoran, oh great leader, you are needed, the meeting is about to begin."

"Sorry my old friend, I must attend to other affairs, but please stay. We have a lot more to catch up on, and there is something I want to show you. Stay as my guest of honour. In a few weeks' time something special is going to happen. You will love it." He instructed Baccarat and Valin to go ahead of him and began to ask a question of Kruno that he had heard from many Kingdoms.

"A Black Knight is a great honour, this Kingdom is incredible, full with ripe opportunities, but we have grown fast and I could use another top ranking Knight." He put his arm over Kruno's shoulders to help with the sale. "I want you to consider joining us. Look out the balcony, this is a great land and my Knights are considered royalty, everything that is mine is theirs."

"To be a Black Knight is something boys imagine and fathers would be proud of. It is honour to be asked, but…"

"Hold on my old friend, don't respond yet. Enjoy Pra and all it has to offer. Stay in one of our best rooms, mingle, enjoy the food, the beer and the women. We have the best of it all."

It was a great offer, and even though he was sure he wouldn't commit to something of this magnitude, he would show his powerful old friend the respect he requested.

The suite was great and it came with everything he could have wanted. The town itself was equally as impressive, but just as Rizzian had mentioned, things started to change over time. Kruno wasn't sure if it was comfort or error, but as time passed he encountered more and more peculiar events. On several occasions he happened by people who were speaking in demonic tongue. It wasn't from a contained few either, a wide range of people from different ends of the city used this tongue. In the SA and most places across the known world, it was pure blasphemy and they would be hung or otherwise punished.

Kruno spent several nights listening to winged creatures fly over the city near his room. He would wait and jump towards the window to see what they were, but every time he looked, he couldn't see anything.

During the time he spent in the company of Zoran, he was amazed by the people's devotion to him. It was mandatory for everyone to bow to the ground the first time they saw him every day. It was also frowned upon if you didn't do the same if his name was just said. Zoran cherished every moment; to the people he was something divine. The Kingdom, its greatness and their fearless leaders, Zoran and Gabriel, were discussed all the time. They were almost worshiped.

Kruno found himself back in the gaudy room of the political building and reflected on his time in Pra. He had been asked by King Deo to figure out if the Dark Realm was a clever name or if it practiced black magic. So far he couldn't conclude anything, other than a vain, aggressive leader, patriotic people and too much use of demonic tongue.

I didn't want to have to ask Zoran directly, but this will be the only way to figure out what, if anything, is going on. I have to be very careful with my words. I am about to accuse a very powerful general, in the middle of his kingdom, of working with black magic.

What transpired over the next few hours blew Kruno's mind. He had privileged seating as he stood on one of the balconies and watched a marvel unfold. He figured out what all the caravans were doing, why they were so secretive and what was in that massive building he couldn't get into. It was all for a military parade. The sides of the streets were packed with cheering crowds. Rooftops, the closest city walls, and any other high point were occupied to witness this spectacle. First the infantry arrived, thousands of men all dressed in light armour and armed with spears walked in perfect unison. A whistle would blow every few minutes and the men would change position from the spear at their side vertical to the ground, to a firing arrangement. It would blow again to signal the infantry back to the original position. It was extremely impressive, especially from an elevated view.

Next the archers entered and then the cavalry, followed by the Black Knights. The cavalry consisted of a large number of heavy horse — Knights in full plate mail with lances, riding fully protected horses. The sheer number of the heavy horse was unheard of and could run over a small army with no support from other military groupings. It was the most terrifying component to any war machine and they made a thunderous noise. The plate mail armour was loud when multiplied, and in conjunction with a chant from the men, caused the building to vibrate. It was an awesome sight and an impressive sound.

The number of Black Knights was never released, but it was more than he could have imagined. These men had to meet years of strict testing and human feats that many couldn't handle for a day. Besides the skill needed to be awarded such status, the cost to build that much plate mail was staggering. How could they afford this?

"Are you impressed yet?" Zoran reached over and grabbed the back of Kruno's neck, obviously very excited.

"It would be hard not to be. I've never seen such a sight."

"This makes my balls tingle. Keep watching, it gets better."

Kruno focused in on his testicles and realized his balls did feel good as well, but it was counteracted by the realization that this army was battle-ready.

Each group was accompanied with advanced mechanical siege and projectile weapons, consisting of catapults and other impressive devices.

A handful of the Black Knights, archers and cavalry stayed and waited, forming a perimeter for a large chunk of vacant land in the middle of the square. They waited for the last of the marchers and the Wizards. No more than a dozen walked slowly toward the centre of the square. They had beautiful black robes that dragged a few inches behind them.

"Let the games begin!" Zoran yelled vigorously.

Kruno noticed everyone enthralled with the parade except for Valin who looked over to him with the same smirk as earlier.

I would love to smack that look right off your face.

The games had begun. Wooden targets were scattered randomly and the Black Knights tossed spears and flicked their swords from great distances with deadly accuracy. Archers had moving targets as the magicians elevated them with simple spells and they easily struck centre. They mock-battled one another to express their tremendous skill with a range of weapons.

A loaded catapult moved into the centre as the first wave of the show moved from the viewing. It was now the Wizards turn to show off. One of them held his hands to his side and released gravity's hold on his body.

Humans' desire to fly rested in almost everyone and this trick was always a crowd favourite. He rose some sixty feet, stopped and motioned for the catapult to release its two-foot diameter rock towards him. It moved with great speed — if it was to hit him, he would be pulverized. Kruno had seen the aftermath of a catapult attack and he hadn't been able to recognize that it was a person. Just prior to impact the Wizard held out his hand and chanted mystical words, stopping the rock dead in its tracks. The crowd roared and the Wizard smiled as it stood suspended in air, slightly spinning. With one point of his finger the rock leapt into motion yet again, but in a perpendicular direction from him, over the city wall, and landing in a field.

The other two Wizards elevated themselves, as did the first, some hundred feet from him. It resembled one of the first stages of modern warfare. Any large army that had Wizards would normally elevate them, giving them an advantage to set spells on infantry, archers or the opposing Wizards.

The lone Wizard fired first with a lightning bolt from his finger tip. It raced forward and engulfed one of his two opponents. He immediately fell from the sky and landed softly on the ground. It was a great acting job — it looked as if he really had been killed and it was enthralling to watch.

The second Wizard chanted mystical words and set his right hand ablaze, and with the motions of tossing a rock, he threw a fireball toward his opponent. The Wizard defensively placed his hands in front of himself as if creating a wedge. As soon as the fireball hit his hands he opened them up, flinging them to the side and split the ball of flame in two; it barely touched him. Impressed with himself he looked for his target after the flame had cleared from his vision, but found only empty sky. The Wizard who fired the fireball had screamed just as it was being defended. It was a loud and spine-chilling screech that made all spectators cover their ears. When they returned their focus, he was no longer in front of the Wizard but had reappeared behind him. With an impressive chop kick, the original Wizard fell from the sky and the crowd went wild.

Interesting, you don't see Wizards attack with hand-to-hand combat. That's exactly why I want Christian to learn how to use his new Clorian staff, it would give him a critical advantage over men of magic. Kruno continued to think, inspired by the impressive show of skill. *One thing they truly have gauged is the advantage an army comprised of Wizards has over one without. The combination is deadly. If you are facing an army that is magically inclined, a military solution is needed or your odds of winning, even surviving, have seriously diminished.*

Kruno looked to Zoran on a balcony adjacent to his and saw him raise his hands to command the excited crowd to be silent. Within a few seconds the crowd was mute. Nobody would dare talk, and with a booming, elegant voice, he called to his people.

"You have just laid witness to the greatest war machine the world has ever seen. This is your army. Our cavalry makes the ground tremble, our archers can penetrate any heart, anywhere, anytime and nothing is stronger than our Black Knights. Black Knights are the key to our future domination. Many cities and towns will just hand over the keys to their land and accept annexation due to the potential decimation that comes from the axe, sword, mace, spear or any other weapon a Black Knight chooses to use." The crowd, with a motion of his hand, released the energy that was building due to the excitement generated by Zoran's powerful words. He loved every second of it, but wasn't finished, and with a gesture silenced them once again.

"I have to thank everyone of the Dark Realm, for you can see where your taxes have gone. This war machine the greatest investment each of you has made. Soon we will run all the land, and riches will flow to each of you." The crowd roared again.

"As you can see, it is not just the Black Knights that will lead us to sustained victory, but the Wizards, commanded by the greatest man of magic in the entire known world. He will be critical to the destruction of all obstacles. Gabriel, you have trained your Wizards well, and I was wondering if you could assist us with something. Mother Nature hasn't blessed us with the best day. Could you teach her to be more cooperative?"

Kruno looked to the sky. It was a relatively warm day but overcast and gloomy.

Okay, what is Zoran asking for now? This is crazy if he thinks Gabriel or anyone is going to change the weather.

Gabriel lifted his hands to the sky and used words Kruno didn't want to hear. He didn't understand everything he said, as it was a hybrid language, but he recognized one of the infused languages. It was demonic tongue that Gabriel used to call on the Netherworld's assistance for the monumental request. It was confirmed; black magic was present here and endorsed by the rulers of this Kingdom.

With his hands raised, he pushed the clouds from the sky, and they rose up like an ocean wave, revealing the sun. Kruno assumed it was done on purpose as Gabriel pushed them toward Dryden. The clouds condensed and precipitation fell on the SA capital and surrounding areas.

This time the crowd didn't cheer, but was lost in awe, as was Kruno. The people of Pra truly understood the power their Kingdom had and pride rushed in.

Zoran jumped in once again and asked for the great unveiling of their new Emperor. Several men pushed a massive covered structure in front of the political building just below Zoran. It stood some thirty feet high and had many points attempting to poke through the blanket covering it.

Things are pretty bad and I have a feeling they are about to get a lot worse. Kruno started to feel as if the walls were closing in on him.

"Everyone… praise… Damascus!"

The men uncovered a great statue of Damascus, a gargoyle. Zoran continued to talk but Kruno didn't hear a word. Whatever little doubt had been in his mind that the city wasn't controlled by pure evil was now removed. A gargoyle, body created by man but life and mind provided by the Underworld. A creature ranked second for its abilities on the battlefield. It was pure evil and used a combination of magic and swordsmanship to destroy most in its path.

Gargoyles started as statues that were created by men. They were originally constructed as decoration or to add an intimidating image to a town or residence. Now they were banned from all areas, including the Silver Allegiance, other human civilizations, Dwarves, Clorians, Northerners, Hedgemen and many others. After a gargoyle was built, eventually they would be turned and become an enemy to anything that breathes.

Zoran's speech continued but Kruno continued not to listen to a thing. The Silver Allegiance needed to be notified. The Dark Realm was a threat that needed to be extinguished. Never had such a massive population submitted to this evil. He had to attempt to keep relaxed. He knew many of the Black Knights didn't trust him and would be examining his body language to get a look at his response.

This is a really bad situation I am in now. Can't see myself riding out of here. Lying to Zoran would be self-preserving, but would deny God and that isn't an option. If I am to die here, then so be it. Nonetheless I have to be careful with my next moves. Shifting from thought to prayer Kruno continued, *God grant me a safe path from this place, and I will gather numbers and destroy this evil.*

The people ran and kissed the feet of the gargoyle. It was disgusting. It explained everything that he had seen in Pra during his visit. He waited for the speech to end and moved into the gaudy room. The crowd cheered with reverence. They yelled Zoran's name as he faded from the assembly and moved towards Kruno with bliss written all over his face.

"Well, Kruno, what do you think? You now know the darkest secrets of the Dark Realm. I want you to be a part of this, you witnessed the legions of men under my control. One of those could be yours to command."

"Zoran… can we speak of this alone?" Kruno said as he attempted to ease the situation about to unfold.

"Everyone goes, except Baccarat and Valin."

The room cleared and the party was going to begin all over the city. The four men stood in a circle and Zoran's eyes began to change. Whatever innocence was within him was dwindling fast. Kruno had to choose his words carefully, but he assumed God would want him to attempt to jar Zoran from a path of destruction.

"What are you doing? You have made a covenant with the Underworld and used a gargoyle to broker the deal?"

"They didn't make a deal with us, we made it with them. It was done on our terms. Damascus is our Emperor who has brought us many great things and soon I will be King."

"Are you crazy Zoran?" Kruno said intensely. The two Knights took the comment as hostile and started to slowly move into a better position to engage him, if needed. "I know you. We studied side by side in Church. This kind of agreement with evil will only send you down a path you don't want to go."

"AM I CRAZY? I will tell you what is crazy — following a God that you can't see, can't hear. Where is he? What has he done for me? I have been told to follow an institution where only a few know the rules. We are told to spend our whole lives sacrificing and then maybe, just maybe, we will have been good enough to be rewarded. Well I am rewarded now. Why wait?" He moved away from Kruno and then turned and looked at him directly. "I am a God!"

The two Black Knights reached for their weapons. Valin placed his hands on the top two knives just below his hips and slowly unsheathed them. Baccarat reached behind his head to grip on to his sword and started to pull it out slowly. Kruno recognized things could get out of control very quickly and instantly put his right hand on his sword. He froze in a position that gave him the ability to heighten his senses. He focused on the floor and used his peripheral vision to guide his sword if it was needed. His skill had reached another echelon, his left hand took control of itself. With his fingers spread, a small blue orb, no bigger than his thumbnail, appeared and started to spin and move leisurely around his thumb, through his index, over his middle finger, past his ring finger and around his pinky and then back again. His subconscious had tapped into a magical element that he didn't have control over.

I have no idea what this is in my left hand, but I know it will do some serious damage. First thing I will do is launch this orb towards Valin. I don't know if it will explode, burst into flames, or shred into little pieces, but whatever it does I have a feeling the man with the eight knives will not like it. Next I draw my sword to defend against Baccarat. He looks to be aggressive and will surely attempt to end me with one strike. Then I will use speed to overwhelm him. His sword is massive and must be close to double the weight of mine. I will take him with agility.

Kruno's thoughts of how the battle would play out were cut off by Zoran who understood that the room was a flinch away from being a bloodbath. He knew Kruno was one of few that had a chance to take everyone down.

"STOP RIGHT NOW! Black Knights, sheathe your weapons... Now!"

It was a pause that seemed to last for hours, yet only a few moments had passed. Baccarat sheathed his weapon but still kept his hand on the handle.

"You should let me take him. He wouldn't have even drawn his weapon before I would have split his head in half."

"Many have assumed a similar conclusion," Kruno responded with a calm confidence, "yet I still stand here, and the last thoughts that trickled from their minds ran down my sword."

Nobody relaxed but just stood there, still ready to engage one another. Zoran attempted once more to bring Kruno over to his side. "Will you change your mind, you could have everything?" he said passionately.

"Will you change yours?" The question wasn't answered.

Zoran told him to leave the room and Kruno's mind wasn't sure if it was a reality. He didn't know if it was a farce. He cautiously backed up through the door, fully expecting an attack, but all he got was a proclamation.

"Kruno, you came here a friend, you leave an acquaintance. The next time I see you, you will be my enemy!"

Kruno moved with haste, but didn't run, mounted his horse and rode toward the gates. He had a few things in his room he decided were casualties and left them behind. During the entire trip through the city he waited for an arrow in his back or a command to take him, but nothing came. His body was still in complete battle mode until several hours' ride from Pra, when he finally relaxed a little.

While he was riding, Baccarat, Valin and Zoran moved to the balcony to watch him leave. Baccarat spoke again, "You should have let us take care of him. He could be a problem."

"Zoran did you a favour." Gabriel appeared out of thin air. He had always been in the room and witnessed the entire event. Baccarat rolled his eyes.

"That man has more skill then even he realizes. If you examined his left hand, he had spell waiting to unleash on one of you." Baccarat asked what would have happened if the spell had been unleashed. The Wizard replied with honesty, "I don't know, that's what frightens me."

"If that was a Predator in the room, would you have been so quick to jump in?" Zoran spoke with intensity. "What if it was the Games Master — would you be so excited to attack? Well that man took both of them out. Show him some respect. Plus, he is still an important part of our plan."

Deo stood on his throne and looked out among dozens of guests, most of whom were political figures. The crowd was dressed in their finest attire to impress the great King of the Silver Allegiance. Some had met with him before, but for most, this was a once in a lifetime event. Just to dine in the Chamber of Deo was a privilege.

Everyone was enjoying their second course when a man with long untidy hair, dressed in light armour and covered in dirt interrupted their meal. The guests were mostly from the upper-class and judged him for his appearance as someone who was in the wrong place or someone who was extremely crass. The man was Kruno and as soon as Deo caught sight of him and could see the duress he had been under, he commanded his full attention.

"Excuse me notable guests, I hope you are enjoying today's meal and I am looking forward to our conversations tonight. I have a matter I must discuss in private. Please feel free to continue your meal and I will be back shortly."

The crowd, for the most part, was upset. Most were enjoying Deo's company for the first and probably the last time unless they made an impression, and didn't want someone to disturb their one shot at his ear. The upper echelons were insulted that a man with a grotesque and offensive presentation was demanding enough to take away the King from them.

Deo signaled to meet in the War Room.

"You really dressed up for the party, didn't you? Ever consider a bath?" Kruno normally would have appreciated Deo's humour, but he was exhausted, covered in dirt and sweat and knew he smelled terrible.

"I have been riding for many days. I've slept the bare minimum necessary to keep on my horse and stay conscious. I've eaten next to nothing."

"Food we can get you and a good place to sleep is around the corner, but something isn't right, that is obvious." As Deo asked what was wrong, Rizzian entered the room with Clinton, one of Deo's proclaimed great SAE Knights.

"Sorry for my appearance and my short attitude, but I am not all here. My eyes sting and my balance is off. Where is Bruno?"

"Bruno's affairs keep him away. The four of us are going to discuss our plan of action based on your findings, so please continue," Deo requested and stared at him, ready to absorb his words.

Kruno's head started to feel heavy. His thoughts were slower than normal and he was thoroughly exhausted. This was a state he avoided as much as possible, but the tension of riding for that long, always wondering when he was going to be attacked, was intense. Struggling, he continued to inform them of his trip to the Dark Realm.

"Well, you were right. Zoran, my old friend, is now the chief commander of the Dark Realm. He has completely flipped sides. From what I witnessed, the entire city, maybe the entire kingdom, is under the influence of black magic."

"Are you positive? This is one heck of an accusation," Clinton spoke out.

The three of them started to talk amongst each other before he had a chance to explain why he drew the conclusion he had. Clinton remained skeptical as the other two seemed to want it to be true, but didn't at the same time. Deo was a person who liked the worst case scenario because he could plan for it and have full support. The worst case scenario made decisions easy. The debate went back and forth until Kruno refocused and jumped in to end the discussion.

"They worship their Emperor. Their Emperor brokered a deal with the Netherworld. Their Emperor is Damascus!" Kruno stopped at that point and watched Deo and Clinton look to Rizzian who knew the name and educated the others, "A gargoyle!"

The words Rizzian used were gentle and soft, but the impact silenced a King. Clinton sat down, Rizzian looked to the ceiling and Deo put his hands on the table. All of them silently imagined the future battles to come. Black magic was one thing, but the support of gargoyles would be horrific. They could tear through a man with ease and enjoyed nothing more.

Kruno waited for the appropriate time and began to describe all that he saw including the massive army, "The ground shook with countless infantry, heavy horse, knights, archers and magicians, many more than I anticipated."

"Yet they let you live! Why would they let you ride back here and inform us?" Clinton interrogated.

Kruno shook his head, baffled.

"They wanted us to understand their power and numbers. They want this information to act as a de-motivator for our people," Rizzian said. Gargoyles and black magic were unquestionably cursed; the mere thought of battling such unknown evil continued to keep the King quiet.

"How do you think the people would respond?"

"Our people… our people will react with excitement, with bravery and will shatter evil of any kind. This knowledge will start a fire in our bellies that can only be extinguished with the destruction of evil," Deo the great King responded in a way few would — with enthusiasm. Even if his mind told him differently, no one would know.

Deo commanded Clinton to make sure the people in the other room were informed that their night would continue but without him. He began pointing to the massive map consisting of the Northern Kingdom, the Dark Realm, the Eastern Dead Lands and past the mountains to the south. It was highly impressive; so few detailed and accurate maps existed. The two discussed the progression of the Dark Realm over the past few years, and more importantly, the past few months. They speculated on its future advancements.

"So there will be an attack. I think I should speed up the talks we had discussed."

Kruno was in the room and tried to focus, but really wanted to leave, check on Ivan and get some badly needed rest. Clinton had re-entered and spoke, "If we are going to seek an alliance with the North, we would have a greater chance at binding the deal if you go, my King."

"I disagree with this idea. The journey is long and could be dangerous. If the Black Knights knew of this, they would throw their entire army at you, attempting to castrate us. Your death would be devastating for Dryden and great for our enemy." Rizzian looked forward with concern.

"Clinton is right. If we want the Northern Kingdom to stand as allies, I will have to go. It would be foolish for the Dark Realm to kill me at this time. That would trigger a war they couldn't handle now. Plus there are a hundred ways to travel to Vard, and few that would know my path."

"I am just saying that if you were to fail or if an attack was to come while you were gone, who would take your place?" Rizzian continued against what he knew would be stubborn resistance.

"Of course my son would have full control," Deo proudly smiled. "Plus the attack wouldn't happen until next spring at the earliest, and would never be on Dryden itself. That would be foolish. No army could smash the walls and would be obliterated by our archers and magicians. You wouldn't even have to leave the city."

"He has greatness in his blood, and is a boy on the cusp of being a man, but he is still a boy," Rizzian responded to the comment about Deo's son.

"My son becomes more impressive every day. He is well skilled and would be a fine leader." The group wouldn't say much more, but it was obvious that at least Rizzian didn't think he was capable of the job. Any more comments that expressed his negative opinion could be construed as insulting to Deo, which was a bad idea.

"For the small chance that this could happen and because it is time for him to get lessons in real life, call to my son and have him join us here immediately." Deo requested Clinton have someone fetch his son and then turned to Kruno. "What do you think, my good man? Is a partnership with the North possible, could men and Northerners work together? I ask you because you have been there, lived there and one of your party members is a Northerner, correct?"

"I think it couldn't hurt." Kruno mustered up energy just to speak. "If you could convince the North to align with the Silver Allegiance, the Dark Realm would never be a threat. I do agree with him," he pointed to Clinton, "that the only shot you have at this is with your presence, but make sure you keep safe, they will come after you if they can… I would if I was in their shoes."

Kruno knew it was his time to leave.

"King Deo, Rizzian, if you don't mind, I would like to be excused. I need to get cleaned up, find Ivan my Northern friend, and I shouldn't be made aware of your final decision to travel north or which route you would take."

Deo walked over and placed his hand on his shoulder, "My good man, I trust you and would even request your advice on the route I should take, but I can see your brain is askew. You would probably lead me south instead of north because of your state of mind."

Kruno smiled at the sense of humour Deo retained even in this serious situation. His personality would jell with the North. His chances of an alliance were bleak, but maybe he could pull it off.

The next words from Kruno's mouth were like magic to Deo and Rizzian, "If you need my sword, you have it." They both knew what an asset he would be as a military leader and in individual combat, and were pleased with his pledge.

"So you will accept my offer to become one of my elites, to become an SAE?" Deo asked and smiled at his salesmanship.

"Sorry King Deo, I am not accepting a lifetime pledge to work under the SA, even though it is a great honour, but I have made a commitment to God himself to make evil, true unabated evil, my enemy. The Dark Realm is now my enemy. My friends will probably join you as well, but I can't speak for them."

Kruno didn't notice Rizzian's odd behavior because he was in a deep conversation with the King. As soon as he had mentioned Ivan's name he pulled his cloak over his hand because it began to glow.

"You mentioned Ivan as your Northern friend. He is a large man, long dirty blond hair and a massive tattoo of a cross on his back?" Kruno nodded his head and the Wizard continued, "Has he been acting strange, distant, lost for a while?" Kruno would have been amazed at the insight by another man, but not by him. He was the most respected and brilliant Wizard in the known world.

"Yes, I have been worried about him. His mannerisms were uncanny for a long while and continue to get worse. Do you know Ivan? Do know what is wrong with him?"

"La Caprata." Rizzian looked at Deo as he said words Kruno had never heard before. The King tightened his face, which communicated a message that made little sense to Kruno. Without a request, Rizzian continued, "It means woman of the sand or Sand Sorceress. They have been considered by many as just a fairy tale, but they are very real. We have never acknowledged their existence and probably never will because fear would spread throughout the cities. It is said that these Sand Sorceresses captivate men subconsciously with spells of charm from great distances. At first it is just a vivid dream, but as time goes on it occupies his every thought, until he seeks to find La Caprata. Like zombies they are non-responsive to friends or even wives. They march off into the desert and are never heard from again. I can't say I know much more than that, except anyone who had attempted to ambush the situation never finds anything, or is never heard from again."

Kruno smacked his head with his palm to try to make sure he heard it all right and kick-start his brain. The only thing he asked was where they were located. Rizzian pointed to the desert about one-and-a-half days travel from Dryden, making a large circle with his hand and offered one last bit of information, "You could catch him if you ride leaving now, but it is a vast desert and even I don't know where they reside." Rizzian stopped Kruno with his hand and with a serious look, "Remember that looks can be deceiving."

Kruno approached the inn. He was focused on finding Christian, Decan and whatever group they could muster quickly, and head out to find his good friend. He wasn't sure how they would locate him if Rizzian didn't know where he was; it would be near impossible for them to find him.

I am coming for you my brother. I am not sure how we will find you, but we will. Larger barriers have been erected, but we have smashed every one of them and sometimes faith gives you a little surprise at the right time.

In mid-thought he witnessed one of faith's little gifts. Outside the inn sat four Gret-chens. They were a sight for sore eyes, really sore in Kruno's case. Gret-chens were massive, grey skinned, hairless beasts that primarily walked on all fours. It was strange because their front legs looked and acted more like arms with similar structure to hands. These beasts only travelled with their masters, and their masters were Northerners.

"Sven!" Kruno said softly with a smile on his face, realizing he had arrived.

One way to find a missing Northerner is to use the instinct and tracking ability of his Gret-chen.

He moved past them and entered the foyer of the inn and saw Sven, Ivan's cousin from Vard. He was talking with two other Northerners and Decan. The Northerners fit the typical description, massive men, extremely well built. As for Sven, he was easy to spot because even though he was only Ivan's cousin, the resemblance was present.

"Sven, you received my letter, great to see you." Kruno announced his presence.

Sven turned and noticed Kruno in a desolate state, struggling to keep himself together.

"Kruno, you look terrible, you look like you have been rolling with the pigs again. Didn't I tell you that they may be easier to have sex with, but they make an awful mess?"

Kruno's exhaustion was at a peak and his body was about to shut down any minute. He normally would embrace Sven and the others with the normal cordial social process, but he was unable to comply. "Sorry Sven, I don't have much time before I pass out. I will explain once I wake up. Strap me to a horse — we are heading out of here to find Ivan."

"Where is Ivan?" Sven inquired quickly. "Your letter you sent via Cardis on the Adas had such intensity about it. I decided the best way to free his mind from a strange place was to introduce him to his Gret-chen." Sven knew something was wrong when a letter arrived by winged messenger. Sven knew Ivan respected Kruno and reaching to the North must have been a last resort and therefore important.

Kruno felt himself fading, his head started to bob, his eyes felt like bags of sand.

"Get Christian… we head out to the desert immediately… Ivan is under a heavy charm and if we don't find him soon we will probably never find him again. Has Ivan's Gret-chen ever met him? We will need his intimate relationship to locate him. Elsewise he is a… a needle in…"

"We don't need Christian, let's pack up now and head out," Decan jumped in. The command was generated because he still had little respect for the Wizard, and also by the fact that Ivan was his responsibility. He needed to locate him immediately. Decan fully expected once Kruno was of sound mind he was going to chew him out and worse if anything was to happen to Ivan.

Kruno, with the last bit of energy, released a command, "Get Christian! We will need him."

Somewhere on the cusp of a dead sleep and reality Kruno dreamt of a woman in a desert. She was physically stunning, with firm yet soft curves, cascading black hair and ice blue eyes. She was dressed entirely in shape-hugging black. She smiled in his direction from what seemed like a mile away one moment and then right in front of him the next. With a strangely erotic and soothing voice, she confidently communicated with elongated speech, and the combination almost sounded like a soft song.

"We look forward to meeting with you warrior... you and your friends..." She slowly turned with a seductive smile, keeping her eyes on him, "Death comes to you soon... at the edge of our blades."

Moments later he felt a thousand little pellets hitting his skin, which brought him back to reality. He couldn't remember where he was and his muscles were still demanding more rest. Opening one eye, he could see stars bouncing around. It was night, he was on his back and looking from side to side he realized he wasn't alone. He noticed two Northerners on Gret-chens riding with at least a dozen men on horses. A few carried torches. The pellets on his skin were from copious amounts of sand being kicked up by the animals. To his left were more men on horses. He saw Christian, and when shifting to call out to him, he realized his body was fastened at his waist and his legs. His hands, when feeling around, expected horse's hair, but found a hard-skinned texture and lots of muscle. He was on a Gret-chen.

"Christian, what is going on?"

"Kruno is up!"

Sven halted everyone for a moment. He got off his Gret-chen and freed Kruno from his bindings.

"Have a nice sleep, my friend?"

Kruno's mind started to recollect what was going on, but was still confused, "What time is it?" Being pulled from an awkward sleeping position he stretched and asked more questions, "Where are we? How are we so many?"

Sven had gathered a crew of thirty.

"Well, it seems La Caprata has drawn in other men just like Ivan. Each of them had lost track of their mates, but Ivan's Gret-chen still has a strong fix on him." He raised his voice to inspire his new company, "This is a good group and whatever lured our men into them, lures our swords and their certain death!" The men all raised their arms and cheered.

"The sun rises in a few hours we should get moving."

Sven nodded, "Kruno, mount Ivan's Gret-chen, he has taken you this far."

Gret-chens weren't very smart but could talk. Very few knew any language except for Northern tongue, and even that was poor, but it was an honour to ride one. Only the Northern men could ride these mono-subservient beasts and only that of high regard. Gret-chens and their Northern riders had been united for centuries.

Many creatures were submissive to Northerners, they had a special bond with most animals, but this relationship was special. Gret-chens didn't live in the wild but were dependent on their masters. They were fierce warriors and the combination of the two in battle was spectacular. A man on a horse has an advantage over many, but nothing compared to a Northerner on a Gret-chen. They were slower than horses, but in battle would snap a horse's legs with one lunge.

Kruno rode beside Sven, but asked his first question to the Gret-chen and did it in Northern tongue, "I hope you don't mind giving a man a ride."

"You are not just man. You speak our speak. You embrace Sven like a brother. Your name is spoken in towns from my home. You are devoted to finding my master."

Kruno was impressed with the comment and felt a strange sensation of pride.

"You can sense Ivan, is he close?"

"Yes, not far."

Impressive, Rizzian the great Wizard couldn't find him, all these men were lost, but a creature with a stigma of poor intelligence has no trouble at all.

Kruno called to Sven but made sure everyone else was out of earshot and spoke in Northern tongue.

"I had a dream."

"That is great Kruno, but if it was about those pigs you were screwing earlier, I have no interest… and some advice, you shouldn't be sleeping with pigs, it is just gross." He tilted his head back and laughed, loud and hard.

Kruno took the conversation in a serious direction. "I dreamt of a woman in a desert. I believe that whatever we are going to face was communicating with me. La Caprata or the Sand Sorceress, whatever their true name, I think they know we are coming and let me know that."

"If they are warning us, then they are scared, and if they are scared, then we have nothing to be alarmed about."

"That's just it, it was almost as if they were coaxing us to fight, they looked forward to battling us."

Sven responded as Kruno should have figured, the same way Ivan would have in that situation.

"Even better, I look forward to meeting these wenches!" His excitement brewed.

The Gret-chen Kruno was riding warned everyone that it sensed Ivan was near, and just at that moment the horses became spooked. As if snakes lay in front of them, they kept rearing on their hind legs and neighing, letting everyone know they weren't going forward. The horses were terrified, but nobody could see why.

One of the Northerners pulled out two glass balls and a leather wrap. Shortly he had them all lined up. Looking through one end he was able to see greater distances through it. After canvassing the path that lay ahead he yelled out, "There, I can see Ivan, I can see the marking of the cross on his back."

"Can you see anyone else with him?"

"No, just him, but you can be sure that wherever he is, your friends are near."

"Leave your horses behind and follow us. The feeble creatures you ride don't embrace challenges like our Gret-chens."

All of the men on horseback dismounted and started to walk. Those on Gret-chens moved a little faster. They started to advance when a deviant light flashed. In an instant, the clouds jumped to a new position and all thirty of them, twenty-seven on foot, looked at each other in confusion. It was very strange. They seemed to move hundreds of feet within a moment's time.

I knew this wasn't going to be easy and that strange things were going to start happening and here we go. He looked back to see the horses some 400 feet away. Not one of them remembered the 400-foot journey as if it happened instantly.

"What just happened?" one of the men yelled out to the group and found his words got caught in the air like a carriage tire in mud slowing them down. His voice was distorted due to the surroundings, it sounded like they were in a small room as opposed to a massive open space.

"We just experienced a time shift," Christian responded.

"What is a time shift?" The question left his mouth with a quiver.

"Time was manipulated, sped up for us. We probably walked all of this way, but don't remember a single step. An impressive spell if I do say so myself."

Christian took out his brand new, untested staff with unusual confidence. He didn't look around to see what anyone else was doing. He was assured of his skill.

Ivan was in sight far away, but able to be seen without the aid of the Northerners tool. He was frozen in his tracks, his back to them all.

"Call out to your man… Come on, get him to turn around." One of the other men made the request with some desperation in his voice. Nobody responded so he decided to say something, attempting to yell, "HEY IVAN, TURN AROUND YOU JACKASS. WE ARE HERE!"

A slender, female figure appeared beside Ivan. She had long dark hair, pearl white skin and was wearing a black cloak. She seemed to float gently in the air a few feet above the ground. Her cloak soothingly fluttered, hanging below her, just caressing the ground. Sand slightly clouded their vision, would clear again and reappear. Ivan and this mysterious woman faded and cleared.

An unnatural voice jumped toward them like a rock skipping on a pond, getting louder as it approached. Her voice elongated each word.

"Who dare calls for what is mine?" The decibel level was way too high to be coming from the lady who was so far from them.

"Release him, or we will take him from you! What you claim is yours, isn't. What you insinuate is your property is a free Northerner." Sven spoke with a commanding voice that still sounded horribly distorted.

Not exactly the way I would have handled it, but Northerners aren't exactly known for their peaceful negotiations in situations like this, Kruno thought. *Personally I would have attempted a diplomatic solution first and then moved to force. A woman, who happens to be suspending herself in air, has captivated the mind of Ivan, tossed us into a time shift — whatever the heck that means — and seems quite confident as one, facing many, might be someone to negotiate with.*

About half the men were afraid of what was to come next, and prematurely unsheathed their weapons. Some had axes, others swords and a couple had spears. It was the last sign the Sand Sorceress needed.

Everything went dead silent. The wind that had been constantly beating sand against their skin since they entered the desert stopped suddenly. She started to shift and move strangely, yet still with grace as she gained altitude. As she floated higher she inhaled deeply and then the reverse exhale could be heard. The clouds began to move at incredible speeds. The clouds shifted in one minute what would normally take two hours. The sun started to move as well, slowly but noticeably. It was a sight no one had ever witnessed. Many of the men started to get nervous and weren't sure what to do. A few questioned why they were there. Had they made a serious mistake? Who or what was the lady rising towards the sky and how did she control nature?

The others, the true warriors, stood strong, never considered retreat, never questioned why they were there. They waited for what was to come.

The Sand Sorceress continued her levitation and gained altitude. The sun's light unnaturally faded fast even though only a thin layer of cloud moved across the sky. It was in midday position but it was dark! She gently twisted and turned with elegance. Silence still dominated even though so much was happening. She rose what seemed to be a hundred feet until the blackness had taken her over. All that could be seen was her outline and her pale white face peering over her arm, which covered her mouth. The sky continued to change, clouds rolled and the now-black sun began to move.

A new shape appeared beside Ivan, who remained still. Another cloaked Sorceress was down on one knee, hands spread forward, touching the sandy ground. She arose slowly. Once standing she pushed back her hood and pushed back the darkness that covered them as well. The day returned to normal. The sun hurt their eyes as they focused on the second mystery female. The clouds slowed down, the sun stopped moving. Everything seemed normal except there was still no wind and no sound.

One Sand Sorceress still floated in the sky, but she wasn't the object of attention. The second woman was everything. Before she took a step forward, she lifted her cloak from her shoulders and let it drop behind her. Even from far away, what was revealed was sheer perfection. Men and women alike would be astonished by the beauty she unveiled. Just like Kruno's dream, this woman had a flawless silhouette.

She moved in their direction, took a few steps, but skipped forward in time, moving a few minutes in a matter of seconds, and getting close fast.

Kruno looked to his side and saw the men's guard start to melt. She got closer and captivated the Northerners as well. All of their minds started to submit to the beauty before them. She breached their perimeter as they stood a scattered five by six.

She moved with absolute seduction, and as she walked in between Sven and his other mounted warriors, she brushed her hand against their legs. As if touched by their master, they immediately dismounted their Gret-chens. Many of the men who had their weapons unsheathed simply let them go.

Kruno felt his mind being asked to give in, and an alluring voice softly whispered temptation in his ear.

"What if I was yours? Imagine my touch, imagine how I feel, how good would I feel with you inside me?" A slight sexual moan sent shivers down his spine. The Sorceress was attempting to enchant all the men into a state of placidity.

He dismounted his Gret-chen in order to pretend he was charmed as well, making him a non-threat. Kruno had been through this before and wasn't falling for it again. His mind was stronger than even he realized. His skill had magnified, and for him to be viewed as just a warrior, even just a great warrior, was a fool's move.

Kruno knew everyone was probably lost or on their way to a docile state, except maybe Christian. He looked over to the Wizard with just his eyes in order not to draw attention. Christian looked back and with a sign asked if he should attack. A small hand motion told him to wait. Continuing their little nonverbal communication, Christian then used his eyes to point to where Ivan stood.

Kruno looked to Ivan and noticed that he stood in an area with wind, where a mini sandstorm brewed just beyond. The perimeter of this storm seemed to just touch Ivan. This was very strange since he looked on from an area of eerie silence without even the slightest breeze. He could barely focus, but could see about a dozen or so shapes. He concentrated hard but still couldn't see.

Christian winked in his direction and mouthed some words. Instantly Kruno's vision was tenfold, he had the eyesight of an eagle, he could see through the cloud of sand and he didn't like what it revealed. What lay beyond the edge of the storm were more Sand Sorceresses.

Some were on horseback — magnificent, black horses gleaming in the sun, a breed he couldn't recognize. All the women were preparing for battle. Every one of them had long black hair that they had tied back in ponytails or in a bun. They examined their weapons which consisted of swords, knives or spears and started to sheath them for the inevitable charge. The last pieces of black armour, which looked to be a type of hard leather, were being fastened. Not only was an attack coming, it was imminent.

The woman who worked the crowd of enchanted men was making her way to the front right position where Kruno stood one back.

Her mind told her they had another group of men, *easy targets to be completely lost with my last words.* Confident that this would seal their victory she said, "With love and lust, I give you, La Caprata."

Kruno watched her walk beside him and couldn't help but notice her impeccable physique. She didn't have the armour that her friends were dressed in, exposing her pure white skin and erotic back.

You are unarmed with traditional weapons and you are a woman, but both rules are about to disappear because it's time to snap our boys back into reality!

She walked by Kruno and smiled to let her friends know she had completed her job with stunning results. These enchanted men would be easily destroyed.

The Sand Sorceress that still observed everything from a bird's-eye view attempted to warn her friend, but it was too late. A strike to the middle of the enchantress's back forced her forward; she lifted off her feet, leapt uncontrollably into the air and landed face first into the sand. The pain of being smashed by something in the back rushed to her brain. She spit out a little blood and lost her breath.

Kruno had thrust-kicked her from behind, with as much velocity as he could muster, stepping forward and pumping his arms back. She didn't weigh much, and since the assault was unexpected, the damage was more severe.

Having experience with charm spells from the Crypton battle of Tristan, he knew that an assault on the spell caster would free the minds of everyone under its supremacy. Most of them snapped out of the enchantment and refocused on the sandstorm in front of them.

"What the heck was that?" Sven asked, dazed and confused.

"It seems our enemy has some interesting abilities. This one charmed every one of you. The spell appealed to your erotic desires."

"Well that was a great spell! It got me all excited." Sven grabbed between his legs. His fellow Northerners and Decan broke into laughter. He then turned to the woman in the sky and said, "Don't just tease me and go. That's not fair. What kind of woman leaves a man like this?"

The comment infuriated the Sand Sorceress floating in the sky. She extended her hand towards the wind and stopped the sandstorm. Visibility returned to normal and it presented about a dozen fully armed women, most of them on horseback.

Men, Gret-chens, and Northerners looked at the sorceresses in silence. Impatience grew among some of the men until someone in the crowd yelled, "We should attack first, let's charge!"

"Don't move! This is their land, their home. Wait for them and take a defensive position. When they charge, and they will, unsheathe and unleash fury." Kruno jumped in because he knew the Northerners would be in support of charging. He needed to make sure he kept command and had shouted intensely.

"But they are just women, small women."

"That is exactly the attitude that will get you slaughtered," Decan commented with uncharacteristic insight.

The commander in the sky touched her chest and extended her arm forward. Immediately the horses snapped into action. The Sand Sorceresses lifted off their saddles, almost as if caught by surprise, but they rode with proficiency. The few on foot exploded with considerable speed, running side by side with the horses.

"Anything in your bag of tricks that will help defend dementia? They are going to attempt to use more of their magic," Kruno yelled to Christian.

They are too small to take us down with just battle skills alone, we need to anticipate the bizarre.

Without answering, Christian raised his hand, palm up and chanted the mystical language calling on a defense spell. A small, barely noticeable field peaked from his raised hand and covered the Northerners, Kruno, Decan and two others. If he'd had the ability, he would have encased the entire group, but it would have diluted over space, and if the Sand Sorceresses detected the defensive shield, they might have a solution. It would be harder to detect if only a small percentage had a barrier from their psyche spell, the most likely to be cast.

The Sand Sorceresses scaled the landscape at a tremendous pace, three times the speed of any normal horse and the ones who ran were only a few paces behind. Before anyone had a chance to either pick up their weapons, which were dropped while enchanted, or unsheathe their swords, the Sand Sorceresses were almost on them!

Instantly the theatre changed. Time slowed down in the reverse; the horses seemed to move at an unnaturally slow speed and every one of the men found they moved even slower. Only the three Sorceresses on foot maintained normal speed as they separated themselves from the pack. The enemy was only forty paces from them and they could barely move, an easy prey, except the six under the defensive spell.

Sven mounted his Gret-chen, pulled his spear from its casing and tossed it with perfect accuracy at one of the Sorceresses charging on foot. As it left his hand something started to happen to the three charging women. Their feet looked as if they snapped at the ankle while in mid-stride. With the next stride, the rest of their legs broke into tiny little pieces and just before the spear hit its intended target, the rest of their bodies did the same; upper torso, arms and head crumbled into fine particles. The path they would have followed still made a trail of shifting sand towards the group and Kruno watched as it went between his legs streaming backward.

"Rear flank!" Kruno yelled to a group that was in disarray and a group that he knew didn't understand the command, but he shouted the warning anyway.

At first, the men were disturbed by the women warriors who broke into sand at will, and then another surprise shot fear through most. The Sand Sorceresses on horseback, which were moving at an oddly slow speed, shot forward. Four of them, with a shift of the hips and pump of the legs, leapt off their steeds straight in the air. They climbed at least forty feet in the air with grace and symmetry, seemed to slow down for a quick moment at their peak, and then viciously rained down.

With a smile on his face, Sven thought to himself, *This attack is brilliant, besides the charm spell, they have a constant ability to manipulate time and gravity. Their attack changes right at the last second, the approach from the sky, the ground and who knows where next? Their death or mine, it will be a great one!*

Kruno called out the first command to Christian, pointing to one of the Sorceresses who had leapt from her horse. She was just about to break her almost-suspended state when he yelled, "Fry that witch, Christian!"

Christian was already prepared. Since the moment Kruno kicked one of them, he started to quietly brew his spell and it had gained brawn over time. He used his staff to release his attack, and pointed toward the first victim of the battle. A stream of fire shot from the end of the staff with scorching intensity. Caught completely off guard she ignited instantly, her skin melted, and a flaming ball of seared flesh struck the battlefield.

She was the first victim. If the battle was to have stopped at that point, it could have been called a victory for the men, but the battle wasn't over and everything was about to change.

The second to hit the battlefield was one of the women who had leapt from a steed; she poured down from the sky and pounced on her victims. The first was a man attempting to pick up his sword, which still lay on the ground from the enchantment. He should have been able to regain a defensive position, weapon in hand before his assassin was on him, but he couldn't move at normal speed. It was like a bad dream he had once when everything else moved in normal motion except him. He was able to bend down but never took his eyes off the sky. His right hand attempted to find the handle of his weapon, but it was a lost cause. She fell fast on him, with sword raised high above her head pointing downwards. She landed perfectly on one knee, and her blade slid deep into his chest.

The second to claim her victim looked down on a man who was attempting to raise his weapon to defend, but he couldn't get it high enough. His mind raced as he screamed to his arm that moved too slowly, "COME *ON*!" With his weapon only at chest level, she fell on him. Using gravity and range of motion to apply enough pressure to kill a man three times over, her blade caught the bridge of his nose, ripped through his jaw, separated it from his face and split his rib cage.

The last airborne Sorceress found a victim who had never come back from the initial seduction. He was an easy kill.

With a loud crack, their hold on time snapped back to normalcy. Most of the men were still disoriented, but if they could pull themselves together fast and forget the fear, they could have equal grounds for war.

The men on the rear flank who hadn't thought about the sand that had shifted under their feet or understood Kruno's warning faced forward, waiting for battle. They could see the women on horseback just breaching their front line.

Only a few feet behind them, three swirls of sand had jumped from the ground, formed bodies with arms tucked into their chests, head down, with eyes closed. The three Sand Sorceresses had rematerialized in a position of extreme advantage. They slowly gained their footing and began to unleash chaos.

The first with a thin, razor sharp sword slid its tip through the surprised victim. Oddly feeling no pain, he looked down as metal ripped through him, saturated with his blood.

The second Sand Sorceress had two blades which she pulled from their position and strategically placed them parallel to the ground, aimed for her prey and eagerly dug them into both sides of his neck. Blood shot out like a stream, hit her hands and splattered backward. The excitement of battle, and blood in her mouth overwhelmed her, apparent by her loud battle cry.

The battle cry shot dread through the last remaining warriors who would submit to fear. They realized they were being attacked from all angles.

The last of the three flanking Sorceresses had two spears which she plunged through the back of her target and out the other side. The motion was quick because she wanted to use her weapons before the group realized she was behind them. She pulled them out and she accurately fired both spears. The first hit mid-back on an unsuspecting fighter, and the second jammed deep into right shoulder of another, which immobilized him for the fight.

The women warriors on horseback had hit the front lines at the same time their sisters in flight landed on the battlefield. Just prior to that, Kruno leapt onto the Gret-chen and charged forward to intercept one of them. His beast gained speed fast and within seconds showed why a warrior and a Gret-chen is a deadly combination, especially versus an opponent on horseback.

Kruno understood the battle tactic for him was to just defend the attack. The two met as her sword crashed against his. The Gret-chen, with one of its powerful arms, smashed the horse's front legs, breaking them in several places. The rider was jettisoned from her horse as it collapsed to the ground. She flew through the air with relative poise, tucked just before reaching the ground, and rolled to her feet. Kruno stopped and turned to watch how impressively skilled these Sand Sorceresses really were.

Sword in hand and battle-ready after being tossed from her steed, she found herself in between a massive Northerner and an enormous muscular creature. The Northerner watched as she landed in his sweet spot. He attacked with his giant axe as his Gret-chen moved in from her other side. She blocked the axe and turned to the massive creature on its hind legs, arms raised like a bear coming down on her. With an open palm she produced a small explosion that forced the creature back a step. The beast was caught off guard but not hurt too badly. Before it could regain awareness, she spun on one foot and smashed its rib cage with a reverse roundhouse. The Sand Sorceress was small compared to a Gret-chen, but its ribs were pulverized and internal organs crushed.

The woman warrior turned to the Northerner who was shocked and upset to see his Gret-chen destroyed. Before he could attack again, she blew sand in his face. Wasting no time she filleted the blinded warrior with three strokes of her sword, slicing through his leg, chest and then removed most of his left arm.

She turned with stunning confidence to seek, find and destroy her next casualty, but was met with a spear to the abdomen and a second to the chest. Sven and the other Northerner finished her off with pleasure.

Christian, at the sound of the battle cry, turned to witness three Sorceresses ripping through his men uncontested and decided to change that. From what he learned from the Clorians, he decided to test his staff and his skills from a physical standpoint. One of the women had just finished cutting down another victim when she felt five two-inch spikes dig into her right side. Christian released five thin metal cords with spikes on them from the end of his new Clorian staff. Two landed in her arm and three down her rib cage. She looked up in pain, attempting to figure out what had happed and saw a young Wizard holding her fate in his hands. The cords tightened and he flung her over his head and out of the battle arena. The spikes ripped free in the air, leaving a little flesh on each one. Badly injured, she wouldn't return.

Kruno on his Gret-chen was impressed with Christian. He had watched him dominate the Sand Sorceress with his new staff. It was a weapon that cost a fortune but was worth it. He then looked across the battlefield and witnessed the slaughter. Men were being cut down rapidly; the white sandy desert was already a crimson blood-red. He looked to see who needed to be taken out, just as one of the Sand Sorceresses did the same. With a blood covered sword she turned her steed from battle and looked his way.

Her horse reared back and broke into a sprint for him. Kruno, still mounted on his Gret-chen, put his hands to his side in a relaxed state to taunt his challenger. He gave no order to move. She raised her sword and was a mere ten feet from him when Sven's Gret-chen leaped from the battle. Sven saw the opportunity and understood Kruno's plan. He threw himself from his beast a moment prior, and commanded him to attack with a shove to motivate. She hadn't seen it and didn't expect the ambush. The Gret-chen attack came perpendicular, and although her peripheral vision did heed a warning, it was without sufficient time. Its massive jaws dug deep into her shoulder and cleared her from her horse. Its leg hit the torso of the horse, causing it to spin in the air, flipping Gret-chen, Sorceress and horse to the sand. The horse lost its footing and slid within feet of Kruno and his Gret-chen. Without even being asked, Kruno's Gret-chen pounded down on the horse with one swift kill shot.

The Sorceress rose warily to her feet with her sword in the only hand she could use. Impressively, she still had some fight in her, even though her fate was sealed with the substantial injury to her shoulder.

Kruno leapt from his Gret-chen and pointed to the severely wounded Sand Sorceress, commanding it to join its brother to encircled and destroy. The two Gret-chens ripped the wounded Sorceress to pieces.

Kruno rushed over to assist Decan, who had been trading attacks with another Sand Sorceress. She was able to defend against his incredible speed with her dexterity. Neither had landed a single blow because they were so closely matched in skill. His double-edged sword danced and spun over his body, but was met with her defensive blocks. Kruno had only seen Decan fight a few times, but thought he was fascinating to watch in battle; he seemed skillfully smooth. Just before Kruno could join in to assist, he dropped to one knee spun his double-ended sword over his shoulder and caught a break. One end of his sword split her ankle. He then rolled up and successfully landed another two slices along the same leg. Her defenses broke down and he exploited it by standing up fast, lacerating her face deeply and finishing with one end thrust into her abdomen.

Decan looked to Kruno, panting, "Are you planning on doing something soon?"

Kruno didn't know how to answer because he realized that he hadn't killed anyone yet. He had been involved in a few deaths, but really didn't have one kill. It was an irritating comment. He thought for a moment to come up with an appropriate response when his concentration was broken. Blood hit his cheek as one of his men shot across the battlefield in between him and Decan. The torso moved with more velocity than even Ivan could muster. Assuming these women were weak was a poor initial deduction.

"We are getting killed out here!" Decan yelled.

He is right! Kruno looked around the battlefield to see dead men everywhere. He remembered that one Sorceress was still floating above them. *Okay, she needs to go.*

"Christian! Go up and say hi to that bitch in the sky!"

"Great Kruno, I love rhymes, do more!" Sven immediately commented on his choice of words while tossing his giant axe. Northerners rarely got frazzled and simply love a fight. Sven had witnessed his friend and a

Gret-chen die. He was surrounded by a powerful enemy and yet still able to make such light, relaxed comments — almost small talk.

The axe Sven tossed met his target with fatal results, removing another Sorceress from the battle, throwing her from her stallion. She was just about to kill a man who stood over a Sorceress's corpse, a corpse he created. His blade was dug deep in her chest. He wouldn't have been able to defend himself. He was mere moments away from being killed.

Christian levitated himself above the battlefield and approached the Sand Sorceress. They floated only a few meters from one another. He expected a great battle, but he wasn't afraid at all — confidence overwhelmed him. He knew he had to be ready for something peculiar. Before he could do or say anything, she spoke with her elegantly elongated speech.

"No thanks Wizard. I wish to see another day." She then bowed and fell from the sky, doing a small flip and landing on her feet. She immediately whistled and tossed a hand full of sand towards the battle. The sand acted like a snowball that gathered momentum downhill and quickly turned into an avalanche. Within a few moments the battlefield was covered in blowing sand, making it impossible for anyone to see.

Kruno understood they would now be at an even worse disadvantage, but instead of an assumed continued assault, the sand settled and they were gone. The battlefield was littered with corpses, but not one Sand Sorceress's body remained.

The few men that survived outside of Decan, Kruno, Christian, Sven and the other Northerner stood in fear. One of them broke into tears.

"Ten of us... ten of us still stand, that's it! That was mayhem. They were outnumbered. They were women and we got our asses handed to us," Decan commented, irritated and confused.

"Thanks for saving my life," one of the men said to Sven.

"You were a man among men. I am glad I could help." He looked for Ivan and yelled, "Where is my cousin?"

The group remembered what this had all been about, Ivan, yet he wasn't anywhere to be seen.

"We will find you Cousin, and we will have our revenge. THAT I SWEAR!" Sven shouted to an empty desert.

One of the men who sat on the ground nursing a broken knee and nose inquired, "How will you find them, they are gone?" His voice was scattered and muffled from the blood.

He is right. How are we going to find Ivan? They surely would have taken him out of range of the Gret-chen. They are far from stupid and I doubt get duped often.

Christian floated down from the sky, "I figured this was going to happen so I gave him a little gift just as the battle started." Everyone looked at him, confused.

"Gave him, who is him and what did you give?" Decan asked.

"Ivan, I gave Ivan a Vita Fairy."

"What in God's green earth is a Vita Fairy?"

"A Vita Fairy is very tiny winged creature, quite beautiful actually. She hid in Ivan's hair. They are very stealthy. When the time is right I will call to her and she will come to me and show me the way to them."

Decan, with little tact, threw his arms up and walked away saying, "Well, so much for Ivan, he is a goner, Vita Fairy! That is the stupidest thing I have heard."

Kruno looked at Christian with absolute sincerity.

"Today was your day!"

CHAPTER 3

MYSTERY OF THE SAND

The wind picked up and blew sand over the men. The battlefield, once so vibrantly charged, was now lifeless as it struggled to regain its synergy. Many had open wounds which were hard to clean in a desert, because they didn't have enough water to remove the sand. The sand didn't bother most of them though, as most were dead, including a Northerner and a Gretchen. The sun was scorching and not helping their dehydrated states. The survivors were silenced by the slaughter and most reflected on the battle. Ten men and three Gret-chens had little or moderate injuries, and the rest were casualties.

Sven bowed to one knee over his Northern companion, and in Northern tongue, wished him a peaceful journey to the other side. Decan sat down, looking up at Kruno and wondering where his mind was, but refrained from making any comment until he figured out what the next step would be. He assumed they would ride back to Dryden, gather more men, re-arm and get enough supplies to last for a long journey over the sand dunes of the desert. He was pretty sure Ivan had already met his fate, but also knew Kruno and Sven wouldn't give up easily. They would search this dry wasteland for months before letting Ivan go. Decan knew he would stand by their side as they searched because the persistence showed tremendous respect. Outside of the admiration, another critical component made Decan's mind up for him. He was responsible for Ivan's surveillance, something he hadn't taken seriously and Ivan had been captured. Kruno hadn't yet given him a well-deserved verbal beating for not following his command.

Kruno canvassed the surrounding area; he looked to the horizon, and with a slow shift, examined the entire 360-degree view. All that could be seen was sand that seemed to go on forever. From this point the entire world seemed to be rolling sand dunes. He then took his focus to a more micro view and looked to the crimson battlefield. This small piece of desert probably never had a living creature walk across its back. Its potential first experience with life was quite the show. The blood-soaked sand would be covered before nightfall and the bodies themselves would be buried by the next day. A week from now no one would even know that this was a spot where a great battle had taken place.

The man with the broken knee and nose looked around like a helpless child. If Kruno had had a chance to get to know him prior to this battle, he never would have allowed him to join them. He had no business being on this battlefield in the first place. His skill wasn't in question. It was his lack of courage that was the problem. Looking up at Kruno, the man made the incorrect assumption that Kruno was also afraid, and by noticing the blank look on his face, he also concluded that Kruno had no idea what to do next. He was the first to break the silence by asking for assistance or at least some direction, but didn't get a response. Everyone ignored him.

Decan cleaned his blades by thrusting them into the desert floor and then pulling them out. The Northerners liked what they saw and did the same. Blood was much easier to clean off before it dried.

Kruno, as always, demanded and received command. Everyone knew he was the decision maker and awaited his orders. Even the few men who had just met him, men who really hadn't known him very long, felt the same way, save the one fool.

Kruno finally broke his silence.

"When it's easier to count the living rather than the dead, you know..." He finished the sentence without words but a shake of his head. Kruno's eyes looked to the distance and not to the men who were listening to him.

"Decan... gather the supplies and the horses and bring them here. Sven, please ask a few of your Gret-chens to assist. Let's bury the dead, send the injured back to Dryden and prepare for our assault."

"You're not thinking about chasing them are you?" the injured man said as he gripped his leg in pain.

The group intently focused on Kruno as he gave a nod to indicate that that was exactly his intention.

"Are you crazy? You'll get slaughtered, at least this time we lived. I am positive that they won't be as nice if you meet them again."

"Doesn't really matter what you think — if Kruno says we go, we go," Decan said as he started to walk towards the horses. He considered stepping on his knee to punish him for the blasphemy spoken to his leader, but chose not to.

"I can't believe what I am hearing. Your man Ivan is dead, along with all of our mates. This is a fool's journey. You don't think you can find and defeat them, do you?"

His negativity wasn't popular amongst the men and it would normally warrant a harsh warning from Kruno, but he did just go to battle with them. He spilt his blood on the same field as men Kruno respected. His response would be gentler.

"We can and we will!" Kruno continued, "Any man that is too injured or doesn't want to follow us will head back to Dryden. Dead men get buried here. No questions asked."

Kruno then looked to the injured man who had been complaining, and with a sharp glance, told him his turn to speak was over.

His mind wandered and thought about his enemy. *Their combination of stealth, magic and skill is impressive. They rely on surprise and deception in order to overwhelm. Well, the element of surprise is gone and deception doesn't work so well when we have a Wizard to defend. We have to rely on a Vita Fairy, and I have to agree with Decan, I have never heard of a Vita Fairy. It does sound ridiculous but it's all we have. If Christian comes through for us here, it's about time he earned his name.*

Only after many great battles did a Wizard lose his given name and receive another. Even though magicians and warriors don't get along for the most part, a warrior is the one who must nominate a Wizard's new name. It couldn't be just any warrior either; it had to be a Knight or someone of equal stature. Kruno and Ivan both had the status to give Christian a new name, but would only elect it when he deserved it. His magic and physical defence skills had drastically improved. The last to come was confidence. He had taken a step in the right direction when engaging La Caprata.

Even after a decorated warrior nominated a man of magic to receive his new name, it had to be approved by a Knight — if not the first to nominate him — a named Wizard and a person with royal blood. It was a great honour and one Kruno was sure Christian wanted.

"Christian, come here."

"That was one crazy battle don't you think?"

The two settled out of earshot from the rest of the group.

"Yes, Decan couldn't have phrased it better. We got our asses handed to us." Kruno sincerely put his hand on Christian's shoulder and said, "You did great. You and I had their enchantment licked, but we might not have had any of the Northerners with us without your defensive block."

Christian smiled, realizing he did well.

"This Clorian staff is impressive, I love it!"

"Well it cost a small fortune, so it should. You did well with it. Close combat is something you don't have to fear anymore. You will learn to embrace it but still work with us close by."

Christian nodded.

"Okay, comrade, make me feel confident about our decision to rely on a Vita Fairy."

"Well, as you know, there are several species of fairies. They are small and ignored, but they are one of the most intelligent creatures on the planet. They are very gifted with a diverse magical arsenal. Fairies are one of the few creatures that are born with their abilities. The knowledge of their ancestors is passed through to them as they are born. Their life expectancy isn't much longer than ours, but they can speak of memories centuries ago."

Christian loved the conversation because nobody else would have cared about it, except Kruno or Dorious, when he was alive. Kruno was always interested in learning as much as possible because it could come to be a critical edge in a future confrontation or decision. He listened to the young Wizard talk for a while as he absorbed the information. They had some time because, until Decan could do an inventory, nothing could be done. The moment everything was ready, Kruno wanted to have his command released.

"What is this Vita Fairy's name?" Kruno prodded Christian in a direction that got to the important part.

"You wouldn't be able to say it, its name isn't in words. I also don't want to call to it before we are ready to go."

"Okay Christian, it's your show — what next?"

"Well, we need to make sure it is in place before we call to it. Once I have bellowed its name, it will come to us and show me where Ivan is. If they aren't settled, then it will come too early."

"Okay, I will tell you when I think enough time has passed. Use your healing spells sparingly, mend as many of the wounds you can on the ones pressing forward, but don't drain yourself too much. Secondly, help the ones in critical condition so they can make it back to Dryden. The ones who can't be healed, the terminal ones, unfortunately can't be helped."

Even though Christian learned that he might have to decide if someone lived or died, a process he dreaded, he still had a quirky smile on his face. Christian didn't really get the exclusive talk with his leader very often. It showed he was becoming more important to the group, further accepted.

His smile and long gaze in Kruno's direction ended quickly as he was commanded with a "Go!" and a strange look from Kruno questioning why he was still there.

Decan and Sven walked over to Kruno and, by patting the sand, he invited them to sit beside him on the peak of a small sand dune.

"I assume you could use some of this." Decan slid a water skin to Kruno.

Kruno slammed half of the contents down his throat, careful not to drop the slightest bit of the liquid gold.

"The only true friend you have in the desert is water, especially when dehydration is kicking in."

"I can't believe how thirsty I am. I don't know a lot about time shifts, but I think it's been a long time since we had a drop of water, even though it didn't feel even close to that," Kruno said with his newly hydrated tongue.

"They should have just shifted time for a few days, then we would have been dried up like a prune."

"I can't imagine a spell like that is easy to cast and for them to hold it for twice as long as they did might be above those sultry wenches' capabilities," Decan responded. They all smiled because the Sorceresses had all been gorgeous.

"I have pictured myself many times surrounded by that many stunning women, and there was always a lot of stabbing and thrusting, but it wasn't with a broadsword, I tell you that." Sven lifted his sword slightly to imitate an erection and made thrusting motions. They all began to chuckle. Even Kruno's hard face cracked. He needed the comic break, even if it was only for a moment.

"It could be a number of things. Decan has a good point. It could have been outside their threshold to continue, like Christian, his stamina with spells has limits. It could also be they wanted to fight, or they were exposed to the same conditions we were. Anyway, talk to me about supplies."

They discussed their inventory and what they assumed lay ahead. Kruno expanded on part of the plan that Sven disagreed with but in the end knew it was the only way.

"Eight of us go. Decan, Sven, Sven's comrade, Christian, myself and three others on horseback."

"Horseback, no way, we aren't abandoning our Gret-chens, plus they are much better than horses," Sven disagreed, shocked.

"How much water does a Gret-chen drink, three times that of a regular horse? Never mind how much they eat! If we want to find Ivan we need enough time to locate him without turning back for supplies. They can transfer the wounded out of here along with the other horses, get a ton of supplies and meet us here."

"I don't think any of the wounded are coming back here, so how is a Gret-chen, which only speaks Northern tongue and not very fluent at that, going to handle Dryden?"

"Don't worry, we have a friend we can trust in Dryden, the Gret-chens will meet up with Zel and deliver a written message." Reluctantly Sven agreed. He loved his Gret-chen, but loved his cousin more and trusted Kruno.

The sun started to set on a day none of them would forget. The cooler night was welcomed with open arms. The wounded and cowardly were sent back to Dryden strapped to horses and led by Gret-chens. Kruno originally thought his team would head out before sunset, but things took longer than expected and sleep could only help.

The men and Northerners alike geared up and mounted their horses just as the sun kissed the sky. Sven was on horseback aside Kruno and engaged in light conversation. Sven respected Kruno's decision to march back into the mouth of an enemy that had almost consumed them, to search a relatively empty desert and to do this for his cousin. Ivan and Kruno weren't blood related, but in many ways their bond was stronger.

"Shall we proceed Kruno?"

"Let's hold on a minute until everyone is ready."

"I love travelling Kruno, but nothing is like home. I must admit I do miss it, especially in a lifeless desert."

"I do love the North as well, it's been a while since I have been up there. Is the weather nice this time of year? How is everything back home?"

"Well the ice is probably close to broken by now, which means the traders are on their way to explore the world and many are finally coming back from their journeys. It's an exciting time. For those returning, some have great stories and a few with vast riches. Others have unique spices, but the best part is when husband and family are re-united. It's a spectacle to watch. Nothing makes you realize how important life is until you first come home after such a long journey."

"I know you leave your two boys and three girls, plus your wife. Not easy I am sure," Kruno mentioned with sympathy.

"I do miss them, but I haven't been gone for too long. Nonetheless, when I get home there will be some serious action time with the wife — I am sure a sixth will be coming about nine months later." Sven started his heavy laugh which put a real smile on Kruno's face. It almost felt weird to smile but great at the same time.

"Have you settled down yet or do you wander from bed to bed?"

"Still looking for the right one Sven. Until then I will do my best to test out as many as I can."

"Just make sure you don't look too long. Your looks will fade and then you will have to rely on charm. Something you are seriously lacking." Sven laughed again.

The putrid smell of the battlefield passed by Kruno's nose. The bodies were gone or buried, but the desert's concentrated heat quickened their decomposition. With pleasure, he commanded the group to start a slow move forward.

"Kruno, you should help yourself to a wife from the North. I have many beautiful cousins, it would be a fine place for a man to settle." The request was one of great respect. Men and Northern women rarely got married. They were by far the most beautiful, maybe now next to La Caprata.

"After we have retrieved Ivan, it will be time to visit the North again. I do love your way of life and your women are spectacular." Kruno insinuated that he would accept his offer, but it was far from that. He loved travelling and couldn't see himself settling anywhere for a long time. That being said, the North was a place he could have seen himself living; great people, great food and a group that never suffered a major defeat. It was cold but that really didn't bother him too much.

The three men on horseback were together behind the rest of the group. Their horses navigated slowly around the graves. None of them knew each other prior to this encounter, but they had a commonality. They were outsiders, had known Kruno for only a short time, and their friends were dead or carried away. They chatted back and forth about their new leaders. Every one of them had heard of Kruno prior to this and they were impressed with everyone's skill. Their conversation seemed to focus on Christian's spells. Most warriors didn't travel the countryside with a Wizard.

"That flame he shot from his staff was amazing!"

"The Sand Sorceress was powerful, but dropped from the sky as soon as Christian levitated himself to meet her."

"The stories we will have when we get back home."

"That's if we get back home, and to tell you the truth, the only way that is happening is if we don't find them."

"You think my brother is dead?" one of the men asked and was obviously upset.

"I am sorry to be so blunt. I search for my brother-in-law, a good man who takes care of my sister and their four kids. I don't see how we would ever retrieve them. These women warriors tore us apart."

"I swore to my father that I would find him or die trying."

"If we find them, die we all will."

"So why did you continue on?"

"I don't retreat, it's not in my nature. Also the chance to travel with Kruno is a once in a lifetime experience."

The third man, who had stayed silent the whole time, had noticed something peculiar under one of the piles of sand where a body was buried. He jumped for a second and grabbed for his weapon. He paused between words and talked slowly as if not to aggravate an untamed animal on the verge of striking.

"Guys... the body... its moving!"

One of them looked over, and after a moment, noticed another small shift in the sand.

"Don't worry, it's just the bodies settling. Haven't you seen a body twitch before?"

Kruno was ahead of them and called to see if it was time to summon the Vita Fairy. Kruno thought to himself that if the Wizard was wrong, he didn't know what to do next.

Christian, with his head tilted to the sky, began to whistle. It was a strong, strange whistle. It started off in one pitch and then changed periodically. Each time it got a little louder and seemed to carry for miles.

"Okay, what do we do now?" Sven asked.

Kruno was usually the man with the answers, but he had no clue and indicated that with a shrug and a facial gesture.

"So tell me more of the North, I am bored waiting and I assume this Fairy will take a while to get here."

"Besides random battles with other nations, we are in peace. All of our internal disputes have been settled. The three states of the North are solidified and have accepted that two religions will exist in harmony."

"Any plans for expansion?"

"We have all the land we need, but the world is fascinating and offers so much. We have plans to explore more and set up camp. If there is an opposing force, we will conquer it, but if they don't mind sharing we are good."

The other Northerner, Sven's comrade, attempted to get used to riding a horse. He had ridden horse years ago but never mastered it. Since then he had always had his Gret-chen. They weren't as smooth to ride or as fast, but Gret-chens, in his opinion, were vastly superior. His mind was made up before riding the horse that he didn't like it. He tried to trick himself into believing he was going to give it an honest attempt, but it was a farce. Under his breath he mumbled comments like "Stupid horse!" and "No good!" and "This is ridiculous, what was Sven thinking?" He was still upset that Sven agreed to let their Gret-chens head back to Dryden. If it was up to him he would have told Kruno to shove it up his ass.

His thoughts were interrupted quickly as he felt his equilibrium disrupted, followed by a painful blow to the side of his head and shoulder. He had been riding in circles one moment and the next he was upside down, face first in the dirt.

STUPID FREAKIN' HORSE, YOU CAN'T WALK OR EVEN STAND UP!

The others weren't paying attention at first, but turned and started to laugh. None of them laughed too loud because he was a big man, one that few of them were thrilled about aggravating. Sven encouraged the group and turned their light giggles into all out hysterics.

"Now cousin, that isn't the way you are supposed to ride a horse. One of the goals is to stay on its back, is it too complicated for you? Should we ride back to town and get a woman or a small boy to teach you?"

He sat up in the sand, brushed his face and joined in with the rest laughing.

The group's positive energy had elevated but it was about to swing in another direction.

The men and Sven laughed and made their own separate jokes which were equally funny, except for Christian whose attempt to be humorous was a failure as always. The Northerner walked around the horse to see if he could get him footed yet again.

Christian caught the look of concern on the Northerner's face and waited for something perplexing to be announced.

He looked down and said, "Is this normal?" Bending down he grabbed one of the front legs of the horse and looked to a hoofless bloody stump. The question was stupid but it was so unexpected.

Sven's laughter had muted the question and he turned to ask him to repeat.

The horse had been in shock at first, but finally felt the pain and let out a loud sign of agony, getting everyone's attention quickly.

"This horse has no freaking leg!"

Silence hit everyone at the same time as their brains pushed hard to come up with an answer. The Northerner scoured the landscape close to him, but didn't move. He wasn't sure what the right move was and wouldn't jump to a premature decision.

Decan pointed to a small area of sand moving some thirty feet from the perimeter of the group. The Northerner had the closest view and could see something grey, smooth and in the shape of a triangle. From the distance it looked to be about the size of a human head and the sand parted around it.

As soon as it had appeared, it disappeared. The group called out to him to describe what he saw.

"Well, to be honest, it kind of looked like a fin." He felt stupid even just saying the words, but it was the best he could do.

One of men in the group of three felt the hairs on the back of his neck stand up. With utter fear he said, "Sand shark!" as if announcing to the world what creature would seal his fate.

"What?" Kruno turned fast and wasn't sure if he heard him correctly.

He had turned just in time to see an explosion in the sand perpendicular to the second man from the end. It was a spectacular sight and happened so quickly the man on the horse didn't have a chance to see what hit him.

With dazzling speed, a creature that looked like a grey blur, blew out from under the sand. About the size of a horse, it leapt through the air, gripped the man around his rib cage with its massive jaw and forced him off the steed. It seemed to wiggle its tail a little as if still pushing its way through the desert floor. It had little spikes all over its body making similar motions.

Its accuracy was magnificent as it cleared the man from his horse instantly, hit the ground on the other side, prey locked in mouth. Its sheer power was displayed as it smashed through the sand on the other side with little evidence of what occurred except for some blood on the sand and a shoe. One of the spikes from the beast's side grazed the horse's backside leaving a deadly laceration — they were wickedly sharp.

"Lift us!" Kruno looked to Christian, commanding loudly. He was asking the Wizard to levitate the group high enough so that this beast couldn't get to them.

"Are you crazy? I can't lift everyone!" He was powerful, but not that powerful. Plus, his magical capabilities were drained after the battle, and most recently, the healing spells. Like a muscle after hard, intense work, he was exhausted.

The suddenly unmanned horse in pain and shock sprinted forward. The group knew they needed to leave instantly and followed in the direction of the fleeing horse, not because it knew where to go but just out of instinct. The Northerner felt the most vulnerable being on the desert floor in the area where another attack was sure to come and ran to intercept the spooked steed.

He was able to grab the reins and pull himself up, remembering his horse mounting training from many years ago, as memories flashed back with fury. He didn't notice the serious injury that the steed had sustained, and within seconds of mounting it, it collapsed to the ground as well.

Rolling on his back he bellowed, "What the heck is going on here? Every freaking horse I get is busted!"

The urgency to get out of the sand was intense and he knew that if he didn't instantly source out another four legs to ride his ass out of there, he would have to draw and fight. This wasn't ideal but he was raised to face anything with confidence. If he couldn't secure a ride, he would embrace his fate.

Decan had led the way and timed things perfectly. With arm extended in mid-stride he reached over, yelled to his new companion and embraced his massive forearm pulling him aboard.

The group, forgetting about the Vita Fairy, Ivan or La Caprata, moved fast and hard in Decan's direction.

Decan's horse was easy to pass as it was severely weighted down. Kruno led the group to a rocky clearing ahead. Maybe it was once a mighty mountain, but the area was perfect. It was a smooth rock landing that could easily hold fifty. He didn't think the creature would have a chance at smashing through such a solid platform.

All of them stopped and rested.

"What just happened?" Decan yelled out.

"Sand shark, ruthless killer. Thick skin, razor-sharp teeth and spikes all over its body. It uses those spikes to move through the sand and explodes on its victims," one of the two surviving men started to explain.

"That is critical information, don't you think? Maybe you should have brought it up to us a little earlier," Decan remarked harshly.

"They don't usually attack a group like ours. They are scavengers, mostly, from what I know. They prey on the weak and injured."

"Well I wonder why they would have been drawn to us. We had buried bloody corpses in the ground and stood around waiting for them. Then this idiot was attempting to learn how to ride a horse and probably drew it in as he stomped around like a jackass." Decan pointed to the Northerner.

"That is one I will give you because you let me ride with you. Make another comment and I will draw this." The Northerner tapped his sword.

The group erupted with accusations and name calling. The foundation for their breakdown was human nature. Being lost in foreign surroundings, defeated twice and having numbers dwindled down had created panic.

Christian called out to the group several times before getting their attention. They finally looked to him.

"Gentlemen, may I introduce our guide." He held up his hand and a very small, multi-winged creature landed in his open palm.

The tiny, dazzling blue creature fluttered in front of Christian's face. Her arms were stretched out fully so she could touch both of his eyelids. The group stood and watched as nothing was said, but his body quivered, indicating a lot was happening. No one in the group, including Kruno, had ever met a fairy before. In all of their travels they never crossed paths. If Kruno really thought about it, he would have questioned why.

Fairies exceeded in the art of stealth and were only social with ones who understood them, and with species that wouldn't be hostile. Kruno himself had passed by hundreds of fairies in his travels, but never knew because they chose not to reveal themselves.

Christian's eyes might have been closed but he could see perfectly. He couldn't see what was around him, but he envisioned the journey the fairy took, both ways and it happened in super speed. It ended with his nose bleeding and she released her projection by simply fluttering back from him.

Christian shook his head to gain perspective, and after a moment, began to describe what he saw, slowly and a little disoriented, as if waking from a dream.

"The vision was different. Their optical abilities are more advanced than ours. If we could see like them, what an incredible advantage that would be."

"Okay, first of all, I don't care about their optical abilities, and second, wipe your nose, it's creeping me out," Decan commented.

The small blue creature shook her head and Christian began to laugh. Kruno also laughed to the shock of the Fairy.

"What? Why are you guys laughing? She shook her head and that is funny?"

The fairy had made fun of Decan's lack of intelligence. Christian or Kruno didn't respond. Fairies didn't have vocal cords and communicated via telepathy. The fairy didn't realize that Kruno could understand. A common miscalculation by most was to underestimate the great warrior. Typically telepathy was practiced by wizards and astute ones at that, but Kruno was a rare exception.

"She showed me everything, they live in an oasis among this lifeless desert, an area full of vegetation and an endless supply of water."

"Is Ivan all right?" Sven asked.

"She stuck with him into their shelter buried deep in rock. I can see it all, as if I was there. For the last few hours they were separated, but he was okay until then. It won't be easy to attack them. They number in the hundreds."

Christian was asked to describe the surroundings and did a piss poor job of it. Everyone was getting irritated. He wasn't great with directions in the first place, and even though he saw what the fairy witnessed, he didn't really know what to look for.

Kruno opened his mind and asked the fairy if she would be so kind to show him what she saw.

"I would like to thank you for your assistance. I am also not sure why you help us, but it is greatly appreciated. May I lay witness to your journey?"

"My dear warrior, it is our pleasure to serve you now, as we have in the past. I would be honoured to show you what I have projected to Christian."

"I think you might have me mistaken with someone else, I must admit I have never crossed the path of a fairy in my travels and know little of your kind," Kruno commented as she fluttered towards him.

"Just because you can't see something doesn't mean it's not there." She changed in a flash as all of her pigment drained from her. From a beautiful blue to completely transparent, she vanished from all of their sights.

"It's not hard for us to hide and no need for thanks. Your group follows you and your motivation to risk life daily has been passed through to each of them. Your foundation for engaging evil rests purely on your love for life and goodness. You can do things we can't, but we can help... Now close your eyes."

His body responded as did Christian's as soon as the now invisible fairy touched his eyelids. His mind opened up and was introduced to an interesting clarity. He travelled as did she. Instead of being overwhelmed by the new pallet of colours and pitches of light that distracted Christian, he focused on defensibility and developed a penetration strategy.

La Caprata's den looked to be populated by several hundred. He laid witness to the oasis Christian had attempted to explain, and saw the old base of a once mighty mountain that was worn away by eons of weather. The rock base was similar to the one they stood on avoiding the sand shark, but was much larger. Caves, brilliant caves, were carved out of the rock interior. Their lair was underground and fortified by rock. There would be no easy entrance.

His nose opened up as did Christian's as she released her grip on his mind.

"Okay boys, mount up, we attack before nightfall. They are very close."

"What is our offensive strategy?" Sven asked as he mounted in tandem with Kruno.

"I will let everyone know when we get closer."

"You have no clue how we are getting in, do you?" Sven said as he examined Kruno.

"No, not really."

"Comforting."

Before they left, the Vita fairy had one more telepathic comment to make, but exclusively for Kruno. *"You know Kruno, Christian is one of a kind. Not many, maybe none, have his potential."*

"I know, I've always known that."

"He loves you, like a hybrid brother-father."

"What we have done for years and will continue to do is train him. Even though it's dangerous, it propels him past any other Wizard who sits in a room and reads all day. If he survives, his skill may be unparalleled. He could be a master of warfare from a magic standpoint, truly understanding what works in battle and having the courage to take action. Two concepts few Wizards have. If he survives, he will live much longer than any of us around here. We are his foundation."

"Your words couldn't please me more."

They stopped just before the edge of a huge sandstorm. Its perimeter was sharp and smooth, unnatural for a storm. Few would question why it looked the way it did, and would either wait for it to finish or head in a different direction.

Kruno knew it would never stop. He asked everyone to be silent many miles back, and as they got close, he made a motion to dismount.

The Northerner — the one who had shared a horse with Christian — put his hands around two of the men, the last to form a group which stood in a circle. He made the motion that he wanted to talk first. Everyone focused intensely, understanding they had to be quiet. They struggled to listen.

"I don't mind sharing a horse with someone, but next time I would like to have someone a little less frisky. I could have been warned that the Wizard was a lover of men."

The setup was seamless and many of them broke into laughter. The timing was completely inappropriate but also perfect. Christian wanted to respond and was angry at the comment, but in all reality he was used to it. For his entire life he had been made fun of. Before he could speak Kruno made the motion to stop talking.

This is what you have to deal with when travelling with Northerners. They can't stop joking. Silence is imperative here and they know that but don't care. I could only imagine teachers in the North have interesting ways of getting them to shut up and pay attention.

"Okay, boys, the game plan is simple," Kruno whispered, attempting to disregard the previous comment and getting serious quickly.

"Why are we talking so low? We are beside a giant sandstorm," Decan whispered.

"Does that look like a normal sandstorm to you? It just sits in the same place," Christian said, looking at him as if he was stupid.

"Sorry, man-loving genius, I apologise."

"They are just beyond this storm. This is the perimeter of their lair. Follow me, no turning back no matter what."

"Hold on, what's the plan?"

"That is the plan."

Decan looked to his leader with disapproval, "That's it? We will just walk through the front door. Hi everyone, we are here. That doesn't sound like a good plan at all."

"I like it, nice and simple," Sven jumped in. He pictured himself walking in, drawing his weapon and announcing it was go time. That was a Northern-type battle plan, but would be foolish because they would be absurdly outnumbered.

"Simple is right. I have a feeling few, if any, have ever breached their perimeter. They won't be expecting us. The fairy snuck in — why can't we?"

"Sure, the fairy is the size of a finger and can be invisible at will. My package alone is bigger than that." Decan grabbed between his legs.

"That is still to be argued." Christian, with his only good insult, mocked Decan's manhood.

The group chuckled, including Decan, for a well-played insult.

"We aren't just going to walk in. I was also hoping our little friend and Christian could help us out with a disguise."

"I would like it to be noted that I think this plan is a stupid," Decan insisted.

The plan was simple but involved a stealth spell. Kruno knew Christian would have a hard time bending the light around everyone, but with the fairy's help it was obtainable. He assumed that the Sand Sorceresses would crack through the spell if they were expecting them, but they weren't. He was willing to bet the thought of anyone attacking them, of walking — as Decan put it — through the front door, didn't even cross their minds. Over-confidence was a weakness to be exploited.

The sand was thick and blew fiercely. It felt like their skin was going to peel right off. They knew they couldn't open their eyes, as the damage would be irreversible.

They only expected a minute or so of sand blasting, as Kruno had speculated, but it didn't seem to end. Everyone started to question in their minds if they should turn back.

"This isn't right. I don't feel good." Decan broke the silence order and yelled because of the pelting sand and clashing winds of the vortex.

"This is fine."

"How do you know, have you ever been in a vortex before?"

"Keep going and shut up."

"It's getting worse, I am telling you this isn't right. Let's turn around."

It was noticeably painful, but nobody paid attention to Decan's suggestion because he had no formal authority. Kruno pushed hard and focused, but he actually started to doubt his decision. He worried that maybe they were now stuck in this sandstorm. Their enemy was very powerful and he wouldn't put it past them.

"We are following a fairy's advice. This is foolish."

Kruno popped through the other side and went from torture to bliss. He, like the others in sequence, found themselves falling to the ground.

Each of them looked up to a new world. In the middle of the Godforsaken desert lay a lush green garden. In the middle of the garden there was a lake. The entire perimeter was a swirling sandstorm and straight up was the blue sky.

"Amazing," one of the men stated and everyone agreed. They all brushed sand vigorously from every orifice.

A few feet from the edge lay waist high, thick elephant grass. It couldn't have been a better place to hide until it was time for a combined stealth spell. A few Sand Sorceresses were strewn about the massive oasis as indicated by the fairy who had flown undetected over the sandstorm wall.

Kruno navigated through the tall grass and peeked through the perimeter to see an impressive, lush sanctuary. A field of crops led to a shining lake and trees were scattered around it.

"So far so good. Now we wait."

The sun's rays weakened and the time to attempt a foolish entry was about to begin.

The fairy sprinkled strange sparkling dust over each one of the men, and as it slowly fell to the ground, their bodies disappeared.

"Okay, the plan is getting better," Decan said softly as he noticed he couldn't even see his own hands in front of his face.

"Ouch who did that?" Christian said and a now invisible Decan chuckled.

"The things I could do being invisible," Sven commented with a smile nobody could see.

"Can you handle your part Christian?" Kruno understood that his defensive spell would be even tougher than the fairy's invisibility spell. La Caprata had unprecedented abilities with magic. Even though they were now blind to the naked eye, they gave off energy that might be picked up by Sorceresses of their calibre. Christian's spell had to block all of their energy. A lot to ask of any Wizard, let alone such a young magician.

"I can hold it, don't worry about me."

"Good luck warriors, and Godspeed." The Vita Fairy opened up her communication to all of them and fluttered off.

The interior of the cave had an eerie blue glow that lit up every corridor. The walls themselves were smooth as if carved from wood by a master carpenter rather than hewn from solid stone. Kruno and Christian were both thinking the same thing. This reminded them of the Games Master and his labyrinth, but even he needed torches to illuminate their path. Here the rock seemed to have its own autonomous ability to produce a form of light.

Each corridor led to different rooms or other corridors. It would be very easy to get lost, but they had an advantage — Kruno remembered every turn as if he had been there himself. The group, unable to talk, moved in silence and each man was equally impressed except for two. Fear started to settle in for them. This was another unfamiliar setting and they expected an attack at any moment. It consumed their minds.

They were surrounded by rock, which made Kruno more comfortable. La Caprata had a keen ability to use sand to their advantage, but there wasn't any in here.

No sand, perfect, that means no sneak attack. Also, the ceiling is too low for them to bring an assault from above.

Dozens of rooms spread out along the passageway, but only a few stood out. One was an armoury resembling a blacksmith's shop. The men could only take a quick peek in as they walked by, but it was obvious that swords and spears were the Sorceresses weapons of choice. Another room seemed to be an internal garden containing not just food items but plants were also being cultivated.

A few women warriors walked by them and the group prepared to be seen, forgetting for a moment they were invisible, but nothing happened. It was a childhood dream for every one of the men. The ability to sneak into a girl's room and watch her undress. In all reality, the dream was very suiting because every single one of La Caprata was stunning, but they were here for a different purpose.

Kruno's plan, which he knew was a real stretch to turn into reality, was to sneak by the Sorceresses, turn Ivan invisible and walk right out. Odds for this to succeed weren't very good, but it was at least a plan.

Something will come to me, I know it.

Their path seemed to descend slowly as they walked. Over time they ended up deeper and deeper underground.

They heard a commotion just prior to entering a great room. It was full of Sorceresses and they were speaking in a strange language. One voice bellowed out and then small chatter amongst what sounded like dozens followed.

None of them expected what they saw as they entered the room. About a hundred or so Sand Sorceresses occupied a massive area. The ceiling was high and covered in stalactites. The walls had strange, crystallized gypsum glittering over their surfaces. It was simply stunning. There was a small pond in the middle of the room, which was fed by water flowing from a gap in the rock near the ceiling. The ground had strange, soft grass on it that acted like a sponge when stepped on. First, it contracted and then expanded, leaving a footprint for a few seconds. A majority of the room's occupants were sitting on the ground facing the other way. Attached to the walls, little balconies held about a dozen or so Sand Sorceress. It was assumed that they were upper class or some form of royalty because of their privileged seating.

The group slowly positioned themselves along a vacant portion at the back of the room. It was an impressive engineering feat and simply magnificent, but the most stunning feature of all was buried among the stalactites that pointed down like teeth from the ceiling. A large diamond-shaped orb seemed to float and emitted a strange blue light. At first guess it seemed to be an energy source. It probably fed the grass-covered floor and potentially illuminated the entire set of paths leading to this room.

Focusing in on La Caprata, they looked to be a species that had perfected aesthetics. Every one of the women was striking. A voice sang from the other end of the room some forty feet up. It was hard to see her from where they were, but she sat in a throne with two others beside her. The throne almost seemed to be bonded to the wall with her feet resting on a foot rest. They couldn't understand what she was saying, but it was motivational as the group responded with clapping.

They assumed the woman must be their leader. Her hair was different than all of the others. It was dreadlocked. Of course she was beautiful and her unique hair added to her look.

She finished her words and opened her hand in the direction of the pond. Two completely naked females emerged from the water. It caught everyone off guard, except for Kruno who didn't lose his focus. The women had flawless breasts, followed by a flat stomach, perfectly curved hips and strong, long legs. One of them tossed her hair back as the other walked seductively beside her. One stopped the other, spun her around slowly, showing her perfect ass. Her hand slid down her back and over her bottom.

Things just got a lot better. Oh my, please don't stop, Decan thought to himself as he stared at the women. He wanted to say something out loud to Sven, but bit his tongue.

Every one of the men couldn't help but be drawn into what was happening. They weren't under any kind of formal spell, but their eyes were locked. The sight was extremely erotic, but ended as the women positioned themselves on a massive ten-foot leaf that seemed to grow from a thick stem in the ground. It moved to meet them as they sat.

Kruno cautiously asked Christian in his mind, *"Can you understand what they are saying?"*

"It sounds like a derivative of common tongue, but no. I can try something, but it will be hard to hold my other spell." Christian understood a lot of languages, but not this one.

Kruno began to think if the risk was worth it. The room was filled with a deadly enemy, but less than two dozen were armed. The surprise would be theirs this time! The problem was that there was no indication that Ivan was alive, and if he was, where was he?

The only chance we have to find Ivan is to attempt to use Christian's spell to help translate. He will no doubt have a real tough time keeping both spells engaged, but how else will we find Ivan? Either way, we will need to reposition ourselves.

He analyzed the situation. Two groups in the rear of the room were armed. They didn't wear full battle gear as they were missing armour, but all of them had two thin swords sheathed along their hips or back.

Kruno repositioned the men behind a group of twelve armed Sand Sorceresses. They slowly unsheathed and awaited his order. With weapons out, they would have an advantage. If they were detected, they needed the first strike to count.

From gibberish to comprehensive understanding of their language, their words started to make sense. Christian used another one of his new spells. It transformed the meanings of words into common tongue for a short time. Nobody but Kruno expected it and at first it was a shock, because as it settled in, it felt like a smack to the head with a twig, not painful but enough to jolt men on the edge of battle.

"Praise yet again to these two warriors." The crowd clapped. "I am proud of our catch. We have one very impressive man, maybe the largest to date. Our battle created the most casualties we have ever sustained. This should make all of you tremendously excited for the next little while. If the friends of such men were strong enough to do the damage that they did, imagine how impressive our prey is."

That was the most casualties they had sustained? We did the most damage? That is ludicrous! We barely survived.

"I call to our commander of the battle to let us know what transpired." The lady on the throne called out to another on the ground level. She raised her voice and began to explain.

"Our spells were inept on a few of them. We assumed they were all easy targets as we moved in, but we were wrong. Some mounted a creature that was vastly superior to horses and they made effective use of the beast. One of them was also a Wizard. He wreaked havoc on us. Sussal was burned to a crisp before she had a chance to draw blood. An intense fire line consumed her from the air. The others had accurate spears and are gifted with handheld weapons like no other."

"Do we have anything to fear from them? Is retribution possible?" One of the women on one of the balconies tossed out the question.

"The few that survived were impressive, but most impressive was their lack of fear. I could sense that they weren't afraid. Our battle plan consists of erotic spells and of course the fear inflicted on our enemies. We couldn't utilize half of our strategy on them as fear never settled in. To answer your question, even after such a positive evaluation, I don't think we will have a problem. There is no way for them to find us and by then we will have disposed of what they seek."

Those sultry wenches think they are going to eat my brother Ivan. I don't think so, Decan thought.

The comment infuriated Sven. His hand gripped his battle-axe tightly. He wanted to unleash havoc with his weapon but held off.

"Thank you commander, we will fully exploit our spoils more than normal because of how taxing it was on La Caprata. May I introduce our finest catch ever." She held her hand out to an empty portion of rock next to one of the balconies. The area started to fade in colour and the shape of a man started to appear. After a few seconds, the wall was transparent and revealed a room behind the rock. Ivan stood there with a massive chain around his neck. The crowd cheered with what could only be morbid excitement.

"I will award shortly the few that will have him. His size is one thing, but his status as a great warrior is what makes him worth so much more. We have others as well." More rooms drained of their pigment and showed another five men chained in a similar manner.

Kruno began to formulate a plan.

Just above their heads, a Sand Sorceress slid down a silk line with her feet from the ceiling like a spider closing in on prey. She slowly moved closer and her eyes changed from shimmering blue to emerald green. She could see them!

Christian's strained spells had provided the release of a little of their energy footprint and a shift of her eyesight gave them shape. With a thin wire in hand in the form of a loop, she descended on them.

Kruno pressed his mouth against Christian's ear and began to whisper. He didn't trust his ability to communicate such an important message via telepathy.

"There has to be a way to get into that room, I am going to…"

Before he could finish he noticed the woman upside down over top one of the men. She moved fast, flipped the noose around his neck, yanked hard and somehow elevated with tremendous speed. The man immediately grabbed for his neck, attempting to put his fingers in between this unknown wire and his neck to protect his vital air supply.

He had little regard for his weapon which fell to the ground with a clank. It happened just as the room fell silent. The ground was covered in grass but it still made a noise.

From across the room the leader on the throne heard an unwelcome clank of metal and looked to see one of her soldiers slide up from the ground with something in her hand. With a blink she intensified her vision and zoomed in. She could see a wire noose in her hand, and even though empty, it seemed weighted. Her eyes also changed from blue to green, altering her vision to see what was dangling from the noose. With this change in optics she could see the men, all of them, a group ready to strike at any moment. She knew they were under attack from an enemy like no other. Her mind didn't have time to deduce how this was possible, just realize that this was a formidable enemy, one able to become invisible and also breach their lair. She looked to the blue orb which lit their world and it changed to a green colour. The change illuminated Kruno and his crew. They weren't invisible to anyone anymore.

The light turned green and Kruno knew their gig was up. The advantage of stealth was gone. The plan was thwarted and a new simple plan was to be activated. Stealth might not be on their side but surprise still was.

"Attack!"

It was music to Sven's ears. He came down hard on one of the dozen armed Sand Sorceresses. All the fury of his cousin's capture and assumed eventual mutilation was turned into raw power. Her small body easily buckled under the pressure.

Speedy Kruno fatally cut a massive laceration down the back of one of them. He then stepped forward as a second turned to see why her partner had shrieked. Before she could comprehend the gravity of the situation, her face was smashed in from his sword.

The Northerner jammed a spear through the back of another. Her legs immediately gave way, she spit blood from her mouth and then collapsed.

The only remaining man from the other group met his target as well. Every one of their targets didn't have time to react.

Decan was a little slower and his moment's pause gave his intended target the right reaction. She didn't look side to side but immediately rolled forward just missing one of his swords. Her roll ended with her on her one knee, weapon drawn and a smile on her face. She had avoided Decan's sword, but just didn't think to look to her side. Before she had a chance to attack, the Northerner had launched his spear striking her upper torso. It replaced her sense of satisfied savvy, indicated with a smirk, to pain and defeat, indicated by a clenching of her teeth and a scream.

The Northerner then reached for his second weapon, a weapon he had specifically brought to this battle after their first encounter in the desert. With flail in hand, he began to swing it around and landed it with deadly accuracy. The spiked, heavy metal ball smashed into a shoulder, shattering bone and then it rebounded, crashing into her head and flipping the destroyed Sand Sorceress.

The initial surprise was over, La Caprata had time to turn and see who was flanking them. The eyes of the massive man with the flail locked eyes with one of them. With sheer swiftness she was able to unsheathe and attempt a defence. The Northerner fully expected her to put her swords over her head to block and he was right. It was a sound defensive if his weapon had a fixed staff, but a flail has a chain connecting the ball and the handle. Moving an extra step forward the chain hit her swords. The ball continued along its path and connected with velocity with the back of her head. Her eyes exploded from the strike, forced her head forward and she collapsed in front of him. The Northerner bellowed with excitement and confidence, echoing fear among all in the room.

Their leader with the dreadlocks stood along with everyone in the balcony to see what was happening. They watched in horror as they were under attack. The thought seemed absurd, an instinctual conclusion created by having too much ego. Their minds attempted to tell each of them that their eyes must be tricking them, but reality set in with a bang. A massive, bright, concentrated white light screamed from the back of the room and an enormous explosion followed.

Christian had shut both spells down in a hurry in order to brew up another. It was time for his favourite spell and one he knew would be perfect. The first stage of his spell, which was now dispensed by his staff, stunned the sight of anyone looking his way. The group closest to him dropped their guard. Four armed Sand Sorceresses had spun around to see several of their comrades on the floor. They immediately focused in on the first of the men they could see and reached for their weapons. Swords unsheathed, two of them took a step forward. The end of his staff emitted a powerful light which stunned their vision, causing them to put their hands to their faces to provide shade. Not that it would have mattered if they kept their position, the explosion to follow decimated. The small orb materialized in between Christian and the four Sand Sorceresses. It exploded with fury, ripping them to pieces by its ferociousness.

The remaining warriors charged Kruno. The first attempted to strike him from above with a chop, but his arm shield easily defended against it. With both her weapons against his shield, he easily placed his sword into her abdomen. Kruno pulled it from her stomach, and with a spin, unleashed his weapon towards the second. His sword was blocked by both of the last Sand Sorceress's weapons. His shield listened to his intentions and magically expanded, covering his fist. With a metal fist he punched her hard, dead square in the nose. The shot exploded parts of her face. Her head cocked back and blood splattered everywhere. Showing his opponent extreme respect for her potential to still fight, even after sustaining such an injury, he followed with his foot. Using his weight, he slammed straight down hard on her unprepared knee, which buckled.

The first dozen were down, most of them slain. They had accomplished more in a few moments than they had with thirty men during their entire last battle.

Their leader, on her throne, watched as some of her troops were slaughtered. This was something their Kingdom of elite women warriors had never witnessed. Men were inferior to them and their lair was impossible to find. How had they done this?

Most of them were unarmed. These men would do serious damage unless she did something.

She was the most skilled of any of them and fear wasn't part of her genetic makeup. She knew the leader of their enemy must fall and wanted to do it herself with no more death of her beloved sisters. She watched Kruno's demeanour and impressive skill as he laid out some of her best and most respected warriors with poise.

With an ear piercing command she bellowed a long drawn out, "Cease!"

Everyone in the room stopped dead in their tracks. The other dozen armed Sand Sorceresses were moving into position to attack but halted. Everyone looked up to her.

Kruno and his crew were waiting for the next round of attackers, but they didn't come after the command was fired from the throne. They too looked up to see what was going to happen next.

The dreadlocked leader stretched her arms to her side slowly with hands waiting for their expected metal friends. The women to either side placed the weapons in her hands with a small tilt of the head, showing deep respect.

She slid the weapons into a sheathe on her back, curled her arms inwards to her chest and leaned forward, letting gravity take control of her. She flipped perfectly and dropped from a fatal height for any man, but did it with confidence. She landed with ease, looked up and started to charge.

Kruno knew she was coming for him. He also knew she would be their best. With no sand to disappear into, the attack would come head on. Their most impressive ability was speed. He knew her two swords would come at him fast. He needed to lighten his weapons to improve dexterity.

She ripped along the ground with unprecedented swiftness. He assumed she would jump over the pond with her supernatural leaping ability, but he was wrong. She didn't change her stride and ran across the pond creating nothing more than a little splash.

Great, she can run across water!

The room went silent in Kruno's mind as he waited for a warrior he knew would be impressive. Everyone focused on the two of them.

He located two Sand Sorceress's swords that used to belong to a now deceased warrior. They were thin and light, but before he picked them up, he grabbed a spear and launched it towards her. The spear spun through the air with precision. The speed of his toss aimed at a target that moved even faster was a good move and he expected an impact.

Kruno watched and was amazed as she flipped backward, kicking the head of the spear which exploded into pieces. The continuous flip spun her landing perfectly back into a running position. He grabbed the two swords from the ground and witnessed her closing in.

Okay, that was impressive, Kruno thought and then commanded, "This one is mine gentlemen."

"No quarrels here my man," Sven said.

She drew her weapons for battle.

With lightning speed, her swords met his as she flipped over his head. Bending backward as far as he could, with weapons in the air, he followed her. Landing behind him she paused for a moment, sized him up and charged once again.

From a distance, all that could be seen were glimpses of steel coming in from all angles. Kruno was on the defensive, as her agility was something he had never encountered. He could feel she was going to overtake him soon if he didn't do something.

She is good. They are coming too fast, I am going to get...

He had done a great job anticipating blows, but was hit with one sword and then the other. One of them opened up his shoulder and the other a small laceration along his chest. Both wounds were insignificant in terms of pain or a distraction, but it showed she had supremacy.

First blood was hers, but her success provided him with his first opportunity. She assumed he would have winced or shied away after being wounded, that his concentration would have suffered, but she was wrong. Kruno had been trained not to feel pain, and wasn't concerned in the slightest with his new wounds. Her assumptions led her to attempt a fatal blow, an early kill, one Kruno blocked with ease.

Her swords rained down on him from above and connected with one of his swords. *My turn, witch,* Kruno thought as her side was unprotected. His one sword held both of her weapons at bay and even though she was fast, she wouldn't be able to properly defend the thrust from his other sword. He started to lunge forward expecting his first successful hit, but another part of her arsenal was introduced.

Initiating the thrust, he didn't pay attention to the fact that she had released one of her swords. She just let it go. His mind told him it would only be a mere moment before she was dangling at the end of his weapon.

With a bare, weaponless hand she opened her palm and forced her arm forward. She didn't physically touch him, but he lifted off his feet and was blown back. The impact felt like he was kicked by a horse and was enough for him to drop both weapons. His mind raced to figure out what had happened. He coughed a little blood and looked up from the ground to see her still in position. Her face was locked in serious focus, arm extended and body erect.

What the heck was that? He gathered his wits fast and didn't bother analyzing the situation. She would be on him with haste. He needed to get to his feet in a hurry, but more importantly, he needed his weapons. Using the ancient trick of great warriors, he called to his weapons with his mind and they slid perfectly into his hands. Out of breath from the impact and dazed, he stood up, swords to his sides. He looked to see where his opponent was, but couldn't see her.

She had leapt above his vision and slammed down on his shoulder with a downward kick. The impact drove him down to one knee. She flipped acrobatically backward, landing perfectly on her feet with a smile.

"It looks to me like you are getting your ass kicked, my man," Decan yelled out to Kruno.

"Don't worry, it is all part of my game plan." Kruno mustered up enough energy to respond

"Love his confidence, but I don't think this is part of his plan. If it is, it is a poor one."

Kruno knew he was in trouble. He needed something fast. Magic was a part of every facet of her attack, surprise was critical.

Time for a little trick of my own. Clorian shield, I could use you a little bigger.

He had never requested his shield to respond that way before, but he needed it to expand in a hurry, and to become translucent would be helpful. He touched his magical arm shield, and pictured what he wanted as she charged him. Within a second, four long pieces of metal shot in opposite directions, two pieces paralleled upward and two down, one set at his wrist and the other at his elbow. Then six similar pieces ran perpendicular to the others resembling a grid. It formed a much larger shield with small spaces in between that allowed him to still see through to the battlefield.

He was shocked, but when he turned to her he could she was amazed, dumbfounded for a moment. He began to charge the shocked Sand Sorceress. The grid shield had one more surprise. During the first few steps towards his opponent several two-foot spikes emerged from the front of his new shield.

It was the most impressive transformation he had witnessed from his Clorian shield. Everyone was flabbergasted.

The dreadlocked Sorceress was completely caught off guard, and had no choice but to drop her weapons, as Kruno was only steps away with a spiked shield leading the way. She didn't have time to flip over him, all she could muster was a launch forward. With the gift of flight, she hoped to knock him over. She hit his shield with hands positioned perfectly, missing the spikes and leaving her body horizontal to the ground.

The impact was hard and almost stopped Kruno in his tracks, but he used every ounce of power from every muscle to continue moving forward. She was completely blown away by his strength, and never assumed he would have been able to fend off the blow and still maintain his stable dominant position.

She was driven backward, unarmed and with spikes too close for comfort. They both knew that his plan was to drive her into the wall, forcing the sharp metal into her.

Her feet hit the wall and the true war began. A war of brawn that was almost evenly matched, but that slightly favoured Kruno. Her arms started to bow and one of the spikes closed in slowly on her shoulder. The tip of the spike penetrated her skin as she looked up almost eye to eye through one of the spaces in the shield.

Even in the moment of battle, Kruno couldn't help but find her stunning. Green eyes that didn't show a hint of fear looked back on him.

She knew something had to change or she would be pinned against the wall, and impaled by a series of spikes. She had to flip out of the way but knew the damage to her shoulder would be severe. Nonetheless there wasn't any other option. The spike dug in deeper and Kruno started to feel the victory at hand. Showing more impressive acrobatic skills and speed, she flipped out of the way. Her shoulder opened up as it tore from the spike. Her landing this time wasn't pretty, as she ended up on her back.

Kruno's shield jettisoned forward and hit the rock wall as metal scraped rock.

Where the heck did you go now? Are you impossible to kill?

He turned, as blood dripped down his upper body from his wounds, and he looked at her through his shield. One of his spikes was red from her wound.

"What do you want to do now?" Kruno shouted to her.

She looked up at the most skilled warrior she had ever seen and decided that the fight had turned on its axis. For the first time in her life she considered defeat as an option.

"What do you mean?" she responded, confused.

Kruno knew that he may be able to defeat her, victory could be his, but he was going to take a few more hits. He also knew that more Sand Sorceresses would flood the room soon, making odds shift in their favour. If a democratic solution could be agreed upon, it would be the right path to follow.

"We have options. Your race, La Caprata as you call yourself, is one of the most impressive I've ever come across, any of us have come across. You're strong, smart and control levels of magic that would impress Rizzian himself. That being said, we are still ready to die for our friends and our weapons are navigated by the best from our world."

Their leader stood up.

"With one shift of my wrist I could have seventy of mine rush this room, hit your group from all angles and tear you apart."

"Think wisely, Sand Sorceress."

"I would be lying if I didn't acknowledge the skill level of your group as well. You are the first to penetrate our lair, the first to destroy so many of ours and you, you are the first to make me bleed."

"We just want our men, Ivan the Northerner and the friend of his." He pointed to the only one of the members that still stood from the original group. "A small token for us to leave with no more death."

Kruno looked up and noticed more holes in the walls had appeared in the chamber, similar to the one that Ivan was in. He noticed many heads looking down on them and understood that this would be the next wave of Sand Sorceresses to descend on them. These ones would be fully armed.

"You can't have him, Ivan, he is the greatest man we have ever lured here. Plus he did decide to come here himself."

"Don't lie to me," Kruno said sternly. "He didn't come here under his own control, he was manipulated by you and it's been going on for months. He is the reason we are here and the only way we would consider leaving. No peaceful negotiation leaves him here, for you to feed on him."

She started to smile for a second, "You think we are going to eat him? That is hilarious. That was never our intention. Come, young man, follow me."

Still not sure what was to come, he followed her. She didn't pick her weapons back up and seemed to be offering some kind of a temporary ceasefire. Kruno looked back to his friends and they looked to him for an answer. He indicated with a shrug that he didn't know what was happening.

Kruno went down a small corridor and was shortly out of sight.

Decan looked around with his lip pinned to his teeth because it was a very intense situation. The five of them stood battle-ready but nobody moved or talked.

"Well, this is officially the most interesting position I have ever been in my entire life."

He looked around and waved, slightly flirting to help break up his nerves, "Hi, ladies!"

The comment and gesture could have been enough to ignite a battle like a flame on dry kindling. The one he waved at flinched forward, but then moved back. Decan tightened up.

Kruno was in a room that was decorated for comfort. The floor had fur on it, which was nice to walk on. It had a few elongated chairs where four or five could sit side by side, with comfortable pillows strewn about. In the corner was a bed.

She was bewitching with green eyes, a curvy athletic body, large lips, and upon closer look, she had artwork on one of her arms, which probably signified her rank. Her mood seemed to lighten and her mannerisms were more relaxed. Kruno didn't let his guard down for a minute and remained quite serious.

"You maintain such confidence even when odds are stacked against you. There is no way you can win the battle."

"Don't be so sure of the outcome, we fully expect victory."

"You really think we are going to eat Ivan, don't you?" She smiled and seemed to relax but Kruno remained tense.

"My name is Kiera. I am the Queen of La Caprata. We are a perfect race, flawless, physically strong, with a deep understanding of magic and our warriors are remarkable. Our lives are perfect and hidden in a place nobody would find us, except for today, of course. We have everything except for one small defect. We can't reproduce. There is no male La Caprata and for the most part it really doesn't bother us. We like women. Men complicate things." As she walked around the room she looked at Kruno with an appeal that was contradictory to what the situation warranted.

"You might like women, but by the way you are looking at me, I would say you're interested in men as well."

"Men have their uses, some of that is sexual, but no one can pleasure a woman like a woman."

"Don't speak for all men." Kruno found himself flirting mildly

"In all reality, your five friends out there have dozens of women ready to rip them apart… but could just as easily rip their clothes off. This time of year, they do get a little antsy, men do offer something new."

She gripped her shoulder and winced a little, blood oozed through her fingers.

"You can put your shield away, we will be parting ways peacefully." She paused for a moment. "You inflicted a decent wound. How are yours?"

Kruno let his guard down a little, and as a gesture of goodwill, commanded his shield to return to its original form, the forearm brace he was accustomed to.

"Impressive hardware you have. I have never witnessed a shield like that."

Time passed and sweat started to accumulate on Sven's forehead. Northerners weren't known for their patience, and his was wearing thin. Each moment that passed gave their enemy more time to prepare for the onslaught.

Decan didn't dare stop his eyes from probing the surroundings, "Sven, I think it's best if we go back to back. They love to flank and I am sure they will come from everywhere. Do you agree?"

Sven didn't respond but started to swing into a new position.

"Christian, how come they can see us now?"

"We had to hear what they were saying so I used another spell. I couldn't hold both spells, so that gave away an energy signature."

"No Christian, how can they see us? I can tell that they notice every part of me, not just a trace of energy."

"I think it has something to do with their light source. The room is now green, it's different."

"So much for the Fairy's spell. Not as impressive anymore," Decan remarked.

"Shut up Decan, the spell was great!"

"Relax, I am not insulting your girlfriend."

They waited and nothing happened except for increased tension.

"Anyone else think Kruno's plan was so great?" Decan said critically.

The two groups stared at one another. From the back, a well-armed group moved slowly forward to replace the unarmed. As time passed, La Caprata's positions bettered and both sides knew it.

The women, even though they stood erect and prepared, showed signs of respect in their eyes, something Sven recognized. He knew they had decimated their group and made a mockery of their defences. Any great intelligent warrior, no matter what race, respects a cunning and able adversary.

Decan understood that the balance in the room was going to shift. Both sides had been halted by their leaders, but something would give soon. The wrong movement, a simple misunderstood comment or dropped weapon could trigger a mass bloodbath. Always wanting to be the leader, he started to prepare as if he was in charge. “Christian, what do you have left in your arsenal?”

Attempting not to move his mouth by locking his teeth, he said quietly, “Honestly, Decan, I am burned out.”

The Wizard had held two spells for a long period of time, and then used his favourite spell, the Sphere of Fire. He was exhausted and incapable of casting anything powerful. He needed to rest before he could drum something up.

Decan’s hands started to sweat and his double sword handle became lubricated. He stood next to massive Sven, a scary sight for any enemy. His sweat beaded and ran down his face several times. Even though it reached his eyes, he barely blinked and just stared forward. He was a muscular man, full of testosterone. His arms stood out the most from his body, fully flexed biceps held weapons ready to crush anyone.

The Sand Sorceresses were confident they could take them down, but fully understood that the first wave would result in many deaths. They also could see that one of their opponents, the other Northerner, was also massive in size and held a weapon that was the most effective against them, a flail. They knew this wasn’t going to be pretty.

The only thing that broke Sven’s concentration was an “mmm”. As if seeing something she liked, one of the frontline Sorceresses accidentally released the sound. It was soft had a sensual tone. She looked at Sven, blood splattered on his pectorals, tall and physically impressive overall. Her eyes passed over his body, bouncing from scar to scar.

“I am not sure if I want to smash them with my axe, or smash her with my other favourite tool.”

Kiera and Kruno re-entered the silent room, one still filled with much tension. Kruno's shield had returned to a docile state and his weapons were sheathed, which indicated that he no longer anticipated a threat.

"My sisters, La Caprata, today we have witnessed something none of us have previously seen. Our precious, well-concealed, beautiful nest has been breached by exceptional warriors. After a long discussion with their leader, Kruno, I have decided it is best to learn from them. They can assist in making our home impregnable. No more blood will be shed, and in return, we will grant them what they desire."

Small conversations broke out amongst the groups and most looked angered or distraught with the decision their Queen had just announced.

The women who stood closest to Sven made another comment with sultry eyes, "I was rather hoping I didn't have to kill you."

"You like what you see?" His voice was deep and seemed to put a shiver down her spine and touch her erotically.

She nodded, "Do you like what you see?"

"I would have to be stupid not to." Sven smiled confidently.

"Is he for real? Is Sven trying to get it on right now?" Decan asked to anyone who wanted to listen.

"That's Sven alright, his mind only has two things on it and that fine ass has occupied one of them."

The few that disagreed with Kiera continued with their isolated arguments. They hoped for a similar view from their sisters in arms. They wanted to make sure there was support if they were to raise their contrary opinion.

"Does anyone in this room disagree with me? Please, may the first move forward. If it takes me more than a few swipes of my weapon to silence you then the decision is yours." Kiera understood what was transpiring and decided to crush the objections with a challenge.

"I have heard that line before. Where the heck have I heard that before?" Decan thought for a few moments and then remembered that Kruno had used something similar when they fought the Cryptons. "Hmm, interesting."

The room silenced quickly. One thing was certain, no one wanted to draw swords against the Queen.

"I don't mean to get harsh, but this is my decision and everyone knows I do what is best for our colony."

"Great Queen, we don't mean to insult you. For as long as I can remember you have given us a blissful existence and all decisions have been well accepted, but I would like to ask you a question that is gentle in nature, but assists us with your decision." From the balcony a woman made a soft inquiry. She waited for Kiera to nod. "These men know our location. They could be devious, leave here under a false treaty and return with vast numbers. A few of these men are illustrious and would have the pull of the Silver Allegiance or the Northern Kingdom."

To Kruno's surprise she had broken a promise made from their discussions and spoke in her tongue. Christian's spell had ceased and none of them understood what was said. Nonetheless, Kruno didn't say anything because he knew the room doubted a decision that was favourable to him and his men. He didn't respond to it, but addressed the crowd himself.

"Men, put your weapons in their sheaths, no more blood is to be spilt. We are guests in a great empire and are honoured to call this a stalemate. We too follow a creed of great honour and are upset at our losses as are you with yours. We wish them well on the other side and embrace these great warriors. La Caprata will have a special place in our minds, but our lips will not form your name after we leave. Silence is our gift along with some consulting on how to defend against another group like ours in the future."

Kiera was impressed with his words and how everyone listened. It was at that moment she was sure this was the right decision.

"To show a sign of commitment, Kruno, please follow me."

Kiera proceeded to the pond. As he got closer, a dazzling sweet smell stimulated his senses. His eyes widened as the exquisite sensuality was quick to take its effect.

"Please, sir, it's time to relieve you of your wounds, disrobe and follow me."

Kruno expressed a little bit of his shyness by looking at her with widened eyes, not sure that she was serious.

"Don't be timid. Many men have walked into this water before you." She walked close to him and whispered the rest, "Just none with me."

She moved away from him and slid her tight black pants off, with a slight ladylike wiggle. Her radiant ass was exposed. She stood up and took her top off. She turned her head without turning her body, keeping her frontal view an enigma and then she asked, "Coming?"

Okay, first we are at war with these women, then we get naked and jump in a pool with them. Interesting, very interesting. I am not normally shy, but this is strange, and my goodness, there is a big focus on me.

"Come on Kruno, there is no reason to be bashful, at least that is what the other ladies have told me. You aren't a Northerner but not many are so well endowed." Sven then turned and smiled at the woman he was flirting with earlier.

The room's response had changed from vicious tension to an angered debate and finally one of sensuality. Peculiar didn't even describe what was happening.

Kiera walked in until the water just hit the bottom of her ass and then she dove forward. She turned and looked back at Kruno. Her dreadlocked hair didn't change much but her eyes seemed to get heavy for a second as if this pool was affecting her senses.

Kruno immediately decided to take his clothes off, all shyness forgotten, and Kiera's eyes opened with excitement. The ladies in the balcony leaned forward to get a look as well.

As soon as his feet hit the pleasant smelling water he understood why she was so insistent on him coming in. An incredible feeling rushed up his legs, one of deep pleasure. His body produced an infinite number of goosebumps, which seemed to have been waiting on the edge of their seats for a moment like this.

He hurried to get the water level above his waist, and as expected, the water illuminated as it touched his testicles.

She swam up to him, stood up exposing her perfect breasts. She took some of the water in her hand and let it run down his chest. The feeling coupled with her extreme sexuality was a rush he wouldn't forget. The water ran down his chest and washed away his wound. He was amazed to feel no pain from a wound that was new. He looked down to see that it had disappeared. She then repeated the process and poured it down his shoulder.

He felt alive and exquisite. He felt as if he was the most beautiful man that ever lived. His muscles felt like armour and sat on him perfectly. She reached forward to whisper in his ear. Kruno's thoughts were of one thing only, an uncontrollable desire to grab the Queen and kiss her. His eyes filled with desire. He held back for a moment, expecting her to invite him take her.

"Don't let your mind travel to places they can't go." She smiled sensually and floated away. "Enjoy the water. Any injuries you have sustained in your life are now gone."

The Sand Sorceress who had been flirting with Sven moved forward. "Aren't you going to ask me for a swim? All of your wounds will be healed."

"I am not really wounded."

She slowly slid her finger down his massive pectoral muscle and with a quick flick opened up a small wound with her nail. He immediately grabbed her wrist tightly. She flinched ever so slightly, "Now you are."

"So that's the type of girl you are."

She smiled and led him to the pool.

Decan looked around at a room full of beautiful women. The deceased had been pulled away and were now out of sight. He then turned to the other guys and said quietly, "Last one in has to lick a horse's ass." Then spoke for all to hear, "Come on ladies, let's all get cleaned up."

"It has been a long time since these women have seen a man, even longer since they have been with one. Have fun," Kiera said with a smile.

She swam to the other end of the pond. Two of them came up beside Kruno and instantly started to rub his chest and put their hand through his hair. The feeling was like being touched for the first time, but he couldn't take his eyes off of Kiera. His vision followed her to the other side of the pool and watched her enchanting body emerge and leave the room.

"No way, I can do that," Christian said from the back of the room. He decided he wouldn't participate as his nervousness kicked in. What he didn't realize was that he was as desired here as he would be at DSW. Pecs were a draw here like anywhere, but intelligence was also a big turn on for these women.

Sensing his bashfulness, the wounded lady with the broken nose, lip and knee, compliments of Kruno, stopped one of her sisters from helping her and looked to Christian. "I may not be pretty right now, but a moment in the water and I will be all you have ever desired. I could use your help to bring me there."

Christian didn't move at first, his nerves holding him back, but he sucked it up and picked the lady up. She flinched in pain as she sucked air through her teeth.

"I am sorry."

"Don't worry, you are being gentle."

Sven didn't take long in the water before things became hot and heavy. Women seemed to line up near him. The first one pulled back from a passionate kiss. "Damn you are arousing, so arousing that I think I should share. Meet my friend." Sven started to kiss another beautiful girl. She was younger and blushing.

"She has never been with a man. Can you help her with that?"

"Absolutely!" Confident and excited, he answered the easiest question of his life. While sexually pleasing one and kissing the other, they switched over and over. The feeling was one of pure bliss.

Christian's foot submerged in the water and an explosion of pleasure hit him hard. He carried the broken woman to the water. His excitement was overwhelming because even though she was still soaked with blood, and damaged, her body was fantastic. Small perky breasts and a flat stomach caused a rush of pleasure. This, combined with anticipation of what was probably going to happen, was too much for him to handle. He dunked her in the pool. He had pleasure written all over his face, but it turned into embarrassment when he prematurely ejaculated. Thank goodness nobody laid witness except for the girl.

"Don't worry. Just tell me you have more of that precious gold for me. It will take me a minute for my knee to heal anyway. Why don't you work on reloading?"

The water embraced every good pleasure at once. He felt like he was finally worthy of a woman. "I am beautiful," Christian, drunk on pleasure, stated.

"Yes you are, my love." The transformation was spectacular. The woman he brought to this magical water was beaten badly, but now it was as if she had never been in battle. She was slender with big eyes and she approached him like a gator. He could see her ass and legs as she swam near the surface and his mind battled with him.

She submerged and his pleasure intensified as she slid his penis in her mouth. After a few minutes she resurfaced pressed against him. Excitement made his heart beat so fast that she could feel it with her hand.

"Now, now, why so excited? I am not the prettiest girl in here, especially for a Wizard as great as you."

"I've... I've... never been with any woman before, but don't tell the guys, please?"

She didn't say a word but smiled.

The men were suited up and ready to go. Everyone still smiled after such a concentrated dose of pleasure. Kruno was the only one of them who hadn't engaged in sexual activity because his mind was focused on Kiera. She had left the pool and he hadn't seen her since.

He looked around. It was evident that La Caprata didn't want them to leave, but Kruno insisted. The Gret-chen would be arriving soon and would end up waiting in a desert with sand sharks potentially looming.

"Listen, Kruno, I think the Gret-chens will be fine. I mean look at all of these ladies. This place is like a utopia."

Kruno looked down at his ankle and noticed that the scar he had from years ago when attacked by wolves was gone. He examined his entire body. All scar tissue was healed.

I can see why they don't want anyone to find this place.

"You promised never to talk of this place and never to return," one of the elder ladies uttered.

"We are men of our word. We just need our men and need to see Kiera."

Retrieving Ivan and the other man was a necessity, but seeing Kiera wasn't essential for anyone, except for Kruno. He couldn't wait to lay his eyes on her.

"I am sorry, Kiera isn't available," one of the Sand Sorceresses said to Kruno's dismay.

"It's okay, Monique, I am here. I am going to take these men away from here."

"Why would you do that? They found this place, they can find their way back."

"They still have to live up to their end of the bargain. They must tell us how they breached our perimeter. They can tell me on the way."

"Well, we can tell you in no time, it's not necessary…" Christian had jumped in, but was cut off by Kruno with a look that told him to shut his mouth.

"Actually, we really do have to leave now. Kiera, I think you should join us so that I can explain to you fully how we penetrated your fortress. It will be invaluable information you can use for future protection.

The sun set only a few hours from La Caprata's lair. Nobody had slept much in days and their bodies demanded rest. Everyone fell asleep almost instantly. Kruno told them he would have first watch. Finally a time he could talk to Kiera.

They had chosen a spot to camp based on Kiera's recommendation. Nuzzled between sand dunes they were out of the eyesight of potential predators. Astutely, Decan mentioned they would have a disadvantage if something did find them and they would have little time to prepare a defence. With poise and charisma that only a Queen could pull off, she explained that Decan had nothing to worry about. This was her desert and nothing would dare challenge her.

"Aren't you tired warrior?" Kiera asked.

"If you only knew what I have been through in the last few days, you would think I would be exhausted."

"Well, the elation experienced from our pool usually has an exhausting effect on people, as you can see." Looking around, Sven and Ivan were both laid out in a weird sleeping position. Both Northerners lay flat on their backs with hands on chest as if in a coffin. They slept with sword in hand to add an extra few moments in case they were woken up with the call to battle.

"I have to admit I have never seen anyone sleep like they do. Is this a family thing? Are they related?"

"Actually, all Northern barbarians are trained to sleep in such a manner. Look at the third." Kruno pointed to the other Northerner sleeping on the other side of the circle.

Kiera laughed a little while putting her hand against her face to maintain a certain composure.

"You're not tired, warrior?" she inquired further.

"My name is Kruno, you don't have to call me warrior. I believe we have seen each other without clothes, that usually removes a layer of formality."

"You saw me naked, yet did nothing about it, why?" She looked at him with a grin and pulled her focus away as if shy, obviously flirting.

"Believe me, I wanted to, but you swam away."

"How many have swam away from you and not wanted to been followed?"

Kruno, oddly at a loss for words, attempted a response, but his lips were silenced by her finger. She pressed her index finger against his mouth with a delayed retraction. The sun sprayed its last few rays from the horizon. It was getting harder to see and Kruno didn't want to blink or he would miss a moment of her beauty.

"The question was rhetorical. I call you warrior because you deserve the name. Any creature with your skill desires to be called as such, but if you want me to address you as Kruno, I will." She continued, "I wish to hear of your past few days. Tell me why you should be so tired. Tell me about anything you wish, warrior Kruno. Before you do, we need to do something about this light. Your story, I am sure, is interesting, but my eyes would yearn for more of such a beautiful sight."

She ripped my line off.

He was wondering how she would be able to improve the light. She raised her hand, fingers cocked and snapped. Directly following the sound, a fire burst into life in the centre of the men. There was no wood, but the fire looked as real as the thousands he had laid his eyes on. It even crackled as if it were burning logs.

He thought about asking but decided against it. Creating a fire from a snap of the fingers was miniscule in comparison to what he had witnessed from both battles.

He began to speak about his past, but was drowned out way too often by Ivan who was snoring too loudly. Kiera only waited a few moments before pressing her finger against her mouth, turning toward Ivan, "Shhh…"

The snoring disappeared, and all noise had actually ceased. Ivan's chest still moved up and down but in silence.

"Oops, I liked the sound of the fire." Instantly the crackling resumed.

"Very impressive Queen, or should I call you Kiera?"

"Hmmm, no, I think Queen is appropriate," she replied unexpectedly with a straight face, a statement she knew would slightly shock a man who didn't want to find a reason to dislike her.

She waited a moment, savouring his attempt at a strong card face and began to laugh again. "You are too serious my warrior — I mean Kruno. Please continue and call me whatever you wish."

Kruno talked of the Cryptons, King Deo, the Black Knights with Zoran and continued up to the moment of their meeting. The conversation lasted what seemed like hours, but also minutes at the same time. She listened intently but interjected appropriately.

"I am not usually that much of a talker," Kruno stated.

Kiera broke focus from his tales, "Well, I loved it. Our lives are great in many ways, but we miss the interaction with other races and the thrill of battle comes too seldom for my liking. I can see your stories when you tell them. Your mind opens up and I can catch some of your thoughts as though I was there with you."

"Your magic skills are unprecedented."

"Ah, young Kruno, you are more impressed with my ability to read part of your mind than anything you have seen La Caprata do thus far? How can this be? In battle, Monique stopped and sped up the clouds, surely a spell you have never witnessed and yet this impresses you."

Kruno explained that she was right and why, "Great magicians I've met, but not one has been able to crack through my skull to read my thoughts unless I let them. I can't fully explain why, but they can't."

"You have a great magical presence within you. The choice of becoming a warrior was one of many options for you. Either way, you can and have developed some of your magical ability. I could teach you how to exercise more of it if we had more time, but we don't." She paused and then started to speak again, "This has nothing to do with my ability to use magic or your ability not to use magic, we are connected in a way few are. Your natural defensive block is transparent to me."

Kruno felt a strange tingle rush across his skin. It was a creepy revelation but exhilarating. Tension was starting to build, he could feel it. His eyes sensually walked down her exposed skin — first her neck, then her stomach and finally her legs, which lay straight out in front of her. A small burst of pleasure started to mount as he looked over her loose, two-piece black garment.

Okay, what am I doing? Let's get my mind away from these thoughts. I am misreading the situation, it's inappropriate to think of a Queen this way.

Attempting to regain control he tried to change the subject. It would be appropriate to ask her about her people. He needed to talk more, to drive his mind clear of a collision course.

"I should tell you how we were able to breach your fortress, this is our part of the bargain." He phrased it in a way that was constructed as a statement but really was a question.

There was an awkward pause as she got closer. The tension started to build again.

He attempted to start explaining when she said, "I am having trouble hearing you." He started to speak louder and she stopped him. "Don't change your voice level, I will get closer."

She moved in about six inches from his face, following a leisurely figure-eight pattern from his eyes, to nose, to lips and back again. His body started to feel symptoms of sexual activity just based on its own desire.

"Continue, warrior, but with even softer words so I can come a little closer." She spoke gently.

Kruno had time for one more question before all of his senses started to ring and tingle, "You don't know who I am, do you?"

He longed to hear her answer, an answer he wasn't sure he was going to hear. Since he had gained fame with the destruction of the Predator, he was well known by most.

The sexual tension heightened, it was set in motion with such velocity that it couldn't be stopped. They both waited for the threshold to be cracked and then the answer came.

"No, warrior, I didn't know you, not until you showed up..."

Her words seemed to sink into his head. For the first time, he wasn't just going to have sex with a female, it was going to be different. Something in his loins told him that his life was about to change, that this was a pivotal point.

Some people start off with small kisses and touches, others jump into something they don't understand, but work through it. In Kruno's and Kiera's case, they waited until the last second of self-control, holding back until the breaking point and then an explosion occurred.

His hand gripped her by the back of the head and pulled her forward. They kissed passionately. Her hand slid down his exposed chest. A hand that was used to the soft touch of a female, expressed joy at touching the rock hard male body and couldn't wait to find the most important part of the male anatomy. She reached in and grabbed onto him in the most delicate of places. His endowment was revealed and the forecasted pleasure to come made her wet.

Back against a sand dune with the dark sky above and the light ricocheting all around them, he leaned back, sliding his hands down her back and easily manoeuvred around her loose outfit, grabbing onto her perfect ass.

Anticipation took hold of them, releasing unprecedented pleasures. She leaned back and pulled off her top revealing her flawless breasts. His hands reached up to caress them, which intensified his desire to have her that moment. His hands wanted to rip the rest of her outfit away.

Just before he got into position, she stood up and stepped back for a minute.

"Where are you going?" His voice fluctuated, expressing concern.

"Don't you want these off?" She jockeyed the bottom part of her outfit slowly, teasing him. The sight was something out of a dream.

She slowly slid her outfit off and stood, the light of the fire behind her.

She mounted Kruno and both experienced a new level of sexuality and pleasure. They continued slowly, staring eye to eye, then cheek to cheek, hair was pulled, skin stroked, rolling every so often to change who dominated.

They made passionate love for what seemed like hours, a majority of it in a dazed dream world, compliments of intense sexual bliss. The night was relatively cool, keeping their sweat just light enough to glisten with the fire's light.

The two lay side by side. Kruno looked up to a perfect sky scattered with decorations. The moon sat almost directly above them, trying to peak at two of the Earth's finest engaging in something beautiful.

"Amazing," Kruno said as his vision started to return to its normal ability.

"Amazing," Kiera agreed.

"I feel as if my entire body is buzzing," Kruno commented, breathing in the sweet air that surrounded this enchanted moment.

After several minutes of silence, Kruno's eyes were heavy, but he was on watch and needed to stay awake or get someone else up. It had to be their turn anyway.

It feels like we have been here a long time. How long has it been?

"I am dead tired and the sun must be coming up soon. I need to get Decan up to be the lookout."

"Do you want the sun to come up? Do you want this to end?" Kiera asked, giving him a small surge of energy.

"No, I want this to last for days. I haven't even begun to learn about you, and once we are separated, I am not sure we will see one another again, but exhaustion is winning this battle."

"It seems like the pool knocked your friends out, but you needed a little extra to do the same. Don't wake anyone up, I will watch. Actually, you have nothing to be afraid of, nothing would dare touch us, this is my desert remember. Sleep, my love."

Kruno's gut told him she could be trusted, but if anyone had witnessed what had occurred they would have disagreed. In a matter of moments he leapt into a dream world.

Kruno awoke from sleep with wonderment. His dream was reality. Looking to the fire he saw the Queen of the La Caprata standing near it. Now fully clothed, she turned and walked over to him.

"How long have I been asleep?"

"How do you feel?"

"Spectacular, I am blown away by how rested I feel. It was the perfect sleep."

"And what did you dream of?"

Kruno had to get past his haziness, but then started to remember that his dream had been an extension of their night. She was there but not just in vision — she was undeniably a part of his dream.

"We continued to talk, you were there!" He was astonished.

"But of course I was. You mentioned our time was limited, you mentioned you wanted this to continue. To be apart while we sleep is foolish. We may as well play all night." She switched back to probing questions. "What did you think of my past?"

The question unlocked an explosion of detail. He could see many moments from her life; her childhood, her first day as Queen, an average day in her life and her understanding of internal peace.

"That is amazing!"

"Most only understand verbal and physical communication. Some go a step further and use telepathy, but few understand the most intimate of communication, through our dreams."

"My dreams have always been fragmented, foolish really."

"That's because you haven't trained for it. You have an innate ability to see things others don't and your dreams are a great place to access them."

They explored this new discovery for a long time and changed subjects into defensibility of the Sand Sorceresses' lair. This was something he owed her, it was part of the deal.

"You have an almost impregnable lair. The sandstorm is brutal to pass through and there isn't a trace outside of it that anything lays behind it. We had some help locating you." He talked about the Vita Fairy and its pivotal role, then moved on to recommendations. "You need a gate at the entrance, also more guards with their sole mission of monitoring of the area outside the entrance. It also wouldn't hurt to have a patrol outside."

Kiera quickly declined his last idea, but with respect, and asked him to continue.

"The most important thing would be to have your chamber covered in sand. The attack from the ground is spectacular and would have enabled your warriors to inflict serious damage on us."

She attentively listened and released some bad news. "Our time is running short, the sun will rise soon. Thank you for completing your end of the bargain. You are a man of your word. Do you have any more questions for me?"

The words struck him harder than the blow of a club to the side of his head. He was upset that the night was coming to a close, but needed to appreciate what he had and not focus on the negative. He also had one more question that needed answering, "Yes, what of Ivan? He seems really out of it. Is there going to be permanent damage?"

"You are concerned because he hasn't talked yet?"

"Kind of, yes. I normally can't shut him up and I really expected the old Ivan to bounce back with a blink of your eye."

"The lure spell we cast on him is a consuming spell, but has no permanent ramifications. I am sure he will wake up back to normal, more normal than he has been for months."

She read how pleased Kruno was that his friend was back and loved the camaraderie.

"I think it's time to wake your friends."

CHAPTER 4

DEO'S EXIT

The landscape of the Silver Allegiance's eastern border was simply stunning. It boasted some of the most fertile land and was a source of envy for outsiders, but a source of pride for the Allegiance. It was full of lush vegetation only rivaled by the southern tip of the Kingdom. The best wine was grown there, making the area quite wealthy.

"Hot dry summers, perfect for making the greatest drink created by man," Deo said with a smile. "Although we do have to give some credit to God. He surely has blessed the soil here."

Deo enjoyed the scenery and loved the open road. Normally he would have travelled by flamboyant armed caravan, designed to show his greatness but also to provide protection. This mission was different, and because of its secrecy, the highly protective and flashy convoy wasn't needed. Attention was the last thing they wanted. For the King to leave Dryden without a guided escort of at least 150 was unheard of; they had much less than that.

Small numbers, this was what Deo loved best about the journey. The simplicity of it all took to Deo's heart, even though he was inclined to embrace all the fame that comes with being a King, the few chances he had to take a trip like this were truly treasured. Riding on horseback through the countryside as equals with a small group of men was something he embraced with delight.

Deo felt like he could finally relax. Since they didn't resemble royalty, if they were to pass by anyone, they probably wouldn't realize he was the King. No crown was on his head, lavish outfits weren't worn and the horses lacked armour. Since he wasn't going to be recognized, he didn't have to be wary of his demeanour. He could relax on the open road. It had been too long since he felt this way.

They had left Dryden under the cover of darkness a long time ago and not a single soul had passed by them. The trip's strange, twisting path was chosen with this in mind — avoidance of interaction. This was accomplished by using old vacant paths far from civilization and trade routes. The only accidental contact might be farmers of vineyards. Deo wanted to visit some of the vineyards, but understood it could compromise their stealth strategy.

The Northern Kingdom was still a fair distance away, but Deo thought about the times to come. He had visited the North many years ago and the King of Vard had been to Dryden a few times over the past decade. Deo and Erikson, King of the North, got along well. Erikson, like his people, loved to have a carousing time and loved to talk about battles; both were of interest to Deo, providing endless hours of conversation. The trip to the North had an objective and anyone could determine what its primary goal was. Deo wanted as much support as he could from the great and powerful Northern Kingdom if the Dark Realm was to attack next spring as anticipated, or any time after that.

He had decided to leave the last few days of the trip to start working on the words and strategy of how to broach the subject with Erikson. Until then he would let his mind enjoy the hiatus.

The group that Deo travelled with was light in terms of numbers, but they were some of his most skilled. Deo never felt nervous about the outcome of his trek northwards, as he had faith in his men lead by Clinton, second only to Bruno, who didn't accompany them on this journey. The men in his company had an ability that was second to few when it came to wielding a weapon, analyzing a battle situation and simply taking down any threat. It was what they trained for all day, every day.

Deo had no choice about riding position and always had someone to his right, left, front and back. This rule stood day and night and it even remained under the most personal situations, including defecation.

"What a beautiful day my good man, don't you think?" Deo commented to Clinton while riding his steed, with a smile spread across his face.

"It is great King, I hope you are enjoying your adventure through your lands."

Clinton, even though he rode only partly battle-ready, could in a moments flash be dressed in full battle gear. His upper torso was fitted with plate mail but his sword, helmet and shield were strategically placed within arm's reach on his horse. All of the men had prepared similarly. Anything that resembled an attack would set them off. The group knew exactly what to do. A warning sign would be called verbally or via signal. The closest to the King would enclose him and everyone would reconfigure and be armed within thirty seconds.

"I am, I miss the open road. What I would truly love to do is visit some of the towns or even a few farmers along the way. They are the backbone of the Silver Allegiance. It would be great to hear what is on their minds."

"Another trip, my King. We must stick to our plan. If we wanted to have that kind of a tour we would have needed to buff up our head count. Stealth is imperative."

"I know we don't want to draw attention. Where we are, with so few, could create a perfect opportunity for our enemy, an enemy I fear will strike our lands early next spring, but I am sure they would love a chance at my head earlier."

"Are you worried about them, my King? The Allegiance is much stronger than they are. We have more men, more land and more precious metal. To me, that spells victory."

"They are a big enough threat to take seriously. Can they defeat us? Very unlikely… but carnage will be on both sides, our people will suffer and that upsets me. The allies they have chosen, a gargoyle and black magic, are a terrible combination, one that will bring upon us horrific, unimaginable battles."

"What kind of strategies do you think they will use?" Clinton inquired further.

"I guess you're too young to have experienced the last small group that was driven by black magic. I won't bother with the details, primarily because it is too disturbing to bring up." Deo had a look of concern and obviously was imagining some future battle. "The things they will do without regard for humanity, it makes me want to empty my stomach into my beard."

"Lovely."

"I guess the best way to describe it is war without rules... no that doesn't do it enough justice. Warriors without a conscience — yes, that is better. To toss an infant to the ground and smash it with a boot wouldn't even make them flinch. Pain of others actually creates pleasure for them."

"Is it really that bad? I don't mean to question your words, sir. I just haven't witnessed anything like that, ever. I know some good people that live in the Dark Realm."

Deo looked at his prized Knight seriously, as he bounced up and down on his horse. "There will be a time soon when it will be blasphemy to make such a comment. It would not be a good idea to bring them up any more. Two things could happen to the people you know in the Dark Realm. The first and most likely is that they will conform, accepting the Devil himself as their leader. The second possibility is that they will become slaves of the nation whose creed is immorality. They will either hide their true feelings and devotion to God, which would create a life of lies, or they could let it be known that they are sticking with God, and then be sentenced to hard labour and eventual death."

Deo realized he might have chosen better words and expressed himself with more sensitivity. Clinton was a Knight but might still be bothered by the finite harshness of his comments.

He continued, attempting to soften the impact, "Clinton, I have many friends that lay under the blanket of the Dark Realm and I am bothered as well. I know you probably want to attempt to save them, but that would be difficult and counterproductive. They are our enemy, every one of them, as of right now. I could grant you leave if we were on the eve of war with any other nation, but not one that embraces the black arts."

Clinton nodded his head, deciding to accept the King's comments and rode forward. With precise training, as Clinton advanced from the King's side, another took his place and one would remain at his parameter at all times.

They consisted of eleven Silver Allegiance Elites, twelve in training, five non-military personnel and one Minister, all on horseback. Including the King, they were an even thirty.

A few of the horses pulled supplies of food, water, more weapons and the King's belongings, including his crown. He didn't wear it now, but it would be needed in Vard.

Clinton rode up to the vanguard where two young men, John and Joe, led the company in the direction provided by him earlier that day. For security reasons, Clinton only gave one day's worth of travel at a time. He kept the only fully planned map. Even the King himself didn't have a copy.

The two at the front were both aspiring Elites, but hadn't been granted the honour yet. Things looked promising for them and being asked to join this mission was a great leap in the right direction. All twelve warriors that weren't Elites were handpicked for the journey by Elites.

John and Joe had been friends for years and constantly competed. They both rode on one of the most important missions of their lives, both knew that this was the platform to become what they coveted so much. They were constantly mistaken for one another for most of their youth. To make the distinction clear, Joe had grown his brown hair long and John kept his cropped short. The confusion was understandable because they acted similarly. It didn't take too long for kids their age or a few years older to keep their comments to themselves. Even though they argued like an old married couple they were best of friends and very skilled with close combat — one feeding off the other, acting as if they could hear the other's thoughts. The other kids knew they could be Knights of the Allegiance one day and decided to give them respect for future considerations.

"I am just trying to tell you that I don't agree. It's that simple," Joe said to John with a serious tone.

"It doesn't matter what you think, how could you question him? He knows what he is doing."

"It is a stupid way to travel. I could come up with a dozen better paths than this one."

"Oh great Joe, so smart that he could run this whole mission. Don't be stupid, keep your mouth shut."

"I am great, at least you got that right."

"No, you're not great, Clinton is. You're not. It's that simple."

"What's with all the talking boys?" Clinton rode up and inquired.

"Nothing, no big deal," John answered before Joe, not giving his friend a chance to voice his opinion and attempting to prohibit what he felt was a stupid challenge. As he made the comment, Joe looked to his friend and shook his head. He then mouthed the word *pussy* in his direction.

"How long since we have been in contact with the front team?" Clinton changed the conversation. He was asking about the group of two that would always be ahead to warn of any danger. It was standard procedure for Elites. They had a party of two in front and behind them, usually out of sight. The skill level to master this was spectacular and only certain Elites could perform in that capacity. One such Elite was on the mission, by far the best at keeping ahead and out of sight, a necessity for the trip.

"It's been midday since we saw them last. Should they have returned by now?" John asked. "If only we knew where they were."

"Hmmm, that is interesting. If only we knew where they were at all times. Maybe next time they go out, they should hold a flag up so we know where they are," Clinton said with a serious tone.

"Sure, and you can use that idea if you would like, feel free to take the credit," John responded, thinking he may have just impressed the great Clinton.

Clinton rubbed his head with one hand and attempted to hold back his comment. He murmured something to himself and then spoke, "That is a really stupid idea."

He then turned around and saw one of his companions riding not too far behind him. Clinton whistled to get his attention.

"Hey, this kid has an idea. He thinks our intel groups should have a flag so we know where they are at all times."

John felt blood rush to his face. He made a major blunder, which Clinton totally exploited. John listened as they all laughed, including Joe. Keeping out of sight was critical and a main objective for the forward flank group. Raising a flag was really foolish and John realized the folly of his comment.

"I am keeping that one in the stupid John comments bank and I will be bringing it out often." Joe struggled to talk as he wiped tears of laughter from his eyes. He truly enjoyed the moment. "That would defeat the whole purpose, dumb-ass."

Clinton changed focus and looked to Joe, who was laughing hard, "So you want to be an Elite, do you?"

"Yes sir," Joe responded as the last of his chuckle tapered off.

"Are you going to be able to separate from all of that hair, pretty boy?" Clinton, with his Elite signature bald head, wanted to make a statement that Joe was no better off than his friend, even after the stupid comment.

"Absolutely, I am pretty no matter what," he said with a confident smile.

"Oh, of course. Well both of you are far from SAE status. You will have to prove your worthiness, but I doubt either of you boys will make it." Clinton continued the tradition of insulting potential future Elites. He had gone through the same process when he was their age and courted to become an Elite. It was the job that he and most of them really enjoyed.

Nothing was said for a few moments as Clinton rode adjacent to them. John decided he would keep his mouth shut for fear of further negative outcomes. Both of them didn't like what Clinton had said, and wanted to lash out in their defense but neither did.

"So you boys know where we are headed, right?"

"Yep, but only until nightfall. I would like to see the rest of your planned path."

"Absolutely not. The route is for my eyes only, you know the rules."

Joe knew the rules but couldn't hold it in. He disagreed completely with the way Clinton was leading them.

"I don't need your map anyway, I can figure out where we are headed and I don't think it makes any sense."

John heard Joe's comments and thought to himself, *What a stupid moron, not only does he decide to question the leading SAE, but does so in an insulting way. Way to go, idiot.*

"Oh really! So you think you know our path and question Rizzian's, Deo's and my decision? Please let me know what the right way is." Clinton looked offended.

"Please, I don't mean to insult anyone, but the strategy you guys selected leaves us exposed to ambush in at least three areas." Joe pointed to several spots on a partially completed map, including one which was the planned camping area for the end of today's journey.

"I wouldn't have brought this up, but as you can see, this camping area is flawed. We should move somewhere else."

"All right genius, what is wrong with this camping area?"

"Look how close we are to the border with the Dark Realm. It puts us in danger of random patrols, we could be picked up and then *bam,* we are cooked. If they knew we were here, it would be easy to set up an undetected attack. Camping in any of these areas is by far the most likely for an assault."

Joe paused for a moment and looked up at Clinton. He seemed to be working it out in his head. Joe pointed back to the map and continued.

"Dense wooded area to the east of us all the way to the border. That's not a good idea. We are positioned in an open field with hills to the north and west. Dozens could easily hide, wait and sneak up on us from any of those directions. We are also way too close to the major river that runs through the Dark Realm. They could spring hundreds of troops on us fast."

Joe stopped and waited, his heart started to pound as he realized that his ideas might not be well received.

"Well, do you agree with this?" Clinton asked John, trying to see if he wanted to take part responsibility for his friend's comments.

"Nobody can control his mouth. I try not to be associated with him."

"There is always one who insists on being dissident. I am sorry, do you know what that means?" Clinton was educated and loved to use his vernacular to belittle people. Joe didn't know what it meant but shook his head like he did.

"Your worries aren't worth much because nobody knows where we are. This truly shows how callow you really are. If we wanted, we could travel in the Dark Realm's territory and it wouldn't matter. This area is vacant. There isn't a single person except maybe a farmer in a day's ride of here. Second, if we moved from the border we would be leaving a river that provides us with something I consider important. Have you heard of water? Also moving in any other direction puts us too close to our cities which happen to be full of people, people have eyes and mouths, which is a sure way to spread the news of Deo travelling with thirty men. Your plan is worthless. Leave the thinking to us. Don't mention your plan to anyone if you value a shot at becoming Elite any time in the future."

Clinton pulled back on the reins, leaving the two to themselves.

"Whoa, you just got schooled," John said. "First you make fun of me, and then you say something so stupid I can't even make jokes about because it's too easy."

"Listen Mr. kiss ass, oh you can use my idea and take the credit, let me suck your sword, not that one, the one between your legs. Anyway, enough of this. He is wrong. There are many rivers we could feed off of and dozens of paths that leave us away from our cities, plus..."

"Shut up stupid," John remarked.

The two continued arguing.

The men dismounted and started to prepare for the night. Deo looked around at his men in motion. He was still impressed, after so many years, at how efficiently everyone worked. Few questions were asked as each person knew their role. Some built the quarters, others began preparing dinner and the rest set up the perimeter.

The cooks weren't used to the travelling, but were passionate about their jobs. Deo didn't just take any chef though. When he travelled he enjoyed few comforts of royalty, but food wouldn't be one he would leave behind. He took with him his personal chef. The royal dinners for Deo's son Egon back home would suffer with the loss of the primary chef of Dryden.

"Hello, my good men, what is on the grill for tonight?" Deo called to the cooks.

The chef wasn't that adept at dealing with people, and if it was anyone else but the King asking, he would have stated in a harsh tone to shove it up his ass. Since it was Deo, he attempted to be tactful.

"The deer that was caught yesterday will be the meat with a seasoning that will leave you in awe. I have to prepare tonight's meal so it will be a while before it's ready. I also have the last of the pastry to be served."

Every few days, two would hunt for any game they could find. The area was fertile feeding grounds for deer, but if unsuccessful, rabbits were in abundance.

"No vegetables?" Deo asked, sounding disappointed.

"My assistant will boil up some potatoes if you would like sir."

"Of course I would like. Please make sure you add those spices that you did the other night. It was delicious."

The chef disliked the interaction and being told what to do, but held in his frustrations. He knew how good he was and didn't like having to answer to anyone. His skill with food was undeniably amazing, but his patience with people was terrible. Potatoes weren't going to be on the menu, but the King made demands as he saw fit, demands the chef would grant but that irritated him.

Most wouldn't dare turn from the King, exposing their back, as it was a sign of disrespect, but the chef was different. As he made concessions for the King because of his royalty, Deo made them for the chef because he was fantastic in the culinary arts. All the chef wanted was to get on with his preparations. Sunlight would submit soon and they were already behind schedule.

"Hey!" Deo called to the chef and waited for him to turn. He looked over at Deo but didn't say anything. His eyes indicated his level of annoyance. He didn't want to be interrupted anymore.

"You're doing a great job but please hurry, I am very hungry."

"Are you not always hungry, King?" the Minister called out to him.

"No, I am full for the five minutes after I eat and then I am hungry again. If I eat three meals a day then I am full a good fifteen minutes every twenty-four hours." The King smiled and walked with Simon the head Minister away from the chef. "That's pretty good I think. Thank goodness I am King, food and I get along very well."

"Yes, I can see that." Simon reached forward and touched the King's belly. They both laughed as he in turn pointed to Simon's which was just as big.

"You know the comments you make irritate the chef?"

"Of course, why do you think I do that? I could ask him anytime during the day what we are eating, but I wait until he starts to prepare. He gets so upset and it's purely entertaining." Deo acted more like a kid sometimes. He was a brilliant political leader but with a twist of immaturity.

Simon was around to give food blessings, help with questions that some of the men may have about faith and to give a few sermons. This trip would have more than one Sunday. Dryden, even though accepting of many faiths, was based, founded and run by one. The King ensured that wouldn't change.

Simon wasn't the most appealing man to females. He had lost most of his hair, wore typical clothes of a man of the cloth, which was made of a type of burlap. He was pudgy but tall and not particularly funny.

"How do you wear such an outfit? It looks itchy, uncomfortable and unappealing. You are the Head Minister to the King, I am sure we could help you with your attire. Might help you get some action." The King stopped for a second and remembered who he was taking to. "Sorry Simon, I know you proclaimed your creed of, well you know, no…" The King used his open palms and hit them together, attempting to signify sex.

"I don't mind the outfit, as I have given up many of the things that man would want. Remember it is easier for a camel to fit through the eye of a needle than for a rich man to enter the Kingdom of Heaven. I am not here to look good but to assist without distractions."

"Don't you wonder though about women? I can't go much more than a few moments without thinking about sex… hold on… see, there I go again. Now, I think I am a terrible horny bastard, so it maybe an unfair comparison to the average man."

"King Deo, I think you might be confused. I can have sex. I just have to be married first."

"Hold the horses, I didn't know that!" The King grew exuberant after what he'd just learned. He liked to help people. He especially wanted to help Simon because he felt the relationship was one-sided. Simon never took anything from the King except for shelter, basic clothing and food, but Simon had given him so much more. He was his connection to God and assisted with critical advice over his tenure.

"Well, we need to find you a wife then."

"It's not that easy Deo."

"Damn right it's easy, are you kidding me? I am the King. I could point to the lady and she would marry you just like that." He meant well but Simon was growing offended.

"I am all right sir, God will introduce me to the lady if and when he chooses to."

Deo continued with what he did best, to convince people he was right, "Listen here, Simon, you have told me that God raises Kings and takes them away. Well I am a King, which means I was put here by God, and maybe I am the one to introduce you to your future missus."

"What are you thinking?" Simon asked, now curious. He always wanted a wife and of course was interested in sexual activity. He was human and his hormones kicked in all the time.

"Let's leave this to God's hand until the outcome of our trip. If we are successful with Erikson and sign some kind of an agreement, I will ask for you to be introduced to one of their women. My goodness, Simon, they have the best women. Maybe I should take one myself. But I digress. When a deal like this is being forged, this kind of request is often a part of it and it is always granted. Just don't bring up your celibate life, they wouldn't understand."

"A human with a Northerner?" Simon was starting to get nervous about how fast this conversation was going. He probably would later learn to embrace the idea and be excited at the prospect of such a prized wife.

"Of course, it is uncommon, which makes it that much more significant. A bond of marriage between a highly regarded member of the SA and a woman of the North would be beneficial for all."

Simon was bombarded with unfamiliar thoughts and responded with a nervous shaky voice, "I will think about it."

"Think all you want, but the decision is already made. That decided, grab me some wine from the storage area, I want to celebrate my remarkable idea."

On the other side of camp, Clinton decided to take a proactive role on defensive strategy because, even though he didn't like that kid Joe and his responses earlier in the day, he was right about them being too close to the border of the Dark Realm. The odds of encountering a patrol were small, but he wanted to develop a strategy to handle it just in case.

Clinton looked for Asgar who would, as always, play the sleeper role for the night. Asgar was by far the best anyone had ever seen at a sleeper role. The job was used over the course of the night, and involved a tremendous amount of self-control. At dusk a sleeper would locate a watch position and not move until morning or if a threat was discovered. The skills needed to be truly great at this position centred in on stealth and focus. Asgar was a strange person and an Elite, which made him perfect for the job. He barely talked and needed very little sleep. He would disappear at night, nobody would have a clue where he was, including any potential enemy. In training he would take every single SAE by surprise. Most would walk right by him without knowing he was there. In combat, his success was outstanding, making him a necessary part of this mission.

Clinton and Asgar didn't get along, which was odd because everyone seemed to like Clinton and everyone respected Asgar. It was tough not to like Asgar because he really didn't say much, ever! Clinton didn't like him though because in training he also was ambushed by Asgar, bruising his ego. Clinton didn't want him on the mission, claiming he would be better off on another campaign, which was the reasoning he stated, but everyone knew that it had everything to do with not wanting to spend months in his company.

Asgar was on one knee, sharpening his blades beside Magnus who stood focused on something else. Magnus was the tallest of any SAE and missed the hair on his head which he lost after accepting the pledge of an Elite, but he made up for the loss with a bushy red goatee. His size was a clear advantage. It instilled fear, something he used all his life.

Asgar and Magnus were best friends. Many would probably deduce the opposite without seeing them together. They would consider it an unlikely bond because Magnus wasn't quiet at all. They were very different. They had been drawn together in battle and caused serious damage to enemies in the past, the pair fighting side by side. Skirmishes had occurred over the years between Black Knights and Elites and the results favoured the Black Knights in most cases, except for a few, including two such events with Asgar and Magnus. They had made a mockery of Black Knights on both occasions, a well-known fact among both Kingdoms.

"Gentlemen, how are we tonight?" Clinton put his hand on Magnus's shoulder. Even though Clinton was a big man, he wasn't beside Magnus. Asgar looked in his direction and then looked back.

"We are good Clinton. What is the good word?" Magnus had no real issues with Clinton and treated him with the respect that their leader deserved.

"Are you guys both going out tonight?"

"Nope, I am staying put, but that is a silly question to ask of my friend."

"Of course Asgar is going out, stupid question, that is what he does best. The only real threat we have, and it is extremely unlikely, is a random Black Knight patrol. Nonetheless, I want to change up the strategy a bit to adjust for this. Why don't you show me where you are going to be tonight and that way we know not to worry about that area?"

Asgar worked on his blade and didn't give the courtesy of looking in Clinton's direction but just shook his head side to side.

"He doesn't even know where he is going to be! It can't be done."

"Hold on. We will have floating patrols tonight and we may mistake you for the enemy, it could be a disaster!"

Asgar smiled and his shoulders moved up and down indicating a little chuckle.

"Don't worry, they won't find him. How many times have you walked right by him and your sole mission was to locate him?"

"Yeah, I remember, I am just trying to be proactive here, boys, help me out."

Asgar just shook his head.

"I think you have your answer, Clinton. No disrespect, but he isn't changing his ways."

"All right, all right, no big deal." Clinton was obviously distraught.

"That being said, what is our plan of attack if we encounter those swine?" Magnus inquired.

"Containment is critical. They won't have a patrol our size and we could easily drop them with our numbers, but if we have to engage, none can escape. Our position must not be compromised." Clinton gave his instructions and walked away.

"He is a bit of a dick, but don't let that get to you." Magnus made the comment as soon as Clinton was out of range. "I hope we do get to run into a few more Black Knights, they are our specialty. Make sure to open that mouth of yours if they are close. Don't take them all for yourself, that's just not fair." Magnus made these kinds of egotistical, confident comments all the time, but he earned the right to brag for both of them.

Magnus continued on as Asgar listened. While talking, they both switched to night armour. It would be impossible for Magnus to sleep in plate male, all Elite's would follow suit that weren't on patrol. They would switch to leather armour, inferior to metal plating when it came to impact resistance, but lighter and more comfortable.

Asgar's night armour was specially designed, created with stealth in mind. Every movement was tested for the acoustic impact it would make. He also really liked knives. He needed short tossing weapons for the moveably and for silent kills, and therefore the armour was designed to hold several blades in non-typical areas.

"Probably another boring night, my friend. Not sure what you do out there, but if I was you I would take a position of comfort, get some extra rest. Remember we are heading to the North. The ladies will be waiting for two great warriors like us." Magnus smiled and raised his arms like a champion welcoming all females to him.

The smell of the venison permeated the camp. Most mouths started to salivate, but the King and a few choice men would eat first. After that, it was all done in shifts. The two most vulnerable times for a camp would be during dinner and through the night.

The King would usually allow different people to eat with him so he could get to know them all. He understood it was a great honour to say they had dined with the King, especially for the non-Elites. SAEs would have spent a lot of time with him as he rarely ate or spent any time without at least one in his vicinity.

Joe and John had the pleasure of sitting with three Elites and the King. They had met with him prior to this, but it had been a formal setting and it hadn't lasted long. Both were nervous but Joe attempted to hide it by acting nonchalant.

Deo sat as if he was nobody special on a log by the fire pit. It was already dark so it was necessary to be near the fire purely for illumination. Soup in hand, the King looked around at his men and future Elites, a feat he was sure Joe and John would eventually achieve. Besides having the necessary skill level to make it past the trials, the Silver Allegiance would be adding more Elites shortly to prepare for the imminent war.

"Are you boys enjoying your food and the trip?" Deo asked to stimulate conversation.

"Yes, sir," John responded, not wanting to say much.

Joe shook his head and rolled his eyes at John's conversation and wanted to take full advantage of this great opportunity.

"My compliments to the chef, this is delicious. I could eat the entire pot myself. I am a growing man, what can I say? I need the meat in order to support my future as an Elite."

"One tongue barely moves and the other flaps around like a fish out of water." Deo's comments were designed to shock the two youngsters. The other men looked at Joe in disbelief.

"I wouldn't make comments about eating all the food, not smart around these guys. They might take you seriously and leave you upside down, naked in a tree. I've seen it before, not a pretty sight."

Joe assumed the comment was directed towards him jokingly, but looked to the Elites who didn't even show a hint of laughter. He waited a few minutes and then retorted.

"I say bring it on but I will warn you, once I am naked you will see my God given third arm and will bow to me as if I was the King." The comment could have been misconstrued, but Joe banked on the sense of humour he had heard the King had.

Deo started to laugh, "Nicely played... Joe, right?"

"Yes sir."

John cleared his throat waiting for Joe to introduce him since he had made some headway.

"Oh yeah, and this is John, my brainless friend."

"Well, I have heard many things of you, John, and a lack of brains was not one of them. Actually, I have heard good things about both of you. Some say you are both a shoe-in for Elite status."

"Not if you asked Clinton," Joe said softly fully knowing that Deo would hear.

"Don't worry about Clinton, he is only doing as was done to him. They will all provoke you, that is part of it." He paused to eat some soup. "You boys must know that we will be focusing on more training for Elite status soon."

Like dogs expecting a treat from their owner, the two of them focused on the King.

"That's good news. I don't want to sound stupid, but why?"

"The war with the Dark Realm is an inevitable reality and it will come soon. We have known this for years and have been investing heavily in the development of our war machine. Developing Elites is an expensive process because so few pass the training. Keeping full time Elites is also very costly, but that is my problem to worry about. Besides Elites, we have invested in anyone interested, even farmers looking to pick up basic swordsmanship or archery. We figure they may be called to a battlefield or find themselves having to defend their property or family. Reality is that front lines will move and ownership of land will change several times. Peasants may be able to fend off or at least cut down a few of our enemy.

Joe and John both stopped eating as they knew they were receiving privileged information. The King trusted them. Wanting more information, John asked, "What else have you invested in?"

Deo loved a few topics of conversation and war was one of them. He put his soup down to explain with more animation. "Everything necessary, the basic weapons are the easiest to come up with. Swords, axes, spears, bows and so on. We have told our blacksmiths we will purchase anything they bring forward. Some of the more ambitious ones use their shops all hours of the day. We have to be more careful with our requests outside of our main cities or from places outside of our dominion. Procuring so much armour and weapons could trigger war prematurely."

"I could only imagine the weapons depots you must have." John's eyes lit up.

"I will show you when we get back. We aren't where we need to be but by mid-winter, latest early spring, we will be there. Even now it would blow your mind, eh Walter?"

One of the SAEs that had been ripping through his second bowl looked up with broth all over his mouth. He wiped his mouth clean with the side of his hand with a flick sideways. His voice was coarse and abrasive, "I could spend hours in there, I will show you when we get back. Especially impressive are the new weapons, they are simply fun."

"Probably the most important investment is development of new weapons. Things change all the time, since I was a boy weapons have advanced so much so you might laugh at what was new then. Wars have been turned on their pivot simply by introducing new weapons. They have shifted battles successfully or negatively as well. Time or gold or relying too heavily on new weapons has also really hurt a battle. Balanced, tested new advancements are the strategy that is needed."

"It doesn't hurt having Xavier's in Dryden," Walter interjected with his objectionable voice.

"Absolutely. Clorians and the people of the Allegiance, well at least Dryden has always gotten along really well together. They are a great race, I really enjoy their company, but it sure doesn't hurt letting them have a piece of our city. They aren't bound to war, but having access to their unique weapons is a great resource in times of conflict."

"Well if Dryden was ever to be under assault, I am sure they would have no choice but to assist," John commented again.

Everyone started to laugh, including Joe, which triggered a rush of stupidity.

"I hope that was a joke," Deo commented. John didn't respond with laughter or with words, so Joe decided to answer for him.

"Nope, he isn't kidding. That was a serious comment." They all started to laugh harder and John was mad and embarrassed at the same time.

"Dryden was designed to be impregnable. Nobody would dare attempt to breach its walls and if they did it would be a massacre. No need to worry if Clorians would assist."

John wanted the laughter at his expense to stop and tossed out a serious question, "Well if they can't attack Dryden, what would be their plan?"

"Walter, if you are done, please show these lads while I finish my food before it is too cold."

Walter knelt beside them and pulled out a map of an expansive area. He explained the assured strategy to be used by their enemy.

"See, they wouldn't attack too far North, especially after our meeting with Erikson or they could make the Northerners nervous and potentially take action. They wouldn't attack Dryden head on either because... well... it should be obvious to everyone. They would probably look to hit remote cities. You see, support would be too far away to provide back-up in a short timeframe. Semi- isolated towns or cities close to their border would be the first stage. Short distances from home would mitigate our ability to cut off of their supply lines. After that their plan would be to move into the remainder of the towns and Dryden would be the last theater of war and they would probably use an anaconda strategy. They would attempt to squeeze us out over time."

Joe jumped in, "They could attempt to open two fronts on us, which would be risky, but is the approach I would take." He stopped, looked around and since nobody said anything he continued. "They have a decent navy. They could, in effect, travel from the south or the north and hit the main port city of Couveer on our west coast. With enough supply ships they could sustain themselves, and it would split our armies to the west and east."

"The south is heavily patrolled, and heading from their north ports would run them past the massive navy of the Northern Kingdom. It could be disastrous for that kind of assault, a very big gamble," another SAE jumped in.

The King sat for a moment. Everyone knew it was his turn to talk. "A big gamble, but one I would consider taking if I was Zoran. All right, let's consider this. Joe, when we get to Vard, write down your notes and have them sent by flying messenger. Let's have our central war planners see this as an option."

The King didn't need to tell him he had done a good job. That was obvious to everyone. Joe felt a rush of pride and couldn't stop thinking about his future as an Elite.

Before they left, Deo made a light comment, which he normally did to motivate his men to stay positive. "Hope you boys saw that dazzling sunset. The sky was a perfect orangey-red, you know that means, tomorrow is going to be a magnificent day."

The night was silent and beautiful, a perfect temperature for rejuvenating rest. Everyone not on duty took full advantage of the conditions, buried in tents they slept like logs. Deo's tent was barely distinguishable. It was designed to look like the others, except it had a slightly different pattern. This was important because he needed to be identified by his men if something went wrong, yet kept the enemy from knowing where he was staying. In most encampments royalty would stay in lavish tents to extend the life they were accustomed to, which was fine as long as there was a bulk of men to defend.

The patrols were out and sleepers in place.

Asgar was intertwined in the branches of a tree. Like always he picked a perfect hiding spot. In the beginning of his career it took him a long time to find the perfect spot, but over the years his skills honed.

Before leaving the camp he had looked at a map of the area, deduced the highest probable area where an attack would occur and then situate himself in the perfect area to ambush. Random travellers might pass over the hills from the north or west but he wasn't worried about them. They would be no threat and picked up by the patrols or someone on watch. Even if they were a detachment of the Dark Realm, like a small group of Black Knights, they would be located and all resources would be utilized to dismantle them. His goal was to stop a premeditated assault.

It was a God given talent as far as he was concerned, because stealth was one thing, but he just always seemed to know which path an opponent would select to attack from. His success rate was undeniably impeccable.

Asgar didn't sleep during the day which baffled everyone. Does he just not sleep? Many would ask that very question, something he found funny. Magnus and the few youngsters he had started training were the only ones who really knew anything intimate about his habits. Sometimes he buried himself in mud or sand, other times he would submerge himself in a riverbank, hide amongst vegetation or live in a tree. What he could do was sleep anywhere, anytime. Comfort didn't matter. Another key to his success was that he was a light sleeper, extremely sensitive to sound.

Asgar dozed off in the limbs, locked in a tree, and would only awaken if something stirred. His heart would slow down and mind close up, virtually eliminating his energy footprint. This hid him from creatures or men with great physical or magical abilities.

Since they left Dryden he went out every night but one. Since they had travelled in or around forests he had spent most of the time in the branches of a tree or in one case tucked away in a massive decaying trunk littered with rodents and bugs. Nothing of any threat had crossed his path. The only things that had passed him were harmless creatures and time. He loved the long stretches alone and really felt connected to his surroundings.

It wouldn't be long before the animals forgot he was there and would start about their nightly activities.

Magnus woke up staring at the cloth ceiling of his tent, a mere arm's reach away. He was slightly upset because he couldn't sleep. The night was ideal, even the annoying crickets were giving it a rest.

His mind started to wander and because of its activity he knew he wasn't going back to sleep anytime soon. When he started shuffling around for the exit, his tent-mate looked over to him. They normally slept in groups of two or three depending on who they were. Magnus, due to his size, would only have one tent-mate.

"Do you have to take a leak?"

"No, I just can't sleep."

"That's crazy. This night is ideal, not a sound in the air."

"Yeah, you're right, but it's almost too quiet. I have been sitting here for a long time and I haven't heard a damn bug or bird or anything."

"Well if you're getting up, tell them to keep it that way. I am out."

Magnus knew he was paranoid; he loved to battle and seemed to find any sign indicating a battle was coming. Nonetheless he wasn't sleeping any more so he left the tent to wander around.

Not wanting to disturb anyone else he walked away from the group of tents. The air was tranquil, it felt almost as if his lungs could taste the sweet smells.

Is there something not right or am I just looking for something? I am pissed off, I could use a good night's sleep. The rest of these jackasses probably won't be getting up until after sunrise and I will probably be still walking around like a fool. Got to admit I miss the lady and my kids in moments like these. Boring, no action, nothing to do except ride around all day and sleep all night. I guess things will change when we hit the North, fine distractions will be everywhere.

Magnus walked around for what seemed like hours until he finally heard something in the bushes. A rustling noise of some sort hit an alarm in his mind. He had his war hammer which had occupied him over the course of his walk. Several times he had imagined just this and crushing whatever adversary came at him. His blood started to pump because it was go time!

"Magnus?" a quiet voice called from the bushes.

"Yes, who goes there?" he said with disappointment.

Two SAE's made themselves noticeable. "What are you doing walking around? Are you next in line?"

"What, I can't walk around? That is ridiculous. No, I am not here to relieve you. You guys need to work on your stealth skills, they are poor."

"Keep the jokes to yourself, we all don't have the privilege of being Asgar's bed mate." They both looked at him, snickering.

Magnus didn't bother to retaliate, and he switched the subjects, "Anything weird out there?"

"Not really, it was very quiet, oddly quiet."

"Not a bird or bug or anything, I noticed that too," Magnus commented as he scanned the dark woods beside him with a concerned look on his face.

"See, I told you that wasn't normal. I noticed it as well, strange not to have any sounds around."

"Tell the next shift I have this patrol. They can sleep. I guess I am relieving you after all."

"Are you sure?"

"I don't feel like sleeping anyway. Let's call it my good deed for the day."

Magnus walked along the perimeter of the camp and started to think about his comrade Asgar who was probably somewhere in the trees. They had been friends for a decade or so, but had bonded quickly, perpetuated by a single battle. Asgar, being so quiet, really didn't have a lot of friends; however, he could wield a weapon like few others. He was great with small throwing weapons like knives and axes.

Magnus reminisced about the battle that had united them many years ago. He thought about how well they worked together, perfectly in sync. He could relive each stroke of his sword and the smell in the air that day. When the Black Knights lay maimed around their feet, that moment made them comrades for life.

Magnus stood, war hammer in one hand and his other brushing his bushy red goatee as his mind still sat in the past.

"Magnus, are you planning on taking my shift?" Clinton called out to him.

"Didn't know it was yours, I guess that scores me some extra points with the boss."

"Funny, but don't worry about it, I will take over."

"I am not just being nice, I just can't sleep. I know what you're going to say, this night is perfect for sleeping, I know but it's just me. Besides wouldn't you rather have this guarding the camp?" Magnus lifted his war hammer, the most menacing of all weapons. "And what about these?" He flexed both biceps.

"Sure, but I would rather have it on a night when we are actually worried about combat. Tonight is a joke." Magnus didn't want to submit to the request and was about to argue back when Clinton commented, "It's a command, Magnus." Magnus knew that his leader was being nice by commanding him to go back to the tents, but he also knew he wasn't sleeping anytime soon. Either way it didn't matter. He had to follow the directive, Clinton was the superior officer.

"All right, my friend, but let me walk with you for a moment."

The two didn't say much at first, just some light small talk but then Clinton pried again, "I wish Asgar was a little more compliant. Please don't be upset. I am just saying he didn't even tell me where he was going."

"Of course not, he didn't even know where he was going. Listen, I know you two guys have your issues but let's put it aside, trust me, he is a great guy."

"I am sure he is. We are all brothers, but because we are brothers bound by Elite stature doesn't mean we have to run through daisy fields holding hands. Our personalities just don't gel and never will." He waited a moment and asked one last time, "So where is he tonight? You must know?"

"Why would you ask me that? Who cares where he is? I don't have a clue." Magnus's tone indicated he was irritated.

"Relax big guy, just inquiring so we don't cross paths. Listen, head back to your tent and enjoy some rest. Even if you can't sleep, lying down and resting is better than nothing."

Clinton made sense and, even though Magnus was irritated at the comment, he was pleased at Clinton's order. As commanding officer he wasn't required to take a shift but he had insisted. Magnus respected him for that.

Magnus listened to his boss and went to his tent but decided against following fully through. Technically he did follow the order, but he wasn't going to be able to relax so he headed to the west side of the camp, found a small hill and slid down onto it.

Relaxing for a moment he heard the silence break, some form of life returned to the forest opposite his position. There was one sound that seemed to dominate. It was a familiar natural knocking noise, similar to a wood pecker but a little different. Magnus was pleased that his paranoia was unfounded. The quick little beats were nice to listen to. Back to the hill, he let his mind relax.

Normalcy added comfort to him at first, but then he really started to listen to the random quick knocking noises. By the second set they sounded familiar, by the third he totally recognized what they were.

Asgar was in a dreamlike state.

Mud covered the small amount of skin that was exposed in between his leather battle armour. In the most unlikely places for a human to sleep, his limbs were locked in tree branches with leaves positioned perfectly. He would be tough to see during the day, let alone at night. He was dreaming of a peaceful childhood memory when he awoke.

Most wouldn't have even noticed the small shuffle of forest vegetation, but most wouldn't be sleeping in a tree. He hadn't moved in hours and at first wasn't sure how long he had drifted off for. He opened his eyes slowly and panned the area looking for anything. It would be expected of most to have their hearts beat a little faster, but not Asgar.

At first he saw nothing, maybe it was a small animal. He started to relax a little when another uncanny noise exposed itself. Being mentally aware this time, he knew what direction it came from and how far away it was. He determined that the sound was a foot rubbing against some kind of foliage.

Who is out there? Be something that I can kill, something challenging. Walk this way and see what happens.

From around the base of a tree a small rabbit bounced by and he smiled.

And I thought you were a big, bad Black Knight. Magnus must have got me all riled up.

Just as he relaxed his mind for a second time he heard another noise, it was a knocking noise with little pops. Vocal cords made them and he knew what creature it was. Two entities made that sound, one harmless and the other the exact opposite. He was sure he knew the difference, but it was confirmed as a massive grey beast came into sight, folding its wings and flexing its muscles.

The moon rays shot through the trees in front of Asgar and struck the most terrifying beast on the planet. It was second in skill only to that of a dragon and compared to Predators in aptitude, but were sadistically evil. Its heart was said to have been molded by the Devil himself. The odds of a gargoyle roaming around were unlikely, along with the odds of Asgar surviving. His primary goal wouldn't be to survive though; it was to protect the King. If this beast could hit the camp while all were sleeping, the results would be devastating. The camp needed to be warned, which he would do, but calling to them now would ensure his death. Even though death was an absolute, he was going to try to kill it and still live. The best way to handle this was to go for the quick kill, but he needed the element of surprise.

The gargoyle could only get to the camp one way and that was through him. He didn't have a weapon in hand but knew exactly where each of them were. His armour had several places that held knives. The knife was the perfect weapon because this strike would have to be fast and silent.

The beast moved toward him, two more steps and he would spring on it. He had to suppress his adrenaline. He would need it shortly but wanted it to explode with him at the perfect moment. Bottle it up and let it pop with its advance. If the beast was facing him, he would have to jump and blow his whistle at the same time, but if it turned around then he could have ultimate striking ability and not have to warn the others until it was dead.

You stupid bastard, wrong forest, wrong tree. You have no idea I am here waiting for you. You're like a bear wandering aimlessly through a forest and just about to walk into a hunter's trap.

He waited, eyes focused. His mind calculated everything. He had full control over all body functions, a drop of sweat wouldn't be released without his approval. The beast stopped a little out of range but it turned around, exposing its back.

Dammit, come on, back a little more. Asgar is waiting for you.

He could blow the whistle now, but that would be a sure-fire way to have him destroyed. Asgar knew he was good, one of the best SAEs, but gargoyles were way too powerful for a human to handle without some advantage. His would be surprise.

Things got worse quickly as another knocking noise was released, and unless this one could throw its voice, there was a second. His eyes confirmed it. The reason the first gargoyle turned around was to greet another.

Come on, tell me someone else knows what this beast's noise sounds like. Magnus, you bastard, stop sleeping and listen, you should recognize something is wrong. Wake up!

Asgar was still careful to not yell too intensely in his mind. Gargoyles were equipped with the gift of magic and might hear a runaway thought.

Two gargoyles, we are in trouble, even if they were all battle-ready. Deo is in danger. Multiple gargoyles can rip through our men.

They were deadly and Asgar had heard of only one man who killed a gargoyle and lived to tell.

Two of them are bad but then things exponentially worsened as Asgar heard a third series of knocks well behind his position. They were under attack and in grave danger! He had no choice but to spring into action.

Its back was still to him. He could see the massive wings lowered and relaxed. They were going to attack but it wouldn't be at this moment. Slowly he slid his right arm from where it had been lodged in dense thick branches, and he reached for a knife on his shoulder. His movements couldn't give a hint of his existence; he couldn't brush the smallest branch, lose his footing or make any noise as he unsheathed his eight-inch knife.

The first stage was a success. He was armed! The next was to free up the rest of his limbs. He was halfway through and everything was perfect when the beast took another step out of range.

Dammit! he thought as the beast was even further from the kill zone. He knew he couldn't wait for the gap to potentially widen even further and quickly analyzed the strike.

Asgar took a deep breath, mind cool and calm and set his body in motion.

See you on the other side, you bastard!

He pulled his left arm free and leapt with one leg toward a large branch slightly lower than his position. He used it to as a springboard with the other leg launching him towards his target. He hoped it would give him the extra distance he needed to strike. His adrenaline popped as he flew towards his enemy. Gargoyles prized themselves on all elements of war, including ambushing and unravelling an ambush, but all they heard was a little shuffle in the tree near them.

Asgar leapt outwards and came down perfectly on the back of the gargoyle closest to him. His left arm wrapped around its upper torso, holding it in position as the beast's knees gave way and his right arm jammed a precise spot. His right hand dug his knife deep into an area between its neck and shoulder. He had to use a lot of strength because he knew its skin was tough. Gravity, years of strength training and a knife sharpened daily was enough to dig right through to the handle.

The second gargoyle had been looking the other way. It caught movement out of its peripheral vision, but by the time it turned back, its comrade was futilely reaching for its neck, a knife protruding from it and its black, sticky blood covered its face.

Nobody was there though. Asgar had hit him and rolled silently out of sight. It was perfect and so smooth that the second gargoyle was confused about what had attacked its friend.

Having full command of common tongue, the gargoyle commented, "Wrong battle to pick. You should have stayed hidden, but I am sure you already realize that. Lucky you got the best of this incompetent fool, but don't get too excited about it, you will perish shortly." The beast glanced quickly at the weapon jutting from its comrade's neck, paused and then smelled the air. "Human! Great, I love human flesh." It then let out short knocking noises indicating its excitement.

Asgar had shifted out of sight and knew he could probably fade away for good if he took the advice of his adversary, but that wasn't going to happen.

He was only a few trees away from it. The first round was his and he started to believe maybe the second would be his as well. He had dropped

Black Knights; maybe gargoyles weren't all they were made out to be. Maybe all the stories were sensationalized.

He moved from tree to tree to get a better view of the situation. Position was everything. He could hear the gargoyle still talking, only a few more moves and he would be able to see it.

Gotcha, you arrogant prick. This one is for all of humanity, for the fact that you think you are better than us.

Asgar took a quick glance and couldn't believe that stupid bastard still stood at the battle site blabbing on about something. With two blades in hand he quickly visualized the attack. His plan was to leap into motion and fire two knives at its chest with as much velocity as he could muster while in motion. Once they left his hand he was going to roll along the ground and rearm.

One, two, three, go!

Just as planned, he turned the corner and fired one, then the other at a helpless target. Nothing was fast enough to avoid his blades coming with such velocity at such a short distance.

Yee-haw! Asgar cheered in his mind as he was assured of his victory. Two gargoyles destroyed by a single human, it was a big win for the human race. The second stage of the plan worked out flawlessly, a quick roll and up to his feet rearmed.

Asgar focused on the victim but couldn't see his knives at first. Then he noticed they were behind the gargoyle wedged into a tree. *How could that be?* His brain started working quickly, attempting to figure out what had gone wrong.

A moment passed with him in battle position, staring at a gargoyle that didn't look his way and was still babbling.

No way I missed, they went right through him. How is that possible?

Asgar was still trying to figure out what had gone wrong when the beast's image seemed to shake a little. It wasn't real! It was some kind of illusion spell!

Dammit!

Asgar knew he had been fooled and needed to sound the whistle quickly, something he should have done before, but he got greedy. He had assumed the fables weren't accurate or that he was great enough to do what no other human had done before.

Asgar dropped his knife and reached for his whistle, his fingers found it and rushed it towards his mouth. He needed to warn the others of the impending attack. Just as it hit his lips so did an impact to his back. With everything it had, the gargoyle struck him so violently that he lifted off his feet and the collision turned his arms into jelly. Having no control of any appendage, he crashed against the ground on his stomach and slid into a massive root. His head bent hard against the tree, his lips were split, mouth full of blood. A moment later he dispelled some of his teeth on the forest floor.

Asgar knew he messed up badly but the collision distorted his thoughts. He tried to pull himself together quickly. The whistle was gone but he needed to warn the others.

"Ha ha ha ha. Stupid human, thought you had the jump on me... guess not. You can't even take one hit. You should have warned your friends. Now they will be massacred and it's all your fault, know that when I send you over." It advanced towards him picking up the blades Asgar dropped. "I am going to enjoy ripping you to pieces with your own weapons."

Asgar used his one arm to flip onto his back. He watched the gargoyle pick up his knives and move toward him. He reached down and pulled the last of his weapons from its sheath, but clearly he had no ability to use it.

I need to warn the others. Lord, I haven't said much all my life and have asked you for very little. Please let me use all of the words I didn't use over the years, let me combine them all, allow me to explode right now!

His jaw was almost broken. The gargoyle had assumed it was, but a small piece of fused bone still bridged it together. With all his might he attempted to put decades of silence into one warning call and yell the loudest warrior's scream he could muster.

He was not able to mouth the word gargoyle because it would have advanced on him once the lips started to form the words. All he could do was attempt to yell, Asgar was granted his wish and he screamed.

Two groups were on patrol that night. Clinton took one of the jobs himself and circled the perimeter to the east and south. Two others had the responsibility of the north and west. The rules were simple: look for anything unusual and if it warranted blow a warning into the whistle.

The fewer the series of blows the more serious it was. Three blows meant to have someone come to investigate, two blows was man down needing assistance, but one continuous blow was the most important and signified an imminent attack.

The men on the north-west patrol were young and hadn't reached Elite status. They were told by their leader that if in doubt, err on the side of caution. To rip one continuous blow would have everyone battle-ready in sixty seconds, including the King himself. They both wanted Elite status and embraced every task with enthusiasm. After talking to Joe and John earlier, they knew that more Elites would be trained soon, which invigorated a lot of excited conversation.

"It must say something that we are out here on patrol. We are doing an important job without an Elite present."

"Yep, won't be long until you and I will be wearing Dryden's crest."

Both armed with a sheathed sword on their hips and a spear housed along their backs, they walked near the forest north of camp. They used leather armour because covertness was important and metal armour would reveal their presence. They weren't supposed to talk, but few followed that rule. They couldn't hold back, especially after hearing the good news from Joe and John.

"Do you think Joe and John were blowing smoke up our asses?"

"I don't know, I don't think so, they did sit with the King."

"Good point!"

"So why are you excited about being an Elite?"

"Are you kidding me? It's all I have dreamed of. I had to kick ass my whole life to get to this point. The honour, the prestige, the adventure."

"Blah blah blah, the women, the food, the women." He cut his friend off and they both laughed.

From an unperturbed tranquil state, the two stopped dead in their tracks as they heard a warrior's scream. They didn't know who it was and if they had a chance to guess, they never would have gotten it right, but it didn't matter.

"What do we do now? We aren't supposed to head back unless a whistle is blown."

"Maybe it's just a test to see how we would react."

The two thought as fast as they could. They needed to get this right and at the moment could only think about the King.

"Forget it. Let's head back, that didn't sound right."

They attempted to break into a run, but didn't get more than a few steps into their stride before a voice inquired from behind.

"Where do you think you are going?"

When they turned they saw the most menacing of sights. Their lives flashed before their eyes. Nothing was said for a moment, giving the emotions of one of them to override his self-control and tear up. Not only did they think about death but they thought about how it was going to come to them. The stories of these vile creatures were terrible; they loved to torture their victims. Hoping to never see a gargoyle face to face, they looked at one only a few moments' charge away.

Why did I have to go on this stupid patrol?

Fear set in as neither wanted to be there. Bravery was one thing, but it would be madness to be fearless in a situation like that. They felt their skin start to oil up, as nerves escalated.

Need to run, need to get back to the others. I need to get back now! His eyes gave in and a tear ran down his cheek.

"Maybe we should run?" his friend whispered to him.

"Oh… now, now, no need to cry. You shouldn't fear me. Do you think I am going to harm you? Look, I am not even armed."

Not being armed wasn't a big deal. They knew it could rip them apart with ease. They also knew it would take great pleasure in disemboweling them.

"Let's turn and run," he said quietly from the side of his mouth.

What they should have done was hit the whistle, but fear had created a gap in logical thinking. Training should have kicked in, but on the off chance the creature wouldn't attack unless they did something to provoke it, they didn't do as trained. They assumed the gargoyle was like a cobra waiting for something it didn't like before the bite.

"I wouldn't run, that would make me upset. I am much faster than you and I have these." It moved its wings slightly and then got serious. "Try not to upset me, it's unwise." The gargoyle spoke with such confidence, playing with its kill before it struck, giving a little bit of hope just to take it away again shortly after.

"What do you want then?"

"You're not even Elites." It laughed and started to move to the side. "Do you know how I know that?"

"We are Elites!" The one with the steadier tongue decided to take a gamble, to see if they could pretend they were more skilled then they really were.

"Hmmm, I say you're not and you shouldn't lie to me." Its voice became harsher, putting a shiver down their spines. "Do you know why I know you're not Elites? Would you like to know why?"

It waited for a moment enjoying how stressful it was for them. The two men stood perfectly erect and thoroughly terrified.

"Well, I will tell you. An Elite would have attacked me by now, even just one would have drawn and charged, but you two stand there as if encased in stone. You are terribly afraid." It started to advance slowly toward them.

"Don't move anymore!" one said with a stutter as the other motioned for his weapon.

The gargoyle put one of its hands up.

"Hold on, reach for that weapon and we won't be friends anymore. I guarantee the full blade won't taste the night's air before you are struck down." They both put the thought of advancing toward their weapons on hold. "Now I am sure we can work something out. Why don't you come over here? Bow down before me and worship me as your God. Kiss my foot and pledge your life to me and then you will be my slave… but live."

"I don't think so, you are everything we hate." They both decided it was time to run, but their minds were playing a game of confidence and then fear. They realized that once they broke into a stride they would set off a series of events that would not be favourable. The steadier of the two men found his knee would start to twitch, as if to start running, but then something inside would freeze up, halting that decision.

"Hate is what I am all about." It turned its head to the side as if straining to listen to something. "I can hear what your thoughts are but I wouldn't do that. Like I said, you don't have to fear me. Have I not told you this already? You don't need to fear me, but it's my friend behind you that should worry you."

"Yeah right, there is nobody behind me." He decided not to look, but instead the young warrior turned and attempted to run. As his eyes focused he realized there was no bluff. A muscular grey beast with its chiseled features took a step forward to meet him as he initiated his run. The gargoyle shoved its hand in his mouth gripping onto his jaw tightly. A feeble attempt to get his sword was made. As he touched the handle of his weapon, its other arm came up with open palm striking his forehead. It had enough force to tear his jaw from his face.

The other soldier just looked to the side as his mutilated friend fell beside him. Fear rushed at him and he started to cry. "Don't kill me, please!"

"On your knees, slave!"

Shaking and afraid of death, he actually bent to the gargoyle's will. He crouched down on both knees close to the ground.

"Now say that I am you master, I am your God."

The words were difficult to come out and he thought about the shame of his family and what he was doing to his faith, but he would ask for forgiveness later. He would make a run for it as soon as the gargoyle wasn't paying attention. His family would understand.

"You are my master, you are my God."

The gargoyle looked down at the human crouched over and shook its head with disappointment. It reached down and slammed the human's head to the ground, pinning him in an awkward and painful position. It knelt beside him to get closer.

With its mouth against his ear it made sure he heard every word. "You have just renounced your religion, you stupid fool. Purgatory is only a few moments away. Your God, who I know of quite well, will be disgusted at your cowardice. Your friend beside you may have tried to run, but he didn't bow down to me, didn't swear allegiance to me." The beast grabbed him by the neck and picked him up, not worrying about being gentle.

Once it had lifted the soldier above the ground it started to squeeze the life out of him. "Neither side wants someone who cries at the first sign of danger, someone who would sway so easily. Enjoy eternity in excruciating pain."

He squeezed out a few words, "But you said I would live if I..."

It stared into his eyes as they filled with blood. "I lied." A few moments later his body stopped fighting and was lifeless. The ever-present strength of gargoyles was evident. It showed its raw power and tossed the motionless body to the side, launching it some ten feet. The body struck a tree and then fell to the ground.

"Come, let's join the massacre. You know I have been looking forward to it." The two leapt into flight.

Magnus's heart started to beat with fury because he recognized the knocking noises from the forest. They were gargoyles!

How is this even possible? Deo. Dammit, I must get to Deo!

His thoughts were jumbled. One or two gargoyles would have a shot at clipping the King. More of them would be an assured slaughter of everyone.

Magnus was lying on his back and hadn't turned over as he attempted to get a fix on how many there were by listening to their knocking sounds.

Okay, how many are you? One, two, three! I hear three different areas you are coming from? Can't be more than that, I haven't heard of a group of more than a couple together... Okay, what do I do now?

He waited for a few moments to gather his thoughts, but a scream rent the night.

The bellow ripped through him. His stomach felt sick as he knew where the scream had come from and from whom. *Asgar!* The man barely muttered a few words every few days and never raised his voice. All of the years Magnus had known him, never once had he heard him scream, but it was unmistakable. That was his voice and he would only yell for one reason.

Why didn't you use your whistle, you stupid bastard? They will be all over you now.

Magnus flipped quickly, but stayed low to the ground and wriggled up the hill to get a perspective of the camp. He could see an outline of tents and a few torches that were lit. Besides that, all that could be viewed was the outline of the trees where he was sure the attack would be initiated.

There is no way this is a coincidence! They will be attacking, they are going after the King, but I doubt they know I am out here. Don't get up yet. Wait for the right moment.

Magnus waited until he could see some movement from the trees. Something took flight and flew towards one of the flanks of the camp. It was hard to focus but it was carrying something, it flew over a tent and seemed to struggle for a moment. The flight wasn't entirely smooth. He watched as it continued for a few moments. He squinted to hopefully see what was really going on, but it didn't attack for some reason. Maybe it was gathering intelligence, maybe it decided it wasn't the best time and just simply flew past the men. As it continued its path it got closer to him and his eyes finally adjusted. His stomach turned, instantly queasy for a second time as he was almost positive he knew what he was seeing. The gargoyle didn't have to descend to attack, because it had some kind of massive steel pole with a hook on the end. It had flown over and jammed it into one of the men. He stared in horror as the lifeless body dangled and was dumped.

Magnus watched as the forest came alive. A few more took to flight with the same plan and had the same results. His men dangled on the ends of this atrocious weapon. He reached down attempting to grab his whistle but it fumbled a few times in his fingers. He was a steady man, a great warrior and going into battle with a gargoyle was something he had dreamed of since he was a child. They were the most loathed enemy of humans that existed, partly because they were great at taking humans apart with ease and relished the process. The anticipation was what made him fluster. In a few moments he would be rock solid again. He finally got the warning tool to his lips, but before he could blow it another whistle sounded.

I just hope that it wasn't too late, please, King, stay hidden, don't come out. Magnus will be joining in real soon.

Magnus knew to run to the battle now would do little good. He needed them to be comfortable, understanding that the battleground was set. Once they believed no back up was coming, he would explode on them!

A loud warrior's scream woke an Elite from sleep. It was off in the distance but enough to arouse him. He immediately got up and wanted to investigate.

"Where are you going?" His partner looked up with squinting eyes.

"You didn't hear that? I heard a battle cry."

"Come on, you're hearing things. I didn't hear anything."

"You wouldn't wake up if a catapult rock smashed a cart full of armour while you were sleeping." He rolled over.

He walked outside with his mace in one hand. His mind was scattered a little from the sleep. The camp was very still and nobody else seemed to be up. He looked around as he stretched.

That felt good... Maybe I didn't hear anything.

He walked around the side of the tent and looked for a torch to examine a little further. He felt at peace, calm and felt no fear, but wrongly so. While he looked around for a light source, he heard a shift of air and out of nowhere his face was impaled by a massive metal hook. The attack came from the air and caught him under the jaw, blowing him off his feet. Instead of falling to the ground he was dragged upward. The metal had jammed up through his jaw and into his sinus cavity. His peripheral vision didn't catch what had hit him and his ears didn't pick up anything besides a shift of air. Having no control over his weapon, he dropped it. With only a few seconds of life remaining, his last thoughts confused.

Slightly curious from inside the tent, his partner called out, "So what's going on?" His tone indicated that he really struggled just asking the question because the last thing he wanted to do was interrupt the best part of his sleep. He didn't hear a response. "Come on jackass, what's happening?" The second stage of silence got him up. Irritated, he commented, "Thanks... you're really loving this, aren't you? Get my ass out of bed. Let me tell you, if you jump out of a corner, I will punch you, so help me."

He stepped out of the tent, looked around and didn't see his friend. "Great, where did you run off too? Was it time for a late night visit to the hole?" He smiled slightly and then noticed the mace lying on the ground. He then turned to see a little blood splatter on the tent canvas. He looked away from the forest into the distance and could see something in the sky, "What the..."

A few thoughts away from putting it all together, he felt an impact from behind. His chest ripped open and then he was yanked upward. He touched the blood lubricated metal hook speared through his rib cage. It had punctured his lung, filling his throat with blood. Having little strength he looked up to see a gargoyle holding a metal pole, lifting him upward. He attempted to speak but couldn't.

God help us!

A few tents away another SAE that rose to investigate was hit hard directly to the stomach. He noticed the attacker a moment before impact, but his brain intelligently deduced he was probably dead, no evasion was possible. He couldn't jump to the side or dive to the ground in time but he needed to help his friends. There was no way that he was able to grab his whistle, but he could let his tent partner know there was something seriously wrong. To yell wouldn't have done much good either except raise a few more weary heads and guide them into a devastating situation. His hand gripped onto the corner of his tent and as he was lifted, it ripped back.

His sleeping partner was on all fours as he was going out to see what was going on as well. He heard a noise he couldn't make out which turned out to be the impalement of his friend and then felt a gust of wind as the canvass of the tent headed towards the sky. He looked up to see a massive metal hook dive towards him. Nimbly he rolled onto his back, getting as close to the ground as he could, just missing being skewered.

"Holy!" he yelled.

With awe, he looked up to see several flying creatures, some with hooked prey. They were under attack! The attack hit them with silence but that was about to end. He grabbed the whistle and let one loud continuous blow rip.

"Get up. We are under attack, weapons, full weapons!"

Everyone woke up, charged! The remaining SAEs leapt into action with primary weapons within reach, most burst out already armed.

The whistle sent in a flurry of gargoyles, unprecedented numbers. Confusion had set in and everyone waited for Clinton to take control, but they didn't realize that he was on patrol.

Walter could hear the chaos and figured the normal exit out of the tent was probably a bad idea. He took his blade and opened up the side of his tent, slipped through it, grabbed his shield and put on his metal helmet. It was a three split helmet, with metal around the back and down the centre, protecting his nose. It looked menacing with spikes on the top of it. The helmet was symbolic, and every time he put it on, his body seemed to excel, it would invigorate him for battle.

Walter knelt beside his tent and put his shield up, just in case arrows were coming down on them. He looked to his right and left on one knee. The sight was horrific. He figured out quickly that they were in trouble. His men were getting jammed on some kind of spikes and air lifted away, gargoyles were everywhere and they were coming from the forest.

He knew this attack was all about the King. His coarse voice yelled out, "Protect Deo, lock shields, this way!"

His booming voice was easy to identify, as Walter charged in the direction of the King. John looked the wrong way coming out of the tent and was about to get speared. Walter pushed his body as hard as he could, demanded intensity from his legs and stretched his shield forward. Walter felt his shield get hit hard by metal on metal. It luckily hit the centre, the perfect spot to deflect and he pushed the deadly hook away from the young warrior.

"Get your shield, weapons, helmet now, defend the King! Defend the King!"

John didn't have time to realize how close he was to being impaled and ignored it as a great warrior should do. Swiftly being first out of the tent, he armed himself.

"The sky, they are attacking from the sky!" John called out to everyone, informing them of this critical information.

"Joe, let's go!" he called to his friend, with shield aimed upward, perfectly angled to defend. The tent exploded as he jumped up through the door and launched a spear. He had peered through, got a target and fired toward an enemy moving in for an attack on one of the men, which it had lined up perfectly. The man had been grazed by one hook and was bleeding from his open shoulder wound. Stunned from the attack, he would have been a goner.

The spear was a true shot and slammed into the unsuspecting gargoyle, digging deep into its arm. The impact forced it to release its heavy weapon. The long metal pole hit the ground with a heavy thud.

"Great shot comrade, we need to follow Walter, let's go, protect Deo!" John yelled enthusiastically to his friend.

Joe grabbed his bow and a quiver of arrows. The two charged towards Deo's tent.

The situation was intense; arguably the best of the human race was getting decimated. Walter eventually had the group in a circle with shields up, but the carnage from the initial onslaught had taken its toll.

Deo, who had been protected by two men, was finally allowed to be lifted up. The attack had stopped. The challenging force had circled back and landed in the trees, no doubt preparing for the second surge.

Deo looked around at the remaining men, five Elites, four other warriors, two cooks and the priest. In a small timeframe over half of his men were dead. Deo was a great leader and motivator but it was a harsh situation. It would be hard to be positive but everyone needed him badly.

"Spread out a little men… let me breathe."

Out of fear and over-protectiveness they were almost on top of one another. He looked to the eyes of the young, some were panicking, but Joe and John didn't. Just like the remaining SAEs, they were ready for his command.

"Are you all right?" Deo asked the man who was saved by Joe's spear, he was obviously injured. He nodded.

"Well I've been in better places than this." He shook his head. "Where is Clinton?" Deo asked and Walter looked back with a shake of the head that told him he had no idea.

"How many are there? Do we have any idea?"

"Could be a dozen, maybe more. It was chaotic, dark and everything had happened so fast."

"All gargoyles, how is that possible? There hasn't been that many in one cluster in decades."

"Maybe there has been, but whoever would have witnessed a grouping like this wouldn't still be alive." Joe made an inappropriate comment.

Deo looked around to see what they had. Everyone focused in on their King with torch lights illuminating intense faces.

"Okay, they are coming back after us, we need to be prepared. Walter, you are commanding officer, what do you think?"

Before Walter could speak, Joe jumped in, "Spears!" He knew it wasn't his place to say anything but he continued, "I hit one with a spear, it did enough damage to force it to drop its hideous weapon."

"He is right, they are attacking from the sky with some kind of metal hook and carrying us away. We need projectile weapons, anything we can toss, our primary weapons will do little good if they are out of range."

"Metal hooks? Like we are fish?" Deo asked in disgust.

"Anyone else?" Walter asked looking for other suggestions.

"One tosses, the other defends. Everyone gets a partner, can you guys toss?" John asked the two cooks, the only two non-military besides the Minister.

The chef's assistant shook his head no with fear, hoping not to get forced into engaging them. He wanted to live and his mind told him not fighting would be the way.

"You are great with knives," the comment was directed towards the chef.

"I am great with knives."

"Okay, you hold the shield and you toss knives."

Deo looked John and Joe in the eyes, "Consider yourselves honorary Elites." It was a strategic move on Deo's part. If they were to survive, they would have passed any training they would have been put through. Also in this perilous situation they had kept their cool and offered strategic defensive advice. Both young men felt invincibility hit them. They were Elites! Deo smiled as he knew they would fight a little harder now.

"Okay, what about weapons?" Deo asked.

"We couldn't have positioned ourselves in a better spot." Walter pointed to the weapons carriage right next to them.

"We don't have long before they take flight from those trees, keep that in mind, fall into position once you see anything. First to see calls it. Anyone without a helmet put one on. Armour would be best but it will take too long."

Joe ran over and got his and John's helmets. The group gathered their weapons and waited. A multitude of things ran through everyone's mind.

"The only true test of bravery is in a person's mind, in a time like this..." Deo commented as he asked for a weapon.

"Sir, you're not to fight."

"I will be damned if you fight alone. We are all brothers, children of God, we are all equal. I may not be much of a spear-tosser," Deo looked to the group with a lifted eyebrow realizing his comment could be misconstrued as being a reference to a homosexual. Everyone laughed. "But if it comes to close combat, I still have a few moves."

Time passed and nothing happened. It wasn't expected. Minutes felt like hours.

"They want us to breakdown. There is nobody close by, they can wait this out for days if they want to."

"We aren't breaking down," John vowed.

They stood focused on the forest. Every movement was sped up to make sure they missed nothing. Wiping sweat, scratching a body part, even blinking was accomplished with swiftness.

The non-military men looked around and realized that death was imminent, but they watched in awe at the steadiness of the Elites. The chef's assistant was holding a shield as directed and he was terrified. He felt the shield's weight push his arm down. He could barely hold it but the others didn't flinch.

"Maybe we should get you out of here?" Walter suggested.

"You know that won't work, they are faster than we are, but it doesn't matter anyway."

"Why is that?"

"Here they come," Deo said calmly. "Time to *battle*!" He yelled the drawn out cry. The group, for the most part cheered, but the chef's assistant, who thought they were nuts, urinated down his leg.

Joe hid behind John's shield with arrow cocked. Everyone had a similar plan. The gargoyles came in waves of five or six, one after the next. The estimate of a dozen was way off, there were a lot more.

Joe fired and struck a target almost every shot. He could see them take the arrows with little effect. One he hit in the forearm, another in the shoulder and a third in the abdomen, but it didn't really seem to have much of an impact.

"Arrows are doing nothing!" Joe screamed.

They came down hard on the shields with the hooks that had some serious weight behind them. The thick metal on metal made for an awfully loud sound. The shields were taking a beating and even the strongest would be shifted off balance almost every strike.

One man took several shots in a row. The first he absorbed with only a slight shift of his ankle, the second forced his shield back in an uncomfortable position and the third knocked him on to his back, with shield to the side. He looked to his side and saw his shield a short distance away. His mind told his body to move fast, pick up the shield and roll to protect himself. That would have been the right move but his vulnerable, exposed position was exploited. Instead of dragging him up, a gargoyle used its weapon like a spear and tossed it downwards through its victim digging deep into the ground right through his stomach.

The man pinned to the ground screamed in pain. He didn't pass out but just stared at his blood everywhere. The shrieking had negative effects on the battle. It fired up and motivated the gargoyles because they loved the torment. It disturbed the remaining men.

Walter listened for a few moments, turned and fatally speared the man.

Some of them looked at him with shock.

"If I am in such a state, do the same to me and I will grant you the same courtesy."

The only real recent success the gargoyles had was a man now pinned to the ground. From a perspective of casualties, the battle had slowed down. Their strategy was to continue to wear down the men, but the gargoyles were taking on damage as well, nothing fatal, but arrows and spears were inflicting unwanted injuries. With all the attacks coming from above, the beasts made a good strategic move and changed things up. Two charged on foot to the unsuspecting men. Eyes were focused above or behind a shield; they didn't think to look to ground level.

One of them swung its massive hooked weapon under a shield and pierced right through an ankle. The weight ripped him off balance and he crashed to the ground.

The shield system worked well but relied on interlocking units, no exposed areas. When the one man hit the ground he left a section of their defense uncovered. The other gargoyle took full advantage of the situation. It tossed its massive metal weapon from the opposite end. It was thick but deadly sharp and moved with velocity. It impaled two soldiers smashing through ribs and splitting internal organs. They slumped over linked together.

The Elite that was ripped off his feet was dragged away. He clawed to get a grip, but to no avail and within a few moments the beast took flight with its catch. He turned and yelled to Walter, "Weapon!"

Walter hastily grabbed a spear and successfully tossed it to him. He knew he was dead but wanted revenge. He needed to make up for his error. Although disoriented, he focused on the gargoyle. Its wings pulled him upward, and it had no idea he was armed. All it could think of was ripping a live human to pieces and the overwhelming joy that would come with precise torture. He jockeyed the spear to a better position but almost let it drop. He held on tight with both hands, aimed and fired. The spear jammed deep into its chest. A perfect shot! It looked down for a second to see a smiling man. Not able to hold on, it let him go. He fell from a fatal height, but hit the ground with a smirk and a feeling of pride. The damage to the gargoyle was severe and it collapsed from the sky, slamming into the ground and pushing the spear right through it.

Although the trade off of one for one should be viewed as a success, the men who surrounded Deo in defense were breaking down. The enemy was too strong and the group's morale had taken a serious dive. The chef's assistant couldn't take it anymore. He dropped his shield and ran away as fast as he could in a straight direction. The chef who was hiding under his shield looked shocked for a moment and realized there was no point to calling out to his friend. He was going to be easily picked off.

They were a mere fraction of the group they once were; only three Elites stood, plus Joe, John, a Minister, the chef and Deo.

"Be sober… be vigilant… because your adversary, the Devil, as a roaring lion, walketh about, seeking whom he may devour," the Minister chanted.

"Creepy line but that might be worth something. Simon! These beasts are created by the Devil himself, right?" John, covered in sweat and splattered blood, asked the petrified Minister.

"Yes, they are!" Simon responded in fear as he clenched his holy book and spread holy water on his forehead in the symbol of a cross.

"Is that holy water?"

"Yes my son. Would you like a prayer?" The Minister felt important for the first time, shifting some of his fear.

An attack forcefully slammed into John's shield, causing him to crack Joe in the side of the head with the end of his shield.

"Watch yourself, jackass! Stop talking and concentrate if you want to get out of this alive!" Joe yelled as he rubbed his head, "Dammit, that really hurt."

"We aren't getting out of here alive and we all know that, but we might be able to take a few of these bastards with us. Soak your arrowhead with the water."

"What? Arrows don't work, they are useless," Joe answered back. He had tossed his bow aside earlier and had been focusing on spears, although conservatively using them as they were in short supply and the gargoyles were getting better at deflecting them.

"Just do it, do it now and put one where it counts!"

Joe ripped the flask away from Simon and doused his arrowhead with the water, aimed and fired. A beast was on an attack run, its weapon ready for impact. The arrow, like always, was a hit, but the results were very different. Immediately it reached for the arrow and screamed as it flew overhead. Tending to the arrow, it dropped its weapon, landing just behind them. Several feet later it crashed into the ground, flipping around on the field, obviously in serious discomfort. The gargoyle ripped the arrowhead from its body. It clawed at the toxic moisture which was burning a hole in its shoulder and pulled some of its flesh off in the process.

"Walter, the same, spear one of those bastards!" Deo said, eyes widened with excitement. "Everyone hand over any water skins to Simon; bless away, Simon."

As instructed, he did just that. Walter hadn't killed one gargoyle over the course of the battle and it drove him mad. He wanted — no he needed —to kill one of them. His King was going to die. No doubt they were all going to die, but gargoyles couldn't leave from the battle and think SA soldiers, including Elites, were an easy victory.

With a spearhead saturated in holy water, he fired a sure thing at a beast flying right over them. It hit the abdomen of the flying monster which dropped its weapon like the last one and started to lose altitude as it clung to the wooden shaft.

Walter, driven by his goal, needed to make sure it was dead. He grabbed a battle-axe and charged away from the group. He didn't bring a shield. He didn't care. All that he needed was to make sure he had killed one of them. Someone yelled for him to stop but he didn't. Racing forward, he leapt over a few bodies and headed directly for the beast, which slid along the ground on its shoulder. He closed in and could smell its death. It screamed on the ground as the holy water burned its tissue. It looked up to see an axe coming down hard. Raising one arm it took a severe shot to the forearm, almost completely severing it. The gargoyle, with whit, pulled the spear from its stomach and jammed it into Walter's leg. He barely flinched as he raised his weapon up for a second and final strike. Nothing was going to break his concentration, even a spear through his leg.

Moments before, two gargoyles sensed how badly Walter wanted the kill and wanted to make sure he died not fulfilling his goal. One with a hole in the shoulder compliments of Joe, moved in for the strike and had him lined up. It was going to split Walter's belly, which was unprotected with his axe above his head. The beast was going to stop the attack and ruin Walter's last wish. Just before contact with Walter's abdomen it was slammed in its side by a war hammer to the ribs. It lifted off the ground to the sound of a human yelling his own name loudly and drawn out, "*Magnus*!"

Magnus had been waiting for the right time to attack and found it. Magnus had watched as Walter had run by him, and watched the gargoyles land with their backs to him. They both didn't have a clue he was lurking in the dark. When the gargoyles moved in to strike Walter, they landed in his wield house. The first was hit hard by the war hammer and tossed aside. Magnus moved fast and launched another assault. The second put its arms up to defend against his second shot. The war hammer connected again and cracked both of its forearms. It hit the ground but scuttled to its feet and jumped to flight, trying to support its busted arms.

At the same time Magnus connected, Walter continued with his axe and hit the target dead square in the chest, splitting open its ribs and extinguishing its life. Black sticky blood splattered everywhere.

"Yeah!" Walter cried out, savouring the small victory. To make sure it was dead, he swung once again severing its head.

Magnus looked up at the sky and he knew a lot more were coming down to finish the job. "Let's go, Walter, move it!"

"I have a spear through the leg saturated in their blood. It moves through my veins and will take me. I make my stand here. You go, protect Deo!"

But Deo wouldn't ever see Magnus or Walter ever again.

Deo watched and understood why Walter left. He looked around at the rest of his men. They attempted to fend off an enemy they were doomed to lose to.

It's just a matter of time now. Good men I have here, a good life I have led. May my son know we fought well and take over for me.

The gargoyles took a few more arrows before realizing they needed a new attack strategy.

The sky emptied as they regrouped inside the forest. Deo knew they would employee a new strategy, one that would surely finish them off. The gargoyles walked from the forest, leaving their horrific, giant hooks behind them. The two groups, humans and gargoyles, were far from one another, but it was easy to see how many gargoyles there were as each carried a torch. From the moment they were lit, a sphere of light illuminated Hell's horrific gift to the world. John and the two Elites grabbed their primary weapons. It would be a close combat with arguably the world's greatest hand-to-hand combat adversaries.

Joe didn't reach for his primary weapon because he was still excited about the strategy involving the blessed water. With his holy water saturated arrowhead he fired a shot at one of the approaching gargoyles. The arrow was true to its mark, even over such a distance, but the target lifted its hand and with a few words in demonic tongue, the direction of the arrow shifted, missing it completely.

"What the heck was that?" Joe said, shocked.

"Black magic. They are intelligent creatures and we don't have any magicians to protect us from their spells. Seems like a stupid decision in hindsight," Deo commented and shook his head.

What I would give for Rizzian or Eclipse right now.

Joe grabbed another arrow, focused on the same target. He was determined to strike it. He concentrated but had trouble seeing, his eyes went blurry. He blinked repetitively and shook his head to clear his vision but it just got worse. He lowered his weapon to fix this untimely issue. Blurriness turned to pain which shot through his eyeballs. Within a few moments they started to bleed. He let go of his weapon and held his hands close to his eyes, yelling in pain. He fell to his knees helplessly.

"What's wrong!" John dropped down to see what was wrong. Joe pulled back his hands smeared in blood and he forced his eyes open. At first they were just bloody, but then John watched them split down the middle and Joe rushed his hands back to his face attempting to soothe the pain.

John's youth was finally present, triggered by emotion, and he got up and charged the gargoyles. Seeing his best friend in such pain precipitated the rash decision. John rushed with no fear towards an illuminated area. The beasts' flame stopped as he approached, it was tough to see what happened. The light jumped back to life a moment later and John lay mangled off to the side. He was easily cut down and tossed aside, no match for a group of gargoyles in midfield by himself.

"Anyone else wish to have a try?" the massive beast yelled out as it approached them. Its hands to its side expressing its cockiness and challenging anyone with its body language and words.

Deo looked to his right and left, realizing he was out of choices. His fate rested with gargoyles. Would he become a prisoner, a slave or perish?

"Two Elites, a Priest and a cook." Deo muttered under his breath, "Sounds like the start of a bad joke." He smiled lightly.

"The great Silver Allegiance Elites, you guys are something special. You are considered the world's best, obviously self-proclaimed." The same gargoyle continued to talk as it closed in on the remaining men.

"What is your name? I assume you are the commanding officer?" Deo inquired sternly.

"Oh, the great King Deo speaks, everyone shall listen and respond," the gargoyle said sarcastically. "You have no power here, it has been removed. Your Kingdom will fall shortly, everyone will succumb to our dominion."

"Foolish gargoyle, you think because you have taken me that Dryden and the other cities will fall? Your victory comes out of luck and you will be no match for our numbers." Deo spoke with confidence.

"Don't move another step — that is close enough," one of the Elites commanded with authority, sword drawn and body in battle position beside the only other remaining Elite.

"So serious and terrifying as well." The beast didn't listen and continued to move.

"I am warning you!" the Elite barked.

The beasts were close enough for the soldiers to see their unappealing faces. They were rigid, carved features, resting on a large jaw. What looked like torches from afar were their left hands burning. Every one of them had a fire spell, their magic was a deadly reason why they dominated on a battlefield and were ranked so highly.

The gargoyle wasn't foolish and didn't let its guard down. These men had no chance at taking them all down, it had never happened in history, but they were still very skilled with a weapon. Most importantly they had no fear; it could be read in both of their eyes. Once an opponent has accepted death as an absolute, he becomes truly dangerous. There was no way they would win this battle but being too confident might possibly create an injury or fatality for one of its own. It stopped for a moment.

"Your precious Kingdom is fractured from within. Haven't you asked yourself how we found you in the first place? How did we mobilize such an assault undetected? Look around you, Deo — no magicians, strange decision. Two dozen gargoyles attacking your secret convoy, a lot of resources allocated to this one area. A lucky guess, I think not."

Deo listened to its comments and he started to think. He wasn't sure what it was getting at.

As Deo's mind searched for answers, the gargoyle tempted the Elites' threat and took a step forward. They would either attack, which he was ready for, or they wouldn't. If they didn't it, showed tremendous weakness.

With the step, the Elites started to move in sync. Both stepping to the side, they started a circular movement, eyes focused on the deadly killer. The gargoyle opened its arms to prepare for any attack from any angle and spread its fingers with exceptionally sharp claws exposed. It looked at them and released its strange knocking noise. Deo watched as the last of his men defended his honour and felt a rush of pride.

A few other gargoyles closed in as well. The only chance to strike was immediately and the first Elite surged forward, his speed took the gargoyle by surprise, but all that did was change its defensive strategy. One hand still flaming, it threw the fire into the face of the charging Elite, burning his skin but also blinding him. A second gargoyle tackled him hard the moment his skin ignited. The mounted beast clamped down hard with its jaw onto his face like a vicious animal. It pinned his arms back and crushed his face. The sight was sickening.

The second Elite sprang into action seeing the exposed back of the beast that mounted his friend. Wasting no time he started to come down hard with his sword aiming for the back of the gargoyle. It was an easy strike, but just before he could hit his target, a spear slammed into his chest and launched him off his feet. He hit the ground and looked in the direction of the spear to see who had hit him. It was uncanny for a gargoyle to use a weapon. His mind started to fog over as his life was close to expiry, but in the distance he could see a man.

"And you want to know, Deo, how we knew you were going to be here? You want to know why your Kingdom will fall? Your covenant with the people you trust the most is worth nothing. Turn and see your Judas."

Deo turned his head in the direction of the spear to see something that made him nauseous. One of his most trusted Elites, a friend, someone he would consider family, presented himself.

"Clinton!" Deo said with shock.

"You got it, didn't see this coming, did you?"

"After everything… You don't know what you have done." Deo looked at him dumbfounded.

"I know exactly what I have done and after everything? What is everything? You give us nothing. You live this fantastic life which we get to watch from the corner. Maybe, just maybe, we can die for you one day. Oh, what an honour."

"What kind of deal did you make? Did they pay you off in gold, houses, women, what is your soul worth?" The head Minister spoke.

"Shut up Simon, you are just as bad as he is. All I know is the rest of my life I will live to the fullest."

Deo shuffled everything in his mind. He realized why Clinton wanted the lead and why he didn't want Bruno on this trip. He argued tooth and nail over the path they should take and also pitched to Rizzian, that he would only draw attention because of his energy imprint. It was Clinton that pushed them to leave their greatest Wizard at home, to not bring any Wizards at all.

"Don't forget, he also took watch tonight," the main gargoyle mentioned as it was obviously able to read Deo's thoughts.

"I have to admit this was way too easy, except for that swine Asgar, it would have been perfect. Way too trusting King." Clinton walked around Deo but wouldn't look him in the eye. Deo picked up on it and challenged him.

"Look me square in the face Clinton. I have something I want to tell you," Deo commanded.

"I don't take orders from you anymore. You take them from me."

"Change of plans, Clinton, he goes down and stays down," the commanding gargoyle said.

"What? No… that wasn't the plan. Nobody was to hurt Deo, that was the deal. He becomes my property." Clinton looked around, angry and growing concerned.

"New rule, Deo doesn't live… and you are going to kill him." Clinton heard the words but didn't want to believe them. He had the stomach to take it this far but he didn't want Deo dead. The others had accepted the life of a soldier. Their whole existence was geared toward dying in battle one day, and he justified their deaths because they would be glorified for defending their King.

The chef moved forward as if he was going to intervene, but Deo placed his hand on his chest and looked him in the eye, "No, my friend, I will make this easier for everyone, even Clinton."

The King bowed down on one knee in front of Clinton, to his and everyone's surprise.

Clinton walked up and said under his breath, "What are you doing?"

Deo said something but Clinton couldn't hear, as he was looking toward the ground, he was obviously ashamed. Clinton got closer and leaned forward, "I can't hear you, Deo. What are you doing? This adds unneeded shame, you are better than this."

Deo looked up at Clinton from his pathetic position. Clinton focused on his lips which were buried in a beard. He knew the King was humiliated and probably would keep his comments quiet, so he needed to try to make out the words. He spoke calmly and not much louder than the first comment.

"You were like a son to me. I probably would have used the word love if asked. You could have had anything, I would have given you anything. You are one of the most skilled I have ever seen, your rank was well earned, and since you are so cunning, I needed you closer to me, close and off your guard."

Clinton was processing the information as he watched Deo's face tighten up around his eyes and forehead.

Just a few moments before Deo kneeled down, he had stopped the chef from advancing and everyone, including Clinton, missed the sleight-of-hand that armed Deo with a knife. Deo's face had tightened as he mustered up the strength he needed to do real damage. He didn't want a flesh wound. He wanted something Clinton would never forget. Deo rammed the sharp cold metal blade deep into Clinton's leg with a grin.

Clinton tightened up and let out a moan as he reached for the knife and hobbled backward. The pain was immense but he could handle that, it was the injury and embarrassment that really hit him hard. The gargoyles broke into laughter.

The chuckling muffled a sound in the forest, a shuffle of leaves.

"Well played Deo... Clinton, not impressed. You want to be a King and you are stupid enough to get stabbed by an old fat man. Maybe you aren't the ruler I thought you were." The commanding officer looked around at its comrades and could see they were hungry, they wanted blood. He waited a moment then focused in on the Minister and chef, "Remove these two, Deo will die alone."

Just as the battle had begun, Rizzian laid in bed in Dryden. He slept on his back in his chamber that was almost as impressive as the King's. It was a red and gold themed room with a beautiful blanket and canopy above his bed to keep falling bugs and rodents away from him. His room had a couch, a writing desk and a fireplace. Few books, gadgets or chemistry mixes were stored here as they were in the room down the hall. He wanted to keep them separate, leaving his sleeping space just for that purpose. The temptation to learn more or practice would keep him away from his critical relaxing time.

A rare and beautiful gem, a Snowflake Obsidian, rested on the night stand beside the great Wizard's head. Besides its rarity, it had a special reason for its high value, it had a perfect twin. They had spent a long time with Rizzian and only on the rarest of occasions did they part. Before the convoy headed north, one of them was given to Simon. With the gem came one instruction. If the King was ever in grave danger, Simon was to stroke the gem. Simon never really knew why, but few ever questioned the great Wizard.

The white spots gave the gem its name and made it different from other Obsidians which were normally solid black. The white parts, the snowflakes, had been glowing for some time, but not enough to wake the old man lying beside it. As time passed it got brighter and eventually started to vibrate until the rock hit the floor. Rizzian finally opened his eyes to see that his room was too bright for any natural light.

"Deo!" His heart started to pound as he rushed out of bed as speedily as he could for his age. He grabbed the stone and stared at it, concerned. He put it in his robe and headed for the window which overlooked the forest. His room had a great view of the city from one window and the other looked over the great series of walls, over the field and to the forest. The trees weren't easy to see, but he could hear the rustling of their leaves.

"I need your help, can you assist?" Rizzian seemed to talk to nobody out the window.

He closed his eyes and listened to the shifting of the leaves. The swishing sound turned from just a calming peaceful noise to something that made sense, a form of communication. It was hard to make out but he concentrated and heard, "We already know what you want, but we aren't to interfere, balance and peace comes from this, these rules of nature, you must understand."

Rizzian didn't really comprehend the way it worked. Trees had no mind, no ability to move on their own, but many years ago he realized they carried secrets. When expanding on his theory that all life was connected he stumbled on a peculiar discovery, a communication medium through the trees. He wasn't exactly sure if it was the trees or something else using them, or disguised as them, but they could tell him things.

"I need your help, we all need your help. Please assist our leader, he is in danger."

Time passed and then the leaves shifted again. "Yes, we know."

Rizzian wasn't sure how to react. He wasn't used to anybody blatantly declining his request. "With his death, war will come, a war that will be fought with fire and many lives will be destroyed, not just man but all vegetation will suffer."

He waited for the winds to push the leaves again, "War comes to you either way. His life won't change that. This is just the prelude to an even greater problem, survive this and something terrible looms, something that will kill us all anyway."

Rizzian didn't understand what was being discussed and normally would have concentrated harder on what was said, but he didn't have time. The rock gem in his pocket was vibrating viciously.

"He matters, I need to be there and now!"

Rizzian waited a moment and didn't hear anything. "I need to know if you will tell me where he is! I need to know if you will assist! If not, I won't forget this, I promise you that."

Rizzian was angry, an emotion he rarely dealt with. He started to consider other options to pursue, ready to take it to levels that he normally wouldn't even contemplate. Anger built as there wasn't a response, he turned and started to walk away from the window. After only a few steps the leaves stirred louder than they had.

"Give us your mind, ride the wind like an ocean's surf."

Few could ever understand the language and even fewer would understand how to give their mind up, to ride wind like an ocean's surf, but Rizzian understood. He released his mind and the leaves rushed forward. Rizzian could see everything and they moved at an incredible speed. It wasn't like he was looking through his eyes, he could see in all directions, 360 degrees. As his thoughts raced over the treetops, he couldn't help but be caught up in the rush. A day's ride passed by in a moment. The feeling almost made him forget about what he was doing, it was elating. His ride abruptly ended and his mind stopped fast and hard in the spot where he needed to be.

Not waiting a moment to gain his perspective, he focused hard and his body materialized to that spot. He had stopped on the top of a tree at the edge of a forest. He balanced himself, only slightly bowing a treetop. His mind levitated his body as if it was second nature.

It took him a moment to focus in.

Where am I? I can see torches, lots of them circling around a camp of some sort. Must be Deo's camp and they must be the Elites with the torches searching for something. Good, just in time to help these boys out. Rizzian focused harder and found Deo. He was on one knee. In front of him was Clinton and to his side the chef and Simon. *Thank goodness Clinton is all right, but why is Deo kneeling? Oh no, not possible!* Rizzian examined further and noted the men with torches weren't men at all. They were gargoyles, lots of them. He scoured the field and could see bodies everywhere. *It's a massacre!*

The commanding gargoyle had a strange look on its face as the rest prepared to take two of the remaining three. They started to move toward the final victims. It inhaled deeply and analyzed the smell in the air. The smell was emanating from the trees behind where it stood, an odour the beast recognized. It turned and looked to the forest. Its eyes scoured, not exactly knowing what it was looking for.

"You can't touch the Minister or you will be breaking the rules of divinity. Back off him, he lives!" Deo bellowed from the ground halting the advancing few. The laws were impervious and great wrath would be bestowed upon anyone attempting to fracture them. Simon felt a strange surge of hope that he would live.

"You are supposed to be wise Deo, but that observation shows you lack the knowledge to run your old Kingdom," the commanding gargoyle said as he continued his attention to the forest. "I am glad you will be dying soon. Let me educate you. The laws of divinity forbid us from striking a man devoted to God, but once he has engaged in warfare he is fair game, he loses his immunity."

With a scared shaky voice caused by a swing of emotions and the horror of what could come to him, Simon spoke, "But I didn't do anything, I didn't strike anyone, you can't touch me." The Minister thought he could convince them. He was sure he was safe until he remembered the holy water that he blessed and was poured on several weapons, and at that moment true fear settled in.

"Oh really, is that so? Anyone who trusts me and attacks the Minister will be rewarded." Still staring off in the distance he presented the challenge.

"You just want to see one of us burn, don't you?" one of the gargoyles said, probing for an answer.

Before it could retort, another one stepped up beside their leader and whispered, "What is wrong commander, what keeps you so distracted? We are about to complete our victory with stunning success."

It spoke quietly, "I don't know, I smell something, something I haven't smelt in a long time and it's bothering me." It then spoke louder, answering to the first inquiry, "I want nothing of the sort, the one who trusts me will be rewarded."

One beast walked up to Simon gradually as the rest watched. It grabbed his face and with one of its claws opened up a small wound along Simon's cheek. He was terrified and didn't know what to do except freeze.

Nothing happened, no divine assistance.

"Very good. You will be rewarded, Deo is yours. The rest of you can fight over and tear the others apart, preferably slowly." As it spoke, its mind started to recognize the smell. A long time ago it encountered the putrid stink, fury set in, then a bit of panic… Rizzian!

The name hit its mind like a ton of rocks. It turned to the gargoyle that was in position to assassinate the King. The honour was overwhelming. It planned on savouring the kill, but heard its commander give a panicked yell.

"Kill the King now!"

As ordered, it didn't waste a second. It gripped the King with the intention of lifting him up and ripping its claws through his chest with a smooth, simple but enjoyable motion. It grabbed on to Deo's face, lifted him to his feet and froze. It didn't move; it couldn't move.

"Now, dammit, now!" the commander bellowed again.

The beast jolted a little, first in the chest and then its leg started to vibrate. Its entire body shook with a series of small popping sounds. There wasn't an open lesion on its body, but its legs gave way and then gravity drove a frameless gargoyle to the ground. Every solid internal structure was pulverized.

Deo smiled at the gargoyle leader, they were the only two that knew what had just happened. From high above the battlefield standing on the trees, the great Wizard used a physics spell, one so powerful few could ever execute it. The spell commanded extreme knowledge of matter, force and motion. Energy was forced into the internal structure of the target until implosions occurred.

"Anyone kill him!"

The two closest advanced fast and hard. As they moved to strike, Deo didn't move. Rizzian was there and he was going to survive the impossible. He would mobilize the entire Silver Allegiance and hunt gargoyles, he would bring a wrath down on the gargoyles they didn't want. Humans outnumbered them exponentially. He relished the opportunity to use all his power to eradicate them all.

The moment after the implosion spell was exercised, Rizzian materialized behind his King and raised both hands. They emitted a glowing bluish light which held the two assailants in position. They couldn't advance even an inch, as if encased in rock.

"Ready to go home King?"

Rizzian knew he needed an exit fast because the rest would jump in soon, numbers he couldn't handle. He had to release one hand and touch the King swiftly.

"Hold on, Rizzian, I can help!" Rizzian looked up with glee to see Clinton who was there to assist him and he was armed. The look on the King's face would have relayed an important development. It would have brought Rizzian up to speed, but he couldn't see it. Assuming Clinton would jump in front of them as a shield or maybe engage the advancing gargoyles, he waited a moment.

Holding off for a second, he watched Clinton do the unthinkable and slide his sword deep into the King's chest. The weapon split his heart instantly ending his life. The look of complete surprise was frozen in

Rizzian's expression, eyes wide, skin pale. He looked into Clinton eyes and without words, without magic, let him know he made a grave mistake.

Rizzian jolted his hands forward in pure anger and full capacity of his magical arsenal. A blue light seemed to spread forward away from him with a surge. The tinted transparent energy moved like a wave forcing anything in its path to be knocked back. The gargoyles' heads were shifted with the force making them close their eyes. Everything felt its push, dead bodies moved, lighter things like arrows or twigs lifted off the ground. The energy went as far back as the forest and even the trees bowed.

When the gargoyles looked back, the King and Rizzian weren't to be found.

"Looks like you regained your position of stature, Clinton. Even Rizzian can't put him back together." The commander spoke the words he wanted to hear, but Clinton didn't feel good at all. It ate away at his insides. He questioned what he had done, but it didn't matter now, nothing could fix it. He would be a hunted man until he died and maybe beyond. The choice was made, he had drawn the line.

Rizzian appeared in the war room holding a lifeless King; his friend, his brother. The travesty was unbearable. The worst part wasn't his feelings, although they were heavily weighing on him, it wasn't the Kingdom that lost a beloved leader. It was Egon he thought of, only a boy, a boy who was about to learn a very painful life lesson.

He opened the door into the main hall. A servant was replacing a torch on the wall. "Call an emergency meeting, first Egon and Bruno, then the Elites. Have them here now, but say nothing to anyone else."

CHAPTER 5

BLOOD SPORT

Deo was dead. The leadership of the great Silver Allegiance rested on the shoulders of a young man. A man who was being groomed for the job, but who never expected it to be so soon. A shock wave of negative uncertainty sped through the city's people, from mouth to mouth, and it was worse than a plague. Like in an outbreak of mass disease, many wanted to flee and depression set in. The plan worked brilliantly for Zoran and the Dark Realm. Deo was well respected. He brought security to Dryden; economically and militarily. With his assassination came a dark gloom over a pivotal component to the Silver Allegiance's defence.

Egon, Deo's son, sat in a room full of the best and most influential minds in all of Dryden. The group included Rizzian who was the head of wizardry defence, Bruno who led the Silver Allegiance Elite, King Deo's political counsel and his defence counsel now under Egon's control. He also added three of his own supporters, all young but people he respected, and by special invitation, Kruno and Ivan were asked to attend.

Tension was high in the room. Everyone looked for Egon to speak, to offer direction, but they had also made up their minds that whatever came from his mouth wouldn't be worth much. What ran through most minds was that he was too inexperienced. His crown still sat on the table, he hadn't placed it on his head yet.

"Shall we place the crown on our new King?" a political advisor suggested. It was a comment that was self-serving and expected from his kind. A man in his position, political in nature, was all about securing good favour.

The news was still fresh in Egon's memory — he would never see his father again. Before Deo left, Egon hadn't told him how he felt. He had always felt that his father was invincible, and even though he discussed ruling the kingdom often, he never expected it for decades. Mostly he commented on it to bed some damsel or to invigorate his status among his friends. It had sharply become his reality, a harsh reality that was combined with the poison of a massive loss.

Egon couldn't cry and he knew that. He wanted to but it would show a weakness he could ill afford. Still the vulnerability of a young man controlled his tongue, "My father's heart just stopped beating and you want me to put this… his crown on my head." The taste of salt built in his mouth as he held back his tears.

"I am sorry Egon, son of Deo, I meant nothing negative of it."

The room went silent again and minds raced, striving to come up with their next move. It was a critical point for Egon. He had to learn to be a King in a matter of hours, to push aside the awful grief that wanted to dominate his mind, wanted to make him curl into a ball in a corner and sob. He had to fill the shoes of his great father and help a Kingdom of so many survive.

"Talk among yourselves," Egon said with his hands supporting his forehead.

"Many people are leaving, many have packed up and are headed out of Dryden."

"Maybe they should leave."

"What kind of a stupid comment is that?" Bruno responded angrily.

The room erupted, people were talking one over another, trying to promote their own agenda. The unproductive conversation went on for too long. Kruno observed and waited for the new King to interject but he said nothing. He just kept his head buried in his hands and stared at the table. It was evident his thoughts were far from lucid.

Kruno looked to Ivan, "Can you get their attention?" Kruno, still smitten over Ivan's return to normalcy, smiled for a second. It was great to have him back.

Ivan, with bulging biceps, lifted a corner of the table a foot or so off the ground. It was extremely heavy and took a while to lift. With each second passing his veins grew thicker and more menacing. Most were distracted by him lifting it and then he let go with a groan. Everyone jolted back a step and looked in his direction with irritation, falling silent.

"Great King, can I speak?" Kruno asked, with strategic respect.

One of Deo's defence council interjected, "Kruno, I don't even know why you're here. Why should you have the floor?"

"I would watch your mouth little man." Ivan decided to respond brashly and out of order, typical of Ivan.

"Easy, big fella, I am not offended to answer the question." Kruno put his hand on Ivan's shoulder to make sure he didn't advance.

"Kruno is one of the most respected men by my father," Egon declared. "He told me to trust only a few and Kruno was one of them. Deo didn't say the same of everyone in this room. Kruno's sword is invaluable and he is now part of us. Don't question him again, but please Northerner, respond with respect."

"Did you hear how I addressed you?" Kruno asked.

Egon wasn't paying full attention, his brain was still scattered. He needed to be jolted and Kruno was about to do just that.

"DID YOU HEAR HOW I ADDRESSED YOU?" Kruno repeated, but louder than he should speak to a King.

"Yes, you called me great King and next time…" He was going to switch from being lectured to the lecturer but was cut off.

"I called you great King because you have no choice but to become great! An entire Kingdom awaits your move! The crown may be heavy but it will get lighter. Your dexterity will improve with it on and soon you would want it fused to your scull. If you still think it's too heavy, look around the room. You have so many friends to help you carry it. Even this guy." Kruno pointed to the man in the defence counsel who had made an earlier comment about him, just to irritate.

"You are the son of Deo. A great man bore an even greater son! He talked so highly of you for a reason. He knew you would be even more powerful than he was, a King that would never bow down, a leader that would laugh in the face of death."

Kruno started to walk around the room and all eyes followed him. "A great enemy descends upon us. The Black Knights will attack us here!" That fact was something few were ready to hear because safety still rested in the fact that it wasn't an absolute. "Turn your despair into anger, use that anger to trigger strength, use the strength to unleash a sword. Have confidence in Dryden, its military, its fortification, but most importantly have faith that God stands at our side. Every enemy soldier that falls will be for Deo."

Egon was definitely paying attention. The comments could be considered a hefty breach by the harshness of his tone, but Kruno didn't care. Egon stood up and looked in Kruno's direction.

"Now pick up that crown and place it where it belongs."

Egon looked around the room and saw many uncertain faces looking back. Bruno and Rizzian each had a chance to communicate via body language and did so with an approving head nod. He then looked to his own advisors, one of them was his best friend. His nod sealed the deal.

Slowly Egon placed the crown on his head. The moment triggered a room full of men with goosebumps.

With a moderate tone Kruno commanded, "Now say 'I am the King.'"

"I am the King."

"Say 'I am the King!'" he repeated, louder.

"I am the King!" Egon's back straightened and confidence filled his face.

"Louder!"

"I AM THE KING! I AM THE KING! I AM THE KING!"

The room broke into excitement and began to chant, "Long live King Egon!" over and over again.

After a while, the room finally calmed down as Egon motioned with his hand for the men to come to order.

"I would ask you to sit down but I feel that would be impossible. Too much energy, good energy remains. Bruno, we must start preparing for war!"

"First things first, we need to turn those little girlie men around. I will ride out and have a nice chat with any potential deserters."

Egon responded, "That I will take care of. I will address everyone. Rizzian, I could use your help to magnify my voice."

"Already a new man." Ivan leaned forward to Kruno. "This must be how you bed so many ladies, with motivational speeches. It's obviously not your looks. I couldn't figure it out, but now I get it." Kruno shook his head and rolled his eyes at Ivan's comments.

One after another the men in the room made suggestions, and like his father before him, Egon delegated.

Ivan had a turn, "I need twenty men."

"Why twenty men, for what?" Paul, Egon's best friend and advisor, responded.

"I can't answer that, I need you to trust me. Even in secrecy I can't tell even you Egon. Just understand this is highly risky, but with great risks comes great rewards."

"Interesting time to ask for twenty men from an already under-manned front, but Kruno trusts you and so I trust you. Paul, see to it that he gets what he needs."

They started to walk down the hallway when Paul spoke, "That is fine, but you will need to find one less — I am your first volunteer."

"I need warriors with great projectile weapon ability."

Paul pulled a knife from his hip sheath and let it fly straight into the air. "Forehead," he promised as he caught the tip of the blade with his fingers and tossed it twenty feet, lodging it into the head of a wooden statue.

"I like your style," Ivan said with a smile.

Ivan rode up to a small old house on the outskirts of Dryden's border. He felt great to be back to normal. Riding his Gret-chen seemed to enlighten his spirits even more.

"War comes to us soon, my Gret-chen, are you as excited as I am?" He spoke in Northern tongue.

The Gret-chen responded with a nod.

"Good boy, but first we have a thrilling task. We are going hunting for the largest of game."

The house was crude in its creation, constructed of daub which bound the wattles. The house looked to be in terrible condition, as if no maintenance had been done on it in years. The walls even had splits in the sides.

Must be lovely here in winter.

Ivan was warned about the person he was going to meet. He was just a shell of a man and the shell was tarnished. He needed to convince him to do something that would go against every grain in his body, but convincing this poor excuse for a man, for a human for that matter, was so critical. Ivan had no choice but to recruit him. This task was more geared towards Kruno's strengths, but Kruno wasn't to be involved in this adventure.

Ivan dismounted his Gret-chen and looked around. This person was probably mad after being isolated for so long with evil dreams circulating around his mind. A quick scan was needed to ensure there weren't any traps. Ivan wanted to make sure nothing was going to surprise him. A massive sword rested in a sheath straight down his back, the handle right behind his head. Not his typical weapon but one he enjoyed from time to time. Ivan was a master of all hand-held weapons, but a sword was the natural first choice for most warriors and one of the reasons he didn't use it often. Flails, maces, axes and war hammers gave him a strategic advantage over most who only practiced sword-to-sword combat. Nonetheless, this was his weapon today.

No stable, no horse, the road from his home has tonnes of grass popping up showing its lack of traffic. This guy might just be a quack. Who knows the last time he has interacted with anyone.

"Elmer, is that you?" a voice inquired from inside the house.

Ivan didn't answer at first as he took in a deep breath from the warming day. He tilted his head to the sun to catch a few of its radiant warm rays, something he hadn't done in a long time. His mind was free from La Caprata and he really hadn't spent much time enjoying his liberty. What he did like was the fact that action was to come with haste and he was thankful for the chance to war soon, but he still needed to appreciate his new freedom, even just for a moment.

"Elmer, if that is you, it's not funny to play games with me." The voice started to crack with fear.

"My name is Ivan and I seek to be heard."

"Leave, Ivan, please leave, you are not welcome here."

"I am coming in if you like it or not."

"Don't come in here, I am warning you."

Ivan unsheathed his sword just in case and pushed the door open with the tip of his weapon. The door creaked with every inch it moved. The inside was dark except for some streams of light that shot in through the spaces in the walls. It took a few moments for his eyes to adjust to the change in light. What was revealed was a disaster. One room cluttered from floor to ceiling with junk.

"Seburg, I am here for you…"

Out of the corner of his eye he saw an object tossed at him. He could tell it wasn't going to hit him and just stood still as it smashed against the floor to his side.

"That wasn't very smart, Seburg."

"I am sorry, don't kill me."

"Who said I was going to kill you?"

"You're a giant man who mysteriously enters my house with sword drawn and the first thing you say is 'I am here for you'. How do you expect me to respond?"

"Good point. Your aim is terrible by the way. Next time be more accurate and try throwing something bigger. If that hit me, it would have only pissed me off!"

Ivan's eyes adjusted fully and he could see Seburg in a corner, curled up on the floor.

This might be more difficult than I expected. How much man is left in him?

"If you're not going to throw anything anymore, I will put away my sword."

Seburg shook his head, identifying himself as harmless. Ivan re-sheathed his weapon and moved to open one of the wooden windows.

"What are you crazy? Don't open that window! Do you want to kill me?" Seburg screamed in alarm,

"Relax, the window can stay shut. What the heck is wrong with you?"

Seburg didn't respond to Ivan's question, but asked, "What do you want?"

"We need your help. We need you to do something vitally important for the Silver Allegiance."

"Nope, I don't think so," he whined.

Ivan was irritated and didn't like being told no. This was why this was a better job for Kruno. He had patience and an ability to use his words to get people to do as he wished. Ivan breathed heavily to release his stress.

"Sit up here Seburg." Ivan pointed to the only table in the little house. He tipped his chair forward, letting all the items piled up fall to the ground.

"No, I don't think so."

"I assume you can deduce that I don't get told no very often. That is twice in a row. Sit up here now!"

The cowardly man slowly made his way to the chair, neatly placed each item that was stacked on it in another pile and sat down. Ivan sat down as well.

Ivan could see that Seburg's skin was bubbled like the effects of leprosy, but with a deep purple hue. One of his cheeks was bad but nothing compared to his arms and neck. He had experienced a terrible burn and probably still felt the physical and emotional pain of something so traumatic.

Ivan paused as his eyes made their final focus and examined his injuries. The man was far from any threat to anyone. He was small, very skinny, badly burnt and an emotional wreck.

"I know what I look like, could you stop looking at me like that?"

"Do you want to tell me what happened?" Ivan knew what happened but wanted to hear it from him. The story had to be exciting.

"No, next question."

Ivan's chair gave a warning of its impending collapse by slightly bowing. It wasn't long enough for him to take action, but at least let him know he was heading to the ground. With a snap, two of the legs gave way and he hit the ground. Seburg chuckled for a second. Pissed off, Ivan stood up, grabbed the broken chair and tossed it hard towards the wall. It was a perfect shot if he was planning to hit a brittle window. The wood exploded through the other side and the daylight hit the mentally disturbed Seburg. As if hit by a beam of fire, he fell to the ground and screamed.

Scrambling to the darkest part of the room, he avoided the light as if it was cursed. He yelled at Ivan, "What's wrong with you? Ahhh!"

Ivan walked up to him and stood looking down at the helpless man. He had had enough of this game.

"King Egon is preparing for war."

Seburg responded pushing the tears away from his voice. "King Egon?"

The news obviously hadn't travelled to his pigsty of a shelter. Ivan educated him on what had happened.

"What… Egon is now King? The Black Knights are going to invade us?"

"That's what I said." Ivan gave him a few seconds to let it sink in then continued, "We don't have much time, so you need to compose yourself right now."

"What does Dryden want with me?" he said with confusion. He was a man with no confidence and a torn, destroyed self-image.

"There is only one thing that you can assist with in your state — information." Seburg didn't understand what he was taking about. He tried to work it out in his mind. Ivan waited as he knew he would eventually get there.

It hit Seburg at once. He knew there was only one thing he could help with, the very thing that kept him hidden, what had destroyed his mind and body. The very thought almost made him vomit. He looked up and shook his head with conviction.

"No, no way! I will never…"

Ivan's patience ran out, time wasn't on his side. He reached down and picked the injured little man up by the neck and lifted him with one arm against the wall. Seburg attempted to defend himself and started to hit Ivan. Ivan barely moved. The impact was nothing more than a small child's punch.

"Look at you! You are so weak. A thirteen-year-old girl could take you down. You are weak because you let yourself be this way. Look down towards your leg. It is all in your head." His bare skin was illuminated by a beam of sunlight and he didn't realize it. "I have the word of Egon, your King, and if that's not good enough to motivate you. I have something that might."

"Are you going to kill me? Fine, kill me, it is a better fate."

"I am not the one you have to worry about. I would kill you clean and with ease, but that kind of death is for brave warriors, not cowards."

Seburg didn't know how to take his words but fear crept in.

Ivan turned with him still locked in one of his hands, took a few steps, opened the door and launched him outside.

Petrified of being outside — something he hadn't done in years — and of the sun, he began to yell. His yelling stopped moments later as his eyes focused on a massive grey beast staring at him with a large jaw.

"He is really hungry but obedient. With a snap of my finger he will start tearing at your flesh."

Ivan's Gret-chen looked at him strangely; he only slightly understood what his master said. It had a tough enough time with Northern tongue let alone common tongue. The Gret-chen was pretty sure Ivan said that he would eat the man, but Gret-chens would never eat a human, they looked too much like their Northern masters.

"I don't see why you would want to go there?" Seburg said carefully, not moving a muscle, attempting to avoid triggering the beast into frenzy.

"Well make up your damn mind. Don't do it just because you are about to be consumed by my beast. It's time to clear your name. This deed will not go unnoticed. Your family will once again hold your name in high regard, as opposed to shame. Regain your manhood. Make a stand and not because you have no choice, but because you challenge your fear."

Hmmm, that was pretty damn good. I must have learned a thing or two from Kruno.

Ivan approached Dryden and saw the city was bustling with activity. The activity wasn't driven by commerce or entertainment. It was the preparation for war that caused so much movement. For whatever reason, the people weren't fleeing Dryden anymore and Ivan had assumed that Kruno had something to do with it. He was partially right, but he had no clue that Kruno was on a mission of his own and was no longer in Dryden.

All surrounding residents were called into Dryden. Military men that were posted close to the city had been summoned and now marched to add to the infantry count. Military planners had scoured the land, discussing a myriad of things from battle structure, to training, to overall strategy.

Dryden had a few challenges, but one of them wasn't resources. Their armouries had massive stockpiles because all central war planning began in Dryden. The city was also self-sufficient. It could survive for months without relying on outside assistance and it boasted impregnable walls.

That combination was always Dryden's defence strategy. An opposing army wouldn't have the time to penetrate before other divisions moved in from other parts of the Kingdom. The Dark Realm wasn't foolish and knew this, and must have had a solution for Dryden's defences. For this reason Kruno and Ivan were on different missions, but with similar objectives.

Ivan and Seburg rode on the back of his Gret-chen toward a group of men armed and battle-ready. Paul, Egon's best friend and advisor, saw the great Northerner from a distance and commanded the group to stand at attention. They were all very young except for two who bore the insignia of SAEs. Every one of them was excited. The energy was tremendous and all were in good shape.

Ivan stopped and commanded Seburg off his Gret-chen.

"Paul, they look like good men, but just barely men at that, except for the two Elites I see."

"They are strong and well skilled in many areas of battle, including weapons like bows and spears. They have no fear and are excited to go to battle with you leading them." Paul defended his choice in men.

Ivan shook his head slowly up and down showing his acceptance. "Good, who here has the best skills with a spear?" Three of them raised their hands but one spoke up, "I am the best!"

Ivan was amused by his comment and liked his confidence.

"That tree." Ivan pointed to a tree well off in the distance.

The young man, full of energy took two steps and fired it. The spear arched up, and even though it had a great line, it landed short of its destination. The man looked disappointed.

"What about you?" He pointed to one of the Elites, "I am sure you could hit that target."

"Nope, I won't even bother tossing it. It would be a waste of energy. Nobody could hit that from here."

"You are a good group, that I can tell." Ivan smiled. "Don't worry about your toss, it was deadly accurate and had great distance. Sometimes you have to know your limits. Where we are going, distance probably won't matter, but we have limitations. We also have some challenges that we mustn't let get to us — pain and fear. There is no room for either."

All focused on the esteemed Northerner. Pain and fear, the two words twisted through each of their minds.

"Every one of these guys volunteers?" Ivan asked.

"Yes, everyone, but they are also handpicked."

"Did you get what I asked for?"

Paul turned and whistled. A covered wagon pulled by a horse was presented. Paul explained, "Everyone is armed well but just in case you wanted something more, I had the blacksmith prepare a little display."

The canvas was removed and a display of weapons was exposed. Ivan's face lit up and Paul knew he had done well. Ivan took a look at his men, did a quick inventory and then started to grab items. Ivan plucked wooden shaft spears, metal spears — which was strange — a war hammer and battle axes.

"Every man has a shield, a primary weapon, daggers and either a spear or a bow. How can they carry any more into battle?" Paul asked.

Ivan didn't answer the question. Instead he remembered that Seburg hadn't been introduced to the group. He grabbed a spear and a shield and tossed to it to him.

"Everyone, I forgot to introduce the twenty-first member of our group, Seburg, our guide and warrior."

The introduction was somewhat bogus, but Ivan knew that Seburg needed it. The group wasn't stupid, but decided against asking any questions.

"Okay, let's hear your names, warriors of Dryden and say them with dignity, because your names will be carved into the walls of this great city, because your families will walk by and point with pride at their son or husband or father with honour."

Each of the nineteen men said their name and Ivan listened with intent. He liked his group. Most of them were rather young, but he could use their energy and lack of understanding of what was involved with the upcoming battle. He knew that many would die, possibly all of them, maybe he himself but it didn't matter. The most feared beast would be the target. The excitement of the battle was building in him like an inferno.

"We march north-east on foot," he said to the group and then continued in Northern tongue, "Sorry my Gret-chen, you must stay here.

I will catch you back on the battlefield. Find Sven, he will instruct you on how to proceed."

Armed over and above what was comfortable, as if facing outlandish odds, twenty-one men marched out to a destination only two knew. The rest assumed they were going to fight many, but they hunted only one.

Paul moved up to Ivan with one of the Elites. They marched at a fast pace, just short of running.

"Ivan, you asked me to get this," Paul said, holding a thick chain with spikes and hooks on it, waiting for an explanation.

"Ah, good, I can't believe I almost forgot about this. That would have been stupid eh?"

Paul continued, hoping for an answer, "I am a little confused. He said that this would hold the strength of two gargoyles. Are we hunting gargoyles?"

"No, we aren't hunting gargoyles."

"Thank God, that would have been one terrible battle." Gargoyles were rated second on the list of most powerful creatures. "Who are we attacking then?"

"I want you two guys to be my commanders on the field. Once I confer with Seburg, I will give you more details, until then, no more information."

Paul was irritated that Ivan didn't respond to him. He wasn't used to people excluding him from any plan, but bit his tongue, knowing full well that an argument wouldn't produce any better results. He stayed silent and faded back.

"You are Dav, correct?" Ivan asked the SAE.

"So the ladies scream."

They talked for a while. Being the elders of the group gave them common ground. Dav waited until they breached the plane of the forest so their voices were a little more muffled, "I know where we are headed, great Northerner."

Ivan looked at him with an inquisitive eye.

"If Seburg is important then there is only one reason why. Most don't know who he is, but I do. Your weapon selections, call for warriors skilled with missile weapons and your elusive behaviour all point in one direction."

"Dav, your ability to deduce my plan tells me you are the right man for the job."

Ivan pushed a branch away from his face as they navigated through the forest, "Don't be misled, Ivan, I just know where we are going. I have no idea how you plan to be successful, but I did bring something that just might assist."

Neither of them confirmed out loud where they were heading, but Dav confirmed he knew their destination when he pulled out a jar with a milky thick paste in it.

"This gel resists flame, I have used it when on battering ram duty. When the main door needs opening and I am the guy for the job. This stuff has helped when the bastards toss burning tar our way. Let me know when you want this applied, just don't ask me to rub it on you. I wouldn't want you to get all excited." They both laughed.

"None for me, thanks."

"Take a look at Seburg and you tell me if you want it on or not? It will help give you an extra few moments before you crisp up."

"No." Ivan let Dav know he wasn't interested in his paste.

Dav changed subjects, "Are you going to tell the men where we are headed? It doesn't go more than a few moments, before one of them questions where we are heading."

"Not tonight, tonight I need everyone to get a good rest. If they knew where we were heading their minds would race and nobody would sleep properly. The task we have before us will be next to impossible, we don't need any disadvantages. Don't tell anyone what lies ahead. I will tell them tomorrow. They need sleep tonight but they will also need to digest and mentally prepare for what is to come. Tomorrow will give them that time."

"You know where we are headed, how are you going to sleep tonight?" Dav asked, figuring he knew the answer, but was excited to hear it anyway.

"Like a baby." The answer was exactly what Dav wanted to hear. No fear from his leader.

Just before dusk Ivan commanded them to make camp. He was extremely elusive and let nobody know where they were going.

"Make a fire to cook our dinner, but it must be extinguished once we are done."

"Why don't we keep a fire for the night? We will be able to see better. It will also keep us warm and keep unwanted creatures away," one of the men asked.

"Nope, no fire, animals are the least of our worries."

"What are we worried about?" Another man jumped in as the entire group listened to Ivan, hoping he was going to shed some light on their destination.

"Fire is a bad idea, we don't want that kind of draw. No fire for the same reason we aren't taking a carved path," Ivan said, not answering the question as they had hoped.

"I have been wondering that myself. I love getting close with nature, but a path would be much easier."

"The Dark Realm's army is moving towards Dryden. It will probably reach battle position in a few days. We wouldn't want to run into them, would we?"

"I would love to meet them, carve me up a Black Knight." With sword raised, a strong declaration emanated from the crowd. The excited soldier swung his sword around his head and smashed it into a tree, mimicking the end of his mock battle with a fictitious Black Knight. Most of the men raised their voice with enthusiasm.

Ivan smiled at the camaraderie.

"You will have your chance and there is nothing more I would rather do than confront them head on, but I have learned that meeting on our terms is a better idea."

"So we hide from Black Knights?" one of the men asked, partly testing their leader.

"No, we wait for them."

Everyone loved his response and respected Ivan for many reasons. Number one was his sheer size. Secondly, Egon had commanded them to follow him, but most importantly was his name. Everyone knew of Ivan or the great Northerner who travelled with Kruno.

They chatted among themselves.

"Make the fire, cook the food and then put it out. Once dark hits, we go silent. Enjoy good conversation until that point." He motioned to Seburg to follow him. "Oh yeah, and don't be cheap when you make my share. I am sure you know you don't get this big on small portions."

Seburg and Ivan sat just beyond earshot. Small talk would probably have been a good approach, but that wasn't his style, so Ivan got right to the point.

"I need to know everything."

"I don't know if I can," Seburg commented and Ivan attempted to exercise patience.

"Well, you don't have any choice."

"You don't understand, I miss my home, I want to go back now."

"You miss the misery of that shack? You miss your confined nonexistence? Snap out of it. That life doesn't exist anymore. You are free now. Now tell me!"

"I don't know if I can do it. I think I have to run, I can't stay, I can't face it."

"You run and everyone dies here and the Silver Allegiance loses critical swords. Actually, everyone will die but me, and I will hunt you down and make you truly understand pain."

Seburg believed every word, and had thought about taking off several times, but that idea was no longer a possibility. He hated where he was but had no choice. He had given up on life a long time ago. He had no family or friends. There was just one person that still helped him, Elmer, a friend from the past who took pity on him and really was the only reason he didn't starve to death.

"You're not very nice."

"I am not overly concerned about that"

"I don't know if I remember it right."

"Don't lie to me, Seburg. It is burned into your memory."

Seburg began to tell him the story. Ivan had no sympathy as he listened. He didn't care when Seburg started to cry. He listened for details and after he was finished, he drilled him for as much information as he could. Their battle plan, the life of twenty-one men, would be based on the scared little man's story and its accuracy.

"I am sorry, that's all I have, I can't remember anymore. Let's see how your memory is in a situation like that," Seburg responded after the inquiries got too detailed.

"I can tell you the weapons of anyone we pass by, just by looking at them once. It doesn't matter what situation I am in. I am always aware." Ivan waited and then asked him to tell the story again.

"AGAIN, why? No, once was enough."

"Again! Now!"

Seburg broke into story once again. When he was done, Ivan commanded the story be told once more. His rationale was to make it flow from his tongue, remove the shock of what frightened him and drain the emotion out of it. He knew it would work. It also had a therapeutic benefit as well.

Darkness arrived. The fire had been completely extinguished. The food was good and even though more inquiries came his way, he didn't reveal any more information.

"After these words, we go silent. Four man contingents, two groups of two, one hour watches, rotate and we rise just before dawn."

The command was set in motion. They moved as trained men should.

Morning came quickly and everyone seemed to sleep well. Ivan knew that was critical to their success and was pleased that his strategy of remaining silent was being exercised by all. Breakfast passed with only a few whispers. Before long they were on the move and getting closer to the point of no return. Most of the men were young, and keeping them silent became a more difficult task as the day moved on. Ivan allowed small chatter to continue, but made sure the decibels were low enough so their voices wouldn't travel more than a few feet.

They maintained their course, parallel to the road just deep enough in the bush to provide cover, but close enough to keep an eye on what marched on it. Ivan always took the vanguard and with each new groove he found a place where they could activate stealth if it was needed. It was part of who he was, always analyzing.

The path they were on elevated for a brief period of time. Ivan's mind conducted defence analysis as he walked, conceptually preparing for battle. As his mind worked, something off in the distance could be heard.

He commanded his troops to stop and pointed to a dense pack of evergreens. With hand motions he instructed another four of them from the rear flank to slide down towards the road on their stomachs and prepare for an up close and personal battle. He in turn did the same with another two men. The rest pushed their way through the dense evergreens, each getting jammed by hundreds of needles. Within seconds the entire group was repositioned and almost impossible to notice. Ivan looked back to see how their ability was to camouflage themselves and he was impressed.

Random sloppy chatter came from a group approaching them along the road. They were either a not a threat, stupid or over-confident. If it was the Dark Realm they were too close to Dryden to have such open communication. Ivan inched to a position where he could see the advancing group. Sudden movement was a bad idea. He used his peripheral vision and even slowed his eye movements. The grass at the edge of the road was more than tall enough, providing excellent cover, perfect for an ambush. Its one drawback was it would be difficult to communicate with the four men on the other flank. Ivan had to signal back to the majority of the men in the evergreens and then they would pass it on. Hand signals were good but nothing like a verbal command, and even verbal communication can get distorted when passing from one to another. All in all it was a great test for his group of soldiers. Ivan passed the message to do nothing until his command.

He couldn't see them yet but by analyzing voices, feet and hooves he knew there were no more than five of them. *Okay... what do we have here? There aren't a lot of you. For your sake I hope you are not part of the Dark Realm. Kruno has commanded that you are our enemy. If you are one of them, then you are in the wrong place at the wrong time. Even if you are Black Knights, which I doubt because of the foolish chatter, we are going to drop you and drop you hard.*

Black Knights were the leading soldiers of Ivan's enemy. Five Black Knights could cause a serious problem. Even though they were outnumbered, flanked from an elevated position, with missile and close combat weapons, they were extremely skilled. He was sure if they were engaged they would kill some of his men, maybe even all of his men. He didn't want to lose even one head. He needed them all.

He waited and watched as five men moved with relative haste along the path. Three of them were on horseback. He heard discussions of Pra and the greatness of Zoran. Ivan could see through the reeds that they were Dark Realm soldiers, making them a target too tempting to let walk by. They were doing something for the impending invasion and it would be a disservice not to attack. At least that's what Ivan told himself. He could see by their apparel that they weren't Black Knights. The two walking were low on the scale, potentially lower than infantry.

One of the men on horseback wasn't paying much attention to his surroundings when he heard, "Drop the horses!"

His mind raced, trying to digest what was happening. Quickly scanning the surroundings, he noticed movement in a cluster of trees and realized he had taken this journey too lightly. He attempted to criticize his decision for accepting this mission and also for not being more alert during it. His thoughts hit a barrier as a bunch of arrows leapt to flight from the trees and flew toward him. His horse took all but one arrow which dug into his leg. Just in front of him one of the other men on horseback hit the ground with deadly arrows planted into his steed. The third horse raced forward with only one arrow in its backside.

His horse collapsed as well, and as he fell he watched a massive man vault from the bush and the polished steel of his blade bounced a ray towards his eyes. On the ground he commanded his men to arm themselves but it was too late. Ivan was already on them. From the trees, Ivan's group watched with awe as he cut two of them down with a few strokes.

Ivan pointed to the man that raced away. The injury to the horse was beneficial in this case for his rider because the pain caused the horse to bolt forward. Ivan pointed in his direction and one of the group of four fired his spear. It happened to be the warrior who had misjudged the tree at the start of this journey. In his mind, he had a lot to make up for. Taking only a moment to adjust the trajectory, he let a spear loose.

The man racing away thought he had cleared enough ground to save him from peril but he was wrong. His beating heart was split by a spear through his back. Death was instantaneous as he slumped from his horse and fell to the ground.

The two remaining Dark Realm soldiers weren't experienced and also weren't used to the very real feeling that death was a moment away and were surprised by the quickness of the battle. They assumed they were protected by their armed escort. They stood each with a small flail to their side, a weapon they really didn't know how to use and watched the Northerner walk towards them, who was supported by another six armed men. Before anyone could speak, they both tossed their weapons aside. One of them dropped to his knees.

"That was easy. It doesn't look like they were Black Knights," Dav spoke.

"No, they would have been wearing different armour if they were," Ivan answered. He then turned to the one man still standing and told him to drop to his knees as well. He put his blade to his neck, "So, anyone else behind you?"

The man was obviously petrified. He didn't mouth a word but just shook his head no.

"Paul, have their hands bound and find out what they were doing."

"What is your destination?" Paul inquired.

"Why should we speak? As soon as we tell you anything you will kill us. Our leverage is gone the minute we answer your question."

"Good point!" Dav whispered to Ivan as they watched Paul.

Paul felt some pressure to be successful at the task assigned.

"Well that may be true, but how you die is something worth negotiating." Paul looked to Ivan who gave him a nod of acceptance.

Leaving Paul to his own devices, he looked to the man who had tossed the spear and waved him over. "Great shot!"

"Thanks, and by the way, we are all impressed with your swordsmanship. You destroyed the want-to-be Black Knights with ease."

Ivan had solidified himself among the group as a truly great warrior. Most had only heard of him, but didn't know if the stories were true — they obviously were.

"Go grab your spear and see if it is still useful."

Ivan looked up to the men in the woods who hadn't moved. He held up two fingers towards the group in the trees, pointed to his eyes with the same split fingers and redirected them down the road. He had commanded them to scout the area.

Dav walked with Ivan as they moved away from the battle group, "Good group of men with strong archery and spear skills but most importantly, they listen."

"I agree and the last thing is the most important. All of the skill in the world wouldn't be worth much if they didn't listen." Ivan pointed to the men they had just engaged. "What do you think of these men?"

"The first three were in training to be Black Knights, but obviously weren't there yet. They were several years away and many milestones from their goal. The other two are nothing to be worried about. They may have some skill but little hand-to-hand combat abilities. I am pretty sure that this was just a scouting mission, intelligence gathering."

"I won't ask how you know all of this and assume you are right. If you are right, what stage of scouting is this?"

"We study the Dark Realm a lot, that's how I know," Dav Replied. "They are our most adept adversaries. If I had to put silver on it, I think this invasion is coming sooner rather than later. This is a late stage scouting mission. They are just checking to see what our final defences will be. If I had to guess, within a few days this road will be occupied by one massive army."

Ivan looked around at the empty road as he processed the information and developed a strategy. "Okay then, we move double time."

"Ivan," Paul called, motioning for him to come. Paul explained what he had learned from his interrogation which confirmed Dav's conclusions. "What shall we do? I am not in the business to kill unarmed, untrained men like this. I say we tie them up and feed them improper information."

"Fine, but make sure they are messed up a little more. Let God choose their fate."

Beaten up and naked the two men were tied to a tree. They would become either food for a wild beast or would be found by the marching army of the Dark Realm, probably only a few days away.

Written in blood on their chests was the taunt, "Hi Zoran, Love Hot House."

Dav could see the look on Ivan's face which was one of confusion. He decided to explain. "When we are weak, let the enemy think we are strong. Hot House is the northern division of our army, and by far our fiercest troops. Zoran assumes he will walk on to our city that has for the most part fled, at the worst he might have to fight all of Dryden's divisions. Nowhere in his battle plan does he assume that Hot House would be here. It might just throw the bastard for a loop."

It was a smart move. Zoran's strategy, like all other great military minds, relied on accurate intelligence; battle compositions, structure and attacking formations are all customized based on their enemy. If Zoran really believed that Hot House was supporting Dryden, it could compromise his entire plan. It was a long shot, but a good solid move and worth a try.

They hiked until late afternoon on a path that was perpendicular to the road. The terrain was thick with vegetation and would have been intense for untrained individuals, but to this unit, save Seburg, it wasn't difficult at all. Seburg struggled on several occasions and wanted to complain but said nothing. He was part of a group, and even though he wasn't involved in conversation, he was in a social setting, something he oddly enjoyed to his surprise.

The group's questions got more intense as they wanted to know where they were headed. Minutes would pass and another question would creep up. Ivan knew he couldn't hold out much longer.

They weren't far from a clearing that led to Rice Lake. Climbing up a small incline, the trees had thinned out leaving a perfect place to stop and hydrate.

"Okay, Ivan, we have had enough with the secrecy, where are you leading us?" The blunt question was asked.

The time was as good as it was going to get because the reason for his secrecy would be discovered shortly. They were very inquisitive, but he assumed some of them would want to take back the question, once they heard the answer.

"Gather round, everyone. Keep quiet and listen to Seburg."

Many had wondered why he was with them, but decided not to bother asking. He didn't fit their mould. Seburg was shy, reserved and not used to talking to anyone but Elmer. He shifted as he knew it was his cue to speak. With respect, the men dropped to one knee to listen.

"Several years ago I marched in your shoes. We had prepared for what was to come. A bunch of us headed up the mountain in search of riches, vast riches. One battle and none of us would ever have to work another day in our lives." He had their undivided attention and continued, "Ten men, foolish mission. Back then I was a lot more of a man, I think. Now I resemble a prune."

"He does sort of resemble a prune," one man whispered; the few that heard him chuckled.

"We hunted a creature that we knew would have hoards of treasure. We searched for the dragon's lair in Rice Mountain." Everyone from Dryden knew that a dragon lived in Rice Mountain, but only a few started to deal with the fact that this might be their destination as well. "The entrance to its lair is easy to find, almost like it wants it that way."

"Of course it wants it that way, stupid prey might walk right into its den and *slam*, they are dragon food."

Dav looked to him and gave a slight head shake, indicating no more interruptions.

"We walked into a dark cavern, our torches lit and pumped for battle. The lair is like a big bowl, tons of gold, jewels and weapons lay strewn about, accumulated from decades of hunting. There is probably enough to buy half of Xavier's Cluster. We charged forward and didn't see it at first, but the dragon knew we were on our way. I don't know how, maybe it smelt us, or heard us or maybe it was magic."

A few more of the men were starting to realize that this might be there destiny, but pulled the thought from their minds in order to focus.

"Anyway, the entire cavern is lit from a huge hole directly above the lair. Inside, our torches weren't needed. One of my friends, I can't remember his name, yelled out, 'Where is the bastard?' It was a stupid move. On the off chance that it didn't know we were coming, it knew then and ambushed us. Within a flash, several of them were burned badly from its intense blast of fire. It was so hot that I felt it meters away. I turned to see this huge winged beast in flight. It didn't attempt to get away. It just wanted a better position to put its tail on a collision course with more of us. I was on the end and for a second just stared at it foolishly. If anyone had a chance to strike it, that was me, but I did nothing. I couldn't move. Its massive jaw had so many teeth and its eyes stared at me with a creepy calm. It wasn't afraid at all. In its mind, killing us was like stepping on rats. He eliminated everyone in a line working his way to me. The last of them was split in several places, impaled by its tail which swung hard along the path where we stood."

"Hold on, what path are you talking about? You are elevated from the ground but on a path?" Paul interrupted.

"Yes we were above the floor several meters, many paths led to this spot. Like a ring around it, they were all connected, like floors if you will."

Ivan was pleased at his composure. Not a tear was shed telling the story. When he told Ivan the story, he had broken down several times by this point; Ivan's plan had worked — Seburg was desensitized.

Seburg noticed the focused attention he was getting. These great warriors looked at him with interest. He could see their minds attempting to see him in this battle. Dragon stories always had this effect because of how terrifying and respected they were.

"Its tail, with long spikes on it, had collided with their legs killing none of them, I don't think, but injuring them badly. We could see it was impossible to hit it with our swords. It was too far back, suspended in flight, we just couldn't reach it. One of my comrades tossed a spear, but with a quick shift of its wings it went right past it. Still I stood frozen. I had a spear but didn't even pull it out. The dragon inhaled and we knew what was coming next. The remaining boys locked their shields, bent down and took the flame. The flame stopped and it was on them. With speed, it closed its jaw around the shield of the man in the centre and bent it with ease, the thick metal-cased shield was no match for its jaw. Then, with power, its arms smashed the other two men backward into the rock. Even though they defended the blow, the strength of the beast lifted them off the ground. The man in the middle found his shield collapsed around him, pinning his arms in hot metal. His scream still haunts me. With a flick up and over its head he went flying into the pit, arms locked and even though dazed, it would have been a painful drop."

A few of them noticed a shift in the trees. It was strange because it wasn't windy at all. A few men broke concentration and let their minds wander. *The leaves seemed to shift in fear.* It appeared that even the trees were afraid of dragons.

"Both men still kept their shields up and were probably dazed themselves. They sat, legs straight out without protection. The dragon smashed its fists down on their knees. Their bones buckled and the noise was terrible. Just to make sure they weren't going anywhere, it torched them. I didn't see what happened after that, I ran like a little girl as fast as possible. It must have seen me run. I made it to the mouth of the tunnel and I heard the dreadful inhale. A moment later I was farther down the path, but all I could feel was the intense heat. The flames gathered around me. The pain was excruciating, but it couldn't overwhelm the fear, so even though I was on fire, my legs kept on moving. I eventually collapsed and fell into a pile of sand which took care of the flames. I knew the tunnel was too narrow for it to fit through, so I waited for the pain to stop, but it seemed to get worse. It never subsided, it still hurt years later, it still hurts now."

The audience was silent. Most of them had figured out why they were told the story, but one wanted it confirmed.

"Great story my man, but what does that have to do with us?"

"That lair is our destiny. We are attacking that same dragon," Paul explained to the crowd as he deduced the plan.

Everyone looked to Ivan, hoping he would correct this assumption, but Ivan said nothing. They were going to hunt a dragon. Even the most courageous had to recheck their bravery. Some accepted their fate in minutes, for others it would take the entire night, for some it wouldn't be accepted at all.

They were silent for a long time, minutes seemed like hours. It was tough for any warrior of any race to come to terms with such an assault. So few could ever talk about encountering a dragon because most were killed. The silence was finally broken.

"Well, this should be a barrel of fun, thanks for the invite," one of the men said aloud.

"Okay… I can accept the challenge but what is the point?" another asked. "How does this help with the war effort?"

"Great question. Anyone want to field the answer?" Ivan asked.

Nobody said a thing, until, "We are here for its blood."

"Does that even work? I heard it's just an old tale."

"Well, I guess we are going to find out if it is real or fake."

"Some gamble, and if you are wrong then Dryden loses our swords. Even if we slay this thing, sorry, *when* we slay it, how are we going to get back in time? I think we have all figured out by the time we will be toe to toe with the dragon, the battle for our beloved Dryden will have already started."

"Don't you know all of the effects when consuming dragon's blood? We will get home a lot quicker than we got here," another called out from the crowd.

Ivan called Paul and Dav to his side. Out of earshot he commented, "Divide them into two camps. Paul you take one and Dav the other. Calm your men down. Get their heads ready for battle and then spell the plan out to them."

"Do we have a plan?"

"No, not yet," Ivan responded.

"Great, perfect." Paul shook his head.

A few of the men had encircled Seburg, and even though they thought he was a coward for leaving, they wanted more information. Most asked unhealthy questions like its size and ability to terrorize. The truth was that the dragon's size was always blown out of proportion and they stood about two and half times the size of an average man. They were big and powerful, but not as big as the storytellers made them out to be.

"What do we know?" Ivan asked.

"We know it's a mean bastard, that is for sure," Paul commented first.

"Not what we are looking for. Come on, look to details that can help us." Ivan was teaching the young lad how to pull useful information from a story. "The battle is won before it starts. Dav, please start."

"Aren't you a Northerner? Don't you just charge into battle?"

"It may look that way, but we have a plan… well most times. Anyway, I have learned a few things from Kruno over the years. Now back to the question."

"His lair is deep with an area that is connected by each tunnel. Shaped like a bowl, it has a significant drop, enough to seriously hurt a man and it's also within his fire range, but taller than the dragon itself."

"See Paul, what we are looking for? We know we can get a height advantage on this beast from the levels. If grounded we have a chance to hit him hard with a barrage of spears and arrows."

Paul attempted to add something, "We also know that the tunnel is lit so we won't need torches."

"Good, this is important and Seburg's friends were stupid for bringing them. The dragon's weakness is in their hearing. They have spectacular sight, a strong sense of smell, but weak hearing. It would have smelt the torches long before they entered its den. Okay, what else?"

Dav jumped in again, "It's fast and nimble in flight and has a spiked tail. It has intense heat, but like most dragons, its first blow is by far the most menacing."

"It likes to use everything, including its powerful jaw," Paul advised, getting the hang of it.

Ivan finished off the discovery period, "The tunnels are about a ten minute walk from the entrance to the middle of its lair. What I know from dragons is they feed almost every day and leave the den at least once a day. The dragon's entire ambush strategy is pivotal on its ability to fly. From the bottom of the lair only its flames can hit us. Here is the plan." Ivan started to draw in the dirt — a picture of the den.

"We will be positioned in these areas, utilizing all entrances. The number one objective is to remove its ability to fly. You guys have to take care of that. Number two is to shut down its two most powerful offensive weapons, flame and its jaw. I will take care of that. Once we have accomplished these tasks, all remaining missile weapons will be used on a fish in a barrel and then we charge."

"You will take care of that?" Dav said with eyebrows raised

"Yes, I will take care of that."

"Okay," Dav looked to Paul, letting him know he thought Ivan was out of his mind.

Ivan spelled out the remaining details for the battle plan and told them to go see their men.

"Okay, sounds crazy, but okay," Paul said to both of them.

"We travel this morning, before sunrise we will be on the fringe of its lair. This is a good time to get some shut eye."

Like magic, Ivan fell asleep. He was always able to sleep. This impressed the men just as much as his earlier ability to wield his sword.

Two men started to chatter, looking at Ivan, "I am shocked that he can sleep at a time like this."

"I guess when you're his size dragons don't frighten you."

"He is big but not standing next to a dragon. Even he must be afraid of the battle to come."

Ivan snored a little.

"Doesn't look like it to me."

"Well, I never thought I would actually fight a dragon. As a kid we acted it out all of the time, but in all reality I didn't really want to do it."

"At least we are going into battle with a leader like him. It is somewhat comforting. The plan sounds strong but could easily be tripped up."

They looked to Seburg who sat against a tree base awkwardly slumped over, twitching chronically. The two continued.

"I tell you what, I don't want to end up like him. I would rather die than live with those burns."

"That wouldn't have happened to you my good friend, you are no coward."

"This challenge will certainly be the test of that."

Over time, the men started to shift their psyche. For these two it had already begun, a transformation from fear to acceptance, from acceptance to confidence.

"Time to get pumped up, let's snuff a dragon! You going to sleep?"

"Not a freaking chance."

Ivan awoke with a tap on his shoulder from Dav.

"Is everyone ready?"

"Just about, can I ask you a question? Why are you doing this? I mean, we are very pleased you're on our side, but you're a Northerner and fighting a battle that even local Silver Allegiance are fleeing."

Ivan squeezed his eyes, transforming back to reality, "Kruno is fighting for you, so I am fighting for you."

"Okay, Kruno is a great guy and all, but we are about to attempt to destroy the world's most proficient killer, in order to rush back to a battle where we will be sorely undermanned. It doesn't make that much sense to me."

"Kruno is my friend, like a brother."

"I have lots of friends."

"Not like him." Ivan was pulled up to his feet by Dav.

"Would you charge off a cliff if he jumped first?" Dav asked, slightly offended.

"Nope, I would stop him if it was certain death, but if he wanted to jump off a cliff to land on the back of a dragon, I would be right behind him."

Ivan changed the subject when he saw some men putting on their leather armour. "No need for that yet soldiers. Actually, no need for clothing. First thing we do is swim in Rice Lake. We smell and a washing will help disguise us from its sense of smell. Stealth is imperative."

Dav thought to himself, *Always pictured Northerners to be dumber than Ivan. His vocabulary is decent and his forward thinking is impressive.*

One of the men shouted, "Good, now I can finally walk beside Walker. He desperately needs to bathe."

The men chuckled and Walker responded.

"Come on, John, you have smelt something worse on a regular basis, how about your wife after I have used and abused her?"

The group found the comment amusing. John charged Walker. The two men fell backward into a shrub. Walker couldn't stop laughing and John eventually smirked and stood up. The noise level wasn't ideal, but Ivan knew it was an important distraction for the men.

"Okay, men, don't take everything off until you are in the water, I wouldn't want you to have penis envy for the rest of your lives. I carry quite the package," Ivan stated with a confident look.

The group continued to laugh and make their own jokes in kind. They had the last of their fun swimming in almost pitch black. Ivan watched the young lads full of life and realized most, maybe all, weren't coming back. He smiled because their deaths would be in glory.

The silence was ever present, nobody had talked for hours. Strict rules were in effect, and they weren't going to be breached. All of the men were camouflaged. Ivan had an idea of where the opening was on the mountain, and he stared at it through thick brush. He monitored every blink, cognisant of every move. He waited for the dragon to appear. A dragon hunts from the sky and swoops down with razor sharp vision on a target that usually didn't see it coming. They can easily see through trees, but Ivan banked on it leaving prior to sunrise. Since they would be under the cover of darkness, he assumed they were safe. The campaign was over if the dragon did a little swoop around the mountain before heading out. It would be a good way to avoid the risk of invasion. He assumed that the dragon, being at the top of the food chain, would leave its chamber thousands of times prior to that day and never worried about an attack.

Lots of luck needed on this one. Would love a great start though. It would give us a shot at this crazy idea of taking a dragon out… This really is insane… I am pleased God, that you have granted me this battle — it will be great. I don't think this is my final hour, but if it is, I will make you proud, Ivan thought to himself.

The sun started to lighten the sky, which upset Ivan. Either the dragon was out night hunting or it was staying in its lair. If it was in its lair they would need another day, but that wasn't possible.

Within the hour we will have to enter your lair, one way or another, and I would prefer to know you are not waiting for us.

The men understood that the increasing sunlight was not ideal, but focused on a broad array of thoughts. Some went over their responsibilities with precision, others had a little nervous bug in them, the rest thought of keeping still.

The sky brightened a little more and something moved up the side of the mountain. It was hard to tell, but it looked like it could be the head of a dragon. Its body became more visible against a dimly lit sky. The dragon was perched on the lip of its entrance, it seemed to stretch, resting on the rock and then lifted into flight. It flew with grace across the sky and out of sight.

Only a few saw it and every one of them had goosebumps rush over their skin, including Ivan. He looked to his arm and focused in on the little lumps that rose to their feet, standing at attention. He looked back to the men as they crept out of their inconspicuous hiding places.

Each of them had their leather armour. It was the worst armour for defending weapons, but the best for defending fire, something each of them were sure they were going to face. The leather was skin tight and tied in the back to make sure it didn't loosen. Leather was like having a second set of skin, but in direct flame wouldn't matter much. Everyone had arm and leg straps covering their appendages, but Ivan's arms were too massive and he couldn't wear armour to cover his biceps.

Dav pointed to his flask with the flame retardant paste in it. Dav was giving Ivan one last chance to apply the paste before tossing the bottle. Ivan shook his head. Dav pointed to Seburg and the terrible burns he had. Ivan grabbed the bottle and smelled it — no scent. He rubbed it between his fingers and didn't really notice any hindrance to his grip. With a nod, thanking Dav, he rubbed it on his arms and the front of his hands. His neck was also exposed, which he lathered as well.

Only one other person could use the paste due to a limited supply, and that was the other commanding officer, Paul. He had over-applied and looked ridiculous. Ivan had to hold back his laughter. Paul attempted to figure out what was wrong, but Ivan didn't bother telling him. The men noticed Ivan's almost joyous mood and felt comforted by it. A few wished they had his attitude. He bounced back and forth from leg to leg as if building his adrenaline and loosening up for a sport.

The dragon would be gone for at least an hour, but he wanted to move quickly, get set, give final orders and wait.

Seburg gave little grief about showing them the way through the mountain. It was a good sign, but Ivan wasn't ready to dispel his cowardice expectations yet. The end of the tunnel was close and many of their hearts started to race. They saw the beast leave, but still, nerves started to set in. Seburg stopped and pointed, but wouldn't go any further. Ivan didn't argue and commanded him to wait. He knew the fear caused by the dragon outweighed Ivan's sword and a chance to regain his honour didn't matter compared to another encounter with the villain, that was the master of his nightmares.

Ivan approached first to confirm it had not returned. The cave of the lair was brilliantly designed; the hole in the roof illuminated the entire room and reflected off all of the sparkling gold and jewels that lay on the ground. It was a perfect lure for stupid, greedy species like man. The bowl-like bottom was larger than Ivan had expected, some two hundred feet in diameter, but it was not enough to change his plans. It was a bit of a drop but in some of the areas it could be a moderately easy slide in. Most of it was 180 degrees, but there were a few areas that offered a better pitch, making it easier to get down, but not so easy to get back up.

Four entrances from separate tunnels led to a walkway around the circumference. The walkway depth was shallow and could only hold one man, but that didn't hinder the plan either.

Seburg did well. This is pretty much how I envisioned this place. I bet there are other chambers below. Not a bone in sight. No bowel movements, the dragon doesn't want to scare anything away. Interesting, I am looking forward to this battle and know it will also enjoy it.

Ivan spoke to nineteen sets of sensitive ears with a whisper. "Okay, last check before you take positions. It may have weak hearing but don't let metal hit metal. Most likely your shield will hit your weapon, avoid that until the battle is on. Most of you are in groups of three for a reason. Once out of that tunnel let your missile weapons loose and then lock shields. One open spot in your connected defence and the fire will rip through. If it is spraying you with flame, the metal on the shield is going to get hot. DON'T LET IT GO!" Ivan smacked one of them in the face to add emphasis. "If you have to switch hands, do it like this," Ivan showed them how to switch slowly. He released his weapon, gripped it with both hands and switched. "Remember it will have to redirect its attention off you, so don't give in to pain. Dropping the weapon is better than getting fried."

"If you are nervous, turn it into excitement," Dav jumped in. "If you don't think we can achieve success, look to the men to your right and left and tell me, have you ever witnessed such talent?"

"He is right, gentlemen, warriors, you are about to become legends, men who are slayers of the most feared beast in the known world." He waited a second to let pride sink in and then it was back to business, "Can I get weapons check?"

"Two dozen spears, three are metal, twelve bows, lots of arrows, twenty daggers, twenty shields, twenty swords, three axes, eight mini axes, one war hammer, these strange daggers and this spiked chain," Walker relayed the information.

"I will take the chain when I am ready, and Walker, you are staying back. You will manage our weapons cache. Only emerge when we are heading into the pit at ground level. Those axes will be necessary to chop it up. Swords will pierce its skin but not enough. An axe will inflict something noteworthy. Nobody goes into the pit until I say so. We will use this elevated position to our advantage. Every last missile weapon will be exhausted before we take it on head first." He was ready to dismiss them from the chat when he turned and said, "Oh yeah, and the war hammer is mine. Walker, make sure I get that."

Minutes seemed like hours. Ivan waited with Walker, whose sole job was to deliver the ordnance to the appropriate people. Two groups waited in each of the other tunnels. The trap was set, but luck was critical, their target needed to descend to its pit and rest somewhere in the centre of the huge bowl. If the dragon grew suspicious at any time it could leave or stay in flight above the path flipping the advantage against them. Their maintained elevated position was imperative to success.

The lair was dead quiet. Neither a bird nor rodent ventured by them, and actually it crossed a few of their minds that they didn't even see a fly or spider.

Even the insects are smarter than we are, Dav thought.

Most of the men had experience with battle and every one of them had defeated a bigger guy in their class, but this was different. A few of them couldn't wait for the battle. They thrived to strike the beast, loved the opportunity, they could stand by Ivan's side any day. On the other side, a couple of men's minds rode a wave, seriously considering leaving over and over again, but they weren't going anywhere. The rest tried not to think about it and were there because their Kingdom commanded them to be.

The moment was near, Ivan could feel it. He was right! As hours had passed the sun's dominance in the lair strengthened. Streams of sunlight shot through the pit, undisturbed until that moment. The light was blocked by something that was in front of the hole in the mountain. With a final flap of its wings, it rested on the lip of the lair. At first it sat in the opening and Ivan's mind tried to tell him that it knew they were there.

C'mon, you bastard, take a knee in your lair, you need the rest, nothing is wrong here.

He had strategically placed himself in the one tunnel that he could observe all other openings. He noticed one of the groups advancing to take a look, barely noticeable, but still visible. He couldn't command them back because he would have to expose himself and use movement to catch their eye. The beast's eyesight was second to none and an alarm would go off. He had to hope that it wouldn't look towards them as it descended.

The damn plan is breaking down already. Back up, you jackasses. Come on, how stupid do you have to be?

They waited. Nothing happened. It was hard to judge time because fear distorted it. Ivan knew that more errors in judgement would occur the longer their target waited. Pressure and autonomous thoughts would get in the way of the pre-set commands.

Frozen and hidden, all Ivan moved was his eyes.

The light pattern changed and the noise of massive claws scratching rock was present as the dragon released its grip on the side of the opening. Wings opened wide, it glided down the cave right past the group.

It had a fresh kill locked in its jaw. It was some kind of large wild swine, maybe a small cow. The animal had bled all over its mouth and let out a small squeal, probably its last. It was a fortunate turn of events for the men.

Blood all over its face hinders its ability to smell us. The noise of the swine will distract its hearing, and the empty belly with dinner in front of it would lessen other senses. Please, let the luck keep coming.

The dragon hit the ground with a clash. Its chamber was stacked full of coins from the kills over the years. Jewels and gold that would be treated with such respect with most intelligent creatures, was nothing more than a dinner plate for a dragon. Even though they were at top of the food chain and one of the most intelligent animals in the known world, they didn't have need for a trading system. Dragons had full use of speech, usually speaking common tongue among other languages, but didn't need to trade. What would they trade for?

Ivan counted to twenty, dropped down to his stomach and cautiously crawled, careful not to make a sound. He made it to the edge and looked down into the pit with one eye. He could see the dragon. It sat in a good spot, perfect for a strike.

You didn't see us and you are sitting in a good spot for us, but not so good for you. Look at you, getting ready to eat your dinner, guess what, we are going to make this your last.

It was a massive beast and looked to stand at least double Ivan's height, but much bigger in mass. Its skin was a scaly green. Not all dragons were green. It was a common colour, but black, white and a golden blue also existed. It jolted its head back. Ivan's first reaction was to pull back but he didn't move. He overrode his instincts. It was just letting the blood of its kill trickle down its throat. It spread its wings and with arms pulled back and stretched again. It was a muscular creature with massive claws on its hands and feet. He could see the tail had a good half-dozen sharp spikes protruding from it. It was simply an impressive killer.

Ivan wanted it to refocus on its meal, rest its wings and then it was time to initiate the battle. Excitement built in him, the plan was working perfectly. Victory was far from guaranteed, but this was a good start.

Little did he know that the plan was about to be disturbed, flipped upside down due to one very poor decision he made, his decision to leave Seburg in the tunnel. He shouldn't have left him so close to the den. Seburg must have heard the dragon which triggered his memories.

"I am burning, Sam, run for your life!" Seburg screamed as he had a flashback.

The dragon had just rested its wings when its head jolted back towards the noise.

Oh no, stupid Seburg! Well who wanted this to be easy?

Seburg's outcry triggered the action but not in the original order of the plan. The first group of three charged forward. They looked down on the beast who, from the moment it had heard Seburg, prepared its main offensive arsenal. It tossed its meal aside, inhaled and primed its most intense fire stream, turned upward and saw three men run from an opening. Ivan could almost see the smile on the dragon's face.

This first group had one of three vital metal spears. Ivan wanted at least two to hit the target and this one wasn't going anywhere near it. The lead man who initiated the advancement not only forgot to run shield first, he actually left it behind. He was so excited his only thought was to jam that metal spear where it counted. The man to his left had his shield only part way up and the man to his right held it properly, charging forward, but it didn't matter. The three shields worked best when locked in a system.

Metal spear in hand, the leading man yelled a battle cry. He forced his weapon into firing position, but he didn't see much of the dragon, all he saw was fire. His head cocked back from the velocity of the flame, eyes burst and upper torso pushed back so hard he flipped off his feet. Instantly on fire, his body had enough momentum to send his corpse into the pit. The leather armour was no match.

The flame hit the side of the face and shoulder of one of them. It flipped him off his feet as well and he too shot forward into the pit. His skin seared to his bone as he crashed into a pile of precious metals.

The third man did as he was told; he stopped, bent down on one knee, putting his entire body behind the shield. It would have worked but the system had broken down. Flames had ricocheted from the middle man, touching his face and his side. The leather armour held its own but it was hot, too hot.

With extreme panic his thoughts rushed through his brain, *My hand is burning, I can't see, I can't breathe!*

The pain in his lungs from the heat, combined with no oxygen and a scalded hand, caused him to toss the shield and run perpendicular from the line of fire.

Ivan saw the first two flip into the pit and the other make a run for it. He then watched the dragon, with a quick shift of its head redirect the flame and blow him against the wall.

Ivan knew that it would immediately look to get airborne and if it could succeed, then the fight was over. He yelled, "Attack!"

Dav led a group of three with a spear toss. They were facing the beast's back. One spear was a direct hit to its wing that had just opened up, looking for the air it would take to elevate it. The dragon spun to see two arrows volleying towards it. With spectacular skill it knocked one of them away in midair with its arm, but the second jammed into its abdomen. The small wince from the arrow impalement gave them enough time to lift shields and lock them together to wait for the fire to come.

They braced for heat but instead were hit with extreme force, tossing them backward. Dav's shield opened up his nose as it crashed into his face. The back of his head hit the rock wall adjacent to the tunnel. Although disoriented, he held on to his shield and pulled his appendages behind the shield, remembering Seburg's story. The other two were flung backward but lost grip of their shields. Dav could see to his side the bloody corpse of some kind of large animal.

The bloody bastard tossed his lunch at us.

"Get your shields up!" he yelled to the two archers in his group of three, but it was too late. The fire followed as the words left his mouth and they were torched. He could see the flame hit one of the young lads and witnessed his extermination, helplessly. Dav wisely closed his eyes and mouth as the flame redirected his way. His hand started to feel the concentrated heat build and every natural instinct told him to drop the shield, open his eyes and breathe, but all would be fatal mistakes. The flames would easily sear his eyes or burn his lungs.

Ivan saw that Dav was in trouble, even with the fire retardant paste, he didn't have long. "Everyone unleash fury!" he yelled and the tunnels opened up. Four teams of three sprung out and let arrows and spears fly. The dragon took several hits to its neck and wings, but not enough to keep it from elevating. It was time for Ivan to enter the battle.

"Walker, metal spear!" Ivan turned to see it delivered perfectly. He grabbed the absurdly heavy spear, aimed, took two steps forward and with momentum, launched it. The dragon was used to the mild injuries from the arrows and wooden spears, but this hit made an impact. The metal spear hit the base of its wing where it met its back. It dug deep and immobilized its ability to fly. It also infuriated the beast.

The dragon now found projectile weapons raining down on it. Arrows pelted its scaly exterior from everywhere and were starting to inflict damage. It also redirected its attention from Dav, assuming he was no longer a threat. Dav sat against a rock wall, struggling for air, face smashed and hand scorched. When the flame stopped, he submitted to his internal instincts and tossed his shield aside. He could see the beast charge on foot in another direction. All the men tossed arrows and spears at an agile yet injured dragon. With impressive speed it ran to the closest group and fired another stream of flame. All six men locked shields, one group on either side of the tunnel. The temperature of its flame was diminishing. The dragon had not put everything into the last stream for a reason, the flame was a distraction. The group figured incorrectly that once its ability to fly was gone, its only ability to attack would be fire. They thought all they needed to do was block the flame as the others emptied their ordnance. The bottom of the pit was too far for it to strike, or so they thought.

The dragon leapt and gripped onto the path with its front claws. It couldn't fly but it could still leap high enough to grab the path. Its spiked tail came over its shoulder and over the shields of one of the groups. Two of the men ended up impaled with spikes through their heads and necks. Their knees buckled and they collapsed. The third man witnessed what happened and lifted his shield to defend another blow from above. The dragon's adrenaline, resulting from the pain of Ivan's spear, created more force. Its tail smashed into his shield. It came down on him hard, resulting in several spikes piercing through the metal. Not many weapons or creatures could pierce a shield with its construction, and the warrior behind it never imagined a first blow would have such brute force. He was a strong, well-built man, but nothing compared to that of a dragon. As the shield fell on him the first spike slammed into his jaw and the second entered his shoulder. They were getting decimated!

The other group of three on the other side of the tunnel glanced to see what was happening. They witnessed the dragon pull back its tail with a shield stuck to it as one of their comrades gripped his mutilated jaw. The dragon grasped the man's leg and tossed him into the pit. What little chance he had to live was eliminated because the drop would certainly take care of any remaining vital signs. The shield was now jammed around its tail, eliminating it as a potential threat.

Paul, one of the three men, yelled, "Swords!" With a metallic sound that draws shivers, two of them unsheathed. The third man opposite Paul had another plan.

The dragon released its grip on the path and let gravity take control, falling into its lair that was littered with dying or dead men. It could feel fewer arrows striking it but with deadlier results. The men were taking their time aiming and pulling the pew back farther to create more force. The dragon looked up to its next three victims, two had drawn their swords, but once it inhaled they locked shields.

Just before the flame hit, Adam on a flank yelled, "Block as two!" That meant not to worry about him, make a V-shape defensive stand, splitting the fire stream in two. The battle had been going on long enough and his fear had dissipated. Something inside Adam grew to a new stratum of confidence. He decided to give the ultimate gift, self-sacrifice.

The dragon couldn't see through its flame. Its intense orange, reds and yellows created an opaque wall of fire. It bounced off shields and rock making its diameter even wider. Focusing from deep within, legs firmly planted on the bottom of its lair, it felt the heat intensify in its throat and it longed for the men to release their shields.

Three arrows struck within seconds of each other and opened wounds on its back. It was enough of a distraction for it not to see Adam on its flank dive out of the flame's path. By the time it noticed him, he had already positioned himself on two feet, tossed his shield aside and released one of the small tossing axes with a warrior's scream. As if knowing the battle would have led him here, he had asked for two small axes during the weapons check prior to the battle. The axe wasn't big, but was deadly; one impact on a human would usually take off a limb.

The first axe was a striking hit and gouged an area near the dragon's ribcage. The second grazed a defending arm, and even though it didn't dig into the beast, it ripped a chunk of its scales off along the outside of its arm up to its shoulder. The two hits caused enough pain for it to make an agonized noise and pull its flame upward.

The sight was impressive and inspired Ivan. He flipped his shield around his shoulders and covered his back like a turtle. He called to Walker to give him the chain, which he wrapped around his right side. The hooked spikes were sharp enough to scratch his exposed arm, and with just a light touch, they opened his skin in several places. He then turned and charged along the path. While charging, he saw Adam reach for a dagger, but the dragon wasn't distracted for long. It continued throwing its flame, but aimed it in the direction of the exposed man. Adam was incinerated without uttering a scream. Ivan knew that if he himself lived, he would describe his valour as a gift from God.

The two men kept their shields locked. They knew it would take a few moments for the dragon to muster another torrent of flame. They had no idea what had happened to Adam and prepared for a misjudged assault.

Moments passed with no flame. All of a sudden their feet were swept from under them. The dragon had leapt yet again, gripped the path with one claw and used the other to swat at their legs.

Paul slid hard along the path, and at first didn't understand how badly he was injured. Moments later he would examine the extent of his injuries, which completely eliminated him from the battle. The thick, razor-sharp claw of the dragon had ripped a massive laceration through his leather armour in his right quadriceps, a cut bad enough to make him flirt with unconsciousness and could result in him to bleeding to death.

The other warrior that was swept from his feet almost flipped into the pit but gripped the edge of the path with both hands, attempting to avoid falling into the pit. The dragon looked at him for a second as they were both in similar positions. From a distance it was a sight that showed the true perspective of proportion. The dragon towered over him.

All missile weapons had ceased for two reasons. One, they were out of arrows and wooden spears, and two, the dragon was too close to their brethren.

There was the briefest pause in the battle as a man looked directly into the eyes of the dragon. The dragon, with full command of the common language, said with a deep, disturbing voice, "Scared? You should be!"

The eyes of the man opened wide with fear. With that, it lunged forward with a massive bite and then simply released him. Its teeth did immense damage and the warrior plunged downward.

The next victim was going to be Paul, who lay defenceless on the path. Ivan knew that he only had a few moments. The dragon would surely eliminate him with ease. Ivan rounded the bend on the path, closing in, and he turned up his speed to a maximum level, drew his curved blades, and just before he got to the burning corpse of Adam, he leapt!

The blades of the daggers spun from the handle up and around so they ran parallel with the handle, weapons designed for blocking and side-gouging.

Walker and the remaining seven watched as the massive Northern warrior, their leader, flew through the air with arms extended and landed on the back of the enormous beast.

Walker knew his job to manage the weapons depot was over. He reached for the last remaining metal spear and commanded, "To the pit!"

It was slightly premature, but Ivan not only jumped into the pit, he jumped on the dragon's back! Walker knew even a Northerner as strong as Ivan would be tossed off without assistance.

Ivan had known Paul was one movement away from extermination and had timed the jump perfectly. It was truly crazy and few would ever even pretend that it was a good idea.

He hit the unsuspecting dragon's back with a thud. His face smashed hard against the beast, which opened up his nose, and his leg hit the feathered end of two arrows, which snapped. He wasn't trying to land smoothly. He wasn't thinking about his face. His primary goal was to dig in for a wild ride. The dragon couldn't believe what was happening and could tell by his weight that this was no average man. Directly following the landing, it felt two sharp pains on the back of its neck, as Ivan dug his blades deep into its scales, locking him into position. The dragon released its grip on the path and landed in the pit, shocked and irate.

The thrashing was vicious but Ivan held on. He needed a moment where the dragon would be more stable, just one moment, before he was tossed into a pit where victory would almost surely be the dragon's. He needed to reach for the chain but couldn't let go. Ivan's legs were lifted off the beast several times. The beast then attempted to swat at him, but connected with his well-positioned shield.

The remaining men flooded the pit, and the dragon was too distracted to notice.

Walker watched Ivan get tossed around and finally figured out his plan. He needed the monster to forget about the Northerner on its back, even just for a moment. He released the last metal spear. It was heavy, but he couldn't miss, or worse, hit Ivan.

Ivan heard the spear dig deep into the dragon's upper leg and it screeched.

With a smirk Ivan thought, *Perfect timing Walker.*

The dragon reared back in an erect position and threw a flame. Ivan knew this wasn't ideal but it was his only chance. He let go of one of the daggers, gripped the chain and slung it around its outer jaw. The flame was hot but his skin resisted the flame, aided by the paste that Dav had made him put on. The beast didn't even notice at first. It foolishly closed its mouth and Ivan locked the chain in place. The chain's hooks slid into position, and once tightened, it couldn't be opened beyond that point and the spikes would make a mess of anything attempting to pry it open.

Ivan knew that it wouldn't be tight enough with just his strength, so he flipped off of the beast while holding on to the chain. His weight was enough to force the dragon to twist its head in his direction, forcing it toward the ground. The chain locked in even tighter! The success came at a price. Ivan's hands had slid along the spiked chain, wreaking havoc to his palms and fingers.

Ivan didn't stay on the ground long. He leapt to his feet and needed distance from the dragon until he could re-arm. His hands took a beating, sliding down the chain tightly over sharp spikes. He didn't want to take his eyes from the dragon and therefor couldn't look to his hands to deduce the damage. He knew the dragon would want revenge, and even a blink of the eye could be enough time to be impaled by its claws. Ivan stared at the beast as he backed up. He wiggled his fingers to make sure that they were all still there.

Need a weapon and need it now.

The dragon realized its jaw was temporarily sealed. It was a devastating shock as it started to realize it might not survive. These opponents had eliminated its ability to fly and now it couldn't breathe fire or lay down its deadly bite. Its back was littered with arrows, a few wooden spears and two neatly placed metal spears. All of these wounds were bad, but could be survivable except for the chain around its jaw.

Ivan backed up slowly as he watched the dragon with rapt attention. It moved back a few steps and reached for the chain. It was a critical blow and it knew it was injured. Open wounds were everywhere, arrows were scattered all over its back. It attempted to pull at the chain, but couldn't get its claws in between it and its jaw. It wouldn't have done much good anyway. It would be impossible to break. It then attempted to force its jaw open, a jaw that has bone-crushing, metal-bending strength when closing, but only a fraction of the force when opening. Its attempt to move its jaw upward was futile and cut deeper wounds into its face, which started to bleed.

Ivan had just started to break into a sideways run to locate Walker and re-arm when the beast realized that the chain wasn't coming off. It understood that a stalemate was the best option at this point. Even if it was able to destroy its opponents, it couldn't feed and would starve to death. A monster of this calibre, realizing it couldn't survive, was a problem. Creatures and men alike fight differently when they know they can't live. They get angry and fear nothing. Ivan knew it would hit them furiously.

"Walker, I could use a little something," Ivan called.

He tried to gather his wits and find out where the men were. While he was riding the dragon's back, Walker had joined Dav with another two men. He distributed the close-combat, deadly axes to Dav, one other and he had kept one. The other three men had positioned themselves spread apart and waited for the opportunity to attack. Walker had left the war hammer where it landed when he tossed it into the pit.

"Over there by the tunnel," Walker screamed to Ivan, knowing which weapon he would want.

The dragon stopped and looked around, getting a perspective on how many men remained. It turned its neck to look behind and could see Dav with three others. It could tell that Dav had little or no fear and was fully armed with one of the deadliest offensive weapons. It looked to its left and could see another three men, armed with swords and shields. It knew they were an easier kill, but what it wanted was the one who jumped on its back. He had to die!

Dav knew dragons were exceptionally intelligent and could see its plan formulate. He knew that it would move for Ivan, so he commanded an attack that was foolish in nature, considering the survivability of the man heading it up, but it would give Ivan time to prepare. Ivan's value was worth more than Duke's.

The dragon was turning its head to locate Ivan and would have charged him once it saw that Ivan was alone and unarmed. Dav could see Duke, the youngest of them all, was anxious to draw blood and was waiting for the command.

"Duke, hit him now!"

Duke turned to the man to his right and said quickly, "It's amazing, I have lived my entire life for these next few seconds."

Duke charged from the group of three. His comrades stayed in their position and watched the skilled young warrior. The dragon stood still as the man charged. It led with a powerful lunge with its arm, attempting to stop him dead in his tracks. With intelligent agility, Duke slid on his knees and raised his shield almost parallel to the ground. The massive claw hit the shield, knocking it right out of his hand, but with little effect to his motion. He hadn't gripped it tightly for a reason and understood it was all a decoy; the shield deflected its blow.

He swiftly popped to his feet, his right hand joined the left to grip his sword, and with a spin, he thrust his weapon into the belly of the dragon. The sword had enough strength to split its scales and do damage, but an axe would have been a more ideal weapon. It stopped with a thud in its abdomen, but Duke didn't care. He pulled his sword out and attempted another assault. Paul knew he was in over his head, but couldn't risk sending the others forward until everyone was ready to attack at the same time.

The dragon had winced when the steel struck its mid-section, but it didn't slow its next strike. It had watched the man about a third its height with fancy acrobatics fool it once, but not a second time. With raw power, using its leg, it crushed him with a thrust kick. His body folded with popping noise. He blew backward and shot along the ground with broken bones, including his spine. He was awake, but blood was spitting from his mouth; he was beyond repair.

The dragon wanted Ivan. It refocused on him and could see that he was scrambling around to find a weapon.

"Forget the hammer! Get over here, regroup," Dav yelled to Ivan.

Dav didn't know Ivan very well. If Kruno had been there he would have charged over in his direction because he would have known Ivan was finding that war hammer.

The dragon also understood that it would be an easier kill to hit Ivan now, but in order to avoid another offensive from the two remaining, it needed a distraction. The dragon motioned as if it were about to attack but didn't act on it. Dav's group flinched as they assumed they were going to be hit.

The dragon pulled the metal spears from its leg and from its back. They were heavy for a human but not for a dragon. It turned and fired them. They weren't tossed as they were intended, but just thrown by the end with a spin. As soon as they left its hands, it charged for the Northerner.

The two men watched the metal spears spin with velocity towards them. The first one put his shield up but far too high. The spear hit the ground sideways just before his feet and collided with his unprotected shins. He was flipped off his feet as the bones in his shins shattered. His upper body headed towards the ground, folding over his legs. Both feet remained attached but they dangled, held only by skin.

The second took the hit right on the shield sideways. It knocked him back with force, but no real harm was done.

Ivan had heard Dav yell to him but didn't turn around. He had to find the weapon he so desperately needed.

"Where are you? Come on, you bastard."

"It's coming! Behind you!" Ivan knew it was a warning he needed to take seriously.

The pit was relatively well-lit from the hole in the mountain, but not broad, unimpeded daylight. After scanning the ground like a mad man, he finally found it. The war hammer, a weapon that he loved, one he mastered unquestionably better than anyone, was now in sight.

He moved toward the weapon. It was in reach when he was hit with a thud, sending him to the ground. The dragon had picked up a dead body and tossed it at him. He was pinned under an unrecognizable comrade.

A moment after, Ivan heard metal hit the ground nearby and from the corner of his eye, back to the dragon, he could see a twisted, perforated shield rocking back and forth on the floor.

Dammit, here it comes. Ivan knew the shield that had been wrapped around the dragon's tail, rendering it useless, was now free.

Ivan turned his head to see the bloody, chain-sealed dragon stop dead in its tracks and start to spin its body swiftly. Its spiked, menacing tail was quickly swinging toward him. With lightning reaction he tossed the dead body off of him, got to his feet, spun the shield from his back and slammed it to the ground, guarding his legs as he attempted to leap above the spikes of the tail.

The tail hit his shield and Ivan flipped over. The spikes, yet again, pierced metal, but only the tip of one caught the heel of his foot. The wound wasn't deadly, but it left him on his back and in a bad position for an inevitable second attack.

Ivan knew how much time he needed to get up. He knew how long it would take Dav, who now charged with the remaining men, to reach his side. It didn't look good. He was going to be hit by the second strike. The impalement was going to be deadly.

He almost made it to his feet when he was lifted off the ground and flung aside. The impact was swift and painful. Yet it wasn't what he expected. All his life he wondered what it would feel like to be penetrated by a sword, spear, or even a dragon, but always assumed it would hurt more.

Ivan, believing he was a fatally injured, looked down to see nothing wrong with him. Perplexed, he touched his torso to see if his eyes were deceiving him, but they weren't. He should be bleeding profusely.

Ivan looked up to see a body only a few feet away slumped over, but sitting up with his back to him. He ran over to see that it was Seburg!

He put his hand on his shoulder and glimpsed at a punctured torso. Seburg couldn't even raise his head or look up and had moments to live. At first Ivan couldn't gauge what had happened. It took him a second to figure out that Seburg took the blow for him.

"Seburg, how, when?" He was astonished by what had just occurred. He thought that Seburg was just a shell of a man, a person who didn't have an ounce of bravery in him. This same man had just jumped in front of a dragon, shattering his life, the same dragon that had haunted his psyche day in and day out for years.

"You saved my life, why?" Ivan crouched over to talk into his ear.

His lungs started to fill with blood and he could barely talk. Each word followed a cough and splatter of blood, "You… just… saved… mine…"

Ivan looked up to see the dragon engaging the remainder of the troops, a mere fraction of what they once were, but maybe strong enough to take it down.

"Go… finish it!" With a small smirk, Seburg felt something he hadn't felt in a long time: pride.

Seburg had waited and contemplated what to do in the tunnel since the battle had started. He thought about his family and how he would love to redeem his name. He thought about the men, but mostly about Ivan, and when he heard a cry from Dav, he just jolted forward with the confidence of the man he once was. He rolled down the side of the pit and jumped in front of the second swing of the dragon. It had happened so fast.

Just as Ivan was lifted off the ground with Seburg as a cushion, a perfectly placed spear had jammed into the back to the dragon's foot, a spear that had lain on the floor of the pit, one that Walker had charged directly into the dragon. The dragon had no idea that Ivan hadn't been exterminated.

With a new sense of purpose he rose to his feet. Seburg's transformation of character left Ivan invigorated. He grabbed his war hammer and knew he had a free shot. A strike he could strategically plan, one which he could drive with mighty power.

Just before Ivan attacked, Walker was tossed backward with a shot from the clenched fist of the dragon. His face looked worse than it was because his lips and nose popped. Disoriented, he knew he had to roll away from the battle until he could regain his awareness.

Five men squared off with the dragon, which looked beaten up, but they all knew it was a tossup as to who would be the victor. Nobody wanted to connect first. Everyone who had struck the creature up close had been hit hard.

The four others were too focused on the dragon and didn't see Ivan move in for a strike. Dav was pleased they didn't because he knew that an eye shift in the wrong direction would set off an alarm for the dragon. Dav saw him move and had the next strike in his mind.

Ivan could see the men spread out in a line. It was time to turn the battle on its axis.

What do you think about this?

With the war hammer raised he struck with all of his strength to the dragon's lower back, right where the tail meets the body and where the fragile spine that controls the tail was located. Ivan gleefully watched the giant war hammer's head strike its back. The noise was as exciting as it was repulsive. The hammer crushed bone and split scales. The dragon reacted by collapsing at the back and had to use its arms to brace it from falling over completely. It limped away due to the several potent strikes.

Dav unleashed another deadly attack with his axe. He hit one of its arms as it tried to flee the battle. The mighty axe severely wounded its arm.

It was a huge victory for them as it immediately defaulted to its other arm to struggle back away from them.

Ivan, Dav and the other three approached, still cautious, as it was severely injured but not dead.

The dragon held its injured arm. Its wings were shattered, tail internally destroyed, leg wounded, and with splits all over its body, it looked broken. It stopped, leaned forward and collapsed to its knee. Moments after, it dropped its head and two men charged forward wanting to end the battle right then. They understood that their names would be known around the world for slaughtering a dragon. The thought of honour over-rode the chain of command and common sense.

"You bastard!" one of them yelled as they charged with weapons up, but the dragon was playing coy, pretending to be more hurt than it was. It wanted more victims.

The dragon looked up, and balancing on one knee, hit the first screaming man in the chest with clenched fist. His sword, which was above his head, fell to the ground without touching the dragon. He was caught off guard and slid under the beast, winded and hurt but not dead. The dragon's strength had diminished.

The second man saw what happened, placed the butt of his sword in his own chest to increase force and ran into the monster. The sword pierced the skin of the dragon and reached far enough in that he couldn't pull it free. The dragon turned and seemed to snicker under the spiked chain. It grabbed the warrior by the ribs and let its claws dig deep into his chest and back. His eyes filled with blood, his hands let go of the sword handle as he slumped over and died.

Ivan waited a moment and then charged. The other warrior beside Dav wanted to follow, but Dav held him back, "This one is his."

Ivan's assault started just as the beast turned and smashed its fist down on the man under it, snapping more ribs, and a second vicious blow punctured his lungs.

Ivan powerfully rained down with the best offensive weapon known to man. The war hammer hit the dragon's collarbone, and with a crackle, its frame broke. He reloaded and struck it hard, not once but twice to the top of its head.

The dragon was dead!

Ivan looked to the sky and let out a boisterous warrior's scream. He let his war hammer slide out of his hand. It was lubricated with his own blood, which covered the handle. Dav and one of the others joined in. Walker stood up slowly and realized they were victors. He mustered up a milder but still excited bellow.

Ivan turned with fists clenched and blood that trickled through his fingers. His eyes told a story of the greatest success of his life. Four stood out of twenty-one. Against any other creature that would be shameful, but against the most cunning adversary, it was a tremendous conquest.

"I can't believe it!" Paul, with his severely wounded leg, looked down from the elevated path. He had slid along on his back and looked over the edge to see the four men standing and celebrating the triumph.

Dav looked over at their Northern leader, someone he would hold in the highest regard for however long he would live.

"You know Ivan, if you had told me your plan was to leap onto the back of the dragon and seal its jaw shut with a chain, I would have called you insane."

"Well it worked!"

"That it did, but it looks like you have a little problem." Dav pointed to Ivan's shredded hands.

Ivan looked down for the first time to see the damage. His heel was injured enough that he favoured it, but that was nothing compared to his hands. The spikes on the chain had split open his fingers and left a couple of massive gashes in his palms.

"Let's wrap them up, but I don't think you will be fighting for a while." Walker offered his diagnosis.

"Don't worry about my hands. They will be fine. Grab the war hammer, look along the shaft and pry off the pieces that don't belong."

Walker did as he was told. He attempted to pick up the war hammer with the same ease as Ivan had, but he had underestimated its weight. It was also covered in blood, making it even more challenging to lift. He looked up to Ivan and without saying a word, indicated how impressive it was to wield such a heavy weapon so effortlessly. About halfway down the shaft he could see that there was something embedded in it. He pried out small tubes with a cap sealed end. All of them were the same size except for one, which was bigger than the others.

"We don't have long. We have to extract the blood of the dragon immediately and my hands won't be of any assistance. If we don't move fast the blood will thicken and won't be ingestible. Fill a small tube and one of you needs to take it back."

Dav looked up at Ivan, he knew the old tale of dragon's blood. It was by far the most expensive liquid to purchase anywhere. Only Kings, the wealthiest warriors and greatest magicians could ever afford it. Taken in small doses it had healing powers, but beyond that it was supposed to have other beneficial effects.

"What's it like Ivan?"

"I don't know. I've never tried it before. Big gamble don't you think?"

Anger filled their minds, but they tried to relax and focus.

Walker filled the first tube full.

"That wasn't easy, it's already thickening... Okay, who wants to try it?"

"Walker, go ahead. It's all yours."

"No way, are you crazy? A cap fine, I have heard of that before, but never has anyone I know or anyone they know, ever ingested that much before. Besides, a cap is supposed to be terrible enough."

"Okay, boys, stop arguing," Paul demanded. "I am useless as it is with my leg. If it has an adverse effect then it may as well be me that bears them. Plus, I didn't do enough to earn this victory."

Ivan didn't agree with his comment. Paul had done plenty. Anyone who had stepped into the lair had done enough as long as they didn't run. He didn't agree but he wasn't going to question Paul now, because Ivan needed a test subject and Paul's injury made him the perfect candidate.

Walker capped it and tossed the tube up on to the ridge. Paul opened it and fired it down his throat.

"Oh my God, that is terrible!"

Ivan would have normally lashed out at him for the blasphemous comment, but he bit his tongue.

Not more than a few moments passed before his body jolted, all limbs shot out, he became uncontrollably erected.

"What do you think is going to happen?" Walker asked Ivan.

"I have heard the same thing as Ivan has," Dav jumped in. "I wouldn't have been here if I didn't. First stage is healing, Paul's body will heal weeks within minutes. Besides physical healing, disease doesn't exist in the dragon's world, so Kings have taken dragon's blood to cure terminal illnesses. Next his body is supposed to go under a physical transformation, muscle tissue triples and the bone structure increases to support it. The next stage…"

"Hold on, are you telling me we are going to be freaks the rest of our lives?" Walker asked, concerned.

"Does it matter? You have sworn an oath," Ivan interjected. "Anyway, no, this is all temporary. It's the magical component to their blood that reacts with ours. The next thing to transform is… watch and see."

They couldn't see Paul because he was lying down on the path above them but that didn't last long. He bellowed in agony and his spasms jolted him. He fell off the path to the bottom of the pit. They stood and watched from a distance. Even Ivan, who usually had a poor attention span, couldn't take his eyes off Paul.

The noise was horrendous, Paul sounded as if his body was being torn in two.

"Doesn't look like its working, do you have another plan?" Dav looked to Ivan who wasn't amused.

Even from a distance they could see Paul's leg was opened up badly from the claw of the fallen dragon. Blood rushed to his face as his veins expanded. He forced himself to look to his leg. Like silk worm threads, two ends of the wounds were being covered from one end to the next. At first it looked like invisible fingers threading the lesion, moving incredibly fast, and it closed up. It then turned to a few old scars which faded away as if they never existed. Smashing his hands backward, the second stage started to kick in and new territory was being treaded. A handful over the centuries had claimed to move beyond this point but nobody in decades.

Paul's leather armour tore with ease. His pectorals, biceps and entire upper torso expanded as his body convulsed. His legs followed; quadriceps and calf muscles grew threefold. He was now taller than Ivan with a lot more mass, it happened so quickly that everyone was astonished.

"What a rush!" Paul stood up. He had a look of relief on his now massive face.

"Not over yet my man," Ivan said, apologetically, knowing what was to come next.

Paul heard Ivan's words just as he was forced forward on to his knees. In a balanced, crouched position his back opened up and what erupted from it shocked even Ivan and Dav who both anticipated it. Paul stood again but this time with the addition of massive wings.

His skin started to turn a light green but faded to his normal peachy white shortly after.

"Okay, that was it. It is the proper amount to take. If he had turned completely green we would have had to dial down the amount."

Walker stared at Paul, a man he had known all his life. He was completely altered, he barely resembled himself.

"What? What is wrong? It can't be that much of a change," Paul said, towering over Walker.

They didn't bother denying it and figured that he would see soon enough. Ivan commanded Paul, "Search the room to see if anyone else is alive. While we repeat what you just did."

"Okay boys, I tell you what, that was terrible, I mean really bad. Now I feel like a thousand platinum pieces, but getting here isn't easy." He stopped and looked at his leg. "Awesome, healed and I am massive. I feel like I could arm wrestle Ivan! I think this is my chance to take you down." He smiled.

"Give me a few moments and we will see about that."

Dav, Ivan, Walker and the other warrior took the blood and waited. Each reacted within moments of each other, but Dav hit the ground first. Ivan decided to sit prematurely.

Paul, who had been through the ordeal, was just as shocked to watch the others convulse and scream. He pulled his eyes away to do as commanded. As he searched, he located a warrior who had been hit by the metal spear from the dragon. He was flat on his face with legs bent the opposite way on the ground. It was revolting to look at.

He was barely conscious as Paul attempted to wake him up. Fumbling to pick up the now much smaller tubes —it took a moment to learn how to use his extra-large fingers — he finally filled it. It was much more difficult as the blood was thickening with haste. Paul flipped the man over. His feet didn't even move, his bones in his lower legs were pulverized and were just holding on by his skin. The movement woke him with a shot of pain putting, him into an instantly lucid state.

"Ahhh, *no*!" The man awoke to excruciating pain and looked at Paul, who resembled more of a creature than anything else.

"Stop freaking out, it's me, Paul." He started to pass out again. "Hold on, not now, stay awake to ingest this." He poured it down his throat and pinned his mouth closed as the gag reflex activated. "Keep this down, it's medicine, it will take away the pain."

Paul turned to see the others transformed, "I don't look like you guys, do I?" The sight would offend everyone, but especially his wife. Nonetheless, it was an impressive group, even if slightly repulsive to the eye. They looked powerful and felt the same way.

"*Yeah*, this is what I am talking about!" Ivan said. "It worked!" He looked to his hands which had been shredded and now didn't have a hint of damage.

"I feel incredible. Is this how you feel all the time Ivan?"

He didn't answer, "Okay boys, we need to learn how to use our wings. It should come natural to us."

Ivan somehow got it right away and was the first to take flight. He landed on the path that encircled the lair, where their assault had come from. "There is one more thing boys, watch this."

Ivan lifted his open hand to the sky and fire shot from it.

"Tell me we can all do that?" Walker asked with joy in his voice.

"Oh yeah, part of this is an understanding of fire. Learn how to fly, learn how to create flame and let's get out of here."

The last to transform was the man with the broken legs. He tried to stand but couldn't.

"Sorry my friend, it looks like the blood couldn't fix all of you, but you will be a great asset. Why walk when you can fly?" His legs were unfortunately beyond even the dragon blood's ability to heal.

Ivan noticed Walker filling the tubes and sealed them.

"Good idea Walker, we can give a few more this gift."

Ivan, Walker, Dav, Paul and two others glided over the treetops with a feeling of invincibility and freedom. The experience was overwhelming, but Ivan knew they had to hurry.

"At best boys, we will get back to the battle when it is just about to start. We need to really test our ability here, no time to learn later."

"My eyesight is spectacular. I can't believe how far I can see." Dav took flank to Ivan who like always was on the vanguard.

"Makes you wonder if the dragon did know we were coming for it. I can easily see through shrubs, right down to the ground."

"Yeah, maybe, but it was the wrong call for it if it did." Ivan laughed as he relived the battle in his mind for a few moments and then continued, "We will remember the dead, especially Seburg. His name will be redeemed, I will meet his family personally."

Dav waited a moment, giving silence to the fallen warriors and then changed subjects asking Ivan, "Did anyone back home have any idea what we were up to?"

"If they did, do you think they would have given me any of you?"

"Good point, it was crazy."

"We need to develop a plan. If I was attacking Dryden, I would immerge from the woods and keep the rear flank covered by the trees. If we fly over the battlefield we want to hit them hard before they have a chance to react. Let's kiss the trees and the first Dark Realm soldier you see, unleash everything you have. Pass that on to each of them, we have some time to practice our flames. Concentrate on direct flames with long distances. The first hit should have no resistance and we can fly low, but after that the higher we can be, the better."

CHAPTER 6

UNEXPECTED ALLIES

Egon burst out of his chamber at ground level in the middle of Dryden on horseback with Rizzian and a dozen Elites. The sudden movement caught everyone's eye, in a town infected with fear. Many were mobilizing to transport their most important belongings out of their homes, to move somewhere else, to avoid certain death. Egon rode in the middle with his Elite soldiers surrounding him. It was hard not to notice Deo's crown, which now rested comfortably on his head. They headed for the front gate.

As Egon rode he noticed the people were in disarray. Confidence was so low in the greatest of all cities due to one man's death. He was twisted with thoughts of pride at how important his father was, but he also negatively wondered if he would be able to live up to his father's legacy. Kruno's speech had enough of an effect on him to push those thoughts aside.

Kruno observed a people that needed reassurance that everything was going to be all right. The Dark Realm had conducted a fantastic strategic move and Dryden's back was on the verge of snapping, with only one battle lost. That was it! They had only lost one group of men, but they were Elites and it had included their King. The Dark Realm could win this war before it was really ever fought, unless the people's faith and courage could be revived. The people were afraid of a dark army that couldn't be defeated, one that would steal their soul. Kruno and the other Elites knew better than that. The enemy was just a group of men, but psychological warfare was a taking its toll.

Horses dragged carriages packed with the personal effects of so many that the exit was backed up. Parents were trying to keep account of their children, who of course, like children, were being uncooperative. People were allowed to leave Dryden freely. That freedom was one of the many benefits that had made it the most coveted place to live and visit for decades.

They got close to the end of the line that led to the exit. Instead of riding to the front, Egon halted his entourage.

"Where do you go?" Egon asked a man who had one horse packed with so many items there was no room for him.

"Who asks me such a question?" Without turning around a man dressed in attire indicating he was low on society's spectrum responded.

"I did!" Egon shouted. He turned to see half of the King's Knights unsheathe their swords. To talk to the King with hostility was a good reason to be battle-ready, but in this case it was more for effect.

"Egon!" The look of petrifaction was present as his eyes started to swell. Fear hit him hard and his posture dropped.

"Good, you know who I am. Why don't you explain to me where you are headed?"

"I am sorry, I… I didn't know... I didn't."

Egon waited a moment as he looked around at the crowd that wanted to be part of a mass exit from his city. He couldn't believe what he was seeing, so many leaving. If they did go and more followed, the Dark Realm will have no issues destroying their capital.

Anyone who had noticed the situation turned with focused intent.

"I am just going to visit some family." He finally mustered up the strength to say something.

"Why?"

"It's been awhile and we are celebrating a birthday."

"Try again, peasant. Lie to me once more and you will face Bruno."

He dropped to his knees as fear set in, fear for his life. "Sorry, Egon, we have to leave. They are coming, a force that laughs at God and he does nothing to them. They will eat my soul, we are doomed."

"Close the gate! Seal the exit!" Egon yelled. His voice wouldn't carry the distance to the exit so one of the Elites rode forward to relay his command.

"If you ever have the pleasure of speaking to the King again you call him *King*, you have no right to use his first name. Your fear is embarrassing." Bruno spoke to the man now crying on his knees with forehead pressed against the ground, pathetically begging for his life.

"Rizzian, Bruno, Kruno, join me up there." The King had canvassed the best possible area to address his people and located a spot on the inner wall, an archer's nest. It was a good place to speak because it was right above the exit.

On the way to the podium they rode past the exit as Egon's order was being exercised. The gate closed and the crowd started to get aggravated. Many started to yell, especially the few that were next in line. The front of the entrance was already heated because a group of citizens had gathered and had been working the King's position on their own accord. They debated with anyone trying to exit. They questioned their manhood, their devotion to the Kingdom.

The argument was spinning out of control when the door closed and the few that were verbally fighting for their choice to leave became distraught. They didn't know that it was Egon who had ordered it shut.

"What is going on here?" Egon roared.

Small fist fights had broken out leaving a couple with broken noses and some sore ribs. Upon hearing Egon's voice, they pulled back.

"They are trying to leave Dryden when we need them the most," one of the men yelled. "They stay and enjoy its bosom when it benefits them, but the second it gets uneasy they want to leave." His shirt had been ripped in the small skirmish defending the city. People from both sides of the argument started yelling at the same time.

"Quiet! What say you?" Egon pointed to a man obviously getting ready to leave. His lip was split from a small altercation. Egon was giving the other side a chance to talk.

"We have every right to leave and we don't have to give a reason. Dryden is built on these principles."

"I will remember each of your faces." Egon pointed to the ones that proactively tried to keep people from leaving. A shot of pride rushed them because they received a personal accolade from their King. He then looked to the group that wanted to leave and said, "Your argument holds water,

Dryden's foundation is as you say, but I am King and I command this gate shut. I have something to say."

Egon rode off but Bruno stayed a moment longer and looked directly at the man who spoke of his right to leave. "And I will remember your face." He said it with disgust. His stomach sank as his pride was hit by a hammer.

"This is the first time I have addressed you since my father's departure." Egon spoke from the strategic elevated position, but it was hard for everyone to hear. The crowd looked up and struggled to figure out his words. Egon then turned to his master Wizard, "Rizzian, could you help please?"

"Sorry my King, I forgot."

Rizzian touched Egon's Adam's apple with two fingers and his throat began to glow blue.

"This is the first time I have addressed you since my father's death." His voice bellowed throughout the city. Many were still in their homes or places of business, but all could hear. His speech reached the far ends of the castle walls.

He stood in the archer's nest and looked onto a massive group who stood in silence. They were afraid, that was easy to deduce. They wanted a reason to stay, but hadn't been given one.

"Nobody hurts more than I do for the loss of Deo, but I know each of you share my pain. I know in many ways he was like a father to all of you, but he was my father. He was the defender of this Kingdom and he did a tremendous job. He was so powerful that our enemy had to resort to horrific tactics to execute him. Why do you leave though? That is the question I ask you?" Egon waited for a few moments but nobody spoke. "Please, someone say something, speak, whatever you say now will have no ramifications on you."

"Deo has left us to fight an army that laughs in God's face and he does nothing," a man yelled from the crowd.

"I have heard this exact comment from another. I assume this isn't the first time you have heard it either. A great army descends upon us, but they are made up of men. They bleed, as does anyone. Put a sword in their hearts and they fall." Egon got louder, "They are just men! Do you understand that?"

"They have gargoyles on their side. They will decimate even our bravest." A random remark came from the crowd.

"I am glad they have chosen gargoyles as a partner." The crowd looked to one another in confusion, not understanding what he could mean. Bruno looked to Kruno and he shrugged his shoulders indicating he didn't know where he was going with this either. "They have Black Knights we have Elites, they come with Gabriel but Rizzian fights for us. They bring gargoyles, well we have men like Kruno who aren't afraid of them."

Kruno was caught off guard by what was said and looked over to the King with shock, *Great, now I am a gargoyle slayer. Sure, no problem, they are nice and easy, thanks Egon.*

"Why am I happy they have chosen to align with gargoyles? With them, comes their last ally, the anti-God. They worship the enemy of our God. Let me ask you who is stronger? Who is stronger, the one who created all of this?" Egon spread his hands indicating all of God's creations as if they never noticed them before. "The sky, the sun, the moon, you, me, everything, or is he stronger, the one who has to sit below the earth in a burning pit?"

The crowd wasn't sold, Kruno could feel it. The boy King was doing an admirable job, but the people needed more. Kruno wanted a way into the conversation but he couldn't just interject.

"Kruno… you will stand with us, you and your men. You will destroy the gargoyles?" a woman yelled from the crowd.

Kruno looked to Egon and Bruno and gave them a look letting them know this was an impossible feat. They knew it was as well, but he didn't have much choice on how to respond. He also knew this was a perfect time to have his shot at the crowd.

He looked to Egon and spoke softly, "May I speak, King?" Egon nodded and Rizzian gave him the same gift with an expanded voice spell. "Will I stand by you? Will my men? Egon has asked me and I say yes. Yes, I will and this sword," he raised his sword to the sky and continued, "has cut down a Predator, now it will slash through the skin and flesh of the gargoyle."

People focused and excitement swelled. Everyone loved the talk of such bravery and confidence. It started to inspire them.

"Your new King is courageous. He has just heard that his father is dead and look at him, he stands here in a position and speaks as if he were Deo himself."

"But Kruno, God does nothing, they mock him and he does nothing."

"You think God is doing nothing? Well then you're not paying attention, you're not listening. I like you people, I love Dryden and I think a lot of Egon, but I don't fight for anyone I mentioned. I would have to be crazy to do such a thing. They come here with a massive army. We will be outnumbered several fold. The battle seems foolish."

Bruno looked to Kruno and said softly, "Not doing such a great job, my man. May want to be a little more positive." Kruno put his hand up to indicate there was more to say.

"Listen to the voice in your head, who do you think that is? That is God speaking directly to you. He speaks to everyone here. He tells us to stay and fight. He tells us not to worry as I am with you. You aren't just warriors of Dryden, you are warriors of God!" A shiver ran over everyone. The crowd was silent as they all listened. Tears built up in many eyes as pride set in. Their backs straightened as feelings of invincibility pushed fear from their minds.

Kruno turned to indicate it was someone else's turn to start speaking. Rizzian spoke with his normal magical voice, "Hot House will be here soon, all we have to do is hold off the army until they arrive. No enemy has ever taken siege of Dryden. No army ever will. The entire school of wizardry stays to fight and I lead them." Rizzian started to levitate, cocked his arms back fast, and as they stopped, a loud boom emanated from him.

The excitement was building in everyone. Egon knew he needed to crack it open. He yelled, "Do you fight with us? Do you want to fight with me? What say you?"

Egon spoke like a King, Kruno's support, referencing God and Rizzian's powerful theatrics broke the crowd into hysteria as they cheered with excitement.

"Say this with me. We are warriors of God."

The crowd responded, "We are warriors of God."

"Again! Louder!"

"We are warriors of God!"

The city cheered over and over again. The sight was awe-inspiring. Egon rightfully let it continue for a while and then calmed them down.

"We have a lot to do. Those who are staying, return to your homes and get ready for instructions from Elites, everyone will be needed."

Egon continued to address his newly inspired people as Bruno chatted with Kruno.

"Very impressive, didn't know you had it in you."

"Neither did I, Bruno."

"Looks like we have a King."

"Reminds me of Deo, we need to protect him. We also need to prepare and that's why I go."

"You're going?" Bruno asked, confused.

"Yes, we will need more swords if we have a shot at defending this city. I will be back in a few days… I hope. Tell Decan and Christian I will return with much needed help. Use Decan. He is a fantastic warrior with a great mind for battle."

They shook hands and grabbed each other on the bicep with the other hand, with a respectful embrace, "I am happy your sword is with us."

The night had a slight chill, with a small shifting wind, which was more pronounced on the lookout point of the outer wall. Guards had been doubled in all areas to watch for signs of war. Everything was to be reported, even though the army was many days away from Dryden, or so their intelligence teams had led them to believe. Nothing was left to chance. The guards were lucid at all times.

Several men above the main entrance overlooked the dark empty field that led to the forest. Much preparation was still needed, but nothing was to be conducted outside the castle walls at night.

Two men moved to the outer area of a lookout den and leaned against the ledge.

"Cool night tonight," one commented. His helmet was off to the side and his hair blew in the wind.

"Yes," the second responded. The two of them were army, but not Elites and never would be. Their skill level was nowhere close to the threshold to even consider that option.

"How long have you been doing night watch?" the younger of the two asked, just trying to hold a conversation and possibly gain some respect.

"Got to be fifteen years or so."

"Really! Don't you miss the daylight?"

"The pay is better and it's usually quiet, not much activity. I am usually out here by myself. I just relax and listen to the river flow by."

"Is this the first time you've had anyone with you?"

"No, no. This isn't the first time the city has been on alert."

"You've been through this before then?" the younger man asked, feeling a little better about the whole situation. If he had been through it and had survived, then that meant that there was some hope of survival.

"Never like this. This is going to be a serious battle, that is for sure. Soon this empty field will be filled with Dark Realm soldiers with only one thing in mind. Soon you and I will find out what we are really made of."

"Soon might be sooner than we think," the young man said.

"What are you taking about? They won't be here for many more days." The older soldier let a rock drop and watched it fall and land in the river, something that had kept him occupied for years.

"Something is out there and it looks like a Black Knight to me... it looks like a few of them."

The older soldier looked up to see figures way off in the distance. The moon lit up the area, but the figures were near the forest and too far away for the watchmen to make a positive identification.

"You must have better eyes than me boy, I can barely see anything. How do you know it's a Black Knight? That is a serious comment to make. Maybe it's just your mind, its playing tricks on you."

They watched until the figures got close enough to be identified.

"Those are Black Knights! They are Black Knights! I can't believe it, here already. Pass on the information. Go, go!"

Kruno sat in the desert. It was the same place he was not too long ago when chasing Ivan. He couldn't believe they had actually rescued him. He pondered the thought with little fear of attack because he sat on the thick rock platform they had used earlier when avoiding the sand sharks. It was a good place to rest for the night.

The fire crackled as its energy helped make the pork on his stick gain flavour. It was late but he was still awake. He knew what he was doing was foolish, but at the same time it made all kinds of sense. He wasn't sure how receptive they were going to be, but it was worth the risk. First, he would get to see her again, which would help satisfy an addiction that had intensified every day since he left. Second, if he could convince them to come on board, even though it was a long shot, the battle would become more reasonable.

He wondered about Ivan and how his journey was going. He needed to be successful. Both of them needed to be.

"Ivan, not sure where you are my Northern brother, but I hope you fair well. My prayers are with you. God please take care of him, he is on a selfless journey. He risks everything for people that aren't his. He fights for you but needs your assistance."

Kruno turned his meat and began to salivate. It was about ready. He pulled it from the fire and peeled a piece off and put it in his mouth. It was as tasty as he had anticipated, but food was always better before a battle. All senses were heightened, his taste buds were no exception. The inevitable fight for Dryden, even though several days away, was already taking effect on him.

"I will see you soon, Kiera. You have no idea how excited that makes me."

Kruno took another bite. The wind shifted and blew sand across the rock behind him, just as he pulled another piece of pork off the stick, and as it touched his lips so did a blade to his throat.

"What do you think you are doing?" a female voice whispered in his ear from behind.

"I was wondering if you took my advice. Looks like you did," Kruno said calmly.

"You didn't answer my question," a Sand Sorceress said, locked in a position that clearly favoured her.

"I need to talk to your Queen. I need to talk to Kiera."

"I have every right to slit your throat. I could leave you right here to bleed to death. I would kick your body off this rock and it wouldn't be more than a few hours before you would be taken under the sand."

"She would know and I bring you no harm."

"You think you bring us no harm?" She paused for a moment, giving Kruno the ability to truly gauge the gravity of the situation. He was strictly at her mercy. "You're right I am not going to kill you, but if you proceed you will be jeopardizing her original decision, the decision to let you leave in the first place. We would have diced you up in our lair, no way you would have won. You weren't supposed to come back, ever. That was the deal."

She pulled the blade away and stood up. He turned and stood up as well.

Damn, are you all this good looking?

Dressed in a tight leather armour suit her beauty was hard not to notice. His male instinct kicked in and his eyes absorbed her striking female form quickly.

"I need to talk to Kiera, this is something that is important to both of our races. She trusted me, you all decided to back that decision, please trust me now."

She started to shake her head. "I shouldn't even be…" He smiled, she continued, "Let's go now and it better just be you. If anyone else is following us I will carve you up and not think twice about it."

Bruno stood hunched over the table in the war room with Egon. It was the middle of the night but there wasn't much time for sleep. Too much planning was still needed. It was just the two of them, but many had been in and out of the room since Egon's speech. He was just a boy in many ways, but he recognized that defect and wisely relied on others to fill that gap.

The late hour was affecting both of them and they knew sleep was inevitably going to overcome them. Rizzian had animated the three dimensional map which showed the layout of Dryden and the surrounding areas. They were talking about defence strategies.

"Bruno, we have gone over so many situations, but they are all contingent on how many they are, their plan of attack and how they are going to place themselves strategically. What battle form are we going to use?" Egon said, with a big yawn, something that was occurring regularly as his brain demanded oxygen.

"We have to think like Zoran and Gabriel," Bruno responded. "They will assume certain things about us as well. One assumption will probably be that we will have fewer men to battle and assume that morale is low due to the loss of our King. Thanks to your speech they will be wrong. This city is ready to fight."

"And who knows Zoran best? We could use as much information as we can get."

"Actually, Kruno knows him best but he is gone right now."

"Gone?" The young King looked to Bruno with a struggled focus.

"He left earlier in the day."

"Great time to leave, is he coming back? All that talk of fighting gargoyles motivated our people, but will be worth nothing if he doesn't return."

"Yes, of course, he mentioned his journey is essential for the battle. I think he has earned the right for us to trust him."

"You are right, exhaustion is overtaking us. How many men can we count on from the adjacent towns and cities?" Egon switched topics and repeated a question that had been previously discussed hours ago. Both men were flirting with utter exhaustion.

Before Bruno could reply, the door behind them flung open. In ran the guard from the wall. Bruno recognized him but couldn't remember his name. He was panting and could barely speak.

"This had better be good, because nobody is supposed to barge in the war room. You're not even supposed to be here, ever," Bruno said with authority.

"You... have to... have to..." His panting was out of control. His lungs demanded oxygen for reasons other than speaking.

"Come on, man, spit it out." Bruno looked to Egon to watch his reaction. He could tell he was irritated, but used restraint to keep from declaring his impatience. "I don't think we keep these guys in good enough shape."

"Black Knights, here." Finally catching his breath, "Black Knights approach."

An alarm went off in Egon's mind. Panic started to set in. *Could they be here now? If so, we have to hold them off for way too long, before relief arrives. This is not good!*

Bruno grabbed his sword that lay in the corner and slid it into its sheath. They raced out of the room heading to the main lookout den, where the man had observed the Black Knights. It was a long trip from where they were, but little time was wasted.

A commotion on all lookout dens along the front of the main wall was underway and the area where the King and Bruno wanted to observe from was overcrowded. Word had spread among those in charge of security. Many had rushed in to get a peek.

Six Black Knights waited on the edge of the moat and looked up for someone to say something. As Egon cut through the crowd, his men in the den dropped to one knee in his honour.

"What do they want?" Egon asked a random soldier as he moved near the ledge.

"We don't know, all they said was that they want to talk to Bruno. I am glad you came. They were getting yelled at pretty harshly by our men."

Egon looked over the edge but Bruno forced him back immediately. His first reaction was to be upset, but Bruno explained, "No disrespect, sir, but I would like to keep you out of their range. Let me do the talking, you can listen." Egon nodded and backed away.

"You looking for me?" Bruno bellowed. His voice had to carry quite a distance and compete with the noise of the river.

"Bruno, is that you?" one of them yelled back.

"Why do you look for me and explain why I shouldn't have these archers place a dozen arrows in your ass?"

With that insinuation, several archers pulled back on their pews, ready to fire on command.

"You don't recognize me? It is me, Bryce. How many times have our families gathered together? I come in peace. We need to chat."

"You might have noticed we are on the brink of war with your Kingdom."

"The brink? The war has already started. Troops are on their way here now, but it's not with our Kingdom. We have denounced our positions, we are no longer Black Knights."

Small chatter started up. Bruno walked to Egon. "Well this is your call. They are going to request entry. What do you want to do?"

Egon started to understand just how many decisions he was going to have to make. Every big decision was his. "Do you trust this man?"

"I have known him for many years, our families are well connected. It would, however, make him the perfect person for a concealed operation. You can't put anything past Gabriel. I actually probably know a few of the men with him. Some I would consider friends, but the reality is the second their brethren killed your father, every one of them became my enemy." Bruno continued, "If they come in, they don't leave."

Egon rationalized that six Black Knights could do little harm. He would mobilize twenty-five Elites and others to escort them through the gates and the gate would be sealed right behind them. "I see little risk bringing them in." Egon gave his nod.

The massive metal gate opened and the drawbridge lowered. Bruno, with ten fully armed Elites, walked to meet them. Being the keen warrior that he was, he canvassed the background for any unwanted surprises. His eyes rolled behind them as far as the darkness would allow. He could see no threat. He then swept over their faces to see what he could read. An ambush didn't hide in their look.

"It's been a long time, my friend." Bryce dismounted to meet with Bruno.

"Don't act too cheerful and stay close to me. A Black Knight is probably the worst thing you could be in Dryden right now."

"I understand Bruno, but we aren't Black Knights anymore." He pointed to his shoulder where the emblem of the Dark Realm used to be, it had been pried off. Bryce then reached into a sack and pulled something out. It was a piece of metal, bent and twisted, but easily recognizable as the emblem. With a toss, he threw it into the river. "I hope you understand this is an act of treason and we would be killed for disgracing the Dark Realm in such a way."

Bruno waved them in. They walked on foot through all four gates and entered the city. A massive crowd had gathered to witness the spectacle. The Black Knights offered to disarm, providing Bruno promised protection. Surrounded by fully armed Elites, they looked around at a lot of angry faces. It didn't take long for the crowd to start tossing out vulgarity. Many citizens started to yell and scream at their enemy.

"Maybe we should move this along faster," Bruno said, fearing the citizens of Dryden would get braver.

"String them up."

"Burn them alive."

"They are demons."

The crowd yelled out. It wasn't often a regular citizen could treat a Black Knight with such disrespect without repercussions.

"Interesting time to come visit, Bryce. As you can see the entire city knows you side with gargoyles and that you practice the black arts."

"Hey, hey, relax, don't use the word *we*. My men don't worship anyone and definitely do not follow the black arts."

"They don't know any different, they are scared," Bruno announced as they navigated through an even denser crowd.

"They should be," he said under his breath. Bruno heard him but ignored the comment. They both knew what was coming to hit Dryden.

The six former Black Knights sat in one of the great halls of the royal building. They were distanced from the crowd, but most of the city knew, or would know by morning, who the new guests were in Dryden. Mixed emotions and many stories ricocheted amongst everyone.

All six men were large, well-built and had long hair. They were wearing Black Knight armour and awaited who would come to see them. Bruno had dropped them off and was coming back shortly or so he communicated. The hall was heavily guarded inside and outside the room.

"Well this is your idea Bryce. I hope you know what you are doing. I could be on my way to a beautiful beach and spend the rest of my days rolling in hay with southern beauties, but instead I am with you, in a place where even the ugliest of ditch pigs wouldn't spit on me," said one of the men

"You want to be spit on?" another asked, confused.

"This is the right move, you know we really had little choice. You would be in paradise, but you would never forget and nor would the Realm," another Black Knight spoke.

"One day we are charging here to destroy our enemy and the next day we are breaking bread with them, strange turn of events, don't you think?"

The door opened and Bruno walked in with a few surprising guests. Rizzian, Decan, Christian and Egon accompanied him. Bruno had listened to Kruno's recommendation to involve Decan in any relevant decisions. Earlier that day he offered some impressive strategic defensive ideas, solidifying his position. Christian had been studying with Rizzian and was with him when he was summoned, and therefore was there by simple logistics.

"So it is true. We have six Black Knights unarmed in a room, I say we gut them." Decan smiled as he made the comment. His walk was one that showed little respect for them as he barely looked in their direction.

"I've heard of you. You are Decan, right?" one of them asked.

"Yes I am, and I am sure you have heard of me," Decan responded with cockiness.

"Yes, I have heard of you, all of the ladies talk about the man that makes threats to compensate for the size of his manhood, or lack of size I should say." He smiled along with the others.

Decan managed a slight grin, turned to the side which was a decoy and drew one of his swords. He moved with speed and stopped the blade right below his jaw. "Sorry, could you say that again?" Decan's blade extended as it did once unsheathed, adding to the effect.

"Real fast Decan, I heard you were quick off the sheathe. Really brave too, drawing on an unarmed man."

"You want your blade? Give him a weapon and let's see who stands." Decan's voice changed as he was getting worked up.

"Fine, give me a blade. I will fight you right here." Both of their faces went flush as blood rushed at the prospect of battle.

"Okay, boys, that's enough. We get it, you are both tough guys," Bryce said.

"Is this what you came here for Bryce, to cause a ruckus?" Bruno asked. Decan put his sword away.

"No, we are here to talk about some serious business. Things you're really not going to want to hear." Bryce turned and looked to Egon. "You must be Egon. I am sorry about your father, he was good man."

"I am struggling right now not to avenge my father. Maybe we shouldn't talk about him." Waiting a moment, he continued, "Actually, maybe we should. Did you have anything to do with his death?" Egon wanted to give the order to slay them, but held back his emotionally charged decision for the rational one. Nevertheless, the guards' grips tightened on their weapons in case they were commanded to use them.

"None of us here had anything to do with your father's death."

"Liars!" Egon shouted as his age and inexperience revealed themselves.

"I am serious. There is no way we would be here now if we did. That being said, we have done some things we regret," Bryce said as he continued to lead the discussion, intelligently changing direction from the dangerous path it was on.

Bruno stepped in, "We have all done things we regret. Egon, you asked me my opinion, let us hear what they have to say."

Egon nodded, "Tell us why you are here, tell us why you left the Dark Realm."

"King Egon, I will tell you exactly why we left, why we have elected to abandon our army as we approached our rival Kingdom, but not yet. It's too disturbing, once I tell you I will be a bit of a mess, I won't be coherent. Let's take things in pace, but know this though, we not only have left them for good, we are willing to fight them, you can have our swords... just ask."

Everyone in the room was focused on every word. They were curious to find out what could be so horrible that it would make them switch sides. The idea of a Black Knight defecting was a foreign thought until that day.

"I don't believe a word, these bastards are trying to use us and exploit our sympathy," Decan interjected, feeding doubt among the Silver Allegiance in the room.

"Kruno told me you would be a good addition to our army, but I am starting to think twice about that." Bruno let Decan know his opinion wasn't asked for.

"We have intimate details of their approach. They will be able to crush your walls and rip through the interior of Dryden. Once they have Dryden, the Silver Allegiance is in serious trouble."

"How is that possible? Our walls are thick and four-fold, it would take weeks of bombardments to puncture a hole in them. By then our entire Kingdom will have destroyed your men."

"Try not to associate the Dark Realm with us. We are not a part of them anymore and disgusted that we ever were." He continued, "They have something I have never witnessed before in my life. I doubt even Rizzian has even seen anything this powerful. Gabriel told us it came from the Underworld, a gift. This gift is actually two harmless liquids. Harmless when separated, but once mixed together they have quite the opposite effect. If just a small dose of each is combined, a fierce explosion occurs. I watched someone who was commissioned to test it out. He only used a few drops in a tube and then inserted a smaller tube of the other liquid inside it. The liquids remained dormant until he tossed them against a wall. The inner tube smashed on impact and boom, a hole the size of a human head was left."

"So what are you suggesting? How much do they have of these substances?" Bruno asked.

"Plenty, barrels full, or so Gabriel says."

"I have never heard of such liquids, but that doesn't mean they don't exist," Rizzian spoke. "So they will fire it via catapult and blast holes in our walls with ease."

Another one of Bryce's men spoke, "That's the plan. They have built a container like a boulder but hollowed it out for the most part. It has two sections and a fragile centre in between. Once it hits a wall or the ground, the two liquids mix and it will rip through anything; bone, rock, stone, mortar, anything."

"How do you know so much?"

"My town was commissioned to build it and we fired it once. My goodness, it is brutally destructive."

"So that's it. They come here expecting to blast through our walls and then run in slaughtering everyone," Bruno commented as he shook his head, attempting to dissolve the visual.

Egon's fatigue was visible as his head nodded. He needed sleep and badly. Bruno knew that and wanted him to get some rest. He could hear the rest tomorrow.

"King, I will handle this from here. I will prepare all information and present it to you in the morning."

Egon got up and walked out of the room. He made it to his bed chamber. He needed sleep, if possible, given the circumstances.

"How many are we talking about?" Bruno asked once the King was gone.

"Seven divisions move here. We rode with one of the divisions and ours brought with it two catapults and dozens of these shells we talked about. Not sure how many more they would have."

"Seven divisions?" Bruno questioned in disbelief. "That has to be half of their total forces!"

"That's about right, I think they will arrive here with just over half of all their forces. They want this to be a decisive battle. They need it to be quick. They have been building for this moment for a decade, stockpiling weapons, training their men and building their army, all for this moment."

"Rizzian, have you ever seen us assemble that many troops?"

"No, in all my years no. It would be very difficult to organize and even harder to support."

"How many catapults should we expect?"

"They are difficult to build and hard to move, but let's err on the side of caution and expect five of them."

Bryce continued with more and more details. The information was overwhelming and helped to solidify his case that he was a deserter. The numbers were staggering and hit Christian hard. He couldn't imagine how they could ever defend such a force. He looked to Bruno and Decan to see if they showed any sign of fear but they didn't. His mind wandered a few times and he wondered how Kruno was doing.

Kruno walked down the rock pathway leading down towards the Sand Sorceresses' den. The last time he was here, his friends accompanied him and he was invisible. This time was very different. Everyone they walked by took serious notice of him. Most of them didn't ask any questions and most followed because they understood the situation was going to be interesting. A range of emotions hit each of the Sand Sorceress he passed as the line grew behind him. They weren't worried about an attack. One man could cause no damage. Kruno was also easily recognized as a man they believed they could trust. He had fought them with great passion, skill and success. That gave him absolute respect.

"Nice to be back here." Kruno attempted to make it sound like he was just passing the time, but reality was he wanted to figure out her frame of mind.

"I could ask you why you are here, but Kiera should be the first to hear your response."

"Looks like you took my advice."

"What do you mean?" Her mannerisms didn't indicate hostility.

"You caught me while on patrol. Prior to our battle you wouldn't have known I was coming."

"Prior to you we never needed patrols, nobody found our domain. You have threatened our security by coming here once, I am afraid you have now illustrated its fragility even more."

Lost for the right words, Kruno stopped talking and waited to enter the main den. He wasn't sure what he was more excited about, seeing her or the speech he was going to have to make. Each had a different type of rush attached to it.

With numerous La Caprata behind him, he entered the room where not too long ago the strangest turn of events had occurred. They battled, negotiated and then a massive sexual escapade broke out. To talk about it was forbidden as per their release agreement, but who would have believed them anyway? Kill dozens, and then have sex with the rest. It would have been a crazy thing to describe and it would discredit even Kruno, giving him a stigma as a fabricator of stories. That was reason enough not to bring it up to anyone, ever.

The feeling he got from the room at first glance was tranquil. Less than half were here this time compared to the last time and most seemed to be relaxing. Light conversations were being conducted in scattered parts of the large room. The waterfall seemed to be more serene since the adrenaline of pre- or post-battle didn't occupy his mind.

Kruno found the odd hue of a green light emitting from the large diamond shape was still a little strange to get used too.

His escort didn't say anything but just stood beside him. She knew it wouldn't take long for everyone to become apprised of their returning guest. As each grouping noticed them, small chatter broke out with a nod or finger pointed in his direction.

Kiera isn't on her throne, the pews of the elders are empty, where is she?

"Fantastic!" Petra, Kiera's second in command, walked towards him from a small cluster in the middle of the room. "It didn't take long for you to break your covenant with us, did it?"

"I need to speak with Kiera," Kruno requested. He had every ear soaking up every one of his words. They were in need of satisfying a heightened level of curiosity.

"I decide who you will talk to, she is unavailable right now." Petra moved in his direction. He could feel her hostility.

Okay… She doesn't really seem to be pleased to see me. Not exactly how I expected this to unfold.

"Do you understand what you have done by breaching our deal? Do you understand the implications you have caused us, our race, our way of life? If I had my way I would…"

"Thank you Petra, I am here." Kiera's voice was quenching. Her words sent a shock wave of endorphins through his body.

She shook her head from side to side as she approached him. Her beauty was undeniable. Every one of them was stunning, but she had uniqueness about her and she had touched a place in him that night in the desert, which was imprinted in his mind forever.

"I am glad you are here, but I am not sure Petra was getting ready to break out the champagne to celebrate my return." He fully expected Kiera to enjoy his comment and respond in a similar manner.

"I am not glad you are here — what are you thinking? Does a deal mean nothing to you?" Her face was cold, as if they shared nothing, as if she didn't care. It made him queasy.

He flipped his approach, "Listen, I mean no disrespect, but what I have to say is crucial for the survival of both of our races."

"You shouldn't be here Kruno, we parted ways like no other. We gave you and your men a respect that concerned many of us. Since you have left, conversations have gone on about whether we made — whether *I* made the right decision."

Well, what was I thinking? I would just pop in, say hello, we would make love on the floor and run into to battle with one another. I am drunk with visions of her nakedness. My decisions have been compromised… Okay, I need to focus on them, need to make them understand how this affects them.

"Kiera, can we speak in private?"

"No, say what you will in front of everyone."

Lovely.

"Dryden is in trouble. It will fall without assistance."

"What do we care about Dryden? What has Dryden done for us?" A random La Caprata spoke out.

"How much do you know about the Dark Realm?"

"To us Kruno, they are a group we take from, that's it. They are of no concern. Your conflict with them has nothing to do with us."

"How much do you know about the black arts?"

The room focused a little more intently after that question.

"Why would you ask such a thing?"

"They have shifted, their leaders, Zoran and Gabriel, have turned towards the black arts. They have been given massive power but given up control of their minds and the right to their souls. They move now towards Dryden and to slaughter everything in their path. No mercy, no rules, just death." He spoke with passion.

"They would never find us here. We will continue to live without any ramifications. This doesn't concern us." A comment was made from a random La Caprata.

"Don't you see, this is blackmail? He is getting ready to tell us if we don't help, he will tell his soldiers where we live. He will command his soldiers, the soldiers of Dryden, to attack us. I bet also, if you don't return, your men are instructed to give them our location. He is threatening to eradicate us." Petra made the assumptive comments and infuriated all in the room. They took stock of her words as if the words had come out of his mouth.

"Wrong! What kind of person do you think I am? I don't want harm to come to you, any of you. I am grateful that you let us leave. We would have fought that day to the death, but every one of you knows we couldn't have won. I wouldn't be here right now, if it wasn't for your gracious decision."

"We didn't let you go out of grace, Kruno. We negotiated with you because you and your men were the best warriors we had ever interacted with. You deserved leniency. Plus, the blood you could have spilt would have left us in a morbid state." She waited for a moment and then gave her decision. "No to you. We will fight another battle another day. Picking the right battles makes sense, I am sure you are aware that this is an intelligent path. This is why we have survived in our utopia for centuries, we do not rush into foolish battles."

A few guards still stood attack ready. They had been that way since he had arrived. Kiera motioned to them, telling them to be at ease. She let them know not to worry about him, to put down their guard.

"That's what this is! This is the right battle! You have to understand that my men or I will never give away your position, but they will find you, this lair will be located. Gabriel is too powerful not to and when he does, you will fight an entire division of men, men with no conscience, an army with no enemies. Fight with us and you stand behind the fortification of the greatest city in the world. You fight with Elites," he paused briefly and quickly thought about their abilities as sorceresses, their battle strategies and decided to bring up something he knew they would be impressed with, "with Rizzian and the Dryden School of Wizardry, and of course Ivan." Being magically inclined, he knew they would respect DSW and Rizzian. This was one of the mutual comparatives between the two peoples. Ivan was brought up for obvious reasons. They had entitled him as the greatest of all men.

Kiera slowly walked around him and noticed, as did he, that every entryway had been filled. The news of Kruno's arrival in just a short time had spread throughout their lair. Everyone wanted to see firsthand what was going on.

"It would take the Dark Realm years to defeat the Allegiance and even longer to locate us. It isn't inevitable that they will even win the battle. It could be decades before they come looking for us. As the war would progress we wouldn't be affected in the slightest," she declared as she moved around his back.

"It is inevitable," he said sternly. "We can't win this battle, they will take out Dryden and the rest will crumble. Don't be foolish. You don't just fight for Dryden, the Silver Allegiance or battle for your home. You fight for your perpetuity. If the Silver Allegiance falls and the reigning Kingdom is the Dark Realm, who will you use to reproduce?" He looked around the room getting louder and more authoritative. "You are one of — if not the most — exceptional races I have ever encountered, but you need men for one thing, well maybe more than one thing." Kruno winked and excited a few of the women that were still revelling in the moments they had with his men. "Shall men with black souls be used for your children? You see you fight for the continuity of your race, you also fight for the very people that we are engaging in battle. Sounds crazy, doesn't it? Do you think that all of the people of the Dark Realm, including even some of their soldiers, want to be under the dominion of the Underworld? Of course not. Help us free them!"

There was a moment's pause. Individually they all pondered over his words... Kruno knew this was still a long shot. They never wanted to be a part of the world; just an enigma, a fable. They lived under a rock, but under this rock was a beautiful place where the mistakes and evils that are a by-product of a large world don't exist. To walk onto the battlefield, as Kruno was requesting, would destroy their secret.

"Sorry, Kruno, we can't help you, this isn't our battle. If they want to charge us, then we will fight them here in the desert, and trust me, they will feel our wrath." The crowd was fired up by Kiera's comment and cheered. Kruno felt a wave of disappointment and knew he would be riding back without a single extra sword. The trip was a monumental waste of time.

Just as he decided to start motioning towards the exit, something hit him in the back of his mind. He felt something breach his skull. It was a voice, a weird mystical voice, "*Come on, my Kruno, you can do better than that. We are still listening, convince them!*" It was Kiera! She had communicated to him without anyone else the wiser. After she spoke, the crowd showed respect for his response. They were listening. From despair to confidence he decided to take another approach.

"I speak on the behalf of an entire Kingdom, an empire that men dominate. In everyday life, and especially on the battlefield, women are less significant, fragile and worth less than men. Yet we men can't win without you. We come here to ask for your assistance, why? Why do we come here?" He waited a moment as energy was building in him. "We come because the best warriors we have ever encountered are La Caprata, a group of women, the top of the chain. A Sand Sorceress's combination of magic, swordsmanship, intelligence and even strength is unparalleled." Kruno stopped and looked to Petra.

"In our Kingdom, a great warrior is venerated as the one that sits atop the hierarchy of all warriors, known as a gladiator," he continued.

"As in ours," Kiera commented quickly. She then opened the channel to his mind again. "*You're doing well, now finish it.*"

"I would put you against our best gladiators," he continued, still looking to Petra. "La Caprata has been in the dark too long. Rise up, fight with us and receive your glory as you deserve. Fight beside tens of thousands of swords. Fight for your future. Battle an evil that has no right to be here on this earth. Show the world that women are just as spectacular as men, even better and demand to be treated as equals. By demonstrating your ability, you do great things for women everywhere."

"Thank you Kruno, let me take it from here." Kiera once again channelled a thought to him.

She levitated to address the entire room and broke into her native tongue. The language sounded like a beautiful song. It was poetic and even though he couldn't understand a thing, he tried to pay attention to the crowd's body language. Over time he read their response and deduced Petra didn't want to follow them to battle. That could be a major problem. His insinuated compliment to her didn't pay off as he had expected, when he singled her out as the top warrior.

The conversation went on longer than he expected. It was out of his control.

I have to ask myself this. Would I fight in a similar situation if roles were reversed?

The conversation continued and then there was silence. A few started to raise their hands. Kruno assumed it was a vote. He watched as several started to follow and put their arms up. He looked on with excitement. It felt as if this was a crowd that was voting for his life. He knew even with La Caprata's support, the Dark Realm was favoured, but the battle was guaranteed to be lost without them. That was a fact. A vote of "no" would probably mean he would meet his creator much earlier than he wanted to.

Hands had raised quickly showing promise but slowly decreased and then halted. It wasn't enough. Well under half had raised their hands. The vote had not gone his way. His journey was a failure.

Dammit! Come on, a few more of you ladies, raise your hands. Don't you have a selfless bone in your body? Well... okay... I need to head back right away, I need another plan and need one fast.

Kruno had to immediately begin to think of a new strategy. They had rejected to offer assistance, but he had expected this outcome. It shouldn't have been a surprise. He had a long ride back to Dryden and would have to come up with another plan in order to balance the fight.

"I will speak in the language that our guest understands," Kiera said while still floating. "I am sorry, Kruno, that I cannot give you what you ask. We won't be able to mobilize our entire army for you. I have asked for volunteers to stand by your side. Some have agreed to go to battle alongside Dryden, alongside you. At first you had less than a handful of soldiers agreeing to support you. Then I told them that you aren't even a part of Dryden, that you fight for them, a noble cause with selfless intent which tipped the scales and many more joined."

He had been wrong in his assumption of the vote. He didn't have everyone's support but he did have some of them. Kruno was overwhelmed, and swallowed heavily to clear his throat.

"I can't thank you enough. The Dark Realm has no idea what is in store for them."

"Arm yourselves. Say your goodbyes. We leave soon," Kiera commanded quickly.

"You didn't expect us to agree to come, did you Kruno?" She had slowly released her control over gravity, landed and walked with him out of the room.

"I thought it was a long shot but we need you and I had to try. Dryden is a good city and the Silver Allegiance is a Kingdom striving towards equality and they focus on a good standard of living for everyone. They're not perfect, but never seem to give up on striving for it."

"I was hoping your main drive to come here had to do with me." She looked over and smiled. Her coldness seemed to have thawed.

"I would be lying if I didn't tell you it was a part of it." He paused for a moment as excitement hit him like a school boy with his first crush. It was silly. He had been with so many women before but none had had this effect on him, not since he was an adolescent. "Did you know that our night in the desert wasn't going to be the last time we were going to see one another?"

"I will answer that question another day."

They entered a large room full of weapons and armour. Having no problem with nudity, the women removed their clothing systematically and put on their leather armour. Although intoxicated with Kiera's presence, he couldn't help but take a few glances at the perfect, dove white skin and flawless bodies.

He noticed that Kiera and a couple of others did not dress themselves. He assumed they were higher on whatever social or military scale they used. Daggers, spears and other small tossing weapons were loaded on them. Swords seemed to follow next. Kruno took the liberty of walking around and thanking several of them. Each nodded or made a small comment.

This is a good group. Would have liked a few more though. Might be three dozen or so, but the way they fight, it will be very helpful. We will need to position them properly. Are they better in one grouping or spread out? I will leave that to Kiera.

Kruno pondered the battle to come and found himself in deep thought. His concentration was broken as the doorway to the armoury was breached. With vigour Petra swiftly walked past Kiera. "What are you doing here?" Kiera asked her second in command.

"Do you really think I am going to let our Queen go to battle while I sit here?" Petra responded with irritation.

"Petra, you…"

"Yes, I do, and with me comes them." In poured more Sand Sorceresses, not the entire army, but their head count swelled. The rest of the group was thankful to see them and so was Kruno.

"Okay, now we have a group to reckon with," Kiera yelled with glee and the group conducted a quick ritual. Several with perfect posture, spun their weapons around their heads to collide with another defending and a beautiful noise of metal on metal ricocheted throughout the room, as they hit exactly at the same time. They switched positions from offence to defence and repeated the action.

Very impressive, I like it. This really fires me up.

Just before they were ready to leave, Petra approached Kruno, "You know what she gave up for you, don't you?"

"Pardon me?" Kruno didn't follow the question.

"Go ask her yourself." It was obvious Petra didn't really like Kruno or at least the disruption he had precipitated, but that really didn't matter. He had fought beside people he didn't really care for and was sure many that didn't like him, but he would rather fight beside someone with skill and passion who he didn't like, than the reverse.

Several armed Allegiance soldiers entered the room with the Black Knights in Dryden.

"Okay, you guys are coming with us," one of them said, looking somberly at the defected Black Knights.

"And where do you think we are going?" Bryce asked.

"Egon has commanded us to detain you."

"You are arresting us?"

"This was Egon's order before he went to his chamber." They started to move into position.

"I told you Bryce, we shouldn't have come here. We should have never listened to you. After everything we've done they are going to arrest us."

"That's true, we didn't have to come here Bruno. We could have ridden off and left Dryden without giving up our valuable information or weapons."

"I know, gentlemen, let me talk with Egon and hopefully we can get you released tomorrow."

"Great, isn't this great. We will be locked in a cage when Dryden is ripped to shreds. You know they will burn us alive." He looked like he was about to get aggressive and the Allegiance soldier's body language indicated a change in demeanour to match.

"Hold on! You're going to try to talk to Egon? Before you talk with your King, you should hear everything. Let me tell you the story I was holding back. Let me tell you why we defected in the first place."

Bruno halted the men and waited with anticipation for Bryce to speak. It was obvious that he was uncomfortable and dreaded reliving the ordeal.

Bryce put his hands through his hair and looked to the others who bowed their heads.

Bruno thought, *These are Black Knights, Bryce has been through many battles, witnessed many things, but never have I seen him or any of his kindred act like this. What could possibly have gone on?*

"We marched toward Dryden with the fifth army out of Pra. The soldiers were more than excited for battle, it was like an infection. They needed it. They hungered for the death of the vermin of the Allegiance. We all thought it was just a clever form of promotion to get all of them into the proper mood. Some, like us, didn't have the same aspirations, but still rode on supporting our Kingdom and its expansion. We followed our leaders, Zoran and now Damascus. The reality is that Zoran and Damascus are more figureheads if you ask me, Gabriel is the puppeteer and he is one scary bastard." Bryce moved to the table and sat on its edge as if to take some of the weight of the story from his back.

"The plan is simple, destroy every town on the way to Dryden, burn it to the ground. We were asked to stay behind until we hit real opposition. By the time we rode through a town, all we witnessed was the aftermath. Buildings smouldered, bodies were being tossed into a pile, but I noticed there were no survivors and asked Gabriel about it. He responded that they were all dead. I then inquired about the women and the children and he told me they were shipped off after battle. The next town we encountered we were close enough to hear the sounds of war. We heard screams from people begging for their lives and then the battle cries in the end, indicating our victory. We were too far away to see anything. We entered the town quicker than the first and again noticed no women or children. Well there were a few women who were held back and gagged and left tied up on the ground. They were obviously kept for entertainment purposes."

"Good God, you guys are really winning me over as great human beings, let the women be kept as sex slaves," Decan commented, inappropriately.

"And you would have done differently?" he asked, but Decan didn't respond because Bruno put up his hand indicating Decan should shut up.

"Anyway, it seemed strange to make it such a priority to have women and children transported out so fast, so I inquired about being a part of the next raid. Gabriel told me that it wasn't going to happen because he wanted me and my men to be available for Dryden. We were to be well rested. It really didn't make that much sense, but I wasn't about to push any harder."

"Hold on, where is Zoran in all of this, why do you seek Gabriel?"

"Zoran is leading another division, probably the fourth or sixth, I am not sure. Gabriel leads the fifth army. Anyway, we decided to advance just behind the battle. We wanted to see what was actually happening at the next town. We knew something wasn't right and that's when it happened." Bryce forced air out through his mouth, expanding his cheeks in an attempt to check his emotions, to buy a few moments before he had to continue.

"Come on man, what happened? We don't have all night here."

"Decan!" Bruno let him know he was really starting to cross the line.

"Okay… okay, please continue, but I don't like you guys very much, I just want that noted."

"Thanks for clearing that up," Bryce said sarcastically, then got serious and continued, "It was late evening with only a little light left in the day. The rain was coming down pretty hard, making everything a mess. There was mud everywhere and nobody was dry. Any opposing men still alive were on their knees, maybe fifteen or so with their hands bound behind their backs. A few women were pinned back by the soldiers. We found out that all the children were locked in the school house and the rest of the women were in an adjacent building. Windows were boarded up and all exits fastened. One of the women in the roadway broke free from one of the soldiers after being sexually taunted and ran for, I am assuming, her husband who was bound in the row with the others. Gabriel stood in the middle of the wide road. It was eerily quiet for all that had occurred. It was like he was basking in his glory, in the victory as the rain came down on him. When she broke free she disrupted the balance. He snapped back from his morbidly blissful state. Irritated that his perfect scene was interrupted, he called for an archer who pulled back on his pew, aimed and placed an arrow in her ribs, a bad place to get hit. It would have easily punctured a lung. The husband got up and ran to his wife who hit the muddy ground a few feet in front of him. He wept on his knees as he watched her cling to life and then die in agony." Bryce understood that everyone in the room probably knew the town, maybe people in the town and each of them would picture their friend as one who died. He wanted to tread lightly, but he needed the pungent effect and continued.

"Gabriel loved it. He watched from a close vantage point to observe the despair and suffering of the man. He reached down and slammed his head to the ground so he was only a few inches from her face. Gabriel then said, 'Hold on, not yet.' She coughed and started to breathe, she was still alive. At first I thought maybe he had some human qualities in him. He watched the joy return to the man's face, but in a matter of seconds she appeared to die again. He wanted to see it all over again for his sick pleasure. He wanted the man to watch his beloved wife die again."

"Oh my God. That is terrible." Christian spoke.

"That isn't the most horrible part. He did it again and again. She was given life, the worst part I am sure of her existence and then made to endure the agony repeatedly. Her husband cried and screamed for him to stop, but that seemed to just fuel Gabriel more. This man stared into his beloved's eyes and endured a torture few have ever in the history of human kind, maybe worse than all others. I couldn't take it. I walked up and jammed my sword into her. Gabriel broke his concentration, as if from some kind of a trance and looked up to me.

"I said, 'That is enough Gabriel, she needs to go, we need karma on our side.' He was furious. Still on one knee, pinning the man to the ground, a man who now oddly thanked me for killing his wife.

"Gabriel rose, staring at me, his hand formed a fist, and with power I have never witnessed, punched down toward the ground and right through the man's head. His fist was inside his splattered skull."

"Not powers like you are thinking, he doesn't possess that kind of strength. It's a spell, an impressive spell nonetheless, but magic," Rizzian jumped in.

"His body twitched as Gabriel pulled his hand from the interior of the very dead man's skull. 'Burn the school, burn it now!' he yelled. I responded, 'Pardon me, what did you say?' Gabriel stood up and looked me straight in the eyes, only a few inches away and yelled, 'You do it, you burn the school!'"

The stomachs of everyone in the room sank hard. Nobody spoke but all prayed that he didn't kill the children, that young innocent children didn't die by burning to death.

Bryce started to get a little emotional. His hard exterior was cracking. "I couldn't believe what I heard, burn the school down. I was frozen at the command. Hundreds of soldiers, including Black Knights that were part of the raid didn't say anything. They looked at me as if asking what was taking me so long to complete the order. They acted as if this was a normal request. Gabriel turned from me and walked up to the remaining men on their knees. They were begging him to change his mind, screaming in a last attempt to save the children of their town, probably for their own kids in the school house. I don't know what they were saying exactly, my mind was a little chaotic. They didn't have a chance to argue long because he ripped through each one them with ease, it was gruesome."

"Tell me you didn't…" Bruno asked.

"Are you kidding me, would I be here now? I mounted up with seven of my men getting ready to get the hell out of there. One of the men handed me a torch. I looked at him and said, 'Are you crazy? You want me to burn down a building with innocent children in it?' Another Black Knight yelled to me, 'Are you crazy? You dare contradict our leader. Those aren't even human children, they are rodents. Burn it Bryce, and burn it now or face my sword.' I looked at the crowd which indicated by the relaxed expressions that they had no problem with the order. I knew it was time to get out and get out fast. I grabbed the torch and let them think I was going to burn it down. We charged in the direction of the school house and many watched in anticipation but we tossed the torch aside."

"That's it, that's all you did? They would have had someone charge over and kill all of those children within moments of your rebellious act. Are you nuts? You may as well have burned it down yourself." Decan shouted furiously, which invigorated the same feeling in many of the soldiers.

"What were we supposed to do? What would you have done?" one of Bryce's men spoke up, obviously upset.

"Something, anything! They were children. You could have turned and fought as many as you could have." Decan continued the bombardment.

"You don't think I think about this every second?" Bryce turned around, grabbed one of the tables and flipped it over. Decan even took a step back from his aggressive reaction, partly because Bryce was obviously upset but also because that table was extremely heavy, and he had lifted it with ease.

Tears started to fill Bryce's eyes.

"If we had fought, we would have died, we would have taken maybe a handful down. Here we can take many more out, many more of those sadistically evil bastards."

"Try to calm down, and please finish the story. Decan, you have been warned enough times," Rizzian commented and then mumbled some words. Decan tried to respond but his speech was temporarily inaccessible. He couldn't say another word. He struggled to figure out what went wrong. He was perplexed and made jerking motions to try to free his tongue. He then looked to Rizzian who pointed in his direction, indicating he was the cause of his inability to talk. He told him to relax or he would be tossed from the room.

Bryce continued, "As soon as I tossed the torch aside Gabriel turned, soaked in blood from the slaughter of the other men and let go several fireballs which raced towards the school and engulfed it in flames. We couldn't do anything but charge in the opposite direction and figure the rest out later. We heard them scream. I still hear them scream. I need vengeance!"

"He burned the school first," Rizzian said with a grave tone.

"Yes. They let the women watch and listen to their children burn. He has gone over the edge. Gabriel isn't human at all. He is completely consumed by evil."

Everyone was in shock. The Black Knights wept a little, a couple of them slid to the ground, one of them even vomited.

"They are all gone, don't you see? None of the soldiers cared, they probably enjoyed it, they aren't human anymore."

"You said you left with eight but there are only six of you," Bruno commented.

"Black Knights cut us off, but we cut through them. You are looking at some of our best, but we lost two men."

"How do we know if this is true?" Christian asked uncharacteristically. "Sorry, this might sound terrible, but how do we know they didn't burn the school down or if that whole story is even true. I mean it sounds true but how do we know for sure?" He started to realize he didn't like the attention and backed off a little.

"I can tell. If these men are infected with the same curse that plagues the one they just described they can't hide it from me." The Wizard walked up to Bryce, looked him in the eyes and examined the white part. "Come out if you are here. God is love, love controls everything, the Devil himself is nothing."

Nobody understood what he was doing, but he wasn't questioned. Rizzian knew the words would give rise to any evil inside them, and if agitated, a black vein would run through the white part of their eye. He continued to taunt, even slapped Bryce. If it remained white then they weren't under the dominion of the Underworld. Doesn't mean they are good men, it just means free will is still theirs and Rizzian didn't believe that any man, good or bad, would ever be a part of such a nefarious act. No one would burn children alive unless they were a part of pure darkness, only harnessed from the Underworld.

"They are okay."

"We still have orders to arrest them Bruno, and you don't have authority to change that," one of the soldiers stated.

"They are right guys, but I will have you out as soon as I can. I know Egon. He will listen to me and Rizzian. Please just follow the men. You will be treated well, not like prisoners. Put them in the temporary cells, get them something to eat and drink, real food, they will not go to the dungeon."

As they walked away, Bruno said to Rizzian, "We have some serious problems coming our way. I am really not sure if we were better off hearing that story or not."

"We are always better off knowing everything Bruno," Rizzian said, using the same tone he usually used when giving advice. "Gabriel is becoming more powerful than I thought. This isn't good. We need to change our defence, we need to prepare with more vigour. A monster hungers for our flesh." The words made Bruno uneasy, primarily because even Rizzian seemed a little nervous. The great and powerful Rizzian seemed like he had a little fear in him. "Ban the use of Gabriel's name."

"Why?"

"Just do it, nobody uses it anymore. Do you understand me? I will burn the tongue from the mouth of whoever utters his name."

The six men found themselves locked in the temporary jail. The conditions were significantly better than the dungeon. It was lit by natural sunlight, spacious and easy to see each other, because there were only vertical bars from floor to ceiling separating the cells. The temporary jail had multiple cells on either side of a corridor. It was obvious they were trusted and their story was believed because they weren't in the dungeon or separated. Bryce and another were on one side and the other four across the hallway in groups of two.

One of the former Black Knights that was the most vocal about disagreeing with Bryce's decision to come to Dryden, found his rage building to fury.

"Bryce, I am angry right now!" He stood up and marched around the cell.

"What in the heck were you thinking? What were we thinking, listening to you?"

"Relax, Bryce is our commanding officer. Whatever he decides, we will follow." Another man jumped in to defend.

"No, he isn't our commanding officer anymore. That dissolved the second we rode away from the town, engaged Black Knights in combat and was solidified when we killed our own."

"You should relax, we're not going to be here long. Bruno will get us out shortly."

"Really, well I don't think so. I think we are thoroughly screwed. Gabriel is going to rip through this city, find us in here and burn us alive. This is if we are lucky, maybe he will torch us to the point of death and keep us alive to feel the excruciating pain." His face turned red and his knuckles turned white from gripping on to the bars, looking straight at Bryce.

"Don't bring up his name, that is a bad idea. You know he can hear us. He might pick up where we are."

"Shut up in there," a guard, out of sight, yelled from around the corner.

"Kiss my ass, you prick," he yelled back. No reciprocating comments followed. He continued yelling at Bryce, staring at him hard, eyes protruding from their sockets, "Gabriel, Gabriel… Gabriel. How does that sound to you?"

Bryce got uncharacteristically fired up and charged the bars as if he was going to rip through them, "Are you that stupid? You are calling him here now after what we did. You know he can probably hear you, you stupid donkey." Bryce waited a moment and then commanded, "Shut him up, before it's too late."

His cell partner, still loyal to Bryce, even though his formal status was really gone, charged him and slammed him against the wall. The two struggled; one tried to keep him pinned, the other attempting to break free. The others yelled different pieces of advice or motivational words like slave owners in a gladiator ring trying to assist their man and help him win.

"It's too late," a voice nobody wanted to hear echoed through the room and rattled the bones of the ex-Black Knights.

A hooded man in a black cloak materialized in the cell where one man pinned another against a wall. Bryce backed away from the bars, retreating to a distant part of the cell. He tried to think fast. He needed a weapon or a way out, but he couldn't think of anything to aid the undesirable situation.

"I am glad you are here, I've been waiting for you." Pinned against a wall, he struggled to speak because his air flow was constricted.

"Well, look who we have here, six swine all ready to be slaughtered." Gabriel shook his head, "Maybe you could back away from him for a moment." His hand was glowing orange indicating a spell was to be unleashed. He took control of the ex-Black Knight who had been pinning the other one. His arms were pulled back without even touching him. He started to yell as if struggling with a heavy weight to keep position. The force was too strong for his muscles and with body locked out of his control, he slid a foot or so back. The other man took full advantage and punched him square in the face, "That's what you get, you prick."

"Violence, excellent. Now let's figure out what is going on here," Gabriel commented, eerily. He then used his other hand to cast a manipulation spell on the one who summoned him. He too lost control of his body and his arms froze in a posture which was spread out, mimicking the other in an awkward position. They both stood close to one another with no ability to move at all. They felt as if their appendages were set in concrete.

Everyone in the jail cell was terrified at the presence of the dark Wizard. The ex-Black Knights knew they were in trouble. Death was around the corner. Other patrons that occupied the cells down the corridor would normally run to see any commotion for entertainment purposes, but in this case, they hid. They didn't want to be noticed at all by the powerful Wizard. Every person in a cell scurried to a corner, except for one group.

Three strange men had a cell to themselves and didn't move at all, but sat oddly on the floor. They all looked similar; pale white skin, wrinkly, very short, and almost underdeveloped in size and height and had childlike characteristics. They obviously weren't children and looked as if they had been in jail for a very long time. Their non-action indicated they either didn't know who Gabriel was or didn't really care if they lived or died.

"Seems like," one spoke, "things just got," the second continued, "interesting," the last one finished the verbalized observation.

"Gabriel, let me go, I called you, I led you here."

Gabriel dropped his spell on him, turned and made an incoherent mumbling towards the hallway. Just as he finished a barely noticeable transparent orange glow covered the entrance to the jail cell corridor like a door.

A guard had heard enough of the noise and walked quickly to see what was happening. His leg breached the orange glowing doorway with ease as if nothing was there. He didn't notice at first but as he passed through the doorway his clothes ignited. His upper body continued forward and immediately burst into flames. It wasn't just his clothes that were on fire, all exposed skin, including his face, was ablaze. Unable to comprehend what had happened, he started to grab at his skin and ran in a panic against one of the cells. The pain was intense and he yelled. The other guards ran to his aid, ready for anything but didn't realize they would meet a similar fate. They each followed and two more burst into flames.

"We are pretty sure"... "Rizzian won't be" ... "very happy." The three creepy looking cell mates spoke in the same format as before, finishing each other's sentences as they looked on but were now standing.

"So tell me what you told them?" Gabriel asked the man who had recently defected from Bryce, his only ally in the room.

"Can't you get me out of here first? More guards could show up. Rizzian could come here."

"Oh my, you do lack intelligence, don't you? I think my reference of a pig was generous, more like the intellect of a rodent."

"What do you mean? Let's get out of here. I can tell you whatever you want to know. I never left the Dark Realm — I was planning this the whole time, you have to believe me."

"How do you think I knew where you were? You called my name several times. Now you call his name, in his Kingdom. Not the sharpest sword of the bunch, are you? I hate stupidity."

"He didn't have to call me, Gabriel, I could smell your vile disposition the second you arrived." The room temperature dropped fast and the fires faded on the burning Allegiance soldiers. Rizzian stood in the hallway, in between the cell Gabriel was in and the cell Bryce was in. He turned towards the glowing doorway and Gabriel's spell disappeared. Without saying a word, Gabriel's fire ambush spell submitted to Rizzian's will.

"You shouldn't have come Rizzian, this isn't our time yet. Our battle is close enough but not today." Gabriel had his back to Rizzian, showing little respect for him.

Bryce had noticed that one of the guards released his spear when he dropped from the flames and that spear now lay against his jail cell. He moved slowly and armed himself. He wasn't sure when he was going to need it, but one thing was for sure — he was much happier having it in his hands.

"I disagree Gabriel, now is a perfect time to battle, no army behind us, just the two of us. Time to settle the question on everyone's mind. Who is more powerful? This event is something that I have anticipated for a long time."

"You have no idea how powerful I have become, you old fool. Your power has limitations and boundaries, mine has none.

"Just say when." Rizzian commented as he prepared a massive offensive spell, assuming he would attack first as Gabriel's back was still to him.

"Okay Rizzian, how about we settle this in the courtyard?" He made the suggestion, but it was just a diversion. The rules of battle between

Wizards were well known among their kind. If one makes a change of theatre request, it is to be accepted as long as it doesn't hinder the other Wizard. Wizards love an open area to do battle so that they are able to use more of their spells and make a spectacle of it. Rizzian knew they were in a confined area and knew that it would be messy. The courtyard would be a much better venue to conduct this test among Wizards and would cause less collateral damage.

"Very well Gabriel, let's head there right now and let's see how powerful you really are."

Rizzian dropped his guard for a moment as he prepared to relocate to the courtyard.

Gabriel, who had no intention of changing the venue, turned and forced both hands forward. His upper body moved as he added power, which forced his hood to fall backward and reveal his face. His eyes were filled with hate and they were the first to hit Rizzian. It was a complicated combination of spells; the first was a hybrid illusion curse, which imprinted horrific thoughts all throughout Rizzian's mind, carved a mark on his heart and punched him in the soul. If he had had more time he would have vomited from the stench of visions that dominated his mind.

It distracted him. He wasn't prepared for a black arts curse of that level and it left him open for the physics spell which forced energy into a condensed area. It created a force that pummelled Rizzian off his feet and jettisoned him backward into the bars of Bryce's cell. The bars bent under as Rizzian hit them. Anyone else would have been split by the metal, but his magic worked on pure instinct. His subconscious mental awareness kept him from being squished through the bars by bending them. Instead they twisted around his arms, locking him and leaving him defenseless.

Even though Rizzian wasn't dead, he was injured. The impact was severe enough to cause him to cough blood. Physically he was hurt but his ego was damaged more. Rizzian was no match for Gabriel's first attack sequence. The combination of spells was spectacular and his foolish decision to assume Gabriel would follow the rules was a novice mistake.

"So you are my greatest adversary? It is very sad, I think. I was hoping for more of a fight, Rizzian." Gabriel didn't move. He just stood and looked at Rizzian in disappointment. "You see Rizzian, I am too powerful for you. Your city will crumble and I will burn your precious school. I will destroy every student and professor. The only way they will be allowed to live is if they bow to me and denounce your silly God."

Gabriel needed to know exactly what the Black Knight traitors had told the Allegiance, and even more importantly, he needed to know all that the traitors knew about the plan of attack. He could see that Rizzian wasn't a threat and could deal with him in a moment. He decided to switch from normal conversation and start to scan the mind of the soldiers. His mind scan would leave the men with the intelligence of a three-year-old at best when he was done. Most who suffered the mind scan lost the ability of motor skills as well. It meant they would basically become a vegetable mentally, but he wasn't concerned with that. Showing no mercy, he decided to start with the one who had summoned him to this prison, the only one that felt some sort of loyalty to him.

Gabriel, with an outreached hand, cracked through his mind and started the process that would drain every part of it in a short period of time. There was no way to hide anything, no secrets could be withheld. The pain was excruciating. Instantly, he started to scream.

The three little weird childlike men stood up and spoke softly, "So"... "you dare insult"... "Rizzian like this?" They moved through the bars, almost liquefying themselves and then rematerializing on the outside of the cell. They stood, staring at Gabriel. A small electrical charge seemed to build within each of them; like lightning bolts sliding up and down their bodies.

Gabriel hadn't noticed them. Only a random nobody prisoner in a cell across from them did and he was shocked, indicated by his bugged out eyes. They had been there for weeks and he thought nothing of them. They were just strange little weird creatures, that somehow just moved through the bars with ease. The prisoner had been very wrong about who they were, very wrong.

"Back"... "Off"... "Gabriel!" they spoke individually, but then unified their voices for the last threat, "This is our house, Tres Nombre!"

Gabriel heard them speak, but didn't pay attention to them. A small burst of white energy snapped against his cheek. It hurt enough to get him to wince and look in the direction it came from. What he saw wasn't as alarming as he expected. It was just three little weird men staring at him.

"Who do you think you are?" Gabriel asked with cockiness.

Another electrical charge leapt from them and hit him in the chest. The pain was real and more intense than the first strike. Gabriel realized he might have misjudged them as more lightning bolts hit him hard in the leg, the face, and then the neck. Without responding they battered him with an intense barrage of white bursts. The bolts flew at him with incredible speed from the little men, who not once lifted an arm or even finger. They just stood and stared. Gabriel raised his hands to defend himself. The light hurt his eyes and the explosions were doing damage. He forced himself into the corner of the cell.

Gabriel knew he could pull himself out of this undesirable position and rematerialize back at the front lines of his army, but he hadn't retrieved the information he needed.

Bryce watched with amazement and waited for Gabriel's response. A few moments passed and Bryce realized that maybe the evil Wizard couldn't respond, maybe he was in serious trouble. The spell looked deadly but this was Gabriel. Bryce assumed he had to leave in a hurry and also assumed he would try to take the traitor with him.

"I don't think so!" Bryce said and released the spear. It dug deep into the skull of the defector just as the two of them disappeared.

"Got you, you stupid bastard!"

The flashes continued for a moment, but simply struck concrete as Gabriel had disappeared as quickly as he had arrived.

A few moments of silence passed, but felt like hours. Nobody was comfortable in the room except for the three little men who somehow managed to toss Gabriel off his game. Bryce moved forward to examine the great Wizard who was entangled in the cell bars. None of the bars were broken, but somehow twisted around him. It was a strange sight. Rizzian was several feet into the cell and leaned on a 45 degree angle from the ground. His upper body had taken most of the impact and sat deeper than his lower appendages.

Rizzian rested for a moment, realizing Gabriel was gone and the threat to everyone had dissipated.

Bryce, only a few inches from his face, asked with confusion, "Are you okay, Rizzian?"

"Physically I've been worse, but mentally I have taken a serious beating."

"How is that possible? I knew Gabriel was good but you are Rizzian. You are supposed to be able to take him down or at least challenge him."

"I got my ass handed to me, that's what happened. Next time it shall be the other way around."

"Do"... "you"... "need our help, Rizzian?"

"No boys, I am okay." Rizzian concentrated and the metal bars started to liquefy.

"Bryce, back up, a splash of this metal on your skin will cause serious damage." Bryce did as the old man advised. His feet were free first and then like wet noodles the bars came down. The red hot material ran down Rizzian's skin, but he shook if off like it was nothing and no damage was done to his person.

"What happened there? I mean you just melted bars with your mind and it rolled off your skin like water. That takes serious skill, but with Gabriel you were sucker punched hard." Bryce changed focus and pointed to the little men. "And by the way, who are you?" He was overloaded with questions and his thoughts were all mixed up with emotion as he tried to digest all that had transpired.

"Are you okay master?" The three spoke at the same time.

"These men are known as Tres Nombre, some of my brightest students, and I will be fine," Rizzian said out loud for all to hear, but then opened a channel to their minds and spoke telepathically, "*but Gabriel did have the jump on me. He has become too powerful. Even for me. The black arts have embraced him like a son, they have invested a lot in him.*"

"Come now Rizzian... As he had the jump on you... So did we on him!"

I saw the evil in him, it's horrific, disturbing. His plans for Dryden are terrible. Everyone will die, everyone. Distraught, he started to walk away.

Before exiting the area he stopped and turned to Bryce and his men. "You fight for us?"

"Just give us the opportunity."

Rizzian looked to several new guards who had reinforced the area.

"Guards, release these men. Get them fitted for armour and introduce them to their commanders."

"But Rizzian, this is not your decision. Egon will have to approve." A random guard disagreed.

Rizzian looked in his direction and his eyes began to glow a bright blue. That's all he needed to see.

"I will talk to Egon. They have proven themselves."

Kruno navigated on horseback through a less travelled road toward Dryden. Behind him, a contingent of Sand Sorceresses followed with thoughts of war occupying their minds, and they moved at an aggressive pace. Not a lot was said, at least not out loud. Kruno's companions didn't need to verbally communicate, but could open a medium in their minds. Even with the freedom of telepathy, conversations were kept to a minimum.

The last of the trees broke into a massive open field which led to the great city of Dryden. Not one La Caprata in the group had ever seen Dryden. Kruno figured such and was excited to see their reaction, but he didn't turn to see their faces. Instead he just imagined what expressions they might have. Every one of them was shocked and impressed.

The river embraced the massive walls, most noticed this first. Others were drawn to the huge statue of a hand which held "Dryden" in silver in the middle of the city. The most impressive of all was its sheer size.

"Surely any Kingdom to call this home will defeat any army that attempts to attack it," one of the leading ladies said aloud for Kruno and the rest to hear.

"Dryden is magnificent, there is no doubt about that, but the army that marches here surely believes they can sack it," Kruno remarked.

Kruno pointed to several groups of men in the field, most of whom were practicing battle techniques. "There," he said to Kiera who was always by his side.

Kruno could tell from the distance that Decan was leading mock exercises. The field had dozens of groups; some as small as ten and a few more than a hundred. Almost everyone was preparing for the ensuing battle. It was assumed a few more days would pass before the Dark Realm would push through the roads in the forest. There was still time for more training.

Kruno rode up beside Decan. He had at least eighty men, all novices from military perspective, possibly men who had never fought before. They were learning the basics with a spear.

"Not a better man to learn from. Consider yourselves very privileged," Kruno called out, making sure everyone could hear.

"Good to see you are back and you have brought with you an exquisite sight."

Kruno had ridden along the open field with numerous battle-ready women. The sight drew a lot of attention. The soldiers on Dryden's walls let out a warning, by blowing a horn as they had been commanded to do, if anything out of the ordinary was to arise.

"We have been blessed with well needed swords, from some of the best." Kruno gave the guests a well-deserved compliment to the bewilderment of Decan's students. They refrained from commenting as they were lower infantry, but most were thinking that it was insulting to have female warriors join them.

"Introduce me to your students," Kruno commanded.

"You are looking at a group of men that used to be farmers and merchants, but are now infantry. I am teaching them three simple but effective moves with the spear and how to work with their shields."

Kruno dismounted and walked up to the group. "Let me see what you have learned. Who wishes to show me?"

At first nobody volunteered because of Kruno's stature; besides having the right to stand by Egon, his fame was well noted. They were nervous to say anything.

"Come on, someone speak."

"Oh great one, I will show you." A younger man, maybe seventeen, stepped forward. Kruno held back his laughter at how he was addressed. Although revered by so many, he never really looked at himself that way.

"Please, son, feel free to call me Kruno, just Kruno. I am just a man as you. Show me what you have learned. Attack position one!" Kruno commanded, knowing full well what they had been taught.

The young boy, enamoured by his interaction with his favourite hero, stepped forward. He was obviously a farmer as indicated by his muscle tone and his permanently stained skin. "Aw!" The boy chanted adding sound effects to his forward thrust.

"Good job, nice posture," Kruno remarked exaggerating a little. "Keep hold of that spear really tight when you strike. This spear could be plunging into Zoran, you know." The group smiled with excitement. Only a few of the old timers understood what the battle would really be like. The others were excited to have Kruno's approval.

"Decan is teaching you well, listen to him. Learn your striking positions, but most importantly, see the victory. Envision your enemy dropping, see them impaled by your spear. Imagine it and it will be true."

From behind, several horses rode up, "Well, what do we have here?" A man relatively highly ranked but not an Elite asked the question as he looked over to the serious and attractive women on horseback. "Is this our entertainment before we go to war?"

"This is La Caprata and they are here to help us fight, show some respect," Kruno stated with irritation in his voice. He had expected this reaction, but still felt disappointed when it happened.

"Kruno, hold on, don't get your undergarments in a bunch. I didn't know this was going to be a beauty pageant. Are we all wearing dresses now to the fight?" The men that rode up with him started to laugh.

"Kruno, we all heard you were going to get us assistance, but this is ridiculous. The word circulated around the city that you were going to bring us warriors. The people were counting on you and you bring us a group to wash our clothes and make us dinner," another man commented.

"Do I know you soldier?" Kruno said, as his lip tightened with irritation.

He was ready to lay down a verbal beating when Kiera asked, "May I respond Kruno?"

"Of course, please, by all means." Any annoyance disappeared when Kiera had volunteered to field the question. Kruno looked to Decan with a hint of a smirk and a wink.

"The gravity of the situation has hindered your ability to see what is in front of you," Kiera stated.

"Oh, don't worry darlin', I know exactly what is in front of me and I really like what I see." The group, which had grown in size, laughed again.

"Time to make an example of him. Petra, would you mind?" Kiera asked in her mind and Petra agreed with a nod.

"It has been said that a man with such disregard for the ability of a woman does so out of a lack of self-confidence and to deflate his embarrassment," Kiera continued.

"Oh, don't you worry honey, I am great with my sword, full of confidence and never been embarrassed."

"I wasn't talking about that long broad sword made of steel in its sheath. I am talking about the pin you have in your pants that you refer to as a penis." The retort was brilliant and everyone broke into laughter. It was obvious that he was upset.

"It is true, how did you know?" one of his group yelled and lifted up his pinkie finger, trying to let all gauge its size and everyone laughed harder.

"Enough talk. Petra, if you please, dismount and prepare yourself with a headless short spear." She did as commanded, walked over to a spear in the ground and snapped its head off with one solid strike of her sword.

"And what is this all about?"

Petra did the same with another spear and tossed it to the ground in front of him.

"You have to be kidding me!"

"Instead of using swords or real spears. This way you won't hurt me too badly." Petra made the comment with a roll of her eyes. Decan and Kruno smiled.

"I am not going to fight a girl." He looked around at his posse who looked back at him. Their expressions indicated they fully supported the fight.

Petra waited in position, holding the wooden shaft as if it was a sword. A few moments passed and everyone waited for something to happen. The soldier finally got off his horse, put his sword on the ground and picked up the wooden staff.

"Okay, little girl, let's see what you have. I am going to turn you around and spank you with this." He wandered around mocking her with gestures, implying she couldn't swing a sword, slashing as an inexperienced woman might do. He looked back to his friends, who found the situation amusing. He was a well-respected warrior, one few would tangle with. Most laughed as he goofed around.

"Come on, this is absurd." He turned around and addressed the crowd.

Petra moved in fast with a quick snap and hit him on the cheek. She wasn't looking for critical damage, just enough to motivate him with pain. The impact made a loud enough noise for the immediate crowd to realize it had hurt him. Most flinched as if feeling the pain themselves.

"You think that is funny? Now look what you have done, now I am mad and have no choice but to hurt you." He was livid at her antagonizing strike and charged. Petra easily defended the strike from above and stuck out her leg to trip him. He hit the ground hard and everyone broke into laughter.

Back on his feet, he brushed the dust from his face and moved in this time with more skill, taking it seriously. Petra stayed defensive for two blows and then thrust kicked his abdomen. He dropped his arms as he moved in to comfort his stomach, exposing his head. The spear forcefully crashed down on the top of his skull. Even though it was much less damaging to be hit with a blunt wooden spear, it still took its toll. He dropped to his knees, letting go of his weapon and gripped his head.

"That's not fair. In a real battle he would have had on a helmet and he wouldn't have felt that," a friend yelled.

"Please, then take his place." Kiera invited him to join the battle with her most decorated warrior.

He dismounted and walked over, never taking his eyes from her. He did not want to be humiliated and decided to be more cautious. He was certain it would be an easy victory but took extra steps. Comparing size he was 50% larger than her, from a distance the fight looked odd.

Petra began to encircle him until the optimum time and attacked with speed. At first her strikes came fast, the fastest opponent he had ever fought, but he defended well. Then she turned it up and the spear was hard to see because of her agility. It was too much for him, all he could do was defend, there was no way to strike back. A few strokes later she took it up one more level. Everyone watching was dazzled by her skill, the wood moved all around him until his defensive wall broke. He took a shot to the ribs and one to the face. They were relatively light shots, but they were just a lead for the final two. She switched sides with a spin and landed a hard shot to the thigh and then to the side of the face.

The crowd cringed, responding to how it would have felt if they were on the receiving end. The swelling started almost immediately, he was down and out.

A third man jumped from his steed from the other end of the temporary battlefield, "How about one more, wench? You better have something really special if you're going to take me down."

Petra could tell he was really skilled with a sword and his build indicated that he would have speed as well. He wasn't tall or very muscular, but thin and lean and he had confidence in his eye. She reached down and picked up the weapon the last victim used, since he didn't need it anymore and tossed it to him. By the time he picked it up she was running toward him. He had a slight smile on his face as he waited. She could see in his eyes his plan was a quick defence and then probably go for her legs. The plan was a good one, but he was fighting a Sand Sorceress and she wanted the result of this blow to ricochet throughout Dryden, so they wouldn't have to conduct this activity over and over proving themselves to other testosterone-charged men.

Just before they connected she split into tiny particles, blew past him and regenerated instantly behind him. Not only was she behind him but she faced him. Everyone was in shock at what had just occurred and most thought they had missed something. A few blinked at the worst time and did miss what had happened. One moment she is in front of him and the next behind him. With ease, she struck her target on the side of the head. She hit him so hard that he flew off his feet and hit the ground. Everyone was flabbergasted.

"Anyone else have any questions about our new allies? Do you think they are a good addition? Do they deserve our respect?" Kruno looked around seriously.

He didn't expect anyone to say anything but heard one from behind, "I have a question." Kruno looked over to see Egon on horseback. He had ridden out to see what all the commotion was. "Will you join us on the battlefield?"

"But of course King, that is why we are here." Kiera had never met him, and although he didn't have his crown on, she knew who he was. When Kruno had told her of stories, she could visualize them in her mind and knew what he looked like.

"I thought it was an important question to ask, for you to hear it directly from me, from the King. Who am I speaking with?" Egon almost seemed to be flirting a little.

"I am Kiera, the Queen of La Caprata, and this warrior is my first commander, Petra."

"I think my first commander, Bruno, would have a hard time with you Petra. We are honoured to have you with us and will show you all the hospitality Dryden has to offer. If anyone questions you again, they will have to speak directly with me. Come, Queen Kiera, follow me."

Kiera rode gently beside Egon, "Why do you put yourselves at such peril for a city you don't know?"

"Oh, we know more of you than you think. We have taken from you for some time."

"So you are looking for atonement?"

"No, that's not it, that's not why we are here."

"Then what is it?" Egon asked with curiosity.

"Kruno asked."

Egon waited for more of an explanation but nothing else was said

"He is something special, that is for sure."

As the two rode away, the third casualty from the battle with Petra walked up to her, holding the side of his face, he grimaced a little and stuck out his hand, "Impressive, I am glad you are on our side. Maybe you could teach me that trick someday." He smiled and she shook his hand.

CHAPTER 7

GABRIEL'S WINDOW

Christian sat on what was once King Deo's favourite couch in a remote part of the castle. It was night and even though he had a lot on his mind, he attempted to wash away his thoughts by staring into the brilliant fire. The battle to come was overwhelming. Life as he knew it was going to change. He had been travelling with Kruno for years, but in all reality nothing they had been a part of would change history as the impending outcome of this war. Still young at heart and green in mind, he questioned his involvement. He couldn't understand why Kruno didn't even consider walking away from this battle. He loved Dryden and the Silver Allegiance, but weren't they just drifters? Why would they risk their own lives? Especially here, where Dryden, as tough as it was, faced the spearhead of an army that vastly outnumbered them, led by an unforgiving power.

His mind then shifted to the new voice in him that was growing stronger, a voice that had little fear and lived for grandeur — one that was a product of being one of Kruno's comrades. His objective was to use this time to release all negative thoughts, to support his leader's decision and fight for Dryden.

The room was one of the most serene man made settings he had ever been in. It was small in comparison to others in the castle but it had character — fur carpets, three absurdly comfortable couches huddled together, a blazing fire encased in a beautiful oak mantel, and the walls were covered in wood panels to give it a perfectly rustic feel.

Christian's mind was unstable to calm down, and even though he was looking for tranquility and attempted to not think about anything, he couldn't help it. In many ways this was a transition point for him. He struggled with selfless thoughts of valour and selfish thoughts questioning his decision to stay and fight.

Slouched on the couch like a child, he sat up immediately and felt mildly embarrassed as Rizzian placed himself on the other sofa beside his. The two didn't say anything at first. Christian pretended to look at the fire with only a few glances at the greatest of all Wizards. His mind, in one way, found peace from his troubled paradoxical thinking as it focused only on Rizzian.

"This was Deo's favourite room, you know?"

"I am sorry, I probably shouldn't be here. I can leave if you would like." Christian asked for permission to stay with the cowardice of child who thought he might have done something wrong. He was attempting to play coy and respectful at the same time.

"I am certain Deo won't mind. He won't be using this room for a while." Rizzian responded with his normal serious tone, but was a little more relaxed than he expected.

Not sure how to interpret the comment, Christian decided to assume it was a joke and incorrectly chuckled a little. He knew as he was doing it he made an improper assumption. He felt like he should say something as tension seemed to build in the room, but as usual, no words left his mouth. His entire life he had held back so many of his thoughts, words that would have changed who he was and how he was perceived. Lack of confidence in social situations caused him to endure many sleepless nights, re-living moments and thinking about what the outcome could have been if he had just opened his mouth.

Christian was wrong about the joke but also about the tension. Rizzian wasn't irritated or mad about the chuckle after his comment regarding the venerated deceased King. Rizzian himself had shared many similar situations as Christian when he had been his age and some to this day. Like most Wizards, they were socially lost, not funny, or really exciting and didn't get along with the ladies especially well.

"You need to learn about your adversary... Gabriel." Sitting down, still staring at the fire in a comfortable yet practical robe, Rizzian dropped an anvil on Christian's lap with the comment.

"My adversary? I am confused, he is their head Wizard and you are ours."

"A general in any army would be a fool if he didn't train someone to be his back up, if he was to fall in battle and no one was there to take his place, it would be a total disaster."

Christian's mind rattled. It sounded like he was going to be the backup if Rizzian fell. That didn't make any sense for several reasons. First, Rizzian wouldn't fall. He was too powerful, and secondly, he couldn't have been referring to him. Too many other great Wizards were in a better position than he was.

Rizzian answered his questions even though Christian didn't vocalize them. "Christian, if I am to fall you must take out our adversary," Rizzian insisted, careful not to repeat Gabriel's name. "He is your primary objective. He is very important to our enemy, his ejection from this world would be most beneficial."

"I don't understand. You have so many talented Wizards that are more experienced, with more comprehensive and powerful spells. You want me to tackle Ga—tackle *him* if you fall?"

"Actually, we shall take him on together. I have dozens of Wizards who are older than you, maybe some who have more stamina or larger volumes of spells, but who has the battle experience that you do?" Rizzian finally looked at Christian, and with a little more life in his face responded, "I want you to learn about him, to review all that we know of him." Rizzian handed Christian a leather binder with pages tied together by a thin velvet string down the side, obviously designed to be able to add and take away pages, a working living document.

"As we have extensive intelligence on him, he will have something similar on all of us. Every one of my Wizards showing any promise would have been noted and studied by the Dark Realm. Then there is you. On the battlefield they have no knowledge of you, which would probably lead to the incorrect deduction that you are a junior and insignificant. They won't know what to expect."

Christian listened to his mentor with his mouth agape. In all reality, he looked foolish and had his thoughts written all over his face. The look told Rizzian that Christian was scrambling to process all that was said.

He wants me to attack Gabriel with him? I don't know about that, who does he think I am? I feel stronger than ever before, I have advanced, but I am not ready for this.

Rizzian didn't read his mind, but his words sounded as if they did. "You are ready for this, you know that, right?" Christian shrugged his shoulders.

"At least you are honest. Most would probably try to lie to me. Christian, I have two things to say to you. The first is that great people do great things when they are out of their comfort zone. Many before you have challenged the impossible and conquered. The result is a radiant, life-changing feeling, a pivotal point in life. Nobody I know was born confident, without fear. They had at least one point in their lives that made them who they are. The second critical thing is your spell, Sphere of Fire. How old are you? I can't even do that spell yet, maybe I never will."

Christian interjected, attempting to argue his incompetence and defend Rizzian's credibility, "That is probably my fault, I haven't written it out properly…"

"Who taught you to speak out of place like that?"

Christian remembered who he was talking to and decided he would really think twice before talking again.

"I am really not good with telling jokes. I shouldn't tell them but I can't help it. Others are so good with them. Feel free to talk as you wish, Christian, when we are here, alone, but in other situations fall back to the rules of conversation. Your spell isn't written wrong, it's complicated. You have a great understanding of physics and I am sure one day I will get it, but that isn't the point. It is one of the world's best spells for close combat and it is unique in nature. It's also a spell that few Wizards would draw upon, as its only benefit is in blunt warfare. Others create spells that can be used for many other things and then adapt them to combat, but yours was created with full intent to be used to decimate an enemy."

Christian had no choice but to feel a surge of pride which added to his confidence. He looked down to the book in his hand and opened it.

"This is everything we have compiled on our enemy. Most of it will focus on the Wizard for obvious reasons. He is vital to their magic arsenal. Read about him, learn as much as you can. The smallest detail may give us our edge. After you have finished reading, come and see me with a plan. I have other details to take care of."

Rizzian got up with a wince, a product of his age. He shifted his back and started for the doorway. Christian stood up as a sign of respect.

Christian was about to ask a question, but Rizzian interrupted before he could say anything, "No. No more questions. One day everyone will stand when you enter and exit a room. One day soon you will be on your way to this kind of respect, which will begin with a name that I will endorse."

Christian's eyes started to water as his sensitive side rose to the surface —something that he had been ridiculed for for many years. Rizzian insinuated that he would get his new name soon. The sheer joy was overwhelming and made him think of nothing but confidence with this daunting task ahead. His mental questioning was over. He was ready for war.

The book was written by magicians and therefore could be processed differently. Simply placing a hand on a page illuminated the mind. Each word didn't need to be read, because it was constructed in such a way that a magician reading it could engulf themselves in the story as if there. The descriptions of people, places and feelings were felt as if they were his own. The reader was actually living those moments.

Once Christian understood that this was the way it was intended to be absorbed, he was excited. It had been several years since he last had the opportunity to experience such a book. Only major cities like Dryden with the DSW would ever have such an inventory of books.

The book began.

Christian was introduced to a child named Michael. He lived in a house just outside of Dryden. At the time, Dryden was part of the Silver Kingdom before the Silver Allegiance was even created. Dryden's source of wealth was its silver mines and took on the name the Silver City — in Christian's time it was still called that name by some. Mines were also located in other towns in the surrounding areas and the group had become the Silver Kingdom. This cluster of wealthy cities became very powerful, boasting a massive army as it allocated monies to build it. By accession, wilfully and by force, the Silver Kingdom grew into the largest, most powerful Kingdom and would become the Silver Allegiance.

Michael lived in the time of powerful, questionable takeovers led by Dryden. Many had chosen to forget about them, to keep the pure image of Dryden intact.

His family's house was modest, easily holding his two brothers, a sister and his parents. His father had been a relatively famous jouster many years ago and now trained the upcoming notable jousters. His position gave the family an easy lifestyle. His father, who Michael looked up to with reverence, was well known and he had met the King on a few occasions.

His problems started at a young age. His entire family had similar traits and were all good looking, athletic and socially adept; everyone but him. He was unattractive, socially lost and far from athletic.

As time went on, it was apparent to his father that his last son was going to be a reject. Michael, even though rejected from the social side of life, was extremely intelligent, but that interested his father very little. Michael could read better than his father by the age of six and he attempted to use that to gain his father's acceptance, but it did the opposite.

His oldest brother had started to win competitions. Spear tossing, archery and short racing were areas he dominated. The more awards he won, the less his father paid attention to his physically impotent, unattractive son.

His other brother was a great horseman and was successful with the ladies, which was another feature admired by his father. Michael, on the other hand, didn't get a second look from women and in all reality didn't care. He didn't really like girls. Concern grew from both parents that he was homosexual. That was where the really painful conversations started to do their damage.

Michael's rejection from his father was something he felt, but he always attempted not to believe it because he had no real evidence. His mother and sister would tell him that they all loved him. Over time, those reassurances came fewer and farther between. The conversations were painful, at first his parents spoke quietly and sporadically about their son's potential sexual appetite and other issues, but eventually they got louder and he overheard everything.

Michael was verbally abused in his sensitive years, driven by the assumption that he preferred the same sex, but the reality was that he didn't like either. That was normal for a child, but as he aged, things didn't change. No interest in men or women, no interest in sex. He just wanted to read and learn more and more. His only friends were his books.

In the beginning he cried. His emotions were triggered by his parents' conversations, omission of love and by his school mates who rejected him at first and then physically beat him.

There was one moment, though, when everything changed. He had enough of the tears and feeling terrible inside. He didn't want the sick, rotting sensation that was tearing him apart like a disease, so he turned off all of his emotions.

He ate, went to school, talked to nobody, slept and read. The only one that showed him any kind of response was his sister, but it was too late. He truly didn't care about anyone anymore.

Problems erupted at home and it caused stress on the family. The verbal abuse shifted from being hidden in a room to right in front of Michael, but like a zombie, he did nothing.

The only glimmer of hope came when he was in his fourteenth year of his life, and a teacher from his school had recognized Michael as a genius. His grades had been sliding over the past year, from top of the class to mediocrity. It occurred in conjunction with when he had turned off all emotions. The reason his grades had slid had something to do with his home life and lack of goals, but it was primarily driven by the fact that class was too remedial for him, it was a joke. Through his own studies, he had learned how to read four languages and his math skills could rival most teachers.

The emotional breakthrough came one day when a new teacher started to teach at his school. He was known as the Professor. He could see Michael's potential and started to talk to him every day after class, and every challenge the Professor threw at him was conquered with ease. Finally he had found someone to talk to, a reason to get up in the morning. Time passed. A full year had gone by and everything was looking up until one day he approached Michael with disturbing news.

"Michael, I have to leave for a while." The comments ricocheted through him with the first pain he felt in years. His only friend, the only person he could talk with, the sole individual who understood him was leaving!

The Professor was different than the other teachers in appearance. He had long greasy hair, was unattractive, skinny and a little creepy. Since he had been spending time with him, the school kids had just let Michael fade into the background. Picking on someone who doesn't care really wasn't interesting, so he was left alone. The kids were also afraid of the Professor.

"Don't believe the rumours you here about me, okay?"

Michael didn't know of any rumours, but he wouldn't have heard them anyway, as he never talked to anyone but the Professor

"This stupid town and the people in it accuse me of such terrible acts just because I am different." The Professor was irate and paced as he talked with a nervous, unappealing look.

"I have to go, and I have to leave now, but I wanted to give you something first." He handed Michael an old black book, with a half black glass sphere on the cover, but no title or words written on the jacket.

"I wanted to give this to you in the future when you were ready, but I know you will treat it with great respect. I wish I could guide you through it, but I can't. Just understand that when I was given this book, it was the most important day of my new life." The Professor started to look around nervously as if something could tackle him at any time.

"Don't tell anyone you have it. Don't let anyone read it. This will be your new best friend. I hope I will see you soon."

The Professor ran down the hall, his departure triggered by the sound of a crowd in the distance.

For the first time in a long time, Michael felt a surge of anger. He was mad and wanted to find out who or what caused him to leave. It wouldn't be long before that was answered.

The accusations had spread through the city like an avalanche down a mountain. Everyone was trying to find the elusive Professor who had been accused of some of the most atrocious crimes anyone could commit.

"You have disgraced our family, you stupid little bastard!" Michael's father yelled as he entered the house. Michael could see the look of fury in his eyes, something he had never witnessed before.

The Professor was accused of having sex with little boys and everyone assumed that Michael was one of them. Even if it was true, Michael would wonder why his own father didn't consult him first. He was just presumed guilty. If he had been sexually assaulted, his father's response would be to yell at Michael. What kind of father was he?

"Your Professor lover disgusts me, I hope he dies!"

"He is more of a father, a mother, a brother than any of you!" Michael screamed, deciding to speak to his father for the first time in months.

His father, who had turned away for a second, slowly turned back with rage and clenched his fist. He hit Michael harder than he had ever been struck. The strike came in from the side and made his head swell under the pressure. The impact

eliminated what little love he had left for his father. With the emotion of love now completely void, he found a new feeling to replace it as his book slid before his father's view.

Michael looked up to see his mother. She did nothing. She just stood there. He needed her now but she didn't intercede. He then watched his father toss the book in the fire. Michael screamed, as it was the only treasure he cared about. He attempted to run to it, but his father called to his brother to intercept him and he did. His strength was nothing compared to his brother. Pinned down, Michael's anger at his family and at himself for not protecting the treasure better and for not having the strength to fend off his brother hit a boiling point. Emotionally charged, he was dragged into the cellar.

Michael sat in a dark place literally and figuratively. Rage continued to build. He hated his family, the city for sending his only friend from him and wanted revenge, but he was no one. He couldn't do anything, he was too weak!

The cellar door was left ajar and he left late that night and walked over to the fire that had destroyed his book. Hoping to at least find the emblem on the front cover, he poked around the ashes, and he hit something. Lifting it from the fire it was impossible but true, the book looked untouched!

How could this be? This is impossible, what is with this book?

As he brushed off the book, he discovered it was perfect. The turn of events charged him with joy, but also made him realize this was more than just a book — whatever lay between the covers would change his life.

Michael waited until the morning light sun illuminated a new world for him. The cover opened as if it was made of lead. He struggled to pry it open and found it would start to give a little and then snap back. Examining it, he discovered there was no lock on it and no reason why it wouldn't open. Eager to investigate its contents, he tried with all his might and yelled, "Open!" The book popped open at his command.

Once opened, he started to read something that he understood was illegal and probably the main reason for the Professor's exile.

Michael hid in the forest for the day and read for as many hours as the sun would allow him. He couldn't stop reading, it was addictive. He barely blinked and rarely took his eyes from the pages.

The sun started to fade but Michael wasn't done. He was upset that he didn't have a candle or torch and didn't want to have to wait until the following morning to read more. He closed his eyes for a second. They burned because they had been opened for too long without even blinking. He opened them to see that the book was glowing a deep orange and it was easy to keep reading. He didn't question why, he didn't want to waste the time on the thought. The book's contents were too enthralling.

The next morning, just before the sun rose, he stood up for the first time and looked around. He saw things differently. It was difficult to explain but things had changed. The white part of one of his eyes had a stream of black running through it. He couldn't see or feel it but it was there. With a calm he couldn't describe, he smiled, a disturbing, spine-chilling smile. He reached forward and touched a tree. Closing his eyes for a second he felt something small hit his shoulder and could hear a few more things hit the ground around him. It felt like it was raining. Michael opened his eyes to see a withering tree, it was winter but the tree was an evergreen. The pine needles turned brown and were falling to the ground all around him.

Michael stopped and looked at his hand, which emitted the same colour of orange as the book from his palm. "Amazing!" He watched the colour on his hand start to fade.

He noticed a small blue bird land on one of the branches. Thinking for a second, he made a choice that most would never consider. He watched it for a few moments and then extended his arm to touch the base of the tree again. Michael closed his eyes and he felt a pleasant jolt. He looked up to see more of the needles falling but no bird.

Stupid little bastard got away.

While in thought, he heard a rustling next to the base of the tree. It was the bird. It flipped a few times and then lay still.

Michael realized he had gone almost a full day and night without food or water. His instincts directed him home. Walking with newfound confidence, he entered his house to a huge shock. The place was packed with people. They were all seated in the centre of the room, surrounding his mother, who must have been crying for some time as her face showed wear.

"Michael!" one of his father's good friends said loud enough, as if to introduce him to the room and with a hint of surprise.

"My baby!" his mother yelled and ran to him. Grabbing on to him with a tight embrace, "Where have you been?" She didn't let him answer. "I am so sorry about before, please tell me, are you hurt?" She pulled back and looked at his face, her hands searched for any wounds or injuries.

The outpouring of emotion made many in the room tear up. All of their friends felt bad about the way they had gossiped about their neighbour's weird child — Michael was often referred to as the strange kid when his parents were out of earshot. They attempted in their minds to retract the awful words that had been said in their homes, especially as of late, with this assumed relationship with the estranged Professor. How could they have judged? If he was their child, they would care for him no matter what.

Michael didn't even raise his arms to reciprocate; he was an emotionally empty shell of a young man.

"You have been gone for almost a week. You must be starving."

Gone for almost a week. She must be losing her mind. Stop hugging me, get out of my way, I need food, water and a little rest so I can read more.

The others started to call in the search party that had been scouring the land for days. He had been gone for almost six days and he didn't even realize it.

How is that possible? How could I not drink for that long? It seemed to be only twenty-four hours at the most. No water for that long would leave me dead.

Once water hit his tongue, he couldn't get enough. The food came next, which he devoured in a few moments. The message was passed throughout town that the weird boy was found. His father was introduced to the news in that manner as he was on horseback, still looking for his son with his eldest two beside him.

"What did you just say?" Michael's father said with a little bit of irritation in his voice to a man chatting with another in the city.

"That weird kid is back home, probably back from an escapade with that Professor," one man said to another with a giggle, not realizing who he was talking to.

Michael's father, much to his brother's surprise, leapt from his horse. He bolted the few steps it took to close in on the man with the big mouth and pinned him to the side of the building by the throat.

Staring into a surprised pair of eyes that were filling with a pinky red he said with all seriousness, "Never call him anything like that again. You're going to go around all day today and say nice things about Michael." He stared at him with intensity. "Got it?"

The man shook his head and he was released with a gasp. Holding his throat he watched the three men ride away.

It was a moment that confused everyone, including Michael's brothers, even his father himself. Something Michael would never hear about, something that could have changed events to come.

Michael hit the sheets and found himself in a dazed new world of controlled dreams. They were ambiguous and confusing, but controllable. While he slept, the neighbours in his house cleared and all of his family returned.

The talk amongst the family was very different than it had been for a long time. Michael was the topic, but this time it was not all negative. The prospect of losing their son weighed heavily on their minds. It was discussed more so by the women, but it was evident that the father cared as well.

Michael missed all of it. The love that was expressed could have potentially melted his hard shell if it was focused properly, but unfortunately that love would never reach the target. He was a hardened young man who wanted nothing to do with anyone. All he wanted was revenge, a revenge he wanted so badly it excited him in his dream state. It would all start the next day. Shortly after getting up, he would show a certain someone from his class he was no pushover.

Michael was up before the rest of the family and snuck out of the house without waking anyone. It was a long walk, but with each step, anticipation grew. He was premeditating an attack on a boy that caused him so much grief and embarrassment since he was a small child. Sean, a child who had been born with the prettiest face and God-given physical attributes, was Michael's fiercest tormentor. He was the best at whatever sport he chose. The combination of these things put him in a position of great popularity. All of this didn't bother Michael. It was what he had done with those attributes that angered Michael, he had abused them.

Michael thought about some of the humiliating moments that Sean put him through over the years, adding fuel to his focused plan. He disliked his family, the neighbours, the city, pretty much everyone, but he truly hated Sean.

Michael knew exactly where Sean was going to be on that bright and sunny winter day. The school house held about a hundred students studying at different levels. It consisted of three buildings and in the middle there was a court yard where the kids could gather and play. For most of his life he avoided the area as if it was plagued. It was the spot he had been beaten up many times. Dragged out, for the most part kicking and screaming in the beginning, but after a while he didn't bother to try and break free. Normally he would sneak around and attempt to evade the sight of Sean and his posse, but today he would do the exact opposite.

A group of twenty or so stood laughing and talking, with Sean in the middle. He had his girlfriend beside him and he was saturated with attention. Michael was sure this was shallow attention and was planning to prove it.

A few moments prior, Michael was full of excitement that he hadn't felt in a very long time. Actually he had never been so elated, but he pushed it aside because it was important to be able to think straight.

At first he walked unnoticed into the middle of the field. Michael was wearing a black cloak and the hood was covering his face. Michael knew it would only be a few moments before someone realized who he was.

"Look what the cat dragged in!" one of the boys yelled out to make sure that everyone heard.

Sean, with his debonair looks, saw one of his favourite targets standing across the way. "Well this is too easy, Michael." He started to walk slowly toward him and everyone followed.

"I thought you couldn't become any lower in life. It was hard to lay a beating on someone for the same reason week after week, it loses its fun, but then you go and suck the Professor's dick. I mean, could you give me anymore reason to beat you? I think I have to for the good of everyone. You sick, twisted little reject."

Fully expecting Michael to run, Sean was ready to break into a sprint, but Michael just stood still staring at him through his hood, fists clenched off to the side with arms fully erect.

"Isn't it time to run, you little freak? Come on, you might be able to out-run me." He turned to his friend with a pompous little chuckle. They all responded in a similar manner. Sean walked right up to him and stared at him face to face. Michael didn't even move. He seemed to stare right through him. If Sean didn't know him any better, he would have probably been a little concerned with such a weird, confident display.

Sean waived his hands in front of his face to see if he could get him to blink, but there was no reaction. He turned to his gang, "He is really gone. Hello, anyone home? Anyone want a beating for being a homosexual freak?" Sean spit in his face to get the reaction he wanted, but again there was no reaction... Everyone laughed but Michael didn't move. He just kept staring.

Sean started to circle around the kid who he had beaten innumerable times. He started to feel a rush and couldn't wait to take him down.

"Hey… stupid?" Sean bellowed as he reached out and slapped the back of his head. Michael moved slightly with the impact, and then kept his composure. He didn't even reach up to wipe his face. The spit just ran down in a stream on his cheek.

"This one is for your family that has to live with the disgrace that you are their son." Sean wound up and drilled Michael in the side of the head. He fell to the ground with the direct strike. He positioned himself on his knees ready to get back up when he was kicked off balance and crashed into the snowy ground.

"Great shot!" one of his friends yelled out.

"That was too easy, let's get out of here," Sean commanded and started to walk away. They all congratulated him.

The praise was interrupted by one of Sean's crew declaring, "Look at him, he wants more."

They all turned to see Michael standing again, in a creepy position with one arm extended in Sean's direction. The inside of his palms glowed eerie deep orange. Michael said words nobody understood and did so with extra emphasis pronouncing each syllable.

"What kind of weirdo horse dung is that?" one of the kids yelled out and many started to laugh.

Michael stood still with full concentration and his hand turned more noticeably orange.

The group waited for Sean to say something, but to their shock, he didn't. All attention was drawn to him with a scream from Sean's girlfriend. Everyone turned to see a bizarre sight. Sean was making the strangest face. As if in great pain, his mouth, eyes and nose were locked. His muscles pulled different parts in different directions to the maximum of their ability.

"Sean, what is going on? What is wrong?"

"Sean, stop goofing about," another friend yelled out.

Michael spoke, "Stupid Michael, the freak, the weakling, the bastard. Doesn't that sound about right? Hey Sean? Answer me? Answer your friends, what is wrong with you?"

The crowd started to take a few steps back to comprehend the gravity of the situation.

Sean's face didn't seem to improve, and through the small slit in his mouth he started to scream. The screaming got worse, and the few girls that were there started to cry and one ran off.

"How weak am I am now Sean? Hey captain of every team you play, how come the master of words doesn't have a lot to say now?"

"Stop it! Let him go!" A few girls begged for Michael to cease the attack, as they figured it out, but he had just started.

Sean's situation got worse as popping noises were heard. Sean finally attempted to bring his hands to his face to investigate the disaster and stop something he didn't understand. As if locked in stone his arms stood at his side. A few moments later they were freed suddenly from their position and they rushed to his face.

Sean's best friend spoke up, directed towards Michael, "Time to stop that right now or you will get a beating so bad your mother won't even recognize you." He started to advance slowly toward the boy with the glowing hand. Normally he would have just jumped him, but this was a new situation he wasn't comfortable with, and really wasn't sure how much personal risk was attached to rushing into a decision like that.

"Should I be afraid of your threat? What do you think?" Michael responded, sounding almost as if he were asking himself. "No, I am not afraid. You are the one who fears me because, if I choose to, I would lock your face just like his." He twisted his hand a little to the right, but didn't lose his intensity. A few more pops and snaps started to spook the others. Half of them ran. Sean's face pulled to an unnatural position and twisted his jaw, at which point he fully covered his face and fell to his knees.

The pain was so intense Sean finally passed out, but he didn't fall over, as Michael's spell held him in position. All that collapsed was his arms, exposing a disfigured face.

"You're going to kill him!"

"That would be too easy a fate for him. He will live and he will live in shame."

One of the boys signalled to three others, telling them to follow his lead. "You may grab another one of us, but we are charging in three and the rest will get through, unless you let him go. One… Two… Three!"

He wasn't bluffing and was just about to leap into action. Michael dropped his hand and Sean hit the ground still unconscious. Michael moved with intensity towards the kid who had threatened to charge. The kid was petrified, but attempted to not let it show. Michael got within inches of his face and looked him straight in the eye.

"I should do the same to you. I should tear all the muscles in your face and leave you a freak, but he is your lamb. Your leader falls. Your leader begins a new life of disfigurement. Please give him my regard. I look forward to seeing him soon."

Michael was outnumbered but nobody dared touch him.

Better to let him walk away, better that it only happens to one of us.

Sean woke up a few minutes later and could see the look upon his friends' faces that told him everything wasn't a dream. His face was mutilated. Muscles that once held his perfect beauty together were stretched or tightened. His face was soft and his skin sagged everywhere. The pain would leave over the next few days, but he was now in a world that was a nightmare that had turned into reality. His speech was also affected. He talked with a drawn out retardation. Friends would disappear fast and girls were a thing of the past. His life as he knew it had been altered for as long as he lived. A life he wouldn't endure long, suicide was inevitable.

Michael sat in his room on the edge of his bed with his hands crossed, resting on his knees. He had been in there all day. His family didn't bother him, but they had no idea what had transpired. Day turned to evening and darkness filled the home. Everyone was home. He could hear them in the main room.

He enjoyed reliving every moment of his interaction with Sean. The revenge invoked such a sense of bliss. Even more enjoyment came from thinking about Sean in his new life. It was obvious he would find a level of rejection even worse than his.

Perfect, simply perfect today. I couldn't have asked for anything more. Sean, you will be embarrassed to be alive, shunned by everyone. You have gone from everything to nothing in a few moments at my hand.

He waited for the next stage of his plan to unfold, one he really hadn't thought through too well, but knew it would work.

First your son is strange, then rejected. He isn't an athlete or good with women. He is also accused of being a homosexual and a lover of the Professor. You are all so blessed and it will be taken away from you. You will live a little of the shame I know.

It was inevitable that the townspeople would come. A crowd would amass and want answers and they would demand justice. That's what they would say, but in reality they wanted this misunderstood kid out of their lives. Michael knew they would come and couldn't wait. His family would have to answer for his behaviour.

The crowd could be heard in the distance and Michael smiled. His dark room had shadows leaping around as the torches of many lit the outside of the house and shot through his window.

At first they were relatively quiet, but their footsteps made enough noise to alarm his father, who opened the door to investigate. His eyes laid witness to dozens of townspeople, many he knew. They were armed and held torches. He walked on to the porch and his two eldest sons followed him.

"What is going on here?" his father asked, puzzled.

"You know exactly why we are here. Where is he?"

Perplexed, he inquired further. "Where is who? Is this some kind of joke?"

"Does this look like a joke? Bring your other son here now or we charge your house."

"I wouldn't do that if I was you!" Michael spoke with conviction as he pushed past his father and took a spot on the porch.

The crowd moved back a step in fear.

"What's going on here, son?"

"I got in a fight and the other boy lost."

His Dad wasn't shocked to hear he got in a fight, but was stunned that he won.

"Is that what you call it, we should burn you down," a random man called out.

"BOO!" Michael yelled out and the man jolted back along with anyone near him.

"Listen, we want you gone, you are exiled from this city. The entire family will leave tonight or we will bring a crowd that will make sure you leave." He stopped talking instantly as Michael lifted his hand around belly level and a small but noticeable orange glow told the horde they should fear him. Michael loved the reaction, he fed off the fear.

"Michael, what did you do?" his mother asked from where she stood, looking through the window. He calmed his hands down so she wouldn't see.

"Well, let's just say Sean isn't as pretty as he was." His father looked at him stunned, probably because Sean was a star in the making for jousting and someone his father worked with.

"Oh, don't worry so much Father. Your precious Sean can still joust. He will just have to leave his helmet on all the time."

"You couldn't have beaten him in a fair fight. That would be impossible."

"Thanks for the confidence Father. I simply fought back this time instead of taking the beating. The end result has put Sean on an even playing field with me. I gave him a taste of what he dished out all his life."

"What did you do?" He looked at him with extreme concern.

"You wouldn't understand, you're not smart enough."

"Try me!"

"Okay, I used my mind to take command of certain parts of his anatomy. Focusing on his face I hyper-extended several muscles to the point of no recovery. The others I snapped completely and even tightened a few to give him a beautiful new look."

His father was in disarray. He couldn't think fast enough. Michael was right — he had no idea what he had said. His mind was launched even further into a jumble when the crowd started to yell accusations.

"Death to the evil one. Death to this family!"

"Black magic, black magic!"

"Burn this house!"

"Don't worry Father, they can't even get close to us, I will make sure of that."

The crowd was getting fired up, but Michael was right, they weren't going to attack, but would regroup and come back with larger numbers.

"Leave tonight or be burned at the stake. Leave tonight and never return!"

The warning echoed in all of their heads except for Michael who didn't fret one bit. He knew the town would exile all of them. It was everything he had wanted to accomplish. This was the second stage of his plan. His family would now all understand rejection. They would learn to be like him and he would re-emerge with them once the common denominator was in place — a commonality of rejection. It was a twisted logic, but as intelligent as he was with books and studies, he lacked in social dynamics.

The crowd left. The wooded area around the house returned to its normal silence. His father pulled them all in.

"What did you do, you stupid bastard? This is winter! Where are we to go, what are we going to do?" his older brother yelled out.

"Be careful. The last person who called me that had his head mutilated."

"Well, maybe we can stay with some friends far enough away from here," his mother suggested.

"We aren't going anywhere. I am riding into the city night now and will straighten this out," his father insisted, and moved toward the door.

Michael was sound asleep, lying on his side, curled up like an infant. He was awoken by a burning sensation on his cheek, without opening his eyes he swatted at his face.

A small hot piece of wood flew to the ground. He sat up fully awake and looked around the room. He could see a lantern and three men surrounding his bed. His cheek smoked a little from the singe.

"What the—?" he questioned as he tried to gain perspective.

His eyes focused on his two brothers and his father.

"Why did you burn me?"

"So it's true, you are using black magic. You are a Satan worshipper. This explains so much."

"What are you talking about?" He noticed they were armed with swords and one had a spear. "I don't practice black magic."

"Oh yeah? Then grab this again." His other brother grabbed the piece of wood that singed his skin. He lifted it to the lantern and showed him a cross, a representation of God. A God he didn't believe in.

Michael asked him to pass it to him. His brother tossed it to him. He gripped the cross and nothing happened.

"See, nothing." They waited for a second until the heat increased and Michael was forced to drop it.

"That is a trick piece of wood!" Michael was scared and started to think maybe his own family would actually harm him.

"No it's not!"

"Don't kill me, I am your son."

"I am not going to kill you, but I am going to show you out a door which you may never enter again."

Forced up by the tip of a sword, he was lead out of his room. He walked by his mother and sister who cried fiercely. His mother started to move toward him and his father commanded her to sit, "He isn't our son anymore. He is infected with the Netherworld and he will leave now."

"It's freezing out, I can't survive. You can't be serious!"

"Get him warm clothes and a ration bag, fill it to the top."

"They will come for you, you will be exiled," Michael said with desperation. He couldn't believe this was happening. He didn't like his family, but also didn't think they would turn on him like this.

"We will be fine, I have made a deal that will allow us stay. They only had one request, you must go!"

The door closed on a life he would never be a part of again. After banging on the door for what felt like eternity, with tears streaming down his face, he turned to a cold night and walked into the darkness.

Christian felt like he hit a wall as he struck blank pages. It was very weird. The chapter he read was near the beginning of the book and it had dozens of pages left before the next chapter, but they were left blank.

"Why wouldn't the rest be filled in?" he asked aloud, confused.

He looked around the room to gain some perspective and digest what he had learned. He was adept at absorbing information. He had witnessed Gabriel's early life as if he was there; feelings, sights and smells were real and were now a part of his memory.

Christian knew it would be almost impossible to find Rizzian and ask if there was an explanation for the missing information, which upset him. He demanded more. With a harsh tone and one hand on the blank pages he yelled, "I need more now, show me more!"

At first he didn't notice but his peripheral vision told him to look to his hand, where he noticed movement. His first thought was that there could be ants or small insects crawling on the pages and he pulled his hand away before verifying what it was. The page had started to fill with words. He was amazed! He wondered if he had done it, or if the book had just written itself.

Christian looked around to see if anyone else was influencing the words to magically appear, and after finding no one there, he placed his hand on a page that was now half filled with words and it jumped back to life. The words filled in under his hand, but instead of really analyzing why or how it was happening, he just accepted it and read on.

For the next few years nobody heard of Michael, and as time passed, few thought about him. They assumed he was dead or far away with no intention of returning. The first few months were tough for Michael's family. They had to reintegrate into the Silver City with a major black mark on them all. His father had made a deal that few parents could have made, and it gained enough respect for him to keep his job. Like any group of people, a new story replaced the real one and Michael was forgotten, his true identity effaced.

At home it was a little tougher, but his father commanded that nobody would ever use his name, Michael never existed. It seemed to work for almost everyone except for his mother and his sister. His mother thought about him from time to time, but it lessened as time wore on. The only way she could accept the sin of rejecting a child, sending him off in the wolves den was to override reality and listen to her husband who pretended that he never existed.

The only groups that discussed him were the odd storyteller when someone new was in town, a few behind closed doors and his sister. She couldn't talk to anyone about Michael directly for fear of retribution, so she would take walks with nobody around and pretend he was with her.

Everything seemed normal until the evening exactly three years to the day they closed the door on Michael, the day they sentenced their son to certain death for selfish reasons.

The day's chores were done, dinner had just finished. The two boys, now men, were home with their mother and father. The youngest, the sister, had not come home yet.

All were sitting at the table except for their mother who started to clean the table settings.

"Everyone knows what today is, don't you?" the mother inquired.

"Today is no different than any other. Don't continue or else," her husband sternly commanded.

"Michael, Michael, Michael, what… we can't say his name?" The words started to make the father's blood boil. He was ready to lash out verbally when a simple knock was heard at the front door. He decided to wait until after the visitor had left before responding to her ranting.

He opened the door and looked out to see nothing. The snow had fallen only a few hours ago and not a single track led to their house. He wondered if he had really heard a knock. Just getting ready to dismiss it, another series of small quiet knocks came from the back door.

"Who is at the front door dear?" the mother asked, using the word "dear" hoping to receive less of a verbal blow from him once their guest had left.

"I got it, sit down boys." He walked over and opened the back door, which revealed a similar scene as the front. He felt strange and his stomach churned a little with the uncertainty looming.

He wasn't sure how to handle the situation. As he walked toward the centre of the room, the two boys stood up because they could read an ominous look on their father's face. Both doors were closed. Both started to knock simultaneously. Fear set in like a deep cold on their skin.

"Who is out there? I demand an answer!" The mother was on the fringe of hysterics.

"Tell me boys, is this one of your jokes?" They immediately answered with concerned head shakes.

The knocks continued uncontrollably and then the horses could be heard, bursting into madness. The barn wasn't close to the house, but the horses could be heard unmistakably.

"Hun, in our room and hide. Boys, each get a weapon and get them now!"

The noise got louder and louder and then it suddenly stopped. They had all wanted it to stop, but when it did they weren't as sure. Away from the doors, in the middle of the room they stood in fear.

The silence was broken as footsteps seemed to patter all over the roof. It sounded like a few little feet and then grew to what seemed like dozens of them. The three men stared up to the ceiling, gripping their weapons.

The family was in a state of panic. The mother crouched near the floor to peek through the doorway to see, but hopefully not be seen.

The rooftop steps seemed to fall off the front of the house and everyone turned, expecting something to breach their home from the front door.

"What is going on Dad?"

"Shhh!"

The back door was the one that opened and in walked a cloaked man, his attire resembled something that a female would wear, but it was definitely a man.

"You called for me?"

They turned to see the cloaked figure standing in their back door.

"Who are you and what do you want?" the father said, attempting confidence, but coming across a little shaky.

"You don't recognize your own blood." The hood fell from the cloak and a hairless, pale face with dark circles under his eyes looked back at them.

"Michael, is that you?" the father asked doubtfully because the man before him barely resembled his son.

"I heard Mom call my old name, well soon to be my old name, and I thought I would stop on by."

His brothers didn't say a word as their minds tried to absorb the information. Was that really him? How could he have survived? Where had he been? Most importantly, why was he here now?

"You're not welcome here Michael."

"Start calling me Gabriel. I am about to earn that name." Michael looked at their perplexed faces.

"Who kicks out their young son to freeze to death? What kind of family does that and why? Great questions I thought I wanted answers to, but as it turns out I now want something else instead."

"Who is here with you, who was making all that noise?"

"Nobody, I am here by myself. Is there a reason I should need someone else? This is a family visit, isn't it?"

The comment was comforting to them. In their minds he was the same weakling of a child, and if he wasn't with someone, he was no threat. They disregarded the weird events that had just occurred.

The mother got up from the floor and started to run towards him. She had the best of intentions, but Michael didn't care. With one hand raised in her direction her second step gave way, she tripped and hit the ground face first.

"This isn't about hugs and kisses. It's better you don't touch me."

The two boys were pissed off after watching their mother smash her face on the ground. She looked up and they could see that she was badly hurt. Her face had opened up, spattered blood was everywhere.

"Did you have something to do with that?" the other brother asked.

He attempted to run to his mother's aid but Michael, with a shift of his hand, launched his brother into the air and away from his mother. He slammed into the other side of the house, hit the ground and looked up in disbelief.

"Michael..." His father attempted to say something but was interrupted as he corrected him.

With a pompous attitude and a finger extended he said, "Gabriel!"

"Whatever your name is, you need to leave and now!"

"In some ways I owe you for your selfish, ungodly decision to send me to what could only be perceived as certain death. I landed into the bosom of something great and the power I have achieved is immaculate. The problem is, in order to attain the next level, to have ultimate power, I have to show how malicious I can be. The more horrid the act, the better the reward for me. Hence, you can understand what I am doing here."

They all looked around the room trying to figure out what would happen next. His father had little patience left and was ready to destroy his son in order to protect his family.

"Remember, Father, when you hit me with your fist? I struck the ground so hard with no chance to defend myself. That was the act of a cowardly man. Today I am here to challenge you, but I come without weapons. All I have are these small stones."

Michael, using both hands, pulled out two handfuls of small smooth rocks and dropped them to the floor. They scattered across the floor and everyone stood and watched in confusion.

"Okay little ones, rise up to attention, come and meet my sweet and kind family," he commanded with hands parallel to the ground. All of the rocks floated up to his mid-section and stayed suspended for a moment. His hands had a slight orange glow about them. Everyone was still confused about what was going to happen next and also a little afraid. He had been banished because of his use of black magic, identified when the cross burned his skin. They had no idea how skilled he had become in the intervening years.

Michael smiled for a moment and then jumped into action. His hands moved with his body as he spun around in dramatic fashion, his face clenched with the effort. The stones followed in a cluster just a moment behind his hands. They flew around his body with great speed and with velocity they shot forward, as he finished his spin with arms pointing towards his father. His father stood erect as dozens of small rocks ripped through his body. His body shook as he was hit repeatedly. They didn't just hit him, they ripped through him! His legs, arms and torso popped with little explosions of blood as the stones jettisoned through his body and out the other side. Some of the stones had enough power behind them to dig into the wall behind him as others fell and rolled along the floor.

They all turned to their father in disbelief, it had happened so fast. They all questioned if he was okay. Even though he was badly injured his face didn't show signs of pain, just confusion.

He wasn't okay! One stone through a leg would put a man on the ground, dozens throughout the body would seal his fate. His internal organs were ruptured with no chance at survival, his legs gave way at the knees and he collapsed.

"Well, that felt good!" Michael spoke, elated. He felt a surge of bliss coupled with relief.

"You bastard!" One of his brothers charged him with sword raised above him. Only a few steps into his charge he heard Michael's voice ricochet through his mind with words that were indistinguishable. He couldn't comprehend what was said but it echoed with acrid results. Michael simply moved a step aside and avoided the strike. His aim had been off, really off. His other brother was on the floor against the wall watching his brother and couldn't understand how his brother could have missed his target. He must have done it on purpose, but why?

Michael started to laugh, "Look at this idiot, he can't even strike an unarmed man. Come on, I am right here."

He turned and swung in the direction of the voice as all optics were gone. He was blind.

"I can't see! I can't see anything!" He screamed in a panic.

Leaving the blinded one to his own devices, Michael walked toward the brother who still sat on the ground after being tossed earlier by a flick of his hand. He was afraid and didn't even reach for his weapon. The cloaked figure moved in his direction. His father was dead, his brother screaming in the corner, useless without sight and his mother barely functional because her face was crushed.

He pleaded with his brother, "Listen, brother, you don't have to do this. Let us go, you have had your revenge."

Michael leaned forward on one knee to get face to face with his adversary. "Do you really want your last words on this planet to be ones of cowardice? Your brother, even though an idiot and blinded, doesn't shed a tear. He still calls for me to come to him, a wish I will grant him momentarily. Maybe your God will lay roses out for him for being brave before he dies, but cowardice is a trait that is disgusting to any God, yours or mine."

Michael's eyes, full of black veins, were a frightening last sight. He placed two fingers on his lips, kissed them and then placed them on his terrified brother's forehead. Michael stood up and as he walked away his brother burst into flames. Michael closed his eyes for a moment to enjoy the screaming.

"What is going on, I am going to kill you, what has happened to my brother?" the blinded brother yelled as he frantically swung his weapon to and fro.

"Our brother, you should say. He is a little hot under the collar, if you know what I mean. Question is, what am I going to do with you? That is the question you should be asking."

He took a swing toward the sound and got somewhat close, but Michael evaded the strike. "Not bad, almost." Michael sized him up with ease and struck him with a fist dead square to the nose. He then pulled his hand back and attempted to shake off the pain. "I don't know why you guys use your hands, it's really archaic and quite painful."

"Watch this Mom, you're going to be *so* proud," Michael called to his mother who was still gaining perspective, becoming a little more aware of the situation after receiving her injury.

"Right knee!" he yelled aloud and touched his own knee. A moment later his brother's knee cracked at the exact spot he had touched. He shrieked in pain as he gripped his knee and rolled around on his back.

Michael then looked over to the other brother whose flames had now ignited the wall.

"Oh no, not looking good for you guys in here. Sorry, brother, I shouldn't say things like that, I know you can't see. I wouldn't want to be rude." Michael spoke nonchalantly.

"Left elbow… Right elbow!" he yelled and touched one, then the next. His brother's elbows followed by shattering left and then right, leaving him uselessly sprawled out on the floor adjacent to his mother.

Michael watched the flames' appetite grow and they engulfed the ceiling. He walked over and grabbed his jointless, blind brother. He dragged him across the room and put him on top of his mother, just to make sure she was weighted down. The entire time he hummed a little tune, a tune that someone might hum while taking a leisurely stroll through a park, but instead he had pinned down his mother to seal her in a burning coffin.

"Well, it's been a blast but I have to go."

His mother looked up, barely able to lift her head which was covered in blood from her nose and finally spoke. "Michael, what have you done? What has become of you?"

"I have found a new family, one that would never reject me."

She could feel the building heat from the fire. She knew her husband was dead along with one son and she wanted to say something that would affect Michael. Her only ability to attack was with words. "You are not my son, I hate you!"

"You can't fire someone after they have already quit. Fire someone, ha ha ha, another witty remark. Bye Mom."

He walked out the back door and closed it behind him. Standing a safe distance away, he watched the house burn and the screams that emitted from the house were of the two that still lived. The sounds were like a brilliant orchestra to Michael's ears.

From the dark, a voice echoed in his head. *You will never be known as Michael again. You have earned your name, Gabriel, the youngest Wizard ever to achieve such an honour.*

CHAPTER 8

HERE THEY COME

"Okay, gentlemen, and I use that term very loosely, I want you to learn everything you can about this armour. This is their most advanced plate mail and it has come a long way from the first that was designed many years ago. After today's lesson, come up and touch it, feel it, hit it. Learning everything you can about the enemy is critical," Kruno yelled to a group of men just in front of the gates of Dryden.

"Forget about learning, I have learned enough. Put one of those bastards in front of me and I will teach him a few things," a proud soldier yelled from the crowd.

"I love your enthusiasm and you will need some of that attitude, but don't be foolish. Battles are won with intelligence and smart fighting. If you face a Black Knight, he will be dressed in a combination of the armour before you. Learn how to exploit them now, here, so when the time comes you won't have to think. The thinking will have been done already. It puts you in a better place, giving you the advantage." Kruno pointed to four sets of Black Knight armour that was generously donated by Bryce and his men as they got fitted for Dryden's armour. All four sets were standing upright. They surrounded a body, legs and arms made of wood, and filled with hay, making these suits a great training prop.

"The first is fully armed, nothing more can be added from a protection standpoint. You will see this type of Black Knight riding a heavy horse with legs and arms fully covered, along with the entire head secured with a helmet. This becomes heavy. What they lose in dexterity they gain in protection." Kruno looked out at men who seemed intrigued to learn more.

"On a heavy horse they will probably use a lance as a primary weapon. Full plate mail is rarely seen unless the knight is part of a heavy horse contingent. It's too difficult to be on foot carrying this much weight, especially if they have to charge in battle. The other suits of armour displayed are lighter as we move left. By removing their legs or arms from the burden of heavy metal armour, dexterity improves and using a more open faced helmet improves their sight." Kruno's tone indicated an important statement was coming up. "One thing is for sure, if they have dressed a man in this armour, if anyone you face on the battlefield is wearing full or partial plate mail, you can be assured he is skilled. I don't say that to create fear, just respect." As Kruno spoke to the group of soldiers, they all listened with rapt intent. They were the cream of the crop, learning to advance from infantry to next level of becoming a soldier. All were handpicked by their commanding officers because they had shown great ability.

"Because of your skill level, you will not be the first on the battlefield. Infantry will lead as some of you have done in the past. There is tremendous honour in leading the battle, but the casualty rate is very high. You are no longer infantry, which means you will be squaring off with the enemy on a more personal level. What position you will take will depend on our time together, but one thing is for sure, the spear, the weapon you have been formally trained on, will not be accompanying you. Today we will simply choose the weapon you would like to train with, or even better, one you have had experience with and want to advance your knowledge of." Kruno turned around to introduce numerous weapons, propped up by a crude stand. Everyone looked on with awe. Weapons were like fine gems in many ways and men tended to be enamored by large numbers of different arms.

"Weapons we don't have a shortage of, so besides a few restrictions, you will in a few moments be selecting your first choice. Although I am sure you know a lot about these weapons, let me introduce them to you. Each weapon has advantages and limitations which you should be made aware of." Kruno grabbed a sword, held it up and looked at its beautiful polished steel.

"Of course, as children you have all dreamed of killing many creatures with a sword. It is a fantastic weapon. It is very versatile and the most common weapons used by far. The sizes and shapes of swords are almost limitless. It is as strong a defensive weapon as it is offensive. It has great dexterity but it also has some disadvantages. First, because it is the most common weapon, your enemy understands its characteristics, they understand what you will be able to do with it and are very comfortable fighting an opponent with one in hand. Second, it's not that great against plate mail." Kruno turned and smashed one of the suits of armour in its side.

"As you can see, it didn't even get close to penetrating it. Trust me, he felt the impact, but a good warrior will be able to mount a counterattack only slightly dazed. If you decide to use a sword, we will teach you how to exploit joints in the armour or look to a secondary weapon to use when facing plate mail. A dagger could be used to battle a fully armed enemy." He put the weapon down and walked over to grab another, basically a pipe with spikes on the head and a leather strap for the handle.

"Welcome to the mace, a weapon that you can learn about fast, especially with someone who is familiar with a sword. Ivan loves this weapon almost as much as any other." Kruno's thoughts let him drift away for a moment to his good friend, wondering where he was. His mind wanted to dwell more on Ivan, but he knew it wasn't the time or place. His task of training these men was vital. What they could learn could mean an extra kill on average per man. He knew Ivan was okay, he had to be.

"The mace, also known as the skull crusher is also quite agile and can be moved with ease. It has great striking potential and it works well defensively as well... It's also good at piercing armour. Blow for blow it's usually more deadly than a sword. On the negative side, it can get stuck in armour, flesh or bone. It doesn't have the smooth slice of a sword. For some reason, it doesn't instill as much fear in the enemy as it should, which can be used to your advantage or disadvantage." Kruno took the weapon and smashed it just below the spot he made with the sword. A spike drove through the armour producing a hole. It was obvious that strike for strike it was more powerful than a sword.

Kruno's weapons introduction moved in a natural progression. The next weapon was similar looking but instead of a fixed shaft it had a chain with a spiked ball on it.

"A distant cousin to the mace is my friend, the flail." Kruno spun it slowly over his head, just enough to keep it suspended in air as he talked.

"This weapon has limited defensive ability. This beauty is all offense!" He swung it around and crashed it into the helmet of the target. The impact produced a large clash, launching the helmet from its stationary position. Bits of hay flung up, adding effect. "This weapon rightly adds fear to anyone who faces it, but it is very difficult to use because of its recovery time. If you are skilled with this weapon, most soldiers would rather fight someone else. I have seen men run from it. Good to know, it is feared. And why you ask? Besides massive impacts it also has one fantastic attribute that no other weapon can boast about. Because it is on a chain, this weapon can go around shields or other weapons used defensively. I love it!" Kruno smiled as he put it down, and then reached for the largest weapon on the rack.

"Here is the MOAW or mother of all weapons, the war hammer! It is number one in fear factor and offensive power. Really there is only one way to defend against its blow, you have to avoid it. Armour gives way to it, shields will crack under it and other weapons used defensively are no match." Kruno turned and with a wince, demonstrated. Starting an attack sequence was obviously difficult. The massive weapon connected with a set of plate mail. It had risen like a terror from the ground, striking the middle of a breast plate. The entire structure was knocked over and the helmet blew off. The resulting damage was a massive dent and it left a hole in it. "This guy is dead. It offers better impact than an axe and flail combined but has a major drawback. It is heavy and takes someone with great strength and experience to jockey it. This is a favourite weapon of Northerners, I wonder why?"

"How goes it young man?" Rizzian's unique way of speaking was recognized instantly. Kruno didn't need to turn around to know it was him, but of course he did out of respect.

"These men listen well. They are taking in what they need to hear. The Dark Realm will be getting spanked so hard they will run in the other direction." The crowd of men cheered. They were elated and honoured to have Kruno train them, to have received the promotion above the rank of infantry, and now to have Rizzian inquire about their progress — it was an exciting combination.

"Good to hear. As great soldiers you understand why we are so strong, why Dryden and the Silver Allegiance will never lose. We have the strongest walls and the most skilled men, all of which work in conjunction with our powerful Wizards."

"Rizzian, may I walk with you?" Kruno inquired. He hadn't finished his class, but he knew he could come back to them shortly. He wanted to take advantage of free time with one of, if not the most, in-demand person in the Silver Allegiance.

"But of course, Kruno, you can have whatever you wish, we owe you a lot."

"Everyone, select your primary weapon and start getting used to it, I will be back in a while." Kruno yelled out his order, one that he knew would create excitement. The men still acted like children in many ways, and couldn't wait to play with their new toys.

The two walked away from the castle in the direction of the forest's edge. Kruno had reached a point where he could talk comfortably with Rizzian, the greatest of all Wizards, like an old friend. Few received that honour.

"I am glad you can accompany an old man. I could use the help. Please carry my sachet for me, if you don't mind?" Rizzian pointed to a leather bag that was thrown over his shoulder. It looked like it was quite heavy as he seemed to favour the shoulder it was strewn over. Kruno, to his surprise, grabbed the bag with relative ease and wondered if Rizzian was acting a little to get him to take the load.

"What is it Kruno?"

"Nothing… I just… I don't mind carrying the bag, but you made it seem like it was heavy."

"It is for an old man like me." He waited a moment and could see Kruno didn't believe what he was saying. "So intelligent, gifted with leadership and swordsmanship, but still your age shows itself from time to time. That sachet to me would be like lifting a big bag of rice for you."

"Come on, I am not having it, you can't pull the wool over my eyes. You could toss a boulder the size of a man from here to the forest's edge and I could barely roll it."

"You are incorrect, Kruno, if you think muscle strength has anything to do with tossing a boulder of that size. It's all magic. If I let my guard down, used no magic at all, you could knock me down with one shove. I bet a fourteen-year-old boy could do the same. You are also incorrect about something else." Rizzian smiled, "If you wanted to throw this man-sized boulder you talk of, as you say I can, so can you."

"Yeah, sure." Kruno smiled lightly not understanding what Rizzian was talking about. He wasn't sure if he was trying to blow smoke up his ass, which didn't make any sense, or if he was submitting to some of the mental issues associated with aging, which Kruno didn't believe was the case.

"You will see one day, Kruno, but today is not that day. The future will show you a great number of things. A plan is set in motion that will make a boulder toss a joke. This is, of course, if you don't die beforehand."

Kruno was confused at what he was trying to say, and when asked to elaborate, Rizzian abruptly told him to change subject.

"Okay then, where are we headed?" Kruno figured the great Wizard probably confused most people due to his heightened understanding and just left it alone.

"Almost there."

Rizzian asked Kruno many questions which seemed more like a random conversation. He answered most of them. They started to walk through the forest's edge, away from one of the roadways. He thought about asking why they didn't use one of the paths, but decided against it, knowing he probably wouldn't receive an answer anyway.

"So Kruno, you know Zoran well. Can you tell me how he became so powerful? How does a man like him reach such a level at such a young age?" Rizzian asked, as he walked through an old part of the forest and down a bit of a gully. The trees were tall with leaves forming a canopy above them. The fresh, pleasant smells released by the moist soil surrounded their senses as each step revealed a new fragrance. Kruno loved the forest and all its peaceful beauty.

"Well yeah, I knew him relatively well. We grew up together, except he is a little older than I am. He was a little cocky, but outside of that he wasn't sadistically evil or anything of that sort, if that's what you're looking for."

"Time and circumstance can completely change a man." Rizzian stopped speaking and waited for Kruno to continue.

"He was a modest fighter, did well in mock battles, but one day he took down three men, older and with more skill. He killed all of them, barely had a scratch on him. The men were Silver Allegiance, one was an Elite. I am surprised you don't know this story."

"I was, as I am now then." Rizzian's comment made no sense to Kruno; he shook his head with a few quick snaps trying to understand what he had said. Rizzian continued, "I have of course heard about this encounter, I just wanted to hear you tell it from your perspective."

"Well, there's not much to tell because I didn't see it, but I do know one thing, nobody wanted to touch him after that. He went from a relative nobody to a man recognized everywhere. That was it though, he never fought again in public. He did take down a few others in combat, just not in town."

"Sounds interesting, sounds questionable." Rizzian seemed to be concentrating on something else, which threw Kruno off because it didn't look like he was paying full attention to him. Getting ready to continue, Rizzian stopped and told him this was the place, the perfect spot.

A perfect spot for what?

"The forest is dense here but not too crowded, and we are the perfect distance from the roadway." The area was scenic, Kruno agreed with that. It was also unique with long vines that dropped down from large trees that seemed as high as Dryden's walls. Generations of children, including Kruno, had played here. They would climb the vines as high as they would dare. Kruno smiled at the memory. Rizzian, possibly thinking the same thing, tugged on one of the vines.

"Good. Pass my sachet," the Wizard asked. Kruno had never actually thought about what was in the bag, but found himself uncharacteristically curious.

The Wizard took out a clear vial that held a purple liquid. Inside the liquid, little solid blue specks floated about. Rizzian shook it, which aggravated the contents, exciting the little blue specks. Kruno squinted to focus in on the interesting vial, not sure what was going to happen or what it was used for. He always had a fascination with alchemy.

Rizzian popped the cork, sucked the contents into his mouth, filling his cheeks. He then cocked his head to the sky and blew it straight upward. Kruno looked on with confusion because it seemed like a really strange thing to do.

Most of the liquid shot straight up, clearing way more altitude than it should have, spreading over a massive diameter. Some landed on Kruno. Not sure how to react he fought off the natural urge to wipe it from his face. He figured if Rizzian filled his mouth with it, it couldn't be that bad. He knew that Rizzian wouldn't let something harmful touch him so he tried to relax a little. As the liquid fell from the sky, he listened to Rizzian start to whistle. It was loud but beautiful, almost mesmerizing.

Kruno was confused and damp, but decided not to ask any questions, even though he had a dozen sitting on his tongue. The old man walked toward a series of trees, and with each step, one of his hands began to glow with more intensity. With two fingers glowing blue and extended, he touched a tree and the bark chipped away. He slid them down and the bark leapt from his path. A simple pattern formed. He made an "X".

"Kruno, take the other vial out and toss it as hard as you can above the treeline that way."

Kruno did as commanded and tossed the vial. It just hit its peak and exploded.

"Should I ask? Or will I just be puzzled."

"All you need to know is we left them a little present."

Egon and his top commanders all met in his father's favourite room in a remote part of the castle. It was considered the most comfortable and relaxing room by almost anyone who had spent a moment within it. Thinking like his father, he wanted to have the last conversation with his leaders in a serene setting before beginning the greatest of all battles. The room was an area that might take a little of the edge off.

The room was filled with highly decorated and well respected people in the art of war. There were no politicians or wealthy citizens, and just the top ranking military were invited. Kruno was asked to take command of several units, including the Sand Sorceresses, which he gladly accepted, and for that reason, among many others, he was included.

The finest wine was opened and everyone had a glass of what a connoisseur would consider perfection. It could cross a weaker person's mind that they opened these bottles so that Zoran couldn't, but the room comprised minds that were impervious to such thoughts. Everyone knew that the odds were bleak for victory, but each was confident in their men, their skills and God.

"I guess we shouldn't drink too much of this wine, I hear tomorrow might be a big day," one of the commanders spoke.

"Really, something is going on tomorrow? You guys have to keep me more informed. Nobody tells me anything around here." Several smirks followed the comment.

Egon was uncertain of how to respond and just kept his mouth shut, but it was written on his face that he was confused with the banter. The comments showed how strong minded they really were. The men weren't afraid in the slightest of the war to come or the death that certainly would ride with it. They actually welcomed the battle to come.

"It is confirmed, they will arrive tomorrow," someone announced as they entered the room, something everyone had assumed.

"Yes, and in typical fashion of the Dark Realm, they have attempted to hit our people psychologically. One of our scouts was captured and tortured, then sent back to us. He had one arm removed and they burned the stump to stop the bleeding. They also carved an upside down cross on his chest, he rode like this through the city. Many witnessed what happened, women and children alike." After he spoke he shook his head in disgust.

"They do this to intimidate us, but it will only have a short term effect. In the end it will just make our people want revenge. Stupid strategy, Zoran doesn't know what he is getting into coming here."

"I hope you are right, but I think many minds are soft and this shows them a glimpse of what is to come. I would expect some of our people will leave the city."

Kruno entered the conversation, "What did the scout say?" Kruno knew Zoran could have done worse and figured he was sent to pass on a message as he rode; otherwise all of his limbs would have suffered the same fate. Zoran wasn't stupid and knew that he would have been less likely to agree to pass on a certain message to them, if he had been inflicted with more injuries.

"He was forced as he rode through the city to chant that the new Games Master falls on us, death is inevitable. He was told to yell that and 'Your God is weak.'"

Several conversations broke out as everyone had something to say. Kruno tuned them out and receded to his own thoughts, letting them have their moment to chat. His mind shifted to the comment about the Games Master. He remembered the long and arduous adventure through the labyrinth and the sheer power of the original Games Master, a title desired by so many, primarily due to the fact that that name was feared by everyone.

"Where is your mind, Kruno?" Rizzian asked, knowing the answer but wanting Kruno to tell him anyway.

The room quieted to focus on the one man in the room who had met the original Games Master and the man who knew Zoran the best. His insight was invaluable; he was the most informed man in all of Dryden on these two subjects.

"So many were infatuated with becoming the next Games Master. This is one of their greatest weaknesses." Kruno stopped for a moment

"I would love to hear about their weaknesses because this army has never lost under the leadership of Zoran, not even a stalemate." Another man jumped in. "If they were to trump us here, he would have a great argument to be granted such a title, not that I am suggesting they are going to win."

"There is no doubt they are powerful. They haven't reported a loss in the time you say and under Zoran's leadership, but their issue is in the goal of becoming the Games Master. You see, there can only be one. Zoran assumes it will be him, but so does Gabriel. They both need each other now, but don't be confused. They don't like one another and both have plans to be the only one leading their Kingdom in the future. Then you can add Damascus into the equation. What do you think that gargoyle wants? It won't sit around and share control with Zoran or Gabriel. Gargoyles look at humans, like we do of swine. They all have a future plan of full control. They all have a plan to eliminate the other two."

"The only thing that doesn't work in our favour is they understand that they need each other now, at least for this battle," a commander said.

"That is true, but it's important to understand their motives for war. They will have an internal struggle. Their very foundation is pulling in three different directions. All of their thoughts for the future rest on dreams built on stone and mortar from the Netherworld, not exactly the sturdiest material."

Bruno took over the meeting, "Thank you, Kruno. Here we are, the eve before the battle that will change our world. We have our directives. We have all been over our battle plan so many times we could probably recite it in our sleep. We meet them outside our walls. This will take Zoran by surprise… that I am sure of. I am sure he will expect us to wait behind our walls and he will be foolishly excited at the prospect of facing us significantly outnumbered in such a setting. We really only have one option and that is to take out the catapults! There is no more time for debate on this strategic move. If you don't fully buy into the idea, that is too bad, change your mind and make sure your men know this is the best plan of attack."

"What have you heard of Hot House? When will they be arriving?" one of Egon's appointed council asked from a back part of the crowded room.

"We aren't counting on them anymore, it's doubtful they will arrive in time. The Dark Realm has covered too much ground with haste. We will take them on ourselves."

It took a moment for everyone to let it sink in. *No Hot House!* Most assumed or at least hoped they would just have to hold the Dark Realm off until Hot House arrived, but a new reality was realized. Everyone attempted to digest the news. After a few moments of silence one of the commanders stood.

"I say bring the bastards here. I may die tomorrow but I will take ten before I go." He spoke with confidence, attempting to change the direction of everyone's thoughts.

"And I will take ten as well. This I pledge to you and to God, who looks down on us with favour." Another stepped forward confidently.

"And I as well!"

The room had a surge of energy as they became more and more excited with every pledge that rang out from everyone in the room. Dozens with the same commitment bellowed out.

"Happy to see the enthusiasm Rizzian?" Kruno asked the great Wizard, noticing the smile on his face.

"Yes, I am happy, but that's not why I smile."

"Okay, what is it?"

"I just met my quota, ten already taken." Rizzian stared off into the distance.

"Just now?" Kruno asked confused.

"A present for you." Rizzian mouthed Gabriel's name, kissed his fingers and put his hand up. He spoke, but it wasn't to Kruno, he seemed to talk beyond him.

"Rizzian, you with me?"

Rizzian slowly shifted his mind back into the room and looked to him, "To answer your question, if I take less than one hundred down, that would be considered a bad day."

"Oh… Good."

Glad you're on our side.

Gabriel gave his order to halt. It was the last stop to regroup before pushing through to battle. What lay ahead was a section of forest and then the vast field that surrounded Dryden. He was leading the vanguard of an entire division that would have their eyes set on the ultimate prize — the great city of Dryden. The prospect of the victory created a fire in him, one of pure excitement. It caused a reaction that built up saliva in his mouth. He hungered for all-out war and conquest.

They waited in a clearing in the forest. The dense forest had kindly given way to an area that had only the odd dominant tree. The sky was clear as evening started to set in. Even though every fiber in his body wanted to push through the forest, he had to wait for the scouts to return. Most of the men he was with were experienced Black Knights and they had the same urges as he did. They had waited for this moment for a decade. To engage their enemy and charge through Dryden's walls, to strike, to kill, to win, it raged through their minds. Most would figure this would be a recipe for conversation, but instead of talking about it, there was an eerie silence because they were focused on the battle to come.

The scout's primary task was to reach the edge of the forest and peer in on Dryden and report back their findings, it was critical information. There was a problem, as the first group hadn't returned on time. They weren't far from the forest breaking and the first group had left midafternoon, but never returned. Gabriel sent a second group but they hadn't returned either.

"The second scouts should have returned by now, my master." A Black Knight moved toward Gabriel.

Gabriel had constructed a mini throne out of dead wood. The material he used had been lying on the floor of the forest. He built it in a matter of seconds, and with the extension of his hand, pieces of wood slid from all directions coming together in front of him. Each piece fit perfectly.

Gabriel sat in his throne and looked toward him but said nothing. It was hard to gauge what he was thinking. Nobody wanted to upset him, everyone walked on egg shells when he was around. The Black Knight waited for what felt like an excruciatingly long time. Eventually the Wizard acknowledged the conversation by slightly moving his hand to indicate he didn't really care.

"Well I am just saying it's been awhile, some of the men are starting to talk. We should do something about this now before it spreads." He spoke confidently and calmly to Gabriel, being a Black Knight taught him to project no fear, but uneasiness definitely rested within him.

"I need to know what is beyond these trees. We have a schedule and we will not fall behind. Our division will arrive first, nothing else is acceptable." Noticeably upset, he looked to the Black Knight for his opinion. He asked with an irritated voice, "So what do you think the problem is?"

"My theory is much saner than what is starting to circulate among the lower ranks. They feel that the area is cursed and we won't be allowed to penetrate it."

"Let me guess, God has stepped down to support Dryden?" Gabriel didn't look amused.

"I haven't heard that but it could be on their minds. Personally, I think it's a small ambush that Bruno has set up to slow us down. I am sure that's what it is."

"Our second scouts weren't just basic infantry, they were skilled. If our weak-minded, foolish troops haven't started to think that God has something to do with this, they will soon. I guess I will have to handle this myself." Gabriel stood up and moved a few steps forward.

"Good luck Gabriel," the Black Knight said as he went to examine the chair. He touched it with his fingers to investigate and it fell apart, collapsing into a pile of sticks.

Gabriel turned and looked in his direction with slight irritation, "You will be joining me."

Gabriel, the Black Knight and several others walked through the forest. The men were focused hard, too hard for their own good. The slightest noise — common and innocent sounds of the forest — were misconstrued and their minds started to play tricks on them. The idea that God was on their enemy's side entered into a few of their minds. Most of them just assumed, as did the Black Knights, that there was an ambush awaiting them. That was enough to have their senses heightened to their most acute level. They were in Silver Allegiance territory. They respected the skills of their enemy, and in this case it was their homeland. They were foreigners in a place their enemy knew very well.

The last of the sun's rays covered the sky as the day was about to flicker out. As the light faded it made things more difficult to detect. Although many things had caught the attention of the men, a strange shift in the forest set off an internal alarm to many of them. A few of them drew their weapons in response. It started a chain reaction and all had weapons in hand. Gabriel knew they were close to the edge of the forest and so far there was no sign of his scouts or the enemy.

They stopped and started to spread out to investigate the area as Gabriel had commanded with a hand signal.

"Gabriel, I found something," a soldier called to his leader.

He moved in his direction to see what had been discovered. Although all were intrigued, several of them didn't turn to look, but stuck to their training and kept an eye on the flanks. The Wizard walked over to see a sword and a helmet in the foliage.

"Things got really weird right here." One of the men expressed his expert opinion, having a background in tracking. He started pointing as he talked. "Look, tracks in all directions. We have been following the path that our second group of scouts took. The first group comes in from this way and both sets of tracks end up in this spot, right here! They were spread out like we are and then, pandemonium struck." The comment that they were spread out like the last group made the hairs on the back of their necks stand up. A few of them started to grip their weapons as if the attack was imminent.

"They ran from this point but what were they running from? I don't see any fresh tracks in the other direction. In order to take our men out, it would take a dozen soldiers, at least. I should see some evidence of them in the area." The tracker got closer to the ground to get a different vantage point. "And where the heck are the bodies? They would have had to collect them."

"Over here!" one of them yelled out to get everyone's attention. "Well I found a piece of someone." A mutilated bloody limb was identified.

"We should head back and get more troops, we need more men." One of the soldiers made his suggestion with a little fear in his voice.

"I don't think so, we stay here. Nothing makes me turn around," Gabriel commanded. "Spread out and see what you can find."

One of the men pushed by a vine hanging from a tree to see what looked like a carving on its trunk. He saw the letter X carved into it. He ran his fingers over it and was about to call for his leader, but he was interrupted. Another soldier that stood beside him caught his attention by questioning in a quiet, yet eerie sounding tone.

"Oh no… How is that possible?"

At the same time the tracker put together a theory on what happened and said to himself, "For some reason they have no tracks, how could that be?" The idea rushed to him, a deduction that couldn't leave his tongue fast enough. "Wait a minute, they are in the trees."

They all looked up slowly at the same time. They wanted the mystery solved, but they weren't quite ready to deal with reality. At least a dozen men hung by vines were strung up in the trees. A few of the bodies swayed gently, and the sight was terrifying.

"How did they get them up there? Not a track around here and they are so high. That is impossible."

Gabriel finally noticed what the two men had found. He saw the carving of the X in the tree.

"Dammit… Rizzian!"

"What, why would you say his name?" one of them questioned with panic in his voice. His instincts told him to run, he felt his intuitions challenge his military duty. He started to move backward when his foot got caught in an exposed root. He tried to free it without looking down as he focused in all directions in fear, but it wouldn't come free. He was frustrated that he got stuck, especially at this particular time. It added to his growing fear. After attempting to free his foot, he finally pulled his attention from a potential attack and looked down to see the root firmly surrounding his foot.

How could this happen? How did my foot even fit in there?

He tried to pry it out with his sword and slid it between the root and his leg, but as soon as the metal touched the root, something happened. It moved! The root of the tree seemed to move up his leg and tighten, pinning him in position. He was in complete disbelief, and didn't have time to try to solve this puzzle because the root tightened around his leg and sword.

He screamed in fear and agony, and the others turned quickly to see what was happening. One of the men turned to ask his friend's opinion, and he cranked his head not to waste any time, but his comrade was not there! Then, with panicked disbelief, he turned to the two men on his other side and they were gone as well! One moment here and the next moment they had vanished. He noticed a sword drop beside him and he knew where they were. They were in the trees!

Without even looking he yelled, "Run!" He took off fast and his heart pounded as he charged forward. His mind couldn't keep up with what had just happened, but he knew he was in serious trouble. Just as he hit top speed, he tripped. He hit the ground hard and slid toward two gigantic exposed roots. He would surely smack into them with a thud, but instead, they had somehow moved or lifted. He needed to get up and move in a hurry, but they came down and pinned him to the ground. The pressure mounted, bones buckled and his rib cage and back easily gave way to the force of the root. All that could be heard was the snapping of bones.

The man with his leg locked in a root looked up for help, his vision was cloudy with a red haze because of the pain and the futility he felt. He watched men get strung up by vines that seemed to have minds of their own. He watched the man under the root on the ground and could hear his bones make an awful noise. The root tightened harder, so hard he blanked out, a moment later his leg separated from his body with a pop and blood spewed out of the stump. Unconscious, he collapsed.

Gabriel was hit almost immediately, the attack came hard and fast from an unexpected place. Just before a massive root worked its way around his legs, he said with his normal calm disposition, "Impressive." The root wrapped around him several times, fast enough that Gabriel didn't have a chance to lift his arms.

The Black Knight found himself in a tree with a vine wrapped around his neck. He tried not to panic as he gained serious altitude and his oxygen supply was cut off. His sword had fallen from his hands. He reached for his neck to relieve some of the pressure but it had no give. He stopped rising and reached for his dagger in his boot, yanked it and cut the vine. He knew the fall would be painful, possibly deadly, but it was his only option.

Four others ran as fast as they could. A massive branch, about eight inches in diameter, swung down from a tree and collided with two of them running close to one another. One was struck in the chest, snapping his ribs and the other across the face, killing him by the time his body stopped sliding. The other two thought they had made it to safety, and let hope enter their minds, when a vine somehow lassoed one of them around the neck, snapping him backward. The other found his foot snagged by a vine, tripping him hard and then dragging him backward.

"I am sorry, God! Why did I defy you?"

Roots, branches and vines all worked in unison. They were flying around, working strategically; one would pin a man in position and the other would hit him from above, wreaking havoc on their targets. The remaining men were smashed into pieces.

Gabriel was completely erect with his vision compromised. He stood straight up and the roots closed in like an anaconda. He felt pain start to kick in as his nose snapped and blood followed almost immediately. He was in trouble and knew it. He hadn't had time to prepare a defense and rushed to do so. He knew he needed the inside of his hands to touch the root and he turned them just in time.

He was just a few moments away from being squeezed to a pulp when an orange glow emanated from him. The tree that the root belonged to found its leaves wither and fall to the ground. Its limbs started to dry up and the root lost its grip as it died and began to break into pieces. The tree as a whole experienced ten years of decay in just a few moments.

The forest seemed to respond to Gabriel. Six vines moved hastily in his direction, but he put his hands up and they seemed to hit an invisible wall only feet from him. Gabriel knew it was Rizzian's spell and understood he needed a massive strike immediately. If he didn't strike fast, every animated part of this forest would rush him at once.

Gabriel mustered up a huge charge deep within and used the most powerful spell he had cast in a long time. His eyes burned orange and his veins turned black, which was easy to see against his pigment-free skin. He dropped to one knee, looked to the ground, closed his eyes and yelled with a morbid, drawn out voice, "DEATH!"

A wave seemed to move from him in all directions like the effect a rock has when dropped in water. Everything in a massive radius pushed back and began to die. Leaves fell, branches collapsed, vines turned to dust, and even the foliage broke down, resembling ash. After a few moments, all that stood were partial tree trunks and the original Black Knight who cut himself from a vine — he was the only other person alive. The spell, although made for vegetation, had an impact on the Black Knight. Gabriel didn't know he was there, but it wouldn't have made a difference, he would have cast it anyway. The wave of death hit him and his hair turned grey. He aged several years in a blink of an eye. The stench of the spell turned him inside out and he vomited.

The Dark Realm troops waited for the third scout team to return, and as they waited, a mental infection started and progressively got worse. Every battle for as long as they could remember had been victorious, but now they rested on the fringe of Dryden; the great capital of the most dominant army of their time. If both armies stood in one spot, the Silver Allegiance would outnumber the Dark Realm. That wasn't the case here, but their enemy's power was arguably superior to theirs. That hadn't entered a single soldier's mind until the first two groups seemed to disappear. Now, with two scout groups gone without a trace, they questioned the power of the Silver Allegiance. Was it as powerful as the world saw them? This strike had better be successful because they were awakening a beast.

Before the third group finally returned, a soldier had run back in a panic. He let curiosity override command and had drifted behind the group led by Gabriel to see what was going to happen, but stayed out of harm's way. His mind was jumbled. He talked about the forest coming alive and the annihilation of their troops. Many were on edge and conversations started to build about the possibility that God himself stood with Dryden.

The second to return was the surviving Black Knight. He marched just ahead of Gabriel. His face told a story of fear. His hair had greyed and the pigment of his skin was lighter. The look he had was one of shock. This added to the hysteria among a few, but the third and final to enter camp solidified it. Gabriel moved a little differently, with haste, not his normal nonchalant swagger. He also forgot about something critical. His nose was broken, he had popped it back in place but didn't remove the blood. This was the first time anyone had witnessed or even heard of Gabriel showing signs of weakness. This was their leader and critically important to the Dark Realm. He was their answer to Rizzian, the greatest of all Wizards. He was their hope for dominance and now, before they even entered the field outside of Dryden, he had been injured.

"See, I told you. If you didn't believe me, look for yourself. We are doomed. Even Gabriel is no match for God," a panicked soldier fuelled the fire.

Gabriel, under his breath, acknowledged his enemy, "Well played, Rizzian, I guess we are tied. I may have underestimated you. Even I couldn't have pulled that trick off."

"We need to turn around, who is with me?" the man continued.

Conversations broke out, but what was not said was even more important. Many of them didn't verbalize their negative thoughts that ricocheted through their minds.

Gabriel knew he needed to eliminate these thoughts immediately. As he continued to walk toward his tent, he raised his hand in the direction of the panicking man, and without looking in his direction, a flash burst from Gabriel's hand. What seemed like a lightning bolt slammed into the body of the hysterical man and burned a hole through his midsection. A lifeless body with a massive cavity in it fell to the ground. Most were startled, but everyone got the point.

Dryden, as an impregnable fortress, looked more like an impregnable entity. The sun rose on the four thick walls towering over the river moat that marched around it and was illuminated by the early light. This was normal, but the sun reflected on something else, something special. Its rays collided with tens of thousands of shields. This made it an entity; mortar, rock, nature and now man fused together with one goal, stop anything or anyone that challenged it.

The men had been moving out all night and aligned themselves in perfect unity. Over-armed due to a lack of men and a surplus of armour and weapons, they were an intimidating sight.

All commanding officers were on horseback, straightening out the lines and going over critical details.

Partly for intimidation, almost all of Dryden's available forces were outside the walls. Normal battle tactics would suggest this was a foolish strategy. Text books were created on military strategy, volumes of them, and few, if any, would advise leaving a fortified city and surrendering the increased defensibility that it insured. They gave up the one imperative strength they had, but this was far from a normal situation.

"I couldn't have imagined a prettier sight Kruno." Bruno and Kruno stopped their horses to converse.

"It is fantastic, isn't it?" Kruno smiled as he looked at the troops.

"Pretty. I could think of a better word to describe it," Decan yelled out, totally out of place, as he rode by. "Mostly men, sweaty and hot all dressed up. Maybe you call that pretty? I guess this is why you are without a wife. Maybe you prefer the other side." His horse seemed untrained as it jumped about. It seemed to mock Bruno as well.

"What the heck are you doing on horseback Decan? Get in line like the rest of them. This is only for men of command."

Decan smiled in their direction. Bruno understood what that meant.

"Oh no, who put you in charge and of what? I didn't know that our farm animals would need a leader, is that what you are commanding? Are you in charge of the pigs?"

"Not unless pigs can fire arrows." Decan knew getting any command irritated Bruno, hence he sported a small aggravating smirk.

"He is an excellent archer Bruno, don't worry."

"Oh, I might worry. If you keep this attitude up, I might have to put an arrow in your ass in the middle of battle." Decan smiled.

"You would like that, wouldn't you Decan?"

"No, but I know you love getting things in the ass." Decan made the joke and even Kruno snickered. "Later boys." Decan rode off.

"I don't know how you handle him Kruno," Bruno said with irritation.

"It's just who he is. You start to forgive his foolish comments when you see him in action on the battlefield."

"I will take your word for it."

"This will be quite the sight when those bastards come through the forest. You know, now that I think of it, as their vanguard hits the battlefield it would be a great time to charge. They would have no time to set up. We could push into the forest or wait as they come through. Their heavy horse wouldn't be effective, battle lines would be in disarray and their archers couldn't fire through the trees." Kruno spoke as he thought.

"Great, we could have used that idea before, but it's a little late now. Plus they will have their catapults buried deep. We wouldn't have a chance at getting to them. Eventually they would transfer troops to roadways and focus the battle there, but it would give us more time. It would take days to get through, maybe enough time to have Hot House here and swing the odds in our favour." Bruno realized that might have been a better plan.

"Really doesn't matter, does it? We are sticking with our plan, a good plan." Kruno changed topics, realizing he stirred up some something unwelcome — doubt.

Bruno shook off the comments and focused on their battle plan.

"Let's keep the troops hydrated and make sure we bring out the Ministers. Your speech about God speaking to them was a brilliant idea, but we must keep it up. You know what the Dark Realm is going to bring out here, and they will attack our troops mentally. They have picked one side and us the other. Our side is stronger. Our troops must believe that, every one of them. When they size up the sheer number of our enemy it will be very intimidating. We need God on our side, even if it's only a perception."

Kruno was about to argue that God *was* on their side when Bruno raised his hand.

"Do you hear that?" They could hear something in the distance, a faint noise. They waited a few moments and struggled to figure out what was in the air. Finally, Kruno deduced what it was, what it had to be.

"Here they come!"

It started off as an unclear hum in the distance. As time passed, the sound became clearer and more menacing. It was a chant that the Dark Realm had used for years. A few dozen chanting didn't do much, but tens of thousands of troops repeating the same chant was demoralizing to any enemy. The chant was conducted from the back of the throat.

"OOOOOOOOAAAA OOOOOOOOHHHHH." It was repeated over and over, and incessant chant that grew louder as they approached.

The chant was impressively powerful and had an evil sound to it. The younger troops could hear it first and then it permeated to everyone as the decibel level rose. The chant served several purposes: it showed union, it illustrated the numbers to come and it made them sound like they weren't human. The Dark Realm lead by Zoran, Gabriel and Damascus were true perfectionists of psychological warfare.

Rizzian stood with Egon in one of the archers' dens away from the battlefield. Egon reiterated what he had heard. "They have conquered many people. Many of their opponents found their troops ran from them before the battle even started, many others dropped to their knees to surrender, others trembled with fear as they were charged."

Overlooking the battlefield Egon panned over his troops and looked to the forest where the chant was radiating from. The movement of multitudes shifted the tops of the trees in the distance. From the ground it couldn't be seen, but from their vantage point it was terrifying.

"Do you believe in God, Rizzian?" Rizzian was shocked by the question. He expected the encroaching enemy to have a different effect on the young King. "I mean, really believe in God?"

"Why would you ask such a question, King?"

"Well, you understand the world more than anyone. You can do things that I can only assume are gifts from him, but maybe you have more insight and have concluded that he doesn't exist."

"I don't think it really matters what I think, but everyone's faith is about to be tested. No matter what the outcome of this battle, it will show many a horrific side to humankind. I guarantee you that scores of your people will question how a God, our God, could let this happen."

King Egon absorbed his words and reflected on the horrors to come.

"But to answer your question, my King… yes, I do."

As the Dark Realm advanced, some of the troops were assigned to shake the trees. Several would rock the larger ones as the front line passed. If too big, then someone would climb up and shake them vigorously. It served two purposes — first it intimidated their enemy, and secondly, it kept them in line. It was a way to communicate. They wanted to hit the battlefield with all forward points at the same time.

Zoran lead two of the divisions and was beaming with excitement. His time to reign as the Games Master was close. This battle would put him in the history books. He would become a legend.

Valin and Baccarat, Zoran's two top Black Knights, rode with him.

"Tell me again why we lead two divisions, one on the cut road and the other through the forest, but for some reason you thought it would be wiser to go through the forest?" Zoran asked Baccarat, from his horse.

"My King, don't you enjoy the ride? Fresh air, all the bugs you can eat." Baccarat waited a moment and continued, understanding that Zoran wasn't amused. "The road left a much better chance of being ambushed. They know you are the head of this army and if they could cut off your head, then we would collapse."

"Hmmm, don't you think I can handle an ambush? Anyway, I should survey this land as it will be mine soon. I should be enjoying this more than I am, my march to victory."

"We haven't won yet Zoran. There is still a battle to be fought." Valin, one of few men who had the authority to speak his mind, did so.

"They will be trembling before we fire an arrow. They will be begging for mercy before we unsheathe a sword," Zoran declared and closed his eyes for a second. His eyelids fluttered as if in pleasure. It was strange but nobody said anything.

"And if they want to fight?" They rode slowly behind the front line. Trees shook around them as their men did as they were told.

"Well Valin… that would be even better. If they don't surrender, then we will be able to kill on a massive scale, rip the hearts out of our enemy and leave them on the ground to rot in the sun. Although I would love to have those walls intact, I don't mind blowing them apart."

Another Black Knight rode up to the three of them, "Permission to speak?"

"Of course, go ahead," Zoran answered arrogantly.

"They are in front of their walls."

"Who is in front of their walls?" Zoran asked.

"They are… Dryden."

"Well that is interesting and stupid. How many of them?"

"I don't know… looks like all of them… a lot!"

Completely shocked, Zoran looked to Baccarat, "Are they that stupid? The child King must have decided this. That strike on Deo might have been the best move we could have made. It left Dryden in the hands of an idiot."

"Good news, I think I will be using this." Baccarat reached back and touched the handle of his enormous sword, which rested down his back. "All this talk of them surrendering or running was making me a little upset. That wasn't what I signed up for, I am here to spill their pig blood."

"Have they advanced forward at all or do they sit docile by their walls?" Valin asked.

"They are sitting still across the field, plenty of time and space to set up, but not too far from here, just off a roadway, a note was found. It was from Hot House!" the Black Knight continued. "Is that true? Is Hot House here?"

Hot House was feared as the most ruthless and effective division of the Silver Allegiance's army. Their plan would be in jeopardy if Hot House had arrived, as numbers would even out. Victory would be a much tougher challenge if the Black Knight was correct.

"A note, what do you mean a note?" Zoran asked and thought in a panic, *Hot House better not be here, those pricks. Tell me our intelligence teams are stupid. How could it be? That makes no sense.*

"Well the note was found carved into one of our soldiers who was tied to a tree. What should we do?"

Baccarat jumped in, "What do you think, idiot? Ride back and hide behind Pra's walls, hoping that big bad Hot House won't attack us." He looked at him and waited a moment for him to realize that the comment was full of sarcasm. "Who cares if Hot House is here? More for us to kill!"

Realizing the conversation had ended, he decided to ride away to escape any more ridicule, but Valin stopped him, "Hold on there, did you see the corpses?" He nodded with a wince and Valin continued, "Why did you wince, were they mutilated, did they smell bad?"

"They weren't torn up too bad, but they smelled horrible."

"Don't worry about Hot House, it's just a scare tactic," Valin concluded confidently.

"And how do you know that?" Zoran asked.

"Our intelligence puts their arrival days away still. Maybe their timing could be off by a bit, but those corpses he describes must be several days old at least, maybe a week due to the smell. We wouldn't be off that much. This is just a tactic."

The chant revealed the incredible number of troops that were just beyond the trees. The forest's edge started to shake as if it was trying to tell the soldiers of Dryden to run, to flee.

The intimidation worked for many of Dryden's inexperienced. They had hoped this moment would never arrive, a small voice in their minds had told them not to worry, this would never happen, but it was going to happen. Frustration and anger kicked in for these men, as they wondered why they had to be there. They didn't want to die.

Everything went silent. The chant had continued for a long time and then it just ceased! It was odd and the soldiers could not figure out why it had stopped. The silence was eerie and seemed to have even more of a psychological effect on them than the actual chant. It was like being on a boat all day, when you lie down at night it still feels like you are still moving with the waves; so the chant seemed to continue to flow in many of Dryden's soldiers' minds.

"Why have they gone silent? What is going on here?" a nervous soldier whispered to the man to his right.

"I don't know, maybe they are turning around. Surely, the sight of all of our troops may make them turn the other way."

"Maybe you're right, that would be great!"

"Don't be foolish. We will be fighting today, that is for sure." Another man leaned forward from behind them to announce as he had overheard the silly deductions.

"And how do you know that?" The original soldier turned to ask, irritated that his peaceful thoughts were trampled on. He didn't respond, instead he pointed forward to the treeline.

The forest secreted the first wave of troops. They permeated the entire forefront of the woods. Three massive areas had Dark Realm men stream onto the great field. Many started to draw the conclusion that this would be the hand that would strike Dryden hard and end so many lives, possibly the staging ground for the destruction of Dryden.

Spread throughout the enemy group were flag bearers. The wind exposed an upside down cross imprinted on each of the flags. The audacity was outrageous.

"Those bastards are really playing this role up, aren't they?" Comments like this and others ricocheted through the Elites. They couldn't believe they mocked God so blatantly.

Primarily soldiers without a horse entered through the forest. Men on horseback took one of three roads that lead to the field. With professionalism, they all knew their positions and started to form the battle lines.

It wasn't long before an equal number of troops were on either side, but the Dark Realm had still not introduced all of their troops. More and more men moved onto the field. Knights, cavalry, infantry, and archers all poured out. As each moment passed, nervousness set in for many of Dryden's infantry.

"Oh my, how many of them are there?" an infantryman said on the front line. They had the best view other than the men on the wall.

Once sufficient numbers were on the field, as a buffer to make sure they weren't rushed, Zoran ordered the catapults forward. The key to the outcome of the battle rolled out.

Egon, from a bird's-eye view on top of the wall, used his fingers to count the number of catapults.

"Dammit, we thought there would be four, maybe five, I count a dozen of them. Things just got a lot worse, didn't they Rizzian? We can't win this fight, can we? Have I condemned all of these men and women's lives? I should have let them go, we should have evacuated."

"Not you… Not me… No one on this field chooses who wins this fight. All we can choose is how we react." Before Rizzian could continue, a flag caught his eye from the corner lookout of the castle. Rizzian turned to see that it was a blue flag, meaning that a boat was approaching. These blue flags were displayed all the time to notify Dryden of its approach. The river was used for trade and travel. On busy days it could be overwhelmed with vessels, but today things were different.

An order had been given to not allow any ship to pass down the river. A small fleet was sent up either side to make sure it wouldn't happen. If a boat made it through, that meant they had breached the line and they could be attacked from the water. This could put Dark Realm troops on either side as the river split around Dryden.

"Dammit they are coming from all angles!" panicked Egan said. His heart pounded as the stress started to break his inexperienced mind.

Rizzian knew that traditionally leaders rode out to meet before the battle to negotiate. That would be expected when both armies were in position, but Rizzian couldn't let the Dark Realm see this side of Egon. He was a scared adolescent and knew they would be influenced by power but thrive off weakness.

"Don't worry, Egon, I will take care of this. You have a seat and relax. Someone bring him some water." Egon took his advice and sat as a servant rushed water to their King.

Rizzian moved with haste along the outer wall to get a better look. The entire time he concentrated on a spell letting the pressure build with each step he took. The spell's intensity and eventual devastation it would unleash grew.

Not sure how many ships are coming, but the first one is going to be nothing but splinters.

The Wizard hit the edge with his hand glowing intense blue. He looked down on the massive river and was ready to unleash his fury when a hand grabbed his shoulder. "Don't, it's a friendly boat." A soldier passed on the information.

"Are you crazy? Never grab my arm like that! This could have blown you into a thousand pieces." Rizzian lifted his hand on the brink of releasing a spell. He lectured a man whose eyes started to water, almost in tears. "This could have been a bad day for you." He decided he would never speak to Rizzian again, and if he survived, he would make sure he never even looked in his direction.

The Wizard noticed the ship wasn't military. It was quite simple and only had a handful of people on board. It was strange that the check point up the river would have let them through. Rizzian wanted to check it out for himself.

"Well, all the gates are sealed and the quickest way from one place to the next is a straight line… so." Rizzian stepped off the edge of the wall and raced downwards as gravity took control. A few men ran to the edge to see what would happen.

The old man fell fast at first but then started to slow, unnaturally. His garments reached for the sky in the beginning, but then started to lower. He floated outwards and his first step was beyond the great moat, touching solid ground.

Not as much fun as it used to be. I guess it's been awhile, Rizzian thought to himself. *Maybe I am getting a little old for tricks like that.*

The boat pulled up to shore before Rizzian could get there. He could hear jubilation from the men on the river front. They were ecstatic about something.

Rizzian walked up to the boat and understood what all the joy was about, as a recognizable face walked toward him.

"Magnus, you're alive!"

"Did you think I was going to let you bastards have all the fun without me?"

"How is it possible? I was there, I saw the last minutes of the battle, everyone was dead!"

"Well it's a story for another time. Looks like we have to deal with some unwelcome visitors." The very tall Elite with a bushy red goatee pointed towards the mobilizing Dark Realm. "Get me my armour and a weapon!" He looked to a page who was ecstatic to see him.

"You don't look so great, Magnus. Maybe you should rest a bit," Rizzian remarked.

"I don't look good, what are you talking about? Look at you, you have the oldest balls within a day's ride." Magnus partly joked with Rizzian, one of few that would dare speak to him that way, but they had known each other for years. "Rest, I have spent all kinds of time resting on this floating log." He looked to the boat's owner. "Not that we don't owe you everything."

"Just doing what I can to help, I am not much of a fighter, but I brought you one," the fisherman commented.

"That you did, and we are in your debt, you will be paid for your deed," Rizzian spoke.

"No insults great one, but to receive payment wouldn't be right, I am just happy I could help."

Rizzian was pondering how impressed he was with the simpleton when he heard another voice. "Hey, how about me?" a young man with bandages covering his eyes was assisted off the boat.

"Another survivor from the attack?"

"Yep, this is Joe, he looked evil in the eye and that is the last thing he will ever see."

Rizzian walked over to greet him. "I know of you, Joe, a skilled archer, almost a shoe-in to become an Elite."

"Not any more, those bastards took my sight. They killed everyone, Deo, John, even the Priest. They left me there and told me I would live with my last image of them, I would live with the shame of defeat, never being able to rectify myself."

"Let me see your eyes, maybe I can help."

"No, they are gone, I know that for sure. My eyes are split in half."

The thought of that made a few of the surrounding people cringe.

Rizzian turned to one of the men. "Take him in the castle to Xavier's, take him to Disha and tell Disha I sent him. I am calling in the favour."

"You mean the Clorians are still here? They aren't fighting with us?" Magnus asked.

"They aren't out here, but they will defend their home. If Dryden's walls are breached, God help the first troops that walk through Xavier's. You know they are against war, but will make a mess out anyone breaching their territory."

"Well from what I can see, conflict is an absolute for the Clorians." Magnus took a step forward and favoured his leg.

"Come here, I can help."

"I don't need any help, I just want to get my revenge. Use your spell somewhere else, don't waste it on me." His comment had just as much to do with not liking magic as it did selflessness.

"Don't let manliness get in the way. It will only take a second." Rizzian reached forward with a few words and a blue hand touched his wounds. Each one healed as if weeks passed in moments. "Now, how do you feel?"

Examining his body, he looked for wounds that were once there but now gone.

"Thanks Rizzian, but I don't have time to be astonished, it's time to fight."

Bruno, on the front line, caught wind of the fantastic news of his friend's return. He turned to ride off to meet him. "Follow me boys. Kruno, would you mind?"

"Go see your man. This battle won't be starting for a while."

Bruno and four other Elites rode quickly with anticipation. Bruno bounced off his steed and approached Magnus, who had just been helped by Rizzian.

"Look who is back from the dead," Bruno said with a serious look on his face.

"That's right, Magnus is here!" Magnus announced himself with arms open, expressing confidence. "I checked out the other side, but didn't like it so I came back. Did you think I was going to let you boys have all the fun? Time to kill some Black Knights!" Magnus collided chests with Bruno and embraced, showing their camaraderie. Each of the Elites left their stallions and greeted their friend the same way.

"Okay my man, how did you survive?"

"Walter dropped one of those bastards with his axe right through its chest. While he was finishing it off they tried to sneak up on him but they didn't know Magnus lurked in the shadows. I put a war hammer right dead centre in one and then cracked another."

"What about Walter?" one of the Elites asked. Magnus shook his head.

"Anyone else live?"

"Joe, a young man, but he is down two eyes."

"Come, let's get you suited up. First you can see the wife," Bruno announced and then commanded someone to ride forward and find her.

"I am surprised she hasn't found another man yet." Magnus mounted a horse next to Bruno.

"I tried, but she wouldn't have me."

"Too small below the belt, I think Bruno."

"See your wife and kids and I will see you on the front line."

"Get those boys ready for me."

Magnus rode towards the metal gate which was shut and wasn't opening even for someone as prestigious as him. His wife stood on the other side with tears streaming down her face. Her eyes were swollen because she had cried so much since the news of Deo's death and the assured death of her husband.

He got off his horse and moved towards her.

"I told them you would be alive, I knew it. My heart told me so. My Magnus is too strong."

Magnus was going to make a joke like he normally would, a macho comment, but he didn't, he couldn't. He reached through the bars and touched his wife. His eyes started to swell but his tears didn't drop.

"Open the gate!" she cried out loud.

"They won't open it. It's sealed shut." Magnus understood without asking.

"What do you mean? I want to see my husband," she said, on the edge of hysterics.

"Honey, they won't open it. Enjoy this embrace, I don't have long."

"What! You are going to fight?" She responded was shocked.

"Of course I am."

"But there are so many... too many."

"Never too many for Magnus. You married me. You know who I am and what I do."

"Great… well… what am I supposed to do?" Irritated and a little irrational, she responded.

"Well you could reach through here and…" He took her hand and put it between his legs. She pulled back, "You bastard! What kind of request is that?"

"What? I have been gone for a long time." He smiled and her crying was interrupted by a few moments of laughter.

"I'll tell you what. Don't die today, and I will give you whatever you want for a month." She smiled, trying to act brave, but it was easy to see it was all an act.

"Now that is real motivation. If you offered that to all the boys, I bet you we would win this war for sure." She laughed again.

The last of the Dark Realm soldiers fell into place and the two armies stared at one another. It was midday and it had clouded over, looking like it was inevitable that rain would fall, adding gloom to an already dismal atmosphere. The upside down crosses gaped at the soldiers of Dryden, making some angry and others afraid.

Time had advantages and disadvantages. As it passed, the sheer size of the enemy had a negative effect on Dryden, staring at such masses played on many minds. Time did have one major positive benefit though because it was another moment closer to when Hot House was hopefully arriving. That was when the bad news arrived.

A speeder — a man on horseback stripped down with all unnecessary weight removed — arrived. He was trained to carry only water, ride the horse just below breaking point and pass on a message. He brought news that Hot House was three days out. Normally that wouldn't be a problem; to crack Dryden's four wall system would take at least that long with conventional shells, but the Dark Realm had something unconventional. They were going to be able to tear down the walls much faster.

"Three days, there is no way we can hold them off for three days," Bruno said on horseback, away from the infantry.

These bastards will be sitting in the city… in our city when Hot House arrives and everything will be soaked in our blood.

Everyone had a massive weight land on their shoulders. They felt gutted, without Hot House it would be a slaughter.

"So then we fight them without Hot House," Kruno said without batting an eye. His delivery showed everyone why he was one of the most famous warriors in the known world. His ability to go through the process of understanding the situation and to accept it was second to none.

"Sorry to interrupt boys, but their flag has gone up. Here comes that prick, Zoran."

The flag of truce indicated the leaders from both sides could ride out to the middle of the battlefield with no need to fear an attack. Common to most battle structures, the leaders had one last chance to negotiate a settlement to avoid war. If it wasn't successful, Wizards would rise and archers would move into position.

Zoran rode to the middle of the battlefield with Valin, Baccarat and about a half dozen Black Knights. Zoran's arrogance could be seen in his body language from afar, even his horse seemed to move with a pompous stride.

"Where is Egon? Who is going with him?" Kruno asked.

"Egon's fine where he is. He stays behind the walls." Rizzian passed on the news to Kruno and Bruno.

"What, he's not coming out? That will be viewed as a sign of weakness. They will exploit it!" Bruno responded.

"I recommended he stay. He is too young and I don't believe they would follow the rules of a truce for one moment. If they could kill Egon, they would — it would be worth it. We need him alive, he is the spirit of our city."

"If they even motioned in Egon's direction, I would jam this blade through his face," Bruno declared with flair.

"Okay, Rizzian, are you taking the honour?" Kruno asked, totally not expecting his response.

"No, I can't go. If I was to venture out there, then Gabriel would do the same. Putting the both of us together is a really bad idea."

"Okay, then who is going?"

"You, Bruno, Kelk and a few Elites." Kruno had no idea who Kelk was, but didn't think to ask because he was shocked that he was invited to be a part of this critical conversation. To represent the King of the Silver Allegiance was a spectacular honour, one he never expected.

"Good to have you on board Kruno," Bruno said and looked him straight in the eye.

"I never expected to be a part of this, I am not even Elite."

"You are today, and we are more ferocious because of it."

The group mobilized and moved forward. The area between the two armies was a decent chunk of land and it would take a few minutes of casual riding to meet in the middle.

Bruno announced the pecking order, irritating Kelk. "First me, then Kruno. Nobody else speaks, understood?"

"Hold on, I make the order. I am in charge here!" Kelk demanded. He was one of Egon's top officials, and Bruno had to honour or at least respect that. That being said, he wasn't going to be pushed around.

"Is that so Kelk, and how many of these meetings have you been to? For that matter how many battles have you fought in?"

"Hmmm… well, how many books have you read on politics and negotiation? I am going to guess very few. Can you even read? This battle can be avoided if we use the right diplomatic tactics."

"You think this battle has a chance at being avoided?" Kruno jumped in with a smile. Kelk's forecasted outcome showed he didn't have the right to speak. "It doesn't matter what you say, they are here to fight. This is all just theatre, unless you want to hand over the city to them. That is the only way they aren't going to charge," Kruno continued.

"Pecking order is Kelk, me and Kruno. Are you happy now? You lead the conversation," Bruno said. It was a foolish argument to be having, but necessary. The Silver Allegiance had to show Zoran they were powerful so they wouldn't be as aggressive in their attack. The fact that Egon wasn't with them took them down a notch. They needed a united front to try to build some of it back. Bruno had to concede in order not to look disorderly.

Bruno directed his conversation to Kruno leaving the other topic, "Kruno, I have to thank you for being here. We all do."

"No need to thank me."

"We absolutely do. You might be the best warrior that graces this battlefield. We know it and it makes us stronger, they also know it and it plays in the back of their minds."

Kruno looked over and saw a few of the Elites that overheard the conversation and they nodded with respect.

"There is nowhere else I would rather be. The Allegiance has treated me well over the years. Deo was a friend and didn't deserve what he received. These are all important reasons why I wouldn't be anywhere else, but most important of all is that this battlefield has the highest concentration of true evil. Evil that has somehow permeated a nation of men. This is unacceptable, their black hearts must be split in two. God wants it and I will die trying to answer his request."

He put on his helmet and looked toward the encroaching leaders of the enemy.

"Let me start with the introductions, I am Kelk..."

"Who cares who you are... forget the introductions, the more time we waste here the longer we have to wait to cut through your men, and for me to take Deo's old bedroom. I want to be sleeping there tonight. Bring in some of your finest females and show them what the Dark Realm is all about."

The sheer rudeness of Zoran's comments rattled even a few of the Elites, but they didn't show it. Zoran wanted a reaction but didn't get one.

"You don't want to negotiate?" Kelk, very much out of his league, asked the question as per the text book he studied the prior night.

"Sure, we will negotiate, even though the victory is guaranteed. Some of your men may be lucky and kill a few of our men, which I would rather avoid. So here are my terms. Open your gates, raise our flag and your troops fight for us against the rest of the Allegiance. How does that sound?" Zoran smugly demanded the impossible and started to irritate the Elites on horseback.

"That's absurd! Seems a little one-sided. What do we get for that?"

"Well, you get to live and fight for the greatest army of all time. You also save your women from being raped and your children from being pitched from the walls into the moat. Sounds like you get a lot, actually, I would say I am being rather generous."

Kruno had his battle helmet on, as did a few others on either side. It covered most of his face and he wasn't recognized when he rode up, "We would like to thank you for bringing your army here. How else could we have gotten so many of you in one place? You do seem to be a little confused though as to who the victor will be."

"I recognize that voice, who is behind helmet number one?" Zoran asked.

Kruno lifted his mask to identify himself. Eyes widened, heads shifted indicating his presence made a difference; even the best Black Knights would rather meet someone else on the battlefield.

"I look forward to seeing your back as you run in the other direction, because I know you will run. You will flee rather than man up and fight, but mark my words you will pay for your crimes. You will be hunted down and killed like the dog that you are," Kruno said with perfect solemnity. The Black Knights looked uncomfortable. Their shifts in position gave away their thoughts.

"You remember the last thing I said to you?" Kruno nodded in response to Zoran's question. "You are now my enemy, you will be shown no mercy."

"I wouldn't have it any other way."

"Where is your Emperor, Damascus? Where is your gargoyle support?" Bruno jumped in.

Valin, on horseback, decided to respond. He was dressed in full plate mail except for his arms. He had knives down the side of each leg, sheathed in the custom-made armour. "We don't need gargoyles to get the jump on you Bruno."

"You obviously needed them to take out Deo. By the way, where is that bastard Clinton? I wouldn't mind having a conversation with him."

"We didn't need the gargoyles to kill Deo," Zoran interjected. "They just really wanted to rip him into pieces, shred his men, your friends, to pieces. It was like a gift. Tearing them up was pure joy and how else could we get Clinton back here in time for the battle? They air lifted him in."

One of the Black Knights took off his helmet in a similar fashion to Kruno. The face revealed was Clinton's. The sky opened up and a cold rain started to fall.

"My sword will easily kill forty today, but I would trade thirty-nine of them for your life." With extreme anger, Bruno was the first to speak and he did so with intensity.

"Look for me on the battlefield. I am coming for you!" Bruno drew his sword for effect and pointed it towards Clinton.

Both sides reacted in a similar fashion, which broke the rules of truce. Zoran looked concerned for a moment, understanding that the odds were even in the middle of the battlefield and his life could be in danger. The battle needed to be fought with them having drastically superior numbers between him and Dryden's army.

Bruno knew he crossed the line, and after a few moments, regained his head. He put his sword back where it belonged and the rest followed suit.

"When is Egon coming out?" Zoran asked. "I don't have all day."

"Egon's not coming out."

"What? Is he that afraid? What an embarrassment."

"He isn't out here for one reason. He would have broken the truce and shoved a spear into your face, Zoran." Kruno, on his feet, told a white lie that helped save face a little.

"Just because we killed his father, big deal." Zoran took the bait but mocked him a little. "Well you make sure that he knows his father squealed like a little pig before he was killed, actually like a female pig. He doesn't even deserve to be called a male swine." Zoran waited a moment and then leaned off his steed beyond Kruno, staring at Dryden's troops.

"Looks like your men are starting to lose interest, I think their faith is washing away with the rain. Are you having an issue with morale?"

News had spread through the waves of the Silver Allegiance troops that Hot House wasn't coming anytime soon. They were going to be on their own to face an impossible task. The news activated a gloom that started unhealthy chatter. It was infectious, as some even talked about leaving their post. It got worse each moment, hundreds of conversations broke out and quickly turned into thousands.

The cure for the mental sickness wasn't far behind and broke through the frontline of the Allegiance. Fully suited up and armed on horseback, one of the most charismatic Elites was ready for battle. Almost nobody knew he was alive, let alone battle-ready. He rode along the front line of his men. His horse took the instructions perfectly and took hard strides showcasing power and confidence.

The conversation shifted as Magnus, helmet-free, reintroduced his presence to the crowd. They erupted with excitement.

"Magnus is ready for WAR, are you ready for WAR?" Magnus yelled and said it over and over again making sure he spread his rhetorical question to everyone.

Not having the support of Hot House drained Dryden's hope, the massive number of troops they faced devastated attitudes, but Magnus, one man, flipped everything.

Magnus didn't lose stride but changed direction and headed out toward the group talking in the middle of the battlefield. As he started toward the group, Damascus took flight.

"Looks like our morale is back," one of the Elites said as the crowd cheered on Magnus's presence.

Zoran smiled and then raised his hand signalling to the rear part of his army. "Maybe I can change that."

Magnus rode hard and stopped fast.

"Look who it is, my good friend, Clinton." Magnus focused on him with revenge in his eyes.

"Sorry Magnus, but he is mine," Bruno commented.

"Maybe we can each take a piece of him," Magnus continued as Clinton's balls rose into his throat. He realized that two of the greatest warriors were arguing over who was going to have the pleasure of killing him.

"I thought you were dead, how did you live?" Clinton finally spoke.

"I checked out the afterlife, didn't like it, too boring, so I came back, but you will see that for yourself soon enough, and you too Zoran," Magnus replied and the Elites loved it.

"Always so tough, aren't you, Magnus? Well we are not too worried about you." As Zoran finished, Damascus landed and slid along the ground. Its size was impressive. Most of them had never seen a gargoyle. It was a menacing sight, making most uncomfortable.

"I thought I would join in and see how everything is going," Damascus said as it looked directly towards the opposition. Damascus noticed that every one of them turned as it looked them square in the eyes, except for Kruno who stared right back, and Magnus who smiled. Damascus drew the conclusion that these were two of their best and anticipated the challenge and the upcoming battle with them. Very few humans or any species would dare challenge a gargoyle. These two men were special, worth extra attention.

"The last time I saw something as ugly as you, it was on the end of my war hammer," Magnus said, smiling again. The fact that he killed a gargoyle provided an element of shock.

"So you killed one of my kind. I can't even count how many humans I have slaughtered."

"Humans, well they are easy," Magnus replied instantly. "I couldn't count how many of them I have killed either, my specialty is gargoyles."

Damascus didn't even bother responding, but instead looked to Zoran and in demonic tongue said, "Fire the weapon!"

Every one of the Dark Realm soldiers understood, but only Kruno on the Silver Allegiance side understood.

"I will fight you right now!" Magnus tried to provoke Damascus but it didn't pay attention.

From the rear flank of the Dark Realm, a catapult released its ordnance, silencing everyone on both sides of the battlefield. The spherical shell glided through the air, over the middle of the battlefield, over the soldiers of Dryden and collided with the outer wall. It connected near the top of the wall and a massive unprecedented explosion rocked the city.

It couldn't have been a better shot. Even the most accurate catapults and the best teams operating them would have trouble hitting it again. It was perfect from the Dark Realm's perspective. The wall exploded, sending bits of stone in all directions. The fireball's heat was felt by the closest two archer dens. Only two physical casualties resulted; however, many more than two psychological ones were produced. The deaths were random soldiers on the second wall behind the strike. Both of them were lifted off the path and landed in between the third and fourth wall.

The light of the fire could be seen all throughout Dryden. The people of Dryden from behind the wall reacted differently than the soldiers out front. The citizens started to panic and many were screaming while the soldiers said nothing. They remained mute after flinching, some more pronounced than the others. They all just stared at the sheer power that had been used against them. They watched pieces of the top of Dryden's great wall slide and drop into the moat below. Nobody had ever even dreamed of a weapon like this.

The Dark Realm army cheered, adding more pain to an already tough day.

"Hand over your army or your city will be ours and everyone will be slaughtered, everyone. Go talk to Egon. Give him our terms." Zoran gave his instructions.

Silence fell over the Silver Allegiance representatives. Nobody moved and nobody spoke for a while. Just before Zoran was going to talk again, Kruno spoke. "You may win this battle, you might be sitting in Dryden in the near future, but it won't last long. This army behind me will fight with courage and skill. We will take so many of you down during this battle, your army will be worthless, so thin that when Hot House arrives they will run over you like grass." Kruno stopped for a moment and looked to Bruno, "Sorry, Bruno, I should have let you speak."

"Couldn't have said it better myself."

"Good, we would rather have it that way," Valin declared. "Slaughtering your men will be enjoyable."

The two sides looked intensely at each other, both itching to draw blood.

"Ride backward from these guys. Don't give these rat bastards your back, they don't honour truth." Kelk made the comment and had his horse slowly back up.

As they backed away Bruno said, "So Magnus, you have another one of the speeches up your ass? Like the one that got the crowd all worked up before."

"All I said is 'Are you ready for war?' over and over. It really wasn't that clever."

"Seemed to work just fine, sometimes it's the speech maker not the words itself."

Magnus raised his voice to make sure their enemy could here, "Hey Zoran." Zoran turned. "I am really looking forward to shoving one of those catapult shells up your ass and then giving you a nice hard kick."

"Who is this Kruno fellow? And Magnus? Are they going to be a problem?" Damascus asked seriously as they moved toward their front lines.

"Magnus is an Elite, a big man, and yes, he is skilled, but nothing Valin or Baccarat can't handle. Kruno is just a man who has made a name for himself. Nothing to worry about either, I will fight him if needed... Doesn't matter anyway, they are only two men," Zoran responded.

"Kruno isn't one of them? Why does he fight with them?"

"He wants his name to carry through time, but if you ask him he fights for God. Ridiculous if you ask me. They wouldn't be an issue at all if you put a few gargoyles on this battlefield."

"Don't bring that up again; you know the choice you had. Deo or this battle — you could have used us for one or the other. Prove yourself here and then we can talk about future battles. Understand that you disappoint me when you talk like that, Zoran. It makes me wonder if we are supporting the right man," Damascus said with a belittling tone.

"Never doubt me, gargoyle, without us you wouldn't have the means to strike at them, you don't have the numbers."

"Oh, yes, human's greatest quality, your ability to breed."

CHAPTER 9

WAR

"Archers!" The long, drawn out command was yelled out and the flag was raised.

The Dark Realm's front line condensed in pockets to form a path for their archers to move forward and set up in front to improve their range. Dryden's archers didn't move forward, they had the luxury of altitude. On top of the wall they filled all archer dens and the entire path along the wall.

Kruno rode over to Kiera, jumped off his horse and smacked it on the ass to send it away. He was close to the front, just behind the infantry, an area that was going to be hit hard with arrows. This would be the one time that being on a horse wasn't an advantage. All men on horseback were at the rear of the formation, out of range.

"How did it go? Did you play nice with the other boys?"

"We are pretty much in the same situation. We yelled at them, they yelled at us. We argued over whose dick is longer, and now we fight." Kruno looked over and noticed something was missing from Kiera and all the La Caprata warriors, "Kiera, we need to get you shields, they will be sending their volley this way any moment." He looked concerned.

"Don't worry about us, no need for a shield." She turned and looked to the sky in the direction of where the arrows were going to come from.

"Okay, if you say so." Kruno shook his head and then focused on his Clorian arm shield. His shield reacted and transformed from an arm brace to a large shield, but smooth not graded like it had been in the battle with Kiera.

"Very impressive, I remember that trick," Kiera said with a grin.

Kruno, with shield aside, looked up at the wall and let his thoughts drift to Decan who was somewhere up there running the show. *Come on, Decan, your time to shine.*

The Dark Realm received their order to release.

Thousands of arrows took to the sky, shot high in order to make the distance. At their peak it was hard to see through them. The Dark Realm arrows started to descend and Kruno yelled to his troops a final command which they had practiced many times. His voice calmed them down, "Okay, boys… drop low and put those shields up tight."

Egon watched from the main archers den. He couldn't have imagined a sight like this. His stomach went queasy as he witnessed the barrage of arrows hit his army. They were an inferior army in terms of numbers, a conclusion easy to draw from his vantage point.

Most of the arrows hit shields but many struck flesh. Poorly positioned men took wounds to the trunk of their bodies, misjudging the angles of the arrows. Many of them dropped their shields and gripped the impalement. Others hit the ground in agony. Blood from the wounded splattered over the surrounding men.

Some did nothing wrong. They were just unlucky as arrows ricocheted off one shield, sending them in an odd direction and hit some men in calves, ankles or feet. Most would have difficulty fighting with injuries to these areas which meant success for their enemy. All they needed was to injure a man just enough to have him useless on the battlefield.

Decan sat in the main archers den with Egon and called out his command. His men were untouchable from their archers because of their height. The archers fired but not all of them. Only a small section had fired their arrows. Egon watched and interjected with panic in his voice, "What about the others, why have you only fired our front row?"

Decan looked at him for a second, "Let me do my job, trust me, King, I know what I am doing."

The number of arrows fired was minute in comparison to the Dark Realm's. All of them headed for one layer of their enemy. Their archers were the target! Although Decan had many options, he decided to attack them, leaving the other ranks holding up shields to block only the odd misfired arrow. This was completely abnormal.

The arrows hit the Dark Realm archers. Their shields weren't as good as the others because they were never the main focus of attack; they were rarely even fired upon. Stunned, they tossed up their shields and took on a larger percentage of casualties than their counterparts. One of the senior archers turned and noticed a massive majority of the arrows had been directed at them, "What is going on? They are firing directly at us, those bastards!" Archers had a code not to fire at each other, which was supported by most, if not all, military strategies.

"Don't worry, they have fewer archers than we thought." He canvassed the losses and number of arrows on the ground. "Load… Back… Fire!"

The arrows rose again. Kruno watched and carefully positioned himself to avoid being struck. His shield had strangely taken a convex form, like a bowl with him in the middle of it, which added even more protection.

I love this beautiful shield more and more. Thank you beauty, Kruno thought and then looked over at Kiera who stood alongside the other La Caprata. Her hand was up and lay flat in the direction of the oncoming arrows. Kruno watched as they raced towards Kiera, but hit a dead stop a few feet from impact. Limp arrows landed all around her.

"How the heck? Never mind, why am I under here when you can stop arrows like that?" Kruno asked.

"All you had to do was ask baby. Stand next to me. Get in nice and close."

The bombardment came hard on Egon's army and took a similar toll as the first. Egon was ready to turn and have Decan pulled from command. He had built up a sweat all over his skin, a greasy paste that had been precipitated from stress and confusion.

"Okay, boys, second attack now!" Decan commanded and the first wall let loose again. He counted with his fingers but instead of looking at the battlefield he looked at Egon, a panic-struck young King. One, two, three and then motioned his hands forward. The second wall of archers let loose this time. He then counted again and the third released, did it again and again recycling the series.

"You see great King, they think we only have a quarter of the archers we do. In most battles, firing in order is considered compulsory, fair play. Well I don't think using gargoyles and catapults that explode is fair. So screw them, these bastards are in for a real surprise when they look up."

Decan smiled and moved to the edge of the wall to get the best view of the onslaught.

The Dark Realm archers dropped their bows with more panic, this time realizing they were the primary target. They took cover under their shields waiting for the counterattack. The arrows hit and then they opened up their shields to reach for their weapons. Some looked up quicker than others and of course expected an open sky, but they were wrong! The second wave of arrows struck many of their unprotected faces, necks and chests. Many didn't look up at all, and when they reached back to grab their long bows, they felt the sharp pains slam into their backs. The ones that were lucky grabbed their shields in a panic as the third and fourth wave hit them, but they were in disarray. The casualties were severe.

Decan turned to Egon. "Well that helped with the numbers, didn't it Kingster?" Decan called him a name nobody would ever call any King, let alone the one that rules the Silver Allegiance, but that was him and Egon was so elated at the success he didn't even notice.

"It's going to be really tough for them to fire back, don't you think? They have many advantages on us, take away their archers and that's one for us."

Egon turned and watched their archers take another series without return fire. He looked to Decan with absolute shock.

Zoran was near the rear flank. He had so many troops ahead of him it was hard to see what was going on. He stood on an elevated platform built for him to view the battle from a safe position, but it was still tough to see what was happening, not impossible but difficult. Gabriel was at his side for a few reasons — one, to help with the commands, and two, for protection. If Rizzian or any of the other adept Wizards were to see Zoran in an elevated structure, he would be an easy target.

"Why aren't we firing back?" Zoran asked with only a little concern.

"It seems like they aren't giving us a chance to," Gabriel replied.

"Not exactly playing by the rules are they? Well let's fire back." Like a conductor, Zoran moved his hands through the sky, every so often saying a number and with that number a flag rose. "Ten… two… seven… five!"

Every one of his catapults were loaded and ready to be fired. The numbers were the actual catapults from one end to the next. They were powerful, but the shells were heavy and volatile. It took a while to load them because it had to be done with several men and with extreme caution.

One after the other the menacing shells lifted off the ground from a massive catapult. The machine itself was complex and must have taken teams of engineers years to design.

Decan revelled in his success as he watched the other archers shrink in numbers as they hid behind shields with their bows on the ground beside them. He then turned and commanded half of the men to fire on the infantry.

Decan knew this unchallenged advantage wouldn't last long and wanted to use it while he could. Their men were taking hits from a constant flow of arrows with nothing in return. The Dark Realm archers were rendered ineffective, but their catapults weren't. Four consecutive shells left the battlefield racing toward their desired collision. A few of Decan's archers stopped but Decan yelled, "Don't stop! Continue to fire, stay strong!"

Decan watched the first sail right over all four walls and heard it smash into a building. Most of the city streets were empty, but not the buildings themselves. Non-warriors were told to stay in their homes until the battle was over. The shell hit the roof of a two story residence; the explosion blew out three quarters of the home and killed everyone inside. Neighbouring homes felt windows blow in and the force of the blast caused enough panic to have them rush to the streets. One man, disoriented, walked out with his ears ringing. Stone was everywhere and a cloud of dust took a moment to settle and exposed an annihilated structure.

The next two connected with the outer wall, the desired target of the Dark Realm. One took out a huge chunk of the wall closer to the ground but the structure above remained intact. The other was heading just below the top of the wall. Decan watched the shell lose altitude and tried to will it from connecting with its inevitable target, an archers den. The men were close enough to him so that he could see the looks on their faces as they blew into hundreds of pieces. One moment they were there and the next they were pulverized. He had never witnessed something so disturbing. Chunks of flesh leapt in all directions, but mostly headed backward, littering the evermore populous streets with disagreeable matter.

The fourth shell missed any structure and smashed into a small courtyard placing a huge hole in the ground, killing only one unlucky man. He watched the massive sphere skim the last wall and head right for his location as if he had a bull's eye on his forehead — bam! He didn't even try to run, not because he understood it didn't matter anyway, he just froze.

"Oh my God! We are getting killed. We can't defend against such power," Egon yelled as his eyes shook in his head from one of the explosions.

Decan collected his thoughts and noticed most of his archers had fallen out of sequence — most had stopped firing completely. He yelled with unwavering conviction. "This is completely unacceptable!" He was obviously irate as he kicked over a large basket. "Listen to me… Hey… Listen to me! Don't focus on their assault, we have them pinned, follow my lead. Fire at your targets, but now I want you to fire at will. Fire everything you got!" He yelled to the commanding officers and they spread the word.

"Egon, you should get out of here. Who knows where the next shell is going to strike? You have to be safe." Decan commanded a man who normally couldn't be commanded.

"Nope, I stay here."

Egon finally felt a surge of confidence as he started to accept one thing; in war, death was a guarantee. He had never commanded any large group of men and it bothered him to see his men get shredded, but even the best victories had casualties. It was impossible to protect all his men. He had to look at it differently, turn off a part of his brain that he had never attempted to before. With that came some relief.

"King, I think…"

He was cut off by Egon, "I am King, I decide where I stay. Now continue leading our archers. They are doing a superb job, but need your guidance." Decan noticed the change in him and liked it.

Over two full rounds of catapult fire had been released over some time. Zoran stared with lust as the great walls of Dryden were busting to pieces. He couldn't believe it was happening, the second wall was exposed in some areas and he knew a few more perfect strikes and possibly they would see the third. It would still be a while before they would be able to penetrate the city, but the sheer power at his fingertips was overwhelming, almost erotic.

"Sir, we need to do something about our archers," one of his commanders yelled, but Zoran paid him no attention, so he spoke up trying to make his point, "Sir, our archers are getting destroyed out there and our infantry is taking losses." He waited a moment and then yelled, "Sir!"

"What, what do you want? I will give up infantry and archers for pieces of their wall any day." Zoran looked ahead.

Baccarat made his way up the tower where Zoran and Gabriel stood. He waited a few moments and Zoran spoke, "It's beautiful, isn't it, Baccarat?"

"It is, my King, just as you said it would be."

"We are on schedule, soon we will be dining at the royal table."

"King, we really should assist our archers. I don't mean to be a bother, but they will be needed in the future. Once we are victorious in this battle, we will have to deal with Hot House... our archers will be needed." Baccarat understood how to reason with Zoran.

"Fine, you have made your point. Raise the flag. Pull back our archers, regroup and start preparation for full attack. Stop our bombardment."

The Dark Realm's remaining archers scurried back out of range and they signalled for a cease fire. Everything stopped. This was a common request in major battles in order to pull the dead away. Arrows were surrendered for catapults. It was temporary, and although Dryden had a lot less dead, they wanted the catapults to stop so they could assess and breathe.

Fires were burning the city internally, not out of control, but enough to occupy many citizens who were trying to extinguish them and enough so that the smoke rose from behind the walls.

Dryden's walls were now porous, but far from being fully penetrated. The reality was they had the means to do what they set out to do. If anyone doubted the Dark Realm they didn't any more.

As the Dark Realm frontline infantry had put down their shields they were able to take stock of how many were dead or injured. The number was fairly substantial with over half of the archers seriously wounded or dead.

The Silver Allegiance used empty ships to pile the dead and move them up river to be dealt with later. Many battles of this magnitude would take weeks, even months, for a victor to be crowned and decaying corpses would cause repugnant smells and could lead to sickness. Therefore the battlefield was cleaned after major surges under the flag of truce. This battle wouldn't take anywhere near that time, but the bodies were taken away anyway to clear a path. There were so many men in the battle that the casualties could pile up, making fighting challenging and negatively affecting the soldiers' frame of mind. Climbing over bodies wasn't a desirable scenario.

Rizzian had situated himself near the rear of the army. Around him all of his magicians stood and waited for his order. The one clear advantage Dryden had was their number of Wizards. It was a bit of an illusion, as many of the Wizards that Rizzian displayed were from Dryden's School of Wizardry — mostly professors and a few senior students. Few of them had ever been to, or wanted to go to war. It didn't matter if they wanted to fight. They had no choice.

In DSW, some classes were geared toward war and combat. Everyone had to take a certain number of them. It was mandatory. A few specialized in combat, and they were more important. One of Rizzian's professors who taught advanced military combat classes was Eclipse. He was a named Wizard like Rizzian, identifying him as possessing an extraordinary skill set. Not only was he willing to be on the battlefield, he was excited to be there.

"Not too often we get to bring out four dozen Wizards to a battlefield. This is a great moment, we will tip the battle in our favour." Rizzian made the statement with pride as he looked over his group.

"Too bad we're all going to die out here," one of the professors said out loud, not thinking clearly, not understanding the gravity of the situation and how it would affect the fragile minds of students and professors that had no experience in war.

Rizzian looked at him and with all seriousness said, "You dare question the power of DSW and Dryden's army. We have no place for you here." Rizzian stared directly at him.

It took a moment to process what had just happened. He never expected this kind of response. "But I didn't mean, I just wanted to..."

Rizzian pointed his finger, "Leave!"

"Where should I go?"

"I don't care but you will not remain on this battlefield." Rizzian made his point and everyone understood. Nobody wanted to disappoint him. "Okay, we have wasted too much time on this, back to the situation at hand. This is a great moment, a moment you will never forget for the rest of your lives. This is our time to shine, to let Kings know how powerful Wizards are."

"I count the seconds to battle Rizzian. Tell me what our next move is!" Eclipse looked more like a warrior than a Wizard on this battlefield, maybe on any battlefield. He was built well, different from the standard lanky Wizard. His face had character in it indicating that he didn't live his whole life indoors and he wasn't raised with a silver spoon in his mouth. His total composition was a massive asset.

Comparing battle experience to age, nobody had what Christian had, making him valuable as well. Christian's presence also assisted with motivation. He was a celebrity to many of the students. Rizzian, Eclipse and Christian were a tri-factor that was the core of Rizzian's plan. A few others stood out, but none like these three.

Rizzian was working over his plan when an image struck his mind. It was a blur but he knew it was important. His head shook and he leered with a confused look on his face.

"Are you okay?" Christian asked.

Rizzian didn't fully understand what he had seen, but knew he had to take action.

"Christian, you take control. Get the men into position. I have to go. See you up in the sky. Rise on my command and prepare for all-out war."

Christian, in an unfamiliar place, needed to man up fast. It was odd he was given this responsibility. Surely it should have been Eclipse or another senior Wizard, maybe one that had fought with the Silver Allegiance before, but Rizzian had put it in his hands. Strangely, Eclipse wasn't upset even though Christian thought he had every right to be.

"Okay, Wizards, we have all prepared for this moment. Battles have few rules and with the Dark Realm the few that should probably won't apply here. Don't show them any mercy, we are more powerful than they are. There is an honour in intelligence and it's time to show who reigns supreme." The words left his mouth as if someone else was the author and he was just an actor. Eclipse smiled, the rest felt their spirits lift.

Thank you God, for the assistance, but I am afraid we will need more than just words.

"Take position, remember your orders and follow on Rizzian's lead."

The Wizards spread out to their predetermined positions.

Rizzian knew where he was going, but didn't know what he had to do when he got there, because he had only caught a glimpse of Gabriel's plan. He wasn't sure if Gabriel wanted him to intercept the thought or if it was luck, either way he was going to the front lines to see if he could shut down the evil Wizard. Rizzian pushed through the last group of men, who were pleased to see the greatest of all Wizards beside them.

On the other side, Gabriel's pale complexion could be easily identified even in the dismal weather. He stood hunched over a little, but he still had all the confidence in the world. The rain collected on his cloak as he looked over at the old man on the other side of the battlefield.

In his mind Gabriel sent a message to Rizzian, "*Today is the day you will bow to me or burn. That is the only option you have.*"

"Gabriel, I am and always will be more powerful than you are. I look forward to your death, like no other before you."

"Power... my favourite word... wait until you see what the true definition of that word is. I am about to redefine it for you. Tell me if you have ever seen this before?"

Gabriel raised his bony white hand, and he started to speak in demonic tongue. His words were horrific to those who could understand him. They were sharp, painful and got worse as he spoke louder. His hand turned the predictable orange, his eyes became like black coal as his words intensified.

Any of his men really close to him, who heard more than a few words, felt pain in their ears. The verbiage wasn't agreeing with their nerves. Several tried to hold off from covering their ears, to try not to look weak, but most couldn't take it and covered them quickly to attempt to obliterate the pain. They each grabbed on and then collapsed to the ground. They yelled in pain, begging him to stop but their screams reached deaf ears. The spell wasn't directed toward his men, but they were unfortunately in the wrong place. In his mind they were expendable. Blood squeezed through their hands as their eardrums finally split.

Rizzian waited and looked along his front line. He knew this spell was going to be impressive. He just didn't know exactly what was going to happen. Everyone on the front was afraid and they were right to feel that way. Against the greatest of all warriors, a man has a chance to avoid a sword, dodge something visible and tangible or even run, but a Wizard's spell was unpredictable and unavoidable. There really was no defense, no warning.

"I am not feeling very good," a soldier said with a queasy look to the man beside him.

"I hear you, I didn't want to say anything but odds are not in our favour, there are so many of them." Responding in a manner that showed he didn't understand that his comment was literal.

"I really don't feel normal at all. How do I loo-ook?" His last word was drawn out as it left his mouth and the other man looked at him in shock.

"What, what's wrong?" He touched his face and it felt strange, almost gooey. His skin had twisted into a disgusting configuration causing his vision to blur. Fear set in, followed by a nauseous feeling. He could imagine what he looked like and started to scream and then off in the distance other screams were heard.

Another group of men didn't feel the sickness, but extreme pain in one or more limbs. The pain was strange and didn't make any sense. One man felt it in his arm. He watched his fist clench out of his control and although he attempted to resist it, it had a mind of its own that kept his attempt at bay. He had no control over his fist and forearm which continued to bend beyond any normal capabilities. His bone warped before his swelling eyes. He dropped to his knees, tried to use his other hand to push it back, but it was a futile attempt. He collapsed to his side, clutching his arm and staring at it with disbelief.

Others across the line experienced the same problems with their feet and legs. Almost the entire first row dropped to the ground. Shrieks got louder as the pain worsened; some screamed for help and others for death.

"What is going on? Rizzian, what is happening?" an infantryman to his right asked with extreme panic.

"Gabriel laid down a curse, a massive malicious curse," Rizzian said with repulsive awe as scores fell every second to his left and right.

"Well help our men, fix them."

"I can't."

"Well then curse them back."

"A curse could only be used by Wizards involved with black magic. They are spells that are directly originated from the Netherworld, anti-God, pure evil." His spell had mutilated the entire front line, save a few that stood next to Rizzian, because of his natural ability to defend it.

The men second in line now had a clear view of the Dark army as their comrades in front collapsed. Some broke the rules and attempted to tend to the injured, but many backed off fearing it was contagious. Not one of them kept their eyes solely on the enemy, they couldn't help but look at the disfigured soldiers.

They screamed not just from the pain but also because of pure fear. How would their wives or friends look at them now? They couldn't fight and if they somehow survived they would be the source of the ridicule and social exile the rest of their lives.

The stronger minded soldiers were only upset because they couldn't defend the city properly, they couldn't defend their own lives or that of their family. Most couldn't stand and would be slaughtered when they were attacked.

"Now you see, Dryden is weak! I am only one and have taken hundreds of men. I will curse you all and then unleash fury. Prepare to perish or kiss the ground in front of my feet and I will let you live," Gabriel yelled out to his enemy, attempting to break their will. "We laugh at your silly God and he does nothing."

A few soldiers, to everyone's dismay, couldn't take it anymore, and based on cowardly self-preservation, they broke into a run across the battlefield. They were looking to Gabriel to let them live. Many Silver Allegiance troops yelled at them as they ran, calling them cowards and other similar names.

Rizzian paid no attention to Gabriel's speech. He whispered words and swept his gaze across their front line. His old eyes focused in like that of an eagle and looked up and down the Dark Realm infantry; feet of one, then up to the shins of another, to the knee and then back down like a wave. His eyes burned bright blue.

Without warning, the Dark Realm troops, who Rizzian had scanned, began to fall to the ground. Tibias snapped and cracked, knees exploded and the bones in their feet were instantly pulverized. The leg of a man became instantly useless as their front line dropped in an orderly fashion. It wasn't sporadic at all, one fell after the other with little time for anyone to prepare. They just waited for their turn. As it got closer to the end many started to run, but it didn't matter, the spell had been cast and the end result was unavoidable. One soldier attempted to avoid being hit and grabbed the man behind him, pulled him forward changing positions. It was a futile act as the spell had already been planted in his knee. As he hit the ground the soldier who was pulled into line didn't waste any time. He drew his sword and jammed it in the face of the man who had tried to put him in harm's way.

The few Silver Allegiance soldiers who had abandoned their post got the best view due to proximity. All of them stopped in their tracks as they watched Rizzian's spell take effect. A few of them tried to return to the side of the Silver Allegiance and ran back begging to rejoin them. The few soldiers on the front didn't need any order, but heard it anyway from the leading general.

"Drop them!" The order was released as the cowards were speared while trying to reintegrate.

Rizzian didn't say a word, he didn't need to. He had responded to Gabriel's attack in a big way.

Gabriel knew the spell Rizzian had used very well. He had cast the same one on his brother when he slaughtered his own family many years ago.

"That brings back memories, Rizzian," Gabriel said with a sick grin, under his breath, as the words were meant only for him. "Get these men out of here and will somebody please shell these bastards." Gabriel raised his voice, commanding them to continue the bombardment as he turned from the stalemate.

The ceasefire was over, Zoran answered Gabriel's request with the reactivation of the catapults, which wreaked havoc on Dryden. The shells that missed the wall either fell short, blasting troops, or in most cases, leapt over the wall and devastated whatever it hit.

Zoran wisely pushed some of his troops back into the forest, putting his front line out of reach of Dryden's archers. The battle was one-sided. Only the Dark Realm was inflicting damage. It was a bad situation for Dryden.

Decan ran over to Egon to see what he was doing and found him backed into a corner. The young King was having another breakdown. His thoughts were disorderly, he figured death for all was inevitable. It was an extreme change in attitude from the one he had earlier, when it seemed like he had pulled himself together.

"Hey King, we need you here."

"Need me, need me for what? Look what I have done, this is all my fault," Egon muttered, afraid.

"Yes, you're right — it is your fault," Decan responded in a manner that shocked Egon.

Looking Decan right in the eyes he said, "What, it's my fault?"

"No, it's not your fault."

Confused the King gave his full attention to Decan, "It is or isn't my fault, which one?"

"It doesn't matter King, who cares? All that matters is you get focused and get the heck off out of here. This isn't the best place for you."

"But they need me to give the authority to attack or to retreat. I make that call," Egon said, looking disheveled.

"Give the authority to me, I can do it," Decan suggested. The idea wasn't selfish at first, but he turned with a smile on his face just thinking about the prospect of having that kind of power.

Egon looked back at Decan as if he was crazy and Decan replied, "Okay, well, it was worth a shot. To have the power to control this army — well, let's just say that would have made my day."

"This great army was entrusted to me to take care of by Deo, my father, an army that will be annihilated."

"Don't say stuff like that, are you crazy? Do I need to slap you?"

"You can't talk to me like that, with a snap of my fingers I can have you killed." Egon was right and Decan was way out of line, but that was Decan's style.

"Nobody heard me so don't worry about it, I am just trying to help. Empower Bruno to make the decision, go collect yourself, then come back when you are ready to take command once again."

As if planned, a shell struck close enough to create a loud noise and vibration that helped hammer his point home. Dust from the wall fell on Decan's shoulder and Egon understood that he needed to leave this position immediately. He got up and walked toward the door, "Empower Bruno. I will be back in a bit."

The King was out of harm's way and power would be given to Bruno. Even though Decan didn't really like him, he knew he was a great warrior and knew the army better than anyone.

Decan ran to the front of the wall to observe the battle. He knew that everything was hinged on Egon's command and the city was taking major hits. More importantly, the wall that surrounded it was also taking a beating. He needed to get to Bruno as fast as possible.

"How long will it take me to get onto that battlefield?" Decan asked one of his archers.

"Well, you have to go through that door, head down the stairs, which leads to a..." He continued but Decan didn't listen. Instead he turned and asked another archer, "How deep is that moat?"

"It's pretty damn deep but why do you ask?" he responded to his commander, very confused.

"That's good enough for me." He leapt over the edge to everyone's shock. It happened so fast that the few that were close to Decan had to shake their heads to make sure they actually saw what they had. The two archers who Decan had questioned looked over and watched him fall. Decan hit the water and they said nothing. They were in the middle of the most massive bombardment ever witnessed in history, but they weren't paying attention because of the insanity of what had just occurred!

"That is the craziest thing I have ever seen… I mean ever," one of the men said as more rushed over.

Bruno watched from the back of the battlefield as each shell rose up and smashed into the wall.

"Kruno, this can't go on any longer, what the heck is going on with Egon? We knew if they wouldn't attack we would have to charge them. It's our only option."

"Then give the order. Let's make a run for those catapults," Kruno responded.

"I can't. The order has to come from the King. It's his decision. It's law, these are our rules of war."

"Well maybe we will just sit around here, wait until we have no walls, no archers and let them attack us," Kruno said and then continued with a lowered voice, "Stupid rule."

Decan, who was drenched, ran up to them a little out of breath. "Boys, good to see you. Well, maybe not you so much Bruno."

"What are you doing down here? You should be in position on the wall commanding your archers," Bruno said harshly.

Before Decan spoke, Kruno asked, "You are soaking wet, why are you… what were you doing?"

"I was bored up there, not much to do but get pulverized, so I decided to drop in." Decan smiled as he pushed water through his hair.

"What do you mean drop in?" Kruno said confused.

"I took the short cut." Bruno and Kruno both realized that he might have just jumped off the edge of the wall into the moat, which was sheer lunacy. Their suspicions were confirmed as they looked up and saw several men cheering and waving. Decan waved back to them. "Much faster my way." Decan made a drawn out dropping noise and demonstrated what he had done with his hands

"That is pure Decan fashion." Kruno reached out and they grabbed hands, showing respect.

"We don't need you down here," Bruno stated and looked back at the battlefield.

"Listen here my bald one. I am here for several reasons — first, I have a plan; second, no battle is ever complete without these," Decan touched his two swords, "and third, I have a message you might be interested in."

Two more shells struck the wall causing more damage, adding to a worsening situation.

Bruno didn't acknowledge Decan, but Kruno listened with intent.

"King Egon has granted you authority to run the battle, you make the call to attack. I think it's crazy that he picked you, but please proceed as you see fit."

"Are you lying to me?"

"You think I want you running the battle? I would rather have that guy take charge," he pointed to a solider who really didn't look like he belonged, skinny and awkward looking, "even though he is useless, I would rather have a woman take command, even this horse could do a better job." Bruno looked at him with irritation.

"If I was lying would I have this?" Decan showed him the royal coin. He wouldn't have this unless it was given to him directly by the King. Decan was telling the truth.

Bruno wasted little time.

"Wizards rise!" The command shot up a series of flags that told Rizzian to start his vital stage.

Dozens of Wizards used their power of levitation to lift well above the battlefield. It would be time for them to unleash havoc on the Dark Realm. The feeling let shivers run down Rizzian's and Eclipse's spines as the crowd cheered. The moment of war had arrived.

On the other side, Zoran looked on as the Wizards rose.

"See, here we go, they will have to attack us with no archer support and significantly out-numbered. They attack us when they have Dryden's great walls to support them. This is just as we planned. Gabriel please, do the honour." He was elated to see what was transpiring. He knew the Allegiance had no choice but to attack because they were damned if they did but more damned if they didn't.

The Dark Realm Wizards, lead by Gabriel, mimicked their enemy and rose to similar heights. The two squared off and everyone knew that it was going to be quite the show.

Bruno couldn't waste any time, the walls of Dryden were crumbling away. Normally the battle would have the magicians fight it out and then send forward the first wave of infantry, but they had to take down the catapults. There was no time to waste.

"Infantry… move forward, first wave!" Bruno yelled before the first spell was cast. The men on the front started to move at a slow pace toward their enemy.

Rizzian floated in the air and looked on at an intimidating sight. Eclipse telepathically communicated with him, "*Beautiful, isn't it?*"

"There are so many it's hard to even estimate the numbers. Beautiful is probably not my choice of words."

"The way I see it, lots more to hit, lots more targets, they aren't as lucky." Eclipse responded like a warrior not like a Wizard, like he always did.

Rizzian opened his mind channel to every one of his Wizards. "*Let's rip them apart! Troops or Wizard, leave the shells.*"

Attempting to hit a catapult shell made little sense. Firstly, it would be hard to hit such a speedy object. Secondly, if the strike was successful they could blast one or more of their Wizards and or send a blanket of fire on Silver Allegiance troops from above.

His hands turned deep blue and from them blue flames formed. They created two large swirling blue balls of fire. Rizzian wanted his strike to have guaranteed casualties and was going to do just that. Aiming beyond the front line toward a condensed part of their infantry, two fireballs raced forward.

It was hard for any of the Dark Realm infantry to tell where the fireballs were going to strike and only a few raised their shields, not that it did much good. The assault hit with such velocity that it blew men in all directions. The fire was intense and consumed dozens more. The flames continued to burn whatever or whoever they touched. Surrounded by extreme heat, the temperature of their armour rose so much that it bound metal to skin. Pain turned to agony quickly, but little screaming came from anyone in its direct path, as the second they opened their mouths, their lungs were incinerated; suffocation took many down.

Eclipse was the next to release, and using another physics spell, he spread his fingers open, with arms to his side and a smile on his face. He was forced backward several feet from the sheer power of the electrical current. White energy resembling lightning leapt from him and connected with Dark Realm troops with astounding speed. The current's first point of contact left a crater in the ground, causing a mini explosion and frying everyone it touched, leaving charred corpses strewn about.

"How did you like that?" Eclipse directed his comment at the enemy. His skin smoked from the spell. Like most Wizards, he had to relax for a few moments to build up another.

The infantry marched forward as the sky went ablaze. Lights, fire and explosions could be felt, seen and heard using peripheral vision as well as directly for those who were brave enough to look up.

The men on the walls of Dryden had a great view of Eclipse's second strike which was surgical. It connected with what looked like an invincible wall of enemy troops. The flash was bright enough to cause most of them to squint. When they regained their full sight they noticed many dead soldiers, some with scattered body parts. They were two great strikes, but the feeling of unanswered success didn't last long.

In sync, as if one, the Dark Realm's entire front moved forward a few steps where the carnage had taken place and then moved back and all corpses and injured had vanished. They looked just as they had before, as if nothing had happened. This was

done to play mind tricks on the enemy, making them look invincible.

"That's all you've got old man? You use boring spells, no imagination," Gabriel yelled out.

With hands to his side, palms facing down he called every small rock and pebble from the entire battlefield. They floated around him in a massive circle. The Dark Wizard pointed to a part of the Silver Allegiance's advancing army. With rapid speed, the rocks shot forward in the direction he pointed.

Rocks hit metal so hard it split right through shields and armour, cutting the infantry down hard. Gabriel kept a constant flow of the small projectiles, starting at one end of the infantry and shifting in a smooth systematic motion. The assault moved and men fell to the ground in vast numbers.

They couldn't do anything to stop the bombardment. The frontline was getting absolutely pulverized. If a solider was lucky to survive he would still have a few rocks wedged into his bone. The ones that survived the wave were covered in blood and showered with screams of pain.

A Wizard dropped from the sky to their aid, took position with a defensive spell to do his best job to protect his men. He didn't have a chance. His spell deflected the first few rocks, but he couldn't handle the power of Gabriel. Stress built in his face until they penetrated his spell and he was shredded to pieces.

Gabriel laughed at the feeble skills of his enemy and enjoyed the massive carnage he was responsible for. Skin and flesh blew off bone and many bones themselves were splintered. Gabriel's eyes turned pure black as the sight brought him absolute satisfaction.

He was jarred from his state of bliss as the infantry stopped falling. The rocks somehow stopped at a group of soldiers who braced for certain death. There was no reason why his absurdly successful spell was no longer working. No visible reason, anyway. The rocks seemed to hit a barrier of some sort only a few feet from impact.

He assumed it must be Rizzian, but looked up to see him engaged in another battle. The only other who could challenge his spell might be Eclipse but he was also visible. His anger mounted.

Gabriel doubled the number of projectiles in an attempt to fix the problem

A few moments before, Christian, without regard for the unprecedented abilities of Gabriel, dropped to the battlefield and shoved his way to the front line. He looked to his side and watched his fellow soldiers pop and crack under the barrage. He also noticed the Wizard who had first attempted to shield them was minced on the ground.

The men were so occupied by the assault they didn't pay attention to the fact that a few were shoved out of the way by an unseen force. Christian was invisible to both his men and the enemy.

With his metal Clorian staff in hand, holding it to the sky, he chanted a few words. He looked right toward Gabriel and watched as the rocks raced from the evil Wizard toward him. It reminded him of a hail storm, but one with more deadly results.

They reached his shield spell and hit it hard, causing Christian to bend his elbows a little to compensate for the pressure. He really hadn't thought it out. He just reacted, dropped and ran with confidence to the aid of Dryden's men. If he had a moment to think about it, he would have probably talked himself out of the idea.

For the most part, the rocks struck a few inches from where his staff was and fell harmlessly to the ground. Christian knew he had things under control and looked to his right to see a shocked but happy man.

Nice try you bastard, you can't figure out what is happening, can you? I love it!

Christian looked across the battlefield and saw the enemy soldiers his men were going to face shortly.

Ah ha! I have an idea. Let's see if this works.

Just before Gabriel doubled the assault, the young Wizard put both hands on his staff and began to bend it. It formed the shape of an open "C", and as Christian theorized, so did the spell play out. Instead of having a strait angle for the rocks to collide with, it followed the contour of the concave shape and shot away from them. As if hitting a slide, they launched outward.

It took Christian a few moments to get the angle right, but once he did, they fired back toward the enemy.

Gabriel was vexed at the fact that some unknown Wizard was strong enough to defend against his spell and keep him from his sight, but got infuriated when his assault was redirected at his army. He looked down to see his men get blown backward off their feet and subsequently shredded.

Christian assumed this would be a temporary benefit because surely Gabriel would stop his spell right away, but he didn't! Dismayed that he couldn't puncture Christian's spell, he intensified it even more; not with more rocks but he increased the velocity of them. Christian felt the pressure but knew he could handle it.

Zoran could see from his perched lookout what was happening. "What is he doing? Gabriel, that idiot, is hitting our men. Tell him to stop, right now!" he yelled and the pitch in his voice highlighted the urgency.

The Wizard Zoran was talking to opened his mind to Gabriel and told him to cease.

"I don't think so. This guy is going to fall to my power, he will die, I will double the spell and double it again until he dies."

"You're killing our men, stop it!"

"I don't care, this battle is mine." Gabriel became obsessed to the detriment of many of his army. Pride plagued his mind, which Christian fully exploited.

"He doesn't care about our troops. He wants to take this Wizard out," he said fearfully, as he passed on the message to Zoran.

Zoran angrily yelled his response, "Tell him that if he doesn't stop, I will have his head!"

The Wizard was in a tough place because either of them could kill him in a second, so he did his best to avoid pissing them off, "Zoran commands you to stop, to stop now. Gabriel, please, this isn't sensible."

This jarred Gabriel enough to let rational thought regain control of his mind. Gabriel waited for a moment and then stopped. He couldn't believe what just occurred. He wanted to know who was able to not only hide from him, but stop his ferocious attack.

"Who are you? Reveal yourself," Gabriel said softly while floating in the air. He released his control over the remaining rocks in the sky and they fell harmlessly onto hundreds of bodies, most were casualties of the recent attack.

Christian didn't reveal himself, but just pulled back slowly, staring up at the great malicious Wizard, who looked down in his direction. He had to concentrate on his stealth spell. He didn't want that kind of attention.

Rizzian guessed who it was and was impressed with his ability, but more so in his decision making skills. Not only did Christian stop the attack, he had used Gabriel's own spell against him, against his troops. If any other Wizard could have stopped the rocks and fired them back, which was unlikely, surely they would have sent them back to Gabriel. In this case, he went a step beyond and used Gabriel's ego to his advantage.

Brilliant, young Wizard, brilliant.

Bruno had watched his first line get battered by magicians, most notably by Gabriel's last spell. He needed to repopulate the first wave which marched slowly toward the Dark Realm front.

"Bruno, let me take some of my men and join the eastern flank," Decan asked.

"Why would you do that? This is just to test their defenses, see how they react. The casualty rate alone makes this no place for a commander," Bruno said while occupied with others, asking questions and giving orders.

"It doesn't have to be a test, the eastern flank is the least defended, it has no heavy horse and the fewest troops. Three of the damn catapults are sitting there. I can get through and smash them," Decan declared with excitement in his eyes.

Bruno didn't answer as he was distracted by so many others, and also Decan's idea didn't make any sense.

"Give me this chance," Decan demanded, finally getting Bruno's full attention. "Our right side has taken few casualties. If we reinforce with the same amount of troops as the other areas, we will be only at a two to one disadvantage."

"That is a big disadvantage and your men are archers!"

"Exactly!" Decan said, not giving up too much information.

"No."

"Listen, Bruno, this will work, they will never expect this, we will catch them off guard." Bruno looked over to him as if on the fence. Decan continued, "You can have all the glory, I will give it to you. Plus think about it, if I am wrong we will all be dead, that includes me. That's probably worth it alone."

After waiting a few seconds, contemplating how he should respond, he said, "Fine, do it." Reluctantly, he let Decan have his way.

Decan didn't waste a moment. He jumped on a horse, but needed to make his typical Decan-like comment and turned to Bruno, "Just kidding about the glory thing. It's all mine." Bruno shook his head as he would do to a child making a childish comment. Decan loved it and laughed as he rode away.

Decan popped off his horse just behind the group of men that would advance to reinforce the eastern flank. He had assumed that Bruno would approve his plan and had proactively gathered all archers not on the wall. He approached the commanding officer and his high ranking soldiers of the eastern infantry.

"Gentlemen, we are here to assist." Decan introduced his presence.

"Assist with what?"

"We are coming with you, we double the men you were planning on bringing."

"Why would you do that?"

"Does this upset you? Would you prefer us to sit back and watch you attack that?" Decan pointed to the front line beyond the advancing men. The sight was intimidating due to their numbers. The leading officer paused for a second so Decan jumped in, "Most would gladly accept more men, are you an idiot?" Decan crossed the line, typical for him, but he actually out-ranked the officer and could say whatever he wanted, insulting or not.

"Sorry, sir, I just don't understand why we need your men. They are not used in this kind of role, they have little experience with a sword." The infantry commander looked a little nervous as he waited for Decan's response.

"Just make sure your men follow my plan, no deviations."

Decan and his men stayed back. They were armed with short bows, which lacked the ability to volley arrows for long distances, but what they gave up in distance they made up for in how easy they were to carry, and in this case, the ability to be concealed.

Decan had another plan that had never been tested in any battle anywhere. He had dreamt up the idea as an adolescent and thought about it for years. It was a sound theory but he wasn't sure how it was going to play out.

Zoran watched alongside Damascus from the other side of the battlefield.

"Things seem to be going okay so far," Damascus commented.

"Okay? Maybe you're not watching the same battle I am. They are advancing toward us now, we will slaughter them. Their walls are crumbling, before day's end we will be able to walk through them. I consider that more than okay. Victory is ours."

"My definition of victory is different than yours Zoran. You think we have won, yet their walls are intact and their army stands tall before us. Victory is when I toss the final baby in our new moat, from our new city wall, when the only survivors from Dryden are stuck in kennels until I am ready to feed on them."

The most likely area for victory was the eastern flank, but the Dark Realm still had double the men, which was a strong advantage. Even if they were to successfully break through their line, the Dark Realm would reinforce their troops. Although there was some distance between the eastern flank army and the middle reinforcing army, it wouldn't take too long to reinforce. Decan knew that and that's why he had to move fast. It had to be a surgical strike.

"Okay, boys, let's start jogging, but don't get too excited, just a little faster than their pace."

"Maybe I should stay off the vanguard?" one of Decan's archers inquired, clearly indicating his fear. Typical of an archer, he didn't have any hand-to-hand combat experience.

"You can thank me later, front line gets more action, more blood." Decan wasn't able to relate with him or anyone who didn't see excitement in close contact battle.

The Dark Realm's eastern flank watched the advancing men step up the pace. Many of the men couldn't wait for battle and hated the fact that their officers had told them to stay in place.

"Nobody moves, keep shields locked and stand tall. Let these pricks come to us," the Dark Realm commander bellowed.

"This is horse manure! Why do we wait? Let's charge out there and meet them head on," a soldier made the comment that resonated in the minds of many.

"No, let them come here, those are our orders. We must protect the catapults." As he spoke, one of the shells shot over their heads.

Decan noticed that Dark Realm soldiers didn't move. They stood firmly in position.

"We need them to charge us or my plan will be a disaster," Decan said with uneasiness.

The commanding officer for the infantry division didn't hear Decan, but understood that they needed their enemy to charge.

"We need these bastards to charge us." One of his men heard and took it upon himself to use manly pride to his advantage, "Let's see if this helps. What are you a bunch of girls? Fight us like men! Come on!"

It didn't take long before the entire division of men yelled and taunted the other side. They were toying with and appealing to the testosterone of the enemy to make a poor judgment call.

"This is ridiculous. Why aren't we charging?" another Dark Realm soldier yelled out.

"I agree, they laugh at us. Let's wipe those smiles off their ugly faces," another yelled in response.

"No! Stand strong, nobody moves." Their commander forced the order on them.

The jog started to turn into a light run by the Silver Allegiance and the chanting got louder. They waved swords and yelled out the final words, insulting their sexuality, "You are a bunch of spear tossers!"

One of the Dark Realm soldiers couldn't take it anymore, and totally out of order, yelled, "Charge!"

Most couldn't decipher if the order was real or not, but still broke from their stationary positions. The excitement of finally attacking Dryden, something they had dreamed of all their lives, was too overwhelming.

Decan moved his group forward. They were trying crouch as they ran, attempting to stay unnoticed. He felt the rush of battle. His hands wanted his swords, as flesh and steel couldn't wait to reunite and wreak havoc on many future victims. *Not yet, boys. We don't need you yet, first we have a surprise.* Decan talked to his weapons as if they were able to hear him.

"Now?" someone called to Decan.

"No, not yet, hold on," he hollered. The two sets of infantry moved toward one another.

"Now sir, Decan shall we..." Nervousness set in for a few as they felt he should have activated the plan already.

He cut him off, "No, not now, stop asking, wait for my command."

The two fronts got closer, almost close enough to see each other's faces. Decan counted in his head *one... two... three...* attempting to occupy his mind so that he wouldn't release the order too soon.

This was as big of a moment as it got for him, and if he was wrong, he had sent these men to their doom and the catapults would continue their bombardment. A set that was poking nice big holes in the last and final wall.

"Stage one, lock and load!" His command was repeated throughout to make sure everyone heard. The archers who found themselves in a scenario which they hadn't been trained for, prepared an arrow and pulled back on the pew while in motion. They kept the bows pointed towards the ground.

After a few more steps, giving adequate time for everyone to be in sync, he yelled, "Stage two, aim forward." The archers stopped on a dime and lifted their arrows, aiming for the backs of their own infantry which still advanced. "One... two... three...four... Stage three... let loose.

The Dark Realm front didn't notice the back half of their enemy stop and kept charging, not alarmed in the slightest. Their shields cupped in one hand moved in a jogging position to the side of most soldiers and weapon in the other. They watched the enemy they planned on engaging dive to the ground in a hurry. It hit them as extremely odd and it should have set off a warning, but they didn't have time to think. As they fell, arrows raced forward just skimming the backs of falling men. The timing was impeccable, arrows jammed into unsuspecting faces, necks, torsos, few appendages were saved. Men lifted off their feet, crashing to the ground.

The threat couldn't be conveyed to the next layer of Dark Realm soldiers. No warning was issued to them and as their comrades fell in front of them, collapsing, they continued to charge ahead unabated, assuming that the reason they had fallen was that they had connected with the front line.

Decan watched as the Dark Realm's front fell several layers deep. He could also see that only a few of Dryden's men hadn't dropped in time and had received arrows in their back. The first round was a success. He too had fired an arrow, connecting with the face of some poor sap. Before the first arrows had struck their victims, the more experienced had already reloaded and waited to fire. Decan called to fire again and they watched as another wave of their enemy hit the ground with massive casualties.

"Again!" he chanted. "Again!"

Round after round of arrows struck the unwary soldiers. The bodies left hurdles for many to avoid which worked in Decan's favour. As they avoided the incapacitated bodies, they watched the ground and didn't notice the archers standing in front of them until it was too late.

It turned out to be a spectacular success, never had archers been used like this before, and the surprise paid off in dividends.

"Stage four! Rise up, archers hold."

Several of the men on the ground had hit hard, avoiding the arrows and were covered in dirt from the slide. The scrapes and cuts incurred would have hurt on a normal day, but adrenaline was too high. They watched the plan work brilliantly. Once stage four hit their ears, they gladly rose and charged, sword in hand, ready to take on a much weaker opponent, one they wanted to decimate.

"That was awesome Decan! That really worked." One archer spoke with pure excitement in his voice.

Decan looked around in haste, his mind was working fast. "It's not over for us yet."

The archer didn't understand and figured he was going to head back to the safe side of the battlefield. "What do you mean?"

"Archers, great job, but ready another arrow." They followed as ordered.

"On my command, fire just over the heads of our men."

"What if we hit them?" Decan turned and looked the archer in the eye and said, "Well, at least it's not you." The man looked back at him surprised, not a response he expected from a man of command.

"Fire!" The order left Decan's mouth and the arrows whizzed above their infantry. The risky strategy paid off as well. The two fronts collided with metal hitting metal or flesh. The rear of the Dark Realm, which had assumed they were safe until they had to face a foot soldier, was met with a big surprise. Severe losses mounted as arrows impaled unsuspecting victims with ease.

The Dark Realm's troops started to collapse fast; first the frontline was ripped down and then rear flank wiped out. The advantage had flipped. The numbers were on Dryden's side and momentum had kicked in. They faced a weaker enemy that was in a state of confusion; one that didn't know where to focus their attention. Decan looked to his right and left then back at the battle.

"Cease fire! Cease fire!" The archers put the weapons aside and looked forward, realizing what they had just been a part of.

Someone yelled out. "Let's join them!" Decan smiled and looked to the archer he didn't ever want to forget because he loved his enthusiasm. "Great idea, let's do that!" The command shocked many because they were archers and archers didn't fight in hand-to-hand combat.

"But, sir, we aren't equipped for this. We aren't trained for this," an archer said nervously.

Decan pulled his two swords from their sheath. "Don't really care, we have them on their heels." As he made the comment his blades extended as they always did. It added effect along with his insane smile at the archer.

"We don't have any weapons."

Decan started to run, "There are plenty on the ground, you have your choice." Already a few steps ahead of them, he called back, "Remember, pointy side into the bad guys."

A few of the archers loved the prospect of hand-to-hand combat and raced forward. The others were nervous but followed as commanded. A couple of them stood back trying to think of a reason not to go into battle.

Decan quickly entered into the action with zeal. It didn't take long for him to be engaged and take down his first victim. He stepped on the back of a fallen man and leapt into battle. He came down hard on a defending soldier with both blades forcing him backward. Decan swiftly jammed him in his torso with his hands still raised. He then connected with the necks of two men, one after another. Blood spat out all over one of his swords and up his arm.

Decan was in the thick of the densely populated battle, and weapons were coming in from all angles. He kept his calm wit about him and defended several strikes expertly. He switched back to offence, opening up a man's abdomen. Quickly spinning, he caught a soldier across his jaw, opening a deadly wound. He felt a rush from the results of his precise killing and was exhilarated. He dropped several others, slicing limbs, and a double blade to the chest of another. He then found himself positioned on the other side of the battle.

Well, that was fast, Decan thought as a bit of disappointment hit him. *But fun while it lasted.*

He connected the ends of his Clorian weapon and two became one and the blades grew yet again. An open field was perfect for his double-ended sword. As he prepared to evaluate the next move, he heard a horn rip a message from the Dark Realm. He assumed that it indicated a call for reinforcements and he was right.

It would take time to reinforce the area, not a lot of time, but it was the perfect opportunity to take a run at the catapults.

Okay, what do we have here? There is just a ten-man contingent guarding each catapult, stupid move Zoran. They are about thirty feet from one another in a line. Okay, here we come.

A huge pile of shells were stacked behind each catapult. It seemed that four or five men operated them. A few stopped their duties as they noticed their defensive line becoming quite porous. More Silver Allegiance troops fell through the other side and now stood with Decan.

Both sides could see the reinforcement troops weren't going to make it in time.

"Okay gentlemen, you guys take out the farthest catapult, you take the middle one and you the closest." He stopped and asked a question to see if any of his men were with him. "Are there any archers here?"

"Yes, sir, there are a few of us." Sweaty and bloody the man had a look of satisfaction on his face as he gasped for breath. He obviously loved the battle.

"Okay, you're in charge of this task. Any other archers, position yourselves here and if those reinforcements get in range, start to fire."

"But!" one archer said with alarm.

"But what?" Decan asked.

"But we dropped our bows before we attacked." The archer that answered didn't want to upset Decan who looked like a mad man. His eyes indicated that there was nowhere else he would rather be. He lived for this and this interruption was irritating to say the least.

"Well, go get them." Decan nonchalantly commanded a task that wasn't going to be easy to fulfill. They would have to run back around or through the battle encountering many hostiles. At this point Decan didn't care. It wasn't his problem.

Decan rounded up twenty men and stormed one of the ten-man contingents. Decan figured the group of soldiers that were assigned with the duty to defend these critical catapults weren't average soldiers. Zoran wasn't that stupid and knew if some of Dryden's soldiers somehow got through to them, they would need to be taken down.

Decan was right. As they connected, he was the only one to inflict damage on any enemy soldier without getting injured himself. His double-ended sword spun with precision. He impaled the right quad of a man, opening it up fiercely, and a set of ribs was next, splitting bone and shooting blood backward, and he then severed the arm of another. The arm fell and the soldier right behind it. The first round of the fight went quickly, but as he turned he realized the Dark Realm guards were trained well. They understood the technique of dropping men with one strike, efficient killing. When he had a chance to canvas their situation, he was shocked. Only Decan and one other stood up against five.

"Hmmm, interesting. What happened to our advantage? Pretty sure this should have been an easy battle," Decan said, acting casual. He watched their men encircle him and the other man still standing.

Decan's uneasiness turned to relief as a spear skewered one of the five from behind. A few dozen more men had broken through the line and were about to join him.

"I recommend running." Decan offered the advice to the hopeless soldiers.

"Kiss my ass, you Elite prick." Decan was honoured to be called Elite because he wasn't even a knight. The reality was he wasn't even part of this army until a few days ago.

"Suit yourself." Decan moved toward them, spinning his double-ended sword above his head.

The first and the second catapult were hacked at by men with a variety of weapons, but axes did the most damage to the wooden structures. The team that had operated the catapults lay mutilated next to them. Hatred fuelled by the immense damage they had caused to Dryden had warranted a few extra blows. They were beaten beyond death.

Decan could see the reinforcements getting closer, but took solace in the assumed fact that all the catapults would be destroyed well before they arrived. He assumed wrong! Two of them were destroyed with ease, but his back was to the third where something was going seriously wrong.

The third catapult was charged in similar fashion as the other two. Things happened quickly, but if the Dryden soldier that led the offensive had really paid attention he would have noticed his enemy didn't flinch. They just kept on working. They didn't even grab weapons.

The leading soldier didn't have time to analyze, but had his eye on the prize. He got within ten feet of his target, raised his sword above his head, screamed to conjure up adrenaline, but slammed into something! As if hitting a wall, his body flattened, including his face and he bounced back hard. His nose opened up and blood spewed everywhere.

A second man did the same, flew back and collapsed right behind him.

"What is going on here?" one man said as he stopped before they did. He reached forward and his hand stopped. There was an unseen barrier surrounding the catapult. It felt like a smooth wall but it was invisible. He looked at the catapult crew with a bizarre investigative gaze. One person stood out, a peculiar man dressed differently with his hand to the sky. He had a book connected to his waist rope, and it became clear that he was a Wizard. He was casting a spell to prevent them from attacking the precious last catapult.

Decan finally noticed the third one very much intact. Although two were out of commission, one would still cause a lot of damage. He needed it destroyed and fast.

"Damn it… damn it… what is going on over there?" Decan questioned, as someone told him to look over at the bizarre sight of the men hacking in midair.

Decan was just about to race over and assist them in completing this pivotal task when someone behind him said, "Looks like"... "a defensive spell"… "to me."

"Whatever it is, I have to get over there before the reinforcements arrive. I guess you have to do everything yourself."

"Don't rush off"... "Mister Commander"... "Mister Decan."

Decan turned to see who was talking to him, and at first, didn't see anyone because looked over their heads. A moment later he looked down and saw three really creeping looking midget-sized men.

"You're wasting my time," he stated, judging them based on their peculiar nature and size.

"Don't rush"... "into something"... "you don't understand," Tres Nombre commented. "His spell"... "is too strong"... "even for your Clorian steel." They all smiled at the same time, a creepy childlike gesture, "But not"... "too strong"... "for us."

"You know you talk really weird?" Decan commented with a disapproving look.

He noticed the archers firing on the closing reinforcements. That meant time was becoming an increasing issue.

"Well I don't really have a choice now do I? Since you just wasted my window to attack, I guess I will now rely on you three whatever you are," Decan said with irritation.

"Window"... "great idea"... "sometimes simple minds"... "have the best solutions." They all repeated the last four words in unison.

"You better not be calling me simple minded," Decan commented as two Dark Realm soldiers had broken free and charged him. He knew they could be a problem because they weren't just regular soldiers but Black Knights. Decan settled into position and waited for them to get close enough to go into a striking sequence. He had decided he would do the opposite of what they would expect and initiate the offence.

Okay, Decan, two Black Knights, don't take them for granted, focus and hit them hard with precise strikes.

He understood it would be difficult to get away without at least sustaining some kind of injury. He stood in an odd position facing the charging enemy. He looked down at the ground, bent forward, double-ended sword in one hand behind his back and he crouched almost as if bowing.

Decan heard the first and then the second hit the ground before they got close enough for him to look up. A few of the men in the temporary archer den had spun around and pummeled them before they got to him.

A misaimed shot slid through his legs. One of the arches yelled out, "Sorry, boss." He looked on, wincing, realizing that missed shot could have been a big problem.

"No problem here, boys. Thanks for the assistance, saved me from getting my sword dirty."

Decan refocused on the situation at hand and redirected his gaze to Tres Nombre. They looked like they were in discomfort. Their faces were tense and concentrated.

"Do you guys need a hole somewhere in order to do something?" Decan found himself humorous, but they didn't flinch.

"The Wizard is exposed"… "he can be hit"… "we have opened your window."

Decan turned and looked at the last catapult. He looked at them, then back at the last catapult, confused for a second. It took him a few moments, but he thought he figured out what they were talking about. He needed a bow and fast. The shot that needed to be made wouldn't be easy, and he had the best chance at making it. Looking around for a bow, he couldn't see one around him.

Stupid ass, why didn't I keep my bow with me? Stupid move Decan, he thought to himself. He had to hurry. His peripheral vision noticed the enemy's reinforcements had overrun his archer den and were on their way. He couldn't find a solution, and just when he thought there was no hope, he looked over to the eliminated archer den. One of them had turned and run like a coward. As he ran he dropped his bow in plain sight. The rest of the bows were buried under bodies or at least not visible, but this one was in clear sight.

Decan dropped to one knee, closed his eyes and concentrated on a system that had worked in the past with his swords, one he had used recently when fighting the Cryptons in Tristan.

"Window"… "is closing"... "opportunity fades." It was obvious that Tres Nombre was struggling, their voices suggested labour.

The bow slid along the ground with speed and landed in his sure hands. With ease he stood up, bow in hand and reached for an arrow from his canister on his back and pulled on the pew. "Where do you want this arrow?"

"His head…" Only one of the members of Tres Nombre responded.

"Great… eighty-three feet, in the head. Maybe we could make it a smaller target next time," Decan said sarcastically.

He knew he could make about one out of three from this distance, but needed to be accurate with the first. He concentrated, eliminated all sounds of war, pushed away the thought of the enemy that could be a moment away from his undefended side. Everything went silent. The only thing he could hear was his heartbeat. He used its consistent beat as a countdown to his release. He could see his target.

"Feeling relaxed and safe, Wizard?"

His body locked in position, aiming a little too high to the untrained eye, and froze. The only thing that moved on his body was his fingers, which opened up. The shot, with a slight spin, raced over the battlefield. It easily passed the defensive spell and caught the unsuspecting Wizard square in the jaw. The impact made him leap off his feet, leaving him squirming on the ground, but it didn't last long. The trauma made him pass out and death followed.

One of Dryden's soldiers watched an arrow fly by his face and take the Wizard off his feet. He then watched one of his comrades swing an axe past the point where it had previously consistently ricocheted. He realized that the barrier was down. He and his group could now chop away at the catapult, rendering it useless, but he also saw an advancing problem. The reinforcements were almost upon them with determination to defend their primary offensive weapon. Within moments they were going to be swarmed and easily destroyed. He wasn't sure if they could take the catapult out in time. This was too paramount a task to take a risk. He understood it needed to be destroyed now; there would be no second chance.

He knew he had to think fast. He searched for a section of the catapult that would be damaged with a few blows, but he couldn't see one. Finally, he formulated an idea, something that would work, but it would be the hardest decision he could make. He had no time to wrestle with it and had to move fast. There was no time to think, just react.

"Get out of here right now!" he yelled to his fellow soldiers.

"What are you talking about?"

He turned and grabbed an old friend by the cuff and looked him in the eye, intense and sombre. "For whatever wrong I have done in my life, I will atone for it right now. Now run!"

The other men broke into a sprint away from the advancing men.

The man with the axe didn't run up to the catapult itself but stood right beside it. He stopped next to the pile of shells. He took the pointed side of his axe and swung it into one side of the shell. A hole was punctured and a liquid spewed out all over the head of his axe. He looked down on his axe and his eyes started to swell as tears started to build. The reaction was precipitated from equal part fear and pride.

"Take care of my family God!" he yelled to the sky. He waited until they were almost upon him. They were close because he could feel their eyes burning his skin. A smile was being prepared for the moment to come. Dozens of Dark Realm soldiers closed in on him as he spun the axe around with more showmanship than was needed. It was his moment and that was the way he wanted it. The metal collided with the other side. The lubricated axe head mixed the two liquids together.

The Dark Realm soldiers expected to be gratified with a victory, but were instead blasted into a thousand pieces. Instantly, the first shell exploded and blew the self-sacrificing hero and his enemy into the air. The explosion was so intense that only the smallest body parts would be found dozens of feet away. It was a chain reaction that pulverized the third catapult and ripped a crater into the ground.

A fireball raced to the sky as a once terrifying weapon of war became just hundreds of harmless burning pieces of timber. Dryden took a moment to absorb what happened and then cheered. Everyone stopped, including Bruno who, to his disbelief, witnessed Decan's success. He didn't like him very much, but had to appreciate what he had achieved.

"I'm never going to hear the end of this."

Kruno smiled and responded, "East side of our castle is secure." They both looked back, and although it was beaten up pretty badly, there wasn't a gap for troops to get through. As long as one of the four walls remained intact, they weren't going to be able to penetrate their defenses.

"Well, we are going to have to come up with two more brilliant plans in order to remove the threat and I don't know how that is going to happen. If not, we attack them head on, only choice."

"Sir, our first wave is getting crushed. The western and centre fronts are getting torn apart, there are too many of them. We need to retreat or reinforce." An officer spoke with urgency.

Bruno was on horseback and looked out, knowing he had to pull back. The walls were getting hammered and they could only hold for a few more hours, but there still was some time. He decided to retreat and regroup. It hurt him that he had sent so many to their death for nothing, although it prolonged the inevitable. It had to be done.

"Pull back, full retreat, get our boys out of there," Bruno commanded.

"Wait..." Kruno said softly with a small shake of his head. His eyes looked down indicating a lack of confidence. Bruno didn't really pay attention. "Hold on, Bruno." This time he spoke up, but the doubt was still there, identified by the inflections in his voice.

Bruno turned and looked at him, always giving him the respect he deserved. "What Kruno? This better be important!" He waited for a moment but Kruno said nothing. He looked a bit lost, disoriented. Bruno turned away to focus on the retreat.

Kruno tried to gather his thoughts. He had a feeling that was difficult to explain, but it was familiar and he knew that it was important, even critical. Bruno started to move away from him. The area was crowded with soldiers looking to their commander, many wanting some time with him, time Kruno had been occupying.

"Bruno, wait! Bruno! Don't pull back your troops."

"Why?" Bruno put his hand up, telling others to shut up so he could hear Kruno.

"Do the opposite, reinforce them," he said as if still a little dazed. "Actually, shift all heavy horse to the far western flank." His eyes finally focused as if coming out of a dream.

"Are you crazy? Our heavy horse is the next best thing to our magicians. We shift them to the left and it leaves us wide open for an attack up the middle."

"They won't attack up the middle or they would be in range of our archers. It would be a foolish move to attack before our walls are pulverized," Kruno responded as a shell flew overhead exploding in the city a few moments later.

"Even if they don't attack us, they will shift all their heavy horse to meet ours. We would be outnumbered, and in the end, they would have a critical advantage with the final seizure. This is a bad idea, it has no military sense behind it. No way!" He turned to his commanders who waited for the debate to conclude. "Continue as planned."

The front line troops were getting pushed back as more dead bodies hit the ground. They were heavily undermanned and feeling the results of the mismatch. The troops next in line to reinforce wanted to rush in, wanted to help. Watching their friends get slaughtered was psychologically damaging.

"Bruno, trust me, you should do this. It's a chance to take out the entire western set of catapults." Kruno spoke with more confidence and focused in with intensity.

"Why? Just tell me why, why won't anyone tell me what they are planning on doing?" Bruno spoke with frustration, flinging his arms to and fro.

"It's a feeling I can't explain."

"A feeling, you want me to shift our entire army to a compromising position based on a feeling?" Clearly buckling under the pressure, Bruno's composure started to collapse.

"I'm never wrong on these things. It should work."

"Not good enough Kruno — it *should* work — what kind of suggestion is that?"

Kruno wasn't a completely sure, but this was the same feeling he had when he was surrounded by Cryptons in Tristan. It was the same voice in his head that he had put his life on the line for in the past and it had always paid off. He believed this was a turning point in the battle, one he couldn't let go. He didn't want to talk about this battle — if he lived — later in life and tell others what they should have done, that he should have been more forceful. He didn't want to have to explain to his future children why they lived under the Dark Realm's rule.

Bruno, still paying attention to Kruno, waited for a response. Kruno didn't respond directly, but for some reason, looked to a man only a few feet away from him not on horseback who he had never met before. "Hey you."

The man turned and looked at him, "Me?" He looked back with a confused and slightly concerned look.

"Yes you. We have never met before, have we?"

"No, why?" The man displayed his nervousness to Kruno.

"Your name is Simon, your wife's name is Alexandra and you have two kids, right?"

Simon looked back in bewilderment, "Yes, that's true. How did…"

Looking to another, "Steve a carpenter by trade, you're not married, your parents are Phil and Samantha, but they don't live here, do they?"

Steve smiled, "Yep, you're right."

"I can do this all day if you want."

"You two don't know Kruno? Swear on your ancestors?" They both told him they didn't know him. "How did you do that Kruno?"

"Sometimes I get a feeling and this is the result. Follow my advice if you choose to. I know it's a leap of faith, but we have to take a chance. If you pull back those troops, we are just delaying the inevitable."

"But if you are wrong Kruno, we just helped speed up the process." Bruno paused and contemplated. He had already taken one massive risk following a man he didn't like when he let Decan have his way. Now Kruno, one of the most respected men in the Kingdom, asked him to do the same. The precedence helped make the decision.

"Reinforce the lines, send heavy horse to the west flank… all of them!" Bruno looked sharply in Kruno's direction and gave him a glance that told him he was uneasy about the decision.

Bruno's attention got pulled away by the dozens looking for answers. A random soldier asked Kruno, "How did you do that?"

"I really have no idea," he responded honestly.

"Seems like a big decision to be made on a feeling, doesn't it?"

"Can't disagree with that," Kruno said, not fully understanding what he was even doing.

"What the..." Zoran shielded his face from the explosion, even though he was a fair distance away from it. It was just a reaction triggered by something unexpected and he took a moment to consider what had occurred.

The blast that Decan's men had created had wiped out an entire system of catapults. Up until that moment, Zoran and Damascus were watching the battle unfold and were pleased with the results, not paying much attention to the eastern flank.

"That Zoran, is a victory for our enemy," Damascus spoke looking down on Zoran with disappointment. Its height advantage added to the impact of the comment.

Zoran waited a few moments and then found the words he was looking for. "It doesn't matter, it was the weakest part of our front. It was an area we were going to sacrifice eventually," he said, attempting to water down the severity of what had just occurred.

"Foolish man, that wasn't supposed to happen yet. Either your plan is weak or your soldiers are feeble."

"Watch yourself Damascus! I run this army." Zoran was upset, but also realized that the beast could rip through him before anyone had a chance to come to his aid. He made his point, then softened it up, "I appreciate your observations, but it's neither of what you suggest. We have underestimated our enemy."

"That is on you," Damascus said, unsatisfied with Zoran and pointed directly into his face with its thick, clawed finger.

"Doesn't matter, they are going to try something risky shortly and we are prepared for it. It's only a matter time. Then we will crush them." Zoran turned and looked out at the battlefield, placing his hands on the edge of the railing on his raised platform. His body language suggested he was comfortable with the situation.

After a pause, Gabriel caught his eye. He was a central part of their barrage and one of the most exciting to watch. Floating in the air, he launched an attack on Dryden's troops.

Off in the distance Zoran's attention was redirected as a visible shift occurred on Dryden's front.

"Zoran, they are going after our other flank. They have shifted all heavy horse to that area, they will attack shortly." Panicked, but pleased to offer Zoran such important information, a soldier passed it on to their leader.

"See Damascus? They are going to attempt to repeat success with all of their heavy horse on the western flank. We can rush the centre of their forces. We will be able to annihilate them. Let them penetrate our western army, we will run right up the middle. " Zoran was ready to give his command — the very command that Kruno didn't want. Zoran wasn't thinking about the archers, he really didn't care. With no heavy horse, Dryden's centre would fall fast.

"Hold up Zoran!" Damascus demanded. "I have watched you make too many foolish decisions. We outnumber their heavy horse so we should take them head on. Follow their lead, wipe out every heavy horse from their army, leave them crippled and castrated."

He pondered the strategy for a moment and then spoke.

"Maybe you're right, they don't need another victory. We will crush them and morale will fall to an unrecoverable low. This battle isn't about who will win. We understand the inevitability of the battle, but it's about how many of our troops we will lose. We need to start thinking about how we are going to rebuild once in Dryden. Hot House will arrive shortly after we have taken siege of the city and they will attempt to overthrow it."

Zoran commanded all heavy horse to intercept, accepting the advice of the future Emperor.

"Win this final victory, take Dryden and I will call in dozens of gargoyles to support the annihilation of Hot House." Damascus's promise was music to Zoran's ears.

The reinforcements hit the front of the Dark Realm. The soldiers hammered away at each other, blood-soaked bodies were everywhere. The screams of disemboweled men were horrific, but it just helped fuel a fire of passionate hate for the enemy. Both sides had infantry in battle. The fronts were condensed, and the battle strategy wasn't about charging into the enemy but keeping a united, solid line.

Just away from the front the most intimidating formation stood — the heavy horse. Heavy horse was not just feared on a battlefield because it brought terror, it brought certainty. The horses were of the largest breed, and although not the fastest, they were the most powerful; made for battle by God himself, some would say. These warrior horses became even more menacing when adorned with full armour — legs, trunk and faces covered in plate mail. This made it difficult to drop the horse, and in turn, to kill the man riding it. The rider would also usually wear full plate mail. Little flesh was exposed. The armour was heavy, but the horse carried the load well, so it made it practical. The weapon of choice for the charge was a lance, which was advantageous in the beginning of the battle, but it would be tossed aside once it lost its usefulness and another weapon of choice would be selected.

Heavy horse against heavy horse was really the only way to challenge because, if they were to charge infantry alone, the end result would just be a slaughter.

Dryden's horses and Knights dressed in silver, with shields that had Dryden stamped into them. The Dark Realm wore all black, including their horses' armour. The field from an observers view looked like the valiant verses the malevolent, the beautiful polished sliver verses the dark evil black. Silver Allegiance forces were obviously outnumbered, but Knights rode heavy horse and there wasn't a flicker of fear among the group.

They waited for the command to attack.

"Gentlemen, I am here to lead the charge." An unidentified man rode up beside the general. He wore a full helmet which covered most of his face and he was dressed in Dryden's armour. The helmet itself was intimidating, with spikes projecting from the top.

"And who the do you think you are?" Marcus, the general, asked.

A small pause seemed to centre over all that could hear. "I am Kruno. It's my idea to charge, I had to convince Bruno. You owe me for that, my ass is on the line." Kruno

lifted his mask, exposing his face.

"We are honoured to have you with us and thankful you helped push Bruno to let us charge those bastards, but these are my men and I am leading them. You should be happy the best general in the Silver Allegiance stands before you."

Marcus was well respected and a great warrior. Having fought in many battles, humility was not one of his attributes. He was the oldest man in the group, but he insisted retirement wasn't going to be even considered for many years, and because of the way he moved and fought, nobody questioned that decision.

Kruno looked back to Marcus's men and they didn't flinch.

"Sounds good to me. You do realize we are outnumbered?"

"Yes, but we are Dryden's finest. They are but women compared to us," the general said with a smirk.

A shell leapt over their heads and crashed onto a fully exposed third wall of Dryden, resulting in massive damage and leaving the precious city just a few more accurate shots away from a permeated defense. Kruno scanned Dryden. Its once stellar defense and beautiful walls were battered. Some areas of the walls were only slightly damaged, but other areas had several layers pummeled. It was obvious the Dark Realm had a strategy.

His plan was barely approved because of its risk, but if Bruno would have taken a full analysis of their enemy's progress, he would have realized it was essential. Next to Decan's set of catapults, which were reduced to scorched ashes, no other set had been destroyed. They had to be taken out, and fast. Why were they so successful? It could have been the skill of operators, weaker structure on the western part of the wall or maybe it was just luck. That didn't really matter, what mattered was silencing them.

"There is the fourth wall!" Marcus noted, looking back. "We need to attack now!"

"Hold off!" Kruno's request seemed urgent, but his explanation on why they should hold off didn't come. Kruno just stood as a vision rushed through his head. He struggled to make it out because it was foggy. He paused and it made Marcus a little nervous about his composure.

Kruno found himself in another similar situation as he had been in before with Bruno, not exactly the same but similar.

"I told you, I lead this division, not you. We need to charge and silence those catapults, silence them now!"

Kruno stopped trying to make a confused vision a lucid image. He had to deal with the reality that they were going to charge, at a time he believed was too early. Timing was paramount for the plan to work. It was tough to explain something he didn't understand, but he knew overwhelmingly that it was right. He relied on almost blind faith.

"How do you plan on taking out those catapults, assuming we get through the Dark Knights?" Kruno asked

"Smash, burn, flip or whatever it takes," the general stated, as if it was a stupid question, assuming he was just buying time for a reason nobody understood.

"What about the one which the Wizard is hosting a defensive spell around?" Kruno said. Not having spoken with Decan, he still knew they probably would be protecting at least one with a Wizard. He stood on his horse to get an elevated view over the troops' heads to confirm his suspicions.

"We can figure that out when we get there. First we have to lead this army through them. When we get there, we will deal with that little bastard with a defensive spell."

"I have a better idea." Marcus looked to Kruno with a raised eyebrow. "Instead of figuring it out when we get there, let me present a solution. Everyone, please meet Christian."

The Wizard rode up on a horse. "Hello, everyone." Kruno was taking his time and eating up as much as he could get away with.

The testosterone-filled men looked at the petite man who was supposed to be a solution. They didn't want to accept his help; brawn, swordsmanship, agility and courage were characteristics of great men. Christian was small and feeble in the eyes of the decorated warriors.

"He isn't even dressed for battle, no time to have him suited up." An objection was tossed, attempting to discredit him.

"What do I need?" Christian asked.

"How about a lance, little man. We are a heavy horse division, if you didn't notice. Your staff won't do much."

"A lance? Okay, I can do that." Christian pulled his Clorian staff close to his face and whispered something to it. A moment later it started to morph. Its flat end turned sharp and grew, near his hand it spread over him, shielding him. Within a few moments his staff became a lance.

Everyone was impressed, but still many didn't want him in their group. Kruno was acceptable as a last minute addition because of his stature, but Christian wasn't as well known and physically not up to their standards.

"Don't worry, he rides behind us," Kruno said.

"I do?" Christian said to his leader.

"Yep, if I am right, it will be smooth sailing for you."

"And if you're wrong?" Christian said with doubt in his eyes. Christian assumed his plan had something to do with design and they would puncture the line, ride fast to the catapults and destroy them. They weren't going to be able to defeat all of the enemy's heavy horse just based on basic math. If that was the case it would make more sense for him to ride in the middle of their formation, otherwise he would have to face several heavy horse himself, something he wasn't too thrilled about.

"Then you're in serious trouble," Kruno said with all sincerity. "Three men will stay back with you and charge a few moments after we rush."

Kruno prepared for the battle to come and had some final words with Marcus.

While waiting, one of the Knights rode up to Christian. "By the way, that might have been the best thing I have ever seen." Christian had won over at least one of them and felt a small surge of acceptance.

Zoran signaled to Gabriel to have two Wizards move to the western flank.

"This will shore up our victory, heavy horse supported by Wizards," Zoran said to Damascus. He looked at the damage the catapults had inflicted. "This side might be more important than I thought. We aren't far from creating a usable entry point, maybe we shift more firepower that way, and plan our attack through that area." He pointed to the extensive damage that was created on the western part of the wall.

"Although interesting Zoran, once we destroy all their heavy horse, we will be in good order for a full out charge. We will bring the heavy horse back into this formation and rip through their lines. Their commander made a huge error and we will exploit it."

The horn blew letting everyone know what was about to happen. The heavy horse charge was always an anticipated part of battle, putting knots in the stomachs of the weak-minded and a rush of excitement in the confident. The infantry across the entire front line knew they had to pull back, taking a few steps from each other, chaotic warfare halted. The men looked at each other with hate in their eyes; the sight of so many corpses of fallen friends infuriated them even more.

Just before the horn sounded to indicate a temporary armistice, one of Dryden's soldiers was locked sword to sword with a Dark Realm infantryman. They were probably a move or two away from one of them being impaled. Each man had secured victory in their mind, even though it could have gone either way. They had no choice but to stop fighting, but every fiber of their will was tested to comply with the command to back off. As they walked away from each other their eyes were locked.

"We finish this later," the man from the Silver Allegiance said with conviction, pointing his sword at his enemy.

"I will look for you on the battlefield. My sword is upset because it needs more blood, the dozen it has slashed so far isn't enough."

A soldier from Dryden attempted to leave the area near the two bickering men. He had been knocked down but not badly injured. The horn couldn't have come at a better time. He thought luck must be on his side because if the horn hadn't blown when it did, he would have had to fight while on his back. He could easily get to his feet and fight later, surely to avoid the mistake that put him on the ground in the first place. As he started to get back to his feet, his luck ran out. Under the blanket of momentary peace, he moved nonchalantly, and as he turned on one knee, a sword entered his back.

One of the Dark Realm soldiers had seen an opportunity and broke the temporary agreement. He saw the back of an enemy soldier and charged the five or so steps it took to get to his victim and jammed his weapon fatally into the retreating individual.

This infuriated Dryden's soldiers. The assassin's eyes turned an evil black just as Gabriel's had done before. The ones that could see him realized that their enemy was truly wicked, they had become partly demonic. He was flushed with pleasure but it didn't last long. One of Dryden's soldiers, who had seen the unfair charge, sprang into action with his own plan. Even though he was too far behind to prevent the death of his comrade, it didn't matter. His plan had nothing to do with prevention or intervention, it was about justice.

The eyes of the Dark Realm soldier were black with satisfaction as steel smashed into the side of his face, spilling more blood on the already saturated battlefield. For power, but more for flair, he spun at the end of his strike and connected with precision.

Officers on both sides had to hold back their men from charging each other.

"One for one! One for one!" a Dryden officer yelled, attempting to stop two tidal waves from crashing into one another.

"We would be fine with that all day," his opponent yelled back, hinting at their superior numbers.

The inevitable signal to charge fuelled adrenaline and created invincibility in their minds.

Kruno found himself lined up shoulder to shoulder with the rest of the heavy horse division. He felt a connection with the other men. They were one of the most respected and feared groups; the surge of power was unmistakable. He examined the men to his left and right. The dazzling silver armour and shields looked invincible, but they faced a similar looking enemy, one much larger and adorned in black.

Kruno was sure he needed more time, but knew they didn't have it and he was fresh out of stalling tactics. Not fully understanding the reason for attempting to delay the charge himself, he focused hard by closing his eyes and shouting in his mind "*HURRY!*"

Since he couldn't explain what his plan was because he didn't know himself, Marcus devised his own plan. It was interesting and involved a spearhead design. They would attempt to overload the central part of their enemy's forces, smash through with concentrated numbers and split through to the other side. It would leave most of the Dark Realm heavy horse untouched, but should create penetration.

They watched the infantry move out of their way and the path was clear. The Dark Realm did the same. The two heavy horse systems had an unimpeded view of one another.

"ATTACK!" The anticipated command bellowed from deep within Marcus.

Knights rode with lances held above their shoulders. They wouldn't bring them down until it was time to hit the enemy. The weight of the plate mail moved up and down, as did the riders' focus. Many looked through helmets that covered a large portion of their face, leaving only a small slit to view the oncoming enemy.

Kruno could see the enemy's position and waited for their response, firmly focused on them from a distance. The only way Marcus's spearhead strategy wouldn't work was if the enemy took one of two formations. The first would be to mimic theirs, connecting nose to nose, eliminating any advantage. The second would be to attack with layers. It would seal the fate of most the Dark Realm's first wave, but the others could adjust and respond to Dryden's strategy.

Kruno didn't know the commander of the Dark Realm's heavy horse division, but he was sure he was intelligent and capable.

A moment passed and The Dark Realm released it's his heavy horse in waves.

Son of a bitch! They are layering. Kruno shook his head. *Dammit! We are in serious trouble.*

A realization hit Kruno and hit him hard. His hunch, the one that he used to convince Bruno, had been wrong! He had convinced Bruno to charge, and now his error would cause the death of so many and guarantee a victory for the sadistically evil Zoran.

Was I just used? Did Gabriel implant these thoughts into my head? What have I done?

He could picture Gabriel and Zoran laughing, mocking him and taking a victory stroll through Dryden.

Not being a man that dwelled on negative thoughts for long, he pushed aside the thoughts of Dryden's city being consumed, its people becoming slaves and his friends, including his new love, all being slaughtered. Kruno focused on what he needed to do. He needed to control what he could and that was the fight at hand. He was going to drop as many of them as he could. He would engage them, fighting beside men he considered his brothers. Gabriel might have planted something in his mind, used him as a vehicle to cause Bruno to make a foolishly miscalculated move, but it would not go unpunished. He was going to make it right.

The enemy moved closer as they trotted with haste towards one another. He had convinced himself that the Dark Realm had used him to make a foolish move, but he was wrong. It wasn't Gabriel in his skull or anyone from the Dark Realm. Once his mind relaxed, a delayed message finally broke through and became clear.

"Don't worry little brother, look up!"

It was the voice of Ivan!

Ivan ripped through the sky over the treetops with tremendous speed. His wings were big and wide and easily pushed through the air.

Messages had been unknowingly sent to Ivan from Kruno, but they were broken and choppy; another unique skillset was born but still in its infancy. The messages were sent over great distances between two men who were still figuring out how to communicate properly, which was even more difficult during a battle. The magic that was also being tossed around on the battlefield created issues for telepathy as well.

Dryden was finally visible but it wasn't that close. Their enhanced eyesight allowed them to see great distances, and they didn't like what they could see. The walls were battered, and from a distance, they watched a direct hit to the third wall with an explosion to follow.

"What the heck is that?" Walker exclaimed, unable to believe his eyes. "How have they done so much damage?"

"I think if we find out what that explosion was, we can figure out the answer to your question," Dav said.

"I have been getting mixed messages from Dryden. We will have to figure out what is going on once we hit the battlefield, make decisions on the fly."

"On the fly, witty Ivan."

"It's good to see Dryden. When I heard we were taking on a dragon, I didn't think I would be seeing it ever again."

"I would assume you didn't think you would be flying toward it either?" Dav looked over to Paul.

It was still a shocking sight, as he barely resembled his former self. They didn't look like humans; they looked more like beasts. He caught himself staring and judging, then realized he looked the same.

"You can say that again," he yelled over the wind that screamed by.

"I can't wait to lay a beating on those Dark Realm bastards!" Anger started to build and they couldn't wait to unleash their newfound power on an enemy they had disliked for years, a dislike that was rapidly turning to hate.

With panic, a clear message entered Ivan's head, *"HURRY!"*

The message from Kruno told him they needed help and fast. He assumed that they were on the brink of collapse, and although the situation was bad, it wasn't that bad. Kruno's visions rushed into Ivan's mind. An image of what the formations of both sides were using was clear in his head. He could see through his optical path as he looked at the enemy's position. He then saw Kruno as he turned to his men, the charging Silver Allegiance forces. The information, although choppy, was good information, something he could work with. It was all Ivan needed. He knew instantly what he had to do.

"Gentlemen, the Dark Realm has been kind to us." The comment created a puzzled thought in the other five hybrids' minds. "In the infinite wisdom of Zoran, he has lined up all the heavy horse in one area of the battlefield." Ivan smiled and then yelled his command. "First strike, heavy horse, cook those bastards." The other hybrids couldn't wait. So many had been sacrificed, and they wanted revenge.

"Let's get there quickly, push hard, and now!"

They did as Ivan said and forced their wings to move at top speed. A feeling of bliss hit every one of them. The strength and power of being dragon-like, coupled with the ability of flight, overcharged their senses. They couldn't wait to come to the aid of their great Kingdom, offer revenge for King Deo's death and to let everyone know that they had killed a dragon for the surge of pride and recognition.

The forest canopy was about to give way to the battlefield and anticipation grew. They wanted to locate the charging heavy horse immediately and weren't concerned with much more. They would be able to attack from a reasonably low height to attain maximum casualties with little chance of retaliation. They could do this because it would be a surprise. If the enemy knew they were coming, they would have placed more distance between them and their targets. Since they didn't know they were coming, they could get really close.

"Don't worry little brother, look up!"

The low altitude plan could have backfired if Ivan hadn't looked up at the last second to see two magicians hovering above the battlefield. They would have flown right into their target zone, which meant they could have been hit from above. Ivan shot past the treeline, and with agility, forced himself to gain altitude quickly.

Hundreds of Dryden's archers on the walls watched the two heavy horse divisions charge one another. They had the best view of the battle and usually were positioned in a secure place during this part of the battle, but with the explosive shells tearing down the walls, it left them in a perilous position.

"Dammit… what the… look!" One soldier could see some kind of flying beasts racing over the trees towards the battlefield, and at first, he assumed it would not be to their benefit. They figured that they were another deadly weapon unleashed by the dark realm.

"Look out! Look out!" one of the men attempted to yell down to the troops to warn them. It was foolish to think anyone could hear from that distance, especially with all that was going on.

Depression had set in to many of the archers who had assumed that a terribly bad situation was just made much worse. Of course, they were wrong.

Ivan climbed fast enough to get to the same altitude as the two Wizards who had levitated above the battlefield in a position they thought had no threat of a counterattack. They planned on tossing spells on a heavy horse division that couldn't strike back.

Ivan watched one of the foolish little men floating confidently, directly in his path, and realized he was about to clobber a Wizard. The prospect of killing men that don't fight with weapons, but with their minds, was pleasurable. All warriors loved to take out Wizards. They didn't fight fair, as far as men that fight face to face with brawn were concerned. Many believed it was a coward's way of fighting, but they were extremely hard to get a hold of. Not this time. Not for Ivan!

With hands forward, he focused and released a fire stream. The path of the flame raced forward and engulfed his target. It consumed the Wizard immediately, clothes and hair ignited almost instantly. Ivan knew the flame was searing and it wouldn't take long for his skin to melt. Not having much reaction time, the Wizard grabbed for his face and pulled in his appendages by instinct. Attempting to gasp a breath of air, the fire raced into his lungs and scorched them. Not dead but close to it, his burning body lost control of gravity and plummeted. He didn't die until he connected with the ground, completely confused with intense pain and inability to breathe or see.

The second Wizard took a moment for his peripheral vision to notice the flames, and when he did turn around to see what was going on, he was too late. He felt a massive impact on his back as Ivan, with incredible speed, connected hard with his elbow. The collision snapped his spine and pushed him in Ivan's direction. The Wizard's head cracked backward and Ivan wrapped his arm around his face to secure him. Although the Wizard was injured beyond repair, Ivan used his sharp new claws and ripped the Wizard's throat. He spun away and dropped to the ground with blood shooting out of his wound.

Walker flew several meters apart from the others in a blanketing strategy. Ivan had told them that he would take care of the Wizards and to stay on course. They travelled in unison, same altitude and same distance apart. They ripped over the back part of the battlefield, over many easy targets, but Ivan had told him the mission was to strike the heavy horse. Many infantry focused forward and didn't notice them until they had flown directly overhead. Some ducked as they flew past them. The first conclusion many of the Dark Realm soldiers presumed was that the winged beasts must be on their side. It made sense. They looked similar to gargoyles or Cryptons and they flew from their side of the battlefield. No need to try to warn the forward positions, or so they thought, but they were dead wrong and found out how incorrect the assumption had been.

Walker could see Dryden's heavy horse was riding hard and close to impact with that of the Dark Realm. He realized why Ivan told them to hurry. If they had arrived a minute or so later, it would have been tough to make as severe an impact. Allies would have been mixed with enemy, and instead of a mass attack, they would have had to be more precise.

The Knights on horseback had no clue what was going to happen, especially the layer of heavy horse that was the farthest from the battle. They had their lances on their shoulders and their bodies weren't braced for battle yet.

Three... Two... One!

Walker counted and then unleashed everything he could muster. The flame's radius consumed dozens of heavy horse. They wanted to fly slowly to maximize damage, but they also needed to connect with the first wave, which would be clashing with their forces momentarily. Even though they moved relatively quickly, the fire did its damage.

Many Knights were in mid-breath at the time the flames hit and they inhaled fire instead of air, and they gripped their chests, falling from their horses. For others, the fire heated up their metal armour, creating excruciating pain. The horses' manes and tails caught fire, causing them to panic. The once well-mannered animals broke into survival mode; instinct took over and they scattered in different directions. It didn't help that many smashed into each other, preventing escape.

Marcus, in mid-charge, saw the flames jettison out from these strange flying creatures and torch their enemy. It didn't take long to figure out that this was what Kruno had been talking about. This was the reason for his earlier requests for delay. He had somehow known that these beasts were going to strike their enemy. Marcus immediately called a halt to the attack.

The first wave of the Dark Realm heavy horse division watched with happiness as Marcus commanded his troops to stop and move into an unprecedented defensive position.

Marcus wasn't stupid and didn't want to create any suspicion on the part of the enemy as to why he had stopped his advance, so he commanded his troops to drop lance and lock shield as if bracing for impact of the Dark Realm, which would be striking shortly. It bought time for the flying beasts to really hit the enemy hard.

"Ride, ride these bastards down!" one of the commanders yelled aloud as they charged Dryden's heavy horse. They were happy because their target would be easier to destroy if they weren't in motion. All of them lowered their lances, tucked them in and readied themselves for a collision.

Ivan flew ahead of the rest of his hybrid dragon-men and landed in the path of the Dark Realm's first wave, which were moving toward Dryden's men. He hit the ground with great force, slid along the ground backward and stared at the advancing troops. The sight of this unidentifiable beast with many characteristics of a dragon spooked many of the charging Knights. Their eyes widened and panic struck like a hammer. They didn't know what they were supposed to do or what they were up against. What was this creature that stood before them? Numerous minds asked that very question.

Ivan didn't give them too much time to think about what was happening before his flames launched forward consuming them. With one knee bent and arms forward, as if pushing something heavy forward, his attack hit them straight on. Their forward motion drove them into the perilous firestorm. The decision to hit them straight on took valour, something Ivan had plenty of. It was also an indication of how powerful he felt with his new body.

At the same time, the other five hybrids scorched rider and horse from above and behind. The flames caused pandemonium; horses panicked, tossing their human leaders. The plate mail burned intensely, melting and bonding skin to metal. Some suits of armour got so hot, blood boiled, causing a surge of pressure and body parts to explode.

Ivan turned and yelled to Marcus's troops. "Are you ready for revenge?" The men were stunned at first, trying to take it all in.

Marcus stepped up and yelled, "Answer the question, are you ready?"

The men cheered loudly.

"Kruno, follow me!" Ivan yelled back.

"Shall we Marcus?" Kruno asked with great satisfaction on his face. Not because he was rubbing it in that he was right. He was just pleased at the prospect of the charge.

"On my command… Charge!" Marcus yelled and they did as they were told. Hundreds of heavy horse launched into a jovial surge forward.

Kruno picked up speed and moved his lance into position. A light smoke from the burning carcasses clogged the view beyond the first wave of charred soldiers and it was hard to see what was beyond it. They had little idea what the Dark Realm had done to regroup.

Only a few of their enemy's first wave were still on horseback. He could see one of them partly engulfed in smoke, but somehow barely affected by the fire fight. The Black Knight noticed the overwhelming charging forces as they easily cleared the remnants of the first wave and started to prepare. He attempted to put his shield into position, but couldn't do it in time. Kruno's horse leapt over the corpse of a steed, and with impressive precision, he jammed his lance into the face of the Knight. He flung off and hit the ground, neutralized.

The tides had turned; a major disadvantage became an extreme advantage. Dryden's forces, led by Marcus on the ground and Ivan in the air, broke through the smoke to see the remaining heavy horse disoriented, confused and a few even afraid. It was a terrifying situation for them, and although there were many casualties, it was nothing compared to what was about to come.

The fire blast had hit the once self-confident Dark Realm forces first and was then followed by the lances. It was a massacre!

"Archers, archers, get the archers ready. Hurry!" The panic-stricken general leading the western flank infantry for the Dark Realm screamed. He should have reacted sooner, but everything had happened so fast. He had watched confidently as his overwhelming heavy horse division advanced. What happened since then was a devastating blur. He couldn't believe his eyes. His heavy horse division had been eradicated, leaving his infantry to defend against a practically untouched Silver Allegiance rush.

He knew that not only would the heavy horse rip through his infantry, their infantry would follow right behind them.

He was right. Most of Dryden's men at first assumed that the flying demon-like creatures were going to be fighting for the Dark Realm, but they soon realized it was quite the opposite. It didn't take long for the order to be released and cavalry led infantry along the battlefield. They charged the softened defenses of the Dark Realm, trying to catch up with the heavy horse. Most were so excited they ran as fast as their legs would take them, separating them from the rest of the group.

The Dark Realm's archers scrambled and had one target in mind — the winged beasts in the sky. "Take them out… fire at will!" one of the generals demanded. Fear was written all over his face. A few men looked his way and they weren't sure if he was going to turn and run. Staring at hundreds of heavy horse and strange fire beasts over their heads, coming at them like a tidal wave, actually made him consider the thought.

The last wave of heavy horse cleared with only a handful of casualties on the side of the Allegiance. It was the single most one-sided heavy horse defeat in history.

The archers were sporadic at first but then laid out a consistent volley. Walker and another took a hit, both in the arm. Kruno looked up as he rode and called to Ivan to get out of the way.

Ivan dropped beside Kruno, flying next to him. "Fall behind us," Kruno yelled as the wind raced by him. "Wait for us to take out the archers and then meet us back there." He pointed with his shield hand towards the catapults, which just happened to release another payload.

Ivan listened and called to his five hybrids to fall back and hit the ground. Everyone got the message except for one. Ivan wasn't sure if he didn't hear the command or was too enthralled with the battle. Either way he flew above the charging heavy horse. All archers turned to the one target they all feared, and an inescapable number of arrows inundated the air space, reaching for the doomed dragon-man.

Ivan hit the ground and looked up at his fellow companion who took dozens of arrows in the chest, wings, shoulders and face. He fell from the sky, connecting with two of the Knights.

"Stupid move," Ivan said furiously. "Pay attention to the battle plan. We are too important." Ivan understood that they could be the key to this entire battle and losing one of them was critical. He didn't care about the man who just lost his life, thousands were going to die today, but it was about the overall battle.

Just as he made the comment, he could hear Dryden's charging army. He looked back to see the cavalry rip by them on horseback and beyond them the infantry followed. They cheered.

Breathing heavy, all of them tried to get as much air as possible. Walker pulled the arrow from his arm with relative ease. The damage to his new body was minimal.

"I love our power," Paul said, looking at his hands with awe.

"Did you guys find that the flames started to weaken?" Dav said.

"Yes, I would imagine like a dragon, it's most potent after rest."

"Lots to learn and little time to do so. Paul, do you still have those vials?" Ivan asked.

"Yes, four of them, why?"

"Head back to the front and find whoever is in command and get these vials down four more throats," Ivan commanded as three shells connected with walls. One was a perfect shot to the fourth and final wall, taking out a large chunk of it.

"Wait a minute, what are you guys doing?" Paul asked.

"We have to act fast. One more direct hit from those catapults and they will have an entry point. We have no choice, we are going to have to take them out."

"What about me? You need me. Send the guy back with the busted legs." Paul referred to the one hybrid who had had his legs pulverized by the dragon. He had to use his wings to stay just above the ground.

"Don't be selfish Paul, you have influence with Egon, go back and make sure the right men take this. Train them fast and we will meet up with you for our next raid."

Paul looked irritated but did as he was told. He took off and headed back to the front lines.

"What's the plan Ivan?" Walker asked.

The crash of lances connecting with the enemy echoed back harshly, causing Ivan to squint. Their sensitive hearing came with a few drawbacks. Walker tugged on his ear and widened his eyes wide, indicating he felt it too and didn't like it much.

Without answering Ivan said, "That's our cue. Follow me!" Ivan knew the archers weren't taken out but they were tied up. "Stay low, really low."

Ivan, the largest of them, started to run and then leapt from his feet. His wings took over. The feeling was remarkable. He had dreamt about this all his life, a running leap into flight. It was a dream he never imagined would ever come true, but it had.

They all stayed low to the ground and flew parallel to the front. "Plan is simple boys, let's rip those catapults to pieces."

Paul watched the infantry charge the field with vengeance on their minds. He was upset that he had to head back, but something else turned his thoughts away from being irritated. A series of thoughts plagued his mind.

Why am I giving this away? I want this feeling again. They don't deserve these. He reached down to his purse and felt the four priceless vials. *Dammit, how much would these be worth? I could probably get ten platinum each, maybe more. Sell two and keep two. Nobody would ever question my ass again.*

Paul scanned the field for the command area. He expected Egon to be there, but he wasn't. Instead Bruno was surrounded by the flags that belonged to the chief commander. It looked like Bruno was in charge, to his shock.

He landed and Bruno's guards unsheathed their swords, ready to engage. "Where is Egon?" Paul asked firmly.

"We thank you for help beast, but by what authority can you ask for our King?"

"Who sends you here to defend Dryden?" One of the SAE jumped in out of place.

Paul, even though he flew to this point, forgot about his appearance and laughed for a moment. He realized how tense everyone was around Bruno. They were ready to attack at any wrong move.

"Why do you laugh? What is so funny beast?"

"I guess I look a little different than when I left. I am Paul, advisor to Egon, son of Norbert."

Bruno looked at him and could see a little resemblance. His bone structure was obviously different but similar and his voice was a dead match.

"I guess an explanation is in order, how about the short version?" The city took another shot. "Time isn't on our side." Paul had originally wrestled with selfish greed to keep the vials of dragon blood, but reached in and pulled them out now.

"What the heck is that?"

"What do you think it is?" Paul smirked. He realized that he was about to release to the world a story that might be told for a century to come, and he was a main character in it. His name, if Dryden survived, would be repeated by school children and storytellers for generations; it was a massive lifelong dream for any warrior. "Ivan led us into a dragon's lair, many stood against it, only a handful survived. We are the survivors. We slayed a dragon. We killed it for Dryden."

Most looked on in shock.

"Your name will echo throughout time. What you did was insane, but worth a lifetime of praise."

"God supports Dryden!" a man cheered and many followed.

"Let everyone hear of this, pass it on," Bruno commanded. He knew this would charge up his men. It was a well needed injection of good news.

"We have four vials, we need volunteers. Bring forth those with the best pedigree, the most valiant and skilled warriors. They must take this gift, this responsibility to defend Dryden."

Ivan led his men around the farthest point of the western flank and raced toward the rear. The speed they were flying at gave an incredible sensation of invincibility. Glancing over the battlefield, he could see the heavy horse penetrate deep into the enemy, but not deep enough to hit the catapults. They would probably be able to reload and fire a few more critical shots. On a positive note, they foolishly only had a handful of soldiers guarding the catapults. Never in anyone's mind did they assume an attack would come this fast and from this angle.

"Don't use fire around those shells!" Walker yelled out as Ivan had his mind set on doing exactly that. He was planning to lay a thick flame on the wooden catapults which would have been a disaster. The catapults would have been destroyed, but the shells would have exploded and taken out Ivan and the other hybrids as well. Walker wasn't fully convinced that the shells would explode, but didn't want to take a chance.

Ivan was leading the charge and didn't have a lot of time to think. He wanted to strike with surprise. Since he couldn't use flame, it was all about brawn. He should have approached a little slower and had two choices: he circle around and re-strike at a manageable speed, or come in too fast for a proper landing, but make the best of it. Ivan made his typical decision; he didn't want to miss the opportunity of the first strike as it would catch them off guard, and the excitement of violent justice to these catapult operators consumed his mind.

Ivan centred in on what he assumed was an engineer working closely with the team operating one of the deadly weapons. His clothes gave away his presumed occupation, sophisticated attire and no armour. With his back to Ivan, the astonished man was hit hard, lifted off the ground and driven forward. Ivan had him in his arm, locked over his right shoulder with the intention of using him as a battering ram.

Ivan knew one of the weakest points of a catapult was its wheels. They looked less durable than the rest of the machine.

The engineer had no time to figure out what had happened or what was going to happen. Using his speed, body weight and strength, Ivan locked his shoulder and slammed the two of them into the wheel. He made sure he used plenty of power.

The engineer's chest collapsed with ease as his body drove through the wheel's circumference. The wheel exploded but still had enough resistance to force Ivan in a direction he didn't choose. Ivan crashed into the ground, flipping into a bystander. His shoulder took on some damage, but a lot less than if he didn't use the engineer to absorb most of the impact.

His head spun from the crash. Lying on the ground he had to gather his thoughts quickly. Making his way to his feet, he examined the situation. He watched two of his hybrid men land around the far catapult and start to shred the little resistance the Dark Realm could muster. Clawed hands and pure brawn punctured armour and ripped through flesh.

Ivan looked to the catapult with a pulverized wheel and knew it was out of commission. It couldn't fire with any accuracy and if they were foolish enough to attempt to use it, they were more likely to hit their own troops instead of Dryden's walls.

Wait a minute, that gives me a great idea!

Before Ivan could continue with those thoughts, something strange caught the corner of his eye. The last hybrid to hit the battlefield had attempted the same strategy as Ivan's. He had planned to rush in, connecting with speed and power. What he didn't expect or see was the defensive spell. He smashed into the invisible shield hard. He couldn't figure it out at first. He looked over to see if his man was alright. Ivan shook his head to clear the foggy thoughts. Stumbling to his feet he seemed okay, but he couldn't figure out what had happened.

Everyone was panicking except the men that serviced that catapult. They kept on with their task as if Ivan and his dragon-men weren't around. They didn't even look up for very long; it was like they were oblivious to the inherent danger around them.

Although the strange occurrence with the impregnable catapult was important, he wanted to fall back on the epiphany he had. "Gentlemen, hold up. Walker, Dav, don't destroy it yet." They had cleared all personnel from one of the catapults and were getting ready to smash it into oblivion.

"Is it loaded?"

"Don't worry, Ivan, we will take the shell out carefully before we rip it to shreds."

"I have a better idea." Ivan smiled.

Walker returned the smile, "I can read your mind, let's give them a taste of their own medicine."

Ivan left Walker to do what was necessary, turned and watched the only catapult not in their control continue its arming procedure, ignorant of the impending threat to their lives. He could see they were close to firing another shell, a shell that, if perfectly aimed, could open up a gap into the city. He had to do something and wasn't concerned about what had happened earlier. He planned his offensive strategy and deduced the five men working the catapult would be torn to shreds with his claws in as many strokes.

Ivan ran hard and slammed into an invisible wall and fell backward. Dumbfounded, his eyes searched for answers. He hit the same thing that his other warrior had. It was foolish to think things would be different, but Ivan, as massive as he was, didn't have many experiences with not being able to overpower or run through something!

A small, skinny man with one hand held toward the sky in the middle of the fearless catapult team turned and waved to Ivan with his other hand, with a cocky provoking gesture, letting him know he was the powerful one and good luck getting to him.

"Damn Wizard." Ivan stood, pissed off, and punched the invisible barrier. His hand was shut down, no penetration.

Ivan screamed and anger filled him as he watched the shell release toward Dryden. He watched the shell fly through the air and connect with the wall. It was just off target. Ivan knew he wouldn't be that lucky again. The catapult team began to make their adjustments to make sure the next was a direct hit.

Ivan couldn't figure out what to do. Looking toward the battle, Kruno and Marcus weren't through yet. He needed to come up with an idea to siege the defenses and shut them down. His ideas were always to smash things head on, he wasn't the imaginative one and needed Kruno's creativity.

Ivan looked over to see Walker and Dav. They had spun the catapult, aiming at the Dark Realm's middle army. The eastern flank was destroyed and it was just a matter of time before the west fell, but the middle army was where the bulk of their strength lay. It was a perfect spot for a strike.

"Loose that shell and get over here," Ivan commanded.

"We want to make sure we get this right, Ivan," Dav commented.

"Just fire it. We have more important things to take care of." Ivan was serious and they could tell. With pleasure they fired the shell. The shell leapt into the air and raced toward the centre of their enemy's forces, an area that had seen little threat and whose confidence had been built up too high. The dense formation of the men added to their casualties as scores of men were blown to bits. Most had no idea of what was going to occur before it was too late. The resulting damage sent a powerful message. The army felt secure until that point, and now the opposite riddled their minds. An attack could come from anywhere.

Dav didn't watch the shot for very long. Ivan had commanded his assistance and he wasn't going to deny him. He turned to see the one catapult still operational. "What is going on? Drop this piece of shit!"

"We can't! The one in the middle is a Wizard, the little bastard. He has some kind of a spell. We can't breach."

Walker stopped and looked at the situation, "Well, first things first, let's work with what we can control," Walker philosophically commented. "Dav, help me."

The two of them grabbed the catapult and began to lift its massive weight over their heads. Ivan understood what the plan was and ran under to help. "One, two, three." They pumped with each number and on Walker's command they tossed the catapult toward the one still in commission, testing the power of this Wizard's spell. It was a direct hit, but simply smashed on top of the invisible defensive wall and slid around it. Ivan couldn't believe it and realized they were in trouble. Brawn was his specialty, which in this instance proved to be fully ineffective.

The Wizard smirked at their futile attempt.

"Okay now what do we do? Come on Ivan, you had a plan to take out a dragon. This is just one man," Dav said, expecting something great from their leader.

"This isn't my strong point. I don't deal well with girlie Wizards, with people who hide behind magic instead of fighting like real men," Ivan replied, heatedly.

"Dammit, they are going to hit the right spot this time. Once this gets locked and loaded, it's over," Dav stated and Ivan and he bickered back and forth.

"Wait! What do you do when you are starting a fire, to help it start burning?" Walker said with a look on his face that showed he had a sudden miraculous idea.

"Stupid question, Walker," Dav said, as he watched them get closer to launching the final shell.

"You blow on it or fan it, and why do we do that?" Walker continued because nobody answered, so he finished his thought. "Fire loves air, it feeds off it."

The torch finally lit in Ivan's mind. He understood where he was going with it, "Fry it!"

That is actually a stupid idea. Not sure what Walker is thinking, Dav thought — he still didn't really get it. He assumed they were going to try to melt the spell with fire.

Ivan, followed by Walker and the other hybrid with no legs, turned on the flame. The flames hit the spell of the Wizard and spread around it. The perfectly smooth shape of the defense spell was now visible as the flames made no impact on it.

"Nice try, your flame won't get to us. My spell is too powerful," the Wizard yelled out to them.

Dav followed, even though reluctant.

"Spread out, hit all sides," Walker commanded and they moved around it.

The Wizard realized the fire couldn't penetrate, but there would be a heat transfer and the temperature began to rise. Beads of sweat started to appear on his forehead.

"You think you are going to sweat us out?" The fire built and he couldn't see them anymore, as the flames were everywhere and so thick they created an opaque barrier. "Or maybe you are trying to block our vision. Well, we already know where our next shot is going."

First the sweat came, which he thought was their reason for initiating the firestorm. The noise it made was like a creature, and the fire seemed alive as it swirled around the perimeter, constantly changing. The noise came from the flame's gluttony for food as it consumed oxygen. The spell was porous on a fine scale for oxygen transfer. The flames fed off the air and the Wizard started to realize that he had been outsmarted. It didn't take long before his knee gave way a little, oxygen levels were falling fast. He and his crew were feeling the effects. He knew that not only was he in trouble, he was going to lose his grip on his spell soon.

"Load and fire fast," the Wizard commanded, attempting to be forceful with his tone, but it sounded weak as his lungs didn't have the required air.

Ivan's man on the outside, who used his wings to hold his position, had a quick glimpse inside and could see they were about to fire. The plan was going to work but not fast enough. He knew they would have time to release the shell. His mind raced for a solution, and then he yelled over to his comrade. "Dav, take my position, shift this way."

"What, why?" Dav asked and his friend flew away! "Where are you going? Get back here!" Dav yelled, then turned to Ivan who shook his head slowly, letting him know to let him go. Dav didn't understand, but Ivan did.

The Wizard started to feel faint, but was satisfied knowing he had won, that the shell would be released. His name would be in the history books as the Wizard that opened the hole for the Dark Realm to charge through. He would be rewarded in the afterlife for the carnage, something Damascus had guaranteed. It was a common promise that was driven into every Dark Realm soldier's mind by Damascus, Zoran or any senior leader. Woozy, he mustered his best attempt to yell, struggling for air he gave the order, "Fire!"

The shell took off and raced toward Dryden with a perfect volley. The Wizard could see a little through the determined fire. A slot that Walker made sure was available. He wanted the Wizard to die knowing he had failed.

The shell hit its maximum height and exploded as Ivan's man, Dav's friend, let it smash into his chest. The explosion blew him to pieces, but saved Dryden's last wall on the western flank.

"You failed, Wizard. From fire to fire you will burn for eternity. How does your God reward utter failure?" The spell shut down as disbelief and failure were more of an impact than the actual lack of oxygen. The flames charged forward.

"STOP!" Ivan yelled as the flames kissed the stockpile of shells. A moment longer and they could have blown.

"Dav… the Wizard… he is yours."

Dav was infuriated that he had lost his long-time friend and wanted revenge. The Wizard had fainted from lack of air, but woke up in a hurry due to excruciating pain as Dav stomped on one of his knees, shattering it to pieces. Dav didn't waste any time as he slammed the first one, then the other. The Wizard sat up, wide awake and screaming, with mouth open wide and eyes expanded so far they almost tore the skin. He didn't have long to scream before Dav, at point blank range, engulfed his face with a fire line.

That's for my friend, you stupid prick.

"Ivan, looks like you did it without our help," Kruno said with satisfaction, holding a bloody sword and still mounted on his horse. Blood wasn't just on his sword but splattered all over him. He was one of the first through the back of the infantry on the western flank.

Christian was right behind him and stated, "I guess you guys didn't need me then."

"It wasn't easy, and we almost blew it, but Walker came up with a great idea," Ivan said, favouring his shoulder.

"And another made a great sacrifice. That last shell would have penetrated the wall for sure." Dav, in a somber mood, stood over a charred corpse.

"Well you're not exactly sure if it would have penetrated the wall. It's not an easy shot," Christian foolishly suggested. It benefited nobody. It added doubt to the sacrifice made by Dav's friend.

Dav turned and looked at Christian, "Make another comment like that, Wizard, and Kruno's friend or not, I will break you."

Christian didn't understand why he was so upset, or why Kruno or Ivan didn't say anything in his defense. He felt a rush of red hit his face and looked to Kruno who didn't even look his way.

"Sorry, I didn't mean…" Christian started to apologize, but he let his words fade away.

Ivan looked over to the bulk of the Dark Realm's forces. Their army stood in the middle of the battlefield. He watched hundreds of infantry run from Marcus's assaulting force, attempting to escape the certain death.

"I understand why they are running, but what I don't understand is why that army didn't attack us," Ivan questioned. "Zoran easily could have reinforced the area by now, forcing us back to Dryden. Instead, not a single soldier moved toward us."

"Maybe they are afraid." Ivan offered an answer to his own question.

"No, Zoran isn't afraid at all. He knows he can still knock down those walls with the catapults he has. He knows he still outnumbers us and fully expects to be sitting on Egon's throne with his inevitable push forward."

"What do we do then? How are we going to stop them?" Walker said.

"Grip in and defend," Dav said.

"Hold them off until Hot House arrives," Ivan stated.

"Actually Ivan, we will take a note from your homeland, a page out of Northern military strategy. We will attack them!" Kruno suggested as he gazed at the overwhelming number of Dark Realm forces.

"Figures, the time I don't suggest full out blunt attack is the time you think it's the way to go." Ivan shook his head. He realized his shoulder was already starting to feel better. The healing ability of his new body was incredible.

"Zoran might not be afraid, but I bet you he is pretty pissed off," Walker said to their delight.

"Oh yeah, he is right pissed." They all started to laugh.

CHAPTER 10

ABSOLUTE DARKNESS

Zoran watched his western flank break down when strange creatures came to the aid of Dryden. Creatures he had never seen before. They torched his heavy horse and destroyed his catapults. He watched as his troops fled from a battle they should have won with ease.

Zoran stared forward in disarray, and he was speechless for a few moments until he furiously blasted out, "What are those things DAMASCUS?"

"I think we made a big mistake giving you so much power." Damascus spoke, not answering the question.

"I said, what are those winged beasts? Sure look a lot like gargoyles to me."

"What are you suggesting little man?" Damascus turned to look at him directly. Zoran had spoken loud enough so the important Knights, politicians and others that were near could hear.

"Do I have to spell it out for you?" Zoran's comment was followed by Damascus moving toward him. Zoran drew his sword swiftly, halting the gargoyle.

The two stared at one another for a moment. Damascus moved in closer, and Zoran pushed the tip of his sword mere inches away from Damascus's chest. The large grey beast, with blistering speed, grabbed his sword with its hand on the blade. Damascus gripped it tightly, but neither moved.

"Next time you draw this sword on me, you had better be prepared to use it, and I would recommend being a lot quicker."

"Now now, boys, time to calm down," Valin said lightly, but it was far from a relaxed recommendation. He tapped his knives, suggesting they would be used if the confrontation continued.

"Doesn't matter — we still outnumber them," Zoran said, letting Valin and everyone know he was offering a truce.

"We have no heavy horse. We have lost two battles in a row and they have some creatures which I haven't seen, even read about, fighting for them. Yet you seem quite fine with the situation." Damascus didn't let go of the sword but tightened up as its bicep flexed.

"We outnumber them and once those walls fall, we will penetrate and defeat them," Zoran said with struggling confidence.

Damascus didn't let go of the sword and it was easy to see that all Zoran really wanted to do was sheath his sword and end the confrontation that would not end in his favour. Valin stepped in once again.

"Damascus, we all respect what you have done to get us here, to this point. I respect you as a leader and a warrior. You may be able to take down Zoran with a swipe of your claws, but if you don't let him have his sword back, every one of my knives will be heading in your direction." Valin was known for being fearless and proved it by challenging one of the world's most feared creatures. He knew nobody was better with knives, and he would be able to release at least three toward it before it turned to attack him.

"I don't let it go for fear of your knives Valin." Damascus shed his anger and let the sword go.

"I am sure you don't Damascus. Why don't you two play nice and come up with a plan to breach those pigs we call an enemy and include me. I have been here all day, haven't killed anyone yet and I am starting to get antsy."

"They will do one of two things," Gabriel spoke as he landed on the platform, returning from battle. "Sit back and wait for our attack, attempting to hold off until Hot House comes, which is ludicrous, or they will attack us, attempting to destroy our capabilities of taking out the last of their mighty walls."

Gabriel listened as many tried to speak at once. He rolled his eyes gently, waiting for what he considered the less intelligent to finish their feeble attempts to come up with a plan.

"Are we done yet?" They looked his way, "Good, now first thing we need to do is put a Wizard on each one of the remaining six catapults, good Wizards. I am pulling them from the sky. I am pulling all of them. First we crack those walls and then we unleash our fury. Since the powers-to-be have lost a good portion of our men, including all heavy horse, the charge will be more cumbersome." Gabrielle looked to Damascus and Zoran with an unimpressed expression, and both of them just listened.

"Get Knights back here around the catapults. Both times they have succeeded because there was no real opposition. They have proven they can get to them and dismantle them, so let's protect our key asset."

Bruno examined the situation. All eyes rested on him to make the decision. Marcus and his successful division had made their way back after silencing the Dark Realm's western army.

"We really don't have any choice. Waiting around is just going to delay the inevitable. I just wish we could wait until nightfall. This is our ground, our land and we could have a better chance getting close to those remaining catapults under the cover of darkness. We have the advantage of heavy horse, but against their numbers they will collapse, and eventually, we will lose."

"Yes, but we will lose fighting. We will take down as many of those Godless bastards as we can," Decan spoke, receiving a new level of respect from Bruno. After his performance, dropping the eastern flank, he earned his place even in Bruno's eyes.

"We die in battle. We die defending our great Kingdom." Marcus spoke up, invigorated.

"I have to agree with you Bruno. It's too bad we can't delay the battle and fight under nightfall. I could really light things up." Eclipse showed off his skill as a small bolt of electricity leapt from one eye to the next. Very strange to see, but almost everyone found it stimulating.

"Maybe we could help." Kiera walked up to the men in the huddle, shyly speaking in a situation she was not accustomed to.

"Enter Kiera, Queen of La Caprata," Kruno introduced her with a smile.

"How can you help?" Bruno responded.

"No time for silly games, silly girl, let the men figure this one out." One of the Elites spoke out, but before Kiera or Kruno could respond, Petra took the matter in her own hands. She looked in his direction, jettisoned her arm forward, and although she never touched him, he was blown off his feet. He hit the ground, slid for a few feet and stopped, stunned and a little embarrassed.

Everyone looked on in shock. The Elite on his back commented, calm and relaxed, "Well, that settles that." He decided to give her the respect she demanded.

"You want night, we can give you night. Well, actually, she can." Kiera touched Petra's shoulder. "Let us be with the front line, let us charge," Kiera continued. "Each one of those catapults is now protected by Black Knights and a Wizard with a defensive spell."

"Son of a bitch! The good news just keeps coming."

"How do you know that?"

"Does it matter?" Kiera realized it did by the looks on their faces. "Look to the sky. Where are all the Dark Realm's Wizards? Where do you think they have gone? But don't worry about it, they are ours to take down. Just promise me to hit their frontline hard."

"Like a war hammer to a chest!" Marcus confirmed, Kiera nodded and Ivan smiled.

They stood heavy on the frontline and looked at the impossible odds that lay before them. No speech was necessary. Everyone understood what was at stake. Kruno looked over and saw Magnus.

"Great to see you my friend."

"If you're telling us we aren't charging, I am not going to be happy with you." His comment was derived from the fact that he had been waiting all day, watching his city get pummeled, his people get killed. The first two assaults, although successful, didn't leave him with the chance to use his weapon once. Magnus craved blood, craved revenge.

"We are charging… all of us."

"First?" Magnus asked

"Yes my oversized friend, first."

"Clinton is mine!" Magnus insisted.

Others heard him, and although many wanted the opportunity to take Clinton's life, nobody would say anything to contradict his right to be the one to take him down. His size, skill and position were all part of their reasoning, but he had also been with Deo when he was killed, and that solidified his right to extinguish his former comrade.

Sven looked over to Kruno. "Can we start preparing now?" Kruno nodded with a strange look in his eye, one which Kiera noticed.

Sven and his Northern friend dismounted their Gret-chens and moved in front of everyone else. They approached a vacant area of the field with calmness, almost as if they prepared for meditation. They didn't look at each other but seemed to be distracted by their surroundings, looking to the sky, then the ground, taking deep breaths, then closing their eyes.

"Kruno my dear, what are your friends doing?" Kiera asked what everyone else was wondering.

"If you have never witnessed this, then it is going to get really weird."

Both Northerners paused and then Sven turned to Kruno and Magnus, "You may join us if you want, either of you two."

Kruno responded quickly, "No thanks, you guys continue, I am fine right here as an observer."

"Magnus?" Sven asked him.

"Absolutely!" Being an astute warrior, he was one of few that knew what was about to happen. He was excited and honoured to join them.

Anyone close to them focused in on the three warriors; some were so intrigued that it took their minds from the looming battle for a moment.

"Close your eyes Magnus, relax, breathe in the air that fills this battlefield. Make one with the ground… the sky… Mother Nature's energy. She is about peace… Although we honour Mother Nature most days… she will not be involved in our actions today." With his eyes closed, the last comment changed the direction of the speech, but was said with an unchanged serene voice.

The other Northerner slid a long piece of bamboo wood through his fingers. Everyone could see it but Magnus. He slowly walked toward the massive Elite. He made sure not to disturb the ground or Magnus in his tranquil state, and then he unleashed the pole. With his full strength, he forced it forward and connected with a smack to Magnus's face.

Pain followed surprise as his head jerked sideways. A little blood shot from his mouth and Magnus stumbled to the side and gripped his face. His eyes shot open and he cried out.

"Mother Nature can kiss my ass! She has no place here today," the Northerner yelled in his direction. Anger filled Magnus's eyes and with muscles trained to respond, he moved toward the one who had struck him.

"Take this!" Sven yelled as he tossed him a bamboo stick. Magnus wound up and swung hard at the Northerner's torso. Instead of defending himself, he lifted his arms up, closed his eyes and waited for the impact. The noise of the impact was heard from a distance and many grimaced. The Northerner yelled and turned to Sven who gladly accepted his turn. The three of them started to smash each other over and over again.

"Kiera, you had better start your process now. These boys are on a timeline and they will be heading that way very soon," Kruno said, pointing towards the enemy, "with us or without us."

Kiera signalled Petra, but drew her attention back to the three men, "Are they insane?"

"No, but that is the idea. This form of preparation leads toward one of the most effective battle mentalities. To you and everyone else, it doesn't make any sense. That's what I thought the first time I saw it, but my goodness wait until you see them on the battlefield. They are putting themselves into a berserker frame of mind. They use a blunt weapon, which really only leaves flesh wounds, but hurts like a bastard. When they are ready to attack, they will have no fear, feel no pain and have an unlimited amount of energy coupled with an insatiable appetite for violence."

"Nice friends you have Kruno."

"We are back on track," Zoran stated, watching his catapults load, aim and fire. "It won't be long before those walls are mere pebbles."

"Too bad we lost both flanks from our army," Damascus said, plotting his case for the future.

"It was your decision to line up the heavy horse. Don't forget that, half of the blame is on you," Zoran rebutted.

"It doesn't matter. They were just men and this battle is still ours," Valin interjected.

"Sh! Our enemy stirs," Gabriel whispered.

His creepiness couldn't have been more apparent as he walked in between Damascus and Zoran. A shiver ran down Zoran's spine. "What is it? I don't see anything."

"I feel something uneasy, something different," he responded.

"I don't see or feel anything, you freak," Zoran said.

"There!" He pointed to Petra floating high above the battlefield, with two others beside her.

"She is fascinating, skin that looks as if it has never been brushed by the sun, long dark hair, beautiful," Gabriel spoke.

"Pale skin is right up your alley, but beautiful and female. I thought you liked boys." Zoran smirked as he spoke, but her physical beauty wasn't exactly what he was referring to. "She would make you bow with one glance in your direction, you weak-minded fool."

She lifted higher than any Wizard would dare go, and Gabriel understood that took exceptional skill and respected it. Petra, wearing a black loose cloak, stopped with her two comrades below her. She froze in position but the wind tossed her cloak to and fro. It moved with elegance and beauty as if she controlled it.

"What does this mean? Is this some kind of attack?"

Nobody answered because everyone only had questions. The sky seemed to shift, to change, the light that filtered through the clouds dropped in intensity. The clouds sped up, rolling thick and then thin. The day seemed to move, time seemed to jump, hours into seconds.

"Amazing!" Gabriel smiled first in her direction with an obsessed stare. He then redirected it to look to a petrified Zoran, who thought about speaking but decided against it. Gabriel looked back on the three floating figures. Her silhouette stood out from the sky — an all-black cloak against shifting colours. It only lasted for a few moments as something unprecedented transpired.

Her hand reached forward and then closed with great difficulty. As if pulling a massive door shut with one hand, she slowly pulled her arm toward her, a clenched fist full of nothing, or so it seemed. The day bent to her will, and light no longer had dominion. It seemed as if she pulled night early from its slumber. All that remained was blackness. It was more intense than most had originally thought; darkness was absolute, not the moon or even a single star shone. True blackness engulfed everyone.

"Who are you, fascinating creature? Tell me on whose authority can you control day from night?" Gabriel attempted to telepathically communicate with her.

Almost everyone was panic-stricken; it was impossible to see anything, even their hands directly in front of their faces. Only those who spent time in a deep dungeon could compare, and this was happening outside, not underground.

"Gabriel, don't you think you should do something?" Zoran asked, guessing where he was. "I am not sure if I am blind or if the sun has bowed to the will of that woman. Either way, fix it and fix it now!"

Zoran asked a question and then gave a direct command, but again received no answer. Gabriel was so intrigued by this unknown woman and her impressive power that his mind had lifted from the battle and war for a moment as curiosity and even a little admiration swelled in him. Another reason he didn't answer Zoran was because he had already started to ascend.

He lifted up into the black sky with fascination.

"You are playing in our domain, sorceress, darkness is ours."

"You see Gabriel, this is where you fall short. You probably assume that we have painted the sky, blotted out the sun and the stars, but you are wrong. You can have your dominion over darkness, we will continue our relationship with light."

"You can control the light of this world? You have the sun follow your command and the stars submit to your request? Never have I heard of anyone having such a gift. How is it possible that you possess this power and I don't even know who you are?"

"You know of us Gabriel, just not much of us, we work in a different area of magic than you do and different than your enemy's. We are strong enough to keep us hidden from even your eyes. We are La Caprata and I am Petra."

"Ah, the legendary Sand Sorceresses. You picked the wrong side, foolish girl. This spell ends now and you will burn with it." His telepathy became stronger to emphasize his intention to come after her with all that he had.

"It doesn't matter Gabriel. I don't need the spell anymore."

Gabriel's eyes changed as he activated his magic. The pigment in his eyes fogged over and turned completely grey; a strange smoky grey. He could see without light and had the ability to focus in like that of a hawk. He needed to destroy his target, but also wanted to see her face before he blew her from the sky.

He focused in on her closely, on her beautiful pale face. He thought he would catch Petra off guard. She wouldn't have expected him to be able to see her. It would go unnoticed.

He was wrong. She seemed to be staring at him as if waiting for that moment. As soon as his sight touched her face she smiled in his direction. He didn't understand at first and wanted an answer. She had a confident smile, one of victory, one that told him he had been duped. Canvassing the sky around her, he looked for more threats and to try to gauge why she was so happy. The only others that were in the sky were two Sand Sorceresses and Eclipse. His eyes were closed and he was noticeably shaking as if extremely uncomfortable or using restraint.

The soldiers on the front line of the Dark Realm stood in fear. The sky had submitted to the will of their enemy. They couldn't see anything and they deduced that Dryden might be much more powerful than they had originally thought.

"What is going on?" a random soldier asked

"I can't see a damn thing."

"They are probably hiding or running away from us. They have used this darkness as a cover. They are all gone. I am sure it will clear soon and we will find that they will all be running as far from here as possible," a random soldier explained his theory, one he hoped was true. Others started to chat back and forth, most agreeing with him.

Being completely without sight, their hearing improved. Through the chatter, slight metal clanking could be heard in the direction of Dryden. "What is that noise?" A few whispered along the frontline.

"I think I hear horses," another whispered in panic.

Most tried to focus harder to see, hoping to catch a glimpse of what was happening; what rested before them.

"Why can't we see?" a psychologically disturbed soldier burst out. It did little, except unsettle more nerves.

"Look, what's that?"

"Look up. There is light."

A light in the sky was drawing everyone's attention to it. They strained to see, making many of them forget about the metal and horse noises. Almost everyone looked up to see little arks of light, like mini lightning bolts in one small area of the sky.

What occurred next was unexpected. From a small, barely visible light with no warning or real build up, a super-charged blast, brighter than the sun, ripped through the sky and struck tens of thousands of men's retinas. It was a pure shock at first, but many felt pain and gripped their faces. Screams were heard in concert.

The few that were smart enough not to have looked up or lucky enough to have blinked at the perfect time, opened their eyes to see blackness only for a few moments. Petra's spell disconnected and the sky quickly returned to the bright sunny day that it should have been for that time.

Every single Dark Realm soldier had wanted the light to return, but what it revealed was terrifying.

The entire front line of Dryden had advanced with the aid of La Caprata and was only a few dozen meters from contact. Heavy horse, cavalry, infantry and Elites broke forward with the command from Marcus!

Gabriel looked at Eclipse and noticed his dominant spell was about to be released. Sparks started to connect between limbs, creating the only light in the sky. He could see him start to shake and knew every one of his soldiers would be looking directly at the only source of light. Gabriel turned from the inevitable blast of light and tossed a fast telepathic warning to Zoran and the other leaders, as well as sending it to as many Black Knights as he could communicate with. He was powerful but there was no way could he warn everyone. It would have drained some of the energy he needed for the counterattack, but he also had little faith in any of his army other than the Black Knights, often referring to the rest of them as rodents. They were expendable.

To his disbelief, he finally looked down to see the entire front line of Dryden within striking distance of his.

I can't believe it. They moved here under me, I was diverted, I was fooled. He would have been fine with every one of his men being fooled but not him. His cocky ego created a need to rectify his bruised image of himself and to do it immediately.

Many of the Black Knights were staring up in the direction of Eclipse, most heard a scream in their minds to duck, to cover their eyes immediately! They didn't know the message was from Gabriel, but the warning came just in time. Most of them heeded the warning and pulled back, shielding them from the absurdly bright ball of light which was ten times the intensity of a lightning bolt.

Gabriel knew this would leave Eclipse open for attack and extremely vulnerable, but he needed to take out the more powerful and bigger threat. He deduced that these mystical women, who he knew little about, would be a better target.

The Dark Wizard chanted as his hands burned a bright orange colour. Energy in the shape of spheres jettisoned from his hands. The first came from his right hand, the second from his left and finally a third from both together. He aimed every one of them at Petra.

The two other Sand Sorceresses elevated, but didn't know what was coming. The orange energy ball raced toward their commander. Without thinking, they moved in front of Petra. She was focused on the spell, which needed to be closed off with delicacy, and couldn't defend or move. The first orange energy blast struck one of them without a challenge, like a horse smashing into a child, and she flew backward. The impact crushed her bones and she flipped over the shoulder of Petra, just missing her. Petra avoided the first body with relative ease, but the second torso came right behind the first.

Another self-sacrificing body raced toward her. The body hit her legs hard, forcing her backward into a spin. Shocked, in some pain, and disoriented, she stabilized herself and waited for the inevitable third blast. There was no time to move, an attempt to defend had to be made.

Petra was weakened, drained from the magic she had just used and realized quickly that she would meet her fate. The spell that raced toward her pulverized two of her sisters with ease. Her fate was sealed; she would die in a moment's notice, embracing death, she closed her eyes.

Just before it hit her, Kiera materialized behind her, grabbed her around the neck and body, yanked hard and the two disappeared.

As the sun returned so did Gabriel's eyes from grey to black, a necessary shift to see in the light.

The plan worked perfectly. Under the cover of darkness, a large portion of Dryden's army had advanced, eating up most of the neutral zone of the battlefield. They had positioned themselves far enough from their enemy so that they would not be discovered, but close enough to take advantage of what Kiera referred to as a "first strike strategy".

La Caprata used this strategy as part of almost every battle. Frontline soldiers assumed they would have time to prepare for an army when they charged. Their enemy wouldn't be prepared; their guards would be down, minds not equipped and all men would be stationary. In this situation, the assistance from Eclipse had been a bonus, as most of the enemy was temporarily impaired.

A group of Rizzian's students and junior Wizards had led the army forward using a similar spell that Gabriel had used with the aid of La Caprata. Their eyes had all turned smoky grey and they were able to see in spite of the absolute darkness. One of them held Marcus's wrists which enabled him to have the same ability. The front line moved ahead without the knowledge of the Dark Realm. A time shift from La Caprata was also used, to move a massive number of men over a large field, quickly and quietly.

Sven, his Northerner companion and Magnus, all riding on Gretchens, with Magnus on Ivan's, knew the plan, but were in no state to wait or listen for orders. Their minds were in a complete state of dementedness, brought on by their pre-war actions. They stayed back from the front line, creating a launch pad to gain speed and hit the enemy first. As Marcus gave the order to charge, they were already in full stride and had the timing down perfect.

"Crazy bastards!" Marcus said as they blew past his men who were just starting their attack sequence. He knew that the men on Gret-chens had premeditated their disobedience, but he wasn't really upset with that. He was more upset that they would have first blood.

Craving blood and violence with a feeling of invincibility, the three on Gret-chens hit a stunned and dazed enemy front line. They would have been no match for the three of them even if their sight weren't already impaired, but they were and the carnage was awe-inspiring for Dryden. Getting their wishes fulfilled in a hurry, blood shot everywhere. Steel connected with one face and then to the next. Gret-chens clawed, slashed and simply bulled over anything in their way.

Not too far behind them the heavy horse arrived. Lances hit with precision, tearing chunks of flesh from bodies. It seemed more like a light training exercise, not a battle with an impressive army because very little resistance was present.

Kruno and Decan led the infantry forward, easily picking off the leftovers from the heavy horse. Dryden's men screamed with excitement as adrenaline super-charged their mental states. Kruno conserved energy by wisely using his weapon and didn't scream at all. This wasn't like previous battles. He felt himself changing, evolving to another level.

Blankets of fire charred many of the enemy from the hybrid dragon-men. The carnage was beautifully sickening. Dryden's army pushed deep into enemy ranks.

Kiera rematerialized with Petra in her arms beside a collapsed Eclipse. His entire body sizzled and steamy smoke rose from his skin. He was completely drained, lying flat on his back. Petra was too drained to move her limbs and she lay beside him.

"Are you okay Petra?" Kiera asked, her voice thick with concern.

"I wouldn't have been without the other two taking the hits for me, and then of course for you." She gasped for breath and continued, "Gabriel is too powerful. We duped him, but he won't be fooled long," she explained, panting. "The energy he fired our way was overwhelming. I have never seen that before."

"I bet you he had never seen what you had done either. Don't worry about him, you have been spectacular," Kiera said.

"That was unprecedented. It will be written in the history books for children to read for generations." Bruno rode over with a small contingent of Elites to see the now venerated Sand Sorceresses.

"I know you told us your plan, but I thought you were nuts, I guess not." With effort, Eclipse complimented Petra. As he turned his head to see her, steam rose from his face.

"I could say the same for you." Petra held out her hand and touched Eclipse's. His skin was hot. She pulled back for a second because it was unexpected.

"I hope you like your steak well done!" He smiled and she responded, "My favourite." They both laughed.

"Humans and La Caprata together, what an impressive combination," Kiera said as she looked up to Bruno on horseback.

"You told us to follow your lead and hit that front line hard. We punched them right in the balls and we were extremely successful, but they are just stunned and will recover soon. What's next?" Bruno questioned with a touch of harshness.

The catapults that had been silent were back on mission. Kiera noticed that several shells hit near the same area. She realized that Zoran had decided to concentrate his firepower to expedite the process. It was a solid move, but meant that she had to respond with haste.

"Let me show you, but they stay with her, protect her. This is not a request!" Kiera said with all seriousness, talking about a group of Elites.

Kiera ran to her beautiful black steed, unnaturally jumped on its back and rode away quickly.

The Queen of La Caprata rode swiftly to her mobilized platoon of Sand Sorceresses. They were all battle-ready and mounted. She pulled on the reins hard, canvassed the battlefield and gave her command.

"Okay, let's take out those catapults and let's do it with perfection. Take any man with black armour seriously and if you face Gabriel, don't attack alone, actually avoid him if at all possible." She paused for a moment to add emphasis to her next words. "These men worship the Netherworld, so let's send them there!"

Kiera broke forward with her group of what some would consider the most terrifying women to ever race across a battlefield. They rode fast and cleared an absurd amount of ground in a small period of time. They were focused on battle; excitement rushed through their veins, but was subdued by rational thoughts. They were close to reaching the battlefield. The absurdly successful charge of Dryden's men had finally met resistance. The sight of the Dark Realm's army had returned and a rush of fully capable men had densely boxed in the area.

As they got close to their allies, several Sand Sorceresses leapt dozens of feet from their horses straight into the air, catching the eyes of many of the enemy. Several others rode straight forward. It was to hide their real attack.

Kiera, with a few of her sisters, dove off their horses, jettisoning forward, with their arms out as if diving into water. They hit the ground and burst into sand. They didn't lose any speed as they slid undetected under their enemy's feet.

Gabriel appeared next to Zoran who was completely distraught. Damascus had picked up one of their soldiers and drove him through the floor of the platform. It showed the power and anger of the gargoyle who then walked away, leaving only a few senior officers, including Valin, on the stage observing the battle.

Zoran had been swearing profusely. He was pissed off at another success for his enemy and started to question their victory.

"Somebody had better come up with an idea really fast or heads will be severed, and trust me, I will have no issues with making it happen, I will bathe in their blood!" Zoran shouted.

"Concentrate all firepower to that one spot." Valin calmly pointed and ordered the focused barrage.

"Who told you to release that command?" Zoran questioned his top Knight.

"It's the right thing to do and I could read it in your face, great Zoran. That was your plan, wasn't it? That's what connects us, your ability to project such great plans with a simple gesture." Valin, quick on his feet, managed to manipulate his King.

"Great idea Zoran." Gabriel let his presence be noticed, and although understood Valin just broke the chain of command, he was right.

"Thanks, of course. It only makes sense, open up at least one hole, then work on a second. We only need one, this will take less time." Zoran took credit without hesitation, but the stress was mounting. The physical evidence of greasy skin proved it. Zoran's demeanor was also starting to change due to duress.

Gabriel sat on one of the railings on the platform, resting from his encounter, almost seeming perfectly comfortable with everything.

"What happened?" panicking Zoran asked his top Wizard.

"It was very impressive… what they were able to do, they could be a problem."

"Could be a problem, why do you say this with such ease?" Zoran tried to remember a moment when Gabriel had ever made a comment like that, but couldn't.

"Well, they would be a problem if you didn't have me." Gabriel didn't mince words when it came to his power and confidence. "It won't be long before we are able to shred a hole that is big enough for us to charge through. I will take care of anything or anyone who steps in our way."

Zoran shook his head trying to organize all of the problems facing him.

"Fine, but what about the damn moat?" Zoran asked, understanding that Dryden didn't just have four thick walls, they also boasted a large river used as a moat, one that wouldn't be easy to cross.

"Don't worry about the river," Gabriel responded.

"We have no way to cross the moat and you tell me not to worry."

"Don't worry about the river. I will take care of it when the time is right."

Zoran started to relax a little, letting his heart rate return to normal. He looked over to the catapults and could see that the new strategy was a wise one. He watched as all six remaining catapults seemed to have their aim perfect. The shells were hitting the walls concentrated on the exact same area. They had systematically annihilated a wide area of the first three walls and he could see the fourth and final wall. He knew it was only a matter of time before the path would be clear to his golden prize. Dryden's forces were too far away to damage the catapults now. Victory was almost assured.

"Start to prepare your Knights, Baccarat. Once the last wall collapses, charge forward and destroy the remaining army. I want that little brat Egon as my personal slave, wiping my ass."

Zoran looked to the three catapults to his left and saw that they had more than enough shells to finish the job, and then he glanced to the right to make sure that everything was intact. He also felt confident in their security because Gabriel had one of his Wizards on each, casting an unbreakable defensive shield.

Six dedicated Wizards, nothing is getting through them, not even the strange flying creatures. Egon, I am coming for my glory, and your precious Silver Allegiance will be mine.

Kiera understood what kind of spell each magician would be using. It was a basic defensive spell, powerful but simple in nature. It would defend any attack that struck it from the outside, but its cleverness didn't take a very important fact into consideration. The spell never accounted for particles as small as sand to be any threat. Big mistake!

With ease, the dissolved Queen Sand Sorceress slid under the spell. From mere bits of sand, she rematerialized underneath what the crew of the catapult considered a safe haven; a safe haven that became a blood bath!

With a pair of fine, thin swords, Kiera hastily examined her battle arena, and determined the first to die were the armed soldiers. Moving with incredible speed, a blade decapitated the first, sending a blood geyser from the wound, painting the inside of the defensive spell like an artist working on a canvas. The second soldier turned to find a blade up through his jaw and her other blade across his neck. She paused for a moment, looked him in the eyes and then sliced his throat. His head was removed but stayed on one of her swords.

The Wizard holding the defensive spell had heard something and casually looked over to see a foreign woman, all in black, somehow behind his spell. She boasted two blades and hands soaked in blood — one of the blades still skewered the head of one of his guards. She turned and moved in his direction as blood rained down behind her from the first kill. The sheer horror of the situation made him freeze in disbelief. The look in her eye showed him that his fate was sealed. She moved on the Wizard and disemboweled him, running a blade across his abdomen. His insides spilled out, face drained of all colour and his spell collapsed.

Kiera didn't notice the faces of the other men, who expressed surprise and utter fear. They were no threat, not her objective and therefore of no concern. She turned to the catapult, the reason she was there, and split the basket that held the shells in half. It was simple and effective. That catapult wouldn't be able to fire another shell.

Kiera looked to her side and watched the other two catapults drop in similar fashion. Just past the last one she saw a platform with the leaders of the Dark Realm looking out over the battlefield, clueless to what had just occurred. It crossed her mind that she should charge forward and kill them now and end this battle swiftly by cutting off the head of the dragon. She then noticed the back of Gabriel and off in the distance a gargoyle. She realized it would be suicide and futile to attack.

Gabriel sat, back to the set of catapults that were in the process of being torn to shreds. He felt an energy ripple touch the back of his neck. It was faint, but noticeable. He didn't turn around but concentrated on his sense of hearing and strange noises were apparent. At first it sounded a little like arrows cutting through the air but his mind deciphered what it was. Thin metal blades were moving at incredible speeds, slicing air and dicing flesh.

He knew that the three catapults were as good as gone behind him. He figured correctly that it was La Caprata, and they were about to descend upon the last three. He needed to do something and do it fast! The entire campaign depended on a few more rounds of fire. Gabriel placed his arms to his side and flexed all parts of his body with a clenched face, loosing a drawn out battle cry.

Gabriel used his power to take the position of one of his Wizards, the one defending the middle catapult of the remaining three. This was a spell that few had ever even attempted to use. Magic understood that no two objects can occupy the same spot at the same time. The result was that one would be destroyed. Although the Wizard that Gabriel had to take out was one of his favourites, it didn't matter. He had no concern for anyone but himself, and didn't even consider the other man. He knew La Caprata would be arriving any second and he was the only one that could foil the attack.

The wizard's body exploded; bones, teeth, blood and brains raced from the deceased wizard in particle form. His pulverized body moved in extreme slow motion from Gabriel. It seemed to almost pause, a testament to his power. His mind became lucid, as the soup like human matter hit the ground around him. Gabriel found himself where he wanted to be; hand up, projecting the spell that his Wizard had been manifesting only a moment ago.

He combed the battlefield trying to find out how they had broken through the spell. He was an exceptional problem solver but time was not on his side. He had to speed up his thoughts to figure out their strategy.

Whether it was just pure luck or skill, he noticed sand shift under the perimeter of the spell and run right by him. He knew how they were getting by the spell now!

Clever little vixens, aren't you, but you won't fool Gabriel again.

He turned to see a materialized Sand Sorceress. He waited until she just opened her eyes and he hit her hard with a charge spell. It forced a significant amount of energy into her torso, blasting her backward a dozen feet, pulverized.

Their attacks weren't perfectly simultaneous and that would be the source of their demise. If they had all arrived when Kiera had, Gabriel wouldn't have been able to react quickly enough, leaving the Dark Realm without catapults and no ability to take down the remaining wall. Dryden could have taken on an entirely new defensive strategy and wait for Hot House if that had happened.

Gabriel knew they were fast and he understood he could only save one more. The closest catapult to the platform was already being dismantled, but the farthest attacker had just arrived.

"Drop your spell now!" Gabriel commanded via telepathy to the last remaining Wizard casting a defensive spell.

"Why... Why would I do that?" He quickly questioned not realizing that a Sand Sorceress had easily passed under his spell, materialized a few steps away and was about to split him in half.

"NOW!" Gabriel's screamed at him and he dropped his spell with a dumbfounded look on his face. The master Wizard used a concentrated form of the spell he had used on his most recent victim, one that would injure less surface area, but would move at a quicker pace. An impact the size of a fist connected with the unwary Sand Sorceress, spinning her torso and putting her on the ground. Amazingly she still held on to her swords, but wouldn't be able to recover in time, before the soldiers charged and chopped away at her with pleasure.

Valin had witnessed Gabriel's change in position and he himself leapt forward, hit the ground and charged the one successful sorceress who had decommissioned the catapult. She turned as she sensed his approach. What she didn't properly gauge was his knives. Already in the air, the first was jammed through her left forearm when attempting to protect the original target — her face — but the second dug deep in her chest. She slumped over and he kept running, but changed directions to assist Gabriel; the second blade had done its job.

"More will be coming!" Valin yelled to Gabriel.

Gabriel closed his eyes and used other senses to visualize the battlefield in his mind. He could hear and feel the entire battlefield, but zeroed in on the area closest to him. He was able to single out shuffling sand — several lines of them along the ground. Valin was right, more were coming but this time he was ready.

The typical battle strategy for La Caprata was to send in a contingency wave in case the first wasn't successful. The second wave usually solidified victory, but in this case they were all going to their slaughter.

"Move in front, move there and get as many men ready as you can," Gabriel commanded Valin, who didn't hesitate.

You easily defeated my colleague's defensive spell, exploiting its weakness, but now deal with mine.

Gabriel's eyes rolled back in his head. He spoke in demonic tongue and slammed his staff in the ground. "Nothing passes this spot, above or below, nobody or nothing, not even air."

Valin had a pretty good idea of what was about to happen. "Ready yourselves gentlemen. These pretty little things will be popping up shortly. They can bite so be prepared."

Valin had as many men as he wanted, almost an endless supply. They were on the opposite end of the battlefield from Dryden's troops, and significantly out-numbered their enemy. The front was a long way from reaching his position, if by a miracle the Allegiance troops could slip through his. The Sand Sorceresses were great warriors, but would be entering a theatre that would spell their doom.

Valin watched as swirls of sand hit Gabriel's impregnable barrier and leapt upward, rematerializing short of their intended location and also right in his wheelhouse. His first knife shot through his target, as she hadn't fully solidified, hitting Gabriel's invisible wall and bounced back, but his second shot connected. Gripping her chest she fell to the ground. More of them appeared and realized they were in serious trouble.

Gabriel knew the tides had finally turned in his favour. He understood that although it would take more time with only two catapults remaining, the walls would soon split open. The time was ready for the retaliation assault and he called the order. He didn't care to discuss it with Zoran who had proven to be useless in his mind.

"Stage one. Baccarat, move forward, pierce their front line."

Baccarat was near the frontline and nodded, hearing the telepathic command in his head, and began his planned drive forward.

"Stage two. Seismic… help out our dear friend Baccarat. Make his trip to Dryden's water's edge an easy one. Stage three, Frost, please proceed."

Far away from the battlefield lay a thicket where two of Dryden's soldiers stood watch. Their job was to watch the river to warn if any enemy ships were approaching. A small rustle caught their attention from the tall bushes, causing them to draw their weapons with jittery nerves.

"Show yourself!" commanded one of the men. The bushes moved more as someone or something started to shift through shrubbery.

"Tell us who you are? That is the last warning." Acting without much thought, he charged forward and stabbed into the bush.

"I got something!" He cheered as his sword seemed to impale an object or person. "I got the bastard!" He attempted to pull back but to no avail, his sword was stuck. He noticed the wall of leaves on the bushes, which were only a few feet away from him, seem to turn from a rich green to a pure white. He tugged on his sword with all his might to free his weapon and pull away from the odd situation. The sword, tip to handle, froze in what seemed like an instant. The ice spread down the steel, over the handle and covered his hands before he could let go. The pain flashed intensely through his body and he started to panic.

Confusion consumed his mind and his eyes widened. He couldn't figure out what was transpiring. The unknown concerned him even more then the pain.

Why are my hands frozen? Why won't it let me go? What is going on here?

While searching for answers, his sword was suddenly set free, and because he was pulling so hard, he fell backward.

His sword was free of whatever held it, but his hands remained bound to his weapon in a block of ice. He screamed and stared at his hands, remembering a childhood encounter with frostbite when his tongue was stuck to a sword. This was much worse.

The second soldier watched in disbelief but prepared for battle. Not worrying about his friend, he watched the bush's iced areas move and a man emerge from them, snapping the frozen branches as he passed. He was a young man with a full head of pure white hair. His eyes were also completely white, with absolutely no pigmentation. The strange sight put fear into the soldier.

"Hurts really bad, doesn't it?" Frost said. He was an agent of the Dark Realm who had been given his name due to his special abilities. His breath was noticeably visible. He smiled as he looked to the man on his back, expressing how pleased he was to see the soldier in pain. Frost was attempting to bait the other to attack, which he did.

Arms up, the other soldier charged. He had planned to chop down on the ice Wizard. Frost moved with tremendous, unnatural speed and actually gripped the soldier's face before he could bring his hands down. His face froze as fast as his friend's sword had. His head became a block of ice, causing his body to give way to the weight.

Frost then turned to his first victim who was in too much agony to attempt to stand and fight. The ice had frozen right through his flesh. Frost walked over and gripped one of his legs, forced it straight and froze it through the knee. "Now you can't get away. Normally I would kill you, but I might be here awhile so you will be my entertainment. Is that okay with you?"

"You will die!" the soldier screamed back, an idle threat full of pain and anger, as his eyes watered from the intense pain.

"Well, yes, that is true, one day I will, but it won't be today and not by helpless you." The soldier attempted to call out for help. "We have to do something about that mouth of yours." Frost gripped the soldier's chin, stared right into his eyes and froze his jaw right through. Frost didn't freeze his full skull like he did with his friend. That would be fatal and not what he intended.

The pain hit his body's threshold and shut him down.

"No no, don't pass out. Dammit… oh well, you will wake up soon. I just want to know if you will live. I would say that a good quarter of your body is frozen, but I am not going to freeze your brain." Frost talked to the unconscious man as if he could hear him, "If you do somehow live, I would imagine it won't be for long, frostbite will take out three of your limbs and most likely your jaw. One thing is for sure, if you do wake up from this, the end of your life will seem like an eternity because it will be very painful. You will curse my name and I will relish it every time you do… Well, you would curse it but someone can't speak, can they?" The Wizard spoke with a creepy look on his face, still remaining on one knee examining his subject.

"Oh well, I guess I better do what I am here for." He motioned toward the river and walked out until the water level reached his chest. He seemed to concentrate intensely and his fists clenched, his arms jettisoned out of the water and slammed down hard on the surface, making a strange noise — it was the sound of the water freezing. Normally, smaller and less active rivers would take weeks, if not more, to freeze, and this river had never frozen due to its size and mighty current. History was about to change, compliments of Frost. His body was the epicentre, and ice moved in both directions from the surface right through to the bottom.

Bruno looked out onto his battlefield, a battlefield that he was in charge of — his battle, his war — and the risky manoeuvres had paid off. Conventional, proven military strategies were his normal approach, but today, under pressure, he did the exact opposite. Today he listened to others with outlandish ideas. So far the eastern and western armies of his enemy were vanquished and only two of the original twelve catapults still had firing capabilities, which he assumed were only moments away from being silenced. That could be considered a success, but he was uncomfortable, extremely uneasy. He knew that the area where he stood — the closest to the wall — was too thin.

"Rizzian, we might be in a very difficult situation here," he said to the Wizard who stood at his side.

Most of his forces were on the frontline. Only a nominal number would defend a final charge by the Dark Realm if they were able to pierce his frontline. He struggled to figure out if he had done the right thing.

"La Caprata has had success with the catapults, but unfortunately only limited." Rizzian spoke as his mind was able to see things that the naked eye couldn't.

"Dammit! What do you mean? Where are they?" Frustrated and stressed from the weight of the battle, his mouth seemed to turn to acid.

"Gabriel stepped in. They took out all but two, now they are pinned in an overwhelming, unfavourable situation."

"Dammit!" Bruno yelled as he slammed his helmet to the ground and watched it bounce away. He looked up as a shell screamed over his head and hit the final wall. The explosion ripped a large piece of it away.

"They will have enough space to charge soon." Bruno stated the obvious. "It won't be long before they will have at least one path into the city."

"They still have to pass us, then cross the river, not an easy task for any army, no matter how massive their numbers!" one of the higher ranking men commented. "I also have not seen any siege weapons at all."

Bruno had a momentary bout of optimism, just to have it ripped away a moment later, leaving an even bigger pit in his stomach. A small boat in the river buckled and snapped but didn't sink. Bruno just shook his head as a soldier ran over and yelled to him, "It's frozen, frozen solid!"

"There is their solution, no siege weapons necessary when you can walk right across it!" Bruno yelled.

As if enough things hadn't gone wrong for Bruno, a weird loud noise echoed from a section of their frontline and the ground vibrated. Bruno and the rest of his men in reserves looked out to see hundreds of their men on their backs, looking disoriented to say the least. One of Gabriel's favourite combination Wizards was Seismic, twin Wizards under one name. Their specialty was charge spells and they had released a goliath of a charge spell.

Seismic had stepped forward and threw their hands toward a part of their frontline engaged in battle. Energy seemed to move, forcing everything out of its way. A barely visible wave had smashed into the men, forcing them off their feet. Some Dark Realm soldiers were hit as well. It had been impossible to just hit Dryden's troops, but it did the job.

The concentration of the spell reaching over such a large radius made it extremely impressive, nearly unfathomable. Rizzian understood and could concoct a charge spell, Gabriel had used several in this battle alone, but neither of them could muster one with that kind of punch, affecting so many. The troops didn't see it coming and lay helplessly on the ground, not dead but injured and disoriented.

"Bastard just got his hole. They will be charging through there." Bruno pointed, "Prepare to defend Dryden, draw your weapons." Bruno knew it wouldn't be long before they charged and it would be their best coming forward, Black Knights led by Baccarat, Bruno's counterpart.

"Get the rest of them back here, call a retreat to defend this position," one of the political members shouted. Although he was dressed in armour and had a weapon, he was far from a warrior and was never planning on actually fighting.

"It's too late, our lines are compromised. We will have to do it, take out as many as you can!" Bruno yelled confidently, realizing that self-pity over past decisions didn't do much. He didn't fear death and looked forward to all-out mayhem.

Baccarat watched his enemy thrown on their backs, giving him and his large number of men a clear charge toward Dryden, with only Bruno and the reserves to defend.

Bruno, although foolish for not leaving the number of men he should have, he kept the right category of soldiers; many of them were Elites, making the upcoming battle one of epic proportions. Infamous Black Knights versus the courageous Silver Allegiance Elites. The best of both armies were meeting in battle, both extremely skilled, all vigorously trained.

"Would have been nice if we left some of the heavy horse to defend!" Christian said as he stood back with the reinforcements and waited for the battle to come.

Charging through the line at the advanced part of the front, Kruno had no knowledge of the Sand Sorceresses' limited success or the hole that had been opened, exposing Bruno's undermanned army. After he slashed through an oncoming soldier, he looked to his side to see the super-charged Northerners and Magnus on Gret-chens making a mess of anything that was remotely close to them. He also noticed that their impressive progress had almost ceased. The rapid penetration into enemy territory was also slowing down.

Kruno realized he was so engrossed in the battle that he forgot about the campaign. He needed to get a pulse on their progress. He needed a view. He noticed a horse without a rider and ran quickly to mount the steed, positioning himself in a safe zone surrounded by his men.

The first thing he could see was a catapult shell rip through the sky. He needed to find out what was going on. Looking around he couldn't really see what he wanted to, there were too many soldiers and the battle was too massive.

"Kiera, can you hear me?" Not sure if she could read his thoughts with so much chaos, he attempted anyway.

"Yes my love, are you okay?"

"I am, but what is going on with the catapults? What happened? They should be silenced by now."

"All but two. Two still live. Gabriel cut their path and now my sisters are pinned in between his impregnable spell and hundreds of troops."

"We must take them out! I am sending help," Kruno responded.

"I am afraid it looks hopeless, stay away from there. Their fate is sealed."

Kruno jumped out the conversation with Kiera, although he could tell she wanted to communicate a little longer. He looked for a solution. "Ivan, is that you?" Kruno yelled out to one of the hybrids, but wasn't sure who it was. They were all on ground level fighting; they left the skies for traditional warfare. He didn't respond. Kruno whistled loudly and got his attention, "Ivan, is that you?"

He had just finished torching two men and tore through another, "What's going on, little cousin?" Ivan yelled back with a look on his face that told the story of how much fun he was having pulverizing people.

"We have to concentrate on the primary objective. We have to take out the catapults. Two of them still remain and they are smashing down our walls, walls I would imagine don't have much left to them."

"I thought your girlfriend was taking them out," Ivan responded with a little jab.

"All but two and they are now pinned with Gabriel holding them off. We need support there and now!"

"Gabriel, good, don't worry, he is mine!" Ivan made the impactful statement with surety.

"No, Ivan, don't go after him yourself, get Christian," Kruno said with authority and couldn't get the command off his lips fast enough. Knowing Ivan and his hasty reactions from thought to action, he would charge after Gabriel himself and put himself in serious peril.

"Christian, are you kidding me?"

A soldier attempted to jab him with a spear. Ivan moved and slammed him with unprecedented power directly in the face, he flipped off his feet with a caved in face. Ivan was offended and didn't want to listen to Kruno; he almost took off. Kruno didn't have faith in Ivan taking on Gabriel even in his morphed state. He was too powerful and Ivan was too cocky.

"Ivan, please, overwhelm your enemy with as much as possible. That is Northern military strategy isn't it? He will help."

Ivan looked back irritated. Kruno pulled a masterful card in quoting Northern strategy, although it wasn't ever intended to involve Wizards, yet Kruno had made the point perfectly.

Magnus looked up with a blood-soaked goatee, very little was his own. His berserker state had made him into an animal, with his vision tainted red.

"I love this Gret-chen!" Magnus yelled out to Sven who was in earshot.

"You guys fight well together, they are much better than your stupid horses!"

Magnus and the Gret-chen had ripped through so many soldiers that he couldn't count them all. He found himself in a vacant pocket of the battlefield and he felt his pulse slow down for a second. He hadn't paid attention to his body, and finally did a quick mental and physical check. His vision had a tinge of red to it, which was part of the reaction, but it started to fade a little and his mind cleared.

"Good boy!" Magnus said to his Gret-chen, talking to him like a dog and patting his head. "You are a great compliment to my battle techniques. Looks like I only have minor wounds, are you okay?"

"Fine I be. Fight more," the Gret-chen responded, throwing Magnus for a loop. He had forgotten that they could speak. He asked many rhetorical questions to horses over the years, never receiving a verbal response.

"Okay, where is our next patch of victims?" Magnus asked himself. He then recalled the battles over the course of the charge. The Gret-chen propelled them forward like a horse, but often threw up a fist or used its claws to, at the very least, force the opponent off balance, if not inflict serious damage. These disoriented soldiers would tumble into Magnus and his striking war hammer; skulls were crushed, collarbones snapped and shoulders buckled under his weapon. The first part of the battle had primarily been infantry, but they were now in a part of the battlefield where better soldiers resided.

His enraged state seemed to die off a little and he wanted it back. He wasn't sure how to do it. He was just about to give his order to move in one direction, when he noticed someone. The rage he so desperately wanted surged to its peak. Off in the distance, some twenty men back, he saw the one person he wanted to meet, the one person he wanted to dismember.

"Thank you God, for this moment of revenge, whatever you want from me in the future just ask for it and I shall do it like a good servant. This gift is worth everything to me."

Magnus pulled his vision from the sky as he ended his conversation with the Almighty and focused in on the traitor who had killed his King. He and only one other had survived that night against a flurry of gargoyles. One man had caused such devastation and Magnus wanted his revenge.

"CLINTON!" Magnus roared and charged forward with one focus. The Gret-chen ripped through the first few soldiers with ease, leaving Magnus to focus on his target.

Clinton hadn't fought at all in the battle until this point. He was just getting ready to head back around and take a safer route to the front line. He wanted to be a part of one of the protected waves heading into Dryden. He figured he had done enough for his new kingdom, but knew he needed to have a little blood on his sword.

He heard his name called and looked up to see Magnus on the back of a large grey beast — a Magnus soaked in blood and filled with rage charging in his direction.

How did he survive? Clinton wondered, but realized he didn't have much time to worry about that. *Come here you lucky bastard. Let me finish off what should have been taken care of before.*

Clinton was half-suited in Black Knight armour, and was one of the most skilled Elites. He knew the first step in his defensive strategy was to get Magnus off the Gret-chen; a formidable enemy, one he knew well from his travels north. He charged the oncoming duo, which showed a set of balls. The Gret-chen lunged forward at the perfect moment to catch almost anyone off guard, but with spectacular skill, Clinton ducked, slid on his thigh with knees together. He just missed the lunging right arm of the Gret-chen and avoided the head of Magnus's war hammer which came inches from his face.

Clinton didn't just avoid two strikes, which was impressive in its own right; he unleashed one of his own. His sword somehow connected with and sliced the back of one of the Gret-chen's hind legs. Clinton rose to his feet and watched the beast go down and Magnus with it.

Magnus hit the ground hard on his shoulder with a roll. He needed to get to his feet and fast.

"Back off! All of you back off, we have unfinished business to take care of. I have been waiting for this for a long time." He heard Clinton yell out a command.

Magnus stood up, dusted himself off, moved his shoulder to see how damaged it was and then looked to his Gret-chen, "Are you okay?" The beast shook its head indicating that it wasn't. It had a deep laceration along its leg. "Get out of here, back to our side." Magnus gave Clinton the same respect and challenged him to a fair fight.

"Bad mistake Clinton, you should have had your men attack me, that way you would have had a chance."

"You think you are so fantastic, don't you Magnus? Just because you are big, you must be the best. Well I don't have your size, but I am much faster and tremendously more skilled."

"The only thing you can do better is flap your gums. You killed Deo, you killed our brothers, you will die here today, that much God has promised me."

Magnus's fury built to an all-time high. He wanted him dead and didn't care if he had to trade one fatal blow for another — Clinton was going to die.

Ivan had leapt to flight. He needed to gather up all of the hybrids because as a group they would be powerful support to the trapped Sand Sorceresses. Four of the original were left, but he also expected that four more were now available from the vials of blood that Paul had hopefully divvied up by that point. He needed to find them all. The task was easier than expected. He didn't need his eyes, he could sense where each of them were. They were all connected to each other.

This just keeps getting better.

"Hybrids!" Ivan yelled out and each heard. They were stationed in two groups, one close to him and the other near the front lines. "Regroup near Dryden," Ivan commanded and they followed.

"Good, now there are eight of us," Ivan stated. They were in an area that was out of harm's way, off to the side and elevated in the air. "Welcome to our little kick ass group." The original four were able to keep themselves balanced better, the others were new to flying and weren't as skilled.

"I feel fantastic!" one of the new hybrids spoke up as he breathed in and exaggerated the outward movement of his chest as he exhaled.

"The feeling only gets better, but we don't have time to hang around and talk about our feelings. We need to take out the last of the catapults and take them out now! I need you all with me."

"We should stay here and assist Bruno. They are at the last stand, they will need us."

"Wrong, Dryden's walls are our last stand, if they fall you can get in line for any suicide situation that suits you. This is not a debate. Kruno has commanded me and I am commanding you." Ivan didn't mince words. He knew they didn't have time to deliberate.

"Let me grab someone and follow me."

Ivan dove from the sky and centred in on Christian, following Kruno's advice. Christian was preparing for battle, staff ready and a head full of spells. He was totally caught off guard when Ivan whisked him up, lifting him upward.

"What the?" Christian watched the ground and his feet separated. He looked up to see Ivan with a pounding heart, "Who do you think you are? Put me down!"

"Nothing would give me more pleasure than to drop you right now, but Kruno needs you somewhere else."

"You could have asked me? You are lucky I didn't react and blow your head off with one of my spells."

"Yeah, really lucky."

"Where are we going?" Christian demanded.

"I am going to take out Gabriel and then the catapults. You are here because Kruno said you should come along."

"Gabriel... I think we need Rizzian for this," Christian said with a little panic.

"Do you wear women's or men's undergarments?"

All eight hybrids shot along the sky, racing toward the catapults. "There!" Walker pointed to the encircled La Caprata. "It's a good area to land." Although surrounded, there was sufficient space to reinforce and mount an attack.

They shifted direction but one of the new hybrids heard a scream from the battlefield. With everything going on he was able to pick out an individual, hearing Magnus yell out Clinton's name. With sharp eyes he focused and could see Clinton. He made up his mind and he broke away. He too wanted revenge.

"Get back here, follow us!" Ivan yelled but to no avail. The hybrid obviously didn't care for authority. "I will have his ass!"

The small section of the battle seemed to stop as Magnus and Clinton squared off, everyone in the vicinity stopped and watched. Two great warriors with different characteristics prepared to kill one another.

"Let's settle the age old question of brawn verses agility, speed and better swordsmanship," Clinton said with complete confidence.

"I will take brawn any day." Magnus moved his heavy war hammer around with ease, showing just how strong he really was. "It's not like you have a choice Clinton, you couldn't even lift this."

Clinton motioned for one of the men to surrender their shield. Sword in one hand and shield in the other, he moved toward Magnus. Magnus watched his opponent shift from foot to foot, changing positions quickly, attempting to confuse him. Sick of the dancing, he unleashed the war hammer. With a downward chop, the bone crushing weapon targeted in on Clinton, but he evaded the attack, leaving Magnus's war hammer with nothing but the taste of dirt as it struck the ground. Clinton took advantage to counterattack, slicing Magnus's shoulder and rolling away with grace.

"You better get used to that!" Clinton taunted.

Magnus responded just as Clinton wanted. The big man attempted another finishing blow. He reloaded and came at him with as much speed as he could muster, swinging the weapon about midsection. Clinton leapt backward, missing its head but keeping a firm grip on his sword. Magnus spun around following the heavy weapon, and with a calculated downward slice, his back was opened up.

"Doesn't look like you are doing too well, old friend. If you want to surrender and kiss my feet, I might consider letting you live. If not, I am going to cut you over and over until you fall." Clinton smiled.

"All I need is one hit!" Magnus said with effort because he had begun his strike sequence as he spoke. This time he had a two strike plan, first a planned miss, lowering Clinton's guard for the follow up. The second strike used the momentum of the first and was on a crash course with the trunk of Clinton's body. He had no choice but to absorb the blow with his shield. The impact blew him off his feet and he fell to the ground, shaken up and with a major dent in his shield.

Magnus wasted little time and forced his hammer downward. Clinton looked like he was going to take a major strike, but wisely rolled to the side fast, having the end of weapon Magnus's deadly weapon smack the ground yet again.

Clinton bounced back to his feet, a little hazy, and although he had been duped, he knew he could kill Magnus and was certain that he wouldn't fall for that again.

Clinton's eyes were focused on Magnus, but couldn't help notice something racing down from the sky. The hybrid who had broken away from Ivan came down hard and landed on two Dark Realm soldiers, crushing them. His demeanour identified he was there for Clinton.

"And what are you supposed to be?" Clinton attempted to cover up the concern in his eyes as he examined a large winged beast looking toward him with hate in his eyes.

"I am here for revenge!" the hybrid spoke in its deep voice.

"I don't think so, beast, he's mine. Nobody deserves to kill him more than me, so back off!" Magnus interjected.

"I disagree. I am the only person that has more of a right than you do Magnus." The hybrid spoke with confidence. Magnus and the hybrid didn't look at each other, but just kept staring at Clinton, waiting for the interlude to end. Clinton, on the other hand, did the exact opposite as he eyed each of them back and forth, not sure where the attack was going to come from.

"I was there when Deo died, this death is mine." Magnus, running out of patience, stated his argument.

"Although I don't doubt your claim for revenge, your dedication to Deo or your dedication to Dryden, I am the one who has more right to Deo's retribution. I am also the man who has the right to tell you to drop to your knees, and you would listen. I even have the ability to ask you to give your weapon up and you would do so without question. Which I am not going to do, by the way, keep your weapon, fight as you have so valiantly, but this maggot is mine."

"There is only one man that has that kind of power over me." As Magnus started to speak, he realized who the hybrid was.

"Egon!" Clinton said out loud with a smirk on his face. "By all means, I would love to fight you. First I kill the King of Dryden and then only a short while later I get to kill his son, who is now King. Two Kings with the same sword — this must be some kind of a record."

As soon as Dryden's soldiers in earshot heard who the hybrid was, they instantly moved into position to defend him. Swords drawn, they pushed forward, creating a semi-circle around him.

"This isn't a great idea Egon, although very respectable. Dryden needs its King and wouldn't be able to deal with your loss, not to say that you are going to lose, but…" Sven, part of the group watching, provided his opinion.

"Don't listen to him Egon, fight me, take your father's killer and murder him as you have dreamed." Clinton egged Egon on and then under his breath said, "You stupid little unskilled brat."

"You are very much appreciated Northerner, for your service on our battlefield, but this is my war and I decide who fights, and I am fighting today, right here, right now."

Sven knew he was out of place in this position and needed to do something. He looked across the field and found the man he was looking for. With a loud whistle he beckoned Kruno's attention.

Egon's transformed body was massive, he felt invincible and focused on the internal rage burning inside him. He breathed deeply in and out, his rib cage expanded and contracted.

"You may be bigger, with wings and claws, but you're still that annoying little kid that nobody really likes." Clinton continued to irk.

"Bigger, wings, claws — you are correct, but you forgot fire," Egon said eagerly as he launched fire from his extended hands. He watched Clinton get engulfed in flames and kept the focused blaze on him with satisfaction.

He didn't realize that Clinton had expected the flame and dove to the side, out of harm's way. He had pure talent and cool thinking. He gracefully rolled along the ground and back to his feet with a spear in hand. He let go of his sword during the roll, exchanging it for the tossing weapon. Not wasting any time, he hurled it!

The spear headed for Egon's chest. He just caught site of it out of the corner of his eye. The only thing to do was stop the flame and stick up his arm to take the brunt of the strike. The spear jammed through his forearm. Egon roared loudly as the pain shot through him.

He looked to his speared forearm, pulled it out fast, spun it around, found Clinton and tossed the weapon right back at him. Clinton easily put up his shield to defend the attack. It dug deep into his shield, rendering it unusable. Clinton tossed the shield aside and watched Egon take his hand and place it over the wide wound and shot fire through it. Again he screamed. It was a smart but painful move, cauterizing the bleeding wound.

Clinton jumped at the opportunity as Egon, clenched in pain from self-cauterization. He whistled to a soldier who tossed him his sword and charged the hybrid. Clinton cleared the ground fast and twisted, bringing his weapon over his head as he spun. Egon used his wings to launch himself up and away from the full striking power of the sword. It would have been a deadly strike but he had avoided most of it. The King still took a slice down his chest with the tip of the sword.

Egon felt the tear of his skin as he flew backward. He hadn't fought hand-to-hand with anyone in a true fight, pain was new to him.

Clinton struck and kept charging, not wanting to ease up, attempting to keep the momentum on his side. Egon thought he had the distance he needed. He expected to have time to prepare a defense or counterattack, but as his feet hit the ground, Clinton was almost on him. He was bedazzled by Clinton's speed and persistence. He was right in front of him, sword coming toward his head in an attempt at decapitation. Egon ducked under the blow, but started to realize just how good his Elites were trained.

He wanted to come up with a plan, but he couldn't because he didn't have time to formulate one. He didn't have any time to think. He realized he was completely out-matched.

From the ducking position, Egon attempted to claw at Clinton with two upward motions, but he evaded with relative ease, stepping backward with elegance. Clinton moved forward and dug the tip of his sword into Egon's shoulder. The Knight seemed to hold it for a second, showing his perfect form, as if teaching a class how to strike with poise.

Egon got a lucky break and kicked Clinton in the chest, knocking him back. With the breathing room, Egon leapt to flight and landed some distance from Clinton on the other end of the makeshift arena.

I can't beat him. Dammit, what did I get myself into? Father, I must avenge your death. If I fail, forgive me.

Egon realized he didn't have the skill set to take down what used to be one of the finest Elites. He was injured and his mind struggled with the thought of leaving, flying to safety.

Kruno heard the whistle from Sven as Egon was squaring off. He understood he was needed and needed immediately. What he didn't know was the King was now a hybrid and about to fight Clinton.

Kruno had fought on horseback for a while, but the steed he was riding now lay on the ground, missing one of its legs. With no horse, he launched into a dedicated jog toward Sven.

"It's Egon!" Sven called.

Kruno couldn't believe what he heard and turned his jog into an all-out run. His mind closed off, causing him to miss a warning from Kiera. She attempted to alert him but the warning wasn't received. He ran through a relatively unoccupied part of the battlefield, only navigating around a few men.

Out of nowhere, he felt a massive blunt impact to his shoulder. He flipped off his feet and slid along the ground. Face buried in dirt, he didn't know what had happened. What he did know was his sword wasn't in his hand and he needed to get to his feet fast.

Standing up almost too quickly, he shook his head to flush out the blurriness. He turned and his eyes focused on a sight, a sight he really didn't expect or want to see. Damascus stared at him from a distance. Its shoulders were square to him letting him know that it was the gargoyle that had hit him and it was here for him. Kruno understood the skill level of a gargoyle; it was compared to that of a Predator, and second only to a dragon. He had beaten a Predator, of course, many years ago, but that was using pure wit and definitely some luck. He always knew that if he faced the Predator that day, many years ago, in this type of situation, he would have been destroyed.

Kruno stood weaponless. He needed to change that fact and did. He opened his hand and his sword slid from its stationary position toward him, flipped from the ground and landed in his hand.

"You went down easier than I expected, maybe they have it all wrong," the gargoyle stated. A statement it believed, but was still impressed with the human's ability to call a sword as he did.

"Not sure who they are, but I really don't care." He paused, gained his breath and continued, "I assume you are here to fight me?" Kruno said it with a straight face.

"*They* are the rightful rulers of the world, the Underworld has told me they want your head, so I have come to take it."

"Looks like the Underworld has started something they shouldn't have," Kruno continued calmly. "You better make sure you kill me here today because you will just be the first. I will hunt your kind down, it will be my life's work to kill every gargoyle that exists today, I am talking about all-out genocide." Kruno pointed his sword toward Damascus.

Like Egon and Clinton's battle, everyone in the vicinity created a circle around them. Another epic brawl, one that was going to shape the war, had begun.

"Oh, don't worry, I am going to kill you and someone very close to you — actually, everyone close to you, I just decided that, isn't that marvellous?" Damascus attempted to throw Kruno off his game, to threaten his family, trying to enrage him. It wasn't an idle threat. They both knew that, but it didn't have any effect on Kruno as he just stared forward.

Damascus didn't respect humans, but it saw something different in him — pure confidence dominated his eyes. He understood Kruno was different. Few men on that battlefield, maybe only the Northerners, would look at a gargoyle as Kruno did, with absolutely no fear.

Damascus let its mind slide back to the moments before it took off to destroy Kruno.

Damascus had watched a terrible beginning to the battle, one it knew should have been one-sided. The victories the Allegiance had were impressive; they had out strategized the Dark Realm with clever tactics and surprise. Although things had changed recently and the battle was now in the Dark Realm's control, Damascus didn't want any more surprises. It needed to solidify the victory and decided to open a channel to the Underworld, searching for advice.

Damascus had stepped away from the battle, leaving Zoran to monitor and control the situation. The gargoyle dropped to one knee and placed its hand on the ground. It closed its eyes and waited a few moments. The ground around it started to shake, its skin started to heat up; a strange feeling leapt through Damascus, and with a sudden pop, everything went silent. Not a single noise was present. Damascus opened its eyes and noticed everything was motionless. Not only were soldiers locked in position, but arrows and spears had stopped in midair and didn't fall to the ground. The clouds didn't move; everything was frozen in a time lock.

An appalling smell of sulfur permeated the air around Damascus, a smell it loved and also feared. If ultimate success was ever achieved the smell would be welcomed and spread everywhere. The ultimate success was the Underworld rising to the surface and Damascus would be congratulated, even revered. The only other time this odour would be present would be if it was ever sent to the Underworld due to failure. The horrific gnashing and pure torture was too disturbing to even think about. Failure wasn't an option.

"Damascus, you are most disappointing. You painted a much different picture when you presented the foolish idea of teaming up with one set of rodents to take out another set of rodents." Nobody was in sight, just a deep disturbing voice from below, exactly what Damascus expected.

"Our enemy has presented unforeseen obstacles. Nobody could have predicted their ingenuity." Damascus attempted to respond, speaking in demonic tongue.

"Rats you talk of and you use the word ingenuity. What do you take us for, some kind of FOOLS?" The voice screamed, expressing disappointment. "You have been given the ideal battlefield and your army significantly outnumbers a leaderless enemy. You have been given control over many, and a weapon that turns powerful, sturdy walls into rubble. Yet you have been thwarted by an inferior army. How would you have even survived if things were at even odds, or Satan forbid, you were outnumbered?"

"We have taken the battle and turned it in our favour. At the beginning we were weak, but we have turned the battle around. Our success is assured."

"If that is so, why do you contact us before your victory is sealed?"

"Revenge! I want to know why they were able to mount such a viable assault against us. Who is responsible? You know this answer and I want to crush the larynx of the individuals that have made such an impact," Damascus said tensely, as anger consumed his mind.

"Not individuals, but one individual. The name you seek is Kruno. His is a great warrior, but more importantly, he and his men are the masterminds that held the allegiance together and presented many of the strategies that have wiped out so many of your rats."

"I know this man, just met him. Thank you for this, I will bring you his skull for your collection."

"He needs to die, should have been killed a long time ago. Destroy him and his woman, Kiera, not just for what they have done but what they will do in the future. Kruno is favoured by our mortal enemy, and God has given him many gifts — he has been touched. His death is most important."

"Then I shall see to it myself. Gargoyle verses human should be fun. Then I will seek out this Kiera and she will be mine as well."

"Be aware, Kruno is tremendously skilled and unpredictable. As for Kiera, we know little of her except that she is the Queen of a race that has been hidden from our view. Bring assistance, take them down with numbers. Don't fail us Damascus, this would be most unfortunate for you, your punishment will be severe."

Damascus snapped back to real time and looked at the warrior known as Kruno.

They both leapt into a charge toward one another. As they ran, Kruno's arm shield changed from its normal shape to a more conventional shield, flattening out, allowing it to withstand the assault it knew was to come. The two collided, and to Kruno it seemed like a blur as he was tossed aside, rolling along the ground. Damascus stopped and

turned to see Kruno off his feet yet again.

Dammit, that didn't work very well! How am I going to take the beast down?

Kruno, on his back, did a quick assessment of any injuries he may have sustained, but found nothing to worry about. He got back to his feet quickly and realized this battle would take everything he could muster up to have any chance at victory.

God, I can't do this without you. I don't fear this beast. It is your enemy. It mocks your good word. Let's take it down together.

Kruno broke toward the beast yet again and ended up with similar results. Kruno was tossed aside with ease. His shield took a blunt impact from Damascus and his sword didn't connect. This time he felt the impact and realized the damage would start to add up if this continued.

"You are nothing and will die as nothing. I am not sure your skull has any value to it, but I will take it, I promised it to someone," Damascus said, trivializing Kruno's abilities.

Kruno used every ounce of strength and skill with his next onslaught. He shifted and moved with speed around Damascus, swung for its head and missed a ducking target. He blocked a wicked claw attack with his shield and moved out of the way of another. Damascus was strong and fast, a deadly combination, but Kruno saw an opening and took advantage of it. He struck the beast along the right shoulder. He was able to deliver it with power, enough power to cause a severe injury.

As Kruno watched his weapon strike Damascus's muscular shoulder, he left himself open. He felt his abdomen contract and force him from his feet, into the air and back to the familiar position on the ground. He had been punched hard and it momentarily winded him.

Kruno gasped twice and his lungs finally caught breath, bringing in vital air to a panicked mind. With the air came pain to his ribs, identifying at least one that was broken. Not expecting an attack so soon, Kruno was caught off guard but alerted when his Clorian shield morphed yet again.

It expanded, covering his torso and head. Understanding what that meant, he used all his strength to brace for impact.

Damascus had jumped on the opportunity to attack, not wanting him to get up again. It stomped hard on a shield that expanded before its eyes. The shield compressed but didn't do enough damage. Damascus then lay down a series of blows with clenched fists, standing over Kruno.

Kruno knew his situation was bad, one of complete defense. There was no opportunity for an attack, a terrible position to be in. He needed it to change, and fast. The impacts were causing the shield to hammer down on his body, causing more pain.

The constant pounding stopped. Kruno moved his shield aside to take a quick peek to see his ankles gripped by the massive gargoyle. Damascus had had enough of the game. It had grabbed its opponent by the ankles, spun him and tossed him with all its strength.

His vision blurred as he shot through the sky. The ground came hard and fast and Kruno's injured ribs highlighted themselves yet again, first with a sharp pain, and secondly with blood that he spit out. Things weren't looking very good. He needed help but nobody was going to intervene...

I need to get out of here! Maybe the Northerner is right. Maybe I need to live.

He watched Clinton back up and saw a twinkle in his eye, a smirk on his face and saw the sword that had killed his father.

No, I stay and fight, die I might, but I will fight, Egon repeated in his mind. It was an old creed he had heard many years ago, one he hadn't thought about since childhood, but it came rushing back to him.

He held his claws up above his head and waited for Clinton, who charged. Clinton kept his weapon up wanting to keep Egon's hands high so he could strike below them, knowing that Egon didn't have the skill set or moxie to prepare for a lower defense while he pretended to attack high.

Everyone watched as Clinton laid down a successful heavy blow. His sword dropped with speed which didn't leave enough time for Egon to do anything but deflect the inevitable strike. Clinton connected with a straight thrust, putting all his strength and weight behind it. Clinton's target was his chest, but Egon was at least able to force it away from vital organs. The sword still did massive damage and impaled the King just above the hip.

Clinton attempted to pull his sword out to prepare his final strike and make history; killing two Kings in such a short time period. He lusted for the victory and how he would be venerated. He was a mere few moments away from the greatness that he always knew would be his. He looked into Egon's eyes and read the panic that was in them.

To his surprise, he attempted to pull it out but it wouldn't budge. At first he thought he must have dug into bone and needed to put a little more muscle into it, but instead his sword moved deeper into Egon. His sword actually came out the other side of him. Still looking into Egon's eyes he realized he had misread the panic. Egon had grabbed the sword and yanked it deeper. Clinton didn't think fast enough, never expecting such a strategy and pain tolerance from Egon, the spoiled little brat. He knew he had to release the sword and jump back, but it was too late.

After sliding the sword deeper into himself, Egon, with one of his massive hands, reached out and gripped onto both of Clinton's wrists that held the handle of his sword. He gripped tightly and wasn't going to let go. He had him!

Clinton looked up to what he could only presume was a smile on the hybrid's face. He was flabbergasted that he had been taken. There was no way that the little bastard could take such pain and come up with such a plan. Clinton tried to move his hands in futility. Egon straightened out Clinton's arms by coming up from below. Clinton's face showed pain but nothing like the pain that was going to come. Egon, with all the power he could muster, lifted Clinton up in the air. It wasn't long before his elbow snapped and bent the wrong way. Clinton could handle intense pain, but screamed because it was excruciating, beyond his superior threshold.

Egon, beaten and battered, sliced and diced with a sword through his hip, held his prize in the air. Everyone was in shock and let him have his moment. Vindication rushed through his mind and soul. He had made a warrior's move, took on a skilled Knight, faced death, but most importantly, had defeated the man who murdered his father. Egon tilted his head to the sky and roared.

Clinton screamed with his arms snapped and muscles torn. He was in terrible shape. Egon silenced his opponent with a heavy head butt, knocking him out cold.

Egon dropped Clinton to the ground, and he fell over like a sack of potatoes. Egon looked around briefly at the admiring eyes of his men and ones of fear from his enemy. Not explaining his actions, he grabbed Clinton by the neck and took flight.

Egon flew toward Dryden with Clinton dangling from his claws. He realized he needed to seek medical attention, but he had to do something first. Flying over the battered walls, he landed deep in the city in a town square. It was an area that was far enough from the catapults where no damage had been sustained, yet most people were hiding in buildings.

"People of Dryden, I give you a gift." Egon started to feel faint and had to make it quick. He understood that nobody would recognize him, "I am Egon your King, just in a different form. The blood of a dragon is in me and as a result I can bring this to you." He tossed Clinton on the ground, who started to wake up. "Do what you want with him, just as long as he dies." He knew that anyone who could fight would be in the battle. These would be simple citizens who had little opportunity to feel a part of this battle but they had all felt its wrath. Egon took to flight, feeling woozy.

Clinton was in a groggy state as he rose to his feet with difficulty, his arms dangled, rendered completely useless by Egon. He looked around and watched as older men, women and children slowly came out of their hiding spots.

"It's Clinton, Egon brought us Clinton!" someone yelled. "He killed Deo, our beloved Deo. Let's stone him, let's rip him apart!"

"Hold on. You don't know the full story." Clinton spoke with a blood-soaked face that he couldn't wipe, and his nose bubbled as he pleaded.

"You are going to die Clinton, you bastard." The crowd started to close in.

"Wait, Timothy, I know you, you're with me." He called to a young man. "Stick with me and I will guarantee you great riches. The Dark Realm will penetrate these walls. They will be here shortly and I can give you everything you have ever desired." Clinton attempted to appeal to the only person he recognized. The mob started to close in, some picking up objects.

"You're going to help me, help us all?" Timothy asked.

"Yes, of course, I have this kind of power," Clinton responded. "I just need help with my arms. They are in bad shape.

Timothy looked Clinton seriously in the eyes. He picked a rock up from the ground and fired it almost at point blank range — it collided with Clinton's face. It smashed several of his teeth, many falling to the ground with more blood.

"You're a foolish man who didn't fear God. You are going to beg for death for what we are about to put you through, but when you die, you are going to wish you were still here. This will be pleasurable compared to where you are headed."

Kruno needed to get to his feet but also needed a new plan. This one was obviously not working. He looked across to see a practically uninjured opponent.

How could this be? I hit it solidly. Kruno paused and realized what the problem was. *Wrong weapon for this fight. Its skin is like armour, need a better weapon or this one needs a new characteristic.*

Kruno knew that he had to make an impact and make one on his next strike. He looked to a very confident gargoyle that figured the battle was an exchange or two away from being over. It would be able to claim its prize soon — the skull of the great Kruno.

Kruno closed his eyes for a moment, which looked odd to the spectators. He became calm and relaxed. He pushed the pain of his ribs from his mind and looked deep for an answer. Opening his eyes he knew the right solution was going to present itself. Even he didn't understand how it happened, but it just did. Only the finest warriors, a handful in one generation, had a balance between brawn, skill and special abilities. He had witnessed it before back in Zoran's gaudy room when he squared off with Zoran's two best Knights, where a small blue orb had appeared out of nowhere. He could call a sword to his hand from dozens of meters away — something Decan was also able to do. He knew his abilities swelled beyond that trick, and it was evident as his polished steel sword turned from grey to pink, and as he charged Damascus, it became a bright red.

The two clashed and the results at first glance were disappointing for Kruno's supporters because he was tossed aside again and this time without his sword. The disappointment changed abruptly as Kruno rolled gingerly and ended up on his feet swiftly with a smirk on his bloodied face.

Damascus roared in the direction of the deep blue sky as pain shot through its quadriceps. It looked down with complete shock as Kruno's sword was now in its leg, jammed right through to the other side. It reached down with full intentions of pulling it out, but let go immediately because it burned.

"What is this?" Damascus said out loud, not really asking anyone, and it roared again. It could hear and smell its flesh sizzling.

Understanding now that the sword was blistering hot, it prepared for the pain. It reached down and pulled it from its leg. The sword, covered in the black corrosive blood of a gargoyle, was rendered useless. Damascus looked over to Kruno in disbelief and shock.

Kruno, also shocked and impressed, gazed a little too long and should have found another weapon but didn't. The gargoyle had a trick up its sleeve and cast a version of a stun spell. It only disoriented Kruno for few moments, but it was enough to get the jump on him even with an impaled leg. Kruno was smarter than that and shouldn't have let his defenses fall, especially because he was admiring his own strike. By losing his awareness he also let his shield morph to its normal form, just a piece of metal that covered all of his forearm and up his shoulder.

Kruno snapped out of the daze to see Damascus in his face. The gargoyle gripped on to Kruno's arm shield with one hand and with the other hand grabbed him by the throat, lifting him off the ground. Kruno was a large man, but as he dangled from the grip of a gargoyle, he looked small.

"You are tricky! I've never seen anyone heat a piece of metal like you did without fire, never heard of anyone doing it that fast." Damascus looked down at his leg, "But you will pay for it, that is for sure. I have to kill you fast but everyone close to you will die slowly." Kruno's face started to turn red with a loss of oxygen and his head supporting most of the weight of his body.

I can't breathe... going to black out any moment... what am I going to do?

Kruno scrambled for a solution but didn't have one. He looked down to his free arm to see if that blue orb had returned, but it wasn't there. He couldn't call a weapon because he couldn't see anything, even if he could, the second he tried to call one Damascus would snap his neck, something it could do with ease.

"No sword and no shield because I have it locked. Duped by a stun spell, that's like tossing sand in someone's eyes." Damascus smiled. Its plan was to watch Kruno run out of air, put him on the ground and then rip off his head.

That's it, you stupid bastard! Thanks for the idea! Kruno said in his mind and a small smile tried to develop on his crunched, blood-filled face.

The shield that Damascus held so tightly was the solution. Damascus started to roar again as pain shot through its hand. It looked over to see the shield react to Kruno's command. It was now covered with spikes which had jettisoned from it, ripping through the gargoyle's massive hands in many areas, and leaving black blood seeping out of each laceration. It couldn't believe what had just happened. It had sustained more damage than any fight before this and from a human, of all adversaries.

Kruno expected it to pull back and let him go. He needed it to do that as things were getting fuzzy and air was desperately needed. Damascus didn't let go, knowing that the shield was now a weapon. It also knew Kruno was running out of air, and it wouldn't be long before he passed out. Damascus decided to endure the pain and finish the fight.

Panic started to set in with Kruno. His solution wasn't good enough. Things started to get fuzzy and he knew he needed to get air immediately.

Kruno noticed that for no apparent reason Damascus was suddenly in more pain. Its face grimaced for a moment, it was in serious stress.

What both of them missed was a rolling ball of sand rush toward the back of Damascus. With amazing speed it transformed into a Sand Sorceress, but not just any Sand Sorceress, it was the Queen!

Kiera, only moments before, had made a difficult choice. Her sisters, the ones she had protected her whole life, a group closer than family, were being slaughtered. They were pinned down between a circle of Black Knights that closed in on them, as well as Gabriel's spell.

Her ability to transform and jump space was unparalleled. She couldn't have saved them all, but could have taken many out of harm's way. Her other choice was to save a man who she really only just met, a man who had changed her life and one she wasn't going to live without. Her decision was made. Her sisters would fight alone.

Materializing behind the huge beast, she jammed the tips of her blades into its back. She expected more penetration because her blades were razor sharp, but its skin was tough. It was enough to create some damage though. She immediately pulled out with perfect form, inflicted another two wounds and then another.

Damascus dropped Kruno and spun its arm around to attempt to clip whoever was behind it. Its arm connected with nothing but sand. Confused, it watched the sand shift and then reform into a female warrior. She immediately thrust both swords forward, but Damascus grabbed both with its hands and gripped them tightly.

"So you must be Kiera. Kind of hard to fight without these, isn't it?" Damascus said as it held on to her swords.

Kiera jockeyed a little to see if she was going to be able to free them. Realizing that she wasn't going to be able to get her blades, she moved toward the gargoyle, stepped on its abdomen and forced her foot into its jaw as she flipped backward.

Damascus felt the collision force its head back. When it looked down, she was well out of striking distance, but her swords were still locked in its grasp. The gargoyle bent them in half and tossed them aside.

"Glad you could make it, this is like a gift. Now I don't have to find you later. Both of you are going to die here today." Damascus gripped its jaw and shook its blood-soaked face.

Kiera didn't pay much attention, she just looked over to Kruno to make sure he was alright. He had managed to get back to his feet as oxygen returned to his lungs. "Are you okay, my love?"

"Will be a lot better when this beast is without a head. Could use a weapon though."

"Any preferences?" Kiera asked calmly and Kruno responded in a similar relaxed tone, "Impact weapon, please."

Kiera broke away again and ended up in a battle zone a hundred yards away, grabbed a battle axe from a Dark Realm soldier, kicked it free and reappeared beside Kruno almost instantaneously. "My dear," Kiera said, as she presented the axe to him.

"You don't fail to impress me."

"Kruno, are you flirting with me?"

Damascus looked at two opponents, one without a weapon, but that changed quickly. Kiera closed her eyes, concentrating, and the two bent swords in front of Damascus broke down to sand and shifted toward the Sand Sorceress. Kiera put her hands down, opening them up as if to receive something. Sand moved between her fingers and her swords were suddenly in her hands, reformed and straightened.

Damascus started to move toward its opponents with a noticeable limp, slowly preparing a plan to take on both. "Can you heat your swords up?" Kruno asked.

"What?" Kiera responded as she was trying to prepare an assault in her mind.

"Those swords won't be very effective unless you can get them really hot. Its skin is tough, but more manageable the hotter they are."

Damascus got closer, moving cautiously and watched the two of them split up, moving at a similar cautious pace. It noticed more sand circulate around Kiera's swords. The sand moved at tremendous speed, creating friction. Her weapons were getting hotter by the second.

Kruno didn't dare blink as he focused in on one of the most dreaded beasts in the known world and understood that, although injured, it was deadly. Concentrating to make sure another spell didn't take him off his game, he observed its body language to determine when to strike or when to defend. Kruno spun his axe in his hand and realized that the spiked arm shield would be an asset to use once again. The shield morphed yet again and formed a glove over his left hand which had spikes extending from it.

The stand-off seemed to last hours but it was really only moments. They all moved at the same time. Kruno swung his axe, missing the gargoyle. It moved out of the way of the deadly axe but right into Kiera's blades. With spectacular speed, her swords opened up its shoulder.

They continued with similar patterns. The only one making an impact was Kiera, lacerating Damascus's chest, back and legs. She dove and rolled, hitting it from every direction, making it impossible for the gargoyle to understand where she would strike next. A dozen successful strikes were visible and obviously affecting the frustrated gargoyle. Its capacity was dwindling and it looked as if was over-matched.

That all changed as it put all its concentrated effort on one target, in this case the easier of the two — Kruno. It let Kiera have a few easy strikes and launched a barrage of claw attacks on Kruno. Kruno was overwhelmed, avoided a few of them but was caught by the last of the series. On a powerful upswing, Damascus's claw ran along Kruno's chest, lifting him up and off his feet.

Kruno hit the ground and knew he was in trouble. The lacerations were deep. He grabbed for his chest and could feel the deep cut and could see that it was covered in blood. The look in Kruno's eyes indicated to Damascus that he was immobilized and would be no further threat.

He watched Damascus do something cunning. It cupped its own blood from the numerous injuries and tossed it in Kiera's direction. The corrosive liquid spattered over parts of her body and she shrieked as her armour and skin burned. It distracted her long enough for Damascus to close the gap and connect a backhanded clenched fist to her shoulder. It hit her so hard that she lifted off her feet, popping her shoulder out of joint and caused her neck to whiplash

Damascus smiled. It had only one more blow to eliminate both of them.

"Stupid wench, you should never have been in this battle. Not only will we kill you here, we will find your lair and kill every one of your kind." Damascus started to move toward her, only moments away from crushing her under its foot. "This is going to hurt…"

Damascus stopped mid-sentence as it couldn't move any more. Something had hit it hard in its rib cage.

Kruno, although was badly wounded, he had bounced to his feet a moment earlier and slammed the spiked end of the axe deep into the gargoyle's ribs. Kruno's wounds were severe, but he wasn't going to watch Kiera get ripped to pieces in front of him. Calling on all his strength, he moved as if he had no injuries.

He knew he couldn't waste time and had the gargoyle completely off guard. Kruno immediately pulled out the axe head, preparing for another strike. He felt his own chest wounds open up with the motion and more vital blood flowed from him. His body wanted to fall, but his mind overrode his body's request to shut down, and with all his strength, launched the final blow. He pulled the axe head out, caulked and struck with all his might. The same spiked end of the axe lodged into the side of its head. Damascus dropped down to its knees with a lifeless look staring forward.

Just for good measure, Kiera rose up fast and jammed one of her swords into its throat.

"How did you? How are you standing?" Kiera asked, confused and concerned.

He looked down to his chest.

"Well, this is a pretty bad wound, but not as bad as I made it seem, although I am pretty sure I need to sit down."

Damascus's death was more important than just removing a great leader from the Dark Realm, more significant than them losing a great warrior. It made an impact on the entire army. A wave left Damascus as its life extinguished and touched many. The gargoyle was the bond to the Netherworld. It had been one of the main reasons so many had succumbed to dark magic. Zoran also understood this, and although he didn't see Damascus get killed, he felt it. His stomach turned and his self-confidence drained from him.

"GABRIEL!" Zoran cried out. "Damascus, the army!"

"You idiot, don't yell out things like that. Just think, I can read your thoughts and project mine into yours. I know that big grey bastard is dead. I feel it too." Gabriel still stood in front of the last two catapults, watching them fire on Dryden and the successful battle in front of his shield spell.

"How is that possible? How could they take Damascus out?"

"That really doesn't matter anymore, does it?"

"The army, we will lose some of the bond we have over them. If I have already felt it, don't you think they have?"

"Well, I guess you will have to be a King then, won't you? Lead them, have them follow you for other reasons, like fear. You think anyone is stupid enough to back down now? You would burn their families at the stake. We are going to win this battle, that is for certain. Command a full attack from our reserves."

Zoran obeyed Gabriel and gave the order for full attack. They would overwhelm Dryden with this push.

"Look to the wall Zoran."

Gabriel knew the shot from one of the catapults was perfect and watched it hit the fourth wall. It opened up a clear path to the city.

"Dryden's legs are open, charge, charge, charge! Give me that city."

The remaining men in the forest stormed forward.

Christian stood in the midst of a group that was destined to be annihilated. His unit had a lot of firepower and they were second to none in skill, comprising hybrids and Sand Sorceresses. One on one — even five on one — would be child's play for them, but the odds were incalculable. Thousands stood waiting for their opportunity to kill. The enemy had formed a semi-circle around them with their backs up against Gabriel's impenetrable shield spell.

The enemy had many Black Knights, led by Valin, who had taken out a few Sand Sorceresses himself. Gabriel looked on, enjoying the show, clearly noticeable by the smirk on his face.

Flames from the hybrids kept the enemy at bay, but it wouldn't be long before Valin would order a charge. They were being bombarded with projectile weapons, mostly arrows and spears, but Valin's knives had also created damage.

"We can't keep this up forever Wizard," Walker shouted as he launched fire forward.

"What do you want me to do about it?" Christian said.

"You better be joking, you are our only hope."

Oh great, me. It's all up to me.

The catapult let another shell go and it screamed toward a vulnerable Dryden and ripped an open path into the city.

I have to dismantle one of Gabriel's spells. This doesn't look good… what am I going to do? The catapults need to be silenced. The more holes they secure the easier it will be for them to enter our city.

Gabriel looked on and watched one of the hybrids get overwhelmed. A spear tossed with great velocity by a Black Knight finally made a deadly connection, digging deep into his ribs. Three arrows then struck his chest once his guard was down. The Black Knight, who had a plan, ordered five soldiers to charge and they did. A mace, an axe and three swords all found home in the hybrid.

Dav turned to see the commotion, and with urgency, had no choice but to engulf the entire area, including the hybrid. His fate was sealed because it was more important to make sure the fragility of their pocket wasn't exploited than it was to attempt to save one life. The five men's torment from their melting skin and burning hair was definitely a deterrent.

"Wizard, you better come up with something really soon." Dav turned his head to see what Christian was doing. Christian had been trying to decide what the heck he could possibly do. He knew that the moment he started testing Gabriel's shield, he would recognize him as more of a threat. The evil Wizard would then have a chance to thwart his plan. Christian had to hit it with a one-strike strategy; creative, hard and once. He noticed Gabriel took joy in anyone's death and was just as enthused with his own men burning and suffering as his enemy was.

"Listen, they are going to make a run at us soon and we aren't going to be able to hold them off," Dav said just loud enough for Christian to hear.

The commotion and pressure made it hard for him to think, but Christian attempted to shove it to the back of his mind.

This needs to be creative. I can't go through it, can't go under, around or over it. What I need is to hit it from the other side. Christian thought for a moment and had an idea that he hoped would work.

"Dav, I need you and one other to put a direct flame toward Gabriel," Christian called, twitchy.

"Don't you think that we tried that, Wizard?" Dav replied, not impressed.

"Do you trust me?" Christian looked at the massive hybrid and didn't get a response. "Well you don't really have a bloody choice, do you?" He spoke with aggravated passion.

At the same time, Valin realized it was time to end the quarrel and had the men around the semi-circle prepare for attack. Normally commanders would step back from this, but he wanted to be a part of it. He grabbed a soldier and used him as a shield. The soldier reacted with fear, understanding what his role was. If fire came their way, he was going to burn.

"Really bad time for two of us to pull away, this had better work... Is this going to work?" Dav submitted to Christian's request although he believed it lacked logic. He turned and laid a fire stream directly toward Gabriel just as the enemy broke into a charge toward them. The rush came fast and hard. Many were torched, collapsing to the ground, but they got closer and closer, an endless stream of men surged forward. The Sand Sorceresses moved into position toward the men who weren't touched by flames and started cutting them down with agility and skill.

"I hope this works," Christian said under his breath, assuming nobody would hear him, but Dav heard him and gave him a concerned look.

Gabriel had watched the massive number of deaths and had loved every moment of their suffering. He didn't fully understand why they started to aim a flame toward him, but it made it difficult to see and it frustrated him. "You guys aren't that stupid, why put a flame on me? You know this won't work. Maybe you stupid bastards know you are going to die and are denying me the pleasure of watching." Gabriel decided that was the reason and it pissed him off.

Christian turned his back to the onslaught, fully relying on others to defend him. Two Sand Sorceresses knew their role and fell back to guard Christian.

He stared at his hand, locking his fingers tightly in an erect position, so tight that they started to shake. He spoke the magical language, dropped to one knee and jammed his hardened fingers into the ground. Christian repeated the words over and over concentrating more and more. He looked up to Gabriel and his eyes burned deep purple. He focused intensely on the area beyond Gabriel's shield.

Gabriel started to feel something strange, that something just wasn't right somewhere beyond his shield spell, and he didn't like it. He couldn't see through the flame and tried to recollect what he had seen moments before the flame had impaired his vision.

"What is that and what am I missing?" Gabriel could feel the presence of magic but just barely. It meant one of two things — either the magic was weak and far away, or someone was able to hide its true potency from him. "This seems familiar — why?" Gabriel let his mind race. He remembered the energy signature was similar to the invisible force that had defended the attack on Dryden's infantry. A force he couldn't see, but it had been able to foil his deadly rock assault.

He realized that he needed to do something, but it was too late. He knew there would be three potential targets: him, his shield spell or the catapults. He was sure the end goal would be the catapults, and if this hidden Wizard was skilled enough to make any of these things happen, the critical weapons would be destroyed.

Gabriel turned to look at the catapults, and with amazement, he could sense the ground below one of them build up a tremendous amount of energy in a condensed pocket. He didn't have time to yell or react because it blew!

Christian used the same spell that he had to clear out the Cryptons back in Tristan to open the path to the Church. He used a spell that didn't have to travel, but brewed exactly where he wanted it to.

Christian added extra brawn to this spell to make sure it did its job. He got the results he wanted! The pressure built in the ground directly under one of the catapults. The dirt around it started to move as vibrations began to shake the soil. The explosion followed, hurling the massive wooden structure into the sky. He assumed he would have to repeat it to take out the second one, but out of pure luck, he watched the first catapult twist and turn in the air and land directly on the other one, destroying both of them.

Gabriel felt the power of the explosion. It forced him hard into his own shield. The loss of concentration made him lose focus on his own spell and it collapsed only moments after. Christian couldn't help but feel a rush of pride and confidence. Gabriel didn't sustain any permanent damage, but a few of the men working and defending the catapults found themselves one moment with legs and the next without. They had been blown off as a result of the explosion.

The semi-circle had completely collapsed and it was all-out war. Hybrids tore at flesh, as the flame throwing would not be effective at this point because it didn't work in close combat very well. Sand Sorceress severed everything in their path, but knew it was only a matter of time before someone got a lucky break. Valin was one of the first to score a kill as he waited for his opportunity. He watched a Sand Sorceress finish off a fourth soldier in a row. Her blades were up and he attacked low, sticking a knife in her stomach and then one in her chin. He looked her in the eye and winked as blood trickled from her wounds and life from her body.

An overwhelmed hybrid was minced up by two Black Knights. Things looked really bad, and then came the relief that was needed. The explosion was loud and Dav, quick on the command, yelled, "Fall back, spell is down, spell is down!" Everyone understood it was time to exit and fast. Hybrids took flight and La Caprata showed their ability to manoeuvre when there was room.

Dav had watched his flame pointlessly hit an invisible shield and then engulf Gabriel. He was shocked and therefor didn't intensify it. He grabbed an exhausted Christian — now fully understanding his importance — he needed to keep him alive. The prospect of frying Gabriel was tempting, but keeping Christian alive seemed more critical. Dav leapt to flight, clutching a flabbergasted and weary Christian.

"You just saved our lives. You might have just saved Dryden," Dav said with pure respect. Dav looked to Dryden to see really only one path into the city. It would be really tough for the Dark Realm to overtake Dryden with only one path. He was confident Bruno would be able to defend Dryden until Hot House arrived.

Gabriel appeared near Zoran, his cloak on fire and skin singed from Dav's flame. He ripped off the cloak and tossed it aside, clearly infuriated, fists clenched and face pulled tight from pure anger. The veins in his head, face and arms were visible, throbbing under his pale skin, as the blood seemed to turn even more profoundly black.

Zoran jumped from the podium and ran over to him. "What just happened? I give it a few moments before Bruno realizes we can't smash down any more of their walls and pulls back. They will seal that hole, preventing us from proceeding with our invasion."

Gabriel didn't say anything. He just stared forward with malicious passion as smoke seemed to be emanating from his skin. He had the look of a wild animal, ready to snap into a rage-filled attack at any moment.

"King Zoran, sorry to disturb you, but Bruno has pulled back all of his forces. Archers are mounting the walls, they are retreating!" a random soldier said excitedly, but noticed Zoran wasn't pleased with the information. "Isn't that a good thing?"

"No, it's a really bad thing, you idiot!" He waited a moment, stroked his hair and then said, "We have to pull back."

Gabriel turned with a burning look on his face, "We are not pulling back. Do you understand me? Don't you dare make that command."

"I am King, don't you forget that, Gabriel."

"Don't you forget that in the blink of an eye I can burn the skin and flesh off your face." He looked Zoran square in the eyes. Gabriel started to shake as he turned his attention back to the battlefield. His shaking seemed to get out of his control as anger filled him. Gabriel started to levitate with a presence that caught everyone's attention. He floated above the battlefield with his hands to his side. Dozens of catapult shells floated behind him. He looked down and could see Bruno had shifted back and clogged up the clear entry point. Many areas were on the fringe of collapse with an exposed fourth wall, but without the catapults, they would stay strong. One entry point wasn't good enough, he needed more and was going to change that in a hurry.

Gabriel screamed, "I am the catapult!" and he started to laugh, a strange evil laugh. He was ready to start to fire his shells when Rizzian rose to meet him.

"I don't think so Gabriel. You have lost here today, you don't have the power to fire those shells." Rizzian looked over at Gabriel, an impressive sight as dozens of large shells floated randomly behind him. He knew it took a tremendous amount of energy and skill to handle a load of that size.

"Really?" Gabriel asked. He pointed to a section of the wall where archers were bravely attempting to gain a decent foothold. A shell raced towards them with great accuracy and blew them up, taking a part of the wall with them.

Rizzian didn't waste any more time talking and unleashed his fury. The two of them hurled spell after spell toward one another. Fireballs, lightning and charge spells launched and struck their intended targets. From the ground, it resembled a brilliant light show. Rizzian would take a hit, and then he would land a blow.

How is Gabriel taking so many strikes? How is he this powerful? Rizzian couldn't believe it. He believed Gabriel should be exhausted by this point.

He had been heavily involved all day, barely resting. Rizzian started to question how powerful his adversary really was.

They both unleashed purely offensive spells, focusing more on the attack rather than defense. Rizzian took a shot, forcing his head back and he lost some altitude. He regained his control, but took another hit, and then another. He felt that he was losing, like he couldn't hold up anymore.

Gabriel knew that he had him in a corner as he overloaded a charge spell that connected with Rizzian and sent him flying backward. He collided with Dryden's wall and headed for the ground. Rizzian had been defeated, deflating the renewed hope of potentially defending Dryden.

The master Wizard felt his bones break when he connected with the wall, and then rushed toward the ground. Luckily for him, Tres Nombre caught him before he slammed into the ground, using a spell which gently eased him down. It saved further damage but he was still injured badly.

"Get him in here, get him to safety," Bruno yelled as he allocated vital human capital to saving their prized Wizard. "Take him to the road!" Bruno referred to a secret back exit used specifically for the purpose of saving any important person. Bruno understood that they were going to lose this battle now that Rizzian was injured. Rizzian had to be saved! He was an integral part of the defense for the rest of the Kingdom. Dryden would be a major victory for the Dark Realm, but the rest of the Kingdom would hopefully mount a challenge, led by Rizzian.

Bruno looked up and realized that sealing one area was a great strategy, but not when more holes were going to be opened up at any minute. It would also give Gabriel a target of the best soldiers all in one dense area. Gabriel decided to slam the weak parts of the wall, knowing that he was moments away from victory.

He fired one shell and it did extensive damage. The second in the same area would finish the job. "Now you will feel the wrath of the Underworld! You will beg to be killed, bow to me. Even Rizzian is no match for the great Gabriel." He fired the second shot and watched in anticipation with a broad smile on his face. The smile turned to a frown as confusion set in almost immediately. The shell seemed slow down, stopping in midair. It still spun but was frozen in its path. It didn't stay stationary for long as it shot back toward him like it was fired out of a slingshot.

Gabriel moved out of the way as the shell shot over his shoulder and landed on a division of his soldiers, making a complete mess of them. Gabriel saw a young man with a metal staff in his hand, his first real view of the enigmatic Wizard.

"Go ahead, Gabriel, fire another one," Christian challenged confidently.

Only a few moments before, Petra — now rested and back on her feet — had grabbed Christian as Rizzian started to lose the battle and asked him, "What did he tell you a few days ago?"

Shocked and confused he asked, "What are you talking about?"

"In the cottage room, what did Rizzian say to you? I am sure that it was profound." Christian remembered but wasn't sure how she would have known about it.

"He told me that if he was to fall, I am to take his place." Christian repeated Rizzian's words with a look of shock. He felt a rush strike him with a tingle down his spine. He was now the leading Wizard for Dryden! He had to take control and save the precious city. Christian rose to the occasion figuratively and literally.

"You again!" Gabriel called. "You have been a thorn in my side all day. At least this time you're not hiding, you should have stayed in hiding." Gabriel didn't recognize his face but the energy signature was unmistakable. He got his first look at the young Wizard.

Gabriel wasted no time and launched a spell toward Christian, who put his staff up to split the spell in half as it passed around him with relative ease. Christian knew Gabriel was tired, burned out, yet still dangerous. He was also drained but understood that Gabriel was exhausted; coupled with a newborn confidence, Christian wasn't afraid anymore. The great dark Wizard stood before him, someone who should be able to crush him with ease, but he wasn't frightened at all.

"Time for the new to replace the old," Christian said. It was something that he thought made sense at the time.

Gabriel knew he was in a weakened state and also could read that his enemy was someone special. Gabriel needed strength, needed it now and knew where to get it.

He looked down at the ground, and with an arm extended and his eyes rolled in his head, he said. "Grant me the energy I need, the power, stamina and will. I will be your new ambassador. Damascus is dead, give me its strength and I give myself to you."

Christian didn't really understand what was happening but knew it couldn't be good. The ground below Gabriel opened up and black, dirty energy rose upward. Gabriel was rapidly regaining all of his strength. Something needed to be done immediately.

"Petra!" Christian called.

Petra stood still on the ground away from the battle. Ready for Christian's request, she had already been working on something special. Time and space became altered. Uneasiness settled around her — sound built from a distance, a sound like the swishing of water or massive amounts of insects. The sound was not distinguishable, and many focused in on her with frightened anticipation.

The men on the wall could see it — off in the distance something moved toward Dryden at an incredible speed. A large stream moved through the forest creating an even louder noise as the leaves were pelted. It was a sand stream! It left the desert, which should have been a day and a half travel away, but it passed at miraculous speed and focused in on her. Petra did not move or even blink an eye as innumerable sand particles ripped through the soldiers in its path, engulfing her. They started to spin with Petra as the epicentre. More and more gathered, swirling and spinning, becoming larger and louder. The sight shocked everyone, stopping most of the battle out of confusion and fear. Most of the soldiers didn't know who had commanded such a spell.

Petra pointed toward Gabriel and the deluge of particles under her command jettisoned toward him in a torrent and seemed to swallow him up.

Gabriel awoke from his coma-like state during his Netherworld communication, dazed, and could see that he was surrounded by sand. He put his hand up to block the particles from entering his eyes. "This is your plan, little man? You think this will keep me from ripping your city apart?"

"Not exactly, Gabriel."

Christian concentrated, pointed his staff at the sand stream between Petra and Gabriel, and applied massive amounts of heat to it.

Gabriel felt the temperature increase and stated, "Uncomfortable you have made me, but nothing more. You are a foolish Wizard and don't belong on my battlefield." Not concerned about the ineffective attack, he launched one of the shells at the wall.

"Hot sand not doing it for you, Gabriel?" He didn't wait for him to answer. "Do you know what happens when you heat sand and then cool it really quickly?"

Tres Nombre stepped forward and knew what their role was. Using the opposite spell, they laid down a concentrated cold spell, striking the superheated sand.

"It turns to glass!" Christian announced.

The hot sand melted in clumps, and when it cooled, it formed jagged pieces of glass. Gabriel heard what Christian had to say and then felt the impact. The glass ripped through his clothing and then tore at his skin. He tried to go into an evasive manoeuvre by elevating, but Petra redirected her sand. Gabriel started to scream in absolute panic. Some pieces jabbed in deep, lodging into bone, while the rest ripped off chunks of flesh. He was overwhelmed and was being torn apart quickly. He covered his face but the move had little effect. He screeched, realizing he could do nothing but wait for death.

The screaming stopped with eerie finality. They kept the sand blasting on him for a while longer, making sure the job was complete. Christian ceased his part of the spell, followed by Tres Nombre, and finally Petra released hers. Gabriel's body, what was left of it, spun in the air, held up by the vortex of the sand. When the sand ceased moving, a mutilated corpse fell from the sky, along with the shells that Gabriel had had dominion over.

Most of the shells fell on top of the Dark Realm soldiers, and they dropped from the sky causing mass panic below. Dozens of explosions ripped through hundreds of men.

Christian floated in the sky, and many looked to him with reverence. The image of him in the sky would be painted for decades to come by artists and imprinted in the minds of thousands.

Kruno, beside Kiera, looked up at him from the middle of the battlefield. "That is your man, my love," she said. Kruno said nothing in return but just smiled.

Frost knew it was his time to move on, and released the river from his will, disappearing into the forest.

The river almost immediately gave way and started to crack, indicating it was about to become impossible to stand on.

Zoran watched in absolute disbelief. Damascus was gone and now Gabriel. He was now the sole commander and he gave his order, "Retreat! Back to Pra! Back to Pra, now!" He shouted as he ran for the nearest horse, knowing full well he was the last target. Kruno, Magnus, and the rest of the Elites — maybe even the powerful Wizard in the sky who just took out Gabriel — would be looking for his head.

The enemy stopped in their tracks and started to pull back. Dryden was beaten and battered, on the brink of collapse, but its people started to cheer. The people in Dryden didn't know exactly what had happened, but they could tell that something great occurred. They broke into a state of jubilation.

"Bruno, let's get off this ice!" someone yelled. They started to run in an effort to get off, but some fell in as the ice unnaturally converted back to water. The sheer joy of the situation made the circumstances humorous.

Soldiers cheered, others cried, some just stared forward, still dealing with the stress of the battle and trying to contemplate what had just happened.

CHAPTER 11

MYSTICAL

The largest assembly in Dryden's history looked upon a makeshift podium with indefatigable jubilation, as their King walked slowly to the platform. A young man his age should have been able to bound up the stairs, taking them two at a time, but Egon walked with a noticeable limp and used a cane to support himself.

The injury he sustained in the battle with Clinton had healed miraculously with the aid of the dragon's blood, but it could not heal him completely. The limp would probably improve over time, but Egon was sure it would never fully dissipate. At best, maybe one day he could lose the cane. With each impaired step, reverence grew with everyone who looked at him. This was a King who had risked so much after losing his father, a King they couldn't be more proud of. Egon's story would rocket to every corner of the known world, on the backs of travellers who loved to tell of the shattering victory.

He winced a few times as the pain in his body intensified, making him realize that the physician's advice to stay off his feet was probably well warranted. This didn't matter to him, though; he wouldn't have missed this address even if it killed him.

Horns sounded to let the crowd know that he was going to speak. Egon looked out to a massive crowd, filled with every class and age from all parts of the Silver Allegiance and other Kingdoms. So many people showed up that they couldn't hold the address in Dryden, but instead stood on the very battlefield where the Dark Realm had turned and fled back to Pra.

Rizzian touched Egon's throat to magnify his voice.

"Our beloved Dryden faced a fierce and powerful enemy, an enemy that was fuelled by pure hatred. Numbers uncountable, holding robust new weapons, pushed Dryden hard, almost breaking her back, but what they didn't realize was these walls — these strapping walls — were built by God himself. What they didn't account for is our heart." As King Egon spoke, he fanned his hand across the landscape toward the city, which was beaten and battered. The walls were pulverized, along with large chunks of the buildings behind them. Repairs had begun, but it would be many months before it would approach its pre-war splendour.

"Dryden's back didn't break because the enemy didn't account for the Elites, for our army, for each and every one of you." The crowd lost composure and cheered with the energy of a dozen lightning bolts. Women cried with pride, men raised their arms embracing each other.

"What they didn't account for was Bruno your commander, Rizzian the greatest Wizard to ever cast a spell and many others of whom I will talk about today."

The crowd cheered out Bruno's and Rizzian's name with no real uniformity. They just couldn't control themselves, internal pride exploded.

A rider had just returned from Pra, and Egon had asked to be interrupted at any time with news. He motioned the messenger forward. The messenger dropped to one knee to bow in front of his King.

"Well, what word from Pra?"

Exhausted, mentally and physically beaten, the once ever-powerful Dark Realm, the only nation besides the North to pose a real challenge to Dryden and the Sliver Allegiance, had fled back to Pra with their tails between their legs. It was more than just a defeat. The grip that Zoran had on his people came from many sources, all of them now dissolved.

Damascus and his Underworld connection had multitudes that had followed him directly under a spell. That was now gone. Gabriel provided an unmatched arsenal and added tremendous security. As much as Zoran hated Gabriel, he had needed him, but he was now dead. Most importantly, they lost a battle that they shouldn't have lost. His credibility, the faith his people had in him, had vanished the moment he called a cowardly retreat.

With each footstep toward Pra, insubordination got progressively worse. Zoran could feel the eyes of his army looking at him with disdain, with ideas of revenge and possibly justice. He knew they didn't respect him, and even more importantly, they didn't fear him. His mind started to completely unravel and his concern for all-out mutiny, led by Valin or Baccarat, started to grow.

His thoughts of his top two Knights breaking command ended when they foiled an assassination attempt on him. A group of four, probably having planned the attack several days prior, made their move when only half a day from Pra. The only mistake they made was a look of uneasiness as they tried to nonchalantly move into position. Valin recognized their awkwardness, cleared his throat to alert Baccarat and they waited. The fight didn't last long, the would-be assassins being no match for the vigilant Black Knights.

That was the trigger that broke Zoran's perceived cool demeanour. He snapped and a verbal rampage turned into a violent one. Without explanation he did the unthinkable. He charged two innocent soldiers and skewered them with a dagger. The first was easily caught off guard, apparent by the look of utter shock on his face. The second watched with complete surprise as the bloody knife was turned on him. Zoran hacked away well after the point of death, like that of someone who had gone mad.

Valin had to command three Black Knights to pull Zoran from the corpses. Immediately the two of them stood in between their bloody King and the rest of the onlookers. They were letting everyone know that their thoughts of stringing up Zoran would come at a price, a thought that was crossing many of their minds.

"Are you crazy?" One of the Black Knights grabbed Zoran by the face as the others held his arms back. His hand struggled to find a grip because blood lubricated it.

"You think I am afraid of anyone? I can kill who I want, when I want."

"Smarten up Zoran. They are just looking for an excuse to take you down, and if they charge, I am stepping aside," one of the restraining Black Knights said with a forceful whisper.

"Okay, okay, let me go… I said let me go!" As Zoran was released the insanity in his eyes was clearly visible, it couldn't be hidden. He put his arms up and dropped his dagger to show he was relaxed. He attempted a smile but it was forced.

"We have a really big problem here, my brother," Baccarat whispered to Valin.

"More than we know, but that being said, we have one goal. Get to Pra. Once there, we will sort out the future."

"What about our leader who is full of composure?"

"Let's just get back to Pra."

"What's going on here?" Zoran walked up to them pretending as if the absolutely foolish act he had just committed hadn't occurred. He placed his arms on their shoulders. "We will regroup, we will attack those bastards again, but this time it will just be us."

"If you're going to walk into a bear's cave while it's sleeping, you better cut its head off before it wakes. Don't kick it in the balls and run. You won't have to go back to its lair, it will find you." Baccarat pitched his analogy.

"We didn't kick a bear. We slapped God right in the face!" Valin's comment hit them hard.

Zoran mumbled attempts to re-energize his top Knights, trying to re-secure confidence as they walked toward Pra. Nobody paid attention to him and eventually he just started talking to himself.

By the time they reached their final stretch, the field that lay just before Pra, it was well past nightfall. The troops had started to forget about their anger with Zoran. They pushed thoughts of dealing with him to the back of their minds. They were all exhausted, hungry and aching for home. They were consumed by thoughts of their beds, their wives, their children and eating good food.

Baccarat and Valin didn't care much for Zoran at the moment, but didn't want him to be killed. He was still their King and the people back home would still respect his authority. Hopefully the men would eventually follow the same path. They would need to rebuild faith in the Dark Realm or they would lose cities by the day. For protection, Zoran was put on horseback, surrounded by a large contingent of mounted Black Knights. Valin thought that Black Knights would be less likely to defect and turn on the King.

"Almost home, I can't wait," one soldier commented.

"Me neither, my girl is going to get a thrashing." Absurdly tired, one of the Knights attempted a quip that would have normally caused a bigger reaction, but just a few forced a struggled smile.

Heads bobbed up and down, many of them moved with their eyes closed, more than one had actually fallen off their horses during the last few hours, waking up when they hit the ground.

"What about you, Valin, what are you going to do?" the Black Knight next to him asked with a torch in one hand. Valin looked over to a soldier who was probably just trying to keep awake. He could tell by the look on his face that he was at peace. He knew he wasn't far from home.

The peace in the man's face was comforting to Valin, but it was stripped away fast and before he could respond to the question. It was difficult to tell what happened because he had received a practically silent assault to his face. The soldier buckled, slumped over, dropped his torch and slid back off his horse.

Normally Valin could have deduced what had happened, but his brain was too slow to recover. He looked forward with shock, doing his best to get his mind to think faster. Three men in front of him reached for their shoulders or ribs. Then a few more felt their horses give way.

What is going on?

Noticing everyone favouring one side, the silence broke as the air was sliced all around him. He grabbed his shield and put it over his left shoulder just in time to avoid an arrow coming in hard with a taste for his flesh.

"We are under attack!" he warned, as arrows rained from the sky.

Confusion consumed everyone, causing massive casualties; soldiers attempted to run in different directions. Many of their legs felt like rubber due to exhaustion.

"TO OUR LEFT! OUR LEFT!" Valin yelled.

"Get into Pra!" another shrieked, and although he was right, this was just the first stage of the attack. Whoever was out there would be charging at some point very soon.

Baccarat, with shield up, looked to his leg. "Dammit!" he cursed, as he noticed an arrow sticking right through his knee, a difficult wound. "We are sitting ducks out here. We are easy targets."

"Put out your torches!" Valin instructed, realizing it was easy for the unknown assailants to stay hidden but they were illuminated. "We might as well have targets on our backs."

"Who is it? Who is attacking us?"

"It can only be one group."

"Who?" one of the Knights close to Valin asked.

"Hot House!"

Valin was right! Hot House had been a day's ride from Dryden when they were informed about what had happened, and had redirected themselves, waiting for the Black Knights like spiders weaving an ambush.

"We walked right into a trap."

"Protect the King," someone yelled out of instinct.

"Yes, protect me."

"We need to get into Pra, get as many as we can."

"Only one way we are going to do that," Baccarat said. "Someone charges them. We need to occupy them while the rest sneak in."

"Great idea, you lead the charge," Zoran commanded Baccarat.

"No way, someone else goes." Valin shot down his King's command.

"You can't tell me what to do, I rule him and he will do as I say." Arrows continued to pound their men. Something had to be done and fast.

"He is our King still," Baccarat responded, showing his character.

"That's bull. Zoran, watch your mouth."

Zoran, out of character, said nothing. The Black Knights around them, although shocked, had much more respect for Valin, and Zoran knew it.

"The army will only follow you or me now. I do have a score to settle with Hot House, those cocky pricks."

"That's suicide!"

"Well then, I will catch you in the next life!" Baccarat held his sword up and Valin touched tips with his. He nodded with admiration.

Baccarat grabbed a group, composed of less valuable infantry, while Valin, Zoran and most of the Black Knights charged for the gate. The arrows stopped as Hot House charged the hapless army, led by Baccarat.

The morning light rose on copious numbers of slaughtered Dark Realm soldiers, and the entire Hot House division stood strong, full of life and with a thirst for vengeance.

"They aren't going to leave this time, they will bring siege weapons in and attack until they get in here." Zoran projected his thoughts to Valin, a few Black Knights and several political figures who stood on top of the wall.

"This was and is one terrible error. How long can we last?"

"Well, assuming they don't mount a successful attack, a month maybe."

"We will send to all corners of my Kingdom and get every warrior here. We will fend them off and retake Dryden." Zoran spoke but nobody listened, as if he wasn't even there.

"What do you think Valin?" one of the highest ranking political figures asked.

"What does he think — who cares what he thinks!" Zoran spoke yet again but nobody even flinched.

"I think we give them something, something that will make them turn away. Get rid of Hot House. They are their best divisions in their war machine. Get rid of them and then sort out the next step."

"Why isn't anyone listening to me? We have this. Give them nothing!"

"Stop embarrassing yourself and shut up, Valin is taking over. Your words mean nothing." Everyone witnessed a spectacular event, a King who had been admired for years, who had built up one of the most powerful kingdoms, was stripped of all power in one moment.

Zoran started to laugh with a bit of nervousness and expected someone to join him, but all faces looked back sternly. The situation intensified.

"I think you are confused. With the snap of a finger, I could have you killed."

"Valin, what do we give them? You lead us now."

"I warned you, seize him, arrest this man!" Zoran bellowed a command that technically would have been honoured a few moments prior and definitely before the massive defeat, but not anymore.

"I will head out and talk with them, I will cut the deal. Samuel will listen to me — we have a past," Valin stated, referring to the leader of Hot House.

Zoran edged closer to a weapon that lay resting against the wall. He attempted to grab it without notice.

"Don't even think about it, Zoran."

Zoran looked shocked that someone had noticed. He didn't know what to do. Panic set in and the only thing he thought of was to run; where, he didn't know, but this didn't seem like it was the right place to be.

Zoran broke into a sprint. Valin shook his head, grabbed one of his daggers and tossed it forcefully. The weapon dug deep into the back of the fleeing, emasculated man. He hit the ground hard with a slide.

"Stay there. You are still useful," Valin said to Zoran, who didn't have much choice.

Valin had ridden out to meet the commander of Hot House, and they greeted each other cautiously. Valin was accompanied by a modest party in terms of numbers, but the Black Knights he selected were all well known to Samuel, having spent time in the North where Hot House was stationed.

Samuel looked on with four times the number of troops in his immediate entourage and boasted a confident and well deserving smirk.

"You guys really crossed the damn line this time. No going back, Valin."

"I picked a path, just as you did."

"Well, I'm not sure why you are out here, not much to discuss."

"What do you want?"

"Blood, death, dismemberment… I don't know, to rip your walls down and embarrass the name Pra, make the Dark Realm a name that is spoken with shame." The commander's anger was abundantly apparent.

"Well, you aren't getting past those walls and you aren't getting Zoran, so name your price, let's try to settle this without more bloodshed." Valin's plan started to take shape.

"Well… okay… then we should just go then." He turned and looked at his Elites. "We tried boys, he said no, so let's head back and tell Egon." He laughed with the other troops.

Valin waited for him to finish laughing, using silence as a negotiating tactic.

"Well, let's start with Zoran, he is ours."

Valin had no interest in Zoran and was willing to give him up, but pretended like he was more important than he was. "Zoran is the glue that is holding us together, our only asset you haven't slaughtered. You have taken Damascus, Gabriel, Baccarat and now you want Zoran?"

"Don't forget your pride as we shoved our sword right up your ass." He smiled. "We are getting in behind your walls and there is nothing that you can do about it, so let us in and we will be kinder."

"You think that Pra is weak? You think this will be an easy task?"

"We are Hot House, enough said," Samuel responded in his normally cocky manner.

"We can wait as long as you can, winter and beyond, or maybe you want to attack us. How do you plan on doing that?"

"You are such an ass, Valin. How are we going to take you out? Cross your stupid rock moat, scale your walls and unleash everything we have."

"Ever wonder why we filled our moat with rocks? Why we didn't use water?"

Valin turned with a whistle and a hand signal. "Let me show you."

While Hot House looked on, an awful noise, like the very face of evil sighing, emanated from Pra, like a magnified, extended last breath of someone just about to die. The terrible sound was one that everyone wanted to cease, as the noise hit the confident soldiers with confusion, irritation and a little fear.

Timber started to crack, and the sound was easily recognizable. Everyone's eyes searched for what was to follow, attempting to locate the source of the wood and buckling sounds. Then, near the two peaks of Pra, it was seen. Wood splintered and popped. Large pieces fell into the city.

Another series of disgusting noises, groaning and scraping, slowly moved from the city.

"Sounds like what I would imagine the dead to sound like, if they were waking." An Elite spoke and Valin responded not with an explanation but with a smile.

Three Dark figures eerily floated from the two peaks and started to move toward the edge of the city.

"Don't be stupid Valin, we will cut you down first, if you attempt an attack from… whatever they are."

"I am not stupid and neither is your man."

"The dead are waking?'

"Something like that."

The three figures stopped at the edge of the wall, hands moved out to their sides and some form of energy built up around them. The energy swirled and developed. Samuel put his hand on his weapon and was ready to make his move on Valin, but the energy shot downward, connecting with the moat.

With awe, the group looked on. Only a handful of the Dark Realm conceptually understood what was happening. Everyone was drawn in. The rocks changed with the extreme heat, they melted and turned into molten rock.

"Good luck crossing that, Samuel."

"Check it out!" Samuel commanded a few to ride up and inspect the transformed moat.

"Not only will you be unable to lay platforms down because they will burn, if you attack, those evil bastards in the sky will send a wave toward them. It will not be a very pleasant scene." Valin smiled.

"I should cut that smile off your face, Valin."

"Listen. You are the most powerful of all Silver Allegiance divisions. We wouldn't have attacked if you were stationed at Dryden and that's no lie." Although it was a lie, Valin wanted to get respect from them. "We know that you could wait us out and attack us, probably even penetrate our forces one day, but at what cost? The carnage would be unimaginable."

"Go on."

"Although it goes against everything I stand for, and will bring devastation, I will give you two colossal things."

Samuel, still amazed, as was everyone at what just occurred, had to really focus on what Valin was saying. His peripheral vision demanded more.

"Zoran — he is yours. I know how badly you want him. We will hand him over." He looked to the sky with distress to really ham it up.

"Don't make a promise you can't keep."

"I will make it happen if I have to toss him off the wall myself."

"No! Everyone has to know the Dark Realm gave up their King to the Silver Allegiance. Bring him to us."

"Deal. The second term, we will negotiate supervised control of Pra."

The riders came back from inspecting the moat. Samuel nodded in their direction letting them know it was time to speak.

"It's too hot to get near it, felt like my skin was going to melt off."

"Okay Valin, let's talk about this. See if that works with those who control Pra."

Morning came and there was no sign of Valin, Zoran or anyone. All archers' dens were filled and the wall was dense with more men.

"That bastard just used us to buy time."

"Well then, we will bring the pain."

"Hold up, Valin will take time convince them. We are asking for their King — not so easy to give up."

"Not sure about any of that, but all the dead bodies are going to turn. If we are going to be here for a while we should toss them into the moat, burn them up."

"Not a bad idea."

"Hold on, what's that?"

Someone pointed to a bound figure on the edge of the wall.

"Who is that?"

"Who do you think?"

Zoran's arms and legs were tied, and he was freaking out. He yelled, "You bastards, I will reach up from the Underworld and rip you to shreds."

He was pushed, fell from the top of the wall, and with a snap, the rope snagged him.

The great King of the Dark Realm, once revered, undefeated and a shoe-in to rule for decades, hung from the walls of his kingdom, swinging from side to side.

"Well, that is not exactly what I wanted, but it will have to do. Good to see that bastard strung up."

"A bad day for the Dark Realm, good day for the Silver Allegiance!"

"I have word from Hot House that Zoran hangs from the city walls of Pra. Baccarat, their commander, has been extinguished, along with thousands of their men," Egon told the crowd. He didn't have all of the facts about how many had died, but this was a time to brag and thousands was a number that many would be elated over.

"My father, the greatest King to ever control Dryden, looks down on us and smiles from Heaven. If he was here in person, he would tell you all one thing. VICTORY IS OURS!" Egon let the crowd go crazy for a while with a smile on his face. "Our city is beaten up but it will be rebuilt. Dryden will look as if nothing had even happened to it, as if a rock wasn't out of place, but we won't forget. We will remember the souls that were lost, and the sacrifices that were made for our freedom. We will not sit in sadness because none of the people of the Silver Allegiance who lost their lives would want that. They would want us to enjoy what they have given to us. Today we don't work. Today we will have our first festival, one that will be repeated every year on this very day. It will be known as Victory Festival." Music erupted and multi-coloured confetti shot out into the sky.

"We won an outstanding victory today, but the reason we were able to achieve such success is through the special assistance of some very special people. Dryden's highest honour is the Warriors Emblem. Until today it has only been given to extraordinary citizens of Dryden, but today that changes. The first emblem that I will personally hand out is to one of the most recognized warriors in the known world, a man of stupendous skills on the battlefield and off. His stories are told across many nations, and he stood by our side, choosing almost certain death over leaving us to our own battles. A man of God, a friend of my father's and hopefully a friend of mine. Please welcome Kruno!"

Kruno, along with a small group, had been asked to stand near the podium, but they hadn't realized the reason behind that request. Kruno had never been recognized in such a manner and was completely overwhelmed by the crowd's expression of excitement and love. He walked over to Egon and accepted the emblem with an embrace. He understood that Dryden was in good hands, that this young man would be a great King. It was the accomplishments on the battlefield, the speech he was giving today and the speed in which he moved from a scared grieving boy to a King with a backbone that led him to form that opinion.

Kruno smiled and waved to the crowd. Egon gave him the floor to speak but he politely declined.

"Are you sure, Kruno?" Egon said with a smile that showed he loved the fact that he was able to offer him this honour.

"No thanks, this is your day, your moment."

"Next I would like to give out an award to one whose physical prowess is in direct relation to his skill set and bravery. He had the absurd idea to hunt a dragon. He and a few others waited in the dragon's den and took down the fiercest living creature. I have had the pleasure to hear this story several times, and it's one that everyone I am sure has talked about numerous times. Ivan, slayer of dragons, please step forward."

Ivan, not shy to speak, didn't waste any time. The men in the crowd looked up, many with man crushes and the women went wild with anticipation that one day they could bed him.

"This is a great honour and one I accept on behalf of everyone that stepped into that lair with me. First I want to mention Seburg. His information was vital to our success and his bravery saved my life. May his family be recognized and greeted with respect." Ivan, as he had sworn, mentioned every person's name and asked Egon for their names to be inscribed on the wall.

Seburg's family was shocked. He had been an absolute disappointment until this moment. They had been rejected by everyone because of him, and he was the reason they were mocked in life. Their perception had changed instantly with Ivan's words. A surge of pride and mixed emotion swelled in them.

"There will be a marble tablet situated in the centre of the town with a statue commemorating this great act of valour," Egon promised.

"Next, I would like to thank Kiera and her dazzling army, La Caprata. It's not every day a King would bow down to a Queen, especially one not of our kind, but it is warranted." Egon wouldn't actually bow down, of course, but the suggestion spoke volumes. Petra walked beside her and Kruno picked up on a small caress that Egon gave to Petra. He looked to Decan who noticed it as well.

Egon thanked more people for their individual efforts while Kruno and Kiera shared whispered words.

"What was that all about?" Kruno asked.

"What?"

"Petra and Egon, I saw something."

"You think?"

"I do, good for him," Kruno said with a smile.

"Have you been telling all of them how great I am in bed? Now everyone will want to sleep with us."

"Everyone already does. Not sure if you noticed, but you and your ladies aren't exactly hard on the eyes."

The two stopped as Decan was recognized for his creative dismantling of the eastern flank.

"Kruno there is something I have to tell you." Kiera had his attention. "This was my last battle as Queen. From now on I will just be Kiera." It was obvious she desired to know how he felt about one moment being with a Queen and the next just a warrior.

"Why?" He asked but answered his own question. "Because I broke the truce, the agreement to not come back?" She nodded. "Because you followed me into battle?"

"A battle that didn't protect La Caprata, one that I chose to endorse."

"You knew this in advance of course."

"Of course my love and I would do it again, without hesitation. It was time to hand over the reigns anyway."

"Don't be light about the situation. I will talk to them, Egon will talk to them."

"It is done Kruno. Even if they would take me back, we couldn't be together. I am not willing to give us up." She reached out and held his hand.

A feeling of guilt battled a surge of pride. Eventually, the guilt would lose the battle, but for the next while, it would bother Kruno.

"You will always be a Queen in my eyes." She smiled and turned back to the King.

"Rizzian…" Egon attempted to introduce Rizzian but the crowd went crazy at his name. "Rizzian…" Egon attempted again but waited for them to calm down. "Okay, okay he has a special announcement which we will get to in a moment." Egon, instead of being irritated, just smiled and waited for the crowd to die down before continuing.

"The Dark Realm made a horrible mistake. They built an army up for decades, used horrific beasts and submitted to evil to take out my father and move into a position to smash our city to pieces. They should have achieved their goal, but they didn't and they will pay for what they have done. God stood by us and gave us the strength, a power to slam our steel into their faces." The crowd roared. Egon continued a bit longer and then prepared to introduce his most renowned Wizard. "And now for a special presentation from the greatest man of magic… Rizzian!"

Again the crowd erupted, but as Rizzian motioned to talk, not a single soul spoke, because his words were seldom heard by most, many with parchments were ready to record what he said word for word. Their ears thirsted for his speech. Rizzian pulled the voice amplifier from Egon and blew up his own.

"Today is a very special day. I can't say it any better than our new King. Every one of you has been injured in some way. You have lost a father, a son, a brother, your home or you yourself are wounded. You all cheer my name, something I am grateful for, but in my old age I would have been bested. Someone of spectacular skill needs to be recognized. Someone who I am proud to say will train under me and probably in many ways teach me a few things. He was under my nose for years, but it took a warrior to drag him into many adventures to reveal his true skill. He represents a new breed of Wizard, one that is part warrior. He isn't afraid of hand-to-hand combat, making him one deadly ally. The Wizard formally known as Christian, please step forward."

Christian was in shock and didn't know what to do. The moment he had dreamed of, one all Wizards dream of, might be happening to him. His unexpected shock made his stomach turn to nerves, and he looked to Kruno who knew that this was part of the day's agenda.

"Congratulations, Christian," Kruno said with immense pride as he motioned toward Rizzian on centre stage in front of the largest group he had ever seen.

"As my name once was not Rizzian, may the name his parents gave him be forgotten. It was a good name, but today represents his rebirth. His overwhelming skill, heroism and unlimited potential has earned him an unprecedented new name. Everyone… recognize… Mystical!"

The crowd flared up at an event that was always public and was treasured among Dryden. Their close ties with DSW and Rizzian was stronger than iron.

Christian had now reached one of the ultimate status symbols. His position was elevated in Dryden and across the Silver Allegiance. All students would read about named Wizards, everyone respected them, and notoriety, among many things, was to be his. He had a spot in DSW at the head table, and would train with the best minds.

"Well if that doesn't get him laid, I don't know what will." Decan made the suggestion to Ivan, who laughed out loud. A few people looked at him with eyes of disapproval.

"You must be proud of Christian — sorry — Mystical. You are responsible for his growth," Egon said to Kruno.

"I played a very small role, just a vessel for God."

"A humble man you are Kruno," Egon commented, but Kruno didn't respond. Egon wanted to ask Kruno a big question and delayed for a moment, almost starting and then stopping like a boy getting ready to ask a girl out.

Before Egon could say anything Kruno reached his hand out, "All right King Egon, I must go now." Egon looked shocked and a little confused.

"Where are you headed and why in such haste? You should stay for the festival. I also wanted to offer you a permanent position in Dryden. Although this isn't exactly how I wanted to do it, I wanted to grant you Elite status to sit only under Bruno and Rizzian."

It was a great honour for many, but it wasn't where Kruno wanted to be. He had been offered Elite status before, but wasn't interested. He wouldn't fit, needed to control his own life, plus he had something to do.

"I better serve the world in another way. I am privileged to have been offered such a position, but I must decline."

"If it's fame you seek, you will find it here. Your name will echo throughout time. Bruno, Marcus, Rizzian all names that children will read about forever."

"I have no interest in fame, my name can die with me and I would be fine with it."

"Then its blood you seek? Blood you will have, we are going to make the Dark Realm pay for their atrocious crimes against us, against God."

"The war you wage is on humans, the blood you offer is that of men. I agree they have committed heinous crimes, but my war is with the Underworld. They were the reason so many joined the Dark Realm. They have drawn first blood and gone too far."

Egon and the half dozen others that could hear the conversation couldn't believe anyone would speak of the Underworld like that. Everyone had alone time, everyone slept, a time when people were vulnerable and to talk so bluntly and negatively of that Underworld was asking for trouble.

"I am going to stick this sword," Kruno moved his sword for everyone to see, but Egon watched his eyes with locked intensity, "into the belly of the Underworld and split it open. Their most precious asset is gargoyles, and I am going to kill them all!"

His statement had different reactions. Some thought he had gone too far and made an absurd vow, others were blown away with admiration and envy.

"You are talking about genocide."

"Exactly."

Kruno walked away to talk with Ivan and Kiera. The King was in shock but needed to return to his speech as Rizzian was almost finished with the presentation of Mystical.

"Mystical stays with you, he will train with Rizzian, this is where he belongs," Kruno said to Egon to give a little back to the shocked King.

"When do you go?" Kruno just looked at him. "Now?" Kruno nodded.

"But you should stay for the party. You should stay for Mystical's ceremony."

"We should stay for that Kruno," Ivan said. "There will be plenty of time for vengeance. Trust me, we don't have a lot of competition. People aren't exactly lining up to hunt gargoyles. There will be lots of them waiting for us."

"Okay, we stay for Mystical. Then whoever wants to join us can come."

"Kruno, why don't you let go of this fixation for tonight, have fun for once. Remember what we are fighting for and then we can make our move on our enemy." Kiera made a good point. She knew he needed to have a little fun. He had been focused and serious since they had met, and she knew that there was another side to him, one that she wanted to explore.

Ivan walked over and grabbed Kruno. He pulled him away from everyone's ear.

"Kill them all, Kruno? You do realize that they are gargoyles?"

"Didn't you take out a dragon?"

"Yes, but it was insane and we had twenty men."

"So then we get twenty men, and then we kill them all!"

CPSIA information can be obtained at www.ICGtesting.com
Printed in the USA
LVOW06s1308150415

434581LV00002B/72/P